HAMMER
OF THE EMPEROR

ACROSS THE WAR-TORN galaxy, the Imperial Guard are a bastion against the enemies of mankind. From the punishing heat of Tallarn's deserts to the bonechilling tundras of Valhalla, these are soldiers who give their lives in the Emperor's name. Whether shoulder to shoulder or crushing their enemies in vast machines of war, they are unwavering in their devotion to duty. On a thousand stars, they repel the forces of Chaos and the foul xenos in an eternal conflict.

This omnibus collects three novels and three short stories telling tales of savage warfare and heroism on the frontline.

GUNHEADS

Sergeant Wulfe leads his armoured tank company, the Gunheads, to the hostile alien world of Golgotha as part of an Imperial battlegroup. Their mission is to locate and retrieve the *Fortress of Arrogance*, a battle tank that belonged to the legendary Commissar Yarrick, hero of Hades Hive.

ICE GUARD

After the withdrawal of Imperial troops is ordered from the ice world of Cressida, a squad of Valhallan Ice Warriors led by the indomitable Colonel Stanislav Steele is sent on a rescue mission to find a stranded Imperial confessor and bring him off-planet to safety. Stanislav and his troops face a race against time as Imperial battleships in the upper atmosphere are preparing to virus bomb the planet.

DESERT RAIDERS

When an Imperial listening station receives an enigmatic call for help from a far-flung planet, a regiment of Tallarn Desert Raiders are sent to investigate. Their mission soon turns lethal as the Imperial Guard find themselves locked in a desperate battle with a formidable foe: the tyranids.

A WARHAMMER 40,000 OMNIBUS

HAMMER
OF THE EMPEROR

Steve Parker
Steve Lyons
Lucien Soulban

BLACK LIBRARY

A Black Library Publication

Desert Raiders copyright © 2007, Games Workshop Ltd.
Ice Guard copyright © 2009, Games Workshop Ltd.
Gunheads copyright © 2009, Games Workshop Ltd.
The short story *Mercy Run* first appeared in the *Planetkill* anthology
© 2008, Games Workshop Ltd.
The short stories *Waiting Death* and *A Blind Eye*
have not previously appeared in print.
All rights reserved.

This omnibus edition published in Great Britain in 2011 by
Black Library,
Games Workshop Ltd.,
Willow Road,
Nottingham, NG7 2WS, UK.

10 9 8 7 6 5 4 3 2 1

Cover illustration by Chris Bristow and Paul Rudge.

© Games Workshop Limited 2011. All rights reserved.

The Black Library, the Black Library logo, Games Workshop, the Games Workshop logo and
all associated marks, names, characters, illustrations and images from the Warhammer
40,000 universe are either ®, TM and/or © Games Workshop Ltd 2000-2011, variably
registered in the UK and other countries around the world. All rights reserved.

A CIP record for this book is available from the British Library.

UK ISBN13: 978 1 84970 028 3
US ISBN13: 978 1 84970 029 0

No part of this publication may be reproduced, stored in a retrieval system, or transmitted
in any form or by any means, electronic, mechanical, photocopying, recording or
otherwise, without the prior permission of the publishers.

This is a work of fiction. All the characters and events portrayed in this book are fictional,
and any resemblance to real people or incidents is purely coincidental.

See the Black Library on the internet at
blacklibrary.com

Find out more about Games Workshop
and the world of Warhammer 40,000 at
www.games-workshop.com

Printed and bound in the UK.

It is the 41st millennium. For more than a hundred centuries the Emperor has sat immobile on the Golden Throne of Earth. He is the master of mankind by the will of the gods, and master of a million worlds by the might of his inexhaustible armies. He is a rotting carcass writhing invisibly with power from the Dark Age of Technology. He is the Carrion Lord of the Imperium for whom a thousand souls are sacrificed every day, so that he may never truly die.

Yet even in his deathless state, the Emperor continues his eternal vigilance. Mighty battlefleets cross the daemon-infested miasma of the warp, the only route between distant stars, their way lit by the Astronomican, the psychic manifestation of the Emperor's will. Vast armies give battle in his name on uncounted worlds. Greatest amongst His soldiers are the Adeptus Astartes, the Space Marines, bio-engineered super-warriors. Their comrades in arms are legion: the Imperial Guard and countless planetary defence forces, the ever-vigilant Inquisition and the tech-priests of the Adeptus Mechanicus to name only a few. But for all their multitudes, they are barely enough to hold off the ever-present threat from aliens, heretics, mutants - and worse.

To be a man in such times is to be one amongst untold billions. It is to live in the cruellest and most bloody regime imaginable. These are the tales of those times. Forget the power of technology and science, for so much has been forgotten, never to be re-learned. Forget the promise of progress and understanding, for in the grim dark future there is only war. There is no peace amongst the stars, only an eternity of carnage and slaughter, and the laughter of thirsting gods.

CONTENTS

INTRODUCTION

WELCOME TO *Hammer of the Emperor*, the second volume collecting together battle-packed novels and short stories about the brave soldiers of the Imperial Guard. For those of you who are new to the 41st Millennium, it is a dark and terrible era. The galaxy-spanning Imperium of Man is beset on all sides by hostile aliens, heretical traitors and unholy daemons. With battlefronts separated by cosmic distances there is only a single force large enough to stand against the innumerable threats that would see mankind torn asunder: the Imperial Guard – the Hammer of the Emperor.

When asked 'Why do you like the Imperial Guard so much?' my answer is all about heroes. In my opinion, the Imperial Guard contains some of the bravest heroes the Imperium has ever known, and I hope you'll indulge me a little while I explain.

The soldiers of the Imperial Guard are just like you or me. They're human, normal men and women who are subject to the same fears, failings and mortal limitations as the rest of us. This has some pretty dramatic implications on the blood-drenched battlefields of the 41st Millennium. Imperial Guardsmen are not superhuman Space Marines clad in ceramite armour and armed with devastating boltguns. They don't pilot the Titans of the Adeptus Mechanicus, the towering god-machines that can crush battle-tanks underfoot and who carry enough ordnance to flatten a city. No, your average Imperial Guardsman is armed with only a standard-issue lasgun and a pair of boots. Let me remind you what they're up against: lethal tyranid predators that can rip your face off in the time it takes to blink, savage orks who can survive a few dismembered limbs without it slowing them down, warp-tainted psykers who can burn flesh from bones with a mere thought and dreaded Chaos Space Marines, renegades who have waged war for countless centuries and by whose hands thousands have been slaughtered. It's fair to say that a single Imperial Guardsmen is no match for these horrors, but they face their foes nonetheless. With fire in their bellies and honest human courage in their hearts, they stand firm against a galaxy of terrifying enemies – and that's what makes them heroes.

Supporting the underdog has always been a bit of a British pastime. It's David versus Goliath, and we love it when, despite it all, the plucky guys get their one in a million chance and emerge triumphant. It makes their victory all the greater. That's all well and good, a sceptic might say. But why then, if the odds are so highly stacked against an Imperial Guardsman, is the Imperium of Man still standing (albeit only just)? Well, thankfully for the Imperium, the Imperial Guard is a vast, megalithic force composed of billions of soldiers. Simply put, the Imperial Guard is the largest and most diverse fighting force in the galaxy.

To be in the Imperial Guard is to be one amongst untold numbers, all fighting (and dying) as they struggle to defeat the Emperor's enemies. There's a great phrase in Warhammer 40,000 – *Whatever happens, you will not be missed.* In the 41st Millennium warfare is at its most brutal; the lives of individual soldiers are irrelevant and the body-count is so high as to be reduced to mere statistics. However, if it's one thing the Imperium is not short of it is manpower. No matter the problem, and no matter how well armed or heavily defended the problem may be, the solution is simple – keep throwing regiments of Imperial Guard at it until it falls over, stops twitching or else ceases to pose a threat. Senselessly bloody? Yes. Inhumane? Absolutely. But it's also extremely effective. The Imperial Guard grinds its foes to dust in gruelling wars of attrition, and millions of lives are expended for the most trivial gains. Yet even amongst such carnage there are pivotal moments when the deeds of a company of courageous troops can the turn the tide of battle. At such times the actions of even a single soldier can make the difference between victory and defeat and it is then that Imperial Guardsmen show us their true mettle and heroes are born.

You've probably already worked out that the Imperial Guard isn't a subtle weapon. It responds to any threat with overwhelming force, and with an inexhaustible reservoir of manpower it can afford to do so. However, while the focus is on the poor bloody infantry, it would be remiss of me not to mention the other thing the Imperial Guard is famed for – tanks! When the soldiers of the Imperial Guard march to war they are accompanied by the thunderous bombardment of artillery fire and the lumbering advance of heavy battle-tanks. These ponderous metal behemoths bristle with guns and belch a fusillade of death as they grind their enemy's corpses beneath heavy steel treads. Let it not be said that the Imperial Guard don't understand the meaning of superior fire-power! However, don't forget that the crew manning these tanks are expected to combat raging daemon-engines that can demolish entire buildings, and giant alien monsters that can crush steel as if it were tin-foil. Now that takes some guts to do, and as we all know, that's something that heroes have in spades.

I also mentioned that the Imperial Guard are the most diverse fighting force in the galaxy. There are a million worlds in the Imperium, each of which equips and trains regiments from amongst its populace to serve in the Imperial Guard. These regiments have their own culture, language and fighting style, as different as the planets they were born on. We can only show a tiny fraction of the Imperial Guard's true variety, from the resourceful and pragmatic Tallarn Desert Warriors to the doggedly stubborn and stoic Valhallan Ice Warriors. The list goes on: the gung-ho Catachan Jungle Fighters, the disciplined Mordian Iron Guard and, well, a million others. However, for all their differences these soldiers have one thing in common – they're Imperial Guardsmen – heroes of the Imperium.

So if, like me, you love reading stories about heroic soldiers battling in the face of adversity, what are you waiting for? Forwards, for the Emperor!

Robin Cruddace
Author of *Codex: Imperial Guard*

MERCY RUN

Steve Parker

'If any event in recent years highlights the folly of underestimating the ork warlord, Ghazghkull Mag Uruk Thraka, it is the woeful mishandling of the Palmeros incident. That a significant part of the 18th Army Group (Exolon) managed to evacuate the planet in time must be scant consolation, if any, to the anguished souls of the billions who did not.'

Excerpted from *Old Foe, New Threat – An Assessment of Orkoid Military Developments in the Late 41st Millennium*,
Praeceptor Jakahn
of the Collegium Analytica
(Imperial Navy), Cypra Mundi

67 kilometres east-north-east of Banphry, Vestiche Province, 07.12 local (16 hours 35 minutes to Planetkill)

'FOR THE LAST bloody time,' roared Wulfe, 'make way in the name of the Emperor!' He sat high in his cupola, squinting into the morning sun. All around his tank, the highway was clogged with shuffling figures, over-burdened animals and carts piled so high they looked ready to tip over. The closest refugees tried to make way for Wulfe's tank, but there was too little room to move. They were hemmed in by the rest of the human tide.

Shouting was futile, Wulfe decided. The old scar on his throat itched like crazy. Scratching it, he looked east, tracing the broad line of sham-bolic figures all the way to the shimmering horizon. The sky was clear and blue, and the air was warming quickly.

Palmeros. Even after two years of war, much of this world was still rich and green. Clean, fresh air. Pure, crystal waters. He'd thought this world a paradise when the regiment had first landed. What would it be like, he'd wondered, to settle here, find a wife, till the land? Then word of the coming cataclysm had leaked out and things started coming undone. Seventeen massive asteroids, allegedly guided by the will of the ork war-lord Ghazghkull Thraka, were hurtling towards Palmeros on a deadly collision course.

Desperate masses poured from the cities, marching in their millions

17

to the nearest evacuation zones. Those squeezing past Wulfe's tank had come from Zimmamar, the provincial capital in the north-east. They followed The Gold Road west towards Banphry. Neither rich nor skilled enough to secure places on the Munitorum's evacuation lists, they'd find themselves facing lasguns and razorwire when they got there. Every last centimetre of space on the Navy's ships was already accounted for.

Wulfe's own regiment, the Cadian 81st Armoured, were already rolling their tanks into the cavernous bellies of the naval lifters that would carry them to the relative safety of space. Not the entire regiment, of course. Not he and his crew – the crew of the Leman Russ battle tank, *Last Rites*. And not the crews of *Steelhearted* and *Champion of Cerbera*, both of which followed close behind, running escort for those damned Sororitas in their unmarked black Chimera.

What did I do, Wulfe wondered, *to deserve the honour of leading this Eye-blasted wild-grox chase?*

His driver inched *Last Rites* forward, gunning the engine threateningly but to little effect. The refugees were already doing their best to stand aside. To proceed any faster, Wulfe knew, would mean pulping innocent civilians under sixty tonnes of heavy armour.

Sister Superior Dessembra was hailing him again on the mission channel. He didn't feel like listening. She'd already ordered him to roll forward, to lead their tanks off the road by crushing anyone in their path, but the thought of it turned Wulfe's stomach. These people were innocent Imperial citizens, and he was unwilling to stain his hands with their blood.

He watched some of them reach out to touch *Last Rites* as they passed thinking, perhaps, that the hulking machine's holy spirit would bless them with a little luck on this final hopeless day. A few craned forward to plant reverent kisses on her thick, olive-painted hull. The sight stabbed at Wulfe's heart.

He knew the mission clock was ticking. The town of Ghotenz, site of their primary objective, was still almost 200km away. Every second wasted here brought he and his men closer to being stranded, to sharing the planet's imminent annihilation. His laspistol began to feel heavy on his hip, calling for his attention. Dessembra was right; breaking free of the masses by force was the only option left. The tanks had to get off the road.

A warning shot, he reasoned, might get them moving. He didn't want to panic them – many would be hurt – but it would be kinder than crushing them.

He lifted his pistol from its holster and thumbed the safety off. Before he could fire, however, screams of terror erupted from behind him. He spun in his cupola to see *Champion of Cerbera* coughing thick black fumes from her exhausts as she rolled towards the edge of the highway. The old tank pulled dozens of helpless refugees under her, crushing their bones to powder. By the time she reached the roadside, her treads were slick with glistening blood. Cries of anger and grief filled the air.

'What are you doing, Kohl?' Wulfe shouted over the vox-link. 'Those are Imperial citizens!'

It was Dessembra who voxed back, 'They are jeopardising the success of our mission, sergeant. And so are you. I'm ordering you to run them down at once!'

The refugee column fell into utter chaos. People howled in terror. They began barging each other aside, desperate to flee the proximity of the war-machines. Animals brayed and kicked out at the people behind them. The old and weak were barrelled to the ground, begging for help as they were trampled to death. Even through the muffles of his headset and the roaring of engines, Wulfe could hear, too, the heart-rending cries of petrified children.

Steelhearted and the black Chimera were already following in *Champion of Cerbera*'s wake. More refugees fell under their treads. *Last Rites* alone stood unmoving, surrounding by a sea of frantic people. Now, however, broad spaces began to appear in the crowd as people pushed away. Wulfe could see the rockcrete surface of the highway clearing before him. He ordered his driver to get them off the road.

Only a few hours into the mission, Wulfe was already at loggerheads with the woman in command. At least the treads of his tank, like his hands, were unstained with the blood of the Emperor's subjects... so far.

Evacuation Zone Sigma, Banphry, Vestiche Province, 4 hours earlier

WULFE DREW ASIDE the heavy fabric of the entrance and stepped into Second Lieutenant Gossefried van Droi's command tent, keenly aware of how dishevelled he looked. Only moments ago, he'd been fast asleep in his bunk.

He cleared his throat, and the three men present turned to regard him.

'Sergeant Wulfe reporting as ordered, sir,' he said, throwing van Droi as sharp a salute as he could manage.

The second lieutenant snapped one back. He looked rough around the edges himself. Deep lines radiated from his eyes, coarse grey stubble covered his cheeks and chin, and there was an unlit blackleaf cigar in the corner of his mouth.

Bad news, then, thought Wulfe.

Van Droi only ever chewed unlit cigars when he was especially troubled.

'Did we interrupt your beauty sleep, sergeant?' asked van Droi. 'When I call a briefing, I expect my men to be punctual.'

Wulfe winced.

Van Droi indicated a steaming pot on a low table in the corner and said, 'Caffeine.' It was an order, not an offer. Wulfe walked over to pour himself a cup while the other two sergeants turned back around in their chairs.

One of these men was Alexander Aries Kohl, broad-faced and flat-nosed, commander of *Champion of Cerbera*, and a notorious martinet. With six years more experience than Wulfe, he'd proven himself a tough, reliable tank commander on battlefields from here to Tyr, but his personality, or lack of one, had so far barred him from advancement.

Sergeant Mikahl Strieber, on the other hand, seated on Kohl's right, was a hit with almost everyone in the 81st. Good-humoured and optimistic, the tall redhead took particular delight in anything that got under the skin of old Kohl. Some thought him reckless, but his survival suggested a certain talent, too.

Wulfe guessed he was somewhere between the two men; more experienced than Strieber and less detested than Kohl. Maybe that was why van Droi liked to dump so much crap on him.

The second lieutenant indicated a chair, and Wulfe sat, apologising for his tardiness. '*Last Rites* isn't due to board until oh-nine-hundred, sir, so the crew and I had a few drinks before lights out.'

'Not a crime,' said van Droi. 'By the time you've heard me out, you'll be needing a few more.'

Wulfe raised an inquiring eyebrow. His commanding officer sighed and perched himself on the edge of his desk. He took the damp cigar from his mouth, looked down at it and said, 'You're astute men, all of you, so you know I haven't called you here for a smoke and a glass of *joi*. Tenth Company drew the short straw tonight, gentlemen, and when I say Tenth Company, I mean *you*.'

Wulfe felt a sinking sensation in his stomach.

Still staring hard at his cigar, van Droi continued. '*Last Rites*, *Champion of Cerbera* and *Steelhearted* are being refuelled and reloaded. Your crews are being ordered to prep for duty as we speak. They'll be waiting for you at staging area six by the time we're finished here. *Foe-breaker* and *Old Smashbones* will be sitting this one out. They've been under heavy repairs since the breakout at Sellers' Gap. Given the losses we suffered there, your tanks have been chosen by default.'

'You're sending us back out?' exploded Strieber. 'You can't be serious, sir!'

'It's not something I'm likely to joke about, sergeant,' van Droi snapped. 'I've made my opinion clear to Colonel Vinnemann, but the top brass are having it their way.'

Sergeant Kohl muttered darkly to himself.

Wulfe's mouth had gone dry. This is a bad dream, he told himself. Wake up, Oskar. Wake up! He took a bitter swig of caffeine, gulped it down and said, '*Last Rites* can't roll without a driver, sir. Corporal Borscht is still listed as critical. I checked on him myself about six hours ago.'

A few days earlier, Borscht had been bitten by some kind of local worm. He'd been in a coma ever since. His throat had swollen up like a watermelon, his limbs were turning black, and he smelled like rotting meat.

Van Droi nodded grimly. 'I've taken care of it. Got you a replacement. It wasn't easy on such short notice, so you'll understand my choices were limited.'

The second lieutenant's nested apology set Wulfe even further on edge. Before he could ask van Droi to elaborate, however, Strieber interrupted. 'What's it all about, sir? Why send us back out now? By midnight tonight, the whole bloody planet will be spacedust!'

The voice that answered was female and unfamiliar, and came from the entrance of the tent. 'Time enough, then, to salvage some glory from this mess.'

Wulfe turned in his seat. A short, rotund woman in flowing white robes walked past him to stand beside Second Lieutenant van Droi.

'Planetkill,' she said, 'will occur at exactly twenty-three forty-seven hours. Of course, with the Emperor's blessing, gentlemen, we'll all be far away by then.'

98 kilometres east of Banphry, Vestiche Province, 09.12 local (14 hours 35 minutes to Planetkill)

LAST RITES SPED east, treads gouging dark furrows in the earth, throwing grassy clods of dirt up behind her. Her driver, Metzger, was pushing her over the plains with everything she had. The Gold Road was out of sight now, hidden from view by the shallow hills to the north. Wulfe had ordered the hatches open for ventilation, but he wasn't riding up in his cupola as he usually preferred. Instead, he was down in the turret basket, perched on his cracked leather command seat, cursing under his breath as he was lambasted by the voice on his headset.

'If you ever put civilians ahead of our objective again,' raged the sister superior through a crackle of static, 'I'll strip you of escort command. Sergeant Kohl has proven capable of grim necessities. I'm sure he'd be willing to take over.'

Wulfe wasn't about to argue with her. He'd seen her papers. They bore all the relevant signatures and seals, some from individuals so high up the ladder he'd never heard of them. *Exolon*'s top brass had issued the woman absolute authority over the mission and, while she was smart enough to leave vehicular management in the hands of experienced tankers, she clearly wasn't about to let something as trivial as human compassion jeopardise her success. Sergeant Kohl apparently felt the same.

'Listen carefully, sergeant,' Dessembra continued, 'because I won't be repeating this. While I admire your sense of morality, I warn you there's no place for it on this mission. The life of a very important man depends on how quickly we reach Ghotenz and return. And all our lives depend on catching the last lifter out of Banphry, so do not test me again. Are we clear?'

Wulfe mentally blasted her with a string of insults, but he knew better than to verbalise them. 'Understood, sister,' he said, and broke the vox-link.

That black-hearted sow, he thought. What the hell was High Command thinking? And isn't all human life supposed to be sacred to the Order of Serenity?

At the same time, however, he couldn't deny a certain uncomfortable relief. Weighing duty against personal honour had always been difficult for him. While he'd wrestled with his conscience, Dessembra's cold disregard for the lives of the refugees had put the mission back on track. Whether he liked it or not, ultimately, she'd been right.

Very well, he swore. It won't happen again.

He'd stow his humanity for now. He could be stone-hearted, too, if necessary.

Keying the tank's internal vox, he said, 'Metzger, keep her running full ahead, eight degrees east-south-east. We'll rejoin the highway south of Gormann's Point. Shouldn't be many refugees so far out. We'll make some time up there.'

'Aye, sir,' replied the driver.

Wulfe rose from his seat and climbed into his cupola, immediately enjoying the warm wind on his face.

Last Rites rolled along at the head of the column. Twenty metres behind her, *Champion of Cerbera* followed, turret facing south-east. Kohl was in his cupola, but he didn't return Wulfe's nod.

Following *Champion of Cerbera*, the unmarked black Chimera purred along with an easy grace, capable of twice the speed of the Leman Russ tanks, but hobbled by the need for their protection.

Steelhearted brought up the rear, her massive cannon pointing south-west. Seeing Wulfe, Sergeant Strieber threw him a casual salute.

Wulfe did likewise then turned to survey the land ahead. The plains north of here were still regarded as safe zones. Naval reconnaissance put the nearest orks just to the south, in the province of Drenlunde. If the mission group were to encounter any greenskins, they'd come from there.

Wulfe was gazing at the low, tree-crested hills to his left when a nasal voice spoke through his headset. It was Metzger. 'Could you check your panel, sir? The auspex is picking up a signal. Looks like a civilian SOS beacon about fifteen kilometres away, just north of our current heading.'

Wulfe ducked back down into the turret to check his station and found that Metzger was right. Someone was signalling for help.

His first instinct, he knew, was the wrong one. Even so, it took him a moment to overcome it. With an unpleasant twist in his gut, he voxed, 'No detours, corporal. We don't have time. Keep her at full ahead, please. Whoever they are, the Emperor will decide their fate.'

'Aye, sir,' replied Metzger, 'full ahead.'

There was no hint of judgement in the man's voice, but Wulfe heard it anyway.

Evacuation Zone Sigma, Banphry, Vestiche Province, 3.5 hours earlier

WULFE KNEW SOMETHING was wrong the moment he reached the staging area. Standing in a pool of electric lantern-light, Viess, Siegler, Holtz and Garver were huddled together, slightly stooped in the way of all long-serving tankers, whispering and passing a single lho-stick around. With the exception of Siegler, the set of their shoulders told Wulfe they were in a foul mood.

As Sergeants Kohl and Strieber left him to greet their own crews, Wulfe breathed in the smell of promethium fumes on the night air. The field was almost empty. The last few engineering tents were waiting to be taken down. And there, just beyond the final tent in the row, sat the shadowed forms of three hulking monsters. They belched oily smoke from their twin exhausts as they sat with their engines idling. To Wulfe's eyes they were familiar, beautiful things. One, in particular, held his eye. He smiled as his gaze followed the sweep of her hull and the noble line of her powerful battle-cannon.

Last Rites.

A trio of robed figures, each grotesquely misshapen by the mechanical appendages that sprouted from their backs, performed final checks on her track assemblies and external fixtures.

Helmut Siegler was the first to spot his sergeant. He came racing over like a hyperactive puppy. After a brief, jittery salute, words began gushing out. 'Viess says it isn't right, sir,' he panted. 'Garver and Holtz won't do it, either. They said they won't ride with him, sir. The Eye is on him. That's what they said, sir. The Eye!'

Wulfe blew out an exasperated breath and walked past his loader, who fell into step behind him. He stopped a few metres in front of his men and returned their stiff, sullen salutes.

Viess the gunner. Holtz and Garver, the sponson men. He'd known them for years – as good a crew as any when the fighting started, and just as troublesome when they were idle. 'What's all this crap about not riding with the new man?' Wulfe demanded.

'It ain't right, sir,' said Garver glancing at the others for support.

'I heard that already,' said Wulfe. 'Let's have some details.'

Holtz, the eldest of the three, took a step forward. 'A man like that ain't nothin' but bad news, sarge. It's wrong enough we're going back out, but to have a cursed man on crew… You'll be wanting him swapped out.'

Wulfe scowled. 'Are you speaking for me now, Holtz? I don't think so. And if you mean to complain about someone, you'll furnish me with a bloody name first.'

Holtz tipped his head by way of apology, but his blue eyes continued to blaze. Once upon a time, those eyes had won him his share of female hearts. That was before so much of his face had ended up looking like hashed groxmeat. Anti-loyalists back on Modessa Prime had hit the tank's left sponson with a shaped charge. Holtz had been inside. These days, the women he bedded fell into two categories – the charitable and the desperate – and Wulfe often found himself cutting the embittered man some slack.

Footsteps sounded on the grass and a nasal voice said, 'The man they're talking about is Corporal Amund Metzger, sir. It's me.'

Wulfe turned to face a tall, skinny man with dark eyes and a long, curving nose. He was dressed in standard-issue tanker's fatigues and, unlike the rest of Wulfe's crew, who mostly smelled of oil, sweat and propellant powder, he smelled of Guard-issue soap.

'Don't be too hard on your men, sir,' Metzger continued. 'They're not wrong. Hell, my own company wouldn't have me.'

'Lucky' Metzger, thought Wulfe. Thanks a lot, van Droi.

Everyone in the regiment knew the story of 'Lucky' Metzger. He had a reputation for climbing out of burning tanks unscathed while everyone else roasted to death. Among the crews of the 81st, that made Metzger about as popular as crotch-pox. Just twelve days ago, he'd survived yet another tank fatality. Now the whole regiment, including officers who should have known better, believed that riding with Metzger was a death sentence. It had nothing to do with his driving ability, of course. He'd been considered exceptional by his instructors back on Cadia.

Unlike his crew, Wulfe knew curses for cudbear crap. Death claimed everyone sooner or later. All a man could hope to do was fight it off for as long as possible and sell his life dear. Only the Emperor Himself was immortal, after all.

All the same, his crew was spooked, and Wulfe knew he had to squash it right away. He glared at the new man. 'Listen up, corporal. This so-called curse of yours is a load of bloody ball-rot. Everyone knows that if the turret takes a hit, nine times out of ten, the driver walks away. I've seen plenty of men crawl unharmed from burning tanks.'

Plenty, he admitted to himself, was stretching things a bit.

He pointed to his own tank and said, 'That big beauty over there is *Last Rites*. Finest in the regiment. Thirty-eight confirmed tank-kills and plenty more besides. And if you take care of her, she'll take care of you. That's how it works. Give me any less than your best, I'll have you up in front of "Crusher" Cortez on more charges than he has metal fingers.' Wulfe turned to the rest of his crew. 'That goes for all of you. The commissar isn't nearly as forgiving as I am. Now get to your damned stations.'

Wulfe's men were about to move off when the clanking of cast-iron treads made them stop. An unmarked black Chimera, workhorse troop-transporter of the Imperial Guard, ground to a halt near the waiting Leman Russ tanks. Its rear hatch opened, spilling orange light onto the dark ground, and disgorged three female figures clad in the long white robes of the Order of Serenity.

'Women,' gasped Viess. 'And one of them looks good!'

'They're not *women*,' barked Wulfe, 'they're Adeptus Sororitas, so don't even think about it, Viess. I don't need the hassle.'

Viess groaned and mumbled something euphemistic about firing his 'gun'. Garver and Siegler chuckled. Holtz managed a grin. Metzger's mouth barely twitched.

With Sister Superior Dessembra leading them, the women approached the crew. 'Sergeant Wulfe,' said Dessembra, 'we should be under way as soon as possible, but perhaps a quick introduction. Just as a courtesy. I doubt you'll need to communicate with my subordinates once we're under way. My driver, Corporal Fichtner, will introduce himself via vox-link.'

Wulfe shrugged. 'Then the courtesy is unnecessary, sister superior. But to show my respect for your order…' Offering shallow bows to the two sister-acolytes, he said, 'Sergeant Oskar Andreas Wulfe at your service, as are my crew, the men of the Leman Russ *Last Rites*.'

Dessembra's smile didn't reach her eyes. She gestured to the tall, grim-faced woman on her right and said, 'This is Sister Phenestra Urahlis.'

Wulfe smiled genially at the imposing acolyte, but her expression remained fixed like a mask.

'And this,' said Dessembra with a wave of her hand, 'is Sister Ahzri Mellahd.'

Sister Mellahd smiled and gave a shallow curtsey. Her robes, cinched tight at the waist, accentuated a striking figure. She was young, curvaceous and excruciatingly pretty.

Viess took a step forward. 'You must see my cannon, sister. It's huge!' Wulfe's hand flashed out, clipping the gunner on the side of his head. 'Ow!'

'Get to your bloody stations, all of you,' he growled. 'Internal systems check. Four minutes.'

'But, sir,' Garver moaned, 'the cogboys have already run two full sys–'

'Don't make me repeat myself, soldier. Move!'

With a mixture of muttered complaints and angry scowls, the crew jogged off towards the tank. Siegler raced over to it with his typical abundance of child-like energy. Dessembra followed him with her eyes.

'That one seems a little *Throne-touched*, sergeant,' she said, nodding in Siegler's direction.

'Injured in the line of duty,' replied Wulfe, tapping the side of his head with a finger. 'And yet, without doubt, the best man on my crew. He's the fastest loader in the regiment, and that's merely one measure of his worth. Sister Mellahd here, on the other hand, possesses the kind of beauty that makes trouble among men. Best she stay out of sight during the operation.'

At the word *operation*, Dessembra flinched. She turned back around to face Wulfe. 'My sister-acolyte is quite without sin, sergeant. It is undisciplined minds that are to blame for such troubles. I'm speaking in general terms, of course.'

'Of course,' said Wulfe, brushing off the mild insult.

Sergeants Strieber and Kohl were already sitting in the cupolas of their respective tanks. 'You can confess your depravities later, Wulfe,' Strieber called out. 'Let's get our arses into forward gear.'

Dessembra frowned. 'Crude though he is,' she said, 'Sergeant Strieber is quite right. Time is not on our side, sergeant. Get us to Ghotenz. Someone there requires our immediate attention.' She made the sign of the aquila on her chest then turned and led her subordinates back to the Chimera.

Wulfe strode over to his tank. In the sky above, vessel after overcrowded vessel was pulling away from the planet's orbit, and here he was, about to roll out on a last-minute mercy run, probably for some damned incompetent blue-blood who'd gotten himself into hot water.

He clambered up the hull of his tank, swung his legs over the lip of the cupola, slid through the hatch and dropped down into the turret basket. As soon as he was seated, he pulled on his headset, activated the tank's intercom, and issued instructions to his new driver.

With their headlamps throwing stark light out ahead of them, the four Imperial war-machines rolled off into the night.

82 kilometres west-north-west of Ghotenz, East Vestiche, 13.09 local (10 hours 38 minutes to Planetkill)

THEY REJOINED THE highway about sixty kilometres south of the abandoned outpost at Gormann's Point. There were no refugees in sight. Perhaps the locals knew they'd never make it to Banphry in time and had opted to die at home. Or perhaps they'd already passed through. Wulfe hoped their absence wasn't a sign of something more sinister.

The surface of the highway dropped gradually, easing its way down into a deep sandstone canyon known as Lugo's Ditch. Wulfe rode high in the cupola, warm winds whipping his lapels as he scanned the area for threats. Craggy, sandstone walls rose high on either side. Wulfe marvelled at the natural beauty of the place, fascinated, in particular, by the rich and varied hues of the rocky strata.

It hadn't escaped his notice, of course, that the canyon was an ideal place for an ambush. There was no word that the orks had spread this far north, but he put his men on high alert anyway. Sergeants Kohl and Strieber, he saw, were equally uneasy. Both sat in their cupolas, peering through magnoculars at the rocky outcrops on either side.

Taking his cue from them, Wulfe dropped down into the turret basket to retrieve his own pair. While he was there, a light began to wink on the vox-board. It was Sergeant Kohl.

'Wulfe,' he said, 'we're well out from the naval patrol routes now.'

'I know that, Kohl. What's your point?'

'My point, *sergeant*, is that *Last Rites* is the only vehicle here with a decent vox-array. Hasn't there been any kind of intelligence update from regimental HQ?'

It was a fair question, but the answer wasn't likely to satisfy. 'No updates,' replied Wulfe. 'If they've anything to tell us, they'll get in touch. But you said it yourself; we're outside of the patrol zone. The fighter wings have their hands full running defensive sweeps for the lifters. I think we can forget about aerial reconnaissance updates.'

Kohl was quiet. A moment later, he signed off.

Though Wulfe's tank boasted a crew of six, only two other men shared the discomfort of the turret basket with him. Viess and Siegler sat within arm's reach of their commander, backs ramrod-straight, eyes pressed to their scopes, scouring the terrain for the first sign of trouble. Wulfe hoped Garver and Holtz were being equally vigilant, tucked away in their cramped, stifling sponsons. Metzger, up front in the driver's compartment, had more space than anyone else, but not by much.

The tank's intercom, usually alive with dirty jokes and crude banter during long journeys, was silent save the background hiss of white noise. The silence told Wulfe just how tense his crew were.

Having fetched his magnoculars, he was about to climb back up when he heard someone say, 'Stop the tank.'

He wasn't sure he'd heard it correctly at first. The voice came through his headset as little more than a whisper, almost lost against the background rumble of the engine. 'What was that?' he voxed back.

'What was what, sir?' asked Viess.

'Stop the tank,' someone whispered again, clearer this time.

'Do *not* stop the damned tank,' Wulfe barked. 'Who the bloody hell said that? Holtz? Was that you?'

'Don't blame me, sarge,' replied Holtz. 'I never said anything.'

'Garver?' Wulfe demanded.

'It wasn't me, sir.'

Wulfe placed a hand on Siegler's shoulder and half-turned him in his seat. 'Siegler, did you just call for the tank to be stopped?'

'Negative, sir,' the loader replied, shaking his head emphatically.

Wulfe had never known Siegler to lie. He didn't think the man was about to start now. 'Who said to stop the tank? One of you said it, Eyeblast you. Confess!'

'Do you want me to stop the tank, sir?' asked Metzger in obvious confusion.

'No, by the Throne! Keep her steady in fifth.'

'I never heard anyone say to stop, sir,' voxed Garver.

'Me, neither,' said Viess.

They sounded worried now. Wulfe was spooking them. It wasn't like him to get flustered this way and it certainly wasn't like him to hear voices.

'When we get back to base,' he told them, 'I'll be checking the vox-logs. Then we'll see which of you smart-arses is having a laugh.' With a scowl, he climbed back up into his cupola. What he saw when his eyes cleared the rim of the hatch turned his blood to ice and jolted him with such a spasm of fear that he dropped the magnoculars.

They struck the turret floor with a loud clang.

A shocking, impossible figure stood on the road up ahead, arms raised, palms out, eerily insubstantial despite the glaring sunlight.

Borscht!

The dark hollows of his eyes locked with Wulfe's. His voice thundered in Wulfe's mind, drowning out everything else. *Stop the tank!*

Wulfe's finger flew to the transmit stud on his headset. 'Stop the bloody tank! All stop! All stop!'

Metzger braked hard on command and Wulfe was slammed forward, ribs hammering against the rim of the hatch. He winced in sudden flaring pain. When he opened his eyes a split second later, the figure of his old friend had completely disappeared.

'By the bloody Golden Throne!' gasped Wulfe.

Panicked voices tumbled over each other through his headset.

'What's wrong, sir?'

'Where are they, sir? I have no targets. I repeat, no targets.'

'Give us a bearing, sarge!'

Wulfe dropped back into his seat, shaking, chilled to the bone. No, he thought. No way. It's nerves. It wasn't Borscht. It can't have been. It's me. I must be cracking. It's the pressure. It's the damned mission clock. It's…

The vox-board was blinking furiously with calls from the other vehicles. On reflex, Wulfe reached out and keyed the mission channel.

'What in the warp are you playing at, Wulfe?' bellowed Sergeant Kohl. 'You bloody fool. If my man wasn't so alert we'd be halfway up your exhaust by now!'

'Why have you stopped, sergeant?' demanded Sister Superior Dessembra.

Wulfe didn't know what to say. He felt numb. He sat rigid, eyes wide with fear and confusion. Siegler and Viess stared back at him, deeply discomfited. He forced himself to answer the uproar over the vox. 'I… I thought I saw something,' he said. 'But it's gone now.'

'What did you see?' Sergeant Strieber asked.

'I don't know, damn it!'

Typically, Sergeant Kohl's meagre patience ran out first. 'You don't know? Throne curse you, Wulfe! Planetkill is just hours away and you're braking for shadows? We don't have time for this.'

'I know that,' Wulfe snapped.

'Enough!' voxed Dessembra. 'I want someone else on point. Sergeant Strieber, your tank will move up and lead us on. *Last Rites* will guard the rear.'

'Sister superior,' said Strieber cheerily, 'I thought you'd never ask.'

Before Wulfe could protest, *Steelhearted* broke formation, rumbled past the other vehicles and accelerated up the highway.

'Wait!' Wulfe shouted over the vox. 'I said *wait*, Throne damn you!'

But it was too late. Strieber's tank hadn't gone two hundred metres when the road bucked under her with an ear-splitting boom. A pillar of fire erupted from the surface, ripping away her left tread, spinning heavy iron links off in all directions.

'Landmine!' shouted Metzger over the vox.

'Strieber, respond!' demanded Kohl. 'By the blasted Eye!'

'*Steelhearted*, respond!' voxed Wulfe.

Groaning and cursing, Strieber answered a moment later. 'Bloody orks mined the road!' he hissed.

'Don't be stupid,' snapped Kohl. 'They haven't got the brains for that.' He didn't sound at all convinced.

Through his vision blocks, Wulfe saw dark, ugly shapes pour from the shadowed gullies on either side of the canyon. The air filled with the growl and sputter of countless throbbing engines.

'Button up, *Gunheads*!' he yelled over the vox. 'Lock hatches! Safeties off!' He reached up and slammed his own hatch shut, locking it tight in one practiced motion.

'He's right!' voxed Strieber, panic charging his voice. 'It's a warp-damned ambush!'

61 kilometres north-west of Ghotenz, East Vestiche, 13.51 local (9 hours 56 minutes to Planetkill)

THERE WERE HUNDREDS of them.

Wulfe's heart was pounding in his chest as he watched them spill out onto the canyon floor. 'Close ranks,' he ordered on the mission channel. 'Form up on *Steelhearted*. Defensive pattern *theta*!'

Metzger gunned *Last Rites* into action. *Champion of Cerbera* and the black Chimera leapt forward a second later, speeding towards Sergeant Strieber's crippled tank.

Steelhearted lay utterly immobilised, track-links scattered around her in a forty-metre radius. Her left sponson was still burning. The shrivelled, blackened body of its occupant, Private Kolmann, hung from its twisted hatch. The other vehicles reached her side now, slid to a halt, and spun on their treads to face outward in a defensive, four-pointed star.

'Stinking greenskins,' spat Wulfe. 'It's a wonder we didn't smell them.'

Among the myriad enemies of mankind, it was the *old foe* he hated most. An image flashed through his mind; the blazing red eyes of one particular ork he'd encountered on Phaegos II. The scar on his throat was a memento of that day – the day he'd almost bled to death.

'Holy Throne!' voxed Kohl. 'How many of them are there?'

Wulfe wasn't about to count. Buggies and bikes of every possible description roared into the canyon. They were gaudy things, painted red, with fat black tyres that churned up the dirt. Many were decorated with crude skull motifs or images of tusked deities. Some boasted far grislier forms of decoration – strings of severed human heads and banners of flayed skin. But the ugliness of the machines themselves was nothing compared to that of their riders and passengers. The orks were hideous, malformed brutes that waved oversized blades and pistols.

Their bodies were twisted and hunched with overgrown muscle. Their eyes and noses were miniscule, but their mouths were wide and full of massive, jutting yellow teeth.

The throaty roar of each engine merged into a cacophony that filled the air. Thick black fumes spewed from exhaust pipes as the orks raced over the sun-baked land, kicking up clouds of dust behind them. But they weren't surging forward. Not yet. They surrounded the Imperial tanks and began circling them at range, moving anti-clockwise.

'What the hell are they doing?' voxed Strieber.

The answer came all too quickly. From random points in the massive circle, small groups of ork vehicles suddenly broke formation and sped inward towards their prey.

The hull of *Last Rites* rattled under a heavy barrage of stubber rounds.

'Damn,' shouted Viess.

'They're trying to confuse us,' Wulfe voxed to the other tanks. 'If we can't predict their angles of attack, there's a chance they can close the gap. We have to start thinning them out, now! Siegler, high explosives!'

'Aye, sir!' With thick, powerful arms, the loader hefted a shell from the magazine on his right, slammed it into the cannon's breech, and yanked the locking lever.

The loading light turned red. 'She's lit, sir!'

Through the vision blocks, Wulfe spotted a knot of large, open-topped half-tracks among the smaller, faster ork vehicles. They were filled to overflowing with monstrous green savages. 'Viess,' said Wulfe. 'Traverse left. Ork half-tracks. Four hundred metres.'

Squinting through his scope, Viess spotted them easily. The ork passengers were howling with insane laughter and excitement. Their blades glinted in the sun. He hit the traverse control pedals, and the turret swung around. Electric motors hummed as he adjusted the angle of elevation. 'Targets marked!' he called out.

Wulfe braced himself in his seat. 'Fire main gun!'

Last Rites rocked backwards with the massive pressure of exploding propellant. Her hull shuddered with the thunderous signature boom of her awesome main gun. The turret basket filled with the coppery smell of burnt fyceline.

Through the vision blocks, Wulfe saw the leading ork half-track vanish in a great mushroom of fire and dirt. The vehicles nearby were blasted into the air, spinning end over end. They smashed hard to the ground, spilling some of their foul passengers, crushing and mangling the rest. Shrapnel scythed out from the blast, eviscerating scores more.

It was a fine shot.

Bikes and buggies began swerving to avoid the burning wreckage, and the ork circle tightened. The enemy swerved inwards with increasing frequency to pepper the tanks with stubber-fire, but *Last Rites* boasted front armour 150mm thick, slanted to deflect solid rounds. The greenskins' armament didn't pack enough penetrating power to pose an immediate threat.

The real danger was in letting them engage at close quarters.

A regular drumbeat of deep, sonorous booms told Wulfe that the other tanks were firing round after round into the ork horde. Every impact threw shattered vehicles and torn green bodies into the air. Alien blood splashed on the canyon floor, mixing thickly with the sand. In only the first few minutes of the battle, hundreds of greenskins were blasted apart by the legendary firepower of the Leman Russ's main battle-cannon.

Like her sister tanks, *Last Rites* boasted a powerful hull-mounted weapon, too. Wulfe ordered Metzger to fire the lascannon at will. Seconds later, blazing beams of light lanced out to strafe the ork horde. The scorching las-blasts cut straight through light armour, igniting fuel tanks and sending bikes and buggies spinning into the air on great fountains of orange flame.

A trio of ork bikes swerved just in time to avoid destruction and came screaming towards *Last Rites*. Bolter-fire from the sponsons shredded two of them, but the last veered from side to side, racing unharmed through the hail of shells. Wulfe saw the hideous rider grin and lob a grenade towards his tank.

'Brace!' he shouted, and prayed that the blast wouldn't wreck their treads.

There was a dull boom and the tank shook. Lights flickered in the turret basket. Wulfe's diagnostics board reported trouble with the right sponson. He ordered the crew to sound off.

Garver didn't answer.

Wulfe ordered Garver to respond.

Nothing.

'Damn it all,' Wulfe shouted. 'We've lost the right sponson. Garver's gone!'

'No!' yelled Holtz over the vox. 'Those bastards!'

In his periscopic sight, Wulfe watched the ork bike accelerating away. As it passed the black Chimera, it was blasted apart by a searing spray of multilaser fire. Someone was manning the transport's turret-mounted weapon. The multilaser turned quickly to target an ork truck and fired again, charring wide horizontal slashes in flesh and metal alike. Slaughtered orks tumbled from the back of the truck in limp, lifeless pieces.

Wulfe wondered if Dessembra herself was dispensing the Emperor's judgement. Or was it one of her acolytes? Whoever it was had avenged Garver. He'd have to thank them later.

'They're getting closer,' voxed Metzger. 'They're using smoke from the wrecks to bridge the distance.'

'Stay calm, you dirty fetcher,' snapped Holtz. 'Keep firing. The sarge won't let them get on top of us.'

'You bet I won't,' added Wulfe, but he saw how quickly the gap was closing. There were just too damned many of them. Sooner or later, they'd get close enough to tag the tanks with high-explosives, or some monster with a flamethrower would press the nozzle of his weapon to a ventilation slit and cook them all alive.

We can't keep this up, thought Wulfe. Strieber, you idiot. If you hadn't hamstrung yourself....

But Strieber's tank *was* hamstrung, and Wulfe was quickly realising that this battle couldn't be won. The mission clock kept ticking. There just wasn't time to fight this one out. And Strieber couldn't hope to re-tread his tank under fire. *Last Rites*, *Champion of Cerbera* and the black Chimera had to break through now.

They had to leave *Steelhearted* behind.

Wulfe saw another armoured half-track, overloaded with roaring ork infantry, break from the circle and make straight towards his tank. Metzger fired a blast from the lascannon, but the truck's thick front armour soaked it up. Wulfe called out to Viess and the gunner swung the turret around with no time to spare.

'She's lit,' shouted Siegler.

Viess didn't hesitate. His left foot stamped on the firing pedal. *Last Rites* bounced on her suspension as her battle-cannon spat its deadly payload straight into the driver's cab of the enemy machine.

A flash. A boom. An earthshaking explosion at point-blank range. Metallic clattering sounded on the roof of the tank as a shower of burning junk and body parts rained down.

'Good shot,' voxed Metzger with obvious relief.

'Great shot,' Viess corrected.

Wulfe was more concerned with the dense cloud of black smoke that was rolling over them from the blazing frame of the ruined enemy vehicle. 'We can't see a blasted thing now. They'll be coming straight for us. Sponson gunners, stay sharp!'

He used the plural out of habit, and the loss of Garver suddenly stung him. They hadn't been particularly close, not like he and Borscht, but the sponson gunner had been crew. Love them or hate them, crew was family.

Dessembra's voice sounded in Wulfe's ears. 'We can't stay here. Move out, now!'

'We must thin them out more,' Wulfe voxed back. Adrenaline was surging through him, making his blood sing. 'At least enough to give Strieber a fighting chance.'

'Priorities, sergeant,' hissed Dessembra. 'There's nothing you can do for him. Look to your rear. We have to go at once!'

Wulfe checked the rear-facing vision blocks and felt his battle-rush bleed off in an instant. It was obvious now. The bikes and buggies were just a diversion, intended to harry the tanks and slow them down while the real firepower closed off the canyon at either end. Grinding its way south-east along the road was a loose formation of ork war machines – massive, heavily armoured and bristling with fat-barrelled cannon.

Wulfe was filled with rage as he looked at them – at least half of the enemy armour had been built from the looted carcasses of fallen Imperial machines. The foul xenos had mutilated and desecrated them.

Under thick plates of armour bolted on at all angles, he saw the familiar forms of a Basilisk mobile-artillery platform, three Chimera transports, and a disfigured Leman Russ. Other vehicles in the formation seemed entirely built from scratch to some maniacal alien design.

'By the blasted Eye!' he spat. Demonstrating impressive aptitude for their kind, the orks had managed to outflank him.

The canyon shook with a ripple of ork cannon fire. 'Incoming!' shouted Wulfe. Explosive shells rained down on the highway. The resulting detonations sent up great clouds of dirt and debris, but little else. The ork cannonade was falling far short of its target, but that wouldn't be the case for much longer.

'Emperor above!' voxed Sergeant Kohl. 'They're fielding heavy artillery!'

'We break through now,' voxed Wulfe, 'or we're dead men.'

Strieber was almost screaming over the vox. 'You can't be serious, Wulfe. You can't possibly leave us here. You can't!'

Wulfe felt sick to his stomach as he answered. 'I'm sorry, Strieber. We're out of options.'

'My tank, my crew – we're *Gunheads*, damn you! Don't you run from this fight. Don't you turn away from us, you rotten bastard!'

There was another rumble of thunder from the ork cannons. The impact blasts were much closer this time. *Last Rites* was showered with dirt. The enemy armour continued to zero in.

Wulfe spoke through clenched teeth. 'Lead us out, Metzger. Full ahead. Keep her off the highway. There'll be other mines there. Siegler, load her up. Armour-piercing. Viess, get ready to break a hole in them. They'll not stop us here!'

'Throne blast you, Wulfe!' screeched Strieber.

'I'm sorry, Strieber. I truly am. But you must see that there's no other way. Keep firing. Keep fighting. Help us break through, and I promise the regiment will remember and honour your sacrifice. It's all I can offer you now.'

Last Rites lurched into motion just before another volley of heavy shells shook the canyon floor. With a sudden convulsion of dirt and rock, a great shell-crater appeared where she'd stood only a moment before. The ork armour was now in range, and still the bikes and buggies raced forward with insane abandon, uselessly spraying the Imperial tanks with volleys of stubber-fire.

In subdued tones, Strieber voxed, 'Good luck then, Wulfe. We'll fight on for as long as we can. I… I hope you make it back to Banphry.'

Viess shouted 'Brace!' and fired the tank's main gun. Three hundred metres away, a bastardized ork Chimera was violently peeled apart. Beside Siegler, the cannon's breech slid back, dumping the empty shell-casing in the brass-catcher on the floor. With servitor-like efficiency, the loader slid a fresh armour-piercing shell into the breech, yanked the lever, and shouted, 'Lit!'

Metzger shifted the tank up into third gear, accelerating out past the crippled *Steelhearted*. Viess swung the turret left, zeroing in on a bulky ork battlewagon. He adjusted for elevation, compensated for the tank's forward motion, prayed to the Emperor for a clean kill, and fired. *Last Rites* skewed to the right with the force of the cannon's recoil, but didn't slow. The round slashed brightly though the air, then buried itself deep in the body of the ork machine. It must have pierced the battlewagon's fuel tanks, because the vehicle was blown so high it flipped onto its roof. Flaming wreckage and charred bodies littered the land and roaring fires blazed from its twisted metal carcass.

Champion of Cerbera and the black Chimera followed close behind *Last Rites*. Wulfe saw a tongue of fire flash out from Kohl's battle-cannon. The ork-modified Leman Russ on the far left rolled to a stop, smoke billowing from a large hole in its turret armour. A moment later, flames erupted from inside. Burning alien bodies began tumbling out of the vehicle's hatches, but it was too late for them. The roasted greenskin crew twitched, then lay still on the sand.

'Keep firing,' ordered Wulfe. 'We're almost through.'

They roared past the chugging ork tanks, narrowly dodging a fusillade of high-explosive shells and rockets. Viess fired directly into the nearest, blowing the entire front section up into the air in a fiery spin. Kohl's tank spat again and crippled another with a shot that shredded its right track-assembly. The black Chimera was firing constantly, but her multilaser could do little damage to the enemy's heavy armour. Instead, Dessembra targeted a large, open-topped truck and managed to slaughter a score of ork infantry.

Then they were through. The canyon lay behind them and open lands stretched out ahead.

The heavy ork machines turned to follow, but they were far slower than the well-oiled Imperial tanks. Only the surviving bikes and buggies had the speed to give chase. They charged forward in pursuit, many of them forgetting the mines that their own warband had laid on the highway surface. Those that weren't blown to pieces closed the gap quickly, but their weapons were inadequate. As *Last Rites*, *Champion of Cerbera* and the black Chimera sped away, Wulfe ordered Viess to turn the turret and pick off their lightly armoured pursuers with the co-axial autocannon.

Wulfe noticed a blinking light on his vox-board. It was Kohl. He was calling on a closed channel. Whatever he had to say, it wasn't for Dessembra's ears.

Wulfe opened the link. 'What is it, sergeant?'

'I'm going back,' said Kohl.

'You're *what*?'

'Think about it, Wulfe. The orks will chase us all the way to Ghotenz unless they have a fight to hold them here.' There was a pause. 'Besides, I've got blinking lights all over the place. We took a big one on the rear decking. The cooling system's almost out and so is the extractor. We can break down halfway to the objective, or we can turn back and buy you some time. I'd rather go out fighting, if it's all the same to you. Maybe we can help Strieber and his crew go out in style.'

Wulfe didn't know how to respond. He felt hollow.

'Get those damned women to Ghotenz,' Kohl voxed. 'Complete the mission for the honour of the regiment, if nothing else. You can still make it off-world if you don't mess about.'

Wulfe wished he could believe it. He'd stopped looking at his chronometer. It only offered bad news. The orks had cost them so much, and not just in terms of time. A voice in his head told him to follow Kohl's example, to die honourably alongside his fellow Gunheads. But another told him that the honour of the regiment had to come first. He had to see the mission through.

'What do I tell Dessembra?' he asked Kohl.

'The truth. I'll give those green bastards plenty to do, by the Throne. They won't be missing you.'

Honour and sacrifice. Wulfe saw that he'd been misjudging Kohl for years, blinded to the man's nobility by his icy manner. Whatever Kohl's flaws, he was a true soldier and a man of uncompromising bravery.

If I survive this mess, Wulfe promised himself, *I'll make sure van Droi puts Kohl and Strieber up for the Medallion Crimson. It's not much, but it's something.*

Kohl didn't wait for any kind of approval. Through the rear vision-blocks, Wulfe saw *Champion of Cerbera* peel off and swing back around towards the canyon. Soon, she was lost in her own dust cloud.

Last Rites and the black Chimera raced on in the other direction. Dessembra was hailing Wulfe on the mission channel and, reluctantly, he opened the link.

'I demand to know what's going on! Why won't Sergeant Kohl answer me?'

Wulfe didn't bother to keep the tiredness and frustration from his voice as he replied, 'Sergeant Kohl is ensuring our escape. His tank is badly damaged. He has decided to give his life and the lives of his crew for the success of this mission.'

Dessembra paused. 'That's… acceptable,' she said. 'Let's take advantage of it.'

Wulfe couldn't contain his contempt any longer. 'Listen to me, Sororitas,' he hissed over the vox. 'Whoever we're supposed to rescue at Ghotenz had better be a bloody saint reborn, because you and your damned superiors have a hell of a lot to answer for. Do you hear me?'

He cut the connection before she could respond.

33 kilometres north-west of Ghotenz, East Vestiche, 5.09 local (8 hours 38 minutes to Planetkill)

WITH THE CLOCK driving her hard, *Last Rites* churned up the surface of the highway, but not so fast that Wulfe could outrun his guilt and anger. His thoughts were on the men he'd left behind. The absence of Garver's voice, in particular, pained him as he knew it must pain the rest of his crew.

He was still shaken, too, by his vision of old Borscht. Since the battle in the canyon, Viess had been pressing for an explanation. How had he known to stop the tank? What had he seen from his cupola? Whose voice had he heard?

The others added their own questions now. Wulfe wished they'd let it go, but they wouldn't. In the end, he exploded at them, ordering them to shut their mouths and concentrate on the job in hand. The mention of Commissar Cortez was enough to put an end to it, at least temporarily.

Wulfe didn't grudge them their curiosity. It was only natural. But he couldn't reconcile himself with what he'd seen and heard. Borscht was in a hospital bed back in Banphry. There were no two ways about it. On the other hand, Wulfe wasn't about to concede insanity, either.

Metzger's voice sounded over his headset, announcing their proximity to the primary mission objective. Ghotenz was less than an hour away. That helped Wulfe to centre his thoughts a little.

It was mid-afternoon now, and the air inside the turret was stiflingly hot. Wulfe ordered all the hatches open, making an immediate difference. He rode up in the cupola and, as *Last Rites* and the black Chimera approached the low hills that sheltered the town, he watched his tank's shadow gradually lengthen on the road in front of him as the sun moved ever westwards.

Only eight hours left until the first massive impact shook this world. In the global firestorm, every living thing would be blasted to ash. It would be a quick, merciful death for most, but it was no soldier's death. There was no glory in it.

'There's something on the road up ahead, sir,' reported Metzger.

Wulfe scanned the highway and spotted the object in question. Metzger had good eyes. There was something approaching, large and dark, but indistinct. As the two Imperial machines sped closer to it, the shape resolved itself into the form of a great, shaggy boviath, three metres tall at its massive, hunched shoulders and just as broad. Six curving black horns framed its leathery face. It dragged a large cart, filled with people, up the highway towards them. Wulfe counted twenty passengers, most of them adults.

Last Rites pulled up beside the cart and Wulfe ordered its driver to halt. The cart's driver shouted something to his beast and, with a deep, resonating moan, the boviath slowed to a stop. Every man, woman and child in the cart turned their eyes towards Wulfe, but it was a tall, ugly woman in the gaudy robes of the Palmerosi merchant class who addressed him.

'You've come, then,' she said. 'You've come to stop it.'

Wulfe locked eyes with her. 'To stop what, *udoche*?' As was proper here, he used the local term for a woman one doesn't wish to court. A short, bearded man seated beside her, presumably her husband, nodded his approval.

'The madness, of course,' answered the woman. 'Ghotenz is in utter chaos. The riots. The killings. We were lucky to get out alive.' At these words, some of the men in the cart patted old civilian-model laslocks.

So the townsfolk are rioting, thought Wulfe. Great!

'Thank you for your warning, udoche,' he said. 'We'll do what we can. But where are you going?'

'We're going to evacuate. We've heard of vast ships at Banphry and intend to buy our passage off-world.'

Just for a moment, Wulfe considered telling them the truth. They'd never make it to Banphry. Even if they had time, even if there were no orks on the road ahead, no amount of money would help them. They were doomed. But perhaps it was kinder to let their hopes carry them to the end.

'Be careful on the highway,' he told them. 'There may be greenskins in Lugo's Ditch.'

'I've yet to see one of these *green-kin*,' said the woman. 'But the pamphlets say loud shouting is weapon enough against them.' She jabbed her thumb at a barrel-chested man in the back of the cart. 'Brudegar has the loudest voice in Ghotenz. He'll drive the aliens from our path.'

Wulfe gave an involuntary shake of his head. This kind of fatal ignorance was the Imperial propaganda machine at its worst. Citizens rarely knew the danger orks represented until they were bearing down on them roaring 'Waaagh!' and all the shouting in the Imperium wouldn't do a damned thing.

Conscious of the black Chimera idling impatiently behind him, Wulfe waved the locals on, and the cart-driver cracked his whip. The massive boviath brayed and began hauling its burden off up the highway, and the Imperial vehicles resumed their journey.

Black smoke could be seen now, rising into the afternoon sky from just beyond the next hill. Only a few kilometres separated them from their objective.

Riots, the woman had said. And killings.

Wulfe steeled himself, thinking that perhaps the least pleasant phase of this whole fiasco might yet lie ahead.

Ghotenz, East Vestiche,
16.02 local (7 hours 45 minutes to Planetkill)

HE WAS RIGHT.

Ghotenz, when he saw it, was a town lost to anarchy. Bloated corpses lay strewn about the base of the old-fashioned curtain wall, rotting in the afternoon heat. Flocks of floating maldrothids, indigenous carrion-feeders, had descended from the sky to gorge themselves on the reeking dead. These strange creatures floated three metres above the ground, plucking soft gobbets of human flesh from the bodies below. Their tentacles, each tipped with a sharp beak, lifted morsels of meat to obscene pink mouths while fat flies buzzed around them.

The spectacle was stomach-churning, and so was the smell. Fighting the urge to vomit, Wulfe thumbed his laspistol's safety off, took aim, and fired into the nearest flock.

He struck one of the maldrothids dead-centre, his shot igniting the creature's internal gases. Its sac-like body exploded with a pop.

Others nearby immediately began pushing off from the ground with their long tentacles. They rose into the air to drift away in search of a safer meal.

'By the Throne,' voxed Holtz from his sponson. 'They're foul, unholy things!'

Outside the gatehouse, his back resting against a stone wall, there sat an old, sun-browned man with a wounded leg. Beside him lay a battered laslock. Judging by the number of empty green bottles surrounding him, he was about the business of drinking himself to death.

As the mighty form of *Last Rites* loomed over him, the man reached drunkenly for his weapon, missed it twice, and gave up. 'Wha'dya want, stranger?' he asked, squinting up at Wulfe. 'Have y'come here to die with the folks the Emp'ror forsook?'

Wulfe scowled down at him. 'Watch your tongue, citizen. The Emperor only forsakes traitors and heretics.'

The old man made a rude noise and resumed his drinking.

Wulfe cursed him for a fool and ordered *Last Rites* through the town's open gates with Dessembra's vehicle following a steady ten metres behind.

As they passed into the town, Wulfe swept his pintle-mounted heavy stubber from right to left, covering the corners of the streets and alley-ways they passed. Then he remembered that Garver was dead and that the tank's right flank was open. 'Stay alert, all of you,' he told his crew. 'Holtz, I want that heavy bolter covering side streets, windows, doors. Viess, same goes for the co-ax. I'll keep an eye on our right.'

Fires still burned in some of the buildings. They passed walls bearing hastily scrawled slogans like *What frakking Emperor?* and *Fine day for an apocalypse!* Most of the stores and stalls had been looted. Rows of squat yellow habs sat silent and still, their windows shattered, their doors splintered. Lifeless bodies hung from bloodstained windowsills and balconies. The streets themselves were dotted with so many corpses that *Last Rites* couldn't avoid them. Wulfe ordered Metzger to drive over them, grimacing every time a wet crunch sounded from underneath the tank. Many of the bodies on the street were women, their clothing shredded. The crack of laslocks and autopistols rang out frequently, sending frightened maldrothids up into the air, abandoning the rich pickings until things settled down.

All this carnage, thought Wulfe, *is the work of man. There's no sign of an ork hand in any of this.*

Only recently, Ghotenz had been a town of dedicated, hard-working Imperial citizens. Foreknowledge of their doom had shattered that. Word of the coming end had unravelled their civilisation faster than any xenos invasion ever could have.

Dessembra's voice broke through the static on the mission channel. 'Turn left at the next corner, sergeant,' she said, 'then take your second right. Our objective awaits us in the church at the end of Procession Street.'

Wulfe relayed the orders to Metzger and the tank rolled on. The sound of gunfire was more frequent now. It was getting closer, too.

As *Last Rites* turned onto Procession Street, Wulfe's jaw dropped. Up ahead, in the square at the end of the street, a violent riot was raging. The focus of the mob's ire was a small Imperial church – a black two-storey structure with a proud golden aquila perched atop its central spire. Wulfe watched in horror as some of the rioters fired at the sacred icon. On the wide stone steps below, people shouted and jeered, and launched rocks and bottles at the building's stained-glass windows.

'They're attacking the church!' snarled Wulfe.

From her Chimera, Dessembra must have seen it too. 'Forward, sergeant,' she ordered. 'They mustn't get inside. Kill every last one of them if you have to.'

Last Rites charged down Procession Street.

The rioters turned. Many who saw her bearing down on them fled screaming into the shadowed side-streets, but others were more foolish. They swung their weapons around and began peppering her hull with small-arms fire.

Shots ricocheted around Wulfe, but he stayed in his cupola, anger galvanizing him. Setting his heavy stubber to full-auto, he swept the barrel from left to right, spraying the mob with enfilading fire. A hailstorm of lead cut through the apostate ranks, ripping into their unprotected bodies. Screams of pain filled the air. Those who weren't killed or wounded leapt for hard cover then leaned out from stone corners to take hopeless pot-shots at the tank.

The left sponson rattled back at them, its heavy bolter chewing apart their inadequate defences, killing them in a blizzard of stone chips.

Behind him, Wulfe heard the rapid cracking of the Chimera's multi-laser and the chattering of her hull-mounted gun. Between them, the two Imperial vehicles unleashed an overwhelming barrage on the street and its buildings.

Less than a minute later, Wulfe ordered his men to cease fire. Procession Street was a silent, blood-soaked wasteland. The only thing moving was the smoke that curled from the muzzles of Imperial guns.

With the mission clock never far from his mind, he glanced down at his pocket chronometer. About seven hours left. Whatever the bloody Sororitas have come here to do, he thought, they'd better do it quickly. There was still the return journey to contend with. They couldn't pass through Lugo's Ditch again. That would be suicide.

'Forward,' he voxed to Metzger.

With the immediate threat neutralized, the two vehicles approached the church. Sister Superior Dessembra ordered them to a halt at the bottom of the steps. Seconds later, the Chimera's rear hatch was thrown open and the three sisters hospitaller emerged into the dry afternoon air.

'Secure the area, Sergeant Wulfe,' Dessembra called out as she stepped over a twitching body. Some of the wounded rioters were still alive, but only just. 'Nothing must disturb us.'

Each of the women, Wulfe saw, carried a sealed ceramite case marked with twin insignia: the winged and laurelled Cadian Gate symbol of the 18th Army Group, and the distinctive fleur-de-lys of the Adeptus Sororitas.

'Metzger,' voxed Wulfe, 'get her ready for a hasty exit. Holtz, stay sharp. Viess, use the co-ax. Siegler, get up into this cupola and man the stubber. Cover the blind spots. Nothing gets close enough to threaten the tank or the Chimera. Is that understood?'

With a quick check of the charge-pack in his laspistol, he leapt down from the hull of his tank and strode up the church steps after the three women. Halfway up, he turned to take a quick look at the tank's right sponson. It was a mess of twisted, blackened metal. Wulfe shook his head. If there was anything left of Garver inside, it wouldn't be much.

Loud creaking announced the opening of the church doors. Wulfe continued up the steps, stopped behind Sister Urahlis, and saw a thin, sallow-faced man in a burgundy robe peering out at them from within. Seeing the insignia on Dessembra's robes, the man smiled and opened the door wider, ushering them in.

'Frater Gustav,' said Sister Superior Dessembra. 'Tell me, does the man live?'

'He lives, sister superior,' replied Gustav in a high, scratchy voice. 'I've been ministering to him in the undercroft, but I lack the skills to do much good.'

The sisters moved inside and Wulfe followed, stepping beyond the heavy wooden doors to find the church filled with people. They knelt on low wooden benches facing the glittering golden altar. They were deep in prayer.

The faithful, thought Wulfe. While the town fell into madness, they took shelter in this sacred house. That, at least, is as it should be.

On his left, Dessembra and the thin priest were talking as they descended a dark stone stairwell followed by the two sister-acolytes. 'You did a great thing when you reported his whereabouts, frater,' Dessembra was saying. 'The man is critical to the war effort in this sector.'

Uninvited and unnoticed, Wulfe hurried after them, following them along a short, dark corridor to a gloomy chamber under the church.

There, in a room lit by hundreds of flickering candles, was the answer to a question Wulfe had first asked back in van Droi's command tent: who were they expected to rescue? The man's identity was no longer classified.

Captain Waltur Kurdheim, only surviving son of General Argos Kurdheim, lay groaning and shivering on a makeshift bed.

The captain's ageing father was a High Strategos in the Officio Tacticae. He'd been attached to Army Group *Exolon* for years. If anyone had the authority to send Imperial tanks on such a reckless mission for personal reasons, it was the hawk-faced old general.

Dessembra moved swiftly to the captain's bedside and checked his pulse, then gestured sharply at Urahlis and Mellahd. 'Quickly, sisters. Open the cases. I need 10cc's of paralycium and 15cc's of gamalthide.'

Wulfe crossed to the opposite side of the young captain's bed. 'By the Eye, sister superior,' he said. 'He's in bad shape. What's wrong with him?'

Dessembra looked up as if seeing Wulfe for the first time. 'What are you doing here, sergeant? Get out at once. You mustn't be in here. Get out, Throne curse you!'

Before Wulfe could respond, he felt a weak hand grip his forearm. It was Captain Kurdheim's. Wulfe looked down into wide brown eyes filled with fear.

'The frater betrayed me,' rasped Kurdheim. 'Don't leave me to them, soldier. If you've any honour in you...'

Wulfe looked at the pale white hand on his arm. 'Rest easy, captain,' he said. 'These women are sisters hospitaller of the Order of Serenity. Medical specialists. They've come to save you.'

Kurdheim pulled his hand away. 'Fool,' he coughed. 'They're my father's lapdogs. He's the only man they came to save.'

Wulfe looked at Dessembra, his frown communicating his confusion.

'He's badly wounded, sergeant,' she said, pulling back the bloodstained sheets. Wulfe saw a big wet bandage on the captain's side. 'His company was lost four days ago on the far side of the Yucharian Mountains. It's a miracle that he made it here. Now, please, step outside and let us do our work.'

Wulfe trusted Dessembra about as far as he could throw an auroch, and he liked her even less, but he could find no legitimate excuse to stay. He left as ordered, but a nagging voice remained in his head. Something wasn't right. Captain Kurdheim hadn't seemed confused at all. His eyes had been sharp and bright, despite his obvious pain. And the fear in them... Wulfe knew real fear when he saw it.

Rather than return to his tank, he stationed himself on the other side of the undercroft door. The sisters would need help, he rationalised, in carrying the young captain up to the Chimera.

Moments later, the screams began. The first was so sudden and unexpected that Wulfe almost leapt into the air. He burst back into the undercroft with his laspistol drawn, but what he saw stopped him dead.

Captain Kurdheim lay under his sheets as before, only now they were utterly drenched with blood. The whole chamber stank of it. Transparent tubes snaked out from under the sheets to a boxy medical device that sat in an open case on the floor. The young captain was screaming through gritted teeth as some kind of thick, viscous substance was being siphoned from his paralysed body and collected inside the machine.

As Wulfe stood stunned and horrified, following the flow of the grey-pink fluid down the transparent tubes, he saw four pale shapes in the shadows by the foot of the bed.

It can't be, he thought. Throne above, it can't!

It was difficult to tell in the low light, but they looked uncomfortably like severed hands and feet.

Wulfe raised his pistol towards the ceiling and fired off a shot. The crack of ionised air was deafening in the small chamber. The women started. Frater Gustav let out a frightened whimper.

Dessembra spun to face Wulfe, anger twisting her fleshy features. 'I told you to stay outside, you dolt. Don't interfere!'

'Ball-rot, sister,' Wulfe spat back. 'That man is a Cadian officer and, from the sounds of it, you're torturing him to death. You'd better have a damned fine explanation for this.'

'You're out of your depth, sergeant. I was assured by your superiors that you'd comply.' Dessembra turned to Sister Mellahd. 'Show him our orders.'

'But they're classified, sister superior,' protested Mellahd.

'Do it, blast you, girl!'

The shapely young Sororitas bowed to her superior, then lifted a rolled parchment from one of the ceramite cases and held it out to Wulfe. 'It's all here, sergeant,' she said. 'See for yourself.'

Without lowering his weapon, Wulfe looked over the scroll. What he read filled him with outrage. The young captain was right – these women hadn't come to save him at all.

They'd come to save his father.

The scroll avoided naming General Kurdheim's particular condition – perhaps it was a source of some embarrassment – but it was very specific about the nature of the cure. Fresh marrow had to be extracted from his son's living body. The scroll listed drugs approved for the procedure, but Wulfe couldn't find any anaesthetics among them. A line in bold red script said something about anaesthesium denaturing important elements of the extracted marrow, but the medical jargon was far too deep for Wulfe to tackle. It was clear, however, that *Exolon* High Command had given full authorisation to this horrific operation. Penalties for failure were listed at the bottom. Anyone interfering in the retrieval of the young captain's bone marrow would be executed publicly as a traitor.

'This is sick,' said Wulfe. 'He's conscious, for Throne's sake.'

Dessembra spoke without turning. 'The captain will make this sacrifice for his father, whether he wishes to or not. General Kurdheim is an important man. His survival is critical to our success in this sector. His son, on the other hand, is expendable. Think logically, sergeant, and you'll see that it makes perfect sense.'

Thick fluids continued to drain from Kurdheim's body, sliding down the transparent tubing and into the humming machine. Something clogged one of the tubes and Sister Urahlis moved forward to adjust it. As she did so, the captain howled in agony.

Wulfe's face was twisted with pity and rage. This was too much. He pointed the barrel of his laspistol straight at the captain's head and said, 'I can free you from your misery, sir. Just say the word! Order it!'

In the blink of an eye, Dessembra had positioned herself between the pistol and the paralysed officer, blocking Wulfe's shot. 'The marrow must be taken from a living body,' she said, her eyes boring into Wulfe's. 'Do you want to give him peace, sergeant? Do you really want to cut this operation short prematurely? Think about it. You're gambling with the lives of your crew. You saw the paper. If we don't get back to Banphry before that first rock hits, we die. If we return without the marrow, we die. And if you return without me, I can promise you that the Commissariat will be waiting for you. And you will die.'

Wulfe's hand was shaking. He itched to kill this woman. How could such a monster claim to serve the righteous Golden Throne? Do it, his conscience urged. Kill her. End this man's agony and punish this dreadful woman for the lives she's already cost Gossefried's Gunheads.

But Wulfe knew he couldn't condemn his crew. To kill Dessembra was to kill all of them. And, as Dessembra watched the realisation show on his face, she knew she had him. With an infuriating grin, she said, 'Leave this chamber now, sergeant. We'll be finished shortly. Have the vehicles ready to move out on my word.'

Hating himself for it, Wulfe holstered his pistol and turned from the room. As he walked stiffly up the stone stairs, he tried to block out the captain's screams, but it was hard. The young man was yelling Wulfe's name over and over, cursing him to the darkest corners of the warp.

Ghotenz, East Vestiche,
17.17 local (6 hours 30 minutes to Planetkill)

WULFE EMERGED FROM the church to find the sun low on the western horizon. The sky was filled with a watery glow, casting the ravaged town in hues of reddish gold. In front of *Last Rites*, dozens of townsfolk had gathered, kneeling with their hands on top of their heads while Siegler covered them with the pintle-mounted heavy stubber.

Wulfe climbed his tank to stand on the engine decking, just behind the turret, and said, 'What's going on here?'

'Locals, sir,' said Siegler. 'They presented themselves while you were inside. Waving white flags, they were. They've come to ask for help.'

'After the attack on the church?'

'They say they had nothing to do with the riots, sir. Busy defending their homes.'

A dark-skinned man kneeling at the front of the group eyed Wulfe, spotted the silver pips on his lapels and said, 'Forgive me, sir, but would you be the officer in charge?' He was middle-aged, muscular and wore the uniform of a town custodian.

Law enforcement, thought Wulfe. Where was *he* during the riot?

'I'm no officer,' he replied. 'But I'm in charge, after a fashion.'

'Then, may we stand?' asked the custodian. 'There are elders among us. We've not come to threaten you or your men.'

Without lowering his voice, Wulfe said, 'Keep them covered, Siegler.' Then to the crowd he said, 'Stand if you wish.'

Slowly, they got to their feet. Some needed help to rise. The custodian took a step closer to Wulfe's tank and said, 'Ships have been crossing the sky in greater numbers than usual today. Some of the merchants fled west, talking about evacuation, and we've all heard about the asteroids and the coming end. We thought… Have you come to help us?'

Wulfe had to lie. He knew that much. *Last Rites* still had to make it out of here in one piece. Let these people believe whatever they wanted if it served that purpose. False hope was better than genuine despair, wasn't it?

'We've come to Ghotenz on other business,' said Wulfe, 'but I can tell you that a Naval lifter is scheduled to arrive here later this evening. Have no fear. The ship will come in plenty of time. But you must be ready to leave.'

Excited muttering swept through the crowd. Wulfe tried not to look at them for fear of seeing relief on their faces. In the last twelve hours, his self-respect had been eroded almost to nothing. He had begun to hate himself, and there was more to come.

'You'll each have a personal cargo allowance of twelve kilograms,' he told them, cementing the lie. 'It's not much, I know, but it's better than nothing. No weapons of any kind may be taken aboard. No plants or animals are permitted.'

'Where should we gather?' asked a woman on the right. 'We don't want to waste any time.'

'The bhakra fields south-west of the town seem best suited to a landing,' said Wulfe. 'I recommend that you assemble there.'

'This is wonderful news,' said another woman behind the custodian. 'Praise the Emperor!'

The rest of the crowd took up the cheer.

Automatically, Wulfe did the same, but there was a bitter taste in his mouth. 'You should return to your homes now,' he called down to them. 'Our vehicles will be leaving momentarily and our way must be clear.'

'Why don't you wait to be lifted out with us?' asked the custodian. 'Your men must be tired and hungry.'

'Thank you,' said Wulfe. 'But our work isn't finished. We have another stop to make before we can evacuate.'

More mutters rippled through the crowd, this time filled with respect and sympathy.

The custodian turned to the townsfolk and said, 'Let's disperse, people. Back to your homes, now. We must all pack for the evacuation.'

After saluting Wulfe with something like parade-ground pomp, the custodian led the crowd away from the square. Their excited chatter filled the street until they disappeared from view.

Siegler turned to Wulfe and asked, 'Are we ready to move out, sir?'

Wulfe looked for it, but Siegler's expression was void of any criticism. 'We're just waiting on–'

The old church doors creaked loudly behind him, and the sisters hospitaller emerged into the fading sunlight. Frater Gustav followed them out. Screams and curses, barely discernable over the noise of the idling tank, still issued from within the church. Wulfe leapt down from the rear decking and climbed the church stairs once more.

Dessembra turned at the door and took the thin priest's hands in her own. 'The Emperor will reward you soon, frater,' she said. 'But one last thing, please. Lugo's Ditch is held by the foe, and we must reach The Gold Road some other way.'

Gustav nodded. 'There is an old trade route, sister superior, that we used before the highway was built. Follow the dirt track north at first. A series of switchbacks will take you up into the highlands, ending just east of Gormann's Point. You can rejoin the Gold Road there.'

'How long will it take?' Dessembra asked.

'From what you've told me, sister superior, you'll be cutting it fine, but it will save you the trouble of the canyon.'

Wulfe stormed over to the small group and thrust his face in front of Dessembra's. 'Finished mutilating Cadian officers, are we?'

Dessembra's expression hardened in a flash. 'Watch your tongue, sergeant. We have what we came for, if that's what you mean.'

'Then why in the warp is the man still screaming?'

Dessembra tried to push past him, but Wulfe's hand flashed out and grasped her wrist. She struggled for a moment, but the sergeant's grip was like iron. The sister-acolytes stepped forward to intervene, but the cold fire in Wulfe's eyes made them hesitate.

'Unhand me, damn you,' spat Dessembra. 'Not that it's any of your business, sergeant, but General Kurdheim was quite clear on the matter. His son will be allowed the honour of dying with this planet and its many faithful martyrs.'

Wulfe felt like striking the woman in her fat face. 'The honour of what? He's in absolute hell. Can't you hear that?'

Echoing up from the below the church, the captain's screams were gut-wrenching. 'His suffering will atone for his unwillingness to do his duty,' said Dessembra. 'He'll go before the Emperor with a clear conscience.'

Maybe it was Dessembra's voicing of the word, but Wulfe found he couldn't suppress his own conscience any longer. He'd done far too much of that already today. Releasing Dessembra and shoving Frater Gustav violently aside, he marched back into the church, drawing his laspistol as he moved.

'Get back here, sergeant,' screeched Dessembra. 'The general's orders were very specific. You'll face a court martial for this!'

Wulfe didn't stop. Looking over his shoulder, he called out, 'This is supposed to be a mercy run, you fat grox. And mercy is what I intend to give him.'

Moments later, the sharp crack of a laspistol rang out from the undercroft.

26 kilometres north of Ghotenz, East Vestiche, 17.53 local (5 hours 54 minutes to Planetkill)

THEY FOLLOWED THE frater's suggested route back to the highway without encountering the enemy, but the sky was darkening quickly, and Wulfe felt time slipping away from him like water through his fingers. The road up into the highlands was hard, and lesser vehicles would have struggled – sure-footed boviaths were far better suited to it – but the muscular engines of the Imperial war-machines had enough grunt for the job. There were some hair-raising moments. Twice, while turning hairpin bends, *Last Rites* almost slid from the steep, narrow trail. She would have plummeted, smashing her crew to death inside her, had Metzger not demonstrated remarkable skills. Even Holtz, still convinced that the new man was a doombringer, felt compelled to pay him a terse compliment.

To Wulfe's great relief, the land soon flattened out. They turned westward just six kilometres south of the old outpost under a night sky dusted with bright, winking stars. Some of those stars were moving – naval transports and escort ships leaving orbit with all haste.

Emperor above, thought Wulfe as he gazed up through his open hatch, let the last ship wait for us.

The vox was quiet. Wulfe watched the other men in the turret struggle with their growing sense of desperation. Siegler was rocking back and forth in his chair, muttering mathematical problems in an attempt to divert his mind. Viess was patting the turret wall beside him and cooing, 'Faster, old girl! You can do it!'

Wulfe watched the second hand spinning on his chronometer, willing it to slow down, but it seemed to get faster instead. The background static of the tank's intercom hissed in his ear, broken only by affirmations when he issued occasional orders to Metzger or general reminders to stay on the lookout for any signs of a firefight out there in the dark. The only orks they spotted, however, were the occasional green bodies on the road. They were surrounded by human corpses. Wulfe guessed a warband had swept north towards Zimmamar, slaughtering any refugees caught in its path.

The tank's headlamps occasionally picked out flocks of maldrothids floating silently in the dark, feasting on the recently deceased. Holtz and Viess, either offended by the sight or just eager to distract themselves, requested permission to fire on the eerie scavengers, but Wulfe wouldn't have it. Gunfire and muzzle flashes might draw unwanted attention. He imagined orks crouched by the roadside in the dark, just waiting for a target to come along.

About halfway between Gormann's Point and Banphry, with a little over seventy kilometres still to go, Dessembra voxed him. 'You must realise, sergeant,' she said, 'that at this speed, there's no hope of catching our ride out.'

'I hope you're not suggesting we give up,' replied Wulfe sourly. 'She's not built for speed, but my man is squeezing everything he can out of her.'

'I'm sure he is, but I think you're missing my point. My Chimera is lighter and capable of far higher speeds than your tank. Since I believe we're no longer under direct threat from orks, and no longer require your protection, I'm ordering my driver to break formation and pull ahead of you. It's imperative that our cargo reaches General Kurdheim. I'm sure you understand.'

There we have it, thought Wulfe. I should have expected no less from you, Dessembra.

'Emperor's speed to you, then,' he voxed back coldly.

The Chimera pulled out of *Last Rites*'s slipstream, charged past her on the right, and pulled back in directly ahead of her. Contrary to Wulfe's expectations, however, the black transport didn't accelerate away.

'Stop your tank,' ordered Dessembra.

'What?'

'I said stop your tank, sergeant. Order your man to pull up at once.'

Wulfe did as he was told. Viess and Siegler turned to give him nervous looks. The last thing they could afford to do right now was to lose forward momentum.

The Chimera slid to a halt on the road ahead, starkly illuminated by *Last Rites*'s headlamps. A heartbeat later, the rear hatch opened. Dessembra appeared in the glaring white light, gesturing impatiently.

'Get a move on, sergeant,' she voxed. 'If you and your men aren't onboard in less than a minute…'

Wulfe could hardly believe his ears. 'Everybody out on the double,' he ordered. 'Into the Chimera, damn you. Don't stop to take anything!'

Hatch doors clanged as they were flung open. Wulfe hauled himself up and out of his cupola in time to see Metzger scramble from his hatch at the front of the tank. Holtz launched himself backwards through his sponson hatch and landed on his back with a grunt. No time for graceful exits.

Wulfe raced over to the Chimera's rear door and stood there, yelling at his men to double-time it. Only when they were all inside did he enter, slamming the hatch shut and locking it. He heard Dessembra say, 'Full-ahead please, Corporal Fichtner!' and the vehicle leapt forward with a sudden burst of acceleration.

Dessembra moved through the cramped passenger compartment until she was standing before Wulfe. She nodded to him once, then, without breaking eye contact, lowered herself into the seat opposite him. 'You see sergeant?' she said. 'Perhaps I'm not the monster you think I am, especially when circumstances allow a certain latitude.'

Wulfe wouldn't let her off that easily. He doubted he'd ever be completely free from his terrible memories of the church undercroft. Wordlessly, he looked along the compartment at the rest of his crew and saw his own mixed feelings mirrored on their faces. Even Metzger, with them for less than a full day, looked glum.

Dessembra followed his gaze. 'What's wrong with you all? You should be grateful. Your chances of survival are now markedly improved.'

A sad smile tugged at the corners of Wulfe's mouth. 'We *are* grateful, sister superior, but we're grieving, too.' Speaking for the attention of his crew, he added, '*Last Rites* was the very finest tank I've had the pleasure to command. She was reliable and responsive, accurate and unstoppable.' His men nodded in silent assent. 'With the Emperor's blessing, her indomitable spirit will infuse another great war-machine. May she be reborn to fight on for the glory of the Imperium.'

'Ave Imperator,' the men intoned.

Dessembra nodded. 'Ave Imperator,' she said, then called to the driver's compartment where the youngest of her acolytes rode beside Corporal Fichtner. 'Sister Mellahd? A hymn if you please. Something to speed our journey back.'

The acolyte's beautiful, oval face appeared at the forward end of the compartment. 'What shall I sing, sister superior?'

With the hint of a grin, Dessembra said, '*Sunder All, His Shining Hammer.*'

It was a well-known favourite of the Cadian tank regiments.

As Mellahd's clear, high voice filled the compartment, lifting the tankers' hearts, Wulfe stared numbly at his chronometer, mesmerized by the inexorable clockwise motion of the hands as the minutes bled away.

58,000 kilometres from Palmeros, Darros III System, Segmentum Solar, 11.31 ship's time (0 hours 0 minutes to Planetkill)

THE MASSIVE IMPERIAL Navy starship *Hand of Radiance* swung away from Palmeros, filled to capacity with rescued men and materiel. Most of those onboard crowded into the ship's vast windowed galleries where, together, they bore witness to the death of an Imperial world. For some, the horrific, violent beauty of it was too much. Dozens fainted.

Wulfe opted not to watch, though the rest of his crew did.

When the first of Ghazghkull Thraka's accursed asteroids punched a hole in the planet's surface and ignited the global firestorm, he was alone in one of the starship's many small chapels, kneeling on a cold wooden bench, praying to the Emperor for the souls of dead men.

He prayed for Kohl, for Strieber and for the crews of their tanks. For Jans Garver, who had died well in faithful service to the Golden Throne. And for Dolphus Borscht – tank driver and friend – who had passed away in his hospital bed during the day.

A shiver ran the length of his spine as he remembered reading Boscht's death certificate. The time of his old friend's passing coincided, almost to the minute, with his inexplicable appearance in the canyon.

Wulfe had opted not to mention the chilling apparition in his report. People who spoke of such things tended to disappear without explanation.

Finally, he prayed for Captain Waltur Kurdheim – tormented and sacrificed to prolong the life of his powerful, uncaring father. A mercy run, Dessembra had called it. More like a sick joke. Wulfe hoped the young officer's soul was at peace in the presence of the undying Emperor.

He rose from his knees and sat back on a wooden pew, turning his thoughts to the future. The 18th Army Group was already en route to their next theatre of war. High Command was talking of a major operation on *Planet G*. They wouldn't disclose the true name of their destination until *Hand of Radiance* arrived in-system to rendezvous with the rest of the fleet, but rumours ran that Commissar Yarrick was somehow involved. And that meant orks.

The fighting, the killing, the losses, thought Wulfe. Endless war.

Despite his melancholy mood, his face betrayed the ghost of a smile. *Last Rites II*, he'd been told, would be waiting for him when he got there.

GUNHEADS

Steve Parker

EXPEDITIO RECLAMATUS

The Imperial Guard

General Mohamar Antoninus deViers
  Supreme Commander, 18th Army Group Exolon

Major General Gerard Bergen
  Divisional Commander, 10th Armoured Division

Major General Klotus Killian
  Divisional Commander, 12th Heavy Infantry Division

Major General Aaron Rennkamp
  Divisional Commander, 8th Mechanised Division

Colonel Tidor Stromm
  Regimental Commander, 98th Mechanised Infantry Reg.
  (8th Mech. Div.)

Colonel Edwyn Marrenburg
  Regimental Commander, 88th Mobile Infantry Reg.
  (10th Arm. Div.)

Colonel Darrik Graves
  Regimental Commander, 71st Caedus Infantry Reg.
  (10th Arm. Div.)

Colonel Kochatkis Vinnemann
  Regimental Commander, 81st Armoured Reg.
  (10th Arm. Div.)

Captain Villius Immrich
  Company Commander, 1st Company, 81st Armoured Reg.

Lieutenant Gossefried van Droi
  Company Commander, 10th Company, 81st Armoured Reg.

Sergeant Oskar Andreas Wulfe
  Tank Commander, Leman Russ *Last Rites II*

Corporal Voeder Lenck
  Tank Commander, Leman Russ Exterminator *New
  Champion of Cerbera*

The Adeptus Mechanicus

Tech-Magos Benendentius Sennesdiar
  Senior tech-priest accompanying Exolon during ground operations
  on Golgotha

Tech-Adept Dionestra Armadron
  A subordinate of Tech-Magos Sennesdiar

Tech-Adept Marthosal Xephous
  A subordinate of Tech-Magos Sennesdiar

Munitorum/Ecclesiarchy Personnel

Confessor Friedrich
  Ministorum priest attached to the 81st Reg.

Commissar Vincent 'Crusher' Slayte
  Political officer attached to the 81st Reg.

PROLOGUE

CALAFRAN CREIDES HAD stopped believing he would wake up. The nightmare was real. The monsters that surrounded him were solid, living, breathing things; he'd found out just how solid when one of them had cuffed him for not working fast enough. The power behind the blow was terrifying. Cal had flown backwards and smashed into one of the ammunition crates he was supposed to be loading. He was sure his rib was broken. Breathing had been painful ever since, and sleep, when it came at all, was more of a struggle than ever.

What was a broken rib, though, compared to the things they had done to Davran? Or to poor crippled Klaetas? Or to old Jovas, the pilot, when he'd collapsed from exhaustion? Best not to think about that. Wasn't it enough that he saw it every time he closed his eyes? The images of sickening torment were practically laser-etched onto the backs of his eyelids. Most nights, after he and the others had been pushed and kicked into an empty cargo container and locked there to rest in the stifling dark, he would wake up screaming. Quick but gentle hands would reach out to reassure him then, one always closing insistently over his mouth. Nobody wanted the monsters to return and investigate the noise.

Living in such a constant haze of fear, pain and misery, Cal had lost count of the days. How long had it been – ten? twenty, perhaps? – since the monsters had boarded *The Silverfin*? She and her crew had been contracted to scavenge naval wrecks from old war zones on the periphery of the Maelstrom. That hadn't lasted long. Early in the first leg of the operation, a bizarre ship, its prow constructed in the likeness of a grinning, nightmarish beast, had ambushed her, shooting out her main thrusters and ramming her from the side. Captain Berrin had recognised the profile of the attacking craft immediately. Aliens, he said, man-haters.

Cal never imagined he would see the captain so afraid. Berrin kept calling them *greenskins*, though their massive, leathery bodies were varying shades of brown. When they stormed the ship, the captain had ordered everyone onto the floor. 'Don't look up!' he had told them. 'No eye contact!' he had said. 'Fighting back will only get us killed.'

It was the first time Cal had ever heard a quaver in the big man's voice. Poor Nameth, never the sharpest tool in the box, looked up anyway, and died horribly for it. A glance was all it took – the briefest instant of gaze holding alien gaze – before one bellowing brute charged straight at him, its roar deafening in the tight confines of the ship. It tore Nameth's head from his neck with a single huge hand. Cal had been lying close by. His friend's hot blood had splashed over his back, soaking his clothes while the rest of the crew screamed and cried out for mercy. The monsters laughed at that, then bound the crew's hands, fixed metal collars around their throats, and chained them all together. Minutes later, the captured humans were locked tight in one of the lower holds and the journey to this Throne-forsaken place had begun. They had been brought to this world to live and die as slaves, and Cal wished now that he and the crew *had* fought back. Most of them had already been worked or beaten to death anyway. What was the point of drawing it out like this?

There was no hope of escape. Where would he go? The slavers' settlement sat high atop a plateau of solid black basalt. Beyond the plateau's sheer sides, red sands stretched to the wavering horizon in every direction. There were a few sloping paths down to the desert floor, but, even if he got to the bottom, there was nowhere to hide out there. He would be spotted and slain in short order. He didn't have the energy to run any more. His aching body felt so heavy. Every motion, even the mere act of drawing breath, seemed to take so much more effort on this world. Why? Did anyone even know which planet this was? He had asked around, but none of the other human slaves seemed to have the slightest idea.

There were hundreds of them. Some had arrived shortly after Cal, others had been here longer, but not by much. No one, it seemed, survived for very long. Those who had arrived before him had a dead look in their eyes, as if their souls had already departed, unwilling to stay locked within bodies forced to endure so much. Sometimes, though,

when the monsters in charge were too busy fighting amongst themselves, or when the thick afternoon heat put them to sleep, a little
glimmer of light would return and some of the older slaves would
speak to the newcomers in hushed voices. They told of how they had
been taken, their ships rammed and boarded just like *The Silverfin*.
They told of those who resisted, and the cruel slaughter that followed.
There were children here, too, they said, dozens of them starving to
death in tiny cages. The monsters, communicating to their human
slaves through crude mime, regularly threatened to devour them if their
parents didn't work harder.

Children? Cal didn't want to believe it. He hoped never to see those
cages. He didn't think he could bear it.

A furious roar snapped him back to his senses, and he realised that his
legs had stopped moving. He was so exhausted, he could no longer feel
the festering cuts and scratches that covered his limbs. Not for the first
time, he had almost fallen asleep on his feet.

There was a sharp crack like a gunshot, and blazing pain lanced across
his back. One of the brutish slave masters – a sadistic monster that the
slaves called *Sawtooth* – stood ten metres behind him, bellowing
hoarsely and brandishing a long, barbed whip.

The whip cracked again.

Drowning under a wave of sudden, intense agony, Cal felt the last of
his strength dissolve. His legs buckled and gave way. He collapsed, dropping the crate of fat, gleaming bullets he was carrying. His back hit hard,
dry rock. Bullets spilled from the broken crate, rolling to a stop against
his body. Some of the smaller, skinnier aliens nearby – hideous creatures with leering faces and long, hooked noses – pointed down at him
from atop a pyramid of stacked fuel barrels. They laughed and chittered
to each other, eyes wide with anticipation.

Cal felt the rock tremble under his body as Sawtooth stomped over,
growling with rage. The alien's massive, steel-booted feet halted on
either side of Cal's head, and Cal knew that the greatest pain of his short
life was about to follow. He remembered the terrible screams of Davran
and the others. He could hardly breathe with panic. His heart galloped.
Distantly, he felt a warm wetness spreading through his ragged trousers,
and realised that he had loosed the contents of his bladder. Fear overwhelmed any sense of shame.

Sawtooth bent over him, assessing him, studying him closely with
unsympathetic red eyes. Was this pathetic little human still capable of
work, or only fit to be tortured and pulled apart as another warning to
the rest?

Thick strands of saliva dripped from the monster's jaws onto Cal's
face. Its hot breath stank like vomit.

Cal gagged. Bile burned his throat. This is it, he thought. This is how my life ends.

He had never been a strong believer in the Imperial Creed. He'd attended weekly services with his parents, and learned the mandatory prayers and hymns under the stinging tutelage of a priest's cane, just like every other resentful boy and girl in the Imperium of Man. But he had never really believed, not in any of it. The God-Emperor was just another old legend among so many. No, he was even less than that. He was a legend of a myth of a legend.

All the same, as Sawtooth straightened and began bellowing to the other monsters nearby, calling them over for a bit of fun, it was to the Ministorum's precious God-Emperor that Cal prayed and pleaded.

Lord of all Mankind, Beacon in the Darkness, Master of Holy Terra and all the galaxy, let me die quickly, I beg you. Don't let met suffer as Davran and the others did. I've sinned, I know it, and held no faith. But, in humble prayer, I ask this of You now.

He expected no answer. It was terror alone that made him pray, but what happened next was a striking example of those coincidences that the faithful so often claim as proof of the Divine. Calafran Creides could not have known that a fleet of Imperial ships held position in high orbit directly above him. They had arrived that very day.

Laughing at thoughts of the torture to follow, Sawtooth grasped Cal's arms and hauled him roughly into the air. Cal's limp feet dangled above the bullet-strewn rock. His undernourished bones cracked and splintered in the monster's iron grip, but he didn't scream. He didn't even whimper. His attention was locked on the sky above.

In it, Cal saw a glorious, blazing light that shunted the thick clouds aside. It was so bright that it hurt to look into it, but he couldn't turn away. Tears of joy rolled down his cheeks. Could it truly be? Yes! The Emperor was *real*! He had heard Cal's prayer, and He had answered it!

'Ave, Imperator,' Cal gasped. Gratitude, relief, love, contrition: all these feelings and more swept over him. He took a deep lungful of hot, stinking air and, with everything he had left, shouted upwards, 'Ave, Imperator!'

The confused greenskins looked up, too, but there was nothing they could do. The blazing light struck the plateau, scouring it, purging it, erasing ork and human alike as if neither had existed there at all.

Soon, hundreds of Imperial drop-ships would begin their descent.

Operation Thunderstorm had begun.

CHAPTER ONE

IMPERIAL SPACESHIPS, MASSIVE and ornate, comparable in size and baroque beauty to the largest cathedrals of Holy Terra, hung together in the infinite dark. They had slid from the warp almost forty days earlier, bisecting the orbits of the outer planets on trails of blazing plasma until finally closing on their ultimate goal. That goal lay somewhere below, on the world that spun beneath them, a world that glowed bright in the glare of the system's harsh sun.

Golgotha: a planet shrouded in thick, choking cloud, all reds, yellows and browns that swirled and bled together like so many spilled paints. In memoirs dating back thirty-eight years to the last Golgothan War, the celebrated Terraxian Guardsman-poet, Clavier Michelos, had remarked on the planet's ominous beauty, and with good reason. From high orbit, at least, it was a stunning sight, but that beauty masked an uncompromising nature, for Golgotha was not a world that welcomed men. Michelos had died here, captured and tortured to death by orks. He wasn't alone in that. The war had been a costly and embarrassing disaster. The orks had crushed everything in their path, and even Commissar Yarrick, the lauded Hero of Armageddon, had been unable to turn the tide of battle. He left Golgotha in bitter defeat with very few survivors at his side.

That was almost four decades ago. Yarrick, now an old man, still fought for the glory of the Imperium. The war with his nemesis, the ork warlord Ghazghkull Mag Uruk Thraka, had taken him back to Armageddon, the world that had made his reputation, while Golgotha remained firmly in the hands of the enemy, a dark stain on his record that could never be expunged.

So, why had men returned? The small fleet that hung above the orange sphere lacked even a fraction of the power required to take it back by force, but that was not their mission, not this time. There was something else down there besides orks, something important that had been lost on Golgotha during the last war, something that the Imperium wanted back. It was a holy relic, a symbol so potent that it might turn the tide of Yarrick's new war. Its name was *The Fortress of Arrogance*.

The fleet sent to recover it was a mixed force. In the centre, a ship far larger than any of the others dominated the formation. This was the *Scion of Tharsis*, a Reclamator craft of the Adeptus Mechanicus, the ancient and inscrutable tech-priesthood of Mars without whom none of the ships present would have existed at all. The *Scion* was flanked on either side by the Imperial Navy's Tyrant-class heavy cruisers, the *Helicon Star* and the *Ganymede*, around which swarmed myriad smaller escort ships and armed transports. It was on one of these transports, an unassuming craft called the *Hand of Radiance*, that the men of the 81st Cadian Armoured Regiment, known less formally as *Rolling Thunder*, prepared for war.

'FORM UP, YOU greasy pukes!' roared an ugly, skin-headed sergeant with a pockmarked face. 'You know the bloody drill. By the numbers, damn your eyes!'

The floor of the starboard-side hangar clanged with the sound of men snapping to attention. The troopers stood in formation, company by company from the first to the tenth, while their sergeants prowled back and forth like hungry wolves, eyes sharp, hunting keenly for the slightest signs of sloppiness. Hulking drop-ships sat behind the ordered ranks of men, their boarding ramps lowered, internal lights glaring yellow inside dark, gunmetal hulls.

A loud, hydraulic hiss sounded on the right of the massive chamber, and a thick door split down the middle, each half sliding backwards into the wall with a cough of oily steam. The metal floor rang with the crisp, pleasing tattoo of dozens of booted feet marching briskly into the hangar.

'Officers on deck!' yelled another of the sergeants. Thick veins throbbed at his temple with the effort of projecting his voice unaided to almost two thousand men.

When the officers had halted and turned to face the assembled troops, the oldest of the sergeants – a stocky man with lumpy scar-tissue in place of his left ear – strode forwards and proudly stated, 'All men present and accounted for, sir. Vehicles already onboard, lashed and locked. Flight and tech-crews ready for the go. Companies one to ten awaiting permission to load.'

Colonel Kochatkis Vinnemann stood at the centre of the group of officers, hunched as ever, leaning heavily on his cane, but resplendent nonetheless in a smart uniform of deep green with glittering golden epaulets. Today was the last day that he would be able to wear the regimental colours for a while. The duration of the campaign would see everyone clothed in camouflaging fatigues of rust-red.

Vinnemann nodded at the sergeant in front of him and was about to issue the boarding command when Captain Immrich – tall, dark and broad-shouldered – leaned close and whispered a few words in his ear. Vinnemann frowned a little at first but finally nodded his agreement. He stepped forward, accepted a vox-amp receiver from the adjutant on his left, held the mouthpiece in front of his lips, and cleared his throat. The sound echoed back at him from the vast bulkheads.

'Those of you with me long enough know that I dislike long speeches,' said Vinnemann. 'Something best left to your commissars and confessors, I think, to men who have a particular talent for it.'

Commissar Slayte, the regiment's widely despised political officer, dressed as ever in the black and gold of his office, bowed slightly at the compliment. Confessor Friedrich, on the other hand, a flush-faced priest in his late thirties, merely swayed a little as if standing in a strong breeze that only he could feel.

'However,' continued Colonel Vinnemann, 'as Captain Immrich has rightly reminded me, our regiment faces something unprecedented in its history. If a situation ever warranted a departure from my typical reticence, it is this one, for we are about to set foot on a world firmly and completely in the hands of the hated ork.'

It was Vinnemann's particular habit to refer to the *old foe* in the singular. Some of the men did a pretty good impersonation of him, though never with any malice. There was tremendous love and respect for the old colonel among those who had served under him for any length of time. It was well earned. Those men whose jibes contained an edge of genuine insult, especially those that mocked his physical disability, quickly found themselves isolated, cast out by their fellows. Among Imperial Guardsmen, such exclusion was as good as a death sentence.

Vinnemann's distinctive posture was caused by his augmetic spine. Twenty-four years earlier, while just a captain, he had undergone a lifesaving augmentation procedure following the destruction of his Vanquisher battle tank. His body had never fully accepted the implant.

Regular injections of immunosuppressants and painkillers eased things a little, but not much. The injury should have killed him, and so, too, the subsequent operation, but his indomitable spirit had kept him alive, that and the care of the medicae nurse he later married. During his slow, painful recovery, his superiors had offered him the option of an honourable discharge. It seemed to them the only logical choice.

Vinnemann had rejected it without hesitation. 'A rear echelon position, then,' they had suggested, but the old tanker had rejected that, too. 'My duty,' he had insisted, 'is to lead my men from the front, no matter what, and, so long as I am able, that is exactly what I intend to do.'

Twelve years later, he had risen to the rank of colonel, taking command of the entire 81st Armoured Regiment.

He studied them now, his brave troopers, during a short pause in his speech. A slim lieutenant at the rear coughed quietly behind his hand. The sound was magnified in the relative silence. Vinnemann drew a deep breath.

'Some of us have fought the ork before,' he continued, 'and with notable success. Our victories on Phaegos II, Galamos and Indara stand us in good stead, though many of you, I suppose, had yet to be born at the time of the latter. Still, the point is this: we *know* the ork. We know that together, man and machine, tanker and tank, we are *stronger* than the ork. We know that we can *beat* the ork. We've proved it time after time.'

He found himself stunned by how young some of the most recent reinforcements looked when standing next to their more experienced peers. By the blasted Eye, he thought, some of them are practically children! Was I ever so fresh-faced?

Thoughts of his two sons bubbled up in his mind. Both were serving in the 92nd Infantry Division on Armageddon. They had grown into fine soldiers. Was it too much to hope for their safety? Was it foolish to pray for them? Millions would die to stop the foe on Armageddon, tens of millions, perhaps. Yarrick's war demanded it. The very heart of the Imperium was at stake. Why should his sons be spared the fate of their comrades? He knew that glory, victory and a good death were the best he could ask for them. It was all that most good Cadians asked for themselves. Besides, were the men before him not also his sons? That was how he saw them sometimes. They certainly made him feel just as proud.

'Could General deViers be any more fortunate than to have our proud regiment roll out under his command? I hardly think so. Yes, I've heard the mutterings among you. I've sensed your dark mood. Why send us to Golgotha, you still wonder, when our kin are so pressed on Armageddon? What difference, you ask, can we make out here on a planet untouched by the Emperor's light? Well, let me tell you something. Listen closely, now, because I want you to understand it. *I believe in this operation!* Do you hear me? I *believe* in it. Our success will make a difference to our beleaguered brothers that you can scarcely imagine. Our triumphant return will re-energise them as nothing else can. Those of you who doubt it will understand once you lay eyes on the prize. Until that moment, I know you'll do whatever it takes, give your every bead of sweat, your last drop of blood if necessary, for the honour and tradition of our proud regiment, for the glory of Cadia, and for the everlasting dominion of the God-Emperor of mankind.'

He scanned their faces for signs of open dissent and found none. Instead, their response to his words was both immediate and deafening.

'For Cadia and the Emperor!' they roared and, like his own amplified words, the sound echoed back at him from the hangar walls.

He grinned at them, eager not to dwell on the doubts he secretly carried. 'Sergeant Keppler,' he said, 'get these brave soldiers loaded up!'

'Aye, sir,' said the old sergeant with the mutilated ear, and he threw up a salute that was so sharp it could have cut glass. He turned, took a deep breath, and roared at the men, 'Right you maggots, you heard the colonel. About face! Squad leaders, take 'em in nice and clean!'

Vinnemann watched them proudly as they marched up the ramps and into the bellies of the waiting drop-ships, each company to a ship of its own. *Be strong, sons of Cadia,* he thought, *now more than ever.*

He turned and dismissed his officers so that each could go to join his men. Finally, with his personal staff in tow, the colonel moved off to board his own shuttle.

The hangar air began vibrating with the whine of powerful engines as the naval flight-crews began warming up their craft. With a great metallic groan, the massive bay doors slowly opened onto space. Orange light flooded in, reflected from the planet below.

After seven long and troubled months aboard the *Hand of Radiance*, it was time, at last, to return to war.

CHAPTER TWO

GOOD SOLID GROUND, thought Sergeant Oskar Andreas Wulfe. Greenskins or not, he was looking forward to standing on good solid ground. It would be a fine thing to feel dirt and rock under his boot-heels again, the first time in far too long. He was sick of living day-to-day on this damned ship with its maze of gloomy corridors and its endlessly recycled air. With thoughts of dunes and mountains and broad open plains, he marched his crew up the boarding ramp and into the drop-ship that would ferry them down to the surface.

The trip from Palmeros to the Golgothan subsector had been the longest unbroken warp journey of his career, and plenty of tempers had frayed under the strain, not least his own. It wasn't just the journey, however. Warp travel was no picnic, but it didn't help that his mind was still wrestling with the memories of his last days on Palmeros, memories that often woke him in a cold sweat, gripping his bunched sheets and calling out the name of a dead friend.

He suspected that his crew was more bothered by this than they let on. They had to bunk with him, after all, and often got as little restful sleep as he did. He thought he detected it in their eyes sometimes, a loss of confidence in him where once it had been unshakeable. How much worse would matters be, he wondered, if he ever told them the truth about what he had seen in the canyon that day? *Much* worse. It didn't do for a tank commander to see ghosts. Those who reported such things tended to go missing shortly afterwards, marched off by whatever Imperial body had jurisdiction. So far the only man Wulfe had confided in was Confessor Friedrich, and that was how he intended to keep it. Even drunk off his arse, as he often was, the confessor was a man to be trusted.

Wulfe forced his mind back to more positive territory. It would be good to see a sky overhead again, instead of pitted metal bulkheads veined with dripping pipes and tangled cables. It hardly mattered what that sky looked like, just so long as it was wide and open and any colour but the lustreless grey of starship bulkheads.

Following the squad in front, Wulfe led his men through one of the drop-ship's cargo holds, turning his head to look at the tanks and half-tracks that rested there. Beyond them, further back in the shadows, sat the company's fuel and supply trucks. All of the vehicles were covered in heavy brown tarpaulins, lashed down with thick steel cables and bolted to solid fixtures in the floor. But, even with her bulk hidden under a tarp, it was all too easy for Wulfe to mark out his own tank. The Leman Russ *Last Rites II* boasted a Mars Alpha-pattern hull, so she was fractionally longer in the body than the other Leman Russ. She was an old girl, and badly scarred – in Wulfe's opinion, one of the shabbiest tanks he had ever set eyes on. Her armour plating was riveted together, rather than mould-cast, and her turret was all vertical surfaces just begging to be hit with armour-piercing shells or rocket-propelled grenades. He was quite certain that she would get him and his entire crew killed during their first engagement. She was nothing like her predecessor, and he cursed her for that. He remembered seeing her for the first time and wondering if, in assigning him this old junker, the lieutenant had meant to punish him for something. Wulfe had thought his relationship with Lieutenant van Droi perfectly solid up to then, but now he felt he had cause to question it. To make things worse, some of the other sergeants had leapt on the chance to rip him up about it.

'Don't get too far ahead of us all, will you?' they said. 'Let us know if you need help pushing her up a dune.' 'What does she run on, Wulfe? Pedal power?' 'How many aurochs does it take to pull her?'

The list went on. Wulfe scowled over at the covered tank, glad she was cloaked by the tarp so he didn't have to look at her ugly hide. He quickly turned away.

The squad in front of him, Sergeant Richter's crew, stomped up a narrow metal staircase and disappeared from view. Wulfe put his hand on the guardrail and hoisted himself up after them, steel steps ringing under his polished marching boots. His men clambered up behind him, right at his back, silent except for the gunner, Holtz, who was grumbling unintelligibly. Wulfe didn't wonder that Holtz was uneasy, though the man was apt to grumble at the best of times. Emerging safely from the warp was one thing, and Wulfe's relief was genuine enough, but every man in the regiment knew what awaited them on Golgotha. Only the crazies and the liars – meaning most of the commissioned officers – professed to like the army group's odds of success here. To Wulfe's mind, Operation Thunderstorm seemed like the most incredible gamble. Colonel Vinnemann had done his level best to instil a sense of purpose and honour in them, of course, but that was all part of the job.

An entire world overrun with orks. By the blasted Eye! Who knew how many of the filthy buggers there would be?

Without realising he was doing it, Wulfe reached up to brush a fingertip over the long horizontal scar at his throat. Orks. His hatred of the greenskins was as strong today as it had ever been. Probably stronger, in fact.

A doorway led into one of the passenger holds at the top of the metal staircase. It was a long dark space barely three metres across, extending to the left and right like a tunnel. Twin rows of tiny orange guide-lights lined the floor, and numbers in faded white paint marked the walls. Wulfe and his men soon found their seats, buckled themselves in, and reached up to pull metal impact frames down over their heads and shoulders. The frames locked into place with a loud click. It was a sound filled with significance, with a distinct finality. Once you were locked in, there was no getting off this ride.

Only minutes remained until the drop. Wulfe felt a familiar tightness in his stomach. He glanced up and down the compartment, and nodded in friendly acknowledgement to Sergeant Viess.

Viess, only recently promoted, had been Wulfe's gunner for some years and remained a friend, though an undeniable distance had grown between them since he had been given his stripes. He had his own men to lead, and Holtz, formerly a sponson gunner, had taken his place on the main gun. Wulfe was glad for Viess. Most men in the regiment aspired to commanding their own tank. He missed having him on his crew, though. Together, they had notched up a good number of armour-kills.

Once the last squad had filed in to the compartment, the door hissed shut. Almost two hundred men sat in the compartment. They were Gossefried's Gunheads, the 81st Armoured Regiment's 10th Company. Only the lieutenant and his adjutant were absent, seated in the cockpit with the drop-ship's flight crew. The rest sat facing their fellows, trading jokes and nervous banter across the hold's narrow length. Corporal Metzger, Wulfe's driver, sat next to him, typically pensive, with Holtz and Siegler – the latter being Wulfe's long-serving loader – in the opposite seats.

This drop was different from the last, not just in terms of the nature of the mission, but for the smaller crew with which Wulfe was rolling out. His previous tank had boasted sponsons on either side of her hull, two protruding compartments, each housing a belt-fed heavy bolter that made messy work of anything foolish enough to close with her. She had been an awesome war machine, utterly unstoppable, and memories of abandoning her on a dark highway so many light-years away filled Wulfe with genuine longing and remorse. He had mourned her loss every day since then, but what choice had there been? Her top speed hadn't been nearly enough. Leaving her behind, he and his crew had boarded a much faster Chimera APC, and the lighter machine's speed had saved their lives. They had made it onto the last lifter into orbit just before the planet Palmeros was utterly obliterated.

Despite the pain of losing his beloved tank, Wulfe knew he had a lot to be thankful for. Billions of Imperial civilians had not been so lucky.

In any case, the new machine – hah! he thought. What was *new* about her? – lacked the same potent defences. Her flanks were practically naked. Her side-armour might be one hundred and fifty millimetres of solid plasteel, but there were weapons aplenty in the hands of mankind's enemies that could cut through it like butter. An attacker only had to close the gap. Without side sponsons, it would fall to Wulfe to cover the tank's blind spots from his cupola high atop the turret. There was a box-fed heavy stubber there, pintle-mounted with a nice, wide arc of fire, for exactly that purpose. He knew it was a good weapon, but he still lamented the absence of side sponsons.

A crackling voice sounded from speakers set in the ceiling. 'Bay doors open. Locks released. Engines engaged. Activating onboard gravitational systems in three, two, one…'

Wulfe felt his stomach lurch, a brief moment in which his body weight doubled as the grav-field of the *Hand of Radiance* and the drop-ship's field overlapped. Just as quickly the feeling was gone, and the drop-ship's onboard gravity became the only force pulling him into his seat.

'Bay doors cleared,' reported the mechanical voice a minute later. 'Firing thrusters. Beginning descent. Breaching thermosphere in ten, nine…'

Wulfe tuned out the rest of the count.

'What's a thermosphere, sarge?' piped a nervous-sounding trooper a dozen seats to the right.

'Stifle it, *drop-virgin*,' barked his sergeant. 'How would I know? Do I look like a cogboy to you?'

Wulfe grinned. New meat, he thought. This was the first drop for a good number of the men. The 18th Army Group's catastrophic losses on

Palmeros had left it at less than half strength. Senior cadets from the Whiteshields – the tough, teenaged Cadian training regiments – had been drafted in to replenish the ranks, but most of those had been posted to regiments in the 8th and 12th divisions. After promoting suitable men from the tech-crews and support squads, the Cadian 81st had to make up the rest of their numbers with men drafted in from the 616th Reserve Regiment – men who, in most cases, had never crewed a tank in their lives. Lieutenant van Droi had expressed his grave concerns about this in private. He felt that most of the new men didn't make the grade, not by a long shot. The reserves were rarely employed at the front lines, tending instead to be used for garrisoning duties and the like. Wulfe knew that their first taste of front line action would sort the men from the boys.

Thinking about who made the grade and who didn't, he cast an involuntary glance along the opposite row of seats towards a man on his far left.

I've got my eye on you, squigshit, he thought.

The speakers crackled to life again. 'Mesospheric penetration in ten, nine…'

'Sounds dirty, don't it?' quipped a ruddy-faced trooper on the opposite row.

'You're so full of crap, Garrel,' said the young man next to him with a mirthless laugh. He tried to punch his comrade playfully on the arm, but the bars of his impact frame restricted his movement.

The anxious trooper who'd spoken up earlier opened his mouth to speak again, but he didn't get a word out before the same gruff sergeant cut him off.

'Go on, Vintners,' he barked, 'ask me what a mesosphere is. I dare you.' Despite his manner, there was an unmistakable tone of humour in the sergeant's voice. 'You'll be on latrines for the whole frakking op!'

Nervous laughter rippled along the rows. Vintners turned pale and clamped his mouth shut.

All this was mere background noise to Wulfe. He was too busy watching the man on the far left, studying the lines and angles of his hawkish face, watching the way he moved his lips as he talked in an undertone with the crewmen seated around him.

His name was Corporal Voeder Lenck, twenty-eight years old and commander of the Leman Russ Exterminator *New Champion of Cerbera*. He was a tall, slim, darkly handsome man, all poster-boy good looks, easy smiles and warm handshakes. But Wulfe wasn't fooled, not for a second, not like the gang of doe-eyed sycophants that had surrounded Lenck since the moment he had transferred in. Why the rookies all flocked to him, Wulfe hadn't figured out yet. The man had been a bloody reserve, for Throne's sake. What was there to admire? Admittedly, he wasn't typical of the newcomers. He had some prior tank experience, for a start. Perhaps that was it: a combination of being fresh to the regiment, like the rest of the new meat, but being an experienced tanker at the same time. It was as good a guess as Wulfe could make.

The records showed that Lenck had been a sergeant earlier in his career, but something had gone wrong. There had been a trial, a court-martial. He had been locked up for thirty days and demoted to the rank of corporal. Only the commissioned officers knew why and, so far, they weren't telling, but Wulfe planned to find out sooner or later.

The day he and Lenck had first met aboard the *Hand of Radiance*, Wulfe had recognised an icy cruelty behind the man's purple-irised eyes. Lenck hadn't done anything overt to induce Wulfe's dislike, not so far anyway, but Wulfe knew it would come sooner or later. It didn't help that he was the spitting image of someone else, a convicted Cadian criminal by the name of Victor Dunst. Dunst and his gang of tattooed cronies had once tried to rob Wulfe in the under-streets of Kasr Gehr. Wulfe had been a Whiteshield at the time, just a teenage cadet on leave before graduating from basic. He had been heavily outnumbered but, like so many Whiteshields, his belief in his invincibility was so complete that he hadn't even thought to run. Instead, he had told the gang to piss off, and Dunst had decided to kill him. Only the chance intervention of a patrolling Civitas enforcer squad had saved Wulfe's life that day. Dunst's knife didn't get more than two centimetres into Wulfe's chest. Wulfe had been very lucky.

As Wulfe looked along the row, Lenck seemed to realise that he was being watched. He didn't turn his head or shift his eyes, he just seemed to sense it. Wulfe saw a grin creep over the younger man's face and felt a tremendous desire to punch him. The feeling of Lenck's bones cracking under his fist would be supremely satisfying, he imagined. Wulfe was no brawler, not like some of the men he knew, but he was no slouch, either. He was pretty sure he could take Lenck if it ever came down to a fair fight, though Lenck didn't seem the type to fight fair. Such an event was unlikely to occur, of course. For Lenck, striking Wulfe would constitute a capital offence due to the difference in rank. Still, thought Wulfe, if we were to put rank aside...

The ceiling speakers crackled again. 'Particle shields holding at eighty per cent. Entering stratosphere in ten, nine, eight...'

Any jokes or remarks that this announcement might have drawn died in the throats of the troopers as the drop-ship began shaking and juddering. Most of the drop-virgins grimaced. A few started to look peaky, as if they might begin to puke.

'Time to put them in, gentlemen,' said Wulfe to his crew. He reached into the right pocket of his field trousers and withdrew a small, transparent curve of hard rubber. It was a gumshield, the kind worn by troopers during hand-to-hand combat training. With a nod, Metzger, Siegler and Holtz drew identical items from their pockets and fitted them securely between their teeth. All along the facing rows, veteran tankers did the same thing. The new meat looked on with expressions of abject horror.

'By the bloody Eye! Why didn't anyone tell the rest of us to bring gumshields?' demanded a round-faced trooper ten seats to Wulfe's right. He was the newest man on Sergeant Rhaimes's crew, and it was Rhaimes – seasoned commander of the Leman Russ *Old Smashbones* – who answered, removing his gumshield for a moment to do so.

'Company tradition, bug-food,' he said. He grinned, creasing the skin around the deep scar that ran from his left eye to his left ear. *Bug-food* was his personal term of affection for the new guys and, whenever he said it, he managed to make it sound like *idiot* or *arsehole*. Recently a lot of the veterans had started using it, and not just in 10th Company. 'You're still a drop-virgin till you break a tooth on the way down.'

The trooper gaped in disbelief for a moment and then fished in his pocket for something. He pulled out a wadded piece of rag, the type of cloth used to shine boots or buttons before inspection, and stuffed it into his mouth. With a miserable expression, he bit down on it. Wulfe guessed it must taste strongly of polish.

From the corner of his eye, he saw Rhaimes nodding at the young trooper. 'Good thinking, son. Good thinking. We'll make something of you yet.'

'...three, two, one,' buzzed the voice from the ceiling. 'Tropospheric entry achieved. Height, nine thousand metres. All personnel brace for increased atmospheric buffeting. Touchdown in approximately nineteen minutes. Disengaging onboard gravitational systems. Switching to local gravity in three, two, one...'

For the second time since he had come aboard, there was an instant of gravitational overlap that made Wulfe feel twice as heavy as he normally did. Some of the men grunted as their bodies protested against the sudden strain but, once the grav-plates below their feet went dead, they hardly noticed the difference.

According to the thick wad of briefing papers that everyone had been issued – though few but the guys in recon, as usual, had bothered to read – Golgotha's surface gravity was a fairly manageable 1.12Gs. Wulfe, who typically weighed around eighty-five kilograms, now weighed twelve per cent more, a little over ninety-five, but the increase didn't bother him. The tech-crews onboard the *Hand of Radiance* had taken care of that. Since leaving Palmeros, they had incrementally increased the shipboard gravity each day, subtly preparing the troops for their eventual ground deployment. Men like Siegler and Sergeant Rhaimes, usually a little soft around the middle, had hardened up a lot over the last few months. Wulfe had felt his appetite increasing little by little, and had noticed his clothes tightening around his arms, legs and chest. His body had adapted. Now, with the planet's local gravity acting on him directly, he didn't feel any heavier than normal. It would make a big difference to the tanks, though; fuel efficiency, firing distance, trajectory, speed, wear and tear. All of these were matters of serious concern. The enginseers in charge of the regimental tech-crews wouldn't be getting much sleep.

Thinking of the strange cybernetic tech-priests, Wulfe decided they probably didn't need much sleep anyway. Maybe they just popped in some fresh batteries. The image that formed in his mind was, in equal parts, both amusing and disturbing.

The drop-ship was really bouncing around. Golgotha's atmosphere was thicker than most populated worlds, and the pressure differentials between the planet's hot and cold zones reportedly made for some truly ferocious storms. Some of the rookies looked set to soil themselves as the craft was tossed this way and that.

Wulfe fought an instinct to tense his muscles. It was far smarter to relax if one didn't want to suffer torn tendons and the like. Such injuries were all too common during a drop.

'Altitude, seven thousand five–'

The static-ridden voice was suddenly drowned out by the most awful, ringing screech. Wulfe pressed his hands to his ears. He knew that sound, knew it never heralded good news. It was the sound of tearing metal!

The drop-ship suddenly rolled hard to the right. Wulfe's head flew backwards and struck the padded surface of the seat. His stomach felt like it was doing backflips. His vision dimmed. He saw stars. Some of the men on the opposite row were thrown so hard against their restraints that their gumshields flew out. Yelled curses filled the air. 'We're frakkin' hit!' shouted a young trooper in a panic. Wulfe's heart felt like it was stuck somewhere up by his throat.

'We're not hit, Webber,' barked another. 'Don't *say* that!'

'What the hell was it, then?' demanded someone else.

'By the bloody Eye!'

'Quiet!' Sergeant Rhaimes yelled at them around his gumshield. 'That's enough of that! It's turbulence, you kak-eating dung-worms. You heard the cogboy. Buffeting, he said. Now, pipe down!'

Rhaimes's lie was all too obvious. He was trying to keep them calm, but no one was buying a word of it.

The ship rolled hard in the other direction and righted itself, though the juddering was so severe, now, that it was painful. The men gripped their impact frames with white-knuckled hands.

Wulfe chanced a look up the row at Lenck and was irritated to see him sitting quietly, lips bulging over the tell-tale bump of a gumshield, apparently unfazed. The cocky upstart only jumped when a noise exploded from the vox-speakers. It was a deafening, high-pitched whine that cut off suddenly to be replaced by the cold flat tones of the cogboy addressing them once again. This time, the voice was amplified to ear-damaging levels and, whether Wulfe simply imagined it or not, he heard hints of his own panic reflected in the broken sentences.

'...concentrated anti-aircraft... storm... below... off course and... down. All personnel... for immediate...'

Suddenly, a great wave of nerve-searing pain blossomed in Wulfe's head. The whole galaxy seemed to roll over on its axis. Up was down, left was right. Then everything shifted again with frightening speed. He shut his eyes tight, saw fireworks bursting behind his eyelids, felt his muscles cry out in protest as his body's limits were brutally tested, and then, with his heart battering the inside of his chest like it wanted out...

Darkness. Thoughtlessness. Silence.

He sank into an unfeeling void in which even bad dreams ceased to exist.

SOMETHING STUNG WULFE'S left cheek. The pain was sharp, and, slowly, though he struggled against it, it dragged him back from the comfort of his dark oblivion. Half awake, he probed the inside of his cheek with his tongue. The flesh was ragged. He tasted blood. His tongue played over nearby teeth and... *Damn it!* Two of them were much sharper than before. They'd been broken. He wondered idly if he'd swallowed the pieces and decided that he probably had.

Next, there came a shooting pain in his eyes. He wanted to shut them tighter, but the lids were already squeezed together hard. Then a shadow fell across him, and the pain dissipated. Slowly, carefully, he eased the lids apart and saw...

'Holtz? Is that–'

Waves of fire surged through his muscles as he tried to rise. He grunted in pain and sank back down.

'Easy,' said Holtz, leaning over him. 'Siegler's gone to scare up a medic, but they've got their hands full. There were deaths, sarge. Brebner and half his crew. Some of Fuchs's men. Krauss and Siemens both lost their drivers. A score of lads from the support crews bought it, too.'

Holtz paused for a second. Then, with sorrow giving way to relief, added, 'By the bloody Eye, sarge, we thought you were out of the game for good this time. Just lie still for a bit, will you?'

They were wasted words. Wulfe was already moving. With another grunt of pain, he rolled to his left and braced himself with his right hand. His fingers pressed down into warm red sand and he froze.

'Golgotha,' he whispered.

Holtz heard him. 'Aye, sir. Golgotha, for better or worse.'

Wulfe paused, letting the sensation of the fine red grains filter up into his brain. He raised a handful of sand up in front of his eyes and watched it pour like water from between his fingers. He rubbed his forefinger and thumb together and noticed that the sand left a stain there, a thick smear of dark red dust.

'Like blood,' he murmured.

Holtz caught only the last of these words and mistook Wulfe's meaning. 'No bleeding, sarge, except your mouth. You feel like anything's broken? If you'll just wait for the medic.'

Again, Wulfe brushed off this advice. Injured or not, he didn't have time to lie around on his back. He lifted his head towards the horizon and, through his nose, drew a few deep, deliberate breaths of the Golgothan air. He immediately wished he hadn't. The air was thick, stung his nostrils a little, and smelled like eggs. Is that sulphur, he wondered, or something worse? Open sands stretched out all around him, flat and featureless, running all the way to the shimmering distance where land and sky seemed to melt and flow together in a mirage line that hovered above the surface of the desert.

He turned his face and looked directly up. The sky was heavily overcast with rich, swirling reds and browns. Quite beautiful, he supposed, but oppressive, too. The cloud ceiling was very low, and lightning flashed deep inside it, though no precipitation fell. He detected the muted glow of the local star, directly above him, hinting at midday, its light barely managing to struggle through. Then he realised how dark everything was. Even in the middle of the day, the ambient light was only a shade stronger than twilight on Cadia.

Holtz followed his gaze. 'According to the cogboys, we should be glad of them clouds, sarge. They say one clear day is enough to kill a man.'

'A million ways,' Wulfe murmured.

'Again, sarge?'

'That Terraxian poet… I can't remember his name. He said Golgotha has a million ways to kill a man.' Wulfe pulled himself up into a sitting position, wincing as he did so. Holtz watched without comment, giving up on trying to keep Wulfe still, merely shaking his head in frustrated disapproval.

'Is Siegler okay?' asked Wulfe. 'Metzger? Viess and his men?'

'Siegler and Metzger are all right,' said Holtz, 'not a scratch on either of them. Same goes for Viess, though his driver is a bit messed up.' Absently, he reached up and rubbed the ugly, discoloured mass of scar tissue that covered the left side of his face. Seven years ago on a world called Modessa Prime, a secessionist guerrilla had hit Wulfe's tank with a shaped-charge explosive. Holtz had been in one of the sponsons. A fine spray of molten metal had turned him from a handsome, confident trooper into one of the most bitter men Wulfe had ever known. Very occasionally, however, Wulfe saw hints of the old Holtz shining through, a bit like the Golgothan sun.

'Eye blast it!' exclaimed Wulfe suddenly. 'Van Droi was up front with the pilot. He isn't–'

'No,' said Holtz, cutting him off. 'Chipped a tooth, though. Raging about it, he is. He was here earlier with that damned soggy cigar sticking out of his mouth. Seemed to know you'd be all right. Said you were to report to him once you were on your feet. You and the rest of the tank commanders, that is.'

That prompted another question. 'What about Lenck?' Wulfe asked, trying not to sound too hopeful.

Holtz snorted. He had declared his own dislike for the new tank commander early on. Wulfe guessed that Holtz's feelings were based on envy more than anything else, though. Holtz had enjoyed great success with the ladies before his face had been scorched and ruined. Lenck had reportedly enjoyed comparable attention from some of the nurses and female naval officers aboard the *Hand of Radiance*. From what Wulfe had heard, he wasn't shy about sharing the details, either.

'First out the lander, that one,' said Holtz with a scowl. 'He's back inside it now, checking on his tank.'

'Damn it,' muttered Wulfe. He looked up at the sky again, addressing the Emperor. 'Was it too much to bloody ask?'

Holtz gave a dry laugh.

'Look on the bright side,' he said. 'If that Terraxian ponce was right, there'll be plenty more chances for him to snuff it before we pull out of here.'

Wulfe shifted his weight and struggled gingerly to his feet. He was a little dizzy, but he managed to stand under his own power. Once he was up, he turned and cast his gaze over the wreckage of the crashed craft.

It was a sorry sight. The desert was littered for hundreds of metres with fragments of every size and shape. Black smoke poured from the aft section, churning on a hot breeze. Wulfe watched it rise, climbing towards the clouds, and thought, *frak!* Talk about advertising our position. We won't be able to stay here long, not running a flag like that.

He looked back at the crumpled body of the drop-ship. Scores of sweating men moved around it, carrying supply crates out from a tear in the hull. Others worked to manually widen the massive emergency doors at the ship's rear so that 10th Company's vehicles could be extracted. They were having a hard time of it, but there was little choice. There was no way to get the tanks out via the loading ramp. The ship's belly was pressed flat to the ground.

Another smaller group of men handled the grimmest task of all. They knelt in the sand, leaning over lifeless bodies to pull dog tags from their necks.

Wulfe's eyes lingered on the motionless form of a trooper not twenty metres away. The lad looked barely out of his teens. The pale skin of his face was bright against the dark red sand on which he lay.

Bug-food, thought Wulfe. He touched the silver aquila badge on the left breast pocket of his tanker's fatigues and whispered a quick prayer for the young trooper's soul. Such pitiful sights were something he had gotten used to after so long in the field. Life in the Guard: you either dealt with it or you didn't, and if you didn't, the commissars would sort you out, permanently.

A million ways to die here, he thought, and we've already had the first. Welcome to Golgotha, troopers.

'Right,' he said, facing Holtz. 'I'll see a medic later. For now, though, I'd better find van Droi. Get Siegler and Metzger together and see about getting our old junk-heap out of the ship. Come find me when it's done.'

'Right, sarge,' said Holtz, 'but do me one favour, will you? Go easy on the tank-bashing. You'll turn her against us if you keep that up. Besides, you can't judge a tank on shipboard exercises, can you?'

'Maybe not,' said Wulfe grudgingly. 'Maybe not, but you and I both know she's got a heck of a lot to live up to.' He turned and limped off to find Lieutenant van Droi, determined to ignore the fire in his joints and muscles as he went.

CHAPTER THREE

Far to the north of Wulfe's position, things were very different for those elements of the 18th Army Group that had landed safely. Their fourth evening on Golgotha saw General Mohamar deViers descend from orbit in his private aquila lander to personally oversee operations at the Imperial beachhead, located, as the ork slavers' base had so recently been, on the Hadron Plateau.

The preparatory stages of Operation Thunderstorm were already drawing to a close. Construction of the new Army Group HQ was almost complete, well ahead of schedule thanks to the contributions of the Adeptus Mechanicus. Their abundant technologies, the impressive prefabricated structures they had provided, the unceasing toil of their legions of brain-wiped biomechanical slaves, these things and more had seen the laser-blasted surface of the plateau converted and fortified in record time. The 10th Armoured Division was preparing to roll out on the morning of the following day, having been charged with securing the first of a series of outposts critical to establishing key supply lines in the east. So, with his private rooms already constructed and awaiting occupation, it was high time, in the opinion of General deViers, that the men on the ground felt the presence of their leader among them. Time, he thought, to remind them just whose show this was.

The sleek aquila touched down in the early evening, alighting on the base's small rockcrete runway without incident. The last of the day's light was just visible as a ruddy glow in the far west, and the base's floodlights were buzzing to life one by one. The lander's boarding ramp had barely touched rock when the general strode down it and began barking orders. He was a thin man, taller than average for a Cadian, clean-shaven with pomaded silver hair and sunken cheeks. At ninety-one years of age, seventy-six of those spent in military service, he looked surprisingly young, no older, in fact, than sixty. The treatments and surgeries he had undergone to achieve this were both expensive and painful, but never unacceptably so.

He was a man who placed a great deal of value on appearances, an attitude reflected in the tailoring of his immaculate uniform and in the polished sheen of the medals that glinted over his left breast pocket. His voice, when he spoke, was sharp and clear, and he had a tendency to emphasise certain words with little thrusts of his chin. The first order of business, he told his men, was a swift round of interviews and inspections, and no, they could *not* wait until the following morning.

He initiated the inspections, beginning, significantly, with the massive tank-crowded motor pool and progressing anti-clockwise through each area in turn. After two hours spent marching around the base snapping out questions and comments, trying in vain to acclimatise to the thick, unpleasant air, deViers confided to his long-suffering adjutant, Major Gruber, that he was deeply impressed. Things had apparently been proceeding very well without him. With its high curtain walls, towers topped with Manticore and Hydra anti-air defences, and the broad, extended parapets boasting row after row of Earthshaker artillery platforms, Exolon's new Army Group HQ represented a vital bastion of security on an otherwise hostile world. DeViers was quietly convinced that it would hold against even the most overwhelming ork siege. It would have to. In all likelihood, such an attack was mere days away. The Golgothan orks would have seen lights in the sky as the drop-ships had descended. Sooner or later, they would come to investigate. No matter how many came, the base could not be allowed to fall. It was the lynchpin of deViers's whole operation.

The plateau on which Hadron Base was being constructed measured over four kilometres in diameter and lay almost directly on the line of the equator. It had been selected on the basis of two critical factors. Firstly, with its sheer sides and few sloping access routes, it was, even without fortification, eminently defensible. Secondly, and more significantly, at a distance of some six hundred kilometres from the general's ultimate objective it was the closest suitable geological feature to the last known position of *The Fortress of Arrogance*.

His base inspection over, deViers ordered a briefing session with his three divisional commanders, Major Generals Rennkamp, Killian and

Bergen. It was deViers's intention to keep the session short, for he had also arranged a rather splendid banquet to celebrate the auspicious beginning of his ground operation. This beginning, he felt, was marked, not by the descent of the first drop-ships, but by his own arrival planet-side, and he would not let the moment pass without some kind of commemorative function. After all, Operation Thunderstorm, as he so regularly reminded his officers, was a righteous quest the likes of which had rarely been seen in the recent annals of the Imperial Guard. Why should the end of its opening phase not be celebrated in good spirits?

That was the plan, at least, but deViers soon found his good spirits dampened.

'How many?' he hissed. His face was red with rage, and his fists were clenched on the surface of his desk. 'Tell me again!'

'Six, sir,' answered Major General Bergen. 'Six missing, with a seventh discovered fifty kilometres to the north-east, spread across two and a half kilometres of desert. All hands lost. Do you wish to hear a list of the individual elements?'

'Of course I do,' snapped deViers. 'Seven drop-ships on the first day. By the Eye of Terror!'

Major General Bergen's voice didn't waver as he read off the list, but his tone was heavy and his face betrayed a grim mood. 'Drop-ship E44-a, the 116th Cadian Lasgunners, companies one and two, killed on descent. Drop-ship G22-a, the 122nd Tyrok Fusiliers, companies one to four, missing. Drop-ship G41-b, the 88th Mobile Infantry, companies three and four, missing. Drop-ship H17-c, the 303rd Skellas Rifles, companies eight to ten, missing. Drop-ship H19-a, the 98th Mechanised Infantry, companies one to six, missing. Drop-ship K22-c, the 71st Caedus Infantry, companies eight to ten, missing.' Bergen paused for a split second before reading the final listing. The missing ship had been carrying some of his own tankers. 'Drop-ship M13-j, the 81st Armoured Regiment, 10th Company, missing. No contact whatsoever from any of those listed.'

General deViers listened quietly to all this, staggered by the blow his forces had taken just from landing on this damned rock. Thousands of men gone. It was outrageous. The last listing was a tank company? By the bloody Golden Throne! An entire tank company, lost somewhere out there in the desert, most probably killed in the crash. Filthy orks were probably looting the site even now. Men were one thing, and their loss was to be lamented, of course, but life was cheap in the Imperium of Man. There were always more soldiers to be had. That's what the reserves were for. But tanks? Tanks were another matter entirely. There were no replacements waiting in the wings for the war machines that had been lost. Each tank put out of action left a gap that nothing else could fill. The strength of his armoured regiment was absolutely critical given the itinerant nature of the operation. With his mind firmly fixated on the negative, the general's anger got the better of him. He leapt to his feet, throwing his chair backwards and banging his fists down on his desk.

'It's a damned fiasco! How could we lose seven drop-ships on the first day? Was it orks? Storms? What the heck are our naval liaisons saying about this? What about the Mechanicus? I want answers, damn it!' Veins bulged in his neck and his eyes looked ready to pop out of his head.

The three officers seated before him remained as still as statues while their general raged. They had seen it all before, and with increasing regularity of late. They knew better than to interrupt him before his tirade had ended. Attempting to soothe him was just asking for trouble. When deViers finally *did* stop spewing fire and sank slowly back into his chair, it was Killian, the shortest, stockiest and, in the general's eyes, least likeable of the three, who spoke up.

'The tech-priests have a team out in the desert, sir. They're studying the drop-ship in the north-east for the cause of the crash. No word yet, of course, since they're out of vox range.'

Killian winced as soon as he said this, realising immediately that he had just poured fuel on the fire. Predictably, deViers pounced.

'Out of bloody vox range?' he roared, and launched into an entirely fresh diatribe. Imperial communications equipment, unreliable at the best of times in the general's long years of experience, was almost useless on Golgotha. According to the tech-priests, there were profound levels of electromagnetic interference from the constant storms that cloaked this world. The Mechanicus contingent attached to the mission had promised a solution in due course, but, for now, communications at any range greater than a dozen kilometres simply degenerated into white noise. Clear communication at even half that distance required the expenditure of significant amounts of electrical power – more than was required to light the base for a whole day – and contact with the fleet in orbit was kept to an absolute minimum by sheer necessity. DeViers cursed and bellowed like a madman until he had spent himself again. It didn't take long.

Despite external appearances, he was still an old man, and the intensity of his outbursts quickly exhausted him. He knew he should work harder to control his temper. He knew, too, that it had been getting far worse in recent months. There was a time, he thought, when nothing fazed me. What changed? Why do I respond so violently these days? I can't let the pressure get to me like this.

He knew that shouting at his divisional commanders was poor therapy, and achieved very little. He would be relying on these men above all others in the days ahead. They would help him secure his prize, his legacy, his place among the good and the great. No, shouting at them didn't help anyone. He forced his voice back down to normal levels. Ten minutes later, after a brief review of the schedule for their coming deployment, he dismissed them so that they might dress for the banquet. As the three senior officers stood and saluted him, deViers briefly considered apologising for his earlier explosiveness.

No, he told himself. Let my anger stand as a message that I expect far better. I won't have them thinking me weak.

Weakness in any form was something Mohamar Antoninus deViers could not abide, especially his own.

THE GENERAL STOLE an hour of sleep after the briefing, though it seemed to him that only seconds had passed before his adjutant shook him gently awake so that he might wash and dress for the banquet. Two hours later, he found himself standing at the head of a long krellwood table in a bright, high-ceilinged room, ringing his goblet with a silver fork and asking his guests for their undivided attention.

'Officers of the 18th Army Group,' he began, beaming at them with theatrical magnanimity, 'and, of course, my other honoured guests, I thank you all for taking the time to attend. It's only right that we celebrate. Tonight, we mark the true start of our holy quest with the best that our circumstances allow. Look at you; the Emperor must be gazing down on you with pride, seated here, dressed so smartly, so ready and willing to be about His divine work. He'll be prouder still when we find our prize. What a moment that will be! One for the history books, indeed. I'm sure you've all dreamed of it as much as I have: the fame, the glory, Army Group Exolon recovering the legendary *Fortress of Arrogance* from right under the nose of the old foe. Yes! For ever after, men will read of our exploits with awe. Let none of you doubt that. There is no cause greater than that which inspires one's fellow man.'

He scanned the faces around the table, daring anyone to pay him less than full attention, and was pleased to see every eye, including several unblinking mechanical ones, turned in his direction.

'We could not have asked for a higher honour,' he told them. 'I've heard mutterings among the men, just as you have, talk of wishing to join Commissar Yarrick and our Cadian brothers on Armageddon. Such talk is to be expected. Exolon is, after all, a fighting man's army, and our men want to make a difference. I appreciate their eagerness, for I too would see us lend Yarrick's forces our much-needed strength sooner rather than later. But all things in their proper time. We can offer so much more by claiming victory here. Through the successful recovery and restoration of *The Fortress of Arrogance*, this army will provide our

Imperial brothers – not just Cadians, but all men of the Imperium – with a renewed strength of purpose and determination that no amount of reinforcement could possibly hope to offer. *The Fortress* is not just another Baneblade battle tank, as you all should know. She is a symbol of everything the Guard stands for: of strength and honour, of courage and duty, of unbending resistance against the foul traitors and alien hordes that strive to wipe our race from the face of the galaxy. I say her recovery is long overdue. So, join me in a toast. Fill your glasses, all of you.'

DeViers waited as his guests sloshed cool golden liquor into goblets of fine black crystal. They were senior officers for the most part. His three divisional commanders, having changed out of their field tunics and into their finest dress uniforms, all looked splendid. The gold accoutrements on their lapels and breast pockets gleamed brightly in the light of the overhead lamps. The other officers present were regimental commanders from the 8th Mechanised and 12th Heavy Infantry Divisions, some of them colonels, the rest majors. They had also smartened themselves up adequately, though more than a few bore grisly facial scars that somewhat ruined the overall effect.

Even with their battle-ravaged features, they were far easier on the eye than the three hooded, red-robed figures that sat among them: Tech-Magos Sennesdiar, Tech-Adept Xephous, and Tech-Adept Armadron, the three most senior members of the Adeptus Mechanicus present at Hadron Base.

DeViers had felt it only proper to invite them, absolutely certain that they would decline. He would not have asked them otherwise. Propriety had backfired on him, however, as all three had come. He still couldn't understand why. They had expressly told him that they wouldn't be able to eat the food his chef prepared. One of them – the perpetually wheezing, twitching Armadron – seemed to lack anything that even approximated a functioning mouth. From what deViers had glimpsed so far under that shadowy hood, it appeared that the adept's entire head was encased in twin hemispheres of steel, absolutely featureless but for a single glowing green eye. In terms of aesthetics, the other two weren't much better.

Sennesdiar, the highest ranking of the three – though his robes bore no markings to denote this – was also the largest figure in the room, his misshapen bulk nearly twice the mass of anyone else present. His robes were perforated all across his back, allowing a number of strange serpentine appendages to fall all the way to the floor where they coiled around the legs of his chair, their metal segments gleaming in the light. Sennesdiar's face – what little could be seen of it under his cowl – was grotesque, the flesh pale and bloodless, little more, in places, than flaps of skin stapled over dull steel, and his tiny mouth was a lipless slash that reminded deViers of nothing so much as a fresh stab wound. The effect was a mask that made a mockery of human features.

The last of the three, Xephous, was no better. In some ways, he was actually worse, for his complex arrangement of mandibles and visual receptors gave him the aspect of a nightmarish biomechanical crab, and the intermittent clacking sounds that issued from him only added to the effect.

By the Golden Throne of Terra, thought deViers, *between the three of them, they're enough to ruin a man's appetite.*

The more human guests had filled their glasses and were pushing their chairs back so that they might rise to their feet for the general's toast.

DeViers turned his eyes away from the tech-priests, glad that the ever-considerate Gruber had seated them among the men at the far end of the table. Much nearer and, thankfully, much easier to behold, were Bishop Augustus and High Commissar Morten.

The bishop, seated on the general's immediate right, was a tall, almost skeletally thin man in his late seventies with a prodigiously long nose. His tanned skin shimmered with a coating of the most expensive and richly-scented oils, and precious gems glittered from the rings that graced each of his long fingers. Like the tech-priests, Bishop Augustus wore voluminous and finely made robes, though his were a dazzling white, symbolising a spiritual purity far beyond the grasp of other, lesser men. *That was worth a laugh,* thought deViers. If rumours about the bishop were true, he was anything but pure. On Cadia, he would have been publicly executed for his unorthodox predilections, but, perhaps, deViers told himself, the rumours were exactly that: idle rumours. The bishop was a fine conversationalist, already winning smiles and laughter from a number of the officers as they had listened intently to his anecdotes before being seated around the table. It was much more than could be said for his Martian counterparts.

The high commissar, seated on the general's immediate left, was a striking figure of a man, clearly of fine noble stock, dressed immaculately in his gold-braided tunic and black silk shirt. Such were Morten's good looks that the only other man present whose features stood up to any kind of comparison was Major General Bergen, whom deViers always thought looked just as if he'd stepped straight out of a recruitment poster.

As was only proper, High Commissar Morten had dispensed with his stiffened cap while at the table, but it was impossible to look at the man without seeing the ghost of it still perched firmly on his head, such was the strength of his identity. He was, in deViers's opinion, the quintessential political officer. Unswerving and utterly uncompromising in his duty, he had served with the 18th Army Group for the last eleven years and, though he and deViers had never developed anything that could be called a friendship, the general enjoyed the man's professional respect and returned it in kind.

The absence of friendship was no great loss. After all, deViers told himself, one must be careful around these commissars.

All his guests were standing now, their eyes on him, goblets filled and at the ready. DeViers lifted his straight out in front of him, took a breath, and projected his voice.

'To success, gentlemen,' he said. 'To success and victory!'

'Success and victory!' they replied with fervour. Excepting the Mechanicus, each of the guests threw back his glass and drank. When they had finished, deViers gestured them back into their seats, smiling broadly at them.

Look at them, Mohamar, he thought, eating out of your hand. To success and victory, indeed, and to immortality, for I *will* have the glory I seek. And Throne help any bastard that gets in my way.

MAJOR GENERAL GERARD Bergen looked down at his plate with absolute revulsion. What the devil *was* this abomination? The starter had been bad enough – chilled bladdercrab with ormin and caprium – so obscenely rich that he'd felt his stomach churning, though the general's other guests had seemed to enjoy it immensely judging by their praise for the general's personal chef. Now the old man's servants brought out the main course – quivering mountains of dark red meat that looked dangerously undercooked.

The general's adjutant, Gruber, placed himself on the old man's right and proudly announced, 'Lightly roasted auroch heart stuffed with jellied grox liver and dogwort.'

Murmurs of appreciation sounded from around the table, but Bergen studied the thing on his plate as if it were an alien life form. It sat there glistening wetly in the light from the lamps, its pungent aroma clawing at his nostrils. He hoped the expression of delight he was struggling to maintain was enough to fool the general. He looked up the table involuntarily and immediately wished he hadn't. DeViers caught his eye. Bergen put extra effort into his artificial smile and saw the old man grin back, buying into his act.

He turned back to the food. Maybe it tastes better than it looks, he thought, but I doubt it.

Bergen considered himself a down-to-earth man for someone of his breeding and rank – it was, in fact, the thing he liked best about himself – and it required effort on his part to maintain the social niceties so important to his station in the classist upper echelons of the Imperial Guard. Whether on the battlefield or off it, he liked to live as his men did, eating standard-issue rations and sleeping on a standard-issue bedroll, washing and shaving as little or as often as his men were able to. Such things allowed him a better understanding of the condition of his troops, of how far he could push them before they would start to come undone. Such information was critical to a good commander. Some of the old-school officers, a few of the colonels and majors seated around him perhaps, also held to such practices, but they were in the minority. Bergen's regimental commanders – Vinnemann, Marrenburg and Graves – had been allowed to abstain from attending the dinner so that they might continue their preparations for deployment, a concession that Bergen greatly envied them. DeViers hadn't given him that option. The old man had been adamant that *all* his divisional commanders attend.

Lifting his cutlery, Bergen began slicing bite-sized chunks from the undercooked heart. Spearing one with his fork, he lifted it towards his mouth. Here goes nothing, he told himself, and popped it in. The texture was highly unpleasant, but he was forced to admit that it tasted a lot better than it looked.

While the general's guests concentrated on the main course, the level of conversation dropped, stifled by the efforts of cutting and chewing, and of chasing each mouthful down with a sip of amasec. But it wasn't long until most of the plates lay empty save a smear of sauce on each, and a flock of servants emerged from the side corridors to clear them away.

Bergen sat back in silence and watched the others interact. His stomach was threatening to rebel against him.

Bishop Augustus dabbed at the corners of his mouth with a white silk napkin and said, 'Exquisite, general, but quite cruel, don't you think, to acclimatise us to such outstanding fare? I suspect Golgotha offers nothing so delicious or refined.'

General deViers faced the bishop, but gestured down the table to Tech-Magos Sennesdiar.

'The honoured magos,' he said, 'tells me that most of the animal and plant life on this world is fatal if ingested. Is that not so, magos?'

The blaring voice that replied was like a vox-caster unit with the volume turned up too high. Like most of the others, Bergen winced.

'If you'll permit me, general,' boomed the tech-magos, each word toneless and harsh, 'the probability of death would depend on the amount and type of matter ingested, the body-weight and constitution of the individual in question, the availability and quality of medical assistance–'

From Bergen's left, a few seats further down the table, the crab-faced Tech-Adept Xephous emitted a sudden burst of noise, high-pitched and raw, like fingernails scraping on a blackboard. His superior immediately replied with a similar condensed sonic burst. Bergen knew this for what it was. The tech-priests were communicating in Binary, the ancient machine-language of the Martian priesthood. When Sennesdiar reverted to speaking in Gothic a moment later, his voice was pitched just right. 'My apologies, gentlemen. My adept informs me that my vocaliser settings may have caused you some discomfort. Is this setting acceptable?'

'A great improvement, magos,' said General deViers.

'Then I shall continue listing the variables relevant to the question of toxicity in–'

DeViers held up a hand and cut the tech-priest off mid-sentence. 'Thank you, magos, but that will not be necessary. A simple yes or no would have sufficed.'

'It is not a simple matter,' said the tech-priest. 'I shall have an acolyte-logis compile a report for you on the subject. We have significant amounts of relevant data.'

'If you must,' said deViers, winking at Bishop Augustus, 'but I'd rather you just warn me if I'm about to bite down on something I shouldn't.'

You wouldn't want to bite off more than you could chew, thought Bergen automatically.

'Actually,' continued General deViers, turning from the tech-magos, 'I'd like to hear the high commissar's thoughts on this amasec. Commodore Galbraithe graciously donated eighteen bottles of the stuff for our little celebration. Such a pity that he wasn't able to share it with us in person.'

'Wasn't able?' asked Major General Rennkamp brusquely, 'Or wasn't willing? I've heard the old spacer hasn't been ground-side for over twenty years. You'd need a direct order from the High Lords to get him off that *Helicon Star* of his.'

There was a ripple of polite laughter.

'A fine ship, that,' murmured a colonel close to Bergen. It was von Holden, one of Rennkamp's men, commander of the 259th Mechanised Regiment. Bergen was a little surprised. He had privately admired both of the battle fleet's heavy cruisers, but it wasn't often one would hear a ground-pounder praising a naval vessel out loud. There were long-running tensions between the Guard and the Navy, a perpetuation of mistrusts that stretched back as far as the Age of Apostasy and beyond.

At the upper end of the table, High Commissar Morten was answering the general. 'A very fine vintage, sir. The commodore is most gracious. This is very expensive stuff. It has a certain citrus quality, you agree? And the significance of his choice...'

'What significance would that be?' asked Bishop Augustus.

'Its origin, your grace,' said Morten. 'This particular amasec is produced exclusively by the Jaldyne prefectural distilleries on Terrax Secundus. Quite rare outside the Ultima Segmentum.'

'Ah, clever of him,' said a glowing deViers. 'Wonderful stuff.'

Bishop Augustus was frowning. 'I'm afraid I still don't see the connection.'

'Terraxian and Cadian regiments fought side-by-side on this very plateau in the last war,' answered the high commissar. 'Together, they were able to buy Commissar Yarrick and his command staff the time they needed to escape the planet's surface. The orks swarmed this very plateau just as Yarrick's lifter ascended. I believe there were several popular books published about the battle.'

A moment of quiet descended on the table as the fighting men present muttered a quick prayer for the fallen. It was Major General Killian that broke the spell.

'I don't suppose any of you have read Michelos?' he asked. 'I've seen a few of my troopers with their noses in tattered copies.'

'Finally taught your lot to read, eh, Klotus?' said Bergen with a grin.

Killian laughed heartily, chasing off the last of the sombre mood that had momentarily fallen on the table. 'You can talk, tread-head. Your lot still think they need to take toilet paper to the mess tent. Must be all those promethium fumes.'

The colonels seated nearby laughed out loud, prone to engage in a bit of good-natured ribbing themselves at times, but General deViers coughed sharply into his hand, and the sound cut through the laughter like a las-knife. The expression on the general's face sent a clear message: not the time, not the place.

Fair enough, thought Bergen. It's your show.

High Commissar Morten sat forward, ice blue eyes fixed on Killian, and said, 'I'm not sure I approve, major general.' Seeing Killian's face redden, he added, 'Of troopers reading Michelos, I mean. His work has a very fatalistic bent. Not suitable material for front-line troops. Dreadful recruitment material, too. The way he refers to Guard service as "the meat grinder". If it were up to me, I'd have the text prohibited under article six.'

Bergen resisted the urge to roll his eyes. First offences under article six meant the lash. It seemed a little harsh for reading a bit of poetry, he thought.

'Come now, commissar,' said Rennkamp. 'Isn't it quite popular with the civs?'

'Civilians?' said Morten. 'I hardly think so. The last I heard, hivers still prefer their entertainment filled with sex and unstoppable heroes.'

'What have you got against unstoppable heroes?' asked Killian, smirking. 'I like to think you're dining with at least one.'

General deViers lifted his glass and said, 'I'll drink to that!'

His adjutant, Gruber, appeared again from the side door, walked to the right side of the general's chair and, in a deep, sonorous voice, announced the dessert – slices of candied bonifruit with hot caffeine to follow for those who wanted it.

Bergen stifled a groan. He could hardly cope with consuming more food, but there was little choice. Propriety made harsh demands. He doubted he could get away with refusing to partake of the sweetened fruit. The general had had quite a few glasses of amasec, but his eyes were missing nothing. It had crossed Bergen's mind that the whole event might have been orchestrated to serve a double purpose. He didn't doubt that the general wished to celebrate – deViers was voracious when it came to attention and respect – but it wouldn't have surprised him if the old man was also using the banquet as an opportunity to gauge the mood among his officers and to root out potential troublemakers. It was hardly an original method. One of the divisional commanders would have to replace the general one day. Bergen knew that Rennkamp was only too eager to step in and take over whenever the chance came up. He wasn't sure about Killian yet. When the amasec was flowing and the room was filled with chatter, it was easy to let one's guard down, confident that those around you were likewise swept up in the bonhomie. Bergen had been careful to sip slowly, conscious that he would be leading his troops out before dawn. Now, he was glad of that, certain that the old general was watching all of them like a hawk.

Warp damn the old bastard, he thought. Millions of our brother Cadians dead and dying in the Third War of Armageddon, and here he is throwing dinner parties on a world infested with greenskins. What happened to him? There was a time when I looked up to him, a time when he was rock-solid. He's not the same man, now. It's as if some kind of panic or mania has taken over. I can't stand what he's become.

He stabbed his dessert fork into a slice of bonifruit and, slowly, mechanically, chewed and swallowed, hardly tasting it at all.

At least tomorrow, he would be out of the general's shadow again.

THERE'S A MAN who understands this quest, thought General deViers. Good officer, Gerard Bergen. Look at him, limiting his drink, careful not to gorge himself, mindful of tomorrow and the pressures on him. Not like some of these others. Damn, but I like this one. I like him a lot. Reminds me of myself.

Commodore Galbraithe's fine amasec was really working hard on the general. His head felt as light as air and there was a very pleasant numbness in his muscles. He was warm, just a little dizzy, and supremely satisfied with the way the evening had progressed.

Gruber had returned to his side to lean over and whisper the time to him. Good old Gruber. He did as he was told, no questions asked, and took care of business, even the nasty stuff.

DeViers rose unsteadily to his feet and addressed his guests for the last time that evening.

'Gentlemen,' he said, 'my adjutant tells me that the hour is late and, as you know, the 10th Armoured Division is rolling out tomorrow to secure the first of our waypoints. Major General Bergen should be in his bunk, and I dare say the rest of you need more than your share of beauty sleep, but I have a few words for you before you disperse.'

His guests turned their heads towards him.

'Operation Thunderstorm is off to a fine, auspicious start. I've thoroughly enjoyed your company this evening and I thank you for helping me to mark this occasion in such a fitting manner.'

His eyes settled for a brief moment on each of them, and he nodded in agreement with his own words as he said, 'We've dangerous business ahead. The filthy orks aren't about to make it easy for us. There's nothing they love more than a fight, and they'll come in their millions once they know men have returned to this place. Soon, our Major General Bergen here will be giving them their first taste of Imperial lead in almost forty years, and there'll be plenty more to follow, by Throne! We'll make the bastards suffer. It's time to remind them whose bloody galaxy this is.'

'Hear, hear!' called out one of Killian's colonels, earning him a broad grin from the general. Some of the other officers lifted their glasses.

'Yes,' said deViers, 'lift your glasses, all of you. A final toast.'

Around the table, the necks of tall decanters clinked against goblet rims. Each guest rose from his seat, some less steadily than others.

DeViers turned to Bishop Augustus. 'Through the counsel of the Emperor's most holy Ministorum, may our faith remain strong.'

The bishop nodded sincerely, as if he would personally make it so.

'Ave Imperator,' replied the men around the table.

DeViers turned next to High Commissar Morten and said, 'Through the uncompromising vigilance of our tireless commissars, may our hearts never falter.'

Morten tilted his head in acknowledgement.

'Ave Imperator.'

The general gestured at each of the tech-priests in turn with his glass. 'Through the wisdom and scientific mastery of the Adeptus Mechanicus, may our guns blaze fierce and our engines never stall.'

'Ave Imperator,' said the officers, but the tech-priests replied 'Ave Omnissiah!' and deViers heard Bishop Augustus mutter a quiet curse under his breath.

'Throne above,' the general went on, 'even the Navy is doing its part!'

Some of the colonels and majors grunted in brief disapproval.

'Come now, you men,' chided deViers, still smiling. 'Commodore Galbraithe sends us his best liquor and has promised me a Vulcan close-support wing once our hangars are finished. I won't exclude him from my toast.'

'May we not also raise our glasses to Major General Bergen?' asked High Commissar Morten. He turned to face Bergen down the length of the table and said, 'The very best of luck to you, sir, in your coming assault on Karavassa. The orks will crumble before you and the might of your glorious tanks.'

'Hear, hear!' agreed the other officers noisily.

'Thank you, high commissar,' said Bergen. 'I'm confident my division will more than live up to the general's expectations.'

Bishop Augustus raised his glass in Bergen's direction and said, 'May the Light of all mankind watch over you and your men, major general, and grant you victory in His Name. You go with the blessings of His Most Holy Ministorum.'

'The Emperor protects!' said deViers sharply, irked that the high commissar had seen fit to hijack his toast.

'The Emperor protects!' chorused the guests, and together, excepting the tech-priests as always, they drained their glasses. At a sign from Gruber, the general's servants emerged from the side corridor again to withdraw the chairs from around the table, signalling an end to the general's soiree. As the guests started filing out of the room's broad double doors, each saluting him as they went, deViers heard Tech-Magos Sennesdiar addressing Major General Bergen.

'I miscalculated the probability of your attendance tonight, major general,' said the magos. 'Are your preparations complete? May I assume that your enginseers are performing optimally?'

'They are,' answered Bergen. 'As for my attendance, the general insisted. Perhaps he sought to distract my mind. Time to think is not always a welcome commodity the day before deployment.'

'Epinephrine,' said Tech-Adept Armadron.

'I'm sorry, adept?' said Bergen.

'And norepinephrine,' said Tech-Adept Xephous. 'Armadron is correct. Troopers under study showed greatly increased levels of both hormones prior to engagement with the enemy. Sections of the brain may be excised to inhibit this, major general. Our skitarii legions do not experience the problem.'

Bishop Augustus was hovering nearby. Overhearing them, he interjected acidly, 'That must be a great comfort to them.'

Tech-Magos Sennesdiar turned his cowled head to face the Ministorum man. 'Their comfort is irrelevant, priest. Their efficiency is not.'

General deViers saw the bishop's face flush and moved quickly to intervene. Before the bishop could respond and escalate matters, he gripped the bishop's hand in his. 'I was greatly honoured by your attendance tonight, your grace. I hope you enjoyed it as much as I did. Remember, if there's anything you need from me, you may contact my adjutant, Gruber, directly. He'll alert me to anything that requires my attention.'

Bishop Augustus gaped for a moment, and then, his tone still edged with displeasure, said, 'Most kind, general. I won't forget. And congratulations once again on such a fine banquet. I shall look forward to your next, providing the guest list is a little more... exclusive.'

Throwing a last contemptuous look at the tech-priests, the bishop lifted the hem of his robe from the floor and stalked out of the room. A string of officers moved up to salute the general and thank him. Without further discourse, the tech-priests took this opportunity to leave.

As the other officers moved off, deViers decided to pull Bergen aside just as he was about to depart.

Standing together, he found his eyes level with the younger man's. Like the general, Bergen was taller than most Cadians. He was of a heavier, more muscular build than the general, too, but then, he *was* forty years younger. Rejuvenat treatments could only do so much. Face to face like this, deViers noted how much smoother and tighter Bergen's skin was. Sometimes, when the general was awoken in the early hours of the morning by the need to relieve himself, he would catch his reflection in a mirror and gasp, shocked that his face could look so skull-like in a certain light. He knew that all the rejuvenat in the galaxy wouldn't hold ageing off forever. How long did he have left to achieve his dream?

'A quick word before you go, Gerard,' said deViers. 'Just wanted to wish you the very best out there.'

Bergen gazed straight back at him and, for a second, deViers felt like he had entered some kind of staring contest. It was a strange moment, but then Bergen spoke, and the feeling, whatever its cause, vanished into nothing.

'I appreciate that, sir,' said Bergen, 'but luck is overrated is it not? I've never much liked relying on it.'

DeViers nodded. 'Don't you worry. We'll all come out of this as heroes.' He hesitated, trying to gain control over all the thoughts swimming around in his head. The commodore's amasec was stronger than he had expected. It was difficult to put into order the things he wanted to say. In a rare moment of alcohol-induced frankness, he settled on saying, 'You know, Gerard, my line – my bloodline, that is – ends with me. Perhaps I've mentioned that to you before.'

Bergen's mouth was a tight line. 'You have, sir.'

'Couldn't father any of my own, you know. Not for lack of trying, by Throne, but my seed's as thin as water, so the experts tell me.'

'I'm sure that it's none of my business, sir,' said Bergen.

It was the cold, flat tone in which they were spoken, rather than the words themselves, that surprised deViers. He recovered quickly, however, clapping Bergen on the arm, and saying, 'I suppose not, Gerard. I just wanted you to understand. A man must leave his mark on the Imperium. History must remember me. I've given my entire life to the Emperor's service.'

Bergen stared back quietly for second. 'We all have, sir.'

DeViers nodded, 'Yes, of course. A fighting man's outfit, my 18th Army Group. I've said it before. Good men we lead.'

'Good men, sir,' said Bergen. 'I'm not sure we deserve them sometimes.'

DeViers couldn't explain why, but those words hit him like a smack in the face. He gaped for a moment, unsure of how to respond. Bergen didn't give him the chance.

'With your permission, sir,' he said. 'I should get some rest before I lead my division out. I want to be ready when we meet the foe.'

'Permission granted,' replied deViers.

Bergen snapped his boot heels together and gave a fine, crisp salute which deViers returned. Then Bergen turned sharply, and marched out of the room.

DeViers watched him go. For a few minutes, he stood alone in silence, thinking how remarkable it was that the word *we* could be made to sound so much like *you*.

CHAPTER FOUR

AFTER THE GENERAL'S dinner, Bergen emerged into the hot night air to find his adjutant, Katz, awaiting him in the driver's seat of an idling staff car, ready to take him back to his quarters. Despite the hour and the fact that he was due to lead his entire division out before dawn, Bergen wasn't in the mood to retire quite yet, and waved Katz on, telling him he would return on foot after a short walk. Though he had limited his consumption to a polite minimum, Commodore Galbraithe's rich amasec had numbed his fingertips, and he felt the need to walk it off. His stomach felt uncomfortably full and his mind was restless, awash with conflicting thoughts. He knew that sleep would not come easily. Perhaps a little time in the open air, even air tainted with the smell of sulphur, would do him some good.

He walked without a specific destination in mind, keeping to areas where the ground was less heavily trodden and less brightly lit, bringing him in short order to the southernmost section of the base. This was not the first time Bergen had been posted to a desert region, and he had expected the temperature to plummet at night, as it so often did in the deserts he had visited on other worlds. But the constant cloud cover on Golgotha trapped a layer of heat in the lower atmosphere that would take many hours to dissipate, and he unbuttoned his jacket and shirt collar as he walked.

Rounding the corner of a prefabricated barracks, he almost bumped into a squad of infantrymen on their way to the mess tents. They stopped to salute him smartly, though the colour of their berets said they weren't from his division. He returned the salute without breaking stride, noting absently that he hadn't recognised anyone he had passed so far. Nothing strange in that, of course. There were close to thirty thousand men in Hadron Base: two whole infantry divisions plus his own armoured, each at roughly ten thousand men apiece, not counting the drop-ship losses, and that was excluding the non-combat personnel so essential to basic operations.

Thirty thousand, he decided, was a conservative estimate. Crowded into the space between the towering curtain walls, it seemed like a vast number, an unstoppable military force, but Bergen knew it was nothing of the kind. Despite the difficulties inherent in scanning the shrouded surface of the planet, what little data they had suggested that Golgotha still seethed with the foe. Those few probe-servitors that had returned safely had shown that the more temperate regions north and south of the desert were dotted with vast settlements wherever the terrain allowed. Even now, thought Bergen, legions of orks might be racing through the darkness, crossing the open sands towards the plateau, following grunted reports of lights in the sky on the promise of a good blood-soaked battle.

Vermin, he thought. They're a plague on the galaxy, the damned greenskins.

He reached the foot of the south wall and began to climb a zigzagging staircase that led up to the battlements. There was a powered elevator inside the nearest tower, but he opted to ascend under his own strength, conscious of the excess of calories that General deViers had forced on him. As he moved from step to step, enjoying the steady rhythm of the exercise, his thoughts dwelled on the Golgothan orks.

They'd had thirty-eight years of freedom to spread across the land, turning every scrap of captured or abandoned Imperial technology to their needs. Even taking into account the unprecedented hordes that had left this world and the surrounding systems to join Thraka's onslaught of Imperial space, there had to be literally millions of orks still present, perhaps billions. Who could say for sure how many?

Army Group Exolon was nothing in the face of such numbers and anyone who said otherwise was either a propaganda man, a fool, or both, as they so often were. Despite the general's grand speech about the importance of their quest, Bergen still shared the most fervent hopes of his men that this would all be over quickly so they could join the fight on Armageddon. *That* was a fight worthy of his beloved armoured division, for if Armageddon fell, Holy Terra, the sacred Cradle of mankind, would be under direct threat for the first time since the divine Emperor had walked the stars.

There could scarcely be a greater danger to the preservation of the Imperium in these dark times.

As Bergen reached the top of the stairs, breathing heavily, his forehead damp with sweat and his quadriceps burning, he stopped and turned to look down on Hadron Base. It was quite something, he admitted. It sat shimmering like an island of light in a sea of absolute darkness. His gaze crossed the small airfield in the north-east quarter, its hangars nearing completion and awaiting the arrival of the Vulcan gunships that the commodore had promised. To the south of it, scores of water towers and storage silos stood in tight, ordered rows like men under close inspection. On the east side, next to one of the base's massive reinforced gates, were the motor pool and mustering field. Both were large and well lit, and filled with red-robed enginseers busily tending to row upon row of transports and war machines. There were hundreds of men in rust-coloured fatigues down there, too: troopers from the support echelons hefting ammunition and supplies back and forth, working hard against the clock. Large Guard-issue trucks – the ever-reliable Thirty-Sixers – were being driven into position so that fuel drums and supplies could be hoisted onto them. Scores of Sentinel walkers squatted in groups like flightless birds at rest, legs folded beneath them to allow for oiling and final weapons checks.

To Bergen, all this was a beautiful sight, something he appreciated every time he saw it, and he stood watching, motionless, for long minutes. He felt lucky, in many ways, to be the man he was. From the age of six, from the moment that his mother had explained his destiny to him, that he was already marked for military service, the Imperial Guard was the only thing that had given real meaning to his life. It was the Guard that had shaped and defined him.

He turned from his view of the base below and moved to the parapet wall, looking out into the black of the night. To his left, rows of Earthshaker guns sat silent, their machine-spirits resting until called upon to commit the explosive, long-range slaughter at which they excelled. Some of the gun crews were absent, sleeping in their barracks or getting fed, most likely. Sirens would call them back to their stations in the event of an attack. Other crews had to remain on duty shifts. They sat by their guns, smoking, playing cards, a few of them sharpening knives or practising close-combat techniques with their fellows. Others moved in pairs along the wall, men on patrol duty, occasionally lifting night-vision magnoculars to their eyes and then dropping them again. Nothing to see out there.

Footsteps sounded behind Bergen and he turned to find a short, scruffy trooper looking up at him with a pipe of styrene cups in one hand and a green flask in the other.

'Care for some hot caffeine, sir?' asked the trooper a little nervously, eyeing the bright golden glyphs on Bergen's collar and the bands at his sleeve.

Bergen smiled.

'Are you sure it's hot, son?' he asked. There was no steam rising from the flask's open lid.

The trooper nodded earnestly. 'My sergeant says it's the atmospheric pressure, sir. Stuff doesn't steam here. Not at normal temperatures, least-wise. He says if it's steaming, it'll put you in the med-block with burns. Can't pretend as I understand it myself, but I'll take his word for it, sir. He's a smart one, is my sarge.'

Bergen smiled, but refused a cup all the same. Any more caffeine tonight and he wouldn't sleep at all.

'What's your name and outfit, son?' he asked.

'Ritter, sir. Two-one-five-three-five. With the 88th Feros Artillery.'

'So these are your guns?' said Bergen, jabbing a thumb over his shoulder.

The little trooper looked proud. 'Sure are, sir. Proper beauties, ain't they? I'm hoping to crew eventually. I'm just support right now, though.'

'They're not half bad, private,' said Bergen, glancing over his shoulder at them. 'Not bad at all. You must be proud that your regiment is part of this operation. One for the history books, this.'

'I suppose so, sir,' said Ritter. 'I mean, I just go where the regiment goes. So long as me and my mates are together, I don't mind where. The air here stinks a bit, though. And… well, there's no girls except them Medicae nurses. And it's only the officers have a devil's chance with any of that lot, isn't it? Even the rough-looking ones.'

Bergen laughed. 'Glad you've got your priorities straight. A man has to keep things in perspective, eh?'

'Too true, sir.'

'Well, you'd best get back to it. I bet some of your mates could use a good shot of caff to keep them awake. Keep your chin up, soldier.'

'Right, sir,' said Ritter. 'Thank you, sir.' He fumbled with the flask and cups for a moment so that he could throw up a stiff salute before moving off to serve the gun crews he so hoped to join.

Bergen watched him go and then started walking anti-clockwise along the wall in the general direction of his quarters, gesturing for the men he passed not to rise on his account. Talking with Ritter had lightened his mood. There was an undeniable value, he believed, in taking the time to talk with the rank-and-file. Their answers were often refreshingly honest, unshaped by the hidden agendas that tightly governed the words of most career-minded senior officers. Some of the younger troopers were blessed with a shining optimism – born of blissful naivety, he supposed – that he couldn't ever remember having possessed. Perhaps it was a class thing. Until the day he entered cadet school, his family, saints rest them, had worked tirelessly to prepare him for a life of war. The old phrase 'harder than a Cadian grandmother' was born of fact, as the network of deep scars on his back attested.

As he walked further along the wall his thoughts shifted to General deViers, and the upturn in his mood was suddenly reversed again. Mohamar Antoninus deViers. Alarm bells had been ringing in Bergen's head for months. There were no two ways about it, the general had been swiftly losing his grip on reality since the destruction of Palmeros.

It should have been the old man's crowning glory, the Palmeros campaign. He was long overdue for retirement and, if he had only managed to turn back the orks and save the majority of the planetary populace, he would certainly have received the coveted Honorifica, and would probably have been granted an Imperial title. Lord General Mohamar deViers: that would have gone some way towards satisfying his lust for fame. Instead, Ghazghkull Thraka had smashed the planet apart with seventeen massive asteroids, killing billions of loyal Imperial citizens and wiping a civilised world from the star charts. DeViers had been forced to pull out fast with none of the everlasting glory he had anticipated. Perhaps he had imagined that the Palmerosi people would build statues in his honour. Yes, thought Bergen, he would have been looking forward to that.

Without victory, there were no statues.

Humiliated, the old man had scrabbled for another cause and, in his desperation, had settled on a hopeless one that other, more wily generals had manoeuvred carefully to avoid: a half-mad recovery mission that Sector Command promised would earn the general his place in the history books.

What wouldn't the old man sacrifice, Bergen wondered grimly, for something like that? He was the last of his line. He'd said it himself. His obsession with leaving some kind of legacy had put the entire army group at extreme risk.

Bergen's steps grew heavier as he began his descent from the high battlements eager to return to his quarters. The walk had done its job. Tiredness settled over him like a heavy blanket. As he trudged down one of the south-eastern stairwells, boots ringing on the metal steps, he cast his mind back to the briefing session earlier that day, and the words the general had offered before dismissing his three divisional commanders.

'Expect a fight when you get to Karavassa, Gerard,' deViers had said. 'You can be sure that every damned outpost that Yarrick established during the last war has been infested with the buggers. They've had plenty of time to dig in, by Throne. Let's hope all that time has made them soft and complacent. Regardless, I know you'll get the job done. I *must* have secure supply lines before I set out to claim the prize.'

'You still insist on taking to the field in person, sir?' Bergen had asked, knowing that it was as futile as ever to argue, but ploughing ahead anyway. With a glance at Killian and Rennkamp, he'd added, 'I think all three of us would counsel you against it. It's an unnecessary risk, to say the least.'

'There's nothing unnecessary about it!' deViers had barked, and Bergen had thought another volcano of anger was about to erupt. But it hadn't. Instead, deViers had simply shaken his head and said, 'Things of value *demand* risk. If the damned Munitorum thought I was too precious to risk, they wouldn't have sent me out here, would they? But that's beside the point. I've prayed for something like this to come my way, Gerard. I deserve this chance. It's my destiny to recover that Baneblade. And if any of you think I'm going to command from the rear on this one, you're bloody well out of your minds.'

Well, one of us is definitely out of his mind, Bergen thought as he recalled the conversation, but I'm pretty sure it isn't me.

He reached the rocky surface of the plateau, increased his walking pace, and soon spotted his quarters up ahead – a low, two-storey prefab that he shared with Colonels Vinnemann, Marrenburg and Graves. He was looking forward to slipping between cool sheets. Such comforts would be just a memory once he was on the move.

Tired as he was, though, his mind still churned.

He knew that thousands of men would die in the coming days. Given the unexpected drop-ship losses, it seemed all too likely that over two thousand already had. There would be worse to come. Golgotha would see to that. Scores of men had already reported to the med-block and they hadn't even left the plateau yet. For some, it was the *fines* – particles of red dust so small that they could penetrate the cell membranes of the human body. The medics said there was little they could do beyond prescribing anti-toxic medication, but the real solution was to get off this blasted planet. The medicines induced short-term vomiting and cramps. Then there were the *dannih* – small chitinous bloodsuckers with powerful tripartite jaws. They seemed to get everywhere, even inside machines. If a man tried to pull one from his skin while it was feeding, only the fat red body would come away. The detached head would then burrow down into his flesh dispensing anti-coagulant, homing in on major arteries. A man could bleed to death if he wasn't careful. It was a powerful deterrent against interfering with the creature's feeding cycle. The only way to get rid of them without this happening was to douse the afflicted area of the body in strong alcohol, an unhappy solution on two counts. Firstly, troopers didn't much like the idea of wasting their coveted liquor on shifting stubborn ticks, and secondly, dousing oneself in alcohol was never a good idea. A handful of the heavier smokers had already discovered this first-hand.

There were other challenges, too. Aside from the dannih and the fines, there were numerous minor conditions related to atmospheric pressure, allergies, the unusual but breathable composition of the air, and all the problems caused by living at a constant gravity of one-point-twelve gees. It seemed to Bergen that Golgotha was waging its own war against the Cadians, and the orks hadn't even got started yet.

Bergen had never been a dour man by nature. Quite the contrary, in fact. He had, in his days as a cadet, been selected to feature in a short series of Cadian propaganda and recruitment films, such was his natural warmth and appeal. But as he opened the door to his quarters and saw Katz snoozing in a chair by his desk, he decided there were three things about which he was depressingly certain.

The first was that his commanding officer was coming apart at the seams. DeViers had lost his way. A powerful aura of desperation hovered around him, and it heralded disaster for the 18th Army Group and everyone attached to it.

The second was that Exolon would never find the famous *Fortress of Arrogance*. Holy icon or not, the orks had enjoyed thirty-eight years in which to strip it down to its bare nuts and bolts. If there was anything left of it at all, it would be unrecognisable. No, *The Fortress of Arrogance* was little more than a carrot dangled in front of the Munitorum's nose by the Adeptus Mechanicus. Whatever interest they had in returning to Golgotha, Bergen would wager it had little to do with finding Yarrick's cherished tank.

The third and last thing, the thing that worried Bergen most of all, and the thing that he was convinced of above all else, was simply this: unless the Emperor Himself descended from the heavens to offer them His Divine Protection, not a single man in his beloved armoured division was going to make it off this blasted world alive. The cards were stacked against them like never before. Millions of men had died in the Golgothan War all those years ago. Now, like those men, the fate of Bergen's troopers would be written in the blood-red sand.

He'd fight it all the way of course. He swore it. He had been born and raised to fight, and there was nothing he wouldn't do to see his men through this.

I'll go over the old man's head if I have to. Killian and Rennkamp will back me up. Together, we'll go to Morten and…

The thought went unfinished. Tiredness crashed over Bergen like a tidal wave and he fell back onto the bed, asleep before his head hit the pillow.

* * *

ELSEWHERE ON THE base, about a kilometre west of Bergen's quarters, the three senior agents of the Adeptus Mechanicus had returned to their apartments and were being attended by a flock of child-like slaves. True children would have perished very quickly in such a place – the pungent chemicals that misted the air would have dissolved the tissue of their lungs – but these were not true children. They had once been so, long ago, before extensive surgeries had converted them into ageless amalgams of flesh and metal like the tech-priests they served, though far less sophisticated. Their brains had been cruelly cut, rendering them incapable of independent thought, and their voices had been silenced forever. Their only function was to obey and, as such, they were beyond sin, beyond mischief or evil. Perhaps in recognition of this, their creator had crafted bronze masks for them, faces frozen in beatific smiles, like half-living sculptures of holy cherubim.

They clustered around their masters, disrobing them, removing peripheral devices, pulling data-plugs from flesh-sockets. Then they helped the tech-priests into a deep circular tub filled with a thick, glowing, milky substance that cast its light up to the metal ceiling. When this was done, the cherub-slaves retreated to shadowy alcoves set in the walls. There they deactivated, and became like dolls at rest in upright coffins.

Apart from the area lit by the glowing pool, the Mechanicus quarters were dark and foul-smelling. To the tech-priests, these things mattered not at all. The darkness hid nothing from augmetic eyes that could see in many spectrums of light. The smells registered only as lists of airborne compounds in varying concentrations, neither pleasant nor unpleasant, simply there.

Wading to the far side of the small pool, Tech-Magos Sennesdiar submerged his misshapen, patchwork body all the way to his neck. Adepts Xephous and Armadron followed suit, and the glowing liquid within the tub bubbled and churned like hot soup.

It was Armadron who broke the silence. His words, when he spoke them, were delivered in the same chalkboard screech he had used at the general's table. <Should the general host such an event again, I shall formally petition you, magos, that I may be excused. The experience was disagreeable. The ecstasy those men displayed in the consumption of organic compounds was disturbing to me.>

The tech-magos answered with his own condensed, high-pitched burst. <Though it was centuries ago, adept, you once ate as they did. You have transcended such weaknesses, and may glory in that, but do not forget the past, most especially your own. Those men require our guidance, rather than our disdain. They cannot comprehend the glory of the Omnissiah as we do.>

Armadron did not reply, a sign that he was reflecting on his superior's words.

<I, too, magos, wish to abstain from such events in the future,> said Xephous. His mandibles clacked together loudly at the end of his burst, something Sennesdiar considered an unworthy habit. <I calculated a three-point-seven-nine per cent chance that the matter consumed at the table would lead to one or more of the guests suffering a parasitic infestation of the lower intestine. Yet, you would not allow me to alert them. I find your reasoning most difficult to process. Do you wish them to host intestinal parasites?>

<Of course, I do not!> replied Sennesdiar. <The risk of infestation was acceptably low, adept, and the general would not have thanked you for the information. Neither would his guests. There are many things about which normal men prefer to remain ignorant.>

Xephous shifted, sending slow ripples over the surface of the milky goop, and said, <Ignorance as a preference, magos? The concept is offensive.>

<I agree,> said Armadron.

Sennesdiar turned his whirring eye-lenses from one to the other. <Taking personal offence indicates unacceptably high levels of subjectivity, adepts. Do not forget, either of you, that your next upgrade depends on my review of your performance here. The teachings of the Fabricator General emphasise the need to remain objective in all our dealings. You will both endeavour to uphold his principles in a more fitting manner or you will be subject to a forced adjustment procedure. Let us restrict ourselves instead to an assessment of the general's guests.>

<Of course, magos,> said Armadron. <It was apparent that the Ministorum man, Bishop Augustus, went to great lengths to cover the residual scent molecules of earlier physical activities.>

<Tried and failed,> added Xephous. <I estimate that he engaged in intimate physical congress with another individual not more than four hours prior to his arrival at the general's table. His partner was almost certainly–>

<The specifics of his actions were as apparent to me as they were to you, Xephous,> said Sennesdiar, cutting across his subordinate. <But they are irrelevant at this time.>

<But he is an Ecclesiarch, magos,> countered Xephous. <A man of the Imperial Creed is forbidden from engaging in such practices by the laws of his church. Should we not report this breach of conduct?>

<Not at this time, no. Deeds forbidden in law are often tolerated in life. The man, like all those in his preposterous organisation, is clearly prejudiced against us, and would benefit from a lesson in respect. His

private pleasures do not currently interest me, but the information has been logged. We move on. Let us talk of the others.>

Xephous said, <The military men are predictably uncomplicated types, magos. I judged them typical of the Cadian officer class. They live to serve the Emperor, expect to die in battle, and greatly covet the respect of their peers. I found nothing remarkable in this. Nothing that threatens our plans at this juncture.>

<Armadron?> said the tech-magos. <Do you concur?>

Armadron bowed his near-featureless head, pulling taut the segmented cables that connected his steel-encased brain to the augmetic ports on his naked metal vertebrae. <I found several notable exceptions to the honourable adept's statement. For example, involuntary subtleties of expression made during conversation suggest that Major General Killian bears a strong dislike for General deViers. He was careful to present a contradictory impression.>

<I did not register that,> protested Xephous.

<I concur with your assessment, Armadron,> said the magos, <and I wish to discern the cause of this dislike. The information may be of use to us if General deViers becomes problematic. Klotus Killian is to be observed.>

<I note your use of the conditional, magos,> said Armadron. <Have you revised your projections for our success? Does the general present less of an obstacle than you posited earlier?>

<I am constantly revising my projections. The general presents a complex problem. The strength of his personal ambition is our greatest hope of reaching Dar Laq and the resting place of Ipharod. It is this very same ambition, however, that poses the greatest danger to our success. I cannot rule out the possibility that he will order us removed from his side once the truth becomes known. Should such an event occur, we will need strong allies and a case for overthrowing him. I have selected Major General Gerard Bergen as the officer most likely to accept a compromise with us. His lifelong association with heavy armour means that he has worked closely with enginseers. He may be more sympathetic to our needs than certain others.>

<I observed him closely,> said Armadron. <This Bergen bears the hallmarks of a man convinced of his own impending doom. Is there no other?>

<I have factored this into my calculations,> replied Sennesdiar. <It changes nothing.>

<Then you intend to proceed as planned, magos?> asked Xephous. <We did not account for the worsening of the electromagnetic phenomena in the decades since we last set foot here. The machine-spirits have become highly uncooperative. The logic engines we

brought refuse to function at all. And vox-communications remain–>

<I have already turned my mind to these technical problems,> the magos replied, interrupting his adept. <Armadron, you will deploy tomorrow with Major General Bergen. Make your authority known to Tech-Priest Aurien. He is the senior enginseer attached to the 10th Armoured Division. I will assign you a servitor bodyguard and adequate transportation. I am sure the major general will be pleased to have someone of your skill and knowledge on hand.>

Armadron bowed his head and issued a short burst of noise that expressed his understanding and absolute obedience.

Sennesdiar rose from the pool, broadcasting an activation code to the cherub-slaves in their alcoves. They jerked forwards to tend to him as he stepped out. Thick fluids ran down his bloodless body, along the piston housings and cables that jutted from the pallid remnants of the flesh into which he had been born almost four centuries earlier. Silvery drops rolled from his slender metal fingers to the grille floor below as he waited for the little slaves to dress him.

In his robes once more, he stepped to the door of his private chamber, turned and said, <I leave you to your duties, adepts. I have much processing to do. The blessings of the Machine-God upon you both.>

<Ave Omnissiah,> they intoned dutifully.

<May your logic be flawless, magos,> added Armadron.

<And yours, adept,> said Sennesdiar. <Do not disappoint me.> Then he swept from the room, leaving his adepts to soak in the bubbling pool. They left shortly after him, however, for there was much to be done.

CHAPTER FIVE

'HOLD THEM BACK, you dogs,' bellowed Colonel Stromm. 'Don't let them pass the outer lines!' He fired his hellpistol into the charging mass of orks, but, squinting through the haze and the sweat that stung his eyes, it was difficult to see the level of damage he was causing. With his free hand, he grabbed his adjutant, Lieutenant Kassel, by the collar, yanking him close to shout in his ear. 'Where the frak are my Kasrkin, Hans? Why aren't they shoring up those blasted gaps?'

The air danced with tracer fire as the orks pushed closer, huge pistols and stubbers blazing. The Cadians fired back with deadly intensity, bright las-beams licking out from their sandbagged positions, slicing through the clouds of billowing dust thrown up by the anti-personnel mines that were detonating under the feet of the greenskins' front ranks. Heavy brown bodies spun into the air to land in bloody, mangled heaps. Other orks trampled over them uncaring, undaunted, yelling and hooting, and roaring bestial battle cries with unrestrained glee.

Competing with all the noise, most particularly with the deafening crack and stutter of nearby las- and bolter-fire, Lieutenant Kassel placed his mouth at his colonel's ear and replied, 'Vonnel's platoon is taking heavy losses on the right flank, sir. The Kasrkin have moved across to plug the breach.'

Damn it, thought Stromm. Five days. Five days we've lasted out here on the open sand, and not a single bloody sign of rescue, no vox-comms, nothing. And there's no end to the greenskin bastards. Scores of men are dead or dying. Our perimeter is shrinking with every charge made against us. This looks like the last of it for The Fighting 98th.

His mind turned to his family, safe aboard the naval heavy-transport *The Incandescent*, which was anchored in high orbit with the rest of the fleet. He had a son, still just an infant, who had been born during the Palmeros campaign. Stromm had hoped to watch the lad grow, to see him strengthen and develop, and one day become an officer like his father. No, not *like* his father, *better* than his father. A son should always strive to achieve more than the man who sired him. He had hoped to see it, to live that long despite the odds. But he'd known the second old deViers had brought Exolon to Golgotha that his life expectancy had been suddenly, dramatically reduced. Here today, before his eyes, the truth of it was playing out.

Curse this world, he thought. To the blasted bloody warp with it! We should have virus-bombed it from space. That would have been poetic justice in that – revenge for all the people Thraka's asteroids have killed. If it weren't for Yarrick's damned tank...

The orks were closing. Six hundred metres. Five-ninety. Five-eighty. The Cadians' landmines were barely slowing them. Heavy alien bodies were being blasted high on pillars of smoke and sand, but the enemy far outnumbered Stromm's men. The foe had bodies to spare. Those that escaped the deadly fragmentation and explosive pressure waves created by each blast just kept on coming, not faltering for even a moment.

On Stromm's first day, the day his drop-ship had smashed nose-first into the red sand, he and his officers had decided that it was best to stay put, sure that Major General Rennkamp would send out reconnaissance units to look for his missing men. But vox-comms weren't worth a damn out here, and darkness fell quickly in the desert, so Stromm hadn't wasted any time in ordering makeshift defensives built, though progress was initially slow under lamp and torchlight.

Sand was, of course, in plentiful supply and had been put to good use. The sandbags had hardened like concrete, such was the effect of water on the Golgothan dust, though Stromm was reluctant to spare even a fraction of their precious reserves for anything other than drinking. Scrap metal pulled from the wrecked ship was plentiful, too. With these resources, his 98th Mechanised Infantry Regiment had constructed outer and inner defensive works, reinforcing the heavy-weapons nests with plates from the ship's crumpled bulkheads.

The resulting fortifications were basic in the extreme, but at least they offered better protection than the open sand. As he fired shot after flesh-searing shot into the charging xenos horde, Stromm was damned glad of those defences.

Torrents of fire blazed out from each of the heavy-weapon nests, chewing apart scores of grotesque alien bodies with broad sweeps of enfilading fire. Some of the regiment's Chimeras and halftracks had survived the crash and were entrenched behind walls of compacted sand and steel, adding their considerable firepower to the desperate battle. The Chimeras' hull-mounted heavy bolters chattered deep and low, ripping the enemy into bloody hunks of meat with their explosive ammunition. Turret-mounted multilasers hissed and cracked, scoring the air with blinding brightness. A few of the Chimeras boasted autocannon as their main armament, their long barrels chambered for powerful thirty-millimetre rounds. They made a harsh chugging sound as they spewed shells out in devastating torrents. Over-muscled brown bodies dissolved into scraps and tatters wherever the autocannon found their mark.

The Chimeras and the weapon-nests were not alone in providing heavy support. Thick spears of lascannon fire blazed down from atop the crumpled hull of the drop-ship. The ship's cockpit had folded like a concertina in the crash and the flight crew had been killed outright, but a handful of navy ratings – tech-crew mostly – had survived. They had been insistent about manning the ship's turrets, only a few of which still functioned. Stromm had seen it in their faces: the fear, the panic. When he had agreed to let them man the turrets, their relief had been all too apparent. They were terrified of meeting the orks face-to-face. He cursed their cowardice, but he couldn't hate them for it.

They hadn't been raised on Cadia. They were lesser men by birth.

In his opinion, that said it all.

Despite such thoughts, he was glad to have those turrets manned by anyone. They poured blistering fire down on top of the orks, killing dozens at a time, charring their bodies to shrunken black husks.

Given the weight of combined fire the Cadians were pouring out, it seemed that scores of orks were dropping with every metre of ground they gained, but they were still gaining. Stromm could already see that it wouldn't be enough, not by any stretch. As so often in a straight fight with the orks, it would ultimately come down to numbers, and numbers were something he didn't have.

Each day that Stromm and his men had stayed by the shattered drop-ship, desperately and futilely trying to raise anyone, anyone at all, on their vox-casters, more and more orks had started to show up. They had been drawn to the site by the spectacular trail of fire and black smoke that the falling drop-ship had painted across the sky in a descent that had been visible for a hundred kilometres in every direction.

Stromm regretted entrenching his forces.

I should have moved us out into the desert, he thought, *away from the crashsite. I should have got everyone away from here.*

Even as he thought this, however, he rejected it. Hindsight was a fine thing, but he had made the best choice he could with the information he'd had. Moving off would have left his infantry companies vulnerable. There weren't enough vehicles left intact after the crash to carry everyone. And there were the wounded to think about, too. He had no idea of their exact coordinates, either. No one did. Where the bloody hell was the rest of Exolon?

His hellpistol clicked, another cell spent. On reflex, he hit the power-pack release, let the magazine fall to the ground, tore a fresh one from a pouch on his belt, slammed it home and resumed firing. His first shot left a smoking black hole where one monster's ugly face had been. That he could now see the damage his shots were causing was not a good sign.

'Sir,' said Kassel urgently, 'you need to think about falling back to the inner defences. We're losing key sections of the outer perimeter.'

Stromm nodded and, still facing and firing at the enemy, began walking slowly backwards in the direction of the wrecked hull.

'Give the order,' he told Kassel. 'I want all our lads falling back to secondary positions at once.'

He chose his targets carefully, firing always at the biggest and darkest-skinned orks. He knew from long years of experience that they were the toughest and most ruthless. Their hides were harder than sun-baked leather, criss-crossed with battle scars and signs of crude surgery. They were veteran killers, relentless, blood-mad savages, and it was they who led the charge.

Throne, but the bastards are ugly, thought Stromm. What kind of universe tolerates such horrors?

It was easy to see why mankind sought the orks' absolute extermination. They were the stuff of nightmares, these greenskins, and they would never stop fighting, never stop killing until there was nothing left to kill. They seemed to wage war for fun, to revel in motiveless slaughter. Or was slaughter motive enough for them? Even now, as they pressed forward, eager to butcher his men, Stromm saw them laughing insanely, as if the whole matter of agony and death in combat was a great game. No, mutual tolerance had never been an option. From the moment the two species had met, the galaxy had set them against each other.

The orks raced closer through the churning dust, and Stromm saw their hideous faces rendered in increasingly sharp detail. He could make out the glint of savage madness in each beady red eye. Each face was a bestial mask. Their noses were small and flat, often pierced with the bones of some luckless animal or with rings or bars of metal. Their mouths were huge and slack, gaping wide and dripping with thick strands of blood-tinged saliva. Those jaws were large enough, in some cases, to close over a grown man's head, and each was crammed full of short, jutting, knife-like teeth dominated by two long, curving tusks that thrust upwards from the lower mandible.

Few things Stromm had ever gazed upon engendered such a feeling of loathing and disgust. The ork race seemed tailor-made to strike fear into the human heart, tapping an ancient vein of primal fear shared by all. It was as if the least worthy traits of his own species had been twisted and magnified a thousand times, and given monstrously powerful bodies with which to wage their bloody and incessant war on Man.

Where had such abominations come from?

Stromm's order to fall back to secondary positions had filtered down to the rank-and-file, and he saw men leap from sandy foxholes and sprint back towards him. Many left it too late. He shouted in frustration as he watched them cut down by sprays of ork stubber-fire. It was a brutal and bloody sight. The large-bore weapons made a real mess of their victims, barking as loud as any bolter, throwing massive metal slugs out in every direction. The orks barely bothered to aim, spraying fire left and right without a thought for accuracy or wasted ammunition. It was only the sheer volume of fire that took such a deadly toll. As the Cadians raced back to the inner defences, many fell screaming, great ragged holes punched into their backs, exit wounds the size of watermelons exploding from their chests and stomachs. Others, more fortunate only in that they suffered less, were struck in the back of the head. Even good, solid Cadian Mark VIII helmets couldn't protect them. Their skulls practically exploded with the impact of the heavy ork slugs, and their headless bodies stumbled and fell, gushing crimson on the sand.

To the last man, thought Stromm, gritting his teeth, firing back until another cell was spent. We'll die here, but we'll fight the bastards to the last bloody man. Damn you deViers! I hope you get your bloody glory.

'Artillery,' someone shouted over the vox. 'Ork artillery coming in from the north. Get down!'

Stromm heard a nerve-rattling whistle on the air, growing to a shriek. *Closer. Closer. Damn it, that's going to hit right on top...*

Both he and Kassel threw themselves to the ground. Great plumes of sand and dust spurted into the air between the Cadians and the orks, and the air shook with a deafening boom. Stromm found himself still breathing. No fatalities. It was a ranging shot, but the next would bring death down on the shrinking Cadian force.

'That's them bringing up the big guns, sir,' shouted Kassel as he scrambled to his feet.

'You don't say, Hans!' barked Stromm. 'Tell those spacer runts in the

las-turrets that I want focused fire on that artillery. Those Navy dogs are
the only ones with a clear line of sight. Do it, man!'

Kassel plucked the mouthpiece of his back-mounted vox-caster from
the clip on his belt, barked out the colonel's orders in a clear, authori-
tative voice and waited for confirmation. He needn't have bothered. The
turret-gunners atop the crumpled drop-ship were already traversing
their turrets to zero in on several massive ork machines – self-propelled
guns that were emerging from a dust cloud about fifteen hundred
metres away. The SPGs had short, fat barrels that sacrificed accuracy for
a higher explosive payload. Their construction appeared so slapdash
they looked as likely to blow themselves apart as to flatten their enemies. By rights, they shouldn't have worked at all, but, as ever with
greenskin machines, their performance defied their appearance. With
great coughs of flame and ground-shaking booms, they launched
another deadly salvo, this time aimed squarely at the las-turrets that had
begun to open fire on them.

Most of the heavy artillery shells went wide of the mark, whining
straight past the wreck and exploding in the sand on the far side. Most,
but not all. Two struck the hull, packed with so much explosive that,
between them, they ripped the superstructure apart. The pressure wave
that sped out from the twin blasts pulverised the turrets and the men
inside them.

Stromm stood gaping for a split second at the terrible destruction,
and then shielded his head as a shower of burning debris cascaded
towards him. By the Emperor's grace, neither he nor Kassel were struck,
but a young trooper on the right fell without screaming, his head caved
in by a turnip-sized chunk of heavy armaplas.

'Try to raise them,' Stromm yelled at Kassel, already knowing in his
heart that it was futile.

Kassel tried. Nothing.

'Again, Hans. We can't lose them now. If they can't knock out those
SPGs we won't last another minute!'

'Nothing,' said Kassel. He tried a third time with the same result.
'They're gone, sir.'

'For Throne's sake! The next bloody salvo will do for us. Can't we get
any of our heavy weapons on them? What about our mortar teams?
They're all we have left that doesn't need line of sight.'

Kassel immediately tried to raise the mortar teams on the vox, but
there was no reply, just hissing static and the sure knowledge that more
men had died.

'Sir, we need to get you away from here. Those greenskin gun-crews
won't take long to reload. We should get you into one of the Chimeras.
The Kasrkin might be able to open a corridor.'

'If you suggest that to me ever again, Hans, I'll pistol-whip you. Do you hear me? You should know better by now. I've never run from a field of battle in my life.'

'I… Sorry, sir.'

'Sod your apologies, man. Just keep shooting. We'll make a proper accounting of ourselves before the end. Get the word out. The Fighting 98th makes its last stand for the honour of Cadia!'

'The Fighting 98th forever, sir!' said Kassel, thrusting out his chest. Determination replaced the fear in his eyes. If they were to die, it would be as only Cadian men could die, strong and true, and unrelenting to the very last. The Emperor would welcome their souls to his glorious hall. Their places at his table would be assured.

The outer defences were swarming with xenos, all jostling for a chance to revel in the slaughter of Stromm's men. They pushed and shoved each other for better position, desperate to claim more kills than their fellows. They were so frantic with battle-lust that savage brawls began to break out here and there among their ranks. Stromm saw one of the beasts – spike-helmed and heavily armoured, its dark skin textured like burned steak – turn to a marginally smaller monstrosity on its right and begin wrestling with it, trying to prise a large axe from its grasp. The smaller ork resisted until the larger rammed the point of a huge, rust-pitted knife right into its belly and unzipped it from sternum to crotch. Thick blood poured out, followed by a tumble of looping intestines that glistened pink as they slid out onto the sand. Then, with the newly won axe in hand, the big one bellowed a battle cry and continued its advance, eager to enter close-quarter combat where it could engage in bloody slaughter.

It took six men firing lasguns at close range to put that bastard down.

By Terra, thought Stromm, they're insane! Death means nothing to them. Whether we have men like Yarrick or not – whether we had a thousand Yarricks, a million even – how can humanity hope to hold back the savage tide?

In Stromm's earpiece, the vox-chatter from his surviving platoon leaders had degenerated into a cacophony of panicked shouts. The gap was closing ever further. Once the fighting went hand-to-hand, it would be over for the Cadians. Nothing could save them then.

'We're losing the inner defences. The bolter-nests are being overrun!'

'What do we do? Fall back to the drop-ship? They're hammering it with artillery!'

'I need heavy weapons support on our right flank, warp damn it! Get me mortars. Get me a heavy bolter. Anything!'

Stromm heard the words as if from a great distance. A strange and unexpected sense of calm had descended on him. All around, the air was churning with noise and heat, whining bullets and cracking las-fire, but, in his mind, everything was supremely clear. The end of his lifelong duty to the Emperor was at hand.

One more time, he allowed his thoughts to return to his family up there on *The Incandescent*, and said a silent prayer to the Emperor:

May my wife remember me proudly, and may our son's achievements exceed my own. To the Emperor's side, I commend the souls of my men, and I ask Saint Josmane to be our guide.

'Hans,' he said, 'the regimental banner.'

'It's here, sir.'

'Then unfurl it, soldier, and give it to me.'

'At once, sir,' said Kassel, and leapt to the task.

Stromm holstered his smoking hellpistol and accepted the heavy banner from his adjutant. Gripping its haft with both hands, he stepped forward, calling to his men as he waved it majestically in the hot, dusty afternoon air.

'Rally to me, Cadians,' he shouted over the din of battle. 'Rally to me, troopers! No more falling back. Here and now, we make our stand!'

The banner was a striking icon of gold and red. The pillared symbol of the Cadian gate dominated its centre and, on either side of it, the image of a grinning skull held a single stalk of wheat between its teeth. The wheat stalk symbolised the regiment's glorious victory at Ruzarch Fields during the infamous Battle of Vogen nearly half a century before. Had the regiment survived General deViers's Golgothan expedition, another symbol of honour would have been added: a stylised cloud and lightning bolt.

The men close enough to hear his voice turned to see their colonel standing there, the banner snapping and fluttering as he waved it over his head. He looked like an image from a propaganda poster, and their spirits burned with fresh pride. Stromm could see it as he looked into their eyes. He saw the fires of determination surging there, the will to die fighting.

'Honour and glory!' shouted a sergeant off to the right.

'Honour and glory!' bellowed his squad.

Something changed in the air, building up like a massive electrical charge. Even the wounded seemed suddenly whole again, though their bodies still bled. They turned from the sight of their colonel and his banner, raised lasgun stocks to armoured shoulders, and met the orks with renewed ferocity, determined to dispatch as many of the slavering beasts as possible before they were overcome for good.

Push through your pain, Stromm willed them. Just a bit further, a bit longer so we know the Emperor's eyes are on us.

Only a few hundred metres, now, until the orks were in among them.

Mere moments until the fighting became hand-to-hand. At that range, the greenskins' massive physiologies would allow them to rip through the Cadians like wet paper. Only the mighty Kasrkin storm troopers, of which Stromm had started with a single company and now had less than three full platoons, had any chance in close quarters, and, even then, not much of one.

'Fix bayonets,' ordered Stromm. Kassel repeated the order over the vox. He might as well have said 'get ready to die.' Against orks, it was essentially the same thing.

The call was taken up by officers and sergeants all along the line as the gap shrank to forty metres, then thirty. Las-fire blazed out in a last, desperate bid to make a difference before the clash of blade on blade. Plenty of orks went down, struck in the face with lethal, short-range blasts. But, if this bought the Cadians any time at all, it was mere seconds.

The ork artillery was rolling forward, too, unable to fire on the Cadians now that their own infantry had closed the gap. The greenskin gunnery crews, in the manner of all their race, were desperate to get closer to the centre of the murder, to stain their hands with the blood of dying men. For this, they kept their machines rolling in.

Twenty metres from Stromm, a massive ork with a broken tusk hacked one trooper to the ground with its cleaver, shoved roughly past another, and raced directly forwards. It was coming straight for the colonel, attracted by the bright, snapping banner above his head. As it closed, it raised its massive stubber with a single hand and fired a burst that caught the colonel on the right shoulder. His tough armaplas body-armour was enough to deflect the shot, but the impact threw him from his feet. He landed on the red sand with a grunt. The force of the bullet's impact had broken his arm, and the banner fell from his hands.

Lieutenant Kassel moved in a blur, catching the banner as it fell, hoisting it high, desperate not to dishonour the regiment by allowing its sanctified cloth to touch the ground. He stabbed the base of the haft into the sand, braced it with one hand, and crouched by his colonel, yelling his name. 'Are you alive, sir? Speak to me, colonel! Please!'

Groaning in agony and clutching his shattered arm, Stromm rolled, and, with Kassel's eager aid, struggled to his feet. He looked around to see men forming a defensive line around him, fighting back desperately with bayonets, pistols, sharpened entrenching tools – anything they had to hand – against the massive chipped axes and cleavers of the orks.

'For Cadia!' Stromm roared, leaving Kassel with the banner and drawing his hellpistol again, this time with his left hand.

'For Cadia!' his men roared back.

They fought with everything they had, but the air suddenly filled once again with the deafening boom of big guns. Stromm tensed, guessing the ork artillery crews had decided to fire after all, whether they killed their foul kin or not. He girded himself for the explosive blast that would bring an end to his life any second now.

Any second...

But it never came. There was no ear-splitting whistle overhead.

'Armour!' cried one of his platoon leaders over the vox-net. 'In Terra's Holy Name!'

'They're fielding tanks, too?' asked another.

'No,' snapped the first. 'Not the blasted orks, man! *Imperial* tanks! Leman Russ battle tanks inbound from the west!'

Stromm heard a second stutter of booming fire and this time, to his utter astonishment, a mob of orks pressing in on the left flank vanished, consumed by a great fountain of dirt and flame.

'Their artillery!' voxed another platoon leader. 'The ork SPGs are burning. All of them. Junked!'

Another sharp stutter sounded from the west, announcing death for more of the foe. The horde was being blasted apart, knots of them disappearing in fountains of dust, raining back to earth as burned and bloody pieces. Those that weren't killed outright by the high-explosive shells were horribly maimed by flying shrapnel. They went down screaming and roaring as tank fire continued to scythe into their ranks.

Even those orks engaged in close-quarter combat couldn't help themselves. The sounds of cannon fire reached them through their battle-lust. For just a second, they turned their heads towards the source, and Stromm's fighters pressed their momentary advantage, downing scores of them, forging a gap across which they could once more employ their lasrifles and surviving heavy weapons. The Kasrkin platoons took this opportunity to press in from the right, shifting closer to Colonel Stromm, the better to protect him and react faster to his needs.

Through the space that had opened, Stromm could see the cause of his company's unexpected respite. There, on the western flank, a great dust cloud rose, churning up from the desert floor. At its head, ten Cadian tanks charged forward in an assault wedge. Behind them, barely visible in their dusty wake, came a line of Heracles halftracks filled to the brim with men and supply crates. It looked like an entire armoured company. For a moment, Stromm thought he was dreaming.

'Colonel,' yelled Kassel excitedly, 'there's an urgent message coming through from... say again... roger that... from a Lieutenant van Droi, sir.'

'Van Droi?' said Stromm. He didn't recognise the name. Most of

Exolon's armour was with 10th Division. He and his men were with the 8th. 'Well, don't keep it to yourself, Hans. What's the message?'

Kassel beamed.

'To dig in, sir. Van Droi says the Gunheads are here.'

CHAPTER SIX

GOSSEFRIED'S GUNHEADS ROARED forward, guns booming like thunder, far more than simple promethium fuelling their charge. Disgust, hatred, the desire for revenge, all of these things and more filled the hearts of the men inside the massive, rumbling war machines as they surged on, desperate to cut the foe down before it was too late for their fellow Guardsmen.

For Gossefried van Droi, the survival of the embattled Cadian infantrymen was paramount. Here at last, after days travelling through the desert without any sign whatsoever that others had survived planet-fall, he had found welcome confirmation that his Gunheads were not alone. Someone else *had* survived and, right now, that meant everything in the world to him. But they wouldn't survive much longer if they didn't get the aid they so desperately needed.

It would be a close thing. He could see that from his cupola. Colonel Stromm's footsloggers were on their last legs. That much was all too clear, despite the dust and black smoke that shrouded the chaos of the battlefield.

'Spread out,' van Droi ordered his tank commanders over the vox. 'Keep your main guns blazing. I want secondary weapons on those hostiles as soon as you make range. Don't spare the treads! Our brother Cadians are dying out there!'

A stutter of cannon fire from the tanks on either side was answer enough for him. Up ahead, still more than a kilometre away, but closer with every passing second, pillars of sand and gore burst into the air. Firing on the move meant a big trade-off in accuracy for the gunners, but, given the sheer number of gargantuan brown bodies in front of them, they could afford to be sloppy. What they *couldn't* afford to be was slow.

No fear of that. Their engines roared, spewing thick black fumes out behind them, powering the sixty-tonne war machines forward over the sand with surprising speed. Between the noise of his engine and the booming of his powerful main gun, van Droi could hear nothing at all of the fighting around the crashed drop-ship. He didn't need to hear it to know how badly it was going. As his tanks crossed the one kilometre line, he gripped the pintle-mounted heavy bolter in front of him and made ready to open fire. Much of the mad alien horde had turned its aggression towards the tanks, knowing they posed a far greater, more immediate threat than the infantry, and a better fight. His eyes picked out the biggest orks, long-tusked, black-skinned abominations wearing huge suits of armour and carrying ludicrously oversized blades. He saw them throw back their heads to bellow battle cries as they readied the rest of the horde to charge.

Bring it on, you godless freaks, thought van Droi. You don't stand a frakker's chance in hell against my 10th Company.

'Break them wide open, Gunheads,' he called over the company command channel. 'Sword, Hammer, move into line formation. Rhaimes, take your squadron out on the left flank. Angle in on their rear. Wulfe, Richter, move your squadrons straight up. Keep the pressure on. Not one of those alien bastards survives. No runners.'

'Spear Leader to company command', replied Sergeant Rhaimes. 'Read you loud and clear, sir. We'll make them wish they'd never crawled out of the dirt.'

'Sword Leader to command,' voxed Sergeant Wulfe. 'Moving into formation.'

Sergeant Richter was the last to vox in. 'Hammer Squadron confirming, sir. Moving up now.'

Van Droi looked to either side and saw his tanks fan out to form a broad fighting line abreast of his machine. *Old Smashbones, The Rage Imperius* and *The Adamantine* pressed left, bearing north-east so that they could swing in on the greenskin flanks and funnel them into the killing zone. As van Droi watched, flame and smoke licked out from their barrels and the air shook with the sound of exploding propellant.

On the right, the tanks of Spear and Hammer squadrons were also keeping the pressure on. Not all of them were fitted with standard battle cannon, of course. Van Droi's company was a mixed force, glad to make do with whatever machines it could get its hands on. As he always impressed on the new meat, what the Gunheads lacked in uniformity, they made up in versatility. Who gave a flying damn if some of the other company commanders sneered? Czurloch and Brismund were the worst for it, those stuck-up pricks. Let them have their nice, ordered companies of identical machines. Specialise too much in one thing, van Droi knew, and you'd be properly stuffed when some bastard suddenly changed the rules.

That didn't happen to his Gunheads.

His machine, *Foe-breaker*, was a rare and highly prized Leman Russ Vanquisher from the forges of Ryza. She was hundreds of years old – the saints alone knew how many kills she'd made since her inception – but she still excelled at taking out enemy machines with her 120mm smooth-bore cannon and its highly specialised, armour-piercing sabot rounds. No other Leman Russ could fire as far and as accurately, and van Droi conscientiously prayed to her machine-spirit every single day, making obeisance in the form of litanies approved by the regimental enginseers.

All this love and attention was repaid tenfold in her performance. She had added another armour-kill to her tally today when van Droi's gunner, 'Bullseye' Dietz, had lit up one of the ugly ork artillery pieces like a bonfire. It was still gushing red flame and thick black smoke into the sky. Dietz hadn't let up, either. Van Droi's loader – a grumpy little shortarse by the name of Waller – was still slamming high-explosive shells into the main gun's breech with all the speed he could manage, and Dietz wasn't wasting them. Every time the gun belched, scores of orks disintegrated, turned into a downpour of red rain that muddied the desert sand.

Seconds now, thought van Droi, his finger beginning to squeeze gently on the heavy bolter's trigger. Just a few more seconds.

He revelled in the rush of hot desert air as it whipped at his collar. Adrenaline surged through him, familiar and welcome. Two and a half decades of this, with combat experience spanning a dozen contested worlds, and still it thrilled him like nothing else ever could. He would never tire of it, never.

In lethal range, he pulled the heavy bolter's trigger back and loosed a flood of explosive shells. The noise was deafening, even with his earprotectors firmly in place. The recoil was wicked, too, despite much of it being absorbed by the pintle-mount. The gun kicked hard in his hands, pouring spent cartridges from its ejector like brass rain.

He strafed the orks in front of him as their return fire danced and sparked on the thick front armour of his tank. Dozens were struck, bolts punching deep into meaty bodies before detonating a fraction of a second later with sickening, yet satisfying effect.

All along the line, his tank commanders were doing the same, manning the heavy stubbers and bolters that graced the lip of each cupola. Those few tanks with sponson-mounted weapons chattered and blazed even louder than the others. Hull-mounted weapons, too, spat deadly torrents into the enemy force, leaving the orks nowhere to run to escape the slaughter.

Van Droi didn't shout or growl or laugh madly like some men did while they fired on the foe. That was for youngsters and fools, in his opinion. Instead, he let go of everything, losing his sense of self, becoming part of a kind of gestalt entity that encompassed the tank and her entire crew. The fighting always seemed to go so smoothly when this happened, as if each man instinctively knew what needed to be done without having to ask. The mark of a good crew, he thought. No. An *exceptional* one.

A sudden crackle of static on his intercom yanked van Droi from his almost trance-like state. The gruff voice of his loader sounded in his ear. 'Vox-panel's flashing down here, sir. Looks like you've got a call coming in from one of the footsloggers.'

Van Droi picked off a few more of the orks nearest *Foe-Breaker* and dropped down into the turret. As he checked the board, he told Dietz, 'Hostiles closing on our two. Get the co-ax on them.' Then, he switched from intercom to vox, and said, 'This is Lieutenant Gossefried van Droi, 81st Armoured Regiment, 10th Company. Go ahead.'

The voice that came back had the sharp ring of the Cadian upper ranks, but it sounded tired and more than a little desperate, too. 'This is Colonel Stromm of the 98th Mechanised Infantry Regiment. Can you hear me, van Droi?'

'I can, sir.'

'Emperor bless your armoured arse, man! You and your men got here just in the nick of time. Bought us a bit of space to fight back, but not much. I've lost a lot of troopers, and it's far from–'

He cut off mid-sentence to issue orders to his men. Van Droi could hear the sounds of intense fighting from the other end. It sounded all too close to the colonel's position.

'Van Droi, are you still there?' asked the gasping colonel a moment later.

'Yes, sir. What's your status? I have a squadron flanking the orks from the rear and two engaging from your left, but you'll need to hold out a bit longer. I can't risk firing any closer to your position. It looked like one of our earlier salvoes was close enough to shave you.'

'I needed a shave anyway,' said Stromm. 'But listen, it's touch-and-go here. The loss of their artillery turned their heads, as did your arrival, and we made them pay. They're fighting on two fronts, and that has split their forces, but there are still plenty of them hell-bent on bloodying us up in a bit of hand-to-hand. I don't need to tell you how long we're likely to last at that range. They grow the bastards tough on Golgotha, and our backs are to the wall, literally. Short of moving inside what's left of the drop-ship hull, there's nowhere else for us to go, and I've no intention of getting trapped in there. It's suicide. If there's any chance you can create a corridor for us, I've a few platoons of Kasrkin that might be able to hold it open long enough to facilitate our escape.'

Van Droi nodded as he listened. 'You'll have your corridor, sir. I'll send one of my squadrons up flush with the drop-ship. They'll cut a path in towards you. Keep your men back until the last moment. There'll be plenty of lead in the air, you understand.'

'The more the better,' replied Stromm. Grunting and shouting almost drowned out his words. Chilling ork battle cries could be heard clearly in the background and, despite the security of his tank, van Droi felt his blood run cold. He knew he had to order Wulfe's tanks forward at once. Sword Squadron fielded the company's only Leman Russ Exterminator, *New Champion of Cerbera*. She would be best suited for the job.

'As soon as you can, van Droi,' Stromm added. 'The Emperor protects. Stromm, out.'

Van Droi immediately switched back over to the company command channel and said, 'Command to Sword Leader. Respond, Wulfe.'

'Sword Leader to Command,' Sergeant Wulfe voxed back. 'Go ahead, sir.'

Van Droi could hear the drumming of a heavy stubber between the sergeant's words.

'Listen up, Wulfe,' he said. 'I have friendlies in urgent need of an escape corridor. I want the *New Champion* on it. Understood? Move your squad up and cut a path flush with the ship's hull. Let the wreck cover the footsloggers' backs. Carve them a path to safety. Colonel Stromm has the vox, F-channel, band six.'

There was only the briefest pause before Wulfe responded – 'Wulfe to Company Command. Sword Squadron is on the move.' – but van Droi could read into it easily enough.

Wulfe was probably cursing. *New Champion of Cerbera* was Corporal Lenck's machine.

'LET'S TAKE IT to them,' Wulfe told his crew over the intercom. 'Metzger, get her in close, three hundred metres, a hull-down position if you can find one. Expect plenty of fire.' *Last Rites II* gunned forward, churning up the desert under her treads, throwing waves of sand up behind her.

Wulfe dropped down into the turret to switch vox channels. Once he had opened the link to his squadron, he said, 'Sword Leader to One and

Two. Orders from van Droi. We're going in. *New Champion*, move up on my right and open a corridor for the infantry. Cut a path in line with the wreckage so their backs are covered. And try not to hit the friendlies, Lenck. *Last Rites II* and *Frontline Crusader* will give supporting fire centre and left. *Frontline Crusader*, stop parallel with me, fifty metre spacing. Hammer Squadron will be supporting us from the rear. Confirm.'

Corporal Siemens came back first. '*Frontline Crusader* confirms, sergeant. Moving up to cover your left. The Emperor protects.'

'The Emperor protects,' Wulfe replied automatically.

'*New Champion* confirms,' reported Lenck a moment later. 'Watch and learn, sergeant.'

'Stow the backchat, corporal,' Wulfe spat back. 'Just do your job.' He had seen enough of Lenck during training exercises in the massive holds of the *Hand of Radiance* to know that he was good – far better, in fact, than could be expected given his level of combat experience – but Wulfe wasn't about to let Lenck know that. The man was already infuriatingly cocky.

With *Last Rites II* just edging in front, the three tanks of Sword Squadron closed with the charging orks. Wulfe scrambled back up into his cupola and grasped the twin grips of his heavy stubber. Looking out at the wall of roaring brown bodies that surged towards him, he realised that he barely needed to aim. Anywhere he fired, he was sure hit something. Hardly pausing to line up along the weapon's iron sights, he pressed his thumbs down hard on the gun's butterfly trigger. There was a deafening rattle as the stubber unloaded on the alien horde, cutting dozens of them to pieces. It was a strange, darkly comical sight, one that Wulfe had witnessed before. The bulky alien savages appeared to dance a deathly jig as they were literally chewed apart by the hail of lead.

Corporal Metzger stopped *Last Rites II* just behind a shallow dune, not much protection, but better than none. It would keep the tank's vulnerable underside covered while the hull armour took the brunt of the enemy fire. Then Metzger manned the hull-mounted heavy bolter, adding his fire to Wulfe's, devastating the press of enemies that were desperately trying to close the gap so they could swarm the tank's hatches.

At this range, Wulfe could see their grotesque faces all too clearly, reminding him of so many other greenskins he had faced over the years. Some men said they all looked the same, but Wulfe knew better. One face in particular was burned into his brain: the wart-covered, lopsided face of the ork that had given him the scar on his throat. The old scar was itching like crazy, as it always did when he was under pressure. Though the Golgothan orks were similar enough to their distant kin to dredge up unwelcome memories, they were different, too. They were brown for a start, discoloured, he imagined, by the red dust to which they had been exposed for so many years. They were also leaner and harder than any he had seen before, their muscles rippling like steel cables. Golgotha had made its mark on them. It had shaped them. Toughened them.

Wulfe stole a glance to left and right, and saw that *Frontline Crusader* and *New Champion of Cerbera* had halted in formation, adding their lethal firepower to the slaughter. The toll on the orks was mind-boggling, and a number of the smallest turned and tried to break from the fight. These few began struggling against the tide pressing at their backs, eager to escape the sweeping arcs of fire that were killing so many of their foul kin. It was hopeless, of course. Wulfe swept his barrel from left to right, cutting them down without mercy.

Suffer not the alien to live.

Down in the turret, Corporal Holtz didn't need Wulfe to tell him what to do. He had plenty of experience to guide him. *Last Rites II*, like so many other Leman Russ tanks, boasted a co-axial autocannon that could chew infantry and light armour apart with ease, allowing the gunner to spare the precious, limited ammunition of the main gun. Holtz employed the co-ax now, traversing the turret slowly in a ninety-degree arc, firing relentlessly, covering the sand in lifeless alien debris. On the other side of the turret basket, Siegler was pulling a fresh ammunition belt from a stowage box. With its incredible rate of fire, Wulfe's heavy stubber would need reloading in a matter of seconds.

'Don't waste any time, Lenck,' Wulfe voxed to the *New Champion*. 'Cut that corridor. Those men can't last much longer.'

'I'm *on* it, sergeant,' Lenck snapped back.

Sure enough, Wulfe saw the Exterminator's turret-mounted heavy bolters blaze into life, stitching a bloody path straight through the foe. They made one hell of a mess, a kill for almost every hit scored.

Wulfe felt someone tap his shin twice. He tore his eyes from the bloodbath, dropped his hand down into the turret, and accepted the ammunition belt that Siegler was feeding up to him. Ork slugs rattled and spanged from the turret armour all around him, sending showers of sparks into the air. Wulfe ducked down, staying as low as possible without abandoning his cupola altogether.

'Sort those bastards out, Holtz!' he yelled over the intercom. 'I'm taking an awful lot of fire up here!'

'If I could just use the main gun, sarge,' Holtz argued.

'Well you can't!' barked Wulfe. 'No high explosives. We're too near the bloody footsloggers.'

Wordlessly, Holtz traversed the turret again, using the autocannon to pour out another lethal hail that bought Wulfe the time he needed to

reload. With quick, practised hands, Wulfe re-threaded the belt into the
heavy stubber, yanked hard on the cocking lever, and was about to
resume firing when something huge and dark leapt high into the air on
a trail of blue fire, curved straight towards him, and landed with a heavy
clang on top of his turret. Just a metre closer and Wulfe would have
been fatally crushed under the heavy body of a monstrous, mad-eyed
brute with a smoking red rocket strapped to its back. It was some kind
of insane greenskin assault trooper!

Wulfe and the ork looked at each other for the briefest instant, blue
eye locked to red, and Wulfe knew that it was over. The ork's rusty
cleaver was already in the air, poised at the start of a sweeping downward stroke that would hack him apart. His heavy stubber couldn't help
him. The ork had one massive foot on either side of the barrel.

Oh, frak, thought Wulfe.

A tidal surge of adrenaline slowed time to a crawl and blocked out
everything but the enormous figure of the monster that was about to
end his life. Wulfe didn't hear the burst of fire from his right. He didn't
hear his name being called over the vox. But he saw the ork's weapon
hand disintegrate in a bloody mist, followed almost immediately by its
massive, razor-toothed head. It burst like a rotten fruit, and he felt the
monster's foul blood spray over his face and fatigues like hot rain.

The creature's heavy blade clattered against the turret armour as it fell.
Then the headless body followed it, falling backwards, slipping over the
tank's track guards to the red sand below.

Wulfe didn't move for another second, confused that he was somehow still alive. He didn't register the ork shells that were whining past
his head.

There was something powerfully salty on his lips, and the foul taste of
it snapped him back to his senses. It was ork blood. He wiped it off with
his sleeve and turned. Looking to the right, he saw Corporal Lenck
standing in the cupola of the *New Champion*, his heavy stubber still
pointed in Wulfe's direction.

For just the briefest moment, Wulfe felt absolutely sure that Lenck was
about to shoot him. There was a look of utter triumph in the arrogant
corporal's eyes. He could end Wulfe's life with the merest pressure of
thumb on trigger.

But the lethal impacts never came. After a tense second, Lenck
laughed, turned his stubber back on the orks and continued firing. He
looked sickeningly pleased with himself.

By the frakking Eye, Wulfe cursed. Now I'm in his debt. Damn it all!
Why did it have to be Lenck?

His eyes followed the line of Lenck's tracers and he saw that the *New
Champion* had cut a deep, broad path in the ork ranks, deep enough and

wide enough to make all the difference to Stromm and his men. The orks were pushing away from the crashed drop-ship, eager to avoid being slaughtered under the torrent of explosive munitions and auto-cannon fire. They left hundreds of their dead behind them in great heaps of reeking meat. Wulfe looked beyond the piled bodies and saw Stromm's infantrymen fighting valiantly with their backs to the crashed ship's hull. Not smart, he thought, to get yourself grounded like that without an exit strategy. It was only by sheer luck, or perhaps the machinations of the Divine Emperor, that the Gunheads had found Stromm's lot in time. If Lieutenant van Droi had picked up the colonel's faint vox-transmissions any later, the Gunheads would have found only dead men and scavengers.

Wulfe had said it before, and he said it to himself again now; he wouldn't have been a footslogger for all the gold on Agripinaa. What kind of madness made men march to battle without at least a hundred millimetres of solid armour between them and the foe? Little wonder that the life of an infantryman was so short. One way or another, most died within their first six months of combat duty. The average for tankers was almost double. He knew some men resented that, but it was tanks and their crews that drew most fire on the battlefield.

Through the veils of churning smoke and dust, Wulfe spotted a man that could only have been Colonel Stromm. His poise, his movements, everything about him radiated strength and leadership. He and the men immediately around him were fighting desperately against those orks that were still pressing in from the far side, protected from the tank fire by the very men they were so eager to kill. At a glance, Wulfe judged that there wasn't much more than a company's worth of men left standing: two hundred, maybe three. The number was dropping even as he watched. The orks kept up a constant pressure, clambering over banks of their dead to fire clumsily-made pistols and stubbers, or to charge forward with blades raised high. The sand under the carpet of dead men and orks had turned into a blood-sodden quagmire.

Wulfe dropped down into the turret and nudged the vox-selector switch to F channel, band six.

'Colonel Stromm,' he voxed, 'you have your corridor, but it won't hold for long.'

Stromm didn't waste time offering thanks. Instead, he answered, 'Understood, armour. We'll make our push. Give us all the cover you can. Stromm, out.'

Wulfe contacted Lenck and Siemens briefly and passed this on. For an instant, he considered thanking Lenck, but he couldn't forget the look in the man's eyes. He decided that they would talk about it later, providing they both lived through this. He scrambled back up into his cupola, intent on doing whatever he could to help Stromm's men. He saw two squads of Kasrkin storm troopers moving out from the colonel's side, swiftly taking up positions that would allow them to hold the passage open for as long as possible. They moved as one, firing clean, disciplined hellgun bursts for maximum effect, and Wulfe found he was profoundly impressed. The Kasrkin were a special breed. He wondered what it took to remain so cool-headed, surrounded by all that death and horror, by alien savages that outweighed you three or four times. He marvelled at their calm efficiency. Like tankers, the Kasrkin drew a certain level of resentment from standard infantrymen. They received special training and superior kit, and commanders tended not to waste them in wars of attrition when there were other options available. Right now, however, that training and equipment was being employed to save lives.

Wulfe wondered how any soldier could resent *that*.

With the corridor momentarily secured, the remnants of the embattled infantry began pouring out, desperately making for the cover of Sword Squadron's tanks. As they ran, some stopped and turned, dropping to one knee to fire back at the pursuing orks. When the men behind had overtaken them, they rose again and ran while someone else covered the rear. It was as well-executed a staggered retreat as Wulfe had seen.

While Sword Squadron's secondary weapons continued to blaze and stutter, helping to hold the orks at bay, Wulfe saw Colonel Stromm run down the centre of the corridor, a wiry-looking comms-officer at his side. The comms-officer was carrying a regimental banner of bright crimson and gold that rippled and waved above his head as he ran. It might have been glorious but for all the bullet holes in it. Wulfe noticed, too, that Stromm's right arm had been strapped to his body. It was probably broken, and yet he moved towards the tanks with as much speed as any of the others, slowing only to turn and fire blazing hellpistol shots back at his howling pursuers.

With men pouring out, racing to the relative safety behind the tanks, it wasn't long before only the Kasrkin storm troopers were left, holding the line until the last man was clear. The orks vented their full fury and rage on them, and some inevitably went down, though they fought to the bitter end through wounds that would have killed lesser men outright.

Sword Squadron gave them all the fire support they could manage. Most of the Kasrkin made it out, but not by much. As they raced towards the cover of the tanks, Wulfe ordered his squadron to keep the fire up but prepare to fall back. Then he contacted Colonel Stromm.

'You have wounded men in your group, sir. Get them up onto the tanks. Use the track-guards and the rear decking, but stay clear of the engine louvres and the radiator. We can carry them out of here and still cover the retreat. Those on foot will have to run. What do you say?'

Stromm began barking out orders immediately, and the track-guards of the three tanks were soon crowded with men in blood-soaked Guard-issue fatigues. Wulfe would have helped them up, but his continued fire was needed to keep the orks at bay.

'Sword One, Sword Two,' he voxed to Siemens and Lenck, 'fall back to Hammer's position. Keep your fire up as we move, but no main guns until van Droi gives the word. We don't want to scatter them.'

A short series of acknowledgements followed and, slowly, steadily, Sword Squadron began to roll backwards. It was then that *Frontline Crusader*'s engine sputtered and died. Wulfe could hear Corporal Siemens swearing over the vox. The panic in his voice was all too clear. 'Oh, Throne! We've stalled. Come in, Sword Leader. *Frontline Crusader* is in big trouble!'

From his cupola, Wulfe saw Siemens slamming his fists on the top of his turret. The wounded men perched on the *Frontline Crusader*'s track guards were looking agitated. The orks coming forward immediately angled straight towards the crippled tank.

Some of the wounded leapt off and started limping through the sand, clearly unwilling to gamble on the engine restarting. Others stayed put, bravely pouring las-fire down at the oncoming enemy. That didn't last long. Wulfe saw them struck by wild sprays of enemy fire. The wounded Cadians fell from the sides of the tank, as lifeless as rag dolls.

Wulfe barked orders over to Lenck, and both the *New Champion* and *Last Rites II* turned their weapons left, desperate to buy Corporal Siemens some time.

Wulfe knew Siemens needed more than time. He needed a bloody miracle.

None was forthcoming.

While the stubbers and bolters were busy raking the charging green-skins, three orks with rockets strapped to their backs suddenly careened upwards on trails of blue fire, landing just metres away from the *Frontline Crusader*'s armoured flanks.

Wulfe barely had time to register the thick, cylindrical weapons the orks were carrying, before they were put to murderous use. The moment they landed, each of the orks raised its tube to its shoulder, took aim at the sides of the crippled tank, and fired.

Three explosions sounded in rapid succession, and a cloud of dust and fire erupted into the air, cloaking the *Frontline Crusader* from view.

'Siemens!' shouted Wulfe over the vox. There was no answer. He immediately turned his stubber on the orks responsible, turning two of

Hammer of the Emperor

them into hunks of dead meat where they stood. Aiming at the third, his shells struck the red rocket on its back, and it detonated, scattering tiny burnt pieces of the ork in every direction.

As the cloak of dust and sand around the *Frontline Crusader* showered back down to the ground, Wulfe saw Siemens's body. It was still in the cupola, slumped forward. His flesh was black. His clothes, hair and skin were still burning. One charred and lifeless arm was draped over the barrel of his heavy stubber.

There were holes in the tank's armour, too. Wulfe could see twin gaping wounds where the plating looked like it had melted straight through. Red flames were boiling up out of them, and out of the hatches the crew had tried frantically to open in their last moments.

Four men, men Wulfe had known, dead. Rage lit inside him like dry tinder. He turned his stubber back on the advancing horde with a vengeance.

'Throne curse you and your entire stinking race,' he yelled at them.

'What are you doing, Wulfe?' a gruff voice demanded over the vox-link. It was Lieutenant van Droi speaking on the company command channel.

'It's the *Frontline Crusader*, sir,' replied Wulfe, breaking only momentarily from his revenge. 'She's been brewed up.'

'I can see that, damn it,' growled van Droi. 'Keep falling back. Spear Squadron is in position. It's time we put a lid on this.'

Wulfe gritted his teeth. Siemens had been all right, not a friend exactly, but a fellow tanker, a Cadian brother. He was one of the few left who had been with the company since before Palmeros. He didn't deserve to be cooked in his crate like that. Wulfe didn't want to think about what it had been like for the crew inside, struggling to free themselves while the flames devoured them. It seemed like every time Wulfe faced the orks, he came away mourning lost men.

He ordered Metzger to keep them rolling backwards, and Holtz to keep the autocannon firing. Moments later, they were back in line with van Droi's *Foe-Breaker* and the tanks of Sergeant Richter's Hammer Squadron. The *New Champion* had beaten them to it. Lenck hadn't wasted time venting anger on the orks. Maybe Siemens's death didn't really bother the cold-hearted son-of-a-bitch.

With the tanks pulling up into a horizontal firing line, Colonel Stromm ordered his able-bodied men to help their wounded brothers down from the track-guards and lead them back to cover behind the vehicles. There was little left for them to do, and it was better for them to stay well back from the main guns if they didn't want their eardrums ruptured.

Rhaimes and the rest of Spear Squadron were visible on the left, pressing the orks into a crossfire. *Last Rites II* and the *New Champion* were ordered to edge right, the better to cover any attempt by the orks to break and run in that direction. The greenskins seemed emboldened by their tank-kill and eagerly charged straight on, a mad howling mass of flesh and metal. Soon, they were exactly where van Droi wanted them. He gave the order.

'Fire main guns!'

What followed was no battle. It was the grisliest sort of massacre.

Against the full, unrestrained fury of the Gunheads, the mindless greenskins never stood a chance.

CHAPTER SEVEN

GOSSEFRIED VAN DROI stood looking up at the ruin of the naval drop-ship, chewing on the end of a damp cigar while, all around him, Colonel Stromm's infantry went about the business of identifying their dead, stripping the bodies of anything that could still be put to use. Grim work, yes, but van Droi knew that it was essential. Out here in the desert, the supplies they had brought with them were all the supplies they would be getting. Speaking over the vox, Stromm had already confirmed van Droi's worst fears: no, there had not been word from anyone else. Exolon's status remained a bloody mystery.

Dark days, these, thought van Droi, and darker ones ahead. Saints guide you, Siemens. You were a good man. I hope you find peace with the Emperor.

The drop-ship that had carried six companies of The Fighting 98th to Golgotha was in a sorry state, even worse than the one that had carried van Droi's Gunheads. It looked like a carcass, the decaying body of a giant beast, huge and grey, landing legs twisted and bent, the bones of its titanium superstructure shining through where the hull had been ripped or blasted away. It was a wonder that any of Stromm's men had survived the crash. It was another wonder they'd lasted out the ork assaults as long as they had. Van Droi wondered how many men and machines he would have lost if he had ordered his Gunheads to dig in back at their own crash site. Might an Exolon reconnaissance patrol have found them? Or would the orks have got there first?

He chided himself. There was nothing to be gained by such speculation. He had made the decision to move out, and he stood by it. Throne
above, if he hadn't, the infantrymen scurrying busily back and forth all
around him would be corpses, probably headless ones, given the greenskins' propensity for taking grisly trophies.

Siemens's death weighed heavy on him. Ten tanks had become nine.
A full crew had been lost. Morale had taken a beating, too, though his
tankers were understandably glad to have found others who had made
planetfall more or less intact.

Van Droi was still looking up at the ruined ship when he heard boot
heels grinding the sand just behind him. He turned and found himself
looking into the scarred and weathered face of a man he judged to be
about twenty years older than himself. He was wrong. There was barely
ten years between them. Even covered in blood and dust, though,
Colonel Stromm somehow managed to look dignified.

'Colonel,' said van Droi.

The colonel was a little shorter than van Droi. He filled his uniform
well – muscular – fit to fight, and van Droi found himself nursing a
hunch that Stromm had once been Kasrkin. That seemed to fit, but he
wasn't about to ask. None of his business. Instead, he gave a sharp
salute and received one back.

Formalities over, the colonel's face immediately broke into a wide
grin.

'You know, van Droi, I'd shake your hand if my right arm wasn't in
pieces,' he said, glancing down at the limb in question. It was cradled in
a white sling stained with dust. 'Bloody orks. Damned good to see you
and your boys come out of the desert like that. Like Saint Ignatius riding into Persipe. I thought I was dreaming.'

Van Droi grinned back. 'You won't find any saints among my lot, sir,
but I'll bet we were as glad to find you as you were to be found. Five days
without a trace of anyone, and we only came across you by sheer luck.'

'Luck or the Emperor's hand,' said Stromm. Gesturing up at the
wrecked ship, he continued, 'A proper mess, this. The cogboys should
have warned us it would be so rough coming down. I know they mentioned the storms, but they didn't say anything about them knocking
our ships out of the sky. And why the hell weren't we told about vox-
range limitations? I'd love some bloody answers.'

'I wish I had some for you, sir. Hundreds of drop-ships launched.
Where the others ended up is anyone's guess, but some of them must
have touched down safely at Hadron. If we could just see the damned
stars clearly for one night, we might be able to navigate our way there.'

Stromm nodded gravely, and then gestured for van Droi to walk with him. Together, they moved off towards a large tent that was doubling as a temporary command centre. Stromm's adjutant, Lieutenant Kassel, was inside. When the colonel and van Droi entered, he turned and saluted.

'Good to meet you, lieutenant,' said van Droi after a brief introduction. The two men, equal in rank, shook hands while Stromm walked over to a munitions crate and sat down.

'Damned heroes, those tankers. Eh, Kassel?'

'Heroes, sir,' answered Kassel with a smile. He produced two glasses of water and set them down on a large crate that was doubling as a table.

'That's the next big problem,' said Stromm, looking down at the glasses before glancing up at van Droi. 'How are you fixed for water, lieutenant?'

Van Droi frowned. 'Not good, colonel. Not good at all. Fuel is another thing we'll have to worry about soon. Food, not so much. I've had my lads on half rations since the crash. But we'll be dead men before long if we don't get water and fuel.'

Stromm nodded. 'You've done a hell of a job keeping your boys alive and on the move. Throne knows, if it weren't for you, my men would be dead. I'd be dead. So, I don't want you to think of me as pulling rank–'

'But you want to fold us into your unit,' said van Droi, finishing the thought. He had anticipated this. It made sense.

'Just for the time being, and for the sake of having a clear command structure more than anything else.'

'No complaints here. Tanks and infantry work a lot better together than they do apart.'

'My thoughts exactly. I'm not a tyrant, van Droi. I'll consult you at every turn. You'll be kept in the loop.'

'You have a plan, sir?'

'It's not much of one, but it's clear that staying here is out of the question. If Army Group Command hasn't found us by now, odds are they aren't going to. It's high time we moved on. The day we came down, I sent a number of scouting parties out. Most never returned, but one of the recon squads that did make it back reported seeing rocky uplands about two hundred kilometres eastwards. The orks started hitting us before we could follow up on it, but I'm sure we'll have a better chance of establishing vox-contact with someone if we can get to higher ground. Thoughts?'

'It could be the feet of the Ishawar Mountains, sir, which would suggest that we came down much further to the south-east than I originally estimated. If it *is* the Ishawar range, following the foothills north-east should take us within a few days' travel of Balkar. Sooner or later, if Operation Thunderstorm is still rolling, the rest of Exolon will deploy near there. *The Fortress of Arrogance* was lost in the north-east Hadar region. So yes, sir. I'd say that's about the best plan we've got.'

'Knew you'd see it my way,' said Stromm. 'Let's talk about numbers. What exactly are you fielding?'

'Nine tanks, all Leman Russ variants, all crewed, plus four Heracles halftracks and eight trucks. Five of those are packed with ammunition and supplies. Most of our personnel are crammed into the halftracks.'

'How many personnel?' asked Stromm.

'One hundred and twenty-nine, sir. Forty of those are tank crew. The rest are reserve crews and battlefield support. Half a dozen are wounded men, two of which are critical.'

Stromm turned to Kassel and said, 'There go our worries about transportation then, Hans.'

Kassel nodded.

'Sir?' said van Droi.

Stromm sat forward and lifted one of the glasses from the top of the crate in front of him. 'We have a few Chimeras, mostly machines from the Kasrkin Armoured Fist squads, and a couple of halftracks and trucks. Seventy per cent of our vehicles were wrecked in the crash.' Stromm looked down at the water in his glass. 'It was one of the factors in my decision to stay put, that and our wounded.'

'Even if we had the transports,' said Kassel, 'it's not much good moving our people out of here if we don't have enough trucks to carry the supplies we're going to need.'

'My support crews are pretty talented, colonel,' said van Droi. 'The vehicles you say are wrecked, are they still in the drop-ship?'

Stromm grinned. 'Think your men can fix some of them up, van Droi?'

'Not like the cogboys could, sir, but I'd say it's worth a try, wouldn't you?'

'Get them on it right away, then. Kassel, make sure they get everything they need.'

'Of course, sir.'

Stromm stood and walked to the entrance of the tent. 'We've got lots to do, gentlemen. Let's be about it.'

Having been dismissed, van Droi and Kassel followed the colonel out into the open air. Van Droi judged that there were just a few hours of daylight left. His crews would have to work under lamps. It would be a long night for them, but there would be time enough for rest once they were under way again.

'If you'll follow me, lieutenant,' said Kassel, 'I'll show you what there is to work with.'

'Lead the way,' said van Droi, and together, he and Kassel moved off, walking around to the far side of the crashed ship to enter via the massive rent in its main hold.

With the two lieutenants gone, an exhausted Stromm let his facade slip, just for a moment. His shoulders sagged and he blew out a deep, exhausted breath. His arm still hurt like hell despite injections of anaesthesium. Sure that no one else was within earshot, he took a tiny, handcrafted icon of the Emperor from a side pocket in his fatigues, raised it level with his face and said, 'Light of all Mankind, there's nothing I wouldn't do for you. You know that. So do you think you might get off your bloody Throne and help us out a bit?'

AFTER CHECKING LAST *Rites II* for outer damage – her headlamps had been shot to pieces, some of her vision blocks needed replacing, and the turret's left-side external stowage boxes were riddled with bullet holes, but these things were easily fixed – Wulfe found himself with a little well-earned downtime. The support squads would take care of maintenance duties. Lieutenant van Droi had ordered the tank crews to rest and recover, knowing they would be crashing hard after the fight. Coming down off so much adrenaline was enough to knock some guys out, but Wulfe didn't feel ready to try for sleep yet. His throat was still itching, though whether it was because of his scar or because of the damned dust, he couldn't be sure. Sipping a little water – a little being all he could afford himself – seemed to help. He pulled a rebreather mask over his mouth and nose and went for a walk. If it was the dust that was bothering him, the mask would stop it getting worse.

Masked or not, his stroll was far from pleasant. The desert sands were cratered, fire-blackened, and absolutely littered with bodies. At least all the bodies were those of the foe. Colonel Stromm's men had finished removing their fallen brothers from the field of battle. Wulfe was glad of that as he weaved between piles of alien cadavers. Many of the bodies wore thick plates of black armour, iron pitted with rust and scored by las-fire. Between the plates, Wulfe saw gaping wounds caked with blood-soaked sand. He was doubly glad of his rebreather now. The stench would have been unbearable without the mask's powerful filter.

Last Rites II had slain many of the beasts, surely over a hundred, though she wouldn't be wearing any new kill-markings for it. To an armoured company, infantry kills counted for little in terms of prestige, even in such numbers. Armour kills were what mattered, the challenge of machine against machine, crew against crew. Such were the fights a tank commander lived for. Until *Last Rites II* bested another tank in combat, she had proved nothing to Wulfe, nothing at all.

Wulfe's crew had a different outlook. After the battle, they had been quick to show their gratitude to her, offering sanctioned prayers to the machine-spirit housed in her metal body. Through the vision blocks, they had seen the *Frontline Crusader* brew up. They had seen Siemens's body roasting in the red fire. Why was it always the most horrific images that remained so clear in one's mind, Wulfe wondered? Why could he never remember a pretty girl's smile or a glorious sunset in the same kind of vivid detail?

The *Frontline Crusader* had stalled and it was all down to the damned dust. In the days the Gunheads had spent crossing the desert, eleven of their machines – five of the tanks, four of the halftracks, and two of the rugged Thirty-Sixers – had suffered the same kind of sudden cut-outs: dust on the contacts, dust clogging the fuel lines. Clean the dust out and you were fine, good to go. It just took a little work, a few minutes' attention. Siemens and his crew had been dead men from the moment it happened. They never stood a chance.

It could have happened to any of them. *Last Rites II* could have stalled just as easily. He knew that. It was a cruel thing that had happened to Siemens, but Wulfe couldn't deny a guilty relief. His crew was alive. He was alive.

His footsteps took him towards the wreckage of *Frontline Crusader*, and he stopped just a few metres from her. She was nothing but a black husk now. Her machine-spirit was gone. She was a corpse like the countless bodies that surrounded her. Thankfully, someone had removed Siemens's remains from the turret. Wulfe hoped the bodies of the men inside had been removed, too. Throne help the support crew who had taken care of that. It was a miserable business. Wulfe had seen some terrible things in his time: turret baskets painted red with blood, equipment caked in bone fragments and gore, blackened bodies fused together by flame so that you couldn't tell where one man ended and another began. Little wonder that infantrymen sometimes referred to tanks as 'steel coffins.' Years ago, Confessor Friedrich had taken it on himself to deal with that kind of mess as often as possible, working quickly, quietly, and without solicitation or complaint. No one had asked him to take on such a burden, but it wasn't right, he said, for tank men to have to see such things. Wulfe hoped the confessor had got down safely with the rest of the regiment. He was a good man. Given the horrors he put himself through, it was no wonder he drank so much.

Moving closer to the black husk of the tank, Wulfe saw again the two great gouges in her side. The armour plating had melted around the wounds, creating a jutting lip of metal under each. He stretched out a hand and found that the metal was cool to the touch.

Walking around to her other side, he found another hole. She had been hit simultaneously on both flanks with three separate impacts. The weapons that had killed her had been rocket-propelled grenades with shaped charges. The implications were grim. Over more than two decades of battle, Wulfe had faced the full gamut of anti-tank weapons, from magnetic mines to man-portable lascannons. He had seen shaped charges employed by armies of rebels and heretics all too often, but he had never seen *orks* field them. He had seen them use simple rockets sometimes, but this was different. Here was a weapon that, with a jet of molten copper, made a mockery of armour up to two hundred millimetres thick.

From now on, he and the other tank commanders would have to be extra wary. The orks had always been dangerous at close quarters, especially to infantry. Now they were just as dangerous to tanks.

Leaving the wreckage of *Frontline Crusader* behind him, he started walking towards one of the wrecked ork artillery pieces that van Droi's Vanquisher had taken out at long range. Ten metres away, he stopped and stared at it, noting the bodies of the greenskin crew that lay around its shredded tracks. They were little more than heaps of smoking bone and gristle. Even before it had been turned into burning junk, the machine had been an ugly thing. It was often hard to believe that these ork vehicles could function at all. Its massive gun was ruptured, peeled back like the skin of a fruit, ragged metal ends twisted outwards from a blast within. Wulfe supposed a round had exploded in the barrel when the turret had been struck. What remained of the track assemblies showed them to be huge, almost as wide as Wulfe was tall, and cruelly spiked, though they hardly needed to be given the nature of the terrain. Flat, open desert was ideal for treaded machines. Wulfe knew that adding spikes was just something orks tended to do. There were other examples nearby, including suits of body armour adorned in a similar fashion. Orks built everything that way: big, heavy, spiky and loud. Laying waste to their misbegotten creations was a duty Wulfe relished.

'Showed the bastards this time, didn't we?' said a rasping voice behind him.

Wulfe turned to see a Kasrkin storm trooper crouching on the sand nearby, leaning over a lifeless greenskin, tugging hard on a pair of metal pliers that were clamped around one of the dead monster's jutting tusks. The Kasrkin had removed his helmet, laying it beside him on the sand while he worked. Clearly, the stench from the ork bodies didn't bother him much. He was younger than Wulfe, though the profusion of crisscrossing scars that marked his hard face added a few years. His skin was swarthy and his hair so blond it was almost white. A south-hiver, then, a Kasr Derth man, or Kasr Viklas, maybe. Back on Cadia, men from the north and south didn't always get on, but the friction usually vanished the moment they got off-world. Cadians tended to stick together in the end, whichever hive they originally came from.

'I reckon we did,' Wulfe replied.

The Kasrkin didn't look up. He yanked hard on his pliers, and the ork tooth came loose with a spurt of thick red blood. He transferred the pliers to his clean hand and shook red droplets onto the sand, muttering an oath.

'Which one is yours then?' he asked.

'Sorry?'

'Which tank?'

'*Last Rites II*. She's a standard Leman Russ.'

'Is that right?' asked the Kasrkin, not looking up. 'What number?' He fixed his pliers to the dead ork's other tusk and began working them backwards and forwards, trying to free the roots from the massive jawbone.

'Nine-two-one,' said Wulfe, slightly suspicious of the soldier's interest. Kasrkin weren't known to be garrulous. Conversation with them was rare.

'Nine-two-one,' the storm trooper repeated between grunts. The corpse's remaining tusk was putting up a bit of a struggle. 'Yeah, I saw you. Carried some of our wounded out, right?'

There was a sharp cracking sound. Wulfe winced as he saw the tusk come free with a gush of crimson. Grinning, the Kasrkin held up his prize so that Wulfe could see it, white as bone, as long as a man's middle finger, and tapering to a nasty point. He dropped the excised tooth into a darkly stained canvas bag by his right knee, and said, 'I saw that one over there brew up. He was your mate, was he? No way to go, burning up like that in a big tin box.'

Right, thought Wulfe bitterly, thanks for that. 'They were good men. They'll be with the Emperor now.'

The Kasrkin didn't speak. He picked up his bag of teeth, rose to his feet, and moved to the next greenskin carcass.

Wulfe didn't need to ask why the soldier was pulling teeth. He had seen it done before. Some said that the orks were superstitious and that finding their dead kin with tusks removed put a terrible fear into them. He doubted that. Fear wasn't something orks seemed prone to. On the other hand, he knew troopers who traded the tusks for packets of smokes and bottles of alcohol. There was usually at least one man in a regiment who could fashion them into charms or trinkets. Sometimes, depending on the planet, civilian traders would offer a high price for them. It was illegal, of course, under the alien artefact laws. Commissar Slayte had executed two men for it a few years back. Repeat offenders. Rather than shoot them, he had chosen to snap their necks. It hadn't helped his popularity much.

The Kasrkin was focussed on his morbid dentistry, and Wulfe decided to head back to his crew. Maybe van Droi had new orders for them. The sooner they left, the better.

Without saying another word to the Kasrkin, he turned and began walking, weaving his way between the heaped corpses, but he hadn't gone ten metres when he heard a shout.

'Hey! Nine-two-one!'

Wulfe turned.

'Souvenir!' called the Kasrkin, and he threw a shining object into the air. It curved towards Wulfe, who reached out a hand and caught it. Opening his fingers, he saw a long, curving tusk with four pointed roots. It was still sticky with blood.

He looked up, expecting some explanation, but the Kasrkin was already moving off towards another corpse, happily humming a tune.

Wulfe rubbed the ork tooth clean on his rust-coloured fatigues, stuffed it into his thigh pocket, and moved off. The muted glow of the sun was nearing the western horizon. There was perhaps another hour before nightfall. He hoped van Droi had a plan. Then again, he thought, maybe the lieutenant was no longer in charge.

VOEDER LENCK WAS lying back, relaxing on one of his tank's track-guards after a good smoke, when Sergeant Wulfe walked by. The rest of the *New Champion*'s crew were sitting on the sand, playing cards and passing around a lho-stick that contained a few ingredients which were not exactly standard.

Lenck heard the sergeant's footsteps in the sand as he approached and raised one eyelid. Here we go, he thought. The uptight prick won't be able to help himself.

Sure enough, the sergeant's nose crinkled and he stopped dead in his tracks, looking down at the gambling crewmen. With their senses dulled by the smoky narcotic, and with the game absorbing their full attention, they didn't even notice him.

'Haha! Frak you, Varnuss,' said a jubilant Private Riesmann. 'That's twice I've had you with the same damned hand. Heretic's gotta pay up, you big grox's arse.'

Private Varnuss, a thick-necked, low-browed man with a shock of bright orange hair, growled and said, 'If I find out you're cheatin', Riesmann, I'm gonna bite your nose off and spit it in your face.'

Despite the threat, he thrust a big hand inside his fatigues and drew out two vials of clear liquid. With a dark look, he passed them to Riesmann, who accepted them with a smug grin, pocketed them, and began to shuffle the cards again.

'You do realise, gentlemen,' said Wulfe sharply, 'that the game of

Heretic is banned by Imperial edict.' The three men seated on the ground gave a start and jumped to their feet, scattering cards everywhere. The lho-stick fell to the sand where it continued to burn, lacing the air with its intoxicating fumes.

'Sergeant Wulfe, sir,' stammered Private Hobbs, the shortest of the men. 'Wasn't playing no Heretic, sir. Just a harmless game of… er…'

Wulfe ignored him. He stepped forward, bent down, and picked up the burning lho-stick. Sniffing it, he said, 'Do I frakking look like I was born yesterday, Hobbs?' He held the lho-stick up in front of the little man's face. 'This groxshit addles the brain, which would explain why you'd think you could lie to me and get away with it.'

Lenck opened both eyes now, turned his head in Sergeant Wulfe's direction, and, with an exaggerated sigh, slid down from the side of the *New Champion*. Time to see if saving the sergeant's life was a mistake or not, he thought. 'My fault, sergeant. My fault. Sorry.'

Wulfe's eyes narrowed. 'You're accepting full responsibility for this, corporal? I find that hard to believe.'

Lenck's shirt had been tied around his narrow waist while he rested, but now he pulled it up, shrugging into the sleeves and buttoning it over his chest. His dog tags clinked together as he did so. 'I taught them a new game while we were still in the Empyrean, sir. S'called… er… Ship-shape. Yeah, that's the one. Isn't that right, lads? It's a good game is Ship-shape. I'll admit, though, sergeant, it does look a lot like Heretic to the untrained eye. I can understand you figuring one for the other.'

Wulfe glared. 'Really, Lenck? Because I could have sworn I heard Riesmann say something about the heretic having to pay up. But let's just say I believe you. What do you have to say about *this*?' For the second time, he raised the dubious lho-stick.

'Ah, now that one's not down to me, sergeant,' said Lenck amiably. 'No. That there was given to us by one of Colonel Stromm's lot. I thought there was something funny about it, to be honest. Didn't I say so, lads? Not like a bloody footslogger to go sharing his sticks with us tankers, is it, sergeant? Suspicious bit of generosity, that. I told them not to smoke it, but it wasn't an order or anything.'

'And did this mysterious footslogger give you his name? Or any more of his smokes? Well?'

Lenck shook his head, unblinking, never breaking eye contact with his squadron leader. 'Just the one, sergeant. Honest. Look, you can have it if you want. Not my business if you like a little smoke now and then.'

He watched Wulfe's face change colour and knew he was stepping dangerously close to the line, but he had to know how far he could push things now that this man, who clearly hated him, owed him his life.

Wulfe dropped the lho-stick and ground it into the sand with his boot.

Private Riesmann winced miserably.

Wulfe stepped in close to Lenck and, in hushed tones, said, 'You thought about it, didn't you, corporal? Earlier today?'

'Thought about what, sergeant?' Lenck replied innocently.

'Don't play the fool. I saw it in your eyes after you killed that ork. Thought about putting a few rounds in me, didn't you? Dangerous weapons, heavy stubbers. They kick like an auroch. Not hard for a few rounds to go wide in the heat of battle. Who knows? The others might have believed you.'

Lenck blinked, feigning a look of horror. Matching his voice to the low level of the sergeant's, he said, 'You're off your *damned* nut, Wulfe. I shouldn't be surprised. You've had it in for me since the day I joined this regiment. Damned if I know why. An inferiority complex, maybe? The only thing I shot today was orks, a lot of them. But, if you want to tell me what your bloody problem is, I'm all ears. If not…'

Wulfe stepped back, fists clenched, and Lenck readied himself to dodge a punch, but the growling sergeant didn't swing. Instead, he said one word. 'Dunst.'

'What?' asked Lenck.

'Does the name Dunst mean anything to you, corporal? Victor Dunst.'

The sergeant was clearly expecting some kind of reaction, but the name meant absolutely nothing to Lenck. He shrugged and said, 'Should it?'

Wulfe stared back. After a moment, the cold rage in his eyes seemed to dim, and he said, 'No, I suppose not. Throne, Dunst would be twice your age by now.'

Lenck stared back. This bastard has a screw loose, he thought. Rattling around inside a tank for so long has damaged the man's brain. He's no better than that idiot loader of his.

'I'll forget what I saw here just this once,' said Wulfe, 'because of what happened today. But now we're square. Got it? You and your men had better shape the hell up, Lenck. Maybe life was a bit more relaxed in the frakking reserves, but let me tell you something about Gossefried's Gunheads. We do our duty. We work for our chops. Start toeing the line or, Throne help me, I'll make it my personal mission to help you regret it.'

The sergeant kept his eyes locked with Lenck's, as if daring him to say something smart, but, if Wulfe had been hoping to see fear in them, he was out of luck. Lenck stared back with a barely suppressed grin. 'You're an example to us all, sergeant. Gentlemen,' he called to his crew. 'Thank the sergeant for putting you straight and saving you from the potential dangerous of suspicious gifts and unsanctioned card games.'

As one and without any trace of sincerity, Lenck's crew shouted, 'Thank you, Sergeant Wulfe!'

Wulfe's gaze didn't shift. 'And you, corporal?' he asked.

'Me, sergeant?' said Lenck, overplaying the innocent. 'I was asleep on the tank. I wasn't playing cards, and I've never smoked a lho-stick in my life, laced or otherwise. That's the Emperor's own truth, I swear.'

Wulfe sneered, but he apparently had nothing more to say. He turned and stalked off, fists still clenched at his side.

Lenck watched the sergeant's back receding for a moment, wondering who in the warp this Victor Dunst was, and thinking that it might be useful to find out.

He drew a lho-stick from the breast pocket of his shirt and flipped it into the air, catching it between his lips. Then he pulled a lighter from another pocket, lit the end of his smoke, and drew in a deep, pungent lungful.

'Have a nice day, Sergeant Arsehole,' he said and turned to join the next hand of cards.

CHAPTER EIGHT

THE LOW CLOUDS overhead flickered like broken lamps, such was the intensity of the fighting outside the walls of Karavassa.

'Watch those gullies to the south-east,' yelled Bergen into the tiny microphone of his vox-bead. 'Don't let them flank those armour companies on the right!'

Basilisk mobile artillery pieces boomed all around his Chimera APC, vomiting clouds of black smoke into the air with every ear-splitting shot. Through his field glasses, the major general watched great spouts of fire and sand burst upwards wherever the massive shells struck. Currently, they were wreaking terrible destruction on the ork foot soldiers.

The 10th Armoured Division had reached the rocky hills around the former Imperial outpost an hour after dawn. It was the eleventh day since planetfall, and Bergen's forces were running two whole days behind General deViers's demanding mission schedule. The conditions on Golgotha were beyond frustrating. Hour after hour, his forces had been forced to interrupt their journey eastward to facilitate repairs. The damned dust was playing havoc with the Imperial machines. It wasn't doing the men much good either. Dozens were sick. Bergen had developed a scratchy cough himself, and his spit was tinged with red.

When 10th Division had left Hadron base six days ago, the major general had been unsettled by the last-minute addition of Tech-Adept Armadron among their number. To his knowledge, no one in the 18th

Army Group had petitioned the Adeptus Mechanicus for such an honour. Bergen took it as another indicator of the hidden agenda he was convinced they were following. So far, nothing Armadron had said in their limited conversations had managed to convince him otherwise. The tech-priest insisted that his superior had ordered him to accompany Bergen's division purely out of concern for their success. Groxshit. The Machine Cult had manoeuvred Imperial forces here, and sooner or later, Bergen intended to find out why. Even so, Bergen had cause to be glad of Armadron's attendance. Despite his unsettling presence, the tech-adept had proved to be a particular asset. He was a member of the priesthood's *technicus* arm and, working closely with senior enginseer Aurien, he had done much to keep the tank columns moving. Without his tireless efforts and expertise, Bergen doubted his division would have made it here for many more days yet. That would really have given old deViers something to rage about.

Despite being fraught with problems, the journey here was still the easy part. Now that they had engaged the orks – whole regiments rushing forward to clash with them as they poured from the outpost's towering iron gates – the damned dust was proving just as problematic in battle as it had been on the move. Since the fighting had begun, a number of Colonel Vinnemann's tanks had been forced to fight from static positions, immobilised early in the assault by engine stalls. The fines penetrated everything. If the brave crews of the Atlas recovery tanks hadn't risked enemy fire to pull those tanks out, the crews would have died where they sat.

Squinting through his magnoculars, Bergen saw greenskin reinforcements pushing and jostling in their eagerness to join the fray.

'Get some fire on the main gates,' he voxed to his artillery commander. 'Hit them while they're bunched up. But don't damage the superstructure! Remember, we need to take the outpost intact.'

His division had been unable to surprise the orks, but then, he hadn't really expected to. The thick sandstone watchtowers of Karavassa had a commanding view from their seat on the basalt bluff up ahead. It wasn't the towers that had raised the alarm first, however. His armour columns had been sighted when they were still about thirty kilometres out from the target. Ork bike patrols had been roaming the area, their powerful headlamps throwing broad cones of light out into the darkness. Some of these patrols had roared out from between high dunes and almost run into the leading Imperial machines. A sudden stutter of gunfire had lit the sands as both sides leapt into action. The bikes were noisy, oversized things with huge wheels and more growling exhaust pipes than they could possibly have needed, but they were certainly fast. Their riders had shown surprising sense for orks, quickly turning tail and racing back the way they had come to alert the rest of the horde. Vinnemann's tanks had managed to take out most of them as they showed their backs, but a few had got away.

As the division had closed on the occupied outpost, with the cloud-smothered sunrise lending the scene a hellish red glow, Bergen had looked out from his cupola to see a huge ork force: a horde of greenskin infantry, numbering in the thousands, supported by tanks, artillery, light armour, and a good number of those ridiculous lumbering contraptions that the orks so loved to build. These dreadnoughts looked like oversized red buckets on piston legs. Their wicked arms flailed to and fro, blades whirring, claws clashing, eager to begin the bloodshed. They were covered in other weapons, too: flamers, rocket launchers, heavy stubbers and anything else that could be bolted to them. They were utterly lethal to infantry, but they were no match for Imperial tanks. Vinnemann's crews had already gunned down at least thirty of them at long range, turning them to burning scrap that rained down on the heads of the orks around them.

'Infantry, keep up the advance!' Bergen commanded. 'Colonel Vinnemann, have three of your companies move forward in support of the infantry on the left flank. Send the rest straight up the middle. We need to knock out their armour support to give our boys a fighting chance. We have to drive a wedge into them.'

Bergen's command Chimera, *Pride of Caedus*, had taken up position on a spur of rock just a few kilometres south-west of the outpost's walls. Even sitting hull down, it was a risky place to perch. Had he been the defender instead of the attacker, he would have put some artillery on the spur, sure that the enemy commander would have chosen this spot from which to oversee his forces. Did such things occur to ork leaders? Bergen didn't know, but his need for a good view of the battlefield overrode his concern.

A series of rippling explosions north-east of his position caused him to turn. One of Marrenburg's mechanised infantry companies, ten Chimeras each carrying a squad of hardened infantrymen, was trying to press forward in support of the troopers on foot. But a phalanx of ork tanks – looted Imperial machines from the last war, disfigured almost beyond recognition by the addition of spikes and strange armaments – had broken free from their engagement with a company of Vinnemann's Leman Russ and were speeding towards the Chimeras with cannons blazing.

Bergen saw two of the Chimeras struck head on, one of them hit so hard that it flipped onto its back. He saw the rear hatch open. Dizzy men began stumbling out, desperate to be away from the burning machine before its ammunition and fuel stores exploded. Most were injured. They fell. Their shaking legs wouldn't carry them. They scrambled desperately to get up again.

Too late. With a great boom and a mushrooming of fire and smoke, the Chimera lifted into the air. Only two of the troopers managed to escape the blast. Bergen cursed and turned his eyes from the sprawled, burning figures that hadn't.

The other Chimera was luckier. The cockpit was aflame, the driver certainly dead, but the hatch at the back had been thrown wide, and the soldiers within were pouring out, lasguns up and ready. Bergen knew those lasguns wouldn't do a damned thing against the ork machines.

He was about to vox Vinnemann for support when a trio of Leman Russ tanks crested a rise just north of the burning Chimeras. They traversed their turrets right, in unison, and blasted the ork tanks at mid-range. One of the ork machines was hit dead centre. The Russ's armour-piercing round must have punctured the enemy tank's magazine, because Bergen saw it explode spectacularly, the entire turret spinning into the air on a pillar of glaring orange flame.

The other two ork machines were still closing on the no-longer-mechanised infantry. The soldiers fired on them in tight, ordered volleys, but it was futile. Las-bolts smacked harmlessly against thick red armour. A second later, however, the three Leman Russ fired again. The ork machines were struck hard, skidding sideways on their treads before halting. Greenskins started to bail out, some of them already howling as flames licked their leathery brown flesh. The Cadian infantrymen moved straight in, pouring las-fire onto the ork crews, cutting them down, blazing away on full charge until there was little left but smoking black hunks of meat.

'Armour Command to Division,' said a voice on the vox. 'Armour to Division. Please respond.' It was Colonel Vinnemann.

'I read you, Armour,' said Bergen. 'Go ahead.'

'I have a visual on enemy light vehicles breaking left to strafe our forward lines. Armour cannot engage. I repeat, armour cannot engage. We have hostile tanks front and right, and we're taking heavy fire from artillery located inside the base.'

Bergen cursed. 'Understood, Armour. Leave it to me. Division out.'

He panned his glasses right until he found the machines in question. There were ten of them: ork war-buggies bristling with heavy stubbers, rocket launchers and more. They were roaring straight towards the Cadian assault line. The men were exposed, busy trying to push the hordes of ork infantry back. They would be slaughtered under the concentrated fire of the buggies unless…

'Division to Recon Two,' Bergen voxed. 'Come in please.'

'Recon Two reading you loud and clear, sir. Go ahead.'

'Ork light armour advancing on our infantry at speed. Look to your two. Those lads need a little Sentinel support, wouldn't you say?'

The man on the other end of the vox was Captain Munzer. Bergen could picture the grin on the man's scar-twisted face as he replied, 'Sentinels moving to intercept, sir. We'll light the bastards up. Enjoy the show.'

Seconds later, Bergen saw Munzer's bipedal machines lope out from behind a rocky hill to the left and open fire. Each of the Cadian Sentinels sported an autocannon, ideal for ripping right through their current targets. Ork bodies were torn apart in the deadly hail. Fuel tanks ignited and the speeding buggies flipped and spun, rolling end over end, spilling the xenos filth onboard.

He couldn't hear them, but Bergen could see the infantry cheering the Sentinel pilots. The cheers stopped dead when five of the Sentinels vanished suddenly in a great ball of flame. A row of ugly black machines had emerged from Karavassa to join the fray. More ork artillery! The surviving Sentinels immediately turned to identify their attackers, but the range was far too great to strike back. Over the vox, Bergen heard Captain Munzer ordering his walkers to scatter so they wouldn't provide such an opportune target again.

'Command to Armour,' voxed Bergen urgently, 'be advised, we have additional ork artillery pushing out from the main gates. What's your status?'

MY STATUS, THOUGHT Colonel Kochatkis Vinnemann, is that my back is bloody killing me.

He cursed his own stupidity. As he and his men had neared the outpost, completely preoccupied with the coming battle, he had neglected to take the vital medication that counteracted his body's immune system. It had been years since the implant surgery, but his body still steadfastly refused to accept the augmetic spine. He needed large, regular doses of immunosuppressants and pain mediators in order to function at his best. But there wasn't time to stop and take them now.

'Division, we are still engaged with hostile tanks. Ninth company is down to half strength. Fourth and Fifth companies have taken multiple losses. We're trying to push in, to flank the buggers on the right, sir, but the damned artillery… I'll ask one more time, sir, will you not put some Basilisk fire down behind those walls? It would make one hell of a difference.'

'That's a negative, colonel,' Bergen answered with obvious regret. 'The objective must be taken intact. We have enemy artillery fire from just outside the main gates. I need one of your companies to knock it out. I know you're up against it, colonel. It's damned messy out there. But do what you can.'

By the blasted Eye, cursed Vinnemann. 'Understood, Division. We're on it. Armour, out.'

He tapped a button on his headset, switching from vox to tank intercom.

'Listen up,' he told his crew. 'Our troops are hurting out there. Not just our tankers, but Marrenburg's lot, Graves's lot. So it looks like the *Angel* gets to enter the fray after all.'

This announcement was met with resounding cheers from his crew. To some extent, Vinnemann's tank, *Angel of the Apocalypse*, was a victim of her own superb design. She was a Shadowsword super-heavy tank, ancient and deadly, but her Volcano cannon, with its nine-metre barrel, had originally been designed for felling traitor Titans and the like. She was far too specialised to warrant being fielded in most conventional battles, including this one.

Today, though, she would get to show what she could do.

The very thought of it was almost enough to overcome the pain in Vinnemann's back.

'Bekker,' he said, addressing his driver, 'get us behind that ridge on the right. Hull down, but leave plenty of clearance for the gun. The rest of you, prep for firing. We're about to make things interesting around here.'

With a great chugging cough from her exhausts, *Angel of the Apocalypse* rumbled into motion.

BERGEN SAW VINNEMANN'S massive Shadowsword roar towards a shallow rise and settle into firing position. The ork artillery pieces had turned their attention to the infantry's forward lines. The bodies of good Cadian men were being blasted apart to rain back down to the ground in ragged pieces. Scores of them were dying with every lethal shot, and the greenskins on foot were using the cover of the artillery fire to bridge the gap, hungry for the slaughter that would take place at close quarters. Elsewhere, Vinnemann's tanks were holding their own against the technically inferior but far more numerous ork machines. Smoking wrecks littered the land, providing cover for small groups of terrified men who had lost their nerve. Through his field glasses, Bergen saw one such group huddled together, eyes shut tight, hands pressed over their ears. It was hard to see through all the smoke and fire, but they were clearly green. New meat.

Where in the blasted warp was their sergeant?

If their regimental commissar noticed them huddled there, frozen in fear and panic, they wouldn't live to become old meat. Executions for cowardice were swift and brutal. There were no appeals. Bergen didn't like executions, but it was the way of the Guard: do your duty and die well, or run from it and die without honour.

He pitied them. It was easy to lose your balance when everything around you was going to hell. He voxed Colonel Graves. 'Division to Infantry Command. It looks like some of your rookies have lost their officer. Check those burning tanks on your ten o'clock, Graves. Get someone over there. Get them back in the fight. If the orks find them first they'll be massacred.'

Colonel Graves's response was brief and affirmative. Seconds later, Bergen saw a squad push left and join the huddled men. His attention was diverted, however, by a high-pitched whine that rose from the right. He had heard its like before, though on regrettably rare occasions. Hearing it now caused a thrill to run through him. He immediately panned his glasses towards Vinnemann's Shadowsword and saw a white glow forming at the muzzle of her huge cannon. Knowing what was to come, he turned his eyes towards the black artillery pieces by the outpost gates. Over-muscled greenskin gunnery crews were hefting shells the size of oil drums into the breech of each huge gun, readying to pulverise the advancing Cadian lines once again.

There was an almighty crack, like a clap of thunder, so close that Bergen felt it resonate deep in his bones. Everything in the area outside the outpost's main gates was engulfed in blinding white light. Bergen thought he saw the shot hit the row of greenskin war machines at an angle, cutting across them diagonally, but he could only watch for a fraction of a second. Looking directly at the beam was painful, and he squeezed his eyes shut.

A glowing afterimage of the Volcano's lethal beam remained behind his eyelids. When he opened his eyes again, he saw that a good number of the enemy machines had ceased to exist. Bubbling pools of liquid metal were the only trace left. Others, though not struck directly, would no longer be firing on his men. Their crews had been roasted to ash. The raw heat of the Volcano beam striking the neighbouring guns was simply too intense to survive.

The Cadian infantry had seen it all happen. A great cheer sounded from the battlefield as their spirits were lifted, and they surged forward, inspired by the incredible display of power they had witnessed from their own side. Bergen could feel it on the air, the special moment that every commander awaited so anxiously. It was the beginning of the end.

He voxed Vinnemann. 'Division to Armour Command. Hell of a shot, Kochatkis. Hell of a shot. That showed the filthy savages.'

Vinnemann answered through gasping breaths. 'Thank you, sir. Great to fire up the old Volcano cannon again after so long. She's drained the tanks, though. And we lost two capacitors. We'll need a Trojan over here for a refuel.'

'Are you all right, man? You sound...'

'Don't worry about me, sir,' replied Vinnemann. 'It's just the usual. I'll deal with it when this is over.'

Bergen was scanning the field of combat, watching his forces surge forward, taking a murderous toll on the foe. 'You won't have to wait long, Kochatkis. Our lads are really pressing forward now. You've inspired them, by Terra. They're cutting into the ork lines like a bayonet through butter.'

It was no lie. The greenskins' brute strength and instinct for battle simply weren't enough to hold off the well-coordinated Imperial forces any longer.

Within the hour, the walls of Karavassa were breached.

CHAPTER NINE

GUNFIRE STILL STUTTERED here and there along Karavassa's narrow streets, but the sounds of battle were little more than faint echoes of the madness and bloodshed that had now passed. The outpost had been retaken. Bergen had achieved his objective. General deViers had the first of the positions that would defend his supply and transport routes between Hadron Base and his intended destination in the east.

One of Colonel Marrenburg's mechanised platoons had found and killed the ork leader, an abomination of preposterous size and musculature, while securing the old Imperial communications building at the heart of the outpost. Bergen had been invited to verify this as soon as the area was judged clear of significant threats. Now he stood in a broad, low-ceilinged room, looking down on the body, marvelling at the size of the creature that lay motionless on the stone floor at his feet. The smell from it was overpowering, like stale sweat and rotting garbage.

He judged the fallen warboss to be at least two and a half metres tall, and not much less from shoulder to shoulder if one included the hunks of iron plate that had been bolted together to form its crude armour. It would have needed to hunch over just to fit inside the building, but then, orks tended to hunch anyway due to the massive slabs of overdeveloped muscle that covered their bodies. There was a poorly painted skull and dagger design on its angular breastplate, the symbol of whatever clan the foul wretch had lorded over. Bergen didn't recognise the glyph.

'Not the best looking bastard I've met, sir,' said Colonel Marrenburg. He stepped forward, stopping at Bergen's side.

'He's no charmer, Edwyn,' Bergen replied, 'that's for sure. Are we certain this one is the leader?'

'It's always the biggest, isn't it?' said Marrenburg. 'He had a bodyguard around him, too. Lost eleven men taking him and his guards down.' The colonel kicked the dead ork's thick forearm in contempt. Bergen watched the huge lifeless hand flop on the floor. The creature's thick fingers looked like they could have crushed a man's bones to powder. 'Made him pay in the end, though,' said Marrenburg. 'Mind if I smoke, sir?'

'Go ahead,' said Bergen. 'Maybe it'll cover the stink.'

'We'll have this place cleaned out in no time, sir,' replied Marrenburg as he pulled a packet of smokes from his breast pocket. 'Offer you one?'

'No, thanks.'

'Sorry, sir,' said Marrenburg with a grin. 'I always forget you don't. Anyway, if you're done looking at this one, the enginseers are waiting to set up some kind of equipment. Don't suppose they've come up with a solution to the long-range vox problem, do you?'

Bergen turned from the dead ork. 'In a roundabout way, I suppose they have. The tech-priests have been laying cables under the sand all the way here, a kind of landline that they insist will do the job. Tech-Adept Armadron has promised to brief us fully once the system is operational. It'll save us having to send any more runners all the way back to Hadron to communicate with the general.'

'Have you sent one to report on our victory here?'

Bergen nodded. 'Two, actually, just in case. Hornet riders with coded parchments. I sent them out as soon as we entered the gates. I expect Tech-Adept Armadron will have his landline system up and running before they reach Hadron Base, but I like to have a little insurance.'

Hornet motorcycles were a variant of the old standard-issue Blackshadow bikes. They were noisy, unarmed, and unarmoured, but they were the fastest machines available to 10th Division. Excepting for any problems, Bergen expected the couriers to reach Army Group HQ the following day.

'Very wise, sir,' replied Marrenburg with a nod.

Bergen didn't feel wise. Today's victory had lifted his spirits – he had seen the raw might of his armoured division overcome a significant enemy presence, and he knew a good number of his men, including no small percentage of those who had died, deserved medals for what they had achieved – but he still railed against the stupidity of the whole operation. Taking Karavassa wouldn't matter a damn once General deViers got to the final waypoint and found nothing left of the legendary tank he so desperately sought.

Bergen intended to be there when it happened, to see the look on the general's face.

'Any word on getting a hospital set up?' he asked, returning his mind to more immediate concerns.

Marrenburg said he didn't know, but Bergen's adjutant, Katz, stepped forward and answered, 'The Officio Medicae staff have taken over a two-storey barracks building close to the west gate. It's been swept for threats. No problems. Their triage teams have already brought in the high priority cases.'

'Good,' said Bergen. 'Make sure they have everything they need. I'm also worried about Colonel Vinnemann. I want him seen by an augmetics specialist as soon as possible. The gravity here, the dust and all the rest of it… From the sounds of it, it's all playing absolute hell with that damned metal spine of his.'

Marrenburg seemed about to comment when Colonel Graves marched in, boot heels loud and sharp on the stone floor. After a momentary glance in the direction of the dead warboss on the floor, he stopped, saluted, and said, 'Just had word from one of my sweeper teams, sir. There's something I think you ought to see.'

THE SOMETHING IN question did nothing to improve Bergen's dark mood. In fact, it had quite the opposite effect.

'Slaves,' he gasped. 'Human slaves.'

He stood in an open square a few hundred metres inside the north wall, looking at a mound of dead men and women. All were stripped. All were chained together, each iron collar linked to the next, every wrist and ankle tightly manacled. The flesh of their skinny chests and buttocks had been cruelly branded with the same glyph that Bergen had seen on the greenskin leader's breastplate. Worst of all, each torso bore broad axe and cleaver wounds. They had been slaughtered like grox. But why? He could only guess. Perhaps, with the battle-lust on them, the orks within the walls had lost control, desperate to share in the blood-letting, and turned on those humans closest to hand. The results were stomach-churning. If Bergen's heart had not already been filled with hatred for the greenskin race, the sight before him would certainly have done the trick. Blood-drinking ticks crawled in swarms over the cooling bodies, searching for the sustenance they craved, but finding little in veins that no longer pulsed.

'We should have expected this,' muttered Lieutenant Katz from behind Bergen's right shoulder.

'Should we, Jarryl?'

'I would have thought so, sir,' answered the adjutant. 'Orks have been raiding the nearby systems unchecked for years. Salvage ships, mostly. The Navy can't do much to protect those that break the spacing restrictions. High risk, high reward and all that.'

'I'm glad my adjutant is so well informed,' said Bergen.

'Sorry, sir,' stuttered Katz. 'I didn't mean to sound–'

'Actually, Jarryl, I was being sincere. You know I value your observations. I just hadn't thought to see something like this.'

'I imagine the poor souls were brought here from Hadron, sir. It was the only ork spaceport in the immediate area before the Navy cleansed it. We know ork clans sometimes trade with each other. These poor souls might have been traded for fuel or ammunition.'

'May the saints guide them on,' said Bergen. He pressed his hands to his chest in the sign of the aquila, and Katz immediately followed suit. Together, heads bowed, they offered a prayer for the dead. When they were done, Bergen said, 'We'll find more of them out there, won't we?'

Katz looked grim. 'I expect so, sir, but not alive. I imagine the other divisions will find some when they take Tyrellis and Balkar, but the orks will kill them before they can be saved.' He gestured miserably at the pile of bodies in front of him. 'There's nothing we could have done, of course.'

Bergen saw the truth of that, but it didn't make him feel any better. These people's lives had been stolen from them by dirty xenos scum. Their spirits, on the other hand, still belonged to the Emperor.

'Make sure the confessors are told of this, Jarryl. I'd like the souls of these men and women to be commended to the Emperor's side as soon as possible. I know the priests are busy with our own dead right now, but these bodies will have to be burned. I don't want the outpost crawling with disease now that we've taken it back. Understood?'

'Understood, sir,' said Katz. 'With your permission, I'll be about it now.'

'Good man,' said Bergen. He listened to his adjutant's footsteps fade behind him.

Above Karavassa, the sky was dimming with the onset of afternoon. The brown-bellied clouds looked almost low enough to touch. They flickered with sheet lightning. Booming claps of dry thunder shook the air.

A crackle of sound in Bergen's right ear announced a short-range vox-transmission just a fraction of a second before Colonel Graves's voice said, 'Graves to Division Command. Are you there, sir?'

Bergen tapped a finger on the transmit stud of his vox-bead and replied, 'Bergen here. Go ahead, Darrik.'

'One of my squads just reported the discovery of primary and secondary ork munitions dumps, sir, plus a significant fuel reserve by the south-east corner. Looks like they didn't get around to scuttling it. Also, I've set up sentry patrols on the walls, as ordered. No room up there for the Tarantulas, I'm afraid, unless we extend the parapets ourselves. One more thing, sir. Captain Immrich is requesting permission to refuel his tanks from the greenskin cache.'

'Immrich?' asked Bergen.

'Yes, sir. He's standing in for Colonel Vinnemann. The colonel is seeing the medicae augmeticist on your orders, remember?'

'Right, yes,' voxed Bergen. 'Tell Captain Immrich to go ahead, but I want the fuel store searched for nasty surprises first, and have him ask one of the tech-priests for a substance analysis before he fills up. Emperor alone knows what the orks put in their fuel tanks apart from promethium.'

'One more thing, sir,' said Graves. 'Tech-Adept Armadron tells me his preparations are complete. A vox-node antenna has been set up and connected to the landlines. We've just opened a link with Army Group HQ. The sound quality isn't too bad at all. General deViers expects you to report personally within the next thirty minutes.'

'Understood, colonel. I'll be back at the comms station in ten. Meet me there. Division, out.'

Bergen turned and began marching back towards the centre of the outpost, retracing his steps along streets filled with rusting junk and reeking of ork blood and excrement. He was glad of a reason to leave the piled bodies of the murdered slaves behind him, but the image of what he had seen stayed with him, a powerful memory that he would draw on later.

It would fuel his hate in the days to come.

THREE DAYS AFTER Karavassa was secured, Major General Rennkamp's 8th Mechanised Division moved up to take the old Imperial supply base, Tyrellis, located in the Garrando region of the desert to the east-south-east of Bergen's position. Resistance was fractionally lighter than at Karavassa, and the troopers might have been in high spirits had it not been for the increase in sickness and parasitic infestation that they suffered. The flesh-boring dannih were a constant nuisance. Orders had gone out for the men to shave their heads and remove any thick body hair in order to help combat the problem. Some troopers, preferring to drink their valuable alcohol rations rather than use them to get rid of the vicious ticks, developed nasty infections. Others reported to the medicae station with skin so saturated by the fines that they looked as if they had been bathing in spinefruit juice. The jokes and taunts didn't last long. The worst afflicted men suffered so badly from the resulting sickness that they died. It was a miserable way to go, organs clogged by accumulating dust, failing one after the other until the whole body shut down. That cast a dark shadow over those who survived, for they knew it was only a matter of time before their own cells became choked with the stuff. The quicker the general gained his prize, they grumbled, the better.

In that respect, at least, things were proceeding well. It was apparent that the greenskin presence between Hadron Base and the last known coordinates of *The Fortress of Arrogance* had been greatly overestimated. It seemed Ghazghkull Thraka's pogrom against mankind had called far more of the orks away from Golgotha than the Officio Strategos had anticipated. This alone remained in Exolon's favour, for if the orks were proving less of a threat, Golgotha was doing her level best to make up for it.

Bergen and the men of his division remained garrisoned in Karavassa, anxiously patrolling the surrounding lands, waiting impatiently for the general's order to move east. That order was expected to come through on the landline once the fortified settlement at Balkar – last of the major outposts needed to secure the route between Hadron Base and the site of the objective – had been retaken by the 12th Heavy Infantry Division under Major General Killian. Until then, there was little to do but wait, and, with time on his hands, Bergen began to notice little things that worried him, such as the subtle change in the tone of his skin. Each time he shaved, he looked into the mirror and noted the deepening pink tinge that coloured the whites of his eyes. He was far from alone in this. Medicae staff had issued everyone in the division with detox packages to help them combat the fines, but they didn't seem to be doing much good. Bergen had pressed Sergeant Behr, the medic on his personal staff, for worst case scenarios.

The sergeant's answers offered little comfort.

There were wildly varying levels of resistance between men. The hardiest would hold out for months, perhaps even a standard Imperial year, but the symptoms would steadily worsen throughout that time. Growing headaches and nausea could be dealt with easily enough; the pills to suppress these were plentiful. For the changes in skin and eye colour, and the damage to organs, nothing could be done with the equipment and facilities at hand. Despite Sergeant Behr's insistence that it would make little difference, Bergen nevertheless issued new orders to his men: they must wear goggles and rebreather masks as much as possible.

If the able-bodied men of 10th Division were suffering, though, it was as nothing compared to Colonel Vinnemann's pain. Day after day

Bergen marvelled at the colonel's resilience. The man rarely uttered a word of complaint, at least not in company, but, between the dust and the higher-than-standard gravity, his augmetic spine was bothering him like never before. The Medicae augmeticist kept Bergen informed of Vinnemann's condition, breaking his oath of patient confidence for the sake of keeping the divisional leader fully apprised. Colonel Vinnemann had been authorised to increase his self-administered injections of immunosuppressants and pain-mediators, but the drugs were problematic if taken in high quantities. Bergen, who held great affection and respect for the resilient little officer, began to offer daily prayers to the Emperor and His Saints that Operation Thunderstorm would come to a speedy conclusion. To lose Vinnemann prematurely would be a huge blow to the expedition. To lose him at all would be a huge blow to the men who knew him.

Finally, on the fifteenth day after planetfall, it seemed as if the Emperor might be listening to Gerard Bergen's prayers.

Reports started coming through on the landline. With Karavassa and Tyrellis securely held and protecting Imperial supply lines, Killian's 12th Heavy Infantry Division had pushed forward, storming the ruined fortress at Balkar, capturing it, and converting it into a front-line stronghold. The fighting had been heavy there, and the casualty figures were high, hinting at a much heavier ork presence closer to the site of the general's ultimate objective. But Killian succeeded all the same, and the forward base so vital to supporting the final leg of the expedition was firmly and fully established. Those officers with a pessimistic bent predicted massive greenskin retaliation, but, for now, Hadron, Karavassa, Tyrellis and Balkar were all back in Imperial hands after almost forty years of enemy occupation. The final stage of the Operation Thunderstorm could commence at last.

Bergen received all this news with a feeling of great relief. He was even more relieved when the 10th Armoured Division's new instructions came through from Hadron Base shortly after dawn on the sixteenth day. General deViers ordered Bergen's forces – minus an adequate garrisoning force – to press east from Karavassa, heading straight for Balkar with all possible speed. Once there, they would link up with elements from the other divisions and await the general's arrival. DeViers would personally lead them out into the Hadar region, to the foothills of the Ishawar range, for the final phase of the operation.

Talking directly to Bergen over the landline, the old man sounded practically ecstatic, like an over-stimulated child on the night before Emperor's Day. Perhaps he sensed his long-sought immortality waiting just beyond his fingertips. He would find *The Fortress of Arrogance*, whatever was left of it, and the operation would enter its closing stage. The

Mechanicus would fire a beacon into the upper atmoshere to signal their position. A lifter would then descend from *The Scion of Tharsis* to haul the holy machine from the desert sands and lift it back into space. Safely aboard the Reclamator craft, *The Fortress of Arrogance* would be restored to its former glory during transit to the Armageddon system. There, it would be presented to Commissar Yarrick, and he would ride it out onto the battlefields of Armageddon Prime, rousing the spirits of his tired soldiers, inspiring in them a glorious new strength. Thus uplifted, they would roll out to crush the foe.

It sounded wonderful, and in Bergen's heart of hearts, he hoped it would be so, but the voice in his head still held to the certainty that it was nothing but a pretty dream. Things would not come to pass that way.

Thirty-eight years, he thought. To imagine that she would still be there…

The moment General deViers closed the vox-link from the other end, Bergen sent out a call to his regimental commanders. When he gave them their updated orders, all three sounded genuinely glad to hear that they would be on the move again within hours. Colonel Vinnemann in particular expressed his relief in no uncertain terms. Bergen had considered ordering the man to remain here, convinced that it would be the best thing for his health. But he knew Vinnemann would only have railed against him, seeing it as the ultimate betrayal. The man was a tanker through and through, just as Bergen had once been, and Bergen knew that, for any real tanker, nothing beat riding out in your crate, treads chewing up the dirt, the hearty roar of a promethium engine vibrating through your whole body. So Vinnemann would stay in command of his regiment despite his suffering, and Captain Immrich would be there to step in if needed.

The regimental commanders broke the link to pass the new orders on to their executive officers and company commanders. From these men, the news filtered down to everyone in the base.

Soon, Karavassa was buzzing with preparations as the 10th Armoured Division prepared to roll out once again.

IN ALL THE scurrying around, the loading, the refuelling, the last-minute checks, and everything else that went on prior to deployment, few men spared a thought for the fate of those companies that had mysteriously disappeared on that first fateful day. Some men did. Kochatkis Vinnemann was one of them. Despite having troubles enough of his own, he prayed regularly for the souls of Lieutenant Gossefried van Droi and his men, convinced that, after so many days without word or sign, they had perished.

As he rolled out of Karavassa at the head of the 81st Armoured Regiment, the long-suffering colonel could not have guessed that, just ten days' journey to the south-east of his position, Gossefried's Gunheads were doing their best to avoid exactly that.

CHAPTER TEN

COLONEL STROMM WAS a man of his word. He embraced the Gunheads as if they had always been part of his outfit, and it pleased Lieutenant van Droi greatly, because, though he admitted it to no one, he had harboured grave doubts about placing his men and machines at the disposal of a man he had only just met. There were those in the upper ranks who might have said he knew all he needed to about the colonel. He had seen Stromm turn aside certain death, after all, and there were surely few better measures of a man than that; but an officer's performance in combat gave few clues, if any, as to how he would command on the move. Then there was Golgotha herself to consider. She was an enemy that couldn't be fought. Her endless sands ground away at the Cadians' morale, and the more time they spent crossing them, the more they seemed to stretch forever.

Van Droi knew his tanks were slowing the whole column down. The Chimeras were much faster, and the Thirty-Sixers were faster still at top speed, but without the tanks the column would have made an easy target for greenskin marauders. Colonel Stromm kept everyone moving together, with the exception of the Chimeras he sent to scout ahead in shifts. Did it frustrate him that the Leman Russ could barely manage thirty kilometres an hour? wondered van Droi. If so, he didn't show it.

For days, the tired, dirty, ragged column had pressed north-east over rolling dunes and, gradually, the landscape began to change, becoming rockier and more uneven in stages. Was the change in terrain a good sign? Van Droi wasn't sure. If it meant they were nearing high ground, it certainly didn't show. The horizon to the north-east remained choked in a pink haze. He saw no jutting spurs of rock, no distant hints of a towering mountain range.

The mood of the men was as dark as the mud-coloured sky and getting darker all the time. Little communication passed from tank to tank. Almost a dozen of van Droi's men had taken seriously ill, and the number was three times greater among Stromm's infantry. There were two medics with The Fighting 98th, two who had survived the dreadful onslaught at the crash site. They took a look at van Droi's sick, consulted with each other, and told him that at least three of the twelve would be dead within a day. Nothing could be done to save them. The dust had poisoned them. Liver, kidneys, lungs, everything was shutting down. The other nine would almost certainly follow soon afterwards if they didn't get specialist medical care. With hopes of finding Exolon having dwindled to almost nothing, that didn't seem probable. Van Droi's anger and frustration got the better of him a few times, and he vented inside the turret of his tank, where his shouts and curses were drowned out by the rumble of the engine.

Colonel Stromm made a difficult decision regarding the seriously ill; he withheld their water and provisions. There was nothing to be gained by spending scarce resources on men who simply weren't going to last much longer. This, of course, did not sit well with friends of the dying men. There were sharp protestations that came near to violence, but the platoon leaders cracked down hard.

Van Droi didn't judge Stromm for the extremity of the measure. Stromm had given him a chance to object, but, to a practical man like van Droi, it made perfect, if unpleasantly harsh, sense. Ultimately, the two medics resolved the issue, administering large doses of anaesthecium to the worst afflicted, letting them die peacefully in a drug-induced sleep.

With the column stopping only briefly, grim, hollow-faced troopers buried their dead comrades in the sand. There was no Ministorum man to pray for them, but one of Stromm's lieutenants, a man called Boyd, had trained briefly as a confessor before abandoning the so-called Righteous Road in order to enlist in the Guard. He said a few words for the souls of the dead, and the column moved on, lighter in number, heavier in spirit.

The mood got even worse when Stromm had his lieutenants issue empty jerry cans and additional water purification tablets to everyone. If they wanted to survive beyond the next few days, he told them, they would have to drink the undrinkable. They would have to drink their own urine.

As IF THE lost Cadians didn't have enough problems, the dawn of the sixteenth day brought more bad news. As the cloud-smothered sun rose once more, casting its dull red glow over the desert, the vox-link began to erupt with anxious chatter. The intercom system aboard *Foe-Breaker* did likewise.

'There must be millions of them!' yelled Bullseye Dietz. 'There's no beating numbers like that, sir. They won't be on foot, not moving at that speed.'

Dietz wasn't wrong. Orks were closing in on them. Judging by the dark line that had appeared in the south-east with the coming of day, there were far too many of them to engage. Raising his head so that he could peer through his tank's vision blocks, van Droi looked again, hoping that somehow his mind had played a trick on him, that it had exaggerated the size of the enemy force.

It hadn't.

The horizon was seething with them. How close were they? Between the heat haze, the dust and the mirage-line, it was practically impossible to tell. That they were visible at all, van Droi decided, meant they were too damned close by far.

The greenskin host had moved up during the hours of darkness, unnoticed by exhausted, overheated, dehydrated men more intent on fighting sleep and sickness than fighting the enemies of mankind.

The Cadians were being chased down. Perhaps this greenskin war party had stumbled onto their tracks, following them out from the drop-ship crashsite, easily tracing them by the deep furrows the tanks made in the sand. Now, the prey was in sight.

'Nails,' said van Droi, 'keep her bloody speed up. And I want to know the moment you feel anything out of order, the slightest jink or engine stutter, any give in the shocks or the drive train. You got that? Let's not have a repeat of what happened to Siemens. We won't have time to frak about with repairs.'

'Don't you worry, boss,' replied Nails. 'We're sympatico, this girl and me. She won't let us down. Sympatico, says I.'

It took a lot to faze Karl 'Nails' Nalzigg. He had earned his nickname the hard way back in the days before he had joined van Droi's crew. He had earned a few medals to go with it, too. Van Droi wished he shared his driver's easy confidence, but *Foe-Breaker* had suffered engine trouble twice already in the days since planetfall. Not her fault, of course. Van Droi's old girl was only as prone to stalling as any of the other machines. With every passing hour, another would stop dead, refusing to start again until the contacts on its engines were properly cleared of the red dust.

To van Droi's knowledge, there was only a single exception.

Wulfe's old crate hadn't stalled once in all the time since the crash. She might look her age, thought van Droi, but *Last Rites II* had already proved that she'd got what it takes under the engine covers.

He hadn't mentioned it to Wulfe, but, of all the tanks assigned to replace the losses from Palmeros, van Droi had hand-picked the Mars-Alpha pattern Leman Russ out for the sergeant personally. Wulfe had taken the loss of his old machine badly. What kind of tanker, after all, could ride into battle time after time in the same tank, come out alive when so many around him died, and not feel some kind of special bond with her? It was exactly the way van Droi felt about *Foe-Breaker*.

His choice of replacement tank for Wulfe seemed to have backfired, though. The rugged sergeant hadn't taken to *Last Rites II* at all. In fact, he seemed to think van Droi had assigned him the new tank out of spite. Van Droi wanted to believe it was simply a matter of time, that Wulfe would come around soon enough, but, with the ork host tailing them, time looked like it might be up. How fast were the ork machines chasing them? There would be buggies in their hundreds. Assault bikes, too, perhaps. Might they even have air support? Bombers? Greenskins were certainly insane enough to fly in such dangerous skies.

A red light began flickering on the vox-board by van Droi's left shoulder. He turned in his command seat, flipped the toggle that turned the light green, and said, '10th Company Command here. Go ahead.'

'Tenth, this is Regiment,' said Colonel Stromm. 'It looks like we're caught between a rock and a hard place. Have you looked south-east recently?'

'I have, sir,' said van Droi. 'Don't like the view much. Very difficult to estimate party strength given distance and conditions, but I think it's fair to say we're a little outnumbered. Assuming the majority of those greenskins are on wheels, they could well catch us by midday.'

'The galaxy does like to stack the odds against us, doesn't it, lieutenant?' said Stromm.

'No glory in easy victories, sir. Still, a man should know his limits.'

'Or in this case,' replied Stromm, 'the limits of his machines. I think... Hold on a moment, lieutenant.'

Stromm cut the link. A few seconds later, the same light on van Droi's vox-board started flashing again. He hit the toggle. 'Sir?'

'Sorry about that, van Droi,' said Stromm. 'Just got word from our scout. I'll let you judge for yourself whether it's good or bad. He's reporting a massive dust storm up ahead. Point your magnoculars a few degrees east of our current heading. You can just about make it out.'

'It's going to hit?'

'Soon, apparently. It's moving fast. If we cut south-east we can probably escape the worst of it, but…'

'But it'll put us within easy striking range of the orks at our back, sir. By the blasted Eye!'

'You said it, lieutenant. I'm not about to order our lads into a battle we won't survive without a damned good reason. I say we head straight into the storm. Take our chances. If anything, it might serve to cover our tracks. We might actually lose the bastards. What do you say?'

It's a ballsy move, thought van Droi. There's plenty that could go wrong. On the other hand…

'The machine-spirits aren't going to like it, sir,' he said. 'I'd put money on mechanical failures. Any estimates on how long the storm will last? We won't be able to see a damned thing while we're in there. If we move at all, it'll have to be very slowly.'

'There's no way to say how long, van Droi,' voxed Stromm. 'The environmental summaries the Mechanicus issued during warp transit painted a pretty bleak picture. Some storms last a few hours, others last days, even weeks.'

'That's one hell of a gamble, sir.'

'Are you much of a gambling man, lieutenant?'

'I guess I am today,' said van Droi.

'That's what I thought. Let's roll the dice and hope for the best. And may the Emperor's luck be with us. Stromm out.'

CHAPTER ELEVEN

COLONEL STROMM ORDERED his column to a complete stop as it was hit by the fringes of the coming dust storm. Visibility had dropped to about fifty metres already. The air around the Imperial machines was dark with veils of gusting sand, and the wind howled, rocking the vehicles on their suspension. The sky was gone from view. On the colonel's orders, anxious men emerged from hatches and cabin doors with their faces goggled and masked, their bodies covered as much as possible against the stinging assault of the hard red grains.

Their voices didn't travel far. Words already muffled by rebreather masks were snatched away by the rising storm. Van Droi was forced to shout at the top of his voice. 'Hurry it up. I want all the tanks chained together before it gets any worse out here. Come on. Only a few minutes left. Work faster.'

The Gunheads hauled heavy steel chains from the stowage bins on the rear of each tank and worked hard to attach them to the towing pegs at the front and back of their machines.

'Twenty metres between each tank,' shouted van Droi. He wished he had a vox-amp handy. The bead he wore in his right ear linked him to his tank commanders, but the crews didn't wear such advanced tech. They took their orders through their tanks' intercom systems. There was no time for van Droi to return to *Foe-Breaker* and dig out a vox-amp now, though. The winds were really picking up. The men worked quickly despite their thirst and fatigue. Some struggled through bouts of coughing that doubled them over in pain and discomfort, but they fought through it to get the job done. It was just as well they did. In the few minutes it took to link all the tanks together, the storm had become incredibly fierce. Visibility dropped another ten metres. Then another. Then another. Van Droi could only just make out the red silhouette of the tanks to the front and rear of his own. The wind was buffeting him so hard that it almost pitched him from his feet as he reached up to climb back into his turret.

After wrestling his way up *Foe-Breaker's* back, he dropped down into her basket, slamming and locking the hatch above him. Hitting the intercom, he said, 'Are we all buttoned up, lads?'

'Tighter than a governor's daughter, sir,' said Waller. He had been van Droi's loader for more than ten years, a compact, ruddy-faced man, good at his work, but a truculent devil when he had a bit of drink in him.

'Right then,' said van Droi. 'We wait for Stromm's lot to finish, then roll forward nice and slow.'

Seated out of eyesight behind his crew, he allowed himself a small shake of the head. This is a bit of bloody madness, he thought. If it weren't for the orks at our backs…

'Van Droi to Colonel Stromm,' he voxed. 'Can you hear me, sir?'

'Not too well, van Droi,' said Stromm, 'but go ahead.' The clarity of the transmission was terrible. The dust-storm had brought with it a shocking drop in the quality of short-range comms. If it got much worse, van Droi thought, they might lose comms altogether. That would ground them here completely until the storm passed.

'My crates are linked and ready. Awaiting your order to move out, sir.'

'Hold on for another minute, van Droi. The last of my lot are getting hooked together now. Can't believe how bad it is out there. Throne help those poor lads in the soft-tops. I hope the extra tarps will be enough to protect them.'

Van Droi grimaced. He was worried too. It hadn't been possible to squeeze everyone from the open-backed trucks and halftracks into sealed cabins and the troop compartments of the Chimeras, but they had done their best. As few men as possible were left to endure the storm in the less protected vehicles. They had been given as much extra cover as was available to protect them, but Van Droi had no idea just how much worse the storm was likely to get.

'I'm sure they'll be all right, sir,' he said, managing to sound far more positive than he felt.

'One moment, lieutenant.'

There was a pause and a flicker of vox-board lights. Then the colonel returned. 'The last of my machines has been linked up, van Droi. Have your tanks lead us out. Keep the speed to a steady ten kilometres per hour, no more, no less.'

'Ten it is, sir. Giving the order now.'

'Very good, Armour. Stromm, out.'

'You all ready for this?' van Droi asked his crew.

The half-hearted grunts that came back to him over the intercom spoke volumes about how his crew felt riding blind. There was no hiding their anxiety.

Van Droi flicked over to the company command channel and said, 'Company Commander to all tanks. Confirm readiness to deploy.'

'Spear Leader confirms,' came the static-riddled response from Sergeant Rhaimes.

Spear One's confirmation followed, then, Spear Two's. So it went until all eight of van Droi's surviving tank commanders had called in.

'Keep your crates absolutely steady at ten per hour. Stay on this heading. I don't want any accidents. *Cold Deliverance* has point. Corporal Muller, lead us out.'

One by one, the tanks of 10th Company started to edge forward blindly, tow chains giving out metallic groans as they went taut.

The rumble of *Foe-breaker's* engine deepened, and she lurched forward gently as her gears caught, feeding power to the massive axle that turned her drive sprocket. The heavy, cog-like wheel turned, iron teeth pulling link after link towards it, driving the tank forward slowly and steadily. The tank directly in front of *Foe-Breaker* – Corporal Fuchs's *Rage Imperius* – was practically invisible now. Van Droi checked the rear vision blocks and found that the tank behind – Corporal Kurtz's *The Adamantine* – was just as difficult to see. The screech of grinding metal sounded over the howling wind and the rumble of the engine as hooks took the strain against towing pegs.

'Keep her real steady, won't you, Nails?' said van Droi.

'Sure thing, sir,' replied the grizzled old driver. His voice was clear. The tank's intercom system wasn't affected by the storm in the same way the vox-link was. 'As steady as Waller's hands after a few bottles of the rough stuff.'

Van Droi frowned. That wasn't very steady at all.

LENCK'S MEN WERE far more worried than he was, and they weren't beyond showing it. As the *New Champion* rolled forward, they grumbled and griped on the intercom, snapping at each other, letting their nerves get the better of them. Lenck tuned them out.

As the storm intensified, gusts battering against his tank, rocking her as if she weighed far less than her sixty-three tonnes, he sat back in his command seat, idly playing with the cruelly serrated knife he kept in his boot. It was a non-regulation blade, officially forbidden, but it had saved his neck a few times back in the reserves, particularly when bigger men came looking for him, burning with anger, ready to pulp him for cheating them out of money or bedding their women. Most lost the will to fight after they'd been cut a few times.

Lenck rated himself with a blade.

He hadn't needed to use his little equaliser since joining the 81st Armoured, but he was sure there would come a time. Sooner or later, someone would come looking for him with a mind to do some damage. He had a feeling it would be Sergeant Wulfe. Most of the men in 10th Company were younger than Lenck, recent reinforcements who looked up to him for one reason or another. It was something different for each, but Lenck could always find it and use it to his advantage. For some, it was his skill with women that they envied. They wanted to share in the secret of his success, not realising there *was* no secret; he was simply better than they were. For others, it was his ability to procure the things without which some men found Guard life unbearable, from extra smokes or booze all the way up to restricted meds. Before that damned drop-ship had ditched him on the red sands, Lenck had enjoyed a nice little arrangement with a certain medicae officer whose sinful appetites he had threatened to reveal to a member of the Ministorum. The man would have faced execution for sure. Throne knew where the bloody clown was now. Maybe he had made it down on another ship. Maybe he was dead. No matter. When Lenck got out of this mess – and he knew he would, for if he believed in anything, it was that he had been born lucky – he would find another source. Everyone could be bent to his will one way or another.

That thought brought him to the curious matter of Victor Dunst, and he felt a rare flash of irritation. Dunst, whoever he was, seemed to be the reason that Sergeant Wulfe had it in for him. Lenck wanted details, sure that the knowledge would give him the upper hand, but he had no idea how to get them. Wulfe's crew seemed to dislike him just as much as their precious commander did, especially that bastard Holtz, the one with the mashed-up groxburger for a face.

'Ain't you listening, Lenck?' growled Varnuss over the intercom.

'No, I'm not,' said Lenck, 'but don't let that stop you.'

The big loader turned to scowl, tattoos on his neck and shoulders rippling as the muscles under them shifted, but he changed his mind when he saw the way Lenck was stroking his knife. He turned back to his station and muttered, 'I said it's getting worse out there, not better. Look through the vision blocks. It's like night-time, only its all red. We shouldn't be moving at all.'

'Least we're not out in front like *Cold Deliverance*,' said Riesmann, chipping in. 'Second in line suits me fine. I wouldn't want to be on Muller's crew for love nor money.'

'And that's saying something,' Lenck quipped, 'since you've always had so damned little of either. Relax, both of you. That's an order. You don't hear Hobbs complaining, do you?'

'He only stopped 'cos you threatened to fix it so everyone in the army group thinks he's a fruit,' replied Riesmann sourly.

'Right,' laughed Lenck, 'and the same goes for you. Think of it like this: so long as we're stuck in this storm, van Droi and that flag-waving fool of an infantry colonel have enough to worry about. We're not out in front. Hobbs is doing all the driving. All we can do is sit back and ride it out.'

The others didn't reply. They listened to the wind for a moment as it screamed around the edges of the tank. Lenck could hear the tow chains creaking. Riesmann and Varnuss glanced at each other nervously.

'What're they saying on the vox?' Riesmann asked.

'Nothing,' Lenck replied.

'You sure? The lights are on. Someone's talking.'

'It's just interference,' said Lenck. He reached into one of the stowage bins and pulled out a green metal jerry can. It was much smaller than the ones they had been given to piss in. He unscrewed the cap, tipped the can to his mouth, and drank.

'Hey,' said Varnuss, 'what's that? If you've been holding back water...'

'It's not water,' said Lenck smugly. 'It's a little something special I've been keeping aside.' He tossed his head. 'Damn it goes down rough. Good kick though.'

Varnus and Riesmann half-turned. It was the most they could manage in the incredibly cramped turret basket. Riesmann sniffed the air and said, 'That's liquor. You'd better share it out, Lenck. We look after you, you look after us, remember?'

'Yeah,' rumbled Varnuss, 'that's what you said, Lenck.'

'I know what I said, you dolts. Give me a bloody break. Would I have shown you at all if I didn't intend to share?'

He lifted the jerrycan and handed it to Riesmann, who took it greedily and raised it to his lips. Before he could gulp any down, however, *New Champion of Cerbera* skidded forward with a sudden surge, and then stopped. Her front suspension strained, groaning as it was compressed to its limits while her rear lifted into the air. Then there was a sharp clang that shook the whole tank, and the front suspension sprang upwards again.

The men inside were thrown from their seats. Lenck just managed to avoid splitting his head wide open on the corner of one of the stowage bins. Varnuss wasn't so lucky. Blood spilled from a deep cut in his crown. Riesmann was thrown painfully against the manual traverse wheel, grunting as the metal handle dug into his side. He spilled Lenck's liquor all over his fatigues.

'What the frak was that?' shouted Lenck. 'Hobbs, what in the bloody warp just happened?'

Fear and shock raised the pitch of Hobbs's voice as he replied over the intercom, 'By the frakkin' Eye, Lenck. I think… I think we just lost *Cold Deliverance.*'

WULFE HAD TO strain his ears to make out the lieutenant's voice as it said, 'All tanks, halt! That's an order. Stop where you are. Do not move an inch.'

He didn't waste any time.

'Dead stop, Metzger,' he snapped over the intercom.

Last Rites II ground to an immediate halt.

'What's going on, sarge?' asked Holtz, pressing his eyes to the main gun's scope.

'Quiet,' said Wulfe. He squinted with effort as he listened carefully to the voice on the vox-link. After a moment, he said, 'It's *Cold Deliverance.* She's gone quiet. From the sounds of it, she dropped.'

'Into what?' asked Siegler, turning to stare at Wulfe.

'We won't know till the storm's passed,' said Holtz. 'Will we?'

Wulfe was listening to the vox again. Then he said, 'The *New Champion* called it in. From the sounds of it, the front tow peg snapped right off. Damned lucky she didn't go over, too.'

'Or unlucky,' grumbled Holtz, 'depending on how you look at it.'

Wulfe knew what he meant, but, if any of Muller's crew were still alive, it was just as well Lenck's tank hadn't gone over.

'What's van Droi saying?' asked Siegler nervously.

Wulfe listened for a another moment. He shook his head miserably as he answered, 'Nothing we can do. So long as the storm continues at this intensity, we can't move a bloody muscle. Muller and his boys will need to wait it out like the rest of us.'

'But they'll need medical attention!' piped Siegler.

'I know that, Sig,' snapped Wulfe, 'but look outside the tank, damn it. You think we can help them in this?'

Siegler looked down at his hands, obviously upset, and Wulfe felt immediately contrite. He leaned forward and patted the loader's broad, powerful shoulder.

'Sorry, Sig,' he said. 'I know you're just worried about them. I am, too.'

Warp-damn it all, he thought. We can't keep taking knocks like this. Where in the blasted Eye are the rest of the army group?

Forcing calm into his voice, he told his crew, 'Let's keep it together. Gunheads never give up, remember? We keep fighting. It's what we do.'

Siegler looked slightly mollified. He said, 'Maybe Borscht's ghost will help us again.'

Wulfe's blood turned to ice-water.

'What did you just say?'

'Damn it, Siegler,' Holtz hissed. 'I frakking told you about that.'

Siegler seemed to realise the gravity of the mistake he had just made. His eyes flashed from Wulfe to Holtz in a panic. 'Sorry, Holtz! It just came out.'

Wulfe turned to Holtz. 'Explain yourself, corporal. And that's not a request. It's an order.'

Holtz shook his head and sighed. 'What did you expect, sarge? Did you think we were too stupid to put it together? That canyon on Palmeros, you losing it and stopping the tank for no reason. Then Strieber's lads getting hamstrung by that landmine. And there was the medicae report. Old Borscht died at almost the exact moment you started hearing a voice on the intercom that no one else could.'

Wulfe slumped in his chair.

'You knew all this time?' he muttered. 'Why the hell didn't you put in for a transfer? Your sergeant thinks he saw a ghost, for Throne's sake. Metzger, did you know about this?'

The driver answered in a sullen tone, 'Afraid so, sarge. It was your warp-dreams mostly. You did a lot of shouting in your sleep while we were between systems.'

Wulfe was dumbfounded.

'We don't think you've lost it,' said Siegler.

'Right,' said Holtz. 'In fact, we were pissed off that you didn't tell us yourself. I mean, the ghost didn't just save you. It saved all of us. We could have prayed for Borscht's soul together. Viess took it pretty badly. Said you should have trusted us more.'

Wulfe saw how foolish he had been to think they wouldn't put two and two together. 'I couldn't tell you the truth. I wasn't sure it was the truth myself. I still haven't come to terms with it. Not really. If it ever got out... I don't want van Droi to think I've lost it. I don't want to lose my command.'

'You really *have* lost it if you think the lieutenant doesn't already suspect the truth,' said Holtz. 'I mean, he never really pushed for a full account, did he? He just accepted that groxshit report you submitted. No questions asked.'

Wulfe thought about that. It was true. He had been too relieved at the time to question the lieutenant's easy acceptance of the report.

'Who else knows?' he asked.

Holtz shrugged. 'No one but us, Viess, and probably van Droi.'

'It *has* to stay that way,' said Wulfe. 'You all know how well it would go down with the commissars.'

'You gonna tell us what actually happened then?' asked Holtz, hoping to bargain.

Wulfe didn't get the chance to respond. The vox-board on his left started blinking. It was the company command channel.

'Sword Leader here, sir,' said Wulfe. 'Go ahead.'

He listened to the lieutenant's transmission. It crackled with static, but he noted how much the vox-signal had improved in the last few minutes. Then he toggled back over to the intercom system.

'Well?' Holtz asked.

'The storm's clearing,' said Wulfe. 'Van Droi wants all vehicles checked for damage. I'm going up front. It's time to find out what happened to Muller and his men.'

CHAPTER TWELVE

THE WIND WAS still howling, and the air dragged at his clothes and hurled sand at him with stinging force, but Gossefried van Droi knew he couldn't wait any longer. If there were men still alive in Corporal Muller's tank, they would need extrication and medical attention as soon as possible. Now if he could just find the bloody thing.

'Here, sir!' yelled a trooper barely visible as a shadow up ahead. The wind snatched at the man's words, but van Droi could just make them out. He hurried over.

'Over here!' said the man as van Droi closed. Others had heard and gathered towards him. 'Careful!' he told them. 'There's a sheer drop.'

Van Droi halted at the man's side and, peering through his goggles, read the name strip above the left breast pocket of his fatigues. It said Brunner, one of Richter's crew.

'Show me, Brunner,' said van Droi.

Brunner moved forward carefully for a couple of metres, guiding van Droi. Then he pointed down towards the area in front of his feet. Van Droi moved level with him and looked down to find himself standing right on the edge of a sheer drop.

Brunner directed his attention to the ground on the left, and van Droi saw two tank tracks leading straight to the edge. Damn it, he thought. Ten kilometres per hour *was* too fast, after all. They'd have been over before they could stop, and the chains weren't made to suspend a tank's full weight.

He squinted down into the shadows, but the drop was too deep to show him anything solid. The storm was still cloaking the area enough to hamper vision at that range, but it was weakening all the time. What would be revealed when it had passed completely? Had the orks followed them in? Were they closing on their backs even now? There was nowhere to run. Forward progress was blocked by the edge of the escarpment. How far did it extend to left and right?

The answers would have to wait. Van Droi needed to speak to Colonel Stromm at once. He ordered everyone back to their tanks in the meantime, and then returned to *Foe-Breaker*. Once he was inside and the hatches were all locked, he flipped a switch on his vox-board and said, 'Armour Leader to Colonel Stromm, come in, please.'

'Go ahead, lieutenant. What's the situation?'

'Not good, sir. As I feared, one of our tanks took a dive. There's a precipice about ten or twelve metres in front of my lead tank. No idea how deep it runs, sir. The bottom isn't visible in all this dust. I'm guessing it's deep. Deep enough to be a big problem, anyway.'

'Do we know its extent? If the orks are right behind us…'

'There's no way of knowing right now, sir. The storm is moving on quickly, though, so I expect we'll have decent visibility in half an hour or less. Suggest we wait it out until then.'

'Of course, lieutenant. I don't want any more accidents. Could any of your men, the ones in the tank… could they have survived?'

Van Droi thought about this for a second before answering. For all the reliability of the Leman Russ – a design that had barely changed in many thousands of years – the turret basket was still a dangerous place to be. The centre of the hot, cramped, noisy little space was usually dominated by the huge mechanism of the main gun. On one side of this sat the gunner, on the other sat the loader. Close behind the gunner, the commander sat within easy reach of everything he needed: maps, comms equipment, small arms and more. What made it so dangerous were the stowage boxes bolted to every surface, their metal edges and corners responsible for more wounds than enemy fire. The locking levers for the hatches weren't much better. They stuck out like blunted metal barbs. Veterans got used to this and reported fewer injuries with each passing year of service, but the new meat learned the hard way.

'Chances are, sir, that most of the men inside are badly injured,' said van Droi. 'More than likely there's at least one dead.'

'But you think there will be survivors?'

'Can't really say at this juncture, sir. It depends on the height of the drop.'

Stromm paused, leaving van Droi to listen to the white noise that filled his right ear for a moment. 'You know, van Droi, that if the orks are close by, I can't give you the time you need.'

Van Droi shook his head. 'I know that, sir. If there's any chance at all, though, that some of them are stuck in there, I owe it to them to get them out.'

He was actually thinking that Stromm's Fighting 98th owed it to them, but he didn't say so. A second later, he was glad he hadn't.

'My boys and I will do everything we can to help, van Droi, but time really is of the essence here. Hold for one second.'

Stromm broke the link, and then reconnected a few seconds later. 'Take a look outside, lieutenant,' he said. 'It looks like the storm has all but passed.'

Van Droi craned his neck and peered through the forward vision block set in the ceiling just above his station. He could see the tank in front of him in sharp detail, the treads on her windward side piled high with red sand. Beyond her, he thought he glimpsed the horizon and... could it be? Was that the pale silhouette of a jutting mountain range? It was difficult to be sure. Behind the thick brown clouds in the west, there were hints of the sun moving lower, but the day was still hot, and the mirage line shimmered. If there really were mountains over there...

Suddenly, something else occurred to van Droi. The orks! He spun to look through the rear vision blocks, but *The Adamantine* was blocking his view.

'Any sign of the orks, sir?' he voxed to Stromm. 'Have you got anyone checking the rear?'

Again there was a pause while Stromm talked to his people. Then, 'No sign of the filthy beasts, lieutenant. I can't believe we lost them so easily, but eyes at the rear report no sign of them. Nothing whatsoever to our backs.'

By the Emperor, thought van Droi. Could it really have worked? Had the storm covered their tracks and sent the orks off somewhere else?

'You still there, lieutenant?'

'Yes, sir. Sorry. I was just wondering where in the warp the buggers went. May I suggest we get scouts out looking for a way down from here, sir? If we want to continue north-east, we'll need a slope or a trail down from this ridge. And, with your permission, I'd like to have some of my men abseil down to *Cold Deliverance*.'

'You have it, lieutenant. Be quick. I want us all moving again as soon as possible. You need anything else, just let me know. Stromm, out.'

* * *

MULLER'S TANK LAY belly up at the bottom of a two-hundred-metre drop, and van Droi knew as soon as he saw her that the chances of any of Muller's men surviving were next to none.

With five other men, all hand-picked, he rappelled down to the rocky desert floor and moved closer to observe the results of the fall. The barrel of the main gun was crumpled and bent, and the secondary weapons had suffered such an impact that pieces of them lay scattered around the inverted hull.

Her turret wasn't even visible, buried deep in sand and loose rock. No one would be crawling from its hatches.

He directed his team to move in and check for signs of life. Sergeant Wulfe was among them and immediately clambered up onto the machine's upturned belly. He removed his laspistol from its thigh holster, lay flat against the tank's belly armour and began tapping out a message in cipher-one. It was an old code, a series of taps and pauses that the Cadian military still taught to cadets in their first year, though there was little cause to use it given the prevalence of vox-comms. Van Droi was amazed that Wulfe remembered the code at all. It had been over twenty years since the man had been a cadet. Reaching back to memories of his own days in training, it took van Droi a moment to unscramble the message. It was the same code, repeated over and over again: *Survivors, respond. Survivors, respond.*

Wulfe pressed his ear to metal for about a minute, after which his movements took on a distinctly urgent quality. Noting this, van Droi moved closer, but he didn't dare speak. This was no time to distract the sergeant.

Wulfe's message changed: *Number of casualties?*

Van Droi saw him press his ear to the armour again, and then, after a short pause, tap a single word: *Wait.*

Leaping down from the belly of the tank, Wulfe marched straight over to van Droi.

'Three dead, one alive, sir. It's the driver, Private Krausse.'

'Status?' asked van Droi.

'Not good, sir. Lots of broken bones. Lacerations.'

'Damn,' spat van Droi. 'I think we both know how this is going to turn out, Wulfe.'

The sergeant looked at the ground. 'Frakking hell, sir. We can't.'

'We both know that's not our call. Stromm's the man in charge. Don't hate him for it. He has to think about the rest of us.'

'Can't we at least try, sir?'

'I wish we could, Oskar,' said van Droi heavily, 'but with our limited resources, it would take the rest of this day and half of the next to cut him out. And that's cutting where the armour is thinnest.'

Van Droi couldn't see Wulfe's face. It was masked and goggled, like his own, against the airborne dust, but he knew the sergeant's expression would be much the same as his: bloody miserable.

'Get yourself and the others back up to your tanks. Stromm will have orders for us to move out soon. His people will have found a trail down for the vehicles by now. Do something else for me, will you? Tell the others... Tell them there were no survivors.'

'You want me to lie, sir?' asked Wulfe. There was a knife-edge of bitterness in his voice.

'I want you to think of what's best, sergeant,' snapped van Droi. 'Morale is bastard low as it is. So you go up there and you tell them no one made it. And we move on. Is that clear?'

Wulfe snapped his boots together. The tone of his voice became flat and hard as he said, 'Crystal clear, sir. My apologies. I should not have questioned you.'

'No, Oskar,' said van Droi. 'No apologies from you. Just... do as I've asked, will you?'

'Of course, sir. You can count on me.'

With that, Wulfe turned, gathered the other four men together and led them back up the ropes to the waiting tanks above.

Van Droi hauled himself up onto *Cold Deliverance*, frowning under his mask at how dizzy the effort made him feel. He wasn't drinking enough water each day, not by far. Who could blame him? The purification kits didn't do much to take away the bitter saline taste of the processed urine. Food rations were also running very low. He must have lost a dozen kilograms over the last ten days, if not more.

He removed a finely-crafted autopistol from the holster at his hip, and lay down on the upturned belly of the tank in the spot Wulfe had occupied a moment earlier. With the heel of his pistol he began tapping a message to the man trapped inside: *Company commander here.*

He listened for a response. After a few seconds, there came a series of clangs. In his mind, van Droi translated the beats and pauses: *Understood. Greetings.*

Van Droi tapped again: *Extrication impossible.*

There was a much longer pause this time before the response came back. This time, a single word: *Understood.*

Do you have a weapon? van Droi tapped.

Yes, tapped Krausse. There was a long pause, then he added, *Will use.*

Van Droi wanted to tap the word *sorry*, but something stayed his hand. Instead, he tapped, *Go with the Emperor, son.*

He listened carefully, ear pressed hard to the thick metal below him, but the tank driver had stopped tapping back. There was only a single last clang from inside the overturned machine. It was the sound of a weapon discharging. Van Droi didn't need to decrypt it to know that it meant goodbye.

As he scrambled down from the tank, walked over to the rope, and began the tiring climb back up, the lieutenant's heart felt like it weighed about sixty tonnes itself. Damn it all, he thought. Who would be a bloody leader of men?

At the top of the rope, arms reached out to help him over, and he stood to find himself facing a row of his tankers clad in masks and goggles. They stood to attention as he rose and dusted off his fatigues.

'Why aren't you lot in your tanks?' he asked them. 'Have Stromm's lot found a way down yet?'

It was the burly Sergeant Rhaimes who stepped forward and said, 'They've found a lot more than that, sir. Switch your vox over to band nine.'

Van Droi huffed impatiently and lifted a finger to his vox bead. He switched it to band nine and froze. He could hardly believe his ears. There was rapid chatter bouncing back and forth. One of the voices was immediately familiar, the gruff but well-educated voice of Colonel Stromm.

The other, however, was new to van Droi, and that in itself was significant.

'Sentinel patrol ident tag nine-theta-nine-six-five confirms your last transmission, colonel. Relaying it back to field headquarters. Standby.'

Van Droi gasped. He moved towards Rhaimes.

'Is that what I think it is?' he demanded.

He didn't need to see Rhaimes's face to know he was smiling as he said, 'Bet your balls on it, sir. A Sentinel patrol! It's Exolon. They must have secured a base nearby.'

Van Droi suddenly felt like leaping into the air. 'By the bloody Golden Throne! They made it down after all. But I can barely hear them on this bead. Everyone back to your tanks on the double. Get ready to move out as soon as we have instructions.'

The men saluted and trotted off at speed. Van Droi felt better than he had in days. Salvation at last. He had been sure they would all die out here one way or another. But now... hope!

Inside his turret, using the more powerful vox-caster there, he heard the communications from the Sentinel patrol coming in much louder and clearer.

'Colonel Stromm,' said the voice, 'I have orders for you from Major General Bergen. You are to move due east, proceed down from the escarpment, rendezvous with this patrol at the base of the cliffs and follow us back to the base at Balkar. Confirm.'

Balkar! thought van Droi. I can't believe we're this far out.

He thought back to General deViers's briefing sessions. From Balkar, it was a short journey eastwards to the last known location of *The Fortress of Arrogance*. From there, the Mechanicus ship in orbit above the planet would be signalled. A recovery craft would be sent for the tank. Then it was back to Hadron base for extrication by the Navy. Throne above, things were looking up!

Suddenly, with the thought of extrication, the lieutenant's mind was yanked roughly back to Private Krausse, the driver trapped inside *Cold Deliverance*.

Extrication impossible.

Van Droi had tapped the message.

Extrication frakking impossible!

There had been no time to save Krausse, no time to wait while fuel and rations were burned up, no time to stop, hoping the orks wouldn't happen across them as they tried to rescue one of their own. It would have put everyone at risk. Van Droi had been sure he was doing the right thing. Only now, suddenly, it seemed that there *was* time. But there was no life left to save.

Van Droi had made that call. Weariness and the weight of his command hit him again like a sledgehammer, and he sat at the rear of the Vanquisher's turret with his hands pressed tight to his face.

By the blasted Eye of Terror!

Absently, with that fraction of his awareness that wasn't drowning in guilt, he heard Stromm's voice again on the vox-link. The colonel confirmed the major general's orders with the Sentinel pilot who was relaying them. Then Stromm contacted each of his officers and gave them his instructions.

To van Droi, he said, 'Damned good news, eh, lieutenant? After all we've been through.'

'It certainly is, sir,' said van Droi. 'My tanks are ready to move out on your command.'

Stromm had served a long time in the Guard. He knew when an officer wasn't telling him something. 'You all right, van Droi? You sound a bit less ecstatic than I would've expected given the circ– Oh! The tank. I'm sorry, van Droi. In all the excitement…'

'That's all right, sir. Of course, I couldn't be happier about making contact with the rest of the army group.'

'Survivors?'

'No, sir,' said van Droi wearily. 'No survivors, I'm afraid.'

'I'm sorry, lieutenant. Of course, they'll be honoured properly when we get to Balkar. I imagine there will be plenty of decorations after the campaign. Throne knows, our lads deserve them. We've had a devil of a time out here, van Droi. Good men lost. But we came through it, man.

We came through. The confessors will organise a service for those that didn't.'

Van Droi knew they would, but it did nothing to comfort him. Once Stromm had signed off, he opened a link to his tank commanders on the company channel. There were only seven of them now, eight tanks left including his own.

'I want a double column. Two fours. *Foe-breaker* front left. *Old Smash-bones* right. We roll east behind the colonel's Chimeras. Keep your eyes open for trouble. You know the drill. I know you're all tired, but we're almost home. See it through.'

When each of the tanks had confirmed and rumbled into position, he gave the order and they all moved out.

CHAPTER THIRTEEN

BALKAR, LIKE ALL of the old Imperial ruins out in the equatorial desert, was a fortified base built on a rocky upthrust that had endured the onslaught of the wind-borne sands. The orks had moved in as soon as the Imperial forces had retreated but, in all those years, they had done little to change the base other than to fill its streets with rusting junk. Several of the structures, mostly barracks buildings and concrete garages, had collapsed in on themselves under the weight of the sand that had accumulated on their broad roofs. Other structures had once been decorated with proud Imperial iconography, but the winds had eaten it away to almost nothing, sandblasting the exposed surfaces smooth. The orks had subsequently covered them in childishly rendered glyphs and impenetrable scrawls of alien gibberish.

Much of the metal used in the construction of the base was flaking away. The rest, anything that the orks had thought to utilise for the modification of their strange war machines, had been stripped out, leaving bunkers without doors and barracks buildings without shutters.

To anyone looking down from the air, the base would have appeared hexagonal in plan, though not symmetrical, designed with uneven sides to take full advantage of all the space afforded by the broad, flat rock underneath. There were a number of wells, cut straight down, very deep into the ground. Unfortunately for the 18th Army Group, they contained no water. They must have dried up long ago. The base's former occupants – the great greenskin horde that Major General Killian's men had fought so hard to eliminate – had been using them as latrines. Killian had ordered them sealed.

It was the topic of water discipline that Colonel Vinnemann was discussing with his staff when a runner from Major General Bergen's office interrupted, bringing him some rare good news. Vinnemann's expression said it all as he sat listening, a mixture of disbelief and joy lighting his battle-scarred features. The look was mirrored on the faces of his staff officers.

'Say that again, son,' he told the runner. The words had gushed out of the gasping lad's mouth. Vinnemann wasn't sure he had heard them correctly.

'Lieutenant van Droi calling for you on the vox, sir. He and his 10th Company are heading towards our position with the remnants of Colonel Stromm's 98th Mechanised Infantry Regiment. The major general thought you would want to know, sir.'

Vinnemann clapped his hands together.

'Did you hear that, Alex?' he asked his adjutant. The young man nodded, smiling. Vinnemann barked out a laugh. 'Fine officer, that van Droi. Fine officer! I knew he'd get his boys through. Come on, you lot. We must welcome them!' He turned to the runner. 'Which direction are they approaching from, son?'

'From the south-east, sir,' replied the young man. He, too, was smiling, infected by the colonel's open joy. 'They're about two hours out. They'll enter through the south gates. The Sentinel pilots who picked up their transmissions are guiding them in.'

'Outstanding,' said Vinnemann. He grasped the head of his cane and struggled to his feet, wincing for a moment with the pain that shot through his back. It would soon be time for more blasted injections, but he wouldn't let the thought of that spoil this wonderful moment. His 10th Company had survived. Gossefried's Gunheads were returning to the fold. Say what you liked about them – and certain officers had plenty to say – they were a bloody resilient lot.

When General deViers ordered Vinnemann's regiment east to secure *The Fortress of Arrogance* at last, every single one of his companies would be accounted for. *Rolling Thunder* would be deploying in full strength. It would do wonders for the regiment's morale.

FROM HIS CUPOLA, Wulfe saw the walls of the base appear through the dusty pink haze in the distance. They rose from atop a rocky mound with a gentle, easy gradient on one side, and they were topped with watchtowers and weapons batteries. He could see long barrels protruding from the old-fashioned crenellations, even at this distance. Home at last, he thought, for home, to him, was with the rest of the regiment. Sure, there was competition, even the odd bitter rivalry, between the companies of the 81st. What regiment didn't endure such things? But they were all tankers together in the end, and all of them were Cadians, and therefore brothers when it came to the fight for mankind's survival. It would be good to see old Vinnemann again, to know that the man was still up front, leading as few other officers of his rank dared to do. Wulfe was surprised at how much that thought suddenly meant to him. Lieutenant van Droi was a great man and company commander in his own right – he was direct, honest and approachable, though he could be bastard hard at times – but Vinnemann was practically a legend among his men. His refusal to lie down and die when other men would certainly have done so epitomised the unrelenting spirit that *Rolling Thunder* was famous for.

'Can't believe we made it back to the rest of the pack,' muttered Holtz over the intercom. 'Never thought we'd live to see this.'

'Can't wait to sleep in a proper bunk again,' said Siegler.

Metzger was typically silent, concentrating on keeping *Last Rites II* in formation behind the tank in front as the walls of Balkar loomed ever larger in his vision slit.

'Do you think they'll have water and food waiting for us, sarge?' Siegler asked.

'They had bloody well better,' griped Holtz. 'I've been running on fumes for the last three days. I'll die if I have to drink recycled piss again. Fit to collapse, I am. Someone'll have to help me out of the hatch.'

'I'm sure the Officio Logistica has taken our supply needs into consideration,' said Wulfe. 'Balkar is the launching point for the general's big gambit, right? He won't have left anything to chance. First thing I'll do after we dismount is find the mess hall. I'll bloody well faint if they try to debrief me first.'

The others laughed at that. Even Metzger. No one would be trying to debrief *him*. Only the tank commanders would have to deal with that, and, as far as fainting was concerned, they all knew that their sergeant had only collapsed once in his life – that day so many years ago when an ork had cut his throat. Blood loss had knocked him unconscious, but the medic that had leapt onto the tank's turret to save him had got there just in time. That very medic, Wulfe later found out, had died a few days later, captured in a raid and tortured to death in a greenskin camp. A mop-up detail had found his body hanging from a makeshift gibbet, hands, feet and other parts lopped off. He had been taken while trying to save a wounded trooper on open ground.

Wulfe was still about the business of avenging him, and only death would ever make him stop. In that sense, he felt a great closeness with

Colonel Vinnemann, though he had only ever spoken to the man twice in person. Vinnemann's never-ending quest to avenge his wife was well known.

Look at what he endures to pursue it, thought Wulfe, having heard stories of the endless pain the colonel suffered.

As the tanks and halftracks got closer and closer to Balkar, a strange noise began to cut into Wulfe's uplifted mood. It came from the rear of his tank, and Wulfe knew at once that something had gone wrong. Metzger reported over the intercom a moment later that the engine's temperature was increasing rapidly. Wulfe checked the rear vision blocks and saw thick black smoke pouring out of the back of his tank from beneath the metal engine covers.

'The blasted radiator has packed in,' he told his crew. 'Metzger, warp damn it, can we at least make it inside the gates? Tell me we can!'

Before the driver could answer, *Last Rites II* gave a great shudder and stopped dead in her tracks. Wulfe cursed so long and loud that he almost went hoarse. He watched the other vehicles move up from behind, come abreast of him, and then overtake. *New Champion of Cerbera* passed within a metre on the right. The vox-board started blinking. Wulfe, thinking it must be van Droi, immediately opened the link.

'Oh dear, oh dear, sergeant,' said a smug voice. 'Looks like you've pushed the old girl too hard at last. Time she was put out to pasture, don't you think?'

'What the frak do you want, Lenck?' Wulfe growled back. 'Just calling to gloat? Frivolous use of vox-communications during an operation… that's a punishable offence. Old Crusher would love to hear about that.'

'Get over yourself, sergeant. I was just voxing to see if you and your men would like a lift into base. There's room on the track-guards. Can't have you sitting out here like idiots, embarrassing the lieutenant and the rest of the company like that.'

Wulfe gritted his teeth. He would rather dance naked at the general's next banquet than let that weasel-faced son-of-a-bitch gloat over this for the rest of his hopefully short life. *Last Rites II* had been running smooth ever since they had left the crashed drop-ship. All the other tanks – *all* of them – had needed to stop sooner or later for field repairs, but not her.

So why in the warp had she chosen now to break down?

Wulfe smacked a fist against the inside of her turret and said, 'Damn it, girl. Couldn't you have waited a few more kilometres?' Then he hit the transmit stud and said to Lenck, 'Move on, corporal, before my gunner blows you into the hereafter.'

'Such hostility, sergeant. Save it for the greenskins, why don't you? *New Champion* is moving on. Maybe we'll see you in the mess hall.

We'll try to leave some food for you, but no promises. Lenck, out.'

Wulfe cut the link and roared with frustration in his turret. 'This stupid old bucket! She couldn't have picked a worse time! We'll be the laughing stock of the whole damned base.'

'Yes she could,' said Metzger. His voice was almost a growl.

'What?' said Wulfe. It was rare for Metzger to speak up, but it was the confrontational tone of his voice that really caught Wulfe by surprise.

'She could have picked a far worse time to give out on us, and you bloody know it, sarge. In fact, this old girl has lasted out longer than we had any right to ask. She's the last crate in the whole damned company to give out, and she waited right up until now, the safest moment since we crashed on this rock. So, I don't give a five-copper back-alley frak whether we're a laughing stock or not, I'm bloody glad to be her driver. And I reckon you ought to shake yourself.'

Wulfe was stunned.

'Yeah, I think so, too!' said Siegler with a firm nod of his head.

Wulfe looked at Holtz. 'Well?'

Holtz scratched his chin. 'Three against one. I wouldn't change her for any other crate in the company, and that includes the lieutenant's Vanquisher. I can't think of any other way to put it, sarge: they just don't make them like this any more. She ain't no beauty, but she'll do for me.'

Wulfe leaned back against the turret wall, looking at the crewmen who shared the tiny space with him. Everyone on this crew had served in Wulfe's previous tank, though Metzger had only rolled out with her once before they'd had to abandon her. The first *Last Rites* had been something special, at least in Wulfe's eyes. It was easy to get attached to a machine that had saved your life so many times. Only her speed had let her down on that final day, when the clock was against her, and they had been forced to leave her behind. Wulfe realised now that his close affinity with the original *Last Rites* had blinded him to the worth of her replacement. *Last Rites II* might look like hell, but she was tougher than old boots. She had got them this far.

'Seems like this old girl has found a few fans,' he said, 'and I've been a bit unfair.'

'Just a bit, sarge,' said Siegler. Of the four-man crew, he had served with Wulfe the longest and the trust between them was strongest, not least because of Siegler's child-like loyalty. '*Last Rites* was a hard act to follow.'

'She was,' said Wulfe, 'but you're right; I reckon this crate is overdue a bit of respect from me. One of you idiots should have told me I was out of order.'

The looks both men gave him said they wouldn't have dared. Had his mood been so bad recently? he wondered. He had always believed himself an approachable man. Was he blind to the truth in that respect as well?

A light began blinking on the vox-board. Wulfe dreaded opening the link. No doubt another of the Gunheads was calling in to gloat. Maybe it was Rhaimes. The company's longest-serving sergeant was never short of a quip.

What would it be this time?

As Wulfe reached over to the board to open the vox-link, he told his crew, 'I'll say a litany of thanks to the old girl's machine-spirit when I get a bit of downtime.'

The men in the turret smiled, and he turned from them, hit the toggle on the vox-board, and said, 'Who the frak is it and what do you want?'

The voice on the other end was not amused.

'Well you could show some damned decorum for a start, sergeant,' snapped van Droi over the link. 'The next man who speaks to me like that gets thrown to Commissar Slayte.'

Wulfe blanched.

'Sorry, sir,' he told Lieutenant van Droi. 'Thought it was someone else. What can I do for you?'

'For a start, you can sit tight until we get an Atlas out to you. It will tow you into Balkar. I've voxed ahead for it already. Damned unfortunate time to break down, Oskar, what with all those people on the walls to greet us. Colonel Vinnemann is up there, and Major General Bergen, too, no doubt.'

Looking across the turret, Wulfe met Siegler's gaze and winked. To van Droi, he said, 'With respect, sir, I can't think of a better time to suffer a breakdown, can you? *Last Rites II* is the only machine in the company to have lasted this long without serious engine trouble. I'd rather it happened here and now than back there in the desert with the orks at our backs.'

Van Droi was silent for a moment. When he replied, a touch of his usual good humour had returned to his voice. 'Fair comment, sergeant. Glad to hear she's finally grown on you. Took bloody long enough, mind you. Anyway, what's this about refusing Lenck's assistance?'

Wulfe knew van Droi was probing with that last addition. Wulfe's contempt for Lenck was still a matter of concern to the lieutenant, then. 'Didn't want to hold him up, sir,' he said. 'We've been on quarter rations and bog-water for so long, I figured that rookie crew of his would fall over if they didn't get some proper provisions.'

'You're a damned poor liar, sergeant,' said van Droi. 'And there are no rookies in my company, not any more. They bled and sweated like the rest of us, and they killed their share of greenskins, so let's drop the whole *them and us* bit, shall we? I'm moving through the gates now. Find me in the officers' mess when you've been fed and watered.'

'Understood, sir.'

Van Droi signed off, but another light was blinking on the vox-board now. Wulfe hit the switch and said, 'This is *Last Rites II*. Go ahead.'

'*Last Rites II*, this is Atlas recovery tank *Orion VI*. We're pulling up to you now. Give us a minute to get tow-lines hooked up and we'll be under way, over.'

The Atlas commander sounded young, and his voice made Wulfe reflect on van Droi's words: no more *us and them*. He had been obstinate in his refusal to accept the new tank. He had been obstinate in not telling his crew about the apparition in the canyon on Palmeros. Was he being just as obstinate about the new meat? Was Lenck really as bad as he seemed, or had Wulfe cultivated bad feeling between them from the start on account of the man's likeness to Victor Dunst? He was starting to suspect it was the latter.

'Understood, *Orion VI*,' he voxed. 'Let me know when you're ready to take us in.'

CHAPTER FOURTEEN

EVENING FELL QUICKLY over the base at Balkar. The sky turned black just as *Last Rites II* finally reached the motor pool where she would undergo her much-needed repairs. Wulfe thanked the young commander of the Atlas tank, asked him where the mess hall and barracks buildings were, and led his crew off to find them. Their search would have been impossible but for the electric lamps that had been strung up throughout the base, their thick cables running along streets and dangling from rooftops. Even so, it wasn't easy. The lights were kept relatively dim at night in order to avoid drawing attention from itinerant ork bands. Earlier that day, units from the 259th Mechanised Infantry Regiment under Colonel von Holden – part of Rennkamp's 8th Mechanised Division – had been sent out to eliminate a band of travelling greenskin scavengers. The greenskins had been spotted some forty kilometres out from the base by scouts on Hornet bikes as they patrolled the low hills to the north. The scouts had then guided Armoured Fist units in for the attack. The action was short, bloody and decisive, and, importantly, none of the orks had escaped. Even a single fleeing greenskin might have brought a larger force back down on the Imperial camp. The last thing Exolon needed was a full-scale assault on their forward position. The top brass were desperate to avoid anything that might delay success, and a siege more than qualified.

The mechanised units that engaged the orks actually managed

something quite unusual; they brought two of the orks back alive. Naturally, both of them were horribly maimed and crippled, hanging onto their worthless alien lives by virtue of their raw inhuman resilience alone. Even so, the struggle to capture them had been immense. Wounded orks were often even more dangerous than healthy ones.

Wulfe heard of it first from a group of soldiers in the mess tent as he finished off a few slices of cooked meal-brick and a glass of rather tepid, but thankfully clear and salt-free water. He shook his head as he listened. Captive orks? It sounded like the officer in charge of the Armoured Fist unit in question was some kind of show-off. Wulfe wouldn't have brought them back. He'd have executed them on the spot. The top brass, on the other hand, must have seen some gain in the situation – a morale boost, probably – because someone had approved the construction of two cages in an area by the east wall. According to the troopers that told Wulfe all this, the captured xenos were proving quite a draw.

Wulfe was just finishing his meal when word reached him that the men of 10th Company were to pay the caged aliens a visit. Wulfe guessed van Droi wanted the less experienced men to see the foe up close and personal, based perhaps on some notion that familiarity eliminated fear.

Groxshit, thought Wulfe. The closer you got to orks, the more you saw how damned dangerous they were.

Despite his earlier promise to give thanks to the machine-spirit of his tank, he found himself with little time to do so. Stopping briefly at his barracks, he made arrangements to meet his crew by the cages a little later, but his first order of business was to find Lieutenant van Droi in the officer's mess. Thus, after a few moments spent trying to smarten himself up a bit – not easy given all he had been through – he crossed the base and arrived outside a single-storey sandstone building with the appropriate marker-glyph on the door.

There was a surly, bored-looking soldier on guard duty outside.

'Sergeant Wulfe to see Lieutenant van Droi,' said Wulfe. The trooper nodded, asked him to wait, and then popped inside to verify things with the lieutenant. A moment later, he reappeared and ushered Wulfe inside.

The officer's mess had a low ceiling of cracked plaster and at least half of the red floor tiles were missing, leaving large areas of bare concrete visible. Strip-lights hung above long trestle tables, buzzing and flickering, their bright glare somewhat harsh to eyes accustomed to the dull Golgothan day. As he looked around, Wulfe decided this place wasn't much of an improvement on the grunts' mess. He wondered idly if the food and drink was any better.

Even here, inside this building, the orks had painted typically crude images of the things that generally occupied their tiny minds: guns, blades, skulls, strange gods, and much more besides. Many of the scrawls were so obscure, so badly rendered that Wulfe couldn't begin to guess what they might represent. Some effort had been made to cover them up, of course, but there were so many. They were literally everywhere. As he had walked here, Wulfe had seen miserable troopers plastering the walls with propaganda material from the Departmento Munitorum. It was a minor punishment detail. The commissars had ordered it. One of the posters near Wulfe's assigned barracks building had caught his eye. *Check your kills!* it ordered. There was a well painted image of a big, strong Cadian trooper blowing an ork's brains out as it lay limp on the ground. The bottom of the poster read:

Destroying the brain will put most targets down for good!

The ork in the poster was a damned sight smaller than any of the ones Wulfe had met, but there was no denying the artist's talent. His or her work graced a number of other posters, too. Most were concerned with showing proper reverence to the Emperor and the authority of his agents, from the political to the theological. Others yet bore the seal of the Adeptus Mechanicus and offered concise reminders on the proper care and operation of standard-issue field equipment.

It wasn't that the troops needed reminding – their drill sergeants back on Cadia had seen to that with an abundance of cruel enthusiasm – but leaving the walls of an Imperial base covered in ork iconography, no matter how short the intended stay, was tantamount to heresy under Imperial Law.

The mess hall was busy. The air was filled with the constant hum of conversation, and no one paid him much attention. Wulfe soon spotted van Droi at a table on the far left. The lieutenant was sitting with a number of officers from the other companies of the 81st Armoured Regiment. As Wulfe walked over to present himself, he noted how damned tired his company commander was looking. The others didn't look much better. Golgotha hadn't been particularly kind to any of them.

'Sergeant Wulfe reporting as ordered, sir,' he said, saluting stiffly. The men seated around the table looked up.

'At ease, Wulfe,' said van Droi around a mouthful of food. Wulfe glanced at the lieutenant's plate automatically and saw a dark, thick slice of meal-brick. It looked hard and cold. So, he thought, the food *isn't* any better. They're on the same rations as us grunts.

He took no satisfaction in the knowledge. He wouldn't have grudged the lieutenant a better standard of fare.

'Take a seat, Oskar,' said van Droi, indicating an empty chair at the corner of the table.

Wulfe hesitated, looking at the other officers. Most were busy chewing or chatting to their neighbours. A few smiled at him or nodded. Wulfe recognised Captain Immrich among them, Colonel Vinnemann's right-hand man, tipped to replace him if the old tiger ever got bored of his quest for vengeance.

'I wouldn't want to impose on the captain and his companions, sir.'

'None of that, sergeant,' laughed Captain Immrich. 'Sit down at once. Let's not make it an order. You'll find none of that classist crap at my table. Isn't that right, gentlemen?'

The other officers agreed, though some less readily than others. Wulfe bowed a little to the captain, and then sat down, stiff as a board. Immrich noted it, grinned and shook his head. 'We've met before, sergeant,' he said, 'aboard the *Hand of Radiance*. You remember?'

'I do, sir.'

'Just after that blasted mercy run we sent you on.' He turned to the other officers and added, 'The Kurdheim affair,' before turning back to Wulfe. 'Bad business that. You should never have been sent back out there with so little time left.'

Damned right we shouldn't, thought Wulfe angrily, remembering the men who had given their lives that day. Not that it was Immrich's fault.

The captain seemed to read Wulfe's mind. 'Tremendous pressure from *up top* on that one. The damned Officio Strategos were adamant about it. Colonel Vinnemann objected from the start, but it was never going to count for much. Did those posthumous decorations ever come through for the other two? Medallion Crimson, second class, wasn't it?'

This question was directed, not at Wulfe, but at van Droi, who forced down a dry mouthful of meal-brick before answering.

'Sergeants Kohl and Strieber,' he said, sorrow stealing across his face. 'No medals. I must've pushed for them half a dozen times. Damned OS classified the whole operation *Zenith Eyes Only*. Officially speaking, it never even happened. All the normal channels are closed.'

Immrich's smile had vanished.

'Damned Strategos have a lot to answer for,' he hissed. 'How many Imperial heroes have died unsung on account of those pen-pushing bastards, I wonder. I'm sure Sergeant Wulfe here deserves a medal for what he went through.'

'The captain is too kind,' Wulfe said absently. He was thinking, not of medals, but of the ghostly vision he had seen that day.

What I went through, he thought? You don't know the half of it.

Another officer piped up, eager to guide the conversation in a slightly different direction.

'Decorations aplenty,' he said, 'when our General deViers gets his name in the history books, though, what?'

It was Hal Keissler, a sturdy, heavy-browed lieutenant with deep-set eyes. He was commander of the regiment's 2nd Company, Colonel Vinnemann's number three man, and something of an occasional rival to Immrich. Wulfe wasn't overly fond of him – the man's love of extreme physical discipline bordered on sadism – but he knew him for a solid battlefield commander. The ribbons and tin on his chest had been earned fair and square, just like van Droi's.

Immrich laughed, changing his mood in short order. 'We all know how much you and your boys love a bit of decoration, Hal. Tell you what, if you leave now, you could have *The Fortress of Arrogance* back here before breakfast. They might even give you a damned governorship for that.'

The others laughed, and Wulfe joined in politely, though not loud enough to draw attention to himself. In his head, he was thinking, frak your bits of tin. If Strieber and Kohl couldn't get theirs, why in the blasted Eye should anyone else? They served the Golden Throne with honour and courage. They gave their lives.

As the officers embarked on a round of good-natured jibes, Wulfe leaned across to van Droi and said pointedly, 'If you don't mind, sir... What was it you wanted to see me about?'

Van Droi had been chuckling at the banter of the other men. When he looked across at Wulfe, however, the humour quickly bled away from his face.

'Markus is sick, Oskar.'

'Rhaimes?' asked Wulfe, taken aback. His fellow sergeant had been goggled and masked last time they had talked, but he had seemed healthy enough.

'He's in a medicae bed right now. Held out as long as he could. He wanted to see his crew to safety, at the very least. It all caught up with him just as we came in.'

'What's wrong with him?'

'It's the fines, mostly,' said van Droi. He sipped from his glass of water, and then placed it heavily on the table. 'He's having a bad reaction to the build-up in his body. Allergic, apparently. He can't command any more, not in his current state.'

'How long will he be out? Days? Weeks?'

Van Droi locked eyes with Wulfe. 'I won't sugar-coat it, Oskar. We're not talking about recovery. We're talking about death. You saw what happened to those lads who got sick on our way across the desert. You heard Colonel Stromm's medics. Even with the facilities here at Balkar, Markus will die unless he gets off this planet soon. And he's not alone. The beds are full of sick troopers.' He pointed at the back of Wulfe's hand. 'More to come, too. Don't pretend you haven't noticed the colour change.'

Wulfe looked down at his fingers. The reddish tinge was undeniable.

'I don't get it, sir,' he said. 'Golgotha was a Mechanicus world once. They must've had millions of workers here. How did *they* manage?'

'If I get the chance to ask them, I'll let you know, sergeant. Maybe the planet has changed since then. Perhaps the factory-settlements were sealed somehow. I think most of them were in the polar zones, anyway. It hardly matters now, does it?'

Wulfe couldn't miss the bitterness in van Droi's voice. Rhaimes and the lieutenant had been good friends for longer than Wulfe had known either man.

'I'm sorry to hear about Rhaimes, sir,' said Wulfe. 'I'll offer prayers to the Emperor that he pulls through. With luck and a blessing, we'll find Yarrick's tank quickly, and the sick will be lifted out in time. I should visit him.'

'No, Oskar,' said van Droi. 'He doesn't want that. Respect his wishes.'

Wulfe couldn't find anything to say to that.

'General deViers is expected tomorrow,' continued van Droi. 'He's flying in. According to Major General Bergen, he's keen not to waste any time. The major general has been in regular contact with him via a cable-based communications system that the tech-priests set up. Didn't quite get the gist of it myself, but at least it seems to be more reliable than the bloody vox. Anyway, the general wants all forward elements to be ready for deployment on his arrival. Gives you about fourteen hours, Wulfe. How serious are the repairs you need?'

'She just needs a new radiator, new fuel lines, new filters, and a bit of love from the cogboys, sir. She'll be good to go after that. I'd say eight or nine hours, give or take.'

'Good,' said van Droi, 'but it's not just the condition of your tank that concerns me right now.' He stared at Wulfe without blinking. 'Listen, I'm sorry to do this to you, but I have to pull Corporal Holtz off your crew.'

Wulfe felt like he had been slapped in the face. 'Holtz? You must be bloody joking, sir! He's only just mastered the main gun. You already stripped Viess out. Now you're reassigning his replacement? What's it about?'

'War is what it's about, sergeant,' replied van Droi, suddenly brisk. 'With Markus out of the game, you're my senior man. You had better understand what that means. The crew of *Old Smashbones* came in as new meat before the drop. Holtz has plenty of combat experience and he's worked his way up from sponson-man. Plus he's a hard bastard. They'll need someone like that to get them through.'

Damn it, thought Wulfe, if I thought he was ready for command…

'Put me in charge of Rhaimes's crate,' he told van Droi. 'I've got more experience. I can deal with a rookie crew. Put Holtz in charge of mine. He'll be much better off with men he already knows.'

Van Droi shook his head. 'I've thought about that,' he said, 'but, to be frank, Wulfe, your crew is unorthodox, and I'm being kind with my wording here. With you at the helm, they're working out all right, but with anyone else…'

'Unorthodox?'

'For starters, you've got a driver most troopers still believe is cursed. They still call him *Lucky* Metzger. It's damned hard to erase a reputation for being the only survivor on crew after crew.'

'That's all behind him,' said Wulfe. 'His luck hasn't killed me yet, has it?'

'I hope it stays that way. But then there's Siegler.'

'What about him?'

'Come on, Oskar. He's damaged goods. You know what he's like. As hard as it'll be for a new commander to get used to him, it'll be twice as hard for *him* if you leave that crew. The only reason he still functions as a front-line loader is the strength he draws from your presence. I honestly think he'd lose it under someone else.'

Wulfe was quiet while he thought about that. Since the accident that had damaged his brain, Siegler had clung to Wulfe like a lifeline, a rock in a turbulent ocean, one of the few things that remained familiar to the man after so much about his universe had changed. What would he be like without his sarge to watch out for him? Van Droi was right.

'I promise you,' said the lieutenant, 'you're getting the best gunner we could find from the reserve squads, a lad from Muntz's platoon that I've had marked out for a while. Good scores on the ranges and I reckon he's got the right stuff. He only missed out on a front-line posting earlier because of misconduct. Nothing serious, you understand. Commissar Slayte has given him the lash a few times for brawling, but you weren't exactly an angel yourself at his age. You'll like him.'

Wulfe was still angry over Holtz being swapped out, but he was in no position to argue.

'This trooper got a name, then, sir?' he asked.

Van Droi sat back. 'Most of the troopers call him Beans. Heard of him?'

'Beans?' repeated Wulfe suspiciously. 'Why the hell do they call him that?'

'I think I'll leave you to discover the specifics yourself,' said van Droi with a grin. 'It'll give you something to talk about. You'll find him waiting for you at C-barracks. He's expecting you. You'll need to break the news to Holtz, of course.'

'That won't be pleasant,' said Wulfe darkly.

'For you? Or for him?' asked van Droi. 'Trust me, Oskar. Holtz will light up like Skellas Plaza on Emperor's Day. Think about it. If he does well, he could make sergeant by the end of this bloody fiasco.'

Wulfe had never considered Holtz particularly ambitious, but most troopers aspired to having sergeant's stripes sewn onto their sleeves. It was more to do with the perks than anything else. Holtz would certainly enjoy the increased alcohol and tabac rations... if he made the grade.

Having finished with Wulfe for now, Lieutenant van Droi was on the verge of dismissing him when a commotion erupted at a table across the room. A short, silver-haired, red-faced man in a colonel's uniform stood and slammed his palms down on the table's surface. His chair crashed to the floor behind him. 'I will *not* hold my damned tongue, Pruscht. You're not my senior officer. It's about time someone spoke his damned mind around here.'

There were five other men seated at the table. Four of them looked desperate to be somewhere else. The fifth was Colonel Pruscht, commander of the 118th Cadian Lasgunners. He was a heavy-set, dark-eyed man with a neatly trimmed beard. Calmly and quietly, he stood and addressed his angry peer.

'Calm down, von Holden,' he said, hands raised in placation. 'You don't want trouble. Think of your men. You don't want them to see you like this, do you? Let's put this one down to strong drink and forget about it. We can't have you talking like–'

'Like what?' exploded von Holden. 'Like someone with a bloody brain?' He spun and cast his bleary gaze over men at the other tables. 'Who among you has the gall to deny it?' he yelled. 'Where's your damned integrity? You all feel the same. I know you do. Armageddon is where we should be, fighting where it counts, where we can do some bloody good. Not out here on this backwater. Men dying of dust and bug-bites and Throne knows what else. And all for a bit of scrap metal no one gave a flying damn about until now. It's been forty blasted years. DeViers should–'

'Should what?' demanded a sharp, clear voice from the door of the mess.

Wulfe turned his head and saw Major General Bergen standing in the doorway flanked by two commissars. His heart skipped a beat when he recognised one of them: Commissar Slayte.

Crusher!

Some men in the regiment boasted that they were afraid of nothing, but they stopped boasting, all of them, when they met the man known informally as Crusher. He was the commissar attached to Wulfe's regiment, and to say he was unpopular was an understatement of titanic proportions.

By the Eye, thought Wulfe, that colonel has dropped himself right in it. Open dissent in front of commissars? I don't want to be around for this.

'Please continue, colonel,' said Major General Bergen, striding into the room, removing his cap and overcoat. The electric lamplight glinted from the medals on his chest and the golden boards on his shoulders. The commissars stalked silently forward at his flanks, like a pair of sleek attack dogs just barely held in check. 'I'll be happy to pass on any recommendations you or anyone else has directly to the general for his consideration.'

Von Holden, his face turning redder by the second, stuttered and looked desperately at Pruscht for support. Pruscht, though, seemed to know better. He sat back down in his chair and sipped from his glass.

With Major General Bergen in the room, Wulfe felt extremely self-conscious. This was no place for a non-commissioned man, despite Captain Immrich's earlier welcome. It certainly wasn't right for a sergeant to see a decorated colonel like von Holden being dressed down.

But the dressing down never actually came. To everyone's surprise, Major General Bergen walked calmly over to von Holden, picked his chair up from the floor, and politely invited the colonel to sit back down. Speechless, perhaps taking this for the calm before the storm, von Holden did so, all the while gaping at the higher-ranking man.

Wulfe glanced discreetly at Commissar Slayte while this was going on, but the man's face was emotionless and his gaze was fixed straight ahead. If he had noticed Wulfe and van Droi, he didn't let on. Perhaps he was waiting for a cue from the major general, some sign at which he would pounce on Colonel von Holden and drag him away. The sign didn't come, and the only movement Crusher made was the flexing of his metal fingers back and forth into fists. Wulfe knew that the action was habitual. The man probably did it in his sleep.

Van Droi turned his attention back to Wulfe and said, 'Best get yourself away now, Oskar. Go about the business we discussed.'

'Right, sir,' said Wulfe. 'Be glad to.' As he rose, he offered a quiet farewell to the other men at the table, 'Have a good evening, sirs.'

A few, Captain Immrich among them, smiled and nodded back. Wulfe saluted, turned, and walked out of the door, relieved to be away from the officers' mess and the tension inside it. He knew there were some good men in the upper ranks, but they made everything so bloody complicated sometimes, not like the grunts. You could speak your mind among the rank-and-file. There might be the odd punch-up afterwards, but you didn't have to worry about bloodlines, family honour and all that career lark, and the bond of brotherhood shared between the men of the lower ranks was one of those things that made life in the Guard more bearable. Wulfe had always thought so, until Lenck had shown up.

Wulfe was torn over that one. The bastard had saved his life, but he was the antithesis of everything Wulfe valued and respected. He was a boaster and a manipulator. Wulfe could almost smell the cruelty within him. Sooner or later, there would be a reckoning between them. It was inevitable.

Wulfe turned his mind to the new gunner, Beans. Was he as good a shot as van Droi said? Would he fit in with Metzger and Siegler? The lieutenant had a point; they weren't the most typical of tank crews.

He walked towards C-barracks, muttering to himself.

'Beans. I hope it doesn't mean what I think it does.'

WULFE FOUND BEANS waiting for him outside C-barracks with his belongings already packed into a canvas bag. He was sitting on a concrete step, smoking a lho-stick, and examining the red dust that had gathered under his fingernails. Wulfe automatically assessed him as he drew closer. Judging by his smooth, open facial features, Beans was young, no older than twenty standard most probably. His fatigues hung loose on a skinny frame. He had rolled the sleeves of his red field-tunic up to reveal heavily tattooed forearms but, if any of the tats were hive-ganger symbols from his life back on Cadia, Wulfe didn't recognise them. That didn't mean much, of course. There were literally tens of thousands of gangs in the vast, crowded fortress-hives where the men of Exolon had been raised.

'You'll be Beans,' said Wulfe as he stopped in front of the trooper.

'Are you Wulfe?' Beans's voice was high and he spoke with the soft, drawling vowels of a Kasr Feros man.

'I'm *Sergeant* Wulfe, and you can call me sergeant, or sarge. If you call me anything else, I'll break your teeth.'

Beans stood up, dropping his smoke at the side of the step and crushing it under a booted foot. He was a good head shorter than Wulfe and had to look up at an angle to meet his gaze. 'All right, sergeant. Throne above. I didn't mean any disrespect, did I? Don't want to get off on the wrong foot. I'm nervous enough already, by Throne.'

Wulfe nodded. At least the trooper was frank. 'Why do they call you Beans?'

'It's my name, isn't it? Mirkos Biehn. Beans. See?'

Wulfe let the relief show on his face.

'What?' said Beans. 'Thought I was going to stink up the air in your turret? Nah, it's nothing like that, sergeant. Then again, I can't promise I'll be forest fresh *all* the time. I'm only human.'

'I'll make sure the rest of the crew don't shoot you for your first offence,' said Wulfe. 'To be honest, it stinks so bad in there when we're on manoeuvres that no one would notice. You'll learn to breathe through your mouth pretty quickly.'

Beans looked horrified and Wulfe couldn't help but laugh.

'As for being nervous, Beans, don't be. My lot look out for each other. It's the first rule. You'll be seeing proper combat on my crew. Make no mistake about that. But the lieutenant tells me you're a good shot, and he thinks you'll fit in well.'

Beans brightened up on hearing this, as Wulfe had intended. 'The lieutenant said that?'

'He hasn't picked out a bad gunner for me yet. Both of my last two went on to command tanks of their own. That could be you in a few years if you do right by me. Now, if that's your bag there, pick it up and follow. We'll drop it off at A-barracks on the way.'

Beans hefted his bag over his shoulder and fell into pace at Wulfe's side.

'On the way where, sarge?' he asked.

'On the way to see some orks,' Wulfe answered.

QUITE A CROWD had gathered around the cages by the time Wulfe and Beans arrived. Troopers were jostling each other to get closer to the front where a couple of lieutenants from the 303rd Cadian Fusiliers were trying to keep order, largely in vain. Wulfe couldn't see Metzger, Siegler or Holtz among the crowd, so he and Beans hung back until two other sergeants arrived and began shouting at their men.

'Playtime is over, ladies!'

'Back to the barracks! Double-time it, you lot!'

About twenty grumbling men pushed their way to the back of the mob and split off from it. With their sergeants leading them, they jogged off down dark, sand-filled streets. Now, with fresh gaps opening in the crowd, Wulfe and Beans pushed forward, using their elbows and shoulders to gain ground.

What a lot of fuss, thought Wulfe, to see monsters I've had more than enough of, but he kept pushing all the same, moving as if on autopilot.

A few rows from the front, he found himself standing next to Siegler and Holtz.

'There you are,' he said. 'Where's Metzger?'

'Gone for a walk,' Siegler answered. 'Said this was bloody stupid.'

Wulfe turned to Beans and said, 'Which should tell you that Metzger is the smart one.'

'I resent that,' said Siegler looking genuinely insulted.

'Me, too,' protested Holtz.

'Don't kid yourselves,' Wulfe told them with a grin.

'Who's the kid?' Holtz asked, turning a scowl on Beans.

'This is Beans,' said Wulfe. 'He farts a lot.'

'Hey!' protested Beans, but he caught a look in Wulfe's eye and laughed.

'Holtz,' said Wulfe, 'you and I need to have a word. Come with me. Beans, stay here with Siegler.'

'Right, sarge,' said Beans.

Wulfe and Holtz broke from the group around the cages and moved off to stand at the side of an old storage building. Together, they leaned back against the pitted sandstone bricks. Holtz reached into his hip pocket, pulled out a smoke and placed it between his lips.

Wulfe decided not to mince words. 'You're getting your own command, Piter. Effective immediately. Van Droi thought I should tell you myself.'

The lho-stick fell from Holtz's gaping jaw to the ground at his feet.

'You're pulling my leg!' he said.

'I'm not.'

'By the Eye,' gasped Holtz. 'My own crate? You mean that Beans kid is taking over on the main gun?'

'Got it in one,' said Wulfe. 'The lieutenant rates him. He scored high in the standard tests. Apparently he's a good shot. But that's not the point. This isn't about Beans. It's about you.'

Holtz barked out a laugh. 'There's a hell of a difference between being a good shot on the practice course and being a good shot in combat. What if he gets the jinks?'

It was a legitimate concern. Wulfe had known other crews that had taken on a new man only to have him suffer the jinks. It was a nervous condition characterised by sever twitches and spasms, and it seemed to be brought on by the noise of the main gun or the impact of heavy enemy fire on the tank's armour. Once a trooper contracted the jinks, he was as good as useless on the battlefield. It took some men years to recover. Others never did.

'You're not listening, Holtz. Forget about Beans. I'll deal with him. He'll be fine. We're talking about you. We're talking about commanding a tank.'

'What's to say?' said Holtz. 'Show me a man in this regiment who doesn't want his own crate!'

Something in Holtz's voice didn't manage to convince Wulfe.

'Come on, Piter,' he said. 'Some men are happier taking orders than giving them out. I sometimes wish–'

'Which crate?' asked Holtz, talking over him. 'And why now?'

'It's Rhaimes's tank, *Old Smashbones*. She's a good, solid machine. Hell of a service record. Rhaimes is sick with the fines. It's serious. Van Droi is treating this as permanent. Says you might make sergeant if you do your duty.'

Holtz bent down, picked up the lho-stick at his feet, blew red dust off it, and popped it back between his lips. Talking around it, he said, 'Rhaimes. Damn. I'd rather be replacing someone else. His crew aren't gonna like this much. Don't expect I'll get a very warm welcome.'

'They're a young crew. New meat. They didn't have much time with Rhaimes, so you should be all right. Besides, they need someone with plenty of combat experience and the stones to get them through whatever's coming. If not you, then who?'

Holtz had no answer for that. He was too busy processing it all.

'Anyway,' said Wulfe. 'Your new crew is in A-barracks, so you won't need to move your stuff far. General deViers is supposed to arrive tomorrow. You won't have much time to get to know them before we roll out, so you'd best start now.'

Holtz nodded, unable to hide a degree of nerves. The side of his face that looked like hashed grox barely moved any more, and showed little emotion, but Wulfe had had enough practice in reading the other half to know that Holtz saw the announcement for the mixed bag it was.

'Just remember,' Wulfe told him, 'you've been through much more than they have. You're in charge. Tank men live or die by the decisions of their commander.'

'No pressure, then,' Holtz replied with literally half a grin. 'Only joking, sarge. I appreciate your confidence. If it's all the same to you, though, I'll head to the motor pool first. Make a bit of a farewell to *Last Rites II* and introduce myself to the new girl.'

'Sounds like a plan,' said Wulfe, clapping his friend on the shoulder. He returned Holtz's brief salute, and then watched him walk off in the direction of the motor pool, wishing him all the luck in the galaxy. Command was hard on any man, but far harder on those new to it. The lives of the crew and the survival of each precious war machine were heavy burdens to bear. Sometimes, Wulfe envied the men under his command. He remembered the freedom that came with being on the bottom rung of the ladder, of having someone else make most of your decisions for you. It was a good place to be when you had good officers. Wulfe trusted van Droi that way, and knew that van Droi, in turn, trusted Colonel Vinnemann, but the chain of command went much higher than that. Major General Bergen had a good reputation, but was it justified? It was hard to tell. Officers at such a senior level were so distant.

All Wulfe could say for sure was that command would be hard on Piter Holtz. At least in the early days. He would sink, or he would swim. It was as simple as that.

Wulfe walked back over to the soldiers jostling around the cages, noting how the crowd had thinned further now that others had begun drifting away. It took much less effort to get to the front of the crowd where he found Siegler and Beans talking animatedly about the creatures in front of them.

The ferocity of the imprisoned orks was impressive given their pitiful condition. The two monsters sat in their steel cages, legs reduced to tattered stumps, bellowing and spitting at the smaller, weaker humans that surrounded them. Beans was stepping in towards the cages to get a closer look when Wulfe grabbed him by the back of the collar and said, 'No you don't, trooper. This is close enough.'

The new gunner looked disappointed and perhaps a little angry, but he said nothing, merely stepping back into line with all the other men. From the same distance, Wulfe eyed the greenskins coldly. One was larger than the other, though not by much. Its skin was a darker brown, too. Both had the nightmare features that had been burned into Wulfe's brain since his first encounter with their kind: tiny nose, deeply-sunken red eyes, wide jaws rimmed with razor-sharp fangs. Their hides looked as hard and coarse as an adult carnotaur's, covered in red dust, lined with cracks. On their massive shoulders, great patches of dead skin were peeling away. They looked as dry as the desert.

So Golgotha is not being particularly kind to them either, Wulfe thought, though I notice the blasted ticks don't bother them. I wonder why.

Wulfe's first deployment as a tanker had been as part of the operation to defend Phaegos II against ork incursions from the Ghoul Stars. That was more than twenty years ago, a different time, a different segmentum, and here he was still fighting the same foe, still losing more friends to them each time they clashed. It sometimes seemed as if all mankind's efforts, all the blood spilled, all the battles won, all of it might count for nothing at all. In galactic terms, had anything really changed? Had anything he had done ever made a blind bit of difference?

Dangerous thoughts, he cautioned himself. If every Guardsman doubted the necessity of his actions, the Imperium would crumble and die. *Of course* he had made a difference. He had killed thousands of mankind's foes in his time. If every man in the Guard accounted for the same number, the green tide would surely be overcome someday.

Wulfe wanted to believe that, he really did, but it was a struggle. For every victory in the history books, how many losses went unpublicised?

As he studied the darker of the two orks, his eyes locked with the creature's. Immediately perceiving a challenge, it began roaring at him and hammering its head against the bars of its cage. It grunted and hissed and bellowed at him in what Wulfe supposed was the orkish language. Commissar Yarrick, the stories said, could understand this bestial gibberish, but Wulfe had never met anyone else who could. No one ever admitted as much, anyway. It was a horrible sound, something wild canids might make as they guzzled meat from a fresh kill, but there was definitely a syntax in there, however unrefined. Wulfe instinctively knew that he was hearing language.

With the force of its violent motions, the dark-skinned ork's wounds had begun to bleed again, but the flow was slow. The blood that oozed out was thick and sticky. Wulfe thought he understood why. It was the low availability of water here. It changed the blood of those that lived in the desert, making it clot far more quickly: a water-conservation mechanism, a survival mechanism, and that wasn't the only gift the hard desert life had given the greenskins. These two orks were distinctly different from those he had encountered before. They were leaner, almost wiry by greenskin standards, though still far larger and more powerful-looking than any human. Somehow, they seemed faster and all the more deadly because of it.

He was about to turn away, to lead Siegler and Beans off at last, when someone began shouting from the rear of the crowd.

'Make way! Make way at once, you damned fools.'

There was no mistaking the cold, crisp voice. Wulfe knew that it was Crusher even before he saw the stiff peak of the man's black cap moving towards him over the heads of the others.

Crusher violently thrust his way to the front row.

'Commissar Slayte,' said Wulfe with a nod. 'Come to view the exhibits?'

'Hardly, sergeant,' hissed the commissar, clocking Wulfe's stripes. 'I'm here to put a bloody stop to this nonsense.'

The commissar swept back the folds of his long black coat and drew a bolt pistol from the holster at his thigh. The motion was smooth, well-practiced. Wulfe knew what was coming. He stepped away.

One of the lieutenants from the 303rd saw it coming, too. He protested. 'Come now, commissar. You can't mean to spoil the fun prematurely. It's good for morale to see our enemies caged and helpless. You must agree.'

Crusher didn't even glance at the man. Instead, he took aim at the smaller, lighter-skinned alien, eased a black metal finger back on the trigger of his pistol, and loosed off a barking shot.

Wulfe had been about to shout, 'Stand back!' to Siegler and Beans, but it was too late. The bolt punched a coin-sized hole in the ork's skull and detonated there, showering the closest men with a foul spray of blood and brain matter. The men behind them, shielded from the spray by their luckless comrades, laughed out loud. The headless ork body slid down to the floor of its cage.

Seeing the slaughter of its foul kin, the darker ork began thrashing madly. Slayte calmly turned towards it and repeated the exact same procedure. Those in the front rows of the crowd pushed backwards. There was another loud crack as the bolt pistol fired and, again, the air filled with a bloody mist.

Crusher holstered his pistol, turned and addressed all those present. 'Damn your eyes, the lot of you. Have you forgotten the principles of intolerance set forth in the Imperial Creed? Perhaps the sting of the lash would help you all to remember.'

The crowd parted wide for him as he stalked off, calling out as he went, 'Suffer not the alien to live!'

'Damn it,' said one of the lieutenants from the 303rd as he dabbed at his bloodstained tunic with a handkerchief. 'Which regiment is that bastard attached to? I feel sorry for them.'

'That would be my regiment, lieutenant,' said Wulfe grimly, 'the 81st Armoured.'

'Colonel Vinnemann's lot?' asked the other officer. 'Throne help you, sergeant. You've got a bad one there. Execute many, does he?'

Wulfe shook his head. 'He likes his punishments, does old Crusher, but the colonel can usually talk him down from a killing. The alternative isn't much better, mind you. He gives out a hell of a beating.'

'Is that why you call him Crusher?' asked the first man.

'You didn't notice, sir?' said Wulfe, surprised. 'His hands. Augmetic replacements, both of them. He lost his organic pair to the jaws of a bull carnotaur some years back. Not that he complains. He caught a deserter back on Palmeros in the first months of the campaign and forced us all to watch the execution. The boy was nineteen. New meat. He saw his cousin get killed and lost it. Commissar Slayte crushed his skull with one hand. Broke it like it was an egg.'

The officers from the 303rd both frowned and shook their heads.

'Those boys in the 259th Mechanised aren't going to be pleased,' said one. 'They had the kill-rights to these two. They made the capture.'

'Might as well disperse, you lot,' shouted the other to the grumbling crowd. 'Nothing much to see now.'

The troopers moved off trailing a palpable air of disappointment and resentment. For a short time, the imprisoned enemies had offered a distraction from the biting of the ticks and the coughing and sneezing caused by the dust. Wulfe stayed a moment longer, staring in silence at the headless alien bodies. Siegler and Beans waited for him a dozen paces away, also silent.

It's not enough, thought Wulfe. No matter how many we kill, it's never enough. They keep coming. We send troops to purge them from one world, and another falls at our backs. Can we ever break the stalemate? Will we ever do more than just survive against them?

He reached a hand up and stroked the scar on his neck. Where had all his faith gone? Aboard the *Hand of Radiance*, Wulfe had always turned to Confessor Friedrich for spiritual strength. *There* was a man he could talk to. Despite being a year younger than Wulfe, the priest had a calm wisdom about him that Wulfe envied, though he wasn't prepared to drink quite as much as the priest did to achieve it. As he led Beans and Siegler back to the barracks, he considered seeking out the priest, but it was already late. He would have to wake his crew at sunrise tomorrow. General deViers wasn't about to let them rest up. That was fine with Wulfe. The hardest part of any soldier's life was downtime: too much time to think, to notice the little things. Typically stoic men would begin to grumble. Colonel von Holden was a stark example and he wouldn't be alone. Dissidence was far from exclusive to the officer class. Fights would start breaking out. There would be more incidents of drunkenness. Some would turn to less legal distractions. Before you knew it, the commissars would be executing men left, right and centre.

It was just as well that the bulk of the 18th Army Group would be moving out soon.

Nothing cleared the mind like going into battle.

CHAPTER FIFTEEN

IT WAS STILL early, but the day was already uncomfortably hot. The Golgothan sky was lighter than Lenck had ever seen it. The chief medicae liaison issued a warning: all personnel at Balkar should stay in the shadows as much as possible until further notification. But it was difficult to follow the Imperial Medicae's advice when Lieutenant van Droi had ordered all crews to run maintenance details. Still, Lenck did his best. He slouched with his back against the *New Champion,* taking shelter in her shadow while his crew griped and whined and ran the necessary checks.

Since daylight had broken over the base, Balkar had been abuzz with activity. Word hadn't reached him why this should be, but it wasn't hard to guess. They'd be moving out again soon. The final leg of Operation Thunderstorm would commence shortly.

Fine with me, thought Lenck. The sooner it's done, the sooner we can get off this blasted ball of dirt. If the next deployment doesn't take us somewhere populated, I'll kill someone.

A scowling Varnuss stuck his head around the rear corner of the tank and said, 'We've finished with the headlamps.'

Riesmann and Hobbs appeared beside Varnuss, both wearing murderous looks that told how much they hated menial work.

'Congratulations,' said Lenck. 'You can start oiling the treads, then. Shouldn't take long with three of you.'

'Sod off,' spat Hobbs. 'Why don't you get off your arse and pitch in?'

Lenck lifted an eyebrow and gazed at his driver coldly. 'Because I'm the one that keeps you lot in extra smokes and booze. Earn it.'

Hobbs spat on the ground and disappeared around the corner of the tank shaking his head and muttering. Lenck got to his feet and dusted himself off.

'I'm going for a wander,' he said.

'Where?' asked Varnuss.

'A little place called none-of-your-frakking-business, that's where. Just have the treads done by the time I get back, all right? Throne knows when van Droi might show up for an inspection or something.'

A FEW HUNDRED yards away, in the south-east corner of Staging Area Four, Wulfe and his crew were likewise engaged with running basic maintenance. Van Droi required all his crews to be able to undertake basic field repairs and the like. If there were problems the crews couldn't handle, the tech-crews took care of them. If it was something even they couldn't manage, the enginseers and their mindless, half-human servitors took over.

'Make sure they're locked down tight, Sig,' said Wulfe, pointing at the spare track links that Siegler was fixing to the armoured sides of the turret. At the rear of the turret, Beans was working, fatigues soaked in sweat as he packed and sealed the stowage boxes that extended backwards from the turret bustle.

Metzger was at the front of the tank, seated in his station with the hatch open, running checks on the remote control system he used to operate the hull-mounted lascannon. He had already checked everything else he was responsible for, working with a wordless efficiency that Wulfe appreciated.

It was their first day with Beans on crew, but the new gunner seemed to be fitting in well enough. Early days, of course, and Wulfe was yet to see how Beans handled the main gun, but he worked without complaint despite the heat and heavy lifting. He may have found Metzger a little cold – the driver took a long time to warm up to people and, even then, he was far from talkative – but Siegler had taken a shine to him. He laughed loudly at even the worst of Beans's jokes. Wulfe cracked the odd smile himself at how bad they were. The one about the two-headed whore on Emperor's Day had been going around since Wulfe's days as a Whiteshield. It hadn't been funny then, either.

Footsteps approaching from the right made Wulfe turn, and a smile spread over his face. A man in simple brown robes was approaching, a heavy, gold-leafed, leather-bound copy of the Imperial Creed swinging from a bronze chain at his belt.

'Confessor!'

The priest smiled back, came to a stop beside Wulfe, and stretched out a hand. 'Damned good to see you, sergeant. I prayed you would make it back to the flock. It seems that the Emperor was listening.'

Wulfe had the sudden impression that Confessor Friedrich had been about to add 'for a bloody change' before he stopped himself.

'I think you might be right, confessor,' said Wulfe. 'It certainly seemed like a miracle when we heard the voice of that Sentinel pilot. I doubt even van Droi believed we would actually make it out of the deep desert alive.'

The priest nodded. 'I heard about Siemens and Muller, Throne rest them. I've already had their crews listed for remembrance at the next honours service.'

Wulfe shuddered as he recalled Siemens's limp body burning atop the turret, but he said, 'They died doing their duty, confessor. I hear Golgotha hasn't exactly been a sightseeing trip for the rest of the army group.'

'Then you heard right. The things I've seen... Sometimes I think the Guiding Light of all Mankind is testing me, sergeant.'

'Maybe He's testing all of us.'

A look of pain crossed the confessor's face. 'Aye, only dead men are free of that. I pulled ten bodies out of a brewed up Chimera yesterday. You couldn't tell one man from the other. Ten shrivelled black mannequins. Two of them fell apart in my hands as I was trying to lift them out. For them, at least, the test is over.'

Wulfe nodded, his face mirroring the priest's sadness.

Confessor Friedrich raised a hand to Wulfe's elbow and drew him away from *Last Rites II*. 'Let's talk where others cannot hear, Oskar. Just for a moment. I would like to know of your spiritual health.'

They stopped in the shadows at the back of an empty Thirty-Sixer, and Confessor Friedrich took a quick look around to make sure they were alone.

'Tell me,' he said, 'are you still troubled by your memories of Lugo's Ditch? I had hoped that redeployment might give you a new perspective on what you saw there. Perhaps your nightmares have receded?'

Wulfe held the priest's gaze. 'I haven't been sleeping enough to judge, confessor. We've been on the move night and day. I slept well enough last night, but I was exhausted. I think perhaps the worst of the dreams are behind me. It may be that you're right. The mission might be crowding the memories out a bit.'

'I would have your mind at ease, my friend, but forgetting your experience completely would be a mistake. We've already talked of the positive. You've seen something that others wish desperately to see. You've had proof of that which lies beyond death. Does that still give you no comfort?'

'I've told you, confessor. His eyes were so hollow. He did *not* look like a man restored. On the journey here to Balkar, my crew confessed that they had guessed the truth. If any weight has been lifted from me, it's that I no longer need to hide it from them. But can you imagine what others would say?'

'If they knew you had seen a ghost?'

'It sounds like bloody nonsense when you say it aloud. I think I'd rather believe I was mad.'

'I don't think you are, but believe that if it helps. There are those who say even Yarrick is mad, driven beyond obsession. Many of the Imperium's heroes would be judged mad by the standards of normal men. It's no bad thing to be different,' he grinned. 'To a degree.'

'That's some choice, confessor, mad or haunted.' Wulfe went silent for a moment as other ghosts rose in his mind. 'If you had seen Siemens…'

The priest closed his eyes and bowed his head. 'It doesn't get easier.'

'Sorry,' said Wulfe. 'You've seen more than your share of horrors. I didn't mean… I wish I had your fortitude. Why do you do it? Clearing the tanks of bodies is a job for the support crews. Why do you continue to torture yourself?'

Confessor Friedrich gazed off into space. 'How could I let those boys face such horrors, Wulfe, knowing that they'll crew tanks themselves one day? They shouldn't have to see the likes of that. They shouldn't have to know how bad it gets before the end. And neither should you.'

'The orks didn't give me much choice.'

They both thought about that for a silent moment.

Changing tack suddenly, the priest said, 'You heard that General deViers has arrived, yes?'

Wulfe shook his head. 'I didn't know. I thought the officers would have had us all lined up to greet him. He likes a big reception.'

'He does, but between them, the major generals decided that preparations for deployment took priority. If deViers wants his forces rolling out before sundown, he'll have to do without the usual pomp this time.'

'He flew in?'

The confessor nodded. 'Touched down just west of the outer wall about three hours ago. He arrived on a Valkyrie transport escorted by four Vulcan gunships. It seems Commodore Galbraithe was as good as his word regarding the close support he promised.'

'Five birds?' asked Wulfe. 'Not exactly a major contribution.'

'Better than four,' said the priest with a wink. 'Anyway, I expect you'll be rolling out very soon, Wulfe. That's why I came to see you. May I bless you and your crew?'

'You're not rolling out with us, confessor?'

'Not this time. The regiment has many sick in the field hospital here.

You heard about Markus Rhaimes, of course. I'm staying to offer last rites to those who need it. But I'm sure your expedition will be over quickly. You'll find *The Fortress of Arrogance* and return. I know you will.'

Wulfe wished he shared the priest's confidence. 'I think my crew would appreciate a blessing, confessor. We need all the help we can get.'

'Excellent,' said the priest. Together, he and Wulfe walked back towards *Last Rites II*.

SQUATTING IN THE shadow of a nearby Chimera, grinning from ear to ear, Lenck watched them go.

'Gotcha!' he muttered.

CHAPTER SIXTEEN

TWO HOURS AFTER Confessor Friedrich had bid them farewell, the crew of *Last Rites II* were nearing completion of their final checks. Together, Siegler and Beans went over every single track link, checking and oiling the heavy iron pins that held them together. Metzger tightened the latches that held the tow cables, entrenching tools, fire axe, bolt cutters and numerous other essentials in place on the tank's hull.

Wulfe, not content to supervise, checked each of the vision blocks and their spares for cracks before turning his attention to the vox-caster. He cycled through each of the listed channels that Exolon would be using in the field until he was satisfied that he could tune into any of them at the flip of a toggle. Finishing this, he took off his headset and sat back in his command seat.

Damn, it's hot, he thought. But once we're under way, the wind should cool us a bit.

It was only now, with his hearing unhindered by the headset's mufflers, that he heard raised voices outside. Recognising them at once, he leapt up from his seat and hauled himself through the top hatch. From his cupola, he looked down to the left and saw Metzger and Siegler standing off against Lenck and his crew. Beans stood off to one side, shuffling anxiously.

'What the frak is going on here?' Wulfe shouted down at Lenck as he

217

climbed from the cupola, and then leapt from the track-guard to the ground. 'What the hell do you want, Lenck?'

'An apology for starters, sergeant,' said Lenck. 'My lads and I were just on our way back from the supply depot when your brain-addled idiot of a loader walked right into us and spilled half our coolant.' He gestured at two jerrycans lying on their side in the sand.

'Siegler?' said Wulfe.

'Groxshit, sarge,' replied the loader. 'They were walking by and started in on our tank.'

'That's right,' said Metzger, eyes locked on Hobbs, who stood directly in front of him, shoulders loose, ready to lunge forward. 'The bastards were at it.'

Wulfe had never seen Metzger like this before. He looked unusually dangerous, as tall and rangy as ever, but with teeth bared in a snarl, long arms ready to lash out. He looked more like a soldier at that moment than at any other time in the months Wulfe had known him. This wasn't the time or place for him to prove his boxing skills, though. Brawling would mean the lash if Crusher found out.

'Lenck,' said Wulfe in a growl, 'get your mongrels away from here before something happens that you'll regret.'

The big one, Varnuss, stepped to Lenck's side, rolling his shoulders and stretching his neck. Wulfe glimpsed ganger tattoos under the collar of his tunic. Was he just posturing, wondered Wulfe, or was he really stupid enough to make trouble with a senior man? Both possibilities seemed equally credible at that moment.

Posturing or not, it was only when Lenck put out a hand and stopped Varnuss from advancing that the big man seemed to reconsider.

'Come on, you lot,' Lenck told his crew in mock exasperation. 'Looks like we'd better go back to the depot and get some more coolant.'

Muttering and cursing, the crew of the *New Champion* turned and fell in behind Lenck as he stalked off. After a few paces, however, Lenck stopped and turned. He pointed at Siegler, though his eyes were locked on Wulfe's as he said, 'With respect, sergeant, you might want to keep your pet moron on a leash in future.'

Wulfe felt something snap inside him. He bolted straight at Lenck and grabbed him roughly by the collar, hauling him up on his tiptoes. Other hands immediately tried to free Lenck, tugging at Wulfe's wrists in vain, trying to break a grip that was like solid steel.

'What're you going to do?' Lenck sneered, looking down his nose at Wulfe without a hint of worry. 'You know the regs.'

Wulfe growled. 'I ought to rip your bloody tongue out, you piece of garbage.'

'But you know you'd pay for it,' said Lenck.

'That's where you're wrong, Lenck. It doesn't go both ways. I could beat you to within an inch of your life, and no commissar could touch me for it.'

Lenck's eyes narrowed. His voice became a hiss. 'I wasn't talking about commissars.'

There was a sudden shout from atop *Last Rites II*. It was Beans.

'Good morning, commissar! How are you?'

Wulfe turned and saw a dark figure emerge from between two tanks about a hundred metres away. His grip automatically loosened on Lenck's collar and the younger man wrenched himself away.

When Wulfe turned around to face Lenck again, the corporal was smiling sardonically.

'I'm sure we'll have a chance to pick this up again sometime, sergeant,' he said. 'In the meantime, my crew has work to do. Excuse us.'

Wulfe watched them go, fists clenched white at his sides. How far would I have gone? he asked himself. Would I have killed him? Could I have stopped myself? He remembered the panic he had felt as Victor Dunst's gang had restrained him all those years ago on Cadia. He winced as he recalled the pain of Dunst's knife being pushed into his torso. He heard the laughter of the gangers, laughter that turned to curses when they heard the siren of the Civitas patrol car.

Lenck's crew cast filthy looks back at him over their shoulders as they went, all of them but Lenck.

He's not Dunst, Wulfe told himself. For Throne's sake, he's not Dunst.

When Lenck was about twenty-five metres away, he turned back towards Wulfe without breaking stride and called out to him. Just five words. Five little words. But they hit Wulfe like a flurry of bolter shells that detonated in his mind.

Wulfe was struck motionless. He saw Lenck laugh, then turn around and lead his men off between two rows of Chimeras.

A hard, sharp voice at his shoulder woke Wulfe from his paralysis. 'What's going on, sergeant?'

Wulfe turned to meet the icy stare of Commissar Slayte, his eyes glittering in the shadow of the brim of his black cap.

'Not sure what you mean, commissar,' said Wulfe readying to move off towards his tank. The commissar moved faster. Wulfe felt a heavy mechanical hand grasp his upper arm.

Crusher turned his eyes in the direction Lenck and his men had taken, but they were gone from view. After a pause, he leaned in towards Wulfe and said, 'You've been away from your vox-set, so maybe you haven't heard, but Colonel Vinnemann has ordered the regiment to muster at the east gate. We leave Balkar in fifteen minutes. Make sure your people are ready, Sergeant Wulfe. I'll make a very memorable example of anyone that isn't.'

Wulfe looked down at the perfectly machined, black metal hand. 'We'll be ready, commissar.'

'Make sure of it,' said Crusher. There was the slightest whirring of gears as he released the sergeant. Then he walked off, taking his threats to other ears.

Wulfe's crew was looking at him wordlessly as he marched past them.

'Get to your stations, all of you,' he said gruffly. 'We're moving out in fifteen.'

Siegler, Beans and Metzger leapt to comply, warned off asking questions by the dark look on Wulfe's face. As always, Wulfe was the last one in.

As he swung his legs over the lip of his hatch, he thought about Lenck's parting words. They had frozen his blood. As he dropped into his command seat, those five words rang in his ears. Did they mean what he thought they meant?

Five little words, each one rocking him like a cannon shell.

'Watch out for ghosts, sergeant!'

CHAPTER SEVENTEEN

Two days east of Balkar, Wulfe and the rest of the expeditionary force entered a rocky region of the Hadar desert known as Vargas. Led by General deViers, riding comfortably in a specially outfitted command Chimera, the Cadians moved in a long column that slowly snaked along the floor of a deep canyon marked on Officio Cartographica charts as Red Gorge.

The gorge ran for almost three hundred kilometres along a meandering path that would eventually lead the men of the 18th Army Group to the site of the largest and bloodiest battle of the last Golgothan War. It was there, at long last, that General deViers expected to find *The Fortress of Arrogance*. It was there, also, that he expected to face the greatest ork resistance to his progress so far. By all accounts, the foothills and low valleys of the Ishawar Mountains were littered with wrecks from the war. What better place for the scavenging greenskins to build a major settlement?

Despite the likelihood of violent confrontation, the mood among the men was mixed. Some were upbeat, seeing the final phase for what it truly represented, an end to their tormented time on a world unfit for human habitation. Others were less optimistic. Some, like Major General Bergen, anticipated great disappointment on arrival at the coordinates the Mechanicus had provided. Even so, the realists in the

221

army group were as keen to get the whole thing over as the optimists were.

On the other hand, few were happy about having the entire expeditionary force negotiate Red Gorge. There was simply no other choice. The rocky clifftops and surrounding highlands were riddled with chasms and crevasses, many of them impossible to spot from the ground until too late. Under other circumstances, Commodore Galbraithe's Vulcan gunships could perhaps have guided the column from the air, but flying conditions were far from ideal over the Hadar. Frequent dust storms threatened to clog air intakes, something that would have sent the Vulcans crashing to the ground. Electromagnetic surges from the thick clouds made mid- and high-altitude flights just as deadly. So the Vulcan pilots were forced to fly low, making slow passes along the canyon floor, just a few hundred metres above the heads of the Cadian troops, visored eyes scanning for signs of ambush.

Wulfe watched the Vulcans from his cupola, black birds roaring as they crossed the strip of red sky overhead. They left trails of grey smoke that moved like ribbons on the wind.

For Wulfe, this phase of the journey was particularly harrowing. The sharp crags and deep, shadowed gullies along which the column moved were a powerful reminder of Lugo's Ditch. As the rock walls rose to fantastic heights on either side, a cold sweat began to soak Wulfe's tunic.

Watch out for ghosts, sergeant!

Even now, with the glow of the second day fading, Lenck's words were still eating away at Wulfe's insides. What had the bastard corporal meant? The most obvious answer was that he knew about Lugo's Ditch. But how? Wulfe was sure that Confessor Friedrich wouldn't have betrayed him. He doubted any of his crew would have, either. Beans didn't know anything about it, so that ruled him out.

Had Lenck simply meant Victor Dunst? A ghost of the past rather than of the dead? That was almost as much of a stretch. All Lenck had regarding Dunst was a name, wasn't it?

Wulfe wracked his brain, desperate to remember who he had told about Dunst. He hadn't recounted the story often – it wasn't exactly one of his favourites – but it *was* an old custom among Cadian troopers to compare scars and tell the tales of how they had been won. Wulfe had shared the Dunst story with a handful of men in his early years with the regiment. Had someone told Lenck? Did the rotten corporal know just how much his appearance troubled Wulfe?

As the day wore on, Wulfe tried to put the matter to the back of his mind. He sat in his cupola, occupying himself with a study of his surroundings as *Last Rites II* rumbled through the dust kicked up by the tanks in front. There was vegetation in the canyon, the first that he had seen since crashing on this world. Not much of it, of course – mostly dry grasses and scrawny, thorn-covered tangles of brush – but it meant moisture. There was animal life, too, and far larger than the biting ticks the Cadians had endured so far. Wulfe saw great, slothful, flat-bodied lizards basking on the rocks. Their skins were armoured with hundreds of small, bony plates, and they were coloured like the land around them. As the Imperial column rolled past, they hissed and slid quickly into the mouths of inky black caves.

Observing these things offered Wulfe only temporary respite from his thoughts. Again and again, he returned to the matters that troubled him most. As the strip of sky above Red Gorge grew dark, he dropped back down into his turret basket, leaving the hatch open above him so that a cooling wind could circulate.

Siegler was dozing in his seat, thick arms folded on top of the shell magazine, head resting in the crook of his elbow. By the glow of the turret's internal lamps, Beans was leafing through a tattered magazine featuring monochrome picts of hard-faced Cadian women stripping out of military uniform. Judging by the state of the pages, the magazine had had a great many owners over the years.

Wulfe smiled to himself and tapped Beans on the shoulder. Speaking low on the intercom so as not to wake Siegler, he said, 'That stuff'll rot your soul.'

'Damage done,' said Beans with a grin. 'I've been through this one so many times I think I've desensitised myself. You want it?'

Wulfe laughed, but his tone was serious when he said, 'Listen, Beans. You and I need to have a talk.'

'What about, sarge?'

'I think you know what.'

Was it Wulfe's imagination, or did the new gunner flush a little?

'The stand-off in the staging area, right?'

Wulfe nodded, frowning. 'A tanker stands with his crew, no matter what. You know the rules. You're lucky Siegler and Metzger overlooked it, but if I ever see you standing on the sidelines like that again, you'll be back on the support crews before you can say "the Emperor protects". What the hell were you thinking?'

Beans shrugged guiltily. 'If it had been any other crew, sarge... But it was Lenck's lot.'

'What difference does that make?'

'Plenty.'

There was a pause, a moment of uncomfortable mutual silence, before Wulfe said, 'Tell me what you know about Lenck.'

Beans looked up. 'I know not to mess with him. The officers might have all the official power in the Guard, but it's guys like Lenck that control the shadows. Every regiment has them, right? The guys who can get you more booze, more smokes, more meds.' He held up his shabby, pornographic pictomag. 'More stuff like this. They make a business of it, and the officers let it go on because the men grumble a little less. Fewer fights break out. I can't imagine Guard life without such guys, can you? Well, that's Lenck. If the price is right, he can get just about anything. He's more like a hive-gang boss than a soldier. And he thinks you're out to shut him down.'

Wulfe knew all this, of course. Beans was still a relative newcomer to the regiment, but he clearly had a good handle on things. Everything he had said was true. Regiments needed their hustlers and fixers. Things became unbearable all too fast without them. It explained a lot about Lenck's mysterious popularity with the newer guys. Still, the idea that Lenck should be allowed some slack on account of this alleged service to the regiment didn't sit well. Wulfe huffed. 'This is the Imperial Guard, not the blasted underhives. Voeder Lenck is a cocky, jumped-up little arsehole and, sooner or later, he's going to wish he'd never met me.'

Beans looked uncomfortable as he said, 'Um… Didn't he save your life, sarge?'

Wulfe spat a curse. 'He killed an ork that was about to kill me. Duty demanded it. Any trooper would have done the same.' His voice had taken on an angry edge, all the harder because, in truth, he was grateful and it bothered him immensely.

Beans raised a placatory hand. 'I'm just saying what I heard.'

Wulfe muttered under his breath. Glancing up through his open hatch, he saw that the sky was almost pitch black. Would old deViers have them pressing on throughout the night again?

Wulfe addressed his driver, 'You need me to take a shift on the sticks, Metzger?'

'I'll be fine for another few hours, sarge,' replied Metzger. 'How about you take a shift then?'

In his long and bloody career, Wulfe had manned every single station aboard a Leman Russ tank. He wasn't nearly as talented a driver as Lucky Metzger, but he was more than capable of keeping his crate in place while Metzger got some much-needed sleep.

'Fine,' said Wulfe. 'Two hours. Let me know if you get tired before that.'

'Will do, sarge,' said Metzger.

Wulfe sat back in his command seat. He wasn't feeling particularly sleepy right now. He mind was running laps. He kept hearing Lenck's words in his head. The old scar on his throat was irritating him, too. He scratched it lightly.

The vox channels were mostly quiet. The only regular traffic was coming from the Sentinel and motorbike scouts up front. After a minute, Beans's voice broke in on his thoughts.

'Want a read?' said the gunner with a grin as he offered his sergeant his magazine.

'Not much reading in it,' Wulfe replied with a half-smile, but he took it anyway.

CHAPTER EIGHTEEN

By the sixth day out of Balkar, General deViers had started to develop a dry, itchy cough. It wasn't nearly as bad as those of some of his officers, but it caused him a certain degree of panic because he was so much older and, therefore, more vulnerable to Golgotha's subtle assaults on his health. He had seen what the red dust had done to some of his troopers. The damned medicae staff were being about as much use as a paper lasgun, in his opinion.

Last night, the high canyon walls of Red Gorge had come to an abrupt end. The column had made it through without incident and had set up camp briefly on the open sand at the canyon's mouth. Dawn had broken only an hour ago, revealing just how fortuitous the decision to halt the column had been. *His* decision, of course. Had the men of Exolon continued pushing eastwards, they would have run straight into the biggest ork fortification that deViers had ever seen.

He was looking at it now.

He stood just outside the doorway of a hastily erected command tent, magnoculars pressed to his eyes, scanning the massive ugly structure that seemed to run from one end of the horizon to the other. Behind it, visible as little more than a faint silhouette in the morning light, he could see the slopes of the towering Ishawar Mountains. Their peaks were invisible, lost in the bellies of blood-coloured clouds.

'Why in blazes wasn't I told about this?' he raged. 'It's colossal. How

Hammer of the Emperor

could the probe-servitors possibly have missed something like this? Get those tech-priests in here. Get Magos Sennesdiar. I want some damned answers at once.'

The ork wall was easily a hundred metres tall. Throne knew how long it was. It was breathtaking in its scale. It was plated with great metal slabs of armour painted red from top to bottom, and decorated with oversized ork glyphs daubed crudely in white. There were sharp, uneven crenellations all along the battlements, and the barrels of huge cannon could be seen thrusting outwards from behind them. But was the wall manned? In the short time deViers had been watching, he hadn't witnessed any signs of life. Could he trust his eyes? The haze of dust and shimmering air made it difficult to discern movement at this range. The gun towers and battlements could, in fact, be seething with the foe.

If they were there at all, however, it seemed that they hadn't spotted the 18th Army Group. Not yet.

Their eyesight, thought deViers, isn't as good as ours, but the longer we watch and wait, the more time we give them to discover us. We can't lose the element of surprise. A sudden thrust is our best chance to get through, and we must get through. Glory and fame await, Mohamar. It won't be long now.

There were vast iron gates, as tall as the wall itself, spaced at intervals all along its length, but none were open. They looked very heavy, very solid.

One of the major generals cleared his throat. DeViers couldn't tell which one.

'And we've no idea how far it extends?' deViers asked. 'No idea at all?'

Bergen, Killian and Rennkamp all stood a pace behind him, staring out at the ork wall through their own magnoculars.

'There hasn't been time to properly reconnoitre it yet, sir,' said Bergen. 'The Vulcan pilots say they're awaiting your order to go up, if that's what you want. There might be a way around it. Best estimates at this time suggest it's over a hundred kilometres long, though.'

'By the Golden Throne,' hissed deViers. 'Over a hundred kilometres.'

He wasn't optimistic about finding a way around. A feeling in his gut, an instinct developed over decades of battlefield command, told him this was all part of his great test. Here was an obstacle put before him to see if he was worthy of everlasting fame. No, there would be no going around it. There was nothing for free in this universe.

The sheer size of the wall suggested it might have been built to keep out Titans. A foolish notion, of course. Nothing could keep out a Titan for long, but it probably made some kind of rudimentary sense to the greenskins. Was the construction of the wall a reaction to Yarrick's assault on Golgotha? The mighty commissar had employed Titans throughout his campaign. Perhaps the greenskins had anticipated an Imperial return all along.

'Gather the officers together,' deViers told his three major generals. 'I want us through those gates by the end of the day.'

'Sir!' protested Killian. 'We have no idea of the enemy's strength. We need full and proper reconnaissance. At least let us get some idea of their numbers before we–'

'I didn't ask for opinions, Klotus,' snapped the general. 'You can see those gates as well as I can, can't you? Reconnoitre all we like, I tell you now, we'll find no way around. We'll have to punch our way through one of them. I will *not* be stopped, not by a damned wall, not by anything.'

Bergen, Killian and Rennkamp dropped their magnoculars and shared a quick look that deViers decided to pretend he hadn't seen.

'Might we not send the Vulcans on a forward sweep, sir?' asked Bergen. 'Order it now and we'll know what we're dealing with. At the very least, they could give us some idea of what's beyond it.'

'We don't exactly have air support to spare, Gerard,' said deViers. 'You know that. They could be cut to pieces by triple-A fire. I don't suppose you'd like to explain that to Commodore Galbraithe?'

'But surely just one, sir,' said Rennkamp.

'It would be better than charging in blind,' said Bergen.

'You know,' said Killian, 'with luck and a prayer, the bloody orks might well have moved on. I didn't see any movement. No signs of occupation at all. I mean, who knows how old that thing is?'

DeViers shook his head. 'No, Klotus. They're there all right. It took a lot of work to make that wall. Our prize lies behind it. And I'm damned sure that the xenos filth who made it are still behind it, too.'

'Honestly, sir,' said Rennkamp. 'A single Vulcan. Just one fast sweep and we'll know for sure.'

'And put the whole damned greenskin horde on immediate high alert? No, Aaron. No aerial recon. The Vulcans can't fly high enough in this accursed weather to evade detection. Give me something else.'

'A Hornet then, sir,' said Bergen. 'A single Hornet reconnaissance bike might be mistaken for one of the orks' own at long range. That's no guarantee they won't fire on it anyway, of course, but if we're lucky, it'll draw a lot less attention and still let us get a man close enough to make a difference.'

DeViers nodded. 'That sounds feasible. Make it happen. Get the best scout we have out there. Someone with experience. I'll want a full report, including a list of as many weak points as possible, within the hour.'

Bergen saluted and moved off to see it done.

* * *

IT DIDN'T TAKE an hour. It was only forty minutes later that the Hornet rider chosen for the reconnaissance run reported back to Colonel Marrenburg. The colonel cut the scout's verbal report short, ordering him to save it for the general's command tent where the army group's senior officers – more than a dozen men ranking colonel and higher – awaited them. Marrenburg then led his man over the red sand and in through the tent flap. The day was already baking hot.

In the cooler shade of the general's tent, Marrenburg introduced his scout to the assembled officers.

'Gentlemen,' he said proudly, 'this is Sergeant Bussmann. He's the best damned scout in my outfit. You can have absolute confidence in his report, I assure you.'

Since Sergeant Bussmann belonged to Bergen's division, deViers asked Bergen to conduct the briefing, giving the general and the others a chance to concentrate on the details and any questions they needed to ask. There wasn't much good news. Judging by the sergeant's account, the wall was more daunting the closer one got to it. Whatever lay inside must have been of great value to the greenskins, for they had expended tremendous resources in its construction, resources that might otherwise have gone into the construction of hundreds, if not thousands, of their war machines.

This bothered Bergen on two counts. Firstly, it suggested that the orks had enough resources to be able to afford such a grand static defence. This led him to suspect they had established ore refineries somewhere. Were they close by? Golgotha had been selected for occupation by the Adeptus Mechanicus centuries ago for the amount and variety of metals deep within its crust. It wasn't much of a stretch to believe the orks were taking similar advantage of the resources. Secondly, the use of so much valuable metal in construction of the wall could only mean that whatever lay on the other side was something the orks considered very important. Yes, they were beast-like and savage, but they could be cunning, too. They weren't nearly as mindless as men believed. They had built a wall, and there had to be a good reason.

As he listened to Bussmann, Bergen found himself wondering if *The Fortress of Arrogance* might not be the thing the aliens were trying to protect. Had they known all along that the Imperium would come back to Golgotha to collect it? Had they planned and built the wall knowing that the fight would come to *them*?

Bussmann reported large amounts of artillery present on the parapets. Some of the barrels he had seen extending out from between the wall's teeth were unnervingly broad, chambered for rounds of such size they might have been more at home on the prow of an interstellar battleship.

That's it then, thought Bergen. They must still be here. There's no way the greenskins would leave weapons like that behind. By the blasted Eye, we've got a fight on our hands.

It had been impossible for Bussmann to gauge the thickness of the wall and how well it would stand up to the weaponry of the 18th Army Group, but it certainly looked like it could take a beating. On the other hand, some of the plates were rusting, and orks rarely built anything with consistent strength throughout. There would be irregularities in the structure that Exolon could exploit if only they could find them.

The question was, would they have the chance? Bussmann had spotted numerous hinged plates set in the wall at apparently random points. A few of them had fallen off, their bolts having rusted, revealing the nature of the others. They were firing ports, and the cannon they hid were massive.

At the end of his report, Sergeant Bussmann cast a somewhat anxious glance at Colonel Marrenburg. Then he took a deep breath and said, 'In my opinion, sirs, a direct frontal assault on the ork wall will result in very heavy losses. If it were up to me–'

'Sergeant,' snapped Marrenburg, cutting Bussmann off. 'You will restrict yourself to answering direct questions.'

Bussmann flushed and an angry look stole across his face, but he said, 'I apologise if I spoke out of turn, sir.'

General deViers cleared his throat and addressed the sergeant. 'We'll overlook it this time, sergeant, but think on this: without hardship there can be no glory. Show me something worth doing that doesn't have its price.'

Bergen wanted to roll his eyes, and, judging by the sergeant's sudden look of disbelief, Bussmann felt the same. Before the scout could dig himself a deeper hole, however, Bergen jumped in and said, 'Thank you very much for your report, sergeant. Your service today has been noted. Unless the general wishes to ask anything else…'

DeViers shook his head.

'In that case,' continued Bergen, 'you're dismissed.'

Bussmann snapped out a sharp salute, turned, and marched out into the light of day.

'We need to focus on the gates,' said Killian. 'From his report, it sounds like they're hinged to open outwards. They're far too big to ram open anyway. How in the blasted warp are we going to breach them?'

It was Colonel Vinnemann, hunched in his chair like some kind of cathedral gargoyle, who answered. 'We all know orks. Chances are, when they see us coming, they'll open the gates and start spilling out like rats from a burning building. We can fight our way through if we don't give them a chance to close the gates again.'

Bergen caught General deViers looking over at the disfigured form of

Vinnemann with an expression of barely concealed distaste, and, for the first time since leaving Hadron Base, he felt a sudden powerful resurgence in his contempt for the old general.

'And if they don't come spilling out?' asked a dark-skinned colonel by the name of Meyers. He was tall and thin, vulture-like, and one of his eyes was a white orb without a hint of iris or pupil. He was one of Killian's men.

Colonel Vinnemann smiled his crooked smile and said, 'Then *Angel of the Apocalypse* will have to roll up and knock on their door.'

Bergen scanned the faces of the men seated in the tent and saw a few smiling at Vinnemann's remark, but the atmosphere was still heavy. No one had really expected this. They weren't prepared for any kind of extended siege. They were hundreds of kilometres from their forward base, and if they entered any kind of stalemate with the orks, their supply lines would be extremely vulnerable. If the orks had any kind of air power, bombing Red Gorge would cut the expeditionary force off from all contact with Balkar. The intelligence guiding the mission had been sketchy from the beginning – a patchwork of Mechanicus probe data, military maps dating back forty years, and Officio Strategos guesswork – but Bergen had never been so sharply aware of the entire mission's free-wheeling, underplanned nature as he was right now.

'So, a full frontal assault,' said Killian unenthusiastically. 'We'll be naked, mind you. All our machines racing forwards across open ground... If the Emperor isn't watching over us, it'll be a bloody massacre at mid-range. You all heard what Bussmann said about the number of cannon on the wall.'

'I think we can discount much of that,' said a scowling deViers. 'Half of the time, ork weaponry doesn't even work.'

'And the other half,' said Rennkamp, his eyes flashing, 'it rips our boys apart.'

DeViers looked suddenly furious, on the verge of throwing one of his rages, but the sheer number of men present and their quiet, concentrated manner seemed enough to quell the outburst before it got started.

That was close, thought Bergen. Rennkamp and Killian are really letting loose on him. Fine with me, but I'm not sure the colonels need to see it.

Bergen didn't disagree with his peers. They had merely voiced the thoughts that had been circling in his own head all this time. Here they all were, after so many days crossing bare sand and rock, chasing a relic that, in all likelihood, no longer existed, and before them was the last and greatest obstacle they would face. Beyond that towering wall of iron and steel, in a rocky valley somewhere at the foot of the Ishawar range, lay the end of this nightmare. Yarrick's tank would either be there or it wouldn't. In either case, breaking through the wall would bring a close to this whole endeavour. They could pull out. They could head for Armageddon, where the fighting really mattered.

'I say we do it,' said Bergen, suddenly committed. Every eye in the room turned towards him. 'A full frontal assault, hammering them with everything we have. If we concentrate our efforts on a small enough section, I think we can pull it off. I think we can break through.'

'Knew you'd see it my way,' said a delighted deViers, leaning across in his chair to slap Bergen on the shoulder.

Bergen fought not to flinch away from the general's hand.

What choice have I got? he thought bitterly. Throne forgive me if I want a quick end to this. It's your fault we're here at all, you glory-hunting old bastard. By the Emperor, I hope this is the last time I serve under you. With a bit of luck, it'll be the last time anyone does.

'Colonel Vinnemann, you'll lead the vanguard,' said deViers. 'I want your Shadowsword right up front, primed and ready. If the orks do rush out as expected, you will pull back to a safer distance and offer fire support under Major General Bergen's directions. But if the greenskins decide to play it safe, I want you ready to show them the Emperor's wrath. Understood?'

'You pick the gate, sir,' said Vinnemann, 'and my old girl will peel it apart. You'll see.'

Bergen felt he had to speak. He faced Vinnemann, but his words were for deViers. 'What the noble colonel is *not* telling you, general, is that such a shot will leave his tank utterly stationary for long seconds both before and after firing. The *Angel of the Apocalypse* will draw heavy enemy fire during that time.'

Vinnemann actually looked hurt, as if he thought Bergen was criticising him and his tank.

'She has more armour than any other machine in the army group,' he said defensively. 'She can shrug off whatever they throw at us. Besides,' he added matter-of-factly, 'if things get too heavy, we'll pop smoke.'

Bergen frowned.

'Then it's decided,' said General deViers, eager to move on. With two fingers, he tapped a sheet of crumpled parchment he had laid out on a small table in front of him. It was the map Marrenburg's scout had drawn. 'Now listen carefully, all of you. We'll be attacking this gate here. It's more isolated than the others, which will give us more time to react to any flanking manoeuvres. I expect they'll send troops out from a number of the nearest gates once we've engaged. Anyway, this is our target and I'm designating it *point alpha*. With the exception of Colonel Vinnemann, all officers ranked major or higher will stay behind this area here.' With a finger, he drew an imaginary line across the map where he believed the ork artillery would be unable to strike. 'I don't imagine the orks have anything that can reach quite this far out. I'll be coordinating the attack personally from my Chimera. Rennkamp, Killian, Bergen, you'll relay my orders to your respective divisions from your own vehicles.'

'Understood, sir,' said Killian.

Bergen didn't speak. He noticed a fresh gleam that had crept into the general's eyes.

'Then let's disperse, gentlemen,' deViers told the colonels in the tent. 'Prepare for the assault. Your divisional commanders will have more specifics for you within the hour. Dismissed.'

The regimental leaders saluted, turned, and marched out of the tent. Bergen considered following Vinnemann out for a private word, but deViers said, 'You three stay a while longer. I want your input on formations.'

What did Vinnemann think he was doing? Bergen wondered. When the orks spotted *Angel of the Apocalypse* sitting out there on the sand, they would hit her with everything they had. She was one hell of a target, easily three times the size of the vehicles that would be escorting her, and, just like at Karavassa, she would be utterly immobile while her capacitors charged for firing. The blast from her Volcano cannon would draw every ork eye on the wall to her, and after the shot, the crew would need valuable seconds to switch the generator back over to power the treads again. Seconds counted for everything when the shells were falling all around you. Popping smoke would only help shield the *Angel of the Apocalypse* if the wind stayed low. If it picked up, it would blow the cover straight off of her.

Vinnemann knew all this, of course. He just wasn't about to let any of it stop him doing his duty. Bergen wondered if perhaps the colonel's pain had become too much for him after all these years. Was the man growing impatient for an honourable death? Throne, thought Bergen, I hope it's not that.

CHAPTER NINETEEN

THE CHAOS OF battle erupted the moment the orks spotted them. The wall *was* manned, as General deViers had known it would be. In fact, there were many thousands of greenskins on it, a huge garrison force, and they leapt to man their long-guns as soon as they noticed the approaching dust cloud of the speeding Cadian armour.

The tanks of the 81st Armoured Regiment moved in loose formation, a broad fighting line with van Droi's Gunheads on the far right flank. Captain Immrich's 1st Company ran escort to Colonel Vinnemann's massive Shadowsword.

It was midday, searing hot, and the thick, muddy sky churned and roiled above the battlefield.

'Charge!' yelled van Droi to his tank commanders over the vox.

The Gunheads roared towards the wall, tearing up the ground that lay between them and their foes. The entire strength of Vinnemann's regiment was being thrown at the wall in one massive surge: ten companies of Imperial tanks, though no company could boast of being at full strength. Every single one had taken losses on the journey east. They were still a force to be reckoned with, however, still something special to see as they tore across the sand. Bursts of black smoke announced heavy firing from the parapets, and the hot desert air filled with deep booming thunder. Great black-rimmed craters began appearing in the sand where the first artillery rounds struck. The orks could hammer the Cadians from this distance with impunity, and the constant barrage soon claimed its first victims. Three of Lieutenant Keissler's 2nd Company tanks were torn apart by tremendous explosions. They were the first of many to fall. Keissler rallied his surviving crews, keeping them in the line.

The men that died at least died quickly. The ork shells were huge and heavy, packed with devastating amounts of explosive. The tanks they struck were smashed apart by the blasts. There was no brewing up, no burning alive in steel coffins, just a sudden, brutal end. Three black husks, barely recognisable as Leman Russ tanks, sat pouring out smoke while other tanks surged past them to continue the push.

The orks had found their range, and Colonel Vinnemann ordered all companies to fan out. Bunching together, with the full weight of the ork defences raining down on them, was suicide.

There was still some way to go before the Cadians entered effective firing range. Even in Golgotha's gravity, a standard Leman Russ battle cannon could take out targets at a distance of over two kilometres, but the ork artillery was pounding them from twice that. Closing the gap at speed was paramount.

Like her sister tanks, *Last Rites II* roared over the low dunes with all her hatches closed. Wulfe sat in the rear of the turret basket, peering through the vision blocks that ringed the rim of his cupola, shouting instructions to his crew. 'That's it, Metzger. Keep her speed up.'

Looking left along the Cadian line, he saw van Droi's *Foe-Breaker* to his immediate right. Beyond her, scores of other tanks raced forwards. It was quite a sight. Suddenly, bright light stabbed at his eyes and he grunted in pain. When he opened them again, he was glad to see van Droi's tank still at his side. He turned to look behind and saw a burning black wreck. Someone else had been hit. Thick black smoke poured outwards and upwards.

That could have been us, thought Wulfe.

Metzger was squeezing every bit of speed he could from the old girl, pushing her forward at full tilt, her engine roaring like a mad carnotaur, her suspension bouncing and juddering, tossing the men in the turret basket around like dolls. There were more flashes of light, more bone-shaking booms. Wulfe saw two more wrecks drop from the Cadian line, fountains of dirt and rock exploding on all sides as the greenskins continued to rain shells on the rapidly advancing Imperial force. Van Droi's Vanquisher had pulled ahead. Wulfe saw her swerve violently to one side, just missing a huge pillar of fire and dust that geysered upwards into the air. Van Droi's driver, Nalzigg, really was good, thought Wulfe. *Foe-Breaker* had escaped destruction by a hair's breadth. Metzger must have seen it, too. A second later, he swerved to avoid ditching *Last Rites II* into the crater caused by the explosion.

Beans banged his head on the metal housing of his gun scope. 'Damn it!'

'Watch yourself,' shouted Wulfe over the cacophony of battle. 'Keep your eyes pressed to the scope's padding.'

Even over the intercom, it was difficult to hear each other. The artillery fire, explosions and engine noise were deafening.

'I want this crate ready to fire the moment we make range,' said Wulfe. 'High explosives. We've got to take out those wall-guns so the infantry don't get minced following us in.'

Up ahead and to the left, some of the tanks from the other companies had pressed forward into firing range, and their guns began to answer the orks'. The tanks were travelling too fast to fire with any real accuracy, but Wulfe saw bright blossoms of fire burst into life as shells hit the wall. It didn't look like they were very effective. The orks' answering barrage, however, managed to destroy a number of tanks from the 5th and 8th Companies.

'By the frakking Eye!' spat Wulfe. 'How can we expect to hit anything in a full sprint? Who conceived this bloody plan?'

Metzger spoke over the intercom. 'We just made range!'

'Beans,' said Wulfe, 'line her up on one of those wall-guns. The bigger the better.'

'Got one,' said Beans. 'Halfway up the wall on our two o'clock. How about it? The gun-port to the upper left of the central gate, sarge?'

Wulfe scanned the wall and found it. It was one of the biggest barrels visible. A good target. The muzzle was so damned wide a man could have sat comfortably inside it.

'Nice,' said Wulfe. 'Siegler, high-explosive. Beans, zero in. It'll be a tough shot. We'll have to fire on the move.'

'I can do it, sarge,' said Beans.

Siegler slammed a shell into the battle cannon's breech, yanked the locking lever and yelled, 'She's lit!'

'Metzger,' said Wulfe, 'drop her down into third but, for Throne's sake, keep us moving. Steady as you can.'

'Aye, sir,' said Metzger.

Last Rites II slowed abruptly, and the tanks on either side began to pull further away from her.

Wulfe barely noticed. His eyes were locked to the target. When he felt that Metzger had her steady in third, he called, 'Fire!'

'Brace,' shouted Beans, and he stamped on the firing pedal with his right foot. *Last Rites II* rocked backwards with the blast. Three plumes of fire burst from her cannon, one from the mouth of the barrel and one from each of the apertures in either side of the muzzle brake.

The turret basket filled with the coppery stink of spent fyceline propellant. Wulfe didn't give it a thought. He was watching the ork wall-cannon. A fraction of a second after *Last Rites II* spat her shell, a yellow ball of fire burst into existence just below the wall-cannon's firing port. Pieces of burning metal showered the sand at the foot of the wall. Black smoke moved on the breeze. When it cleared, Wulfe saw...

Frak!

'It's a miss,' he reported to the crew. 'Metzger! Floor it! Take her back up to full speed. We have to keep moving.'

He took his eyes away from the vision blocks for a second and saw Beans hammering a fist onto his thigh.

'Damn it!' shouted the youngster. 'By the blasted Eye.'

Wulfe leaned forward and gripped his shoulder. 'Beat yourself up later, son. Right now, I want another shot lined up. Siegler? High-ex. Now!'

The loader didn't waste any time confirming. He rammed another shell home, yanked the locking lever and shouted, 'Lit, sarge!'

Come on, Beans, thought Wulfe. Concentrate, boy.

'Metzger,' said Wulfe, 'drop to third.'

'You've got it, sarge,' said the driver.

'Adjust your shot, Beans,' Wulfe told the gunner. 'Up a little. A little more. We're closer now. You ready?'

'I have the shot,' said Beans.

'Take it!' said Wulfe.

There was a deep boom and a rush of pungent smoke. *Last Rites II* reared up on her treads with the power of the recoil, and then hit the sand again with a rough bounce. The main gun's breech slid back and dumped the spent shell casing in the brass catcher on the floor.

Wulfe held on tight, eyes scanning the wall through his vision blocks. The massive gun-port Beans had been aiming for erupted in bright red flame and black smoke. Debris exploded outwards. Whooping and cheering filled the compartment.

'That's more like it!' shouted Wulfe. 'Metzger, back up to fifth, now!'

The engine roared. The base of the wall was no more than a kilometre away. The other companies were already slowing to blast every last gun-port they could see. Fire and smoke poured from the wall's gun-ports and towers. Leman Russ Conquerors and Demolishers from the 8th and 9th Companies were lobbing shells up onto the parapets, too, desperate to take out the artillery pieces before they could shred the infantry vehicles that would follow in the wake of the tanks.

Black smoke billowed up into the sky from all directions. Angry fires blazed all around.

From the corner of his eye, Wulfe saw a light blinking on his vox-board. He hit the toggle. It was van Droi.

'Company leader to all tanks. We've been ordered to peel right. It doesn't look like the orks are coming out of their own accord after all. Colonel Vinnemann is about to kick their door in.'

'Metzger,' said Wulfe, 'take us right, parallel with the wall. *Angel of the Apocalypse* is moving up.'

VINNEMANN'S MASSIVE SHADOWSWORD had so far enjoyed the cover of the dust clouds kicked up by the other machines as it rolled forward, moving into position to attack point alpha.

One shot, thought Vinnemann. We'll have one shot at this. We absolutely must force a breach.

Over the vox, he head Major General Bergen say, 'Are you in position, colonel?'

'A few more seconds, sir,' Vinnemann replied. Then his driver reported over the intercom that they had position. The gunner confirmed line-of-sight. Vinnemann voxed back to Bergen. 'In position now, sir. Readying to fire.'

'We're counting on you, Kochatkis,' said Bergen.

Vinnemann heard Bergen notify all units on the divisional command channel, 'Division to all armour, be advised. *Angel of the Apocalypse* is about to fire. I repeat, *Angel* is about to fire.'

On the tank's intercom, Vinnemann told Schwartz, his engineer, 'Switch all power to main gun. Tell me when she's charged.'

'Yes, sir.'

'Vamburg,' said Vinnemann, addressing his gunner. 'Full blast, full duration. Let's turn that gate to vapour.'

'No worries, sir. Ready to light it up.'

'Capacitors full, sir!' reported Schwartz

'Right, Vamburg,' said Vinnemann. 'You heard him. Do it!'

'Brace for firing!' shouted the gunner.

A hum filled the air inside the tank, like thousands of voices joined in a single tone that rose until it drowned out all else. A charge passed through Vinnemann's twisted body as he felt the space around him vibrate. The pain he usually felt melted away for a moment as the tone rose higher and higher. Then, suddenly, the whole bulk of the Shadowsword shook as if it had been kicked by a giant. Blazing white light burst from her cannon, lancing straight across the battlefield, striking the massive ork gate dead centre.

The air shook with a massive thunderous crack. The iron gate glowed blindingly bright for an instant, and then seemed to vanish completely just as if it had never been there at all. The armoured wall all around it glowed white, then yellow, then orange and red. Gobs of molten metal began to rain down on the ground. Seconds later, the armour plating had cooled again and solidified. It looked like melted wax.

The wall was breached. The 18th Army Group had its passage, but the battle was just beginning. Beyond the hole, ork structures burned, damaged by the destructive energy that spilled through from the Shadowsword's powerful blast.

Vinnemann surveyed the results of his crew's efforts and opened a vox-link to Major General Bergen. 'Objective achieved, sir. Point alpha is open. The wall has been breached. But we must secure it at once.'

Bergen, in turn, voxed the rest of his forces. 'Division Command to all units. Move up and secure the breach at all costs. I repeat, secure the breach at once.'

Through his vision blocks, Vinnemann saw scores of tanks wheel around and race for the gap he had just made.

'Schwartz,' he called over his intercom, 'all power to the main drive. We've got to move.'

Already, the ork artillery had started cutting a deadly path of dirt and fire towards *Angel of the Apocalypse*. More and more of the ork guns swivelled to focus on her.

'Vamburg,' said Vinnemann. 'Fine shot. But get some bloody smoke up, will you? Bekker, pull us straight back as soon as you can. We're a sitting target out here.'

'All power back to main drive, sir,' reported Schwartz. 'Ready to move her on your say.'

'Good man,' said Vinnemann. 'You heard him, Bekker. Get us out of here.'

A trio of heavy shells struck the earth just in front of the *Angel's* hull, making a tight triple-beat of explosions. The blast waves rocked her on her suspension. Vinnemann heard pieces of rock raining down on the roof of the turret. 'Damned close. The next lot will hit us for sure if we don't get the hell out of here. Move it!'

The mighty Shadowsword rumbled and shuddered as her giant drive sprockets started turning in reverse, but she weighed three hundred and eight tonnes. Accelerating from a dead stop wasn't exactly effortless.

As she started rumbling backwards, Vinnemann heard Bergen hailing him again on the vox.

'Division to Armour Command. Can you hear me, Kochatkis?'

'Go ahead, sir,' said Vinnemann.

'You have to pull back faster. Ork fighter-bombers are inbound from the south. They're coming in fast.'

'From the south, sir?'

'Affirmative,' replied Bergen. 'Throne knows where the hell they launched from, but, judging by their angle of approach, they didn't come from behind the wall.'

'You think the orks have long-range comms, sir?' asked Vinnemann. 'Could the orks on the wall have called in an airstrike from somewhere?'

'If they have comms with that kind of range here on Golgotha,' said Bergen, 'then they're a damned sight better off than we are. And I'll be asking the tech-priests why. But listen, Kochatkis, your crate is the biggest thing we're fielding out there. Expect lots of unwelcome attention. I'm sending some of our Hydras forward in support of you. We've already lost one of the Vulcans. They weren't designed for dogfighting. They can't handle anything with that kind of airspeed.'

'Understood, sir,' said Vinnemann. 'We're pulling back as fast as we can, but the anti-air cover would be much appreciated.'

'The Hydras will be with you in a few minutes, Kochatkis,' said Bergen. 'Inform me when they reach you.'

'I will, sir. Armour Command out.'

Bombers from the south, thought Vinnemann. Didn't Stromm and van Droi report a great ork host moving in that direction?

'MOVE IN, MOVE in,' shouted Wulfe over the intercom.

Metzger gunned *Last Rites II* forward, and they passed the melted edges of the ork wall. The sight that greeted Wulfe was of a place in turmoil. Shoddy ork buildings were everywhere, each an ugly mishmash of rusting steel poles and sheets of corrugated metal all bolted together at odd angles, looped by barbed wire and painted with bright glyphs of white on red. Greenskin foot soldiers were everywhere, crowded onto raised platforms or charging in great tides over the sandy ground, blazing away at the intruding tanks with everything they had.

Most of the weapons they carried were heavy stubbers and flame-throwers, oversized cleavers and axes, none of them much good against fifteen centimetres of heavy armour, but Wulfe knew that far more dangerous weapons were available to the Golgothan orks. His eyes scanned the roaring mobs, frantically searching for signs of the thick, tube-like weapons that had brewed up Siemens's tank. It was an impossible task. There were too many of them, and too much movement all around.

Wulfe didn't have time to make a count of how many tanks from the 81st had survived to pass the breach. He had some sense that the number might be around fifty, meaning that fully half of the regiment's armour had been lost in getting this far. As he thought this, trails of bright flame streaked out from one of the tower-like constructions and struck a tank to his left. The tank exploded in a spectacular ball of orange flame.

'Shaped charges,' he yelled over the vox to any of the other tank commanders that might be listening. 'They've got anti-tank weaponry!'

The vox-chatter he heard back told him which tank had been hit.

'*Dark Majestic* is down,' shouted someone. 'Anti-tank fire from ten o'clock high.'

Dark Majestic was a 3rd Company machine, one of Lieutenant Albrecht's.

'Beans,' called Wulfe over the intercom. 'Traverse left. Ork tower. Three hundred metres. High-explosive.'

Siegler heaved a shell into the main gun's breech. 'She's lit.'

Wulfe tapped Beans on the left shoulder, twice, a sign to fire at will.

'Brace!' shouted the gunner.

Last Rites II shook, coughing fire from her muzzle, and the ork tower disintegrated spectacularly. Bodies rained to the ground amid the storm of burning junk.

'Eat that!' shouted Beans.

'That's a kill,' said Wulfe. 'Nice shot, son. But don't get cocky. Traverse right. Target ork tower, five hundred metres. High-ex. Fire at will.'

Siegler slung another shell into place. As the traverse motors hummed, turning the main gun towards the specified target, Wulfe took the briefest second to check the rear. He saw the burning wrecks of Imperial tanks on all sides. Black bodies, too small to be orks, littered the ground, their clothes still on fire. He cursed.

Most of the regiment's tanks were still fighting desperately, however, holding back the seething tide of orks with booming volleys of explosive fire that killed countless hundreds with every passing moment.

Thank the Throne, thought Wulfe, that most of the greenskin bastards only have blades and guns. With the exception of those carrying explosives, the ork infantry were largely powerless against the might of Imperial armour. Their wall-mounted cannon and artillery pieces were useless back here. The Cadian tanks were gradually pushing out from the breach, forming a wide semi-circular perimeter so that the infantry vehicles pouring in behind them had room to deploy. Wulfe saw half-tracks, Chimeras and trucks skid to a halt behind him and start unloading men.

The soldiers immediately added their fire to that of the tanks, and the death toll among the orks mounted faster and faster. Torrents of stubber and bolter fire blazed out from the Chimeras and halftracks, and the Cadians continued to gain ground.

Keep it up, thought Wulfe. We're beating them. By the Golden Throne, we're beating them.

Then he heard van Droi's voice on the company command channel.

Ork armour had been spotted approaching from the north along the inside of the wall. Wulfe turned his head in that direction and caught a glimpse of hulking black machines just as Siegler shouted, 'She's lit!'

'Brace!' shouted Beans.

The tank rocked and the turret basket filled with the sharp stink of propellant once again. Wulfe quickly checked and saw that Beans had made another direct hit. The tower collapsed sideways, spilling green bodies all around it.

'Good work, soldier,' Wulfe told the gunner. 'No time to rest, though. We've got enemy heavy armour coming in. Siegler, I want armour-piercing up the spout. Beans, traverse left.'

Rumbling through the smoke, fire and dusty haze, three hulking metal monsters emerged. Wulfe gaped. The ork machines had been fashioned to look like some kind of carnivorous creature. Their insane alien creators had given them metal jaws with long steel tusks that clanged together as they gnashed. They were bristling with cannon and secondary armaments. Wulfe could only imagine the fear such machines might drive into infantrymen, but, to *Last Rites II*, the ork tanks were big fat targets, begging to be turned into burning scrap.

Wulfe had every intention of obliging.

His fellow tank commanders clearly had the same idea. As the monstrous ork armour closed, all three machines rumbling and spluttering their way along a wide avenue that ran parallel to the inside of the wall, the Leman Russ tanks loosed a stuttering volley of armour-piercing shells.

Most of the shells struck home, and one of the ork machines stopped dead in its tracks. The greenskin crew began bailing out at speed, leaping from high hatches to land on the heads and shoulders of the ork infantry that surged around the treads of their machine. They weren't quick enough. The magazine inside the tank detonated seconds later, and both the escaping crew and the orks on which they had dropped were roasted to death in a massive rush of red fire.

Wulfe heard Captain Immrich broadcasting on the regimental channel.

'Good kill, armour,' he said. 'But the other two aren't taking it very well.'

The other monstrosities brought all their cannon to bear on the Leman Russ machines closest to them and unleashed a ground-shaking fusillade of high-explosive shells. Two Imperial tanks – one a Conqueror, the other a Destroyer – erupted into fire almost simultaneously. The Destroyer's onboard plasma-containment field lost integrity almost immediately. It exploded with a spectacular and lethal burst of energy that turned a dozen Cadian infantrymen nearby into piles of ash.

Wulfe yelled out in protest as he watched. He heard Captain Immrich's voice on the vox.

'Armour down,' the man was yelling. 'I want those bloody abominations taken out, now! That's an order!'

Wulfe wondered who the dead tank crews were. There hadn't been any chance to read the names on their crates before they were brewed up. There would be time to find out after the battle, if he lived through it. For some men, the absence of friends would become brutally, painfully apparent after the fighting was done. Thinking of this, he looked around for Viess and Holtz. Were they still alive? Still fighting?

They were. *Old Smashbones* was blasting away at a sturdy-looking ork tower on the far right. *Steelhearted II* was standing parallel with van Droi's tank, its turret slowly turning to face the ork armour.

Wulfe realised that his own crate had a clear line-of-sight on the right-hand target.

'Beans,' he said, 'target the one on the right. See that plate of armour just right of the main gun's mantlet? The one with the glyph?'

'The skull-looking thing?' said Beans. 'Yeah, I see it.'

'There's a damned good chance that armour is protecting the gunner's station. If we can put one through it...'

Beans didn't answer. He hit the traverse pedal, already busy lining up the main gun. Electric motors hummed as he adjusted elevation. He had to get it right. A miss might very well mean more Cadian deaths.

'Lit,' said Siegler.

Beans was just about to call out *Brace!* when the whole tank was suddenly shunted backwards about three metres. Wulfe shook his head, trying to lose the ringing sound in his ears. They had been hit right on the front armour, the glacis plate.

'Damn,' spat Wulfe, simultaneously checking himself for injuries. 'Metzger, you all right?'

'More armour approaching from front-right, sarge,' reported the driver. 'They look like looted Leman Russ.'

'Try to hit their treads with the lascannon,' ordered Wulfe. 'Buy us some time.'

The vox was filled with reports of the new machines' approach. Beans was already reacquiring his original target. His crosshairs were quickly re-centred on the skull-glyph that decorated the multi-cannoned monster to the north.

'I have it, sarge,' he said.

'Take the shot,' said Wulfe.

'Brace!' called Beans, and stamped on the floor trigger.

The shot hit the ork machine exactly where it was supposed to, and Beans let out a whoop of joy, but there was no explosion, no sudden burst of flame, just a neat black hole the size of a grapefruit right in the centre of the skull-glyph's forehead. The ork tank's turret stopped moving. It stopped firing, too.

'That's a kill,' said Wulfe, slapping Beans on the back. Quickly, he turned his attention to the machines Metzger had reported. Bright spears of lascannon fire were blazing out from *Last Rites II*'s hull-mounted weapon. The Cadian tanks on either side had also turned their attention to the newcomers, while others blasted the last monster in the avenue to the north, reducing it to twisted, blazing metal.

Wulfe was impressed. Beans was doing well. That last kill had been a fine shot. His men were functioning as a unit. This was the way it was supposed to be. Nothing else weighed on his mind but the heat of battle and the drive to win. No ghosts. No gangers. He felt less burdened than he had in a long time.

One of the orks' looted Leman Russ tanks soaked up a lascannon blast and lurched forward, coughing flame from its main gun. Dirt and smoke exploded into the air just a few metres to the right of Wulfe's machine.

'Gunner, traverse right,' Wulfe barked over the intercom. 'Ork armour, eight hundred metres and closing. Armour-piercing. Fire at will!'

CHAPTER TWENTY

'SAY AGAIN, EAGLE Three,' said Bergen into the mouthpiece of his vox-set. 'Say again.'

'Eagle Three to Command,' said the sharp, high voice of the female pilot. 'Eagles One, Two and Four are down. Where the hell is that Hydra support? I can't outrun the damned ork jets. And I can't keep them off the *Angel* on my own.'

'The Hydras are almost there,' said Bergen. 'Listen, Eagle Three. I know you're up against it out there, but just hold on. We'll have triple-A support for you in a few seconds. You should be able to see them now.'

'Two on my tail. Can't shake them. Wait... By the Golden Throne!'

'What is it, Eagle Three?'

'Command, I have visual on a massive ork horde closing in from the south. A huge number of vehicles. The land is black with them, sir.'

'Confirm, Eagle Three. Significant enemy force advancing from the south.'

The vox hissed.

'Eagle Three,' said Bergen, already sensing she wasn't there, 'confirm enemy force in the south. Eagle Three, respond. Oh, for frak's sake!'

Anger welled up inside him. Bergen had fought alongside women before. There were Cadian regiments entirely composed of the so-called fairer sex, though they tended to serve on Cadia's Interior Guard rather than off-world. They were as tough and ruthless as any male

247

soldiers he had known, but his attitudes were still old-fashioned in some respects. The knowledge that a woman attached to Operation Thunderstorm had just been killed by orks stung him with unusual sharpness. Eagle Three was Navy, and there was no love lost between the Navy and the Guard, but she had hung on bravely to the end, as brave as any of his tankers.

If he lived through this, he swore he would try to find out her name, to make sure she and her fellow Vulcan crews were honoured.

Commodore Galbraithe will have to be told, he thought. Throne help the poor bastard tasked with that.

Of more immediate concern, of course, was Eagle Three's last report: a significant ork force moving north towards their position. It had to be the host that Stromm and van Droi had reported. How fast were they moving? When would they arrive? He couldn't know. And all the forces at his disposal were already engaged with the orks on and inside the wall. He had to tell deViers. But first...

'10th Division Command to Armour,' he voxed. 'Are you there, Kochatkis?'

'I'm here, sir,' said Vinnemann. 'Go ahead.'

'You just lost close support from the Vulcans. Thought you should know.'

'I saw that, sir. The fuselage hit just a few hundred metres away. Looks like those bombers are swinging around for a run on us.'

'Can you see those Hydras? They should be all around you by now.'

'They've just joined us, sir,' said Vinnemann. 'We lost two, but four of them are still in the game. The wind is stripping our smoke cover off and the ork artillery isn't missing us by much. But the Hydras will be a real surprise for those bombers the next time they make a pass.'

'Let's hope so,' said Bergen, 'but there's something else I have to tell you. We're being flanked from the south.'

'Flanked, sir?' asked Vinnemann. 'What kind of numbers?'

'Can't confirm that, but from the sounds of it, far more than we can reasonably handle.'

'Our forces have breached, sir,' said Vinnemann. 'There's no way we can fight on two fronts and still push through to reach *The Fortress of Arrogance*. What does the general say?'

'I'm going to report to him now, Kochatkis,' said Bergen. 'Just wanted you to know.'

'Appreciate that, sir. Armour, out.'

DEVIERS EXPLODED WHEN Bergen told him the news.

'They're bloody *what*?' he demanded.

'They're flanking us from the south, sir,' replied Bergen. 'Last transmission from Eagle Three stated the land was black with them. Serious numbers, sir. We're about to find ourselves between a rock and a hard place.'

'By the blasted Eye of Terror!' raged deViers. 'Why now? We've just gained the breach.'

'If I might suggest something, sir,' said Major General Killian.

'Out with it, Klotus,' snapped deViers.

'Well, sir. It seems to me that the only place we can hope to fight them and win would be Red Gorge. We'd be cutting it fine in terms of the time left to us, but, if we could effect a retreat to the canyon just before the second ork force arrives, we could fight them on a much smaller single front.'

Rennkamp nodded. 'Straight out of the Tactica. Engage a superior force at a bottleneck. It would give us more control.'

DeViers's eyes were so wide and bug-like with anger that Bergen thought they might pop out of his head. 'Retreat to the canyon? And turn this whole thing into a protracted fight? I suppose you think we should just let the orks patch their wall up, too, so we can waste time and resources attacking it all over again? You bloody clods!'

Killian and Rennkamp each took a step backwards. 'You can't mean to fight it out on open land, sir,' said Killian. 'It'll be a bloody whitewash. A massacre.'

'I'm afraid I agree with them on that count, sir,' said Bergen. 'Our expedition will end here if we engage in a stand up fight. You can forget your place in the history books if that happens.'

The last sentence seemed to surprise deViers. He looked like he had been slapped. He turned on Bergen, hissing, 'What would you have me do, Gerard? Call a general retreat? Should we run back to Balkar with our tails between our legs? No holy tank? No glory of any kind? I'll die before I let that happen. Nothing will get in the way of my success here. Do you understand? Do you all get it?'

Bergen thought he understood only too well. Whatever happened, it was deViers's obsession with glory that would decide their fate. For a long moment, no one said anything. It was a metallic voice from the entrance to the tent that broke the spell of silence. Tech-Magos Sennesdiar stood there, his huge, angular bulk a dark silhouette. Just beyond him, standing outside in the daylight, Tech-Adepts Armadron and Xephous waited patiently.

'There will be no retreat,' Sennesdiar boomed at them in Gothic. 'There will be no going back to Balkar.'

Bergen turned.

'With respect, magos,' he said. 'That decision rests with the general.'

Sennesdiar stooped a little so that he could fully enter the tent. Then he moved towards them, stopping a few metres away, dominating them with his size, causing them all to look up at him.

'I did not mean to suggest otherwise, gentlemen. But some moments ago, Adept Armadron received a landline transmission from Balkar. Our forward base is under assault. The orks have managed to breach Balkar's walls. The garrison commander does not expect his forces to last another hour.'

'They what?' gasped deViers. 'Balkar is under siege?'

'As are our bases at Hadron, Karavassa and Tyrellis, if word from Balkar is to be believed. Great numbers of orks have assaulted our outposts from the north and south. It is clear that the orks have found a way to communicate effectively over long range and are coordinating their attacks.'

DeViers looked ready to fall down. For all his rejuvenat treatments, he suddenly seemed every bit the ninety-one-year-old man he was. 'Coordinated attacks?' he muttered. 'By orks?'

'I think our current dilemma confirms the possibility quite solidly,' said Killian. 'The orks on the wall called in fighter-bombers, after all.'

'Yes,' said Sennesdiar. 'The attacks are most certainly coordinated. The question I wish to have answered, however, is what the good general intends to do next.'

'We should go to Balkar's aid at once,' said Rennkamp. 'How can we even consider going on with our supply lines interrupted?'

Bergen shook his head. 'By the time we get back to Balkar, it'll be too late to make a difference anyway.'

Killian agreed. 'There'll be no one left, not if the outpost walls have already been compromised. Damn it all. All those medicae personnel, the sick and wounded...'

Bergen scowled. He knew good men back there, men who had been too sick to go on, and women, too. He didn't want to think about all those gentle medicae nurses left to face the savagery of the orks without hope of salvation.

'There will be no retreat,' said General deViers icily. 'Understand that now.'

'We of the Adeptus Mechanicus,' said Sennesdiar, 'wish to recommend that this expeditionary force continues to push east. *The Fortress of Arrogance* has never been closer. The general's glorious quest is still well within acceptable feasibility parameters.'

'You've got to be joking,' said Rennkamp. 'General, please. I think Klotus is right. If we can't go back to Balkar, at the very least we need to fall back to Red Gorge and dig in there. Fight the orks on our own terms.'

Killian nodded emphatically. He looked at the magos. 'Once we've secured the gorge, we could send up one of the orbital beacons to call for evacuation.'

'Absolutely not,' raged General deViers. 'Magos, the beacons must only be used if and when we secure *The Fortress of Arrogance*. Is that clear?'

Bergen studied the general's face, thinking how disappointed he was that the man he had once looked up to had become so self-serving and obsessive. Despite all that, however, he felt that the general was right. To get bogged down in a long-term engagement at Red Gorge would do them no good.

'Neither I nor my adepts have any intention of utilising the beacons until the moment is right, general. You may be assured of that. You do not intend to leave without your prize. So, too, it is with us. No one will be lifted from Golgotha until our objective is met.'

Bergen read between the lines. He heard the unspoken words. At no time had the magos said that his objectives were the same as the general's, but whatever the tech-priests wanted, it suited them to support deViers. He saw that fact give strength to the general now. The old man stood taller, the years falling from him once again.

'Every last damned one of you,' deViers said. 'When you get back to your vehicles, I want you to tell our forward elements to hold that breach at all costs. And get every other man and machine under my command through it before the orks get here from the south. That means the fuel trucks, the water trucks, food, supplies, munitions, every last damn bit of it. I want everything we have, everything we'll need, through that breach and heading east towards *The Fortress of Arrogance* before the ork reinforcements are on us. Is that understood?'

Rennkamp mumbled something incoherent.

'I said is that understood?' hissed deViers.

'Understood, sir,' said the three major generals.

Tech-Magos Sennesdiar didn't wait to be dismissed. He turned and left the tent, saying nothing more.

'You're mad, sir,' said Rennkamp. 'You do realise that?'

DeViers looked at him and grinned. 'Mad, Aaron? Or inspired?'

It's a thin line between the two, thought Bergen. He felt miserable. He had known for a long time that deViers would get them all killed for his own sake: Balkar lost, supply lines cut, every major outpost they had won under siege by the greenskins. It was worse even than he had imagined it would be, but still *The Fortress of Arrogance* pulled the general on relentlessly, and with him, the men and machines of the 18th Army Group.

'You'll see that I'm right, gentlemen,' said deViers. 'It's odds like these that make legends of men. We can still find Yarrick's tank. It awaits us not far from here. And one day, all of the Imperium will know our story.'

No they won't, thought Bergen. Because none of us will survive this to tell it.

DeViers dismissed them, and, after a salute that lacked any sincerity whatsoever, Bergen returned to his Chimera. The men of his division were still out there, fighting for their lives, fighting to hold the breach in the ork wall so that the infantry could keep pouring through, helping to secure more and more ground on the other side.

If he and the other divisional commanders could just get everyone through before the orks from the south moved into range, then maybe, just maybe, they *could* run east. With luck, they might stay ahead of the orks for a while. They might even reach the supposed coordinates of Yarrick's tank.

Bergen hoped he survived that long. He hoped the tank *was* there, despite his doubts. He wanted to know that the dead had fallen for something greater than an old man's self-importance.

In the back of *Pride of Caedus*, he hit a toggle on his vox-caster and opened a link to Colonel Vinnemann.

'Armour, this is Division.'

No answer. Bergen felt his skin crawl.

'Armour Command,' he voxed, 'this is Divisional Command. Respond, please.'

Nothing but static.

'Damn it, Vinnemann, respond. That's an order, you hear?'

Words tumbled over and over in his mind, like a mantra: *don't let it be, don't let it be*.

Perhaps there was just something wrong with the *Angel's* vox.

Emperor, let it be that, he pleaded.

He switched channels, contacting Colonel Marrenburg, who was overseeing the artillery companies not far from deViers's forward command tent. 'Marrenburg, can you get a visual on *Angel of the Apocalypse*? I can't raise Vinnemann on the vox.'

Marrenburg sounded like a different man when he answered, and Bergen realised that his fears were well-founded.

'It was the ork bombers, sir,' said the colonel. 'The Hydras got most of them, but Vinnemann's tank took too many direct hits. We just took the last one down, but not before it managed to deliver a final payload. Not much left of the *Angel of the Apocalypse* now, sir. Throne rest the souls of all those who crewed her.'

Bergen's mouth went dry. He was speechless. He thought of Vinnemann, of the hunched little man who had endured so much pain, so much struggle just to keep on fighting. Few men Bergen had ever met could be said to embody the Cadian spirit of honour and resilience so well. His eyes began to sting, and his throat felt tight. He would miss Kochatkis Vinnemann. The unrelenting colonel had gone beyond the call of duty long ago. Perhaps now, his soul would be reunited with that of the wife he had spent so long avenging. He had more than earned his peace.

The 81st Armoured Regiment's second-in-command would have to take over. That was Captain Immrich.

Bergen would promote Immrich later… if he was still alive.

CHAPTER TWENTY-ONE

CAPTAIN IMMRICH WAS alive, and he was working damned hard to stay that way. He was doing a fine job of it, too, and of gaining ground as he led the tanks of the 81st Armoured Regiment against the ork hordes that swarmed towards them from almost every direction.

Under Immrich's command, the Imperial armour kept pushing out beyond the wall, and the space they created behind them became filled with ever greater numbers of Chimeras, halftracks, Thirty-Sixers full of troops, and Sentinel walkers that added the firepower of their autocannon to the battle, slaughtering hundreds of greenskin filth with great sweeps of fire.

The ground was a carpet of smoking metal, big brown bodies and raw red meat. Ork carcasses covered every inch of sand and rock. The Cadian tanks pulped them as they rolled forward. There was no way to avoid them. The bodies were everywhere. Treads of black iron became slick and shiny and red. Only the filter-masks worn by the Cadians protected them from the stench. Without the masks, it would have been impossible to breathe without vomiting.

Even with all his hatches locked up tight, Wulfe's nose crinkled in disgust as the smell of so much death permeated his turret, competing with the powerful combined stink of oil, sweat and fyceline.

Last Rites II had knocked out three ramshackle ork machines already, and Beans was swinging the turret around on a fourth that was approaching from front-left, when Wulfe heard Immrich's voice on the vox-link. It sounded different, drained, as if something had sapped the life out of the man. He sounded lost. 'All units, listen up. This is Captain Immrich. New orders from General deViers. All tanks are to focus on carving and holding a corridor east. The rest of the army group is coming through behind us. When they're clear, I'll give the word. I want all tanks to fall in behind them and cover the column's rear.'

We're running east, thought Wulfe. Why the frak aren't we solidifying our position here first? The orks will close in behind us and harry our flanks if we run now. Does the general mean to let them cut off our route back to Balkar?

'There's more,' said Immrich. 'I've just been placed in temporary command of the regiment. Colonel Vinnemann… Colonel Vinnemann has gone to meet the Emperor.'

Wulfe reeled backwards in his seat. It couldn't be true. It just couldn't be. Vinnemann *was* the regiment. To every man who knew him, he was as permanent as the stars. What would the regiment be without its guiding light, its living symbol of honour and duty? He felt the news hit him like a physical blow.

The sudden boom of his tank's main gun shook him back into himself. The turret jolted. The smell of burnt propellant tugged his nose. He checked the vision blocks and saw a heap of burning black metal straight ahead. The main gun was still pointing directly at it.

Beans whooped with satisfaction. 'How many points do I get for a truck full of the bastards?'

'Metzger,' said Wulfe, ignoring the gunner's celebration, 'wheel us around to the north. We're to hold a corridor here for the others to come through.'

'Aye, sir,' said Metzger, and the tank started to move.

'Siegler, Beans, keep that rate of fire up,' said Wulfe. 'Armour-piercing. Focus on their armour. Our infantry can deal with their foot soldiers.'

He hoped that were true. So far, they'd given the orks a damned hard time getting anywhere near the Cadian tanks. Every vehicle that careered towards them had been lit up like fireworks at a Founding Festival. The orks were still coming, though, pouring towards the breach from all along the wall, desperate to join the fray where the fighting was at its thickest. As the Imperial tanks steadily thinned down the number of ork machines, the fight became one of lighter weapons: lasguns, bolters, stubbers and the like. Wulfe moved automatically, unlocking the hatch of his cupola without thinking, still numbed by the news of Vinnemann's death. How would van Droi be taking it? The lieutenant had idolised his senior officer.

Shock and numbness bled off the moment Wulfe poked his head and shoulders above the rim of the hatch. There was no time for them. The air was filled with the noise of gunfire, alien battle cries and the screams of the dying. In his peripheral vision, Wulfe saw the guns of the vehicles on either side of him blazing away, cutting down dozens of heavy brown bodies as they charged. Distantly, he noted that one of the tanks, the one to his right, was an Exterminator. Lenck's machine.

Wulfe grabbed the grips of his heavy stubber, knocked the safety off, cocked it, and hit the thumb-triggers hard. He barely needed to line up.

Fire blazed from the stubber's muzzle. The recoil shook him, a deep juddering that travelled right through his body. It was a satisfying feeling. More satisfying still was the sight of a row of massive greenskin warriors in iron plate being literally chewed apart by his hail of fire.

'Beans,' said Wulfe over the intercom, 'if you don't have any armoured targets, get on the damned co-ax. Put some autocannon fire on them. We have to hold them here until the rear elements get through!'

'I'm on it,' replied Beans. Seconds later, the co-axial autocannon rattled to life.

More orks fell.

'Push through,' shouted General deViers over the vox. 'I want every last one of you through that damned gap at once. Don't look back.'

The orks' flankers from the south were closing fast. DeViers had moved the vulnerable machines ahead – fuel and water trucks, all the transports with their critical supplies – and ordered a rearguard of Chimeras to follow, turrets turned to protect the flanks. If any of the ork light armour closed before his rear echelons passed the breach, the Chimeras would have to hold them off. It was far from ideal, but all the heavy armour was up front, holding the corridor eastward. There was no time to reshuffle his forces. Together, the orks behind the wall and those from the south would try to smash his force, like glowing steel between anvil and hammer.

The general's Chimera, *Arrow of Alibris*, moved at the head of the racing column, churning up the dusty ground towards the gap that *Angel of the Apocalypse* had made. Beside him, the Chimeras of his divisional and regimental commanders matched his speed.

We *will* make it, he told himself. If the tech-priests have it right, *The Fortress of Arrogance* isn't more than eighty kilometres east of here. But how will I be able to recover it with all the damned pressure from our rear? How long will the Mechanicus need to send their damned beacon into space and bring down the lifter?

Thinking of the tech-priests, he put out a verification call. Were they still alongside him? What was their condition?

Tech-Magos Sennesdiar answered the call personally. His tinny voice was disturbingly calm. 'Worry not, general. We are still with you. But you must ensure that our vehicles are adequately protected. If anything were to happen to them, your mission would end prematurely. Given atmospheric conditions, only we can signal the fleet for evacuation.'

It almost sounded like a threat to deViers, but that didn't make it untrue.

'We've got a solid rearguard in place,' answered the general. 'The orks at our backs will not take us, even if my men have to die to guarantee our window of escape. And the armour ahead is holding a road east for us as we speak. If you can think of anything I'm forgetting, don't hold your tongue!'

Actually, he doubted the old Martian priest still had a tongue. He doubted he had a soul, either. If only the damned Mechanicus could have been kept out of all this. No doubt they would try to claim some, if not all, of the glory of the imminent recovery. He wouldn't let that happen. He would…

No, Mohamar, he told himself. It isn't the time to think about that.

'General deViers to all divisional commanders,' he voxed. 'Status report. Now!'

'Armour in position and holding the corridor,' replied Bergen. 'North and south parallels secure, sir, but let's not gamble on holding them any longer than necessary. We've taken losses all across the board.'

'Rennkamp here. I've split my infantry to support Bergen's armour on both sides of the corridor. I'm working with Killian to forge east. Forward elements are pushing away from the battle.'

'Major General Killian?' voxed deViers.

'Here, sir. My forward elements report a clean run on the far side of the corridor. No large ork structures to speak of, but the terrain gets rough a few kilometres out. The Ishawar peaks aren't far, sir. If we keep heading east, we'll soon be moving into the foothills.'

'That's exactly where we *want* to go, major general,' said deViers. 'That's where she waits.'

IT TOOK ALL Bergen's efforts just to make sense of the constant vox-chatter that sounded in his ears. The corridor was holding, but the rearguard had been engaged by the orks from the south. Their light armour wasn't a serious threat, but he had seen this all before. The orks used their fast trucks, bikes and buggies to slow prey down while they moved the heavy stuff up for the kill. It wouldn't happen like that today. The 18th Army Group couldn't afford to turn and fight.

DeViers was pushing everything he had left into a desperate dash, but what the devil would he do when he got there? Bergen wondered. The orks would be coming right along behind them, right on their tail.

There would be a face off, sooner or later. It would be a straight, stand-up fight, and the Cadians were looking at bad odds.

Immrich seemed to be holding up, at least. Bergen had worried that the news of Vinnemann's death might undo him, but battle had a way of keeping a man's priorities in order. There would be time for sorrow and mourning later. Right now, the fight for survival was keeping him together.

Bergen's driver, Meekes, called back to him that they were through the breach. Bergen would have known it anyway. The sound of battle was deafening. He moved into the Chimera's turret to get a look through the vision blocks. All around him, he saw Imperial machines blasting away with everything they had. Dead xenos lay in dense heaps all around, but every second, hundreds more clambered over the corpse-mountains to add their fire to the battle. Pistol and stubber fire danced and ricocheted off the Chimera's hull. There were other weapons, too. The orks seemed to have developed las and plasma analogues. Could it be that they were learning from their battles with the Guard?

'Keep your speed up,' he told Meekes. 'There's no time to join the fight. The sooner we're clear and running for the hills, the sooner we can pull our armour back in behind us.' And the sooner deViers will realise that this was a bloody wild grox chase from the start, he thought.

He knew Rennkamp and Killian were thinking the same thing. All three men seemed to have a silent understanding. DeViers was out of control. His ambition had become an obsession, and the obsession had led to madness. Look where his haste, his impatience, had got them: orks left and right, orks at the rear. It was a blasted miracle that Exolon had survived this long.

He saw Vinnemann's tanks – no, *Immrich's* tanks – blasting away for all they were worth, great tongues of flame and beams of las-fire leaping out from their weapons. No, he thought, it's nothing to do with miracles. It's *them*. It's their determination, their refusal to lie down and die.

Vinnemann lived on in them.

They were Cadians, and he was damned proud of them all.

'IMMRICH TO ALL tanks,' voxed the captain. 'The command staff are clear. Rear echelons are through. I want all machines to fall in by company. We run east, but keep your turrets covering the rear. There'll be more ork machines coming through that breach once we move off. Keep your speed up. They'll be chasing us all the way. Let's make it as unpleasant as possible for the bastards.'

Wulfe listened carefully, and then relayed the information to Metzger. In formation with the tanks on either side, *Last Rites II* started rolling again, still firing as she went.

The orks on foot rushed into the space left by the departing Imperial machines, but they couldn't hope to match the speed of the fleeing armour. Wulfe watched the tide of brown bodies grow smaller. He could still see the breach, but the light that shone through from the other side was cut off by massive angular shadows, the first rows of reinforcing ork armour moving through to give chase.

They could only come through three abreast. That'll slow them down, thought Wulfe. If the top brass hadn't been in such a damned hurry to move, we could have used the bottleneck to slaughter the filthy sods. What the hell are the brass thinking? If we come back this way, we'll have to go through this all over again.

Metzger was pushing *Last Rites II* along at full speed, tearing up the ground. There was nothing orderly about the retreat. It was a mad, desperate flight. There was an undeniable sense of panic and disorder about the whole thing. Wulfe hoped someone knew what they were doing, because right now, he couldn't see a good end to any of this.

As the ork wall disappeared behind the Imperial column in clouds of dust, smoke and heat-haze, Wulfe turned his attention straight ahead and saw the Ishawar mountain range rising above him. They dominated the landscape, towering over everything like dark, glowering gods. The foothills were much nearer. The land was already rising to meet them.

We're going up, thought Wulfe?

Looking back the way he'd come, he saw the sun's dull red glow behind the clouds. It was barely visible, just peeking now and then from cracks in the thick cover. Night would be coming soon. That would help. Orks didn't cover so much ground at night. He remembered the Kasrkin he had met earlier – the tooth collector from Stromm's 98th – and the general belief that orks were highly superstitious. Wulfe wondered if that extended to feelings about the dark. Mankind had always held a special fear of the night. It was a primal thing. Even now, Throne only knew how many millions of years since mankind's mastery of fire, it was still deeply ingrained. The darkness was to be feared. Did the orks feel something similar?

Wulfe dropped down into the turret basket, reached up, and locked the hatch of his cupola.

Sitting in his command seat, battle having turned to flight, he allowed his exhaustion to finally settle on him. His muscles ached. Straining against a growing stiffness, he lifted a jerrycan from a rack on the floor and took a mouthful of lukewarm water. Siegler and Beans were looking at him expectantly. Beans in particular looked keen for his sergeant to speak.

Wulfe nodded at them, but he couldn't smile. Colonel Vinnemann was gone. Things already felt different.

On the intercom, he told his crew, 'Good job, you lot.'

'Thanks, sarge,' replied Beans, but Wulfe sensed he was waiting for more, which was only natural given the fact that he had just survived his first front-line engagement. In fact, he had distinguished himself. Wulfe wasn't in the mood to give him his dues right now, though. He felt like he'd had the wind knocked out of him.

'Beans,' he said, 'you and Siegler need to get some rest. Metzger, I'll cover for you as soon as we get a chance to stop, but that might not be for a while yet. Can you go on?'

'I've got a flask of caffeine that'll see me through,' said Metzger. 'Get some rest, sarge. Sounds like you need it.'

Wulfe decided he would tell them about Vinnemann later. He would spare them the grief for now.

He closed his eyes and leaned back against the inside wall. The rumble of the tank rattled his teeth together, but, after so many years of sleeping on the move, he was well used to it. It actually seemed to help him sleep these days.

'Wake me if someting bad happens.'

Raising an eyelid, he checked to see if Siegler and Beans were following his example. Siegler was, but Beans was still looking at his sergeant.

'I meant what I said, Beans,' said Wulfe. 'Get some shut-eye while you can. There's going to be more fighting soon. And if you thought today was bad...'

He never finished the sentence. A warm darkness embraced him, and thoughts of battle slipped from his mind. He dreamed of a blue sky and the green banks of a shimmering lake. There were purple mountains in the distance, each with a perfect cap of white snow, and, on one of the grassy hills at the foot of the mountains, he saw a great structure of white marble, a shining fortress.

To Wulfe's eyes, it seemed close, just a few hours walking distance, but, at the same time, and with an inexplicable surety that can only exist in dreams, Wulfe knew that the fortress was much, much further away than it looked.

CHAPTER TWENTY-TWO

'THEN WHERE THE frakking hell is it?' raged General deViers.

A blood-red dawn found the general and his beleaguered forces in a dry, rocky valley between the foothills of the Ishawar Mountains. It was a scene that held the eye and boggled the mind. Here, at long last, was the reported resting place of *The Fortress of Arrogance*, at least, so the Adeptus Mechanicus had told the Munitorum. General deViers had pinned all his hopes on it.

But there was no sign of Yarrick's tank. In fact there was no sign that it had ever been here at all.

The valley was two kilometres long, curving away to the north-east where its floor gradually rose to meet the mountain slopes. The hills between which it nestled were of loose orange sand and darker orange rock, but much of the land was covered by rusting metal, for it was here that a great battle had once been fought. Yarrick's forces had passed through these foothills, hounded by Ghazghkull Thraka's hordes from the north. It was here that the Imperial troops had truly foundered, sandwiched between their pursuers and a well-equipped secondary ork force that came up from the south-east in a pincer movement. Thraka had surprised Yarrick and wreaked havoc on his army, fielding some of the greatest monstrosities available to any ork commander; massive avatars of war to rival in power and stature the mighty Titans of the Adeptus Mechanicus.

263

For the sake of target identification, the Officio Strategos tagged these towering creations Gargants. Similar designs of a lighter class had been code-named Stompers. They looked much the same but for the difference in size. There were reports of Gargants as tall as the greatest machines of the Legio Titanicus. They were as tall as the orks could make them: massive effigies of their savage gods, dressed for war in great skirts of the thickest armour plating the greenskins could find. Clouds of toxic gas and steam vented from them with every lumbering, earth-shaking step, and they were typically armed with more weapons than was practical.

More often than not, their arms were composed of cannon of outrageous calibre, all grouped together so that they might launch volleys of devastating shells at a single target. Atop each giant body sat a control deck in the shape of a monstrous metal head. The orks designed these to look much like themselves; they had red eyes, albeit glowing ones made up of sensors, and jutting metal jaws that thrust forward, providing a parapet for the insane infantry that manned the gun positions there. Each shoulder was a firing platform bearing everything from artillery pieces to mortars and fixed stubber positions. Nothing else in the ork arsenal embodied their enthusiasm for war like these oversized abominations.

It was the wreckage of one of these Gargants that told General deViers he was looking in the right place.

The Gargant was practically skeletal. Over the years since Yarrick had managed to fell it, ork bands had come, stripping away everything they could use from its mighty carcass. They took the weapons. They took the armour plates. All that lay before deViers and his forces was a rusting frame that barely hinted at the terror of the original machine.

Other, smaller machines lay all around it, also half buried in the sand, also looted. They were mostly dreadnoughts, much smaller than a Stomper, but deadly enough in their own right. There were signs that Imperial Titans had fought here, too. The wreckage of their mighty guns lay half-buried in the hillsides. The valley had seen a great battle, so great, in fact, that few living beings had walked away from it, and few machines had survived it intact.

It was here that Yarrick had lost his Baneblade *and* his freedom. It was here that the greenskin warlord Ghazghkull Thraka finally captured his nemesis, though he released him soon afterwards so that he would have a worthy opponent for his second war on Armageddon.

'Someone answer me,' demanded deViers. He was standing halfway up the left hillside, scanning the valley desperately, and the air of panic he exuded was palpable. Bergen stood close by, shaking his head.

I knew it, he thought. He wasn't gloating. His feeling was one of resignation. Here was the proof that his doubts had been justified all along. There was no need to feel guilty for harbouring such scepticism. He had been right, but he had truly wanted to be wrong. The current question was this: what would Tech-Magos Sennesdiar do now? The ancient tech-priest *must* have known all along that the whole expedition would eventually come to this. He must have known he'd have to answer for the missing Baneblade eventually.

General deViers was thinking about the tech-priests, too. 'Get the damned cogboys over here. I want a bloody explanation. And don't let the men stop searching. I want to know the moment anyone finds anything, absolutely anything at all.'

Bergen looked out over the opposite slope. The day was still new, but the air was already warm. There was no breeze, not yet anyway. Looking westwards, he gazed along the row of tanks and transports that sat waiting patiently for their orders. The tank crews were out, stretching their legs after a long hard run from the orks. The Sentinels were up on the high ground, keeping watch on the gullies below. The greenskins couldn't be far off. The hours of pitch darkness might have slowed them down a little, but Bergen knew it was a temporary reprieve. The orks wanted to fight.

What would deViers do, Bergen wondered? Would he have Exolon make a stand? Or would he urge them on? Where was there left to go after this?

'You called, general,' said a mechanical voice from Bergen's right. He turned his head to see the three senior tech-priests drift forward, red robes rippling around them as they moved. 'May we assume that your men have found *The Fortress of Arrogance*? I shall launch an orbital beacon as soon as I have verified this.'

'No they bloody well have *not* found it,' deViers practically screamed. Purple veins bulged at his temples and up the side of his neck. His eyes were wide, and Bergen saw for the first time that the whites had turned pink, just like everyone else's had.

So, he thought, the old man is suffering the effects of the fines, too.

'Tell me right now, magos,' demanded deViers, 'are we in the right place? Is this not the valley in your reports? These *are* the coordinates I was given!'

'This is the place, general. All our intelligence indicated that *The Fortress of Arrogance* was here.'

'*Was* being the operative word,' deViers exploded.

'Clearly, general,' said the magos with perfect self-control, 'if it is not here, it must have been moved. Do not fret, however. We of the Adeptus Mechanicus come prepared for such a contingency. We have the knowledge and equipment that will allow us to track the movement of the machine. *The Fortress of Arrogance* was possessed of a unique and powerful machine-spirit. Through our ancient arts, we may still be able to commune with that spirit and learn where its vessel has been taken.'

DeViers looked far from placated by this, but his desperation seemed to bleed off a little. Bergen, on the other hand, didn't know what to think. As a lifelong tanker, he had come to believe in the machine-spirits that inhabited each of the tanks he had personally commanded. He had seen how much better they functioned when one observed the proper rites. He had witnessed first-hand the peculiar techno-sorcery of the Martian Priesthood in action. There were so many things he would never understand about it all. Was Sennesdiar speaking the truth? Could he really commune with the spirit of the revered machine?

Tech-Magos Sennesdiar let out a piercing mechanical shriek, and his adepts immediately turned and stalked back to their idling Chimera where it sat atop the southern slope.

'My subordinates and I need to perform a ritual, general,' said Sennesdiar to deViers. 'We shall consult the machine-spirit and bring you your answer. Have faith. I am no lowly enginseer. I would not have opted to join this mission in person had I harboured any doubts about its success. You will have your prize.'

DeViers's jaw was tight. He didn't answer. Bergen suspected that the old man was simply too damned angry for words. Sennesdiar didn't wait for them anyway. With a swish of his robes, he turned his massive bulk and headed back to his Chimera, leaving deViers and his senior officers halfway down the hillside, looking up, watching him go.

'Damned tech-priests,' hissed Killian. He glanced over at Bergen, caught his eye, and said, 'Sorry, Gerard. I know you tankers are close with them.'

Bergen shook his head. 'Not really, my friend. They only let us know as much as they want us to. I don't delude myself about that.'

'Do you think they really can perform some kind of sorcery?' asked Rennkamp. 'If they can't, we've come all this way, lost all those men, for absolutely nothing.'

Bergen shrugged. 'I guess we'll know–'

He stopped short of finishing his sentence. There was fresh chatter on the vox-bead in his ear. The others heard it, too. He saw the same expression steal over their faces as he knew must be present on his own.

'Throne curse it all,' spat General deViers. 'Back to your machines all of you,' he ordered. 'The tech-priests had better perform their rites damned quickly.'

The senior officers turned and marched at speed to their idling vehicles. The Sentinel pilots were reporting orksign. The greenskins were only two hours out.

CHAPTER TWENTY-THREE

<We must be quick,> Tech-Magos Sennesdiar told his adepts in the security of their personal Chimera. <But not so quick as to raise the officers' suspicions even further. This has always been a moment of great risk for us. There will be others to come, but they will hinge on the outcome of what we do here. We must be convincing. The general must believe we lacked all foreknowledge of the situation.>

<Finally we are closing on Dar Laq,> said Xephous. <I am eager to see it for myself.>

<I envy Magos Ipharod his discovery,> added Armadron.

<Do not let anticipation get the better of you,> Sennesdiar told them. <For all we know, Ipharod's discovery may have killed him. I do not know what kind of state we will find him in, if we find him at all. Concern yourselves with matters of the present. Everything yet depends on evading the orks and leading Exolon up into the mountains. The Cadians will not be keen to follow our lead.>

<Then, how do we proceed, magos?> asked Armadron.

<We must convince them that our rites are genuine. At the very least, General deViers must strongly believe that his prize is still within reach. He must believe that we have located *The Fortress of Arrogance* through our communion with the machine-spirit.>

<His anger consumes him,> said Xephous. <He expected the Baneblade to be here. He will not trust us readily.>

<He is desperate,> said Sennesdiar. <We offer the last possible hope of salvaging his quest. Angry or not, he will grasp at anything we offer him, no matter how thin. I am not concerned about General deViers so much as I am about his divisional commanders. Armadron, you spent the most time with Major General Bergen. How much of a problem does he represent?>

Armadron prefixed his sonic burst with a single tone that signified his lack of absolute certainty. <Gerard Bergen lacks confidence in his general. I feel that he longs to be rid of the man, but that his respect for the methods and order of the Imperial Guard override every other instinct he has. I project that he will continue to follow the proper chain of command no matter what.>

<Xephous,> said Sennesdiar. <You have observed Major Generals Rennkamp and Killian. Speak.>

<Neither one, magos, seems the type to advance himself by illicit means. The Cadian code of military honour holds fast. They adhere rigidly to mission protocols.>

<As it should be,> said Sennesdiar. <That is to our advantage. DeViers will follow us out of desperation. The others will follow deViers out of duty. That will be enough to get us to Dar Laq. Once we enter the tunnels, however, there will be questions, questions we do not wish to answer.>

<The veil will be lifted, magos,> said Armadron. <They will sense our deception. Even if they do not, the truth remains. We cannot locate *The Fortress of Arrogance* for them. Ipharod's transmission merely states–>

<I received a copy of the transmission, adept,> said Sennesdiar. <I am well aware of its contents.>

Armadron bowed. <Apologies, magos.>

<I do not need apologies. I need you both to gather the enginseers together. I will lead the ceremony. It will be convincing. The Guardsmen will have no idea that it is a simple blessing rite. They will see what they want to see. They will see us commune with the Omnissiah, and, when the charade is over, we will guide them to *our* objective. Now, disperse.>

WULFE YAWNED. HE was lying on the rear decking of his tank, cap pulled down across his eyes, but true rest seemed out of reach. Perhaps it was the dust. Perhaps he was sick and hadn't realised it. There was an ache in his muscles that would not go away. It had dulled somewhat since he lay down, but it was still there, at the edge of his awareness.

Beans and Siegler were preparing rations of sliced meal-brick and water by the side of the tank. There was nothing else to be had, but at least they weren't back to drinking purified piss.

Would they even live long enough for that to happen again? Wulfe wondered. It seemed to him that the 18th Army Group was practically broken already. Lifting his cap and looking around, he saw crewmen resting on rear decking or track-guards just like he was, but there had been significant losses. Van Droi's 10th Company was down to just five tanks. The lieutenant's crate, *Foe-Breaker*, was still in the game, though the man himself had become extremely quiet since the death of the colonel. Viess and his *Steelhearted II* had made it through. The man was a solid commander. Van Droi had made a good move, promoting him to sergeant on the voyage to Golgotha. Viess had justified that choice back at the wall, taking out his share of the ork armour, and Holtz seemed to be doing all right with *Old Smashbones*. It was a small miracle that he had survived when so many others had not. Perhaps it was beginner's luck. In any case, Wulfe was damned glad van Droi hadn't promoted Holtz just to have him die in his first firefight as a commander.

Then, of course, there was Lenck.

Wulfe hadn't given the bastard much thought during all the madness that had erupted since their passage through Red Gorge. Battle was good that way. One could achieve an almost peaceful state in the middle of all that mayhem.

Wulfe glanced over at Lenck's tank, but if the crew was outside they must've been lying low, because he couldn't see them. Perhaps, like Metzger, they were all sleeping.

Wulfe sat up and swung around to watch the tech-priests. They were down on the valley floor performing some kind of arcane ritual he couldn't begin to fathom. It looked different to the rites he had watched them perform on the regiment's tanks but not much. Every tech-priest and enginseer attached to the expedition was down there, all dressed in the red robes of their cult, heads bowed in prayer. They moved in a clockwise circle, chanting and emitting strange mechanical noises that no human throat could have made.

Some of them carried censers that they swung back and forth, lacing the air with blue smoke that hung above them, gently shifting in slow motion. There was no breeze. The air was thick and warm. He looked up. The tall red peaks of the Ishawar rose so high in the near east that they pierced the bellies of the clouds like tusks.

Why did everything have to remind him of orks? He would be facing them again soon enough. Van Droi had voxed him just twenty minutes ago to say so. The orks were closing in on them, still pursuing from the west. The Sentinels had used long-range scopes to spot them well out from the valley, but, in a little over ninety minutes the orks would be here, and the fighting would start all over again. Would deViers lead them in another run? Or would he have them turn and fight?

Wulfe would have preferred to fight. It had become increasingly clear to him that no one was going to make it out of this alive. The officers still talked of finding Yarrick's lost tank, and they put a lot of faith on the tech-priests' ability to signal for evacuation. A lifter would come for them when the time was right. At least, that was how Wulfe understood it. He just didn't think it was going to be that easy.

The thought of dying here didn't anger him. He had spent his whole life knowing that he would perish in the service of the Emperor. What better way was there?

None, he told himself, but Armageddon would have been preferable. There, at least, his last moments could have been spent fighting to protect Holy Terra, rather than to retrieve an abandoned relic. He told himself that any fight against orks was a good fight. If he and his crew were to die here today, so be it. He would meet his fate head-on.

He turned his attention back to the tech-priests. Their ceremony intrigued him. He was a firm believer in machine-spirits. Nothing strange in that, of course. All tankers came to feel that way, no matter their original outlook on the matter. Throughout his career, he had seen members of the Adeptus Mechanicus achieve things he couldn't hope to explain. It wasn't stretching credence to imagine that the senior cogboys down there might actually come away with some kind of answer.

The Fortress of Arrogance was gone, but how far had it gone? If it was still within reach, then he would like to see it before he died. It was a rare machine, after all, almost unique in the galaxy in that, since its loss thirty-eight years ago, it had been sanctified by both the Ministorum and the tech-priests, and those two august bodies almost never saw eye to optic sensor.

'Grub's up, sarge,' called Siegler from the side of the tank. 'You want to wake Metzger?'

Wulfe slid off the track-guard and landed on his feet by Siegler and Beans.

'Let him rest a little more,' he told them. 'We'll keep some for when he wakes up.'

The three men sat and enjoyed their small repast as chanting lifted towards them from the valley floor.

'I still don't get it,' said Beans. 'They think they can find out where it went?'

Wulfe nodded and spoke around a mouthful of tough, dry meal-brick. 'You'd better hope they can. The orks will be on us soon. I think deViers will give the cogboys enough time to finish their little communion and then lead us off somewhere. He won't give up looking.'

Siegler shook his head.

'And people call me crazy,' he said.

Wulfe grinned and clapped his friend on the shoulder. 'Yes, they do.' Beans laughed.

A burst of vox-chatter from the bead in his ear made the smile suddenly drop from Wulfe's face. He spat his mouthful of meal-brick onto the hard ground at his side.

'What's up, sarge?' asked Siegler.

Wulfe stood bolt upright.

'Get your arses into the tank,' he told them, 'and wake Metzger at once.'

All around them, the air shook with the rumble of engines being turned. A Chimera just ten metres away rumbled noisily to life, coughing blue-black fumes from her exhausts. Siegler and Beans jumped to their feet.

'That was van Droi,' said Wulfe, picking up the remains of his meal and stuffing them into a tin box. 'The tech-priests say they got their answer. We're moving out.'

'But where to, sarge?' asked Beans.

Wulfe had turned and was already clambering up the side of the tank. He didn't stop climbing, but called over his shoulder, 'To the mountains, trooper. We're going into the mountains.'

CHAPTER TWENTY-FOUR

THE PATH THE 18th Army Group took from the valley up into the Ishawar Mountains soon became treacherous, especially for the tanks, most of which weighed over sixty tonnes, but there was no time to be careful. The orks were less than an hour behind them. They had spotted the Cadians rising up into the hills and had turned on a burst of speed. Bergen didn't know how long it would be before the orks caught up to them, but he knew the machines at the rear of the column would soon face the threat of ork bikes and buggies. The light, speedy greenskin machines were far more adept at handling rough terrain like this. The steep gradients and narrow trails that Exolon found itself forced to follow were really challenging the heaviest of the Cadian machines.

For now, though, there was little choice but to push on with all the speed they could muster. General deViers was taking Tech-Magos Sennesdiar extremely seriously. The magos claimed that the almighty Omnissiah, tech-aspect of the Divine Emperor of Mankind, had been roused by their ceremony and had spoken to them directly through their most powerful and sophisticated auspex scanners. The data was irrefutable, the tech-priests insisted. *The Fortress of Arrogance* had indeed lain in the valley for many years, but had been moved in the recent past. Even now, Sennesdiar told them, the orks that had taken it were within striking distance, if only the general would lead his forces up into the mountains exactly as the magos directed.

It sounded entirely too convenient to Gerard Bergen. He was sure the tech-priests had known from the start that Yarrick's lost tank was no longer in the valley. DeViers was still in charge, however, and the old general had become so frantic, so desperate, that he might believe just about anything he was told. Whether deViers was mad or not, Bergen and the other divisional leaders weren't about to protest. Not now. What was the point? Rennkamp and Killian both seemed to feel as he did. Cut off from the rest of the Imperial forces with little hope of ever returning, there was little choice but to follow the path they were on and see where it led them in the end.

Bergen rode high in the cupola of his Chimera, a habit he had developed over his long years as a tank commander. He remembered those times fondly, times before he had been singled out for greater things.

Greater things? That was a laugh. Operation Thunderstorm had gone to hell. The Munitorum wouldn't want to lose face. They'd expunge it from the Imperial records once it was clear how spectacularly it had failed.

It hasn't failed yet, said a tiny voice in the back of his mind, but another, louder voice at the front said, *hasn't it?*

Bergen tried to ignore both and looked up at the sky.

The cloaked Golgothan sun was close to its zenith, judging by the bright patch in the thick red clouds overhead. At this altitude, the clouds seemed so low they might choke him, and he automatically checked that his rebreather mask and goggles were firmly in place.

The expedition force had ascended over a thousand metres already.

Where in the blasted warp are the cogboys taking us, he wondered?

He tried to look back down the mountainside along the route they had followed, but all he could see was the clouds of dust kicked up by the line of coughing, spluttering vehicles behind him. The column was significantly shorter than it had been when it had set out from Balkar. He still didn't know exactly how many had died rushing the ork wall.

He felt two sharp tugs on his trouser leg and dropped back down into the Chimera's passenger compartment. His adjutant indicated a flickering light on the vox-caster.

'Major General Killian wants a word, sir,' he said.

Bergen told his adjutant to patch Killian through, and then spoke through the tiny vox-mic built into his rebreather mask.

'Bergen here,' he said. 'Go ahead.'

'Gerard, this is Klotus. I've just had a vox from my scout captain. Something you should definitely hear.'

'Go ahead. I'm listening.'

'It's about the trail we're following,' said Killian. 'We're not the first to tread it.'

'So the orks *did* bring *The Fortress of Arrogance* this way?' said Bergen in genuine surprise. Whatever he had expected, it hadn't been that the tech-priests might be telling the truth.

'Too difficult to say; the tracks are vague, all but eroded. But the scouts say there is sign of at least one vehicle and a fair number of foot soldiers.'

'It has to be orks. According to the records, we're the first Imperial troops to set foot here since the last war.'

'Maybe. But not everything goes into the records, does it? And it depends on whose records we're talking about. There's no way the tracks are thirty-eight years old. I can tell you that much.'

Bergen sat silent for a moment. It had to be orks. It just had to be, but, if the tracks *were* Imperial, it meant that someone else had got here first. Why hadn't Exolon been told? By all accounts, theirs was the first officially sanctioned mission ever to attempt a recovery of Yarrick's tank. If the tracks they followed belonged to an Imperial force, who the hell were they, and what were they doing here?

'Will you tell me the moment you know more?'

'Of course I will,' said Killian. 'I don't like this any more than you do.'

'You've told Rennkamp? General deViers?'

'About to,' said Killian.

Bergen thought about that. 'Why did you come to me first, Klotus?'

Killian hesitated, perhaps checking for a second that the channel was properly encrypted. 'Because deViers has been losing it for months. We both know it. And he's closer to cracking right now than I've ever seen him. If he has some kind of breakdown, the mission will fall to you. And so will our survival. I want to get off this rock alive, Gerard. I'm not meant to die here and neither are my men.'

'Thanks for the update, Klotus,' Bergen said. 'Keep me posted, won't you?'

'You've got it. Killian signing off.'

The light on the vox-board blinked out.

In Tech-Magos Sennesdiar's specially fitted Chimera, Tech-Adept Xephous hit a toggle and watched a similar green light die. He turned to his superior and said, <They have found traces of Ipharod's force.>

<That was inevitable,> replied Sennesdiar. <It changes nothing. I am far more concerned that orks may have followed Ipharod's unit down into Dar Laq. If so, we may not find Ipharod after all.>

There was a moment of silence as each of the Martian priests processed the ramifications of this. It was Armadron who ultimately broke it. <The fragment may be lost, then. What do you propose, magos?>

<Our plans must cover both eventualities,> Sennesdiar replied. <It may be that Ipharod has managed to protect the fragment. If not, we will need to employ the 18th Army Group in recovering it. They will play their part, whether they wish to or not.>

<You cannot be thinking of telling them the truth, magos?> said Xephous.

<I will tell them whatever I must,> answered Sennesdiar. <We must have the fragment. Even if it costs the life of every last man on the expedition force, we *will* have it. Nothing must stand in our way.>

<We are with you, magos,> said Xephous.

<Ask,> said Armadron, <and we shall serve.>

WULFE GROWLED AS another wave of dust smothered him and his tank. If he didn't know better, he would have said the *New Champion* was churning up the ground deliberately to impair his vision, but all the tanks were suffering the same problem. The trail was so narrow that the Imperial machines had to move in single file. As the convoy climbed higher and higher into the mountains, the danger increased.

Metzger was guiding *Last Rites II* carefully along a crumbling ridge while trying to keep her at a reasonable speed. Everyone knew that the orks weren't far behind, though they couldn't be sighted, hidden from view by the dust and the drop-off.

Wulfe took a look to his right and, not for the first time, felt something flip inside his stomach. A vast chasm yawned between the peak they were ascending and the next. He turned his eyes to the front again and felt his stomach muscles relax.

What the hell are we doing up here, he asked himself? High altitude is no bloody place for heavy armour.

Wulfe and the rest of the Gunheads were near the rear of the column, part of an armour detachment charged with defending the Thirty-Sixers and Heracles halftracks that carried most of the remaining supplies. As such, the orks were snapping at their heels. They were most at risk.

Behind *Last Rites II* came *Old Smashbones* and a few Leman Russ Conquerors from Major General Rennkamp's 12th Mechanised division. Wulfe didn't know the crews, but that didn't matter. Whatever division they came from, the Cadians really had to stick together. There weren't all that many left of them, just a few thousand men packed tightly into a few hundred machines. By contrast, scouts attached to the rearguard reported ork vehicles pursuing in the thousands. Turning to face them was not an option. The Cadians could only keep going while the techpriests insisted that this was the way.

Orks or not, the mountain trail was proving enough of a challenge on its own.

Still looking ahead, trying to guide his driver as well as he possibly could despite the dust, Wulfe decided to vox Lieutenant van Droi. Van Droi had been too damned quiet since learning of Colonel Vinnemann's death. It wasn't like him.

'Sword Lead to Company Command,' he said. 'This is Wulfe, sir. Please respond, over.'

'Company here, Wulfe,' replied van Droi. He didn't sound well. 'What can I do for you?'

Wulfe wondered how to say it without causing offence. 'Just reporting in, sir. Still quiet back here. No sign of the orks so far. I don't suppose it's too much to hope that they called off the chase?'

'How long have you been a soldier, Wulfe?' said van Droi. 'You know better than that.'

'I know, sir,' said Wulfe. 'I know. Just wishful thinking. Listen... about the colonel, sir...'

'What about him, sergeant?'

The lieutenant's tone told Wulfe he was treading dangerous ground. 'I'll miss him, sir. That's all.'

Van Droi was silent for a good ten seconds. Wulfe thought the lieutenant had actually broken the link for a moment, but then van Droi said, 'You know, Oskar, when young men get their first combat posting, it's as if they're suddenly children again. Doesn't matter if they're officers or grunts. They feel inadequate, confused and scared. They feel like they don't belong. And the fear that builds up in them sometimes... Maybe you felt that way yourself.'

'I'm sure I did, sir,' said Wulfe. 'It was a long time ago, but I'm sure I did.'

'I never forgot that feeling,' voxed van Droi wistfully. 'I hated it more than anything, you know. I felt like a burden to those around me. I had so much to learn and they had no time to teach. It was Vinnemann that pulled me out of it. He was just a captain back then. It was before his injury. He was one hell of a leader.'

'He was a good man, sir,' said Wulfe.

'He was a great man,' said van Droi. Again there was a long pause. 'It's not looking good for us out here, Wulfe. But if we have any chance at all to make him proud, I say there's nothing we shouldn't do to honour him. Understand?'

Wulfe thought he did. It wasn't about nice neat plans any more. Things had gone way beyond that. Van Droi was looking for something to hold on to, something solid, and, in the honour of the regiment and his duty to Colonel Vinnemann, it was clear that he had found it, despite the mess they were in. Wulfe hoped he might draw a little strength from that himself. If it worked for van Droi, it could work for him, too.

He was a soldier. He was a Cadian.

'For the colonel, sir,' he told van Droi, 'and for the regiment. If we go out, we'll go out with a hell of a bang, sir.'

Van Droi sounded a little brighter when he answered. 'That's the stuff, Oskar. Not many of the Gunheads left now, but we'll make our mark, by Throne.'

'You bet, sir,' said Wulfe. 'You can count on me and my crew.'

'I know I can, sergeant. Van Droi out.'

'MAJOR GENERAL KILLIAN would like to speak with you again, sir,' said Bergen's adjutant over the intercom.

Bergen, up in his cupola again, immediately changed the channel on his vox-bead and said, 'News, Klotus?'

'I'll say. My scout leader just reported in. This trail takes us up into the clouds just a few hundred metres around the next curve and ends shortly afterwards. Visibility is poor, and the going is extremely treacherous. But that's not all. The scouts... they've found something strange. I thought you ought to know.'

'Strange? What are we talking about exactly?'

'They had difficulty describing it to me. Look, Gerard, I'm not sure what we're getting into here, but I know I don't like it and neither do my men. According to my scouts, it's something we'd better see for ourselves.'

CHAPTER TWENTY-FIVE

'HUMAN?' ASKED GENERAL deViers.

'I wouldn't want to bet on that, sir,' replied Rennkamp. 'I suppose it could be. Difficult to tell with all the erosion. All the same, it's damned strange, if you ask me. What in blazes is it doing up here?'

The Cadian senior officers – deViers, his division commanders, and various attached staff – stood at the very end of the mountain trail, surrounded by anxious scouts from the 88th Mobile Infantry Regiment, the men that Marrenburg had sent forward to lead the column. Massive spurs of dark rock curved around them on either side, and the upper reaches of the mountain stretched high above them, peaks lost in the roiling clouds. The eyes of the Cadians barely lingered on any of these things, however. Instead, they were locked to the sight that lay straight in front of them.

It was ancient, that much was certain, and it was something that none of the Cadians had been prepared for.

A great rectangular space had been excavated in the side of the mountain, forming an alcove so wide and deep that one could have parked an entire Naval lifter inside it. The edges looked like they might once have been angular, squared off by the tools or machines of the masons that had carved it, but they weren't very square now. Thousands of years of harsh weather had smoothed and rounded them, as it had also done to the twin god-like figures, cut from the same stone, which knelt below the alcove's roof, taking the immense weight of it on their broad rocky shoulders.

The figures were vast and strange. They looked immensely powerful, but were they supposed to appear so distorted? Or had they just been badly rendered? Their huge block-like heads were preposterously over-sized by comparison to their sturdy torsos. Each arm and leg seemed likewise exaggerated in its thickness, presenting the beings as having impossibly heavy musculature, and their hands and feet, much like their heads, seemed so big as to make the statues appear like some kind of grotesque caricatures. They were a strange sight indeed, and they looked like no statue of a man that Bergen had ever seen.

He wondered what had they looked like in their heyday. Had they been intricately carved? Had their faces been rendered in exquisite or terrifying detail? Had they been covered in glyphs or precious metals? How long had they knelt here, locked in a battle with gravity to prevent the side of the mountain from burying them? A great many millennia, surely.

The surface of each was pitted, their features long gone, lost in time. They were utterly faceless. In the millennia to come, they would crumble altogether and the roof of the alcove would collapse, burying all evidence that they had ever existed.

Thank the Throne, thought Bergen, that all that rock hasn't come down already, or we'd be facing a dead end. The orks would have us properly trapped.

The expedition force *wasn't* trapped. There *was* a way ahead.

The cavernous black mouth of a tunnel gaped between the two huge figures. It looked wide enough to take four or five Leman Russ tanks driving abreast of each other. This ancient structure was a gate, a doorway into the belly of the mountain. The mighty statues were its guardians.

'Abhumans, I'd say,' said Killian. 'Maybe some kind of mutated human colonists. Who knows how old this is. It might date back to pre-Strife times.'

'Gruber, get the tech-priests up here,' snapped deViers. 'We don't have time to stand around discussing it, but I'll be damned if I'm going to lead us all down there before I know what we're looking at.'

The general's adjutant put out a hurried call for the senior Martian priests to move up the column.

Yes, thought Bergen, let's see what the cogboys have to say about this. I'm sure this is where they've been leading us the whole time. Whatever the Mechanicus wants, I'll bet my boots it's in that tunnel somewhere, or on the other side of it, perhaps. One way or another, though, we're going in. Emperor protect us.

He knew that the men wouldn't like it. He didn't like it much himself.

Alien things were anathema. From the moment a child of the Imperium could understand Low Gothic, he or she was drilled to hate all xenos and everything they stood for and, from the moment they joined the Guard, that hatred was fed and nurtured and beaten into them until, for many, it became a consuming passion.

Suffer not the alien to live.

Wonder not at its works, thought Bergen, reciting from the Imperial Creed. For such things weave their corruption into the minds of men and make us weak in the face of our foes.

Many a man with too much curiosity had been burned at the stake by commissars, members of the Holy Inquisition, or even by outraged civilian mobs. Heresy carried a high price.

A monotone voice, like metal rasping on metal, sounded from behind Bergen. He turned to see Magos Sennesdiar approach, face shadowed under his cowl, long red robes snapping at his ankles. In his own way, he was even more alien than the grotesque stone twins. The metal tendrils that sprouted from his back and his monstrous machine-bulk made the kneeling stone giants seem so much more human. He was flanked, as usual, by the equally disturbing Adepts Xephous and Armadron.

'Fortune favours us, general,' said Sennesdiar.

Bergen noted that, unlike the Cadians around him, the tech-priests did not wear goggles and rebreathers. They didn't need them.

How fragile we must seem to them sometimes, he thought to himself. Do they pity us, or do they view us with contempt?

The officers had turned to greet the tech-magos, and he stopped in front of them. Raising his dark, unblinking eye-lenses, he gestured with long metal fingers towards the ancient structure up ahead. 'Dar Laq lies open before us. Why do we not proceed? The ork legion will be upon us soon.'

'Dar Laq?' asked Killian. 'Is that what you just called it?'

'May I assume, magos,' said deViers testily, 'that this... this *place* is known to you?'

'In name only, general,' replied the magos. 'Dar Laq was long rumoured to be somewhere in this region, though it was never located and catalogued while Golgotha belonged to us. At this altitude, the clouds render auspex scanners almost entirely useless and, as you can see for yourself, we are shrouded from view up here. There were tales of other ancient settlements too, of course, but though my revered brothers searched, it seemed that time had hidden them too well. It is remarkable that this gateway still stands, and it pleases me that our expedition has led to its accidental discovery.'

'Gateway to what exactly?' asked Bergen.

The magos turned and looked straight at him. Bergen tried to read him, to search for some sign of deceit, a twitch perhaps, some hint of conspiracy, but the magos's body language was impossible to read, for there simply was none. Bergen felt he might as well have tried to read the emotions of an automatic sentry-gun.

'We do not know the name of the sentient race that occupied Golgotha before us, major general,' Sennesdiar answered. 'We found no remains of their dead, no written records. They were long gone when the Great Crusade came this way, and where they went remains a mystery. We of the Mechanicus do not like to posit suppositions without adequate data.'

'Meaning you can't really tell us what lies ahead, right?' said Rennkamp, cutting in. He shook his head and turned to General deViers. 'We could be walking into anything, sir.'

'I said they were long gone, major general,' said Sennesdiar, 'and I meant it. I doubt we shall find any cause for alarm within. If your concern is greenskins, on the other hand, perhaps I may offer some reassurance. By their extremely superstitious nature there is a very high probability that the orks will not pursue us. There is no sign that they have entered here. If they ever discovered it, they did not deface it as they usually do. No glyphs. No spoor, unless your scouts have uncovered some. I recognise that there may be some resistance to proceeding this way among the troopers. This is a xenos place, but I project that the most we shall encounter is rubble and ruins.'

'And an exit that will get us out on the other side,' said Bergen. 'Or what's the point in going down there at all?'

'I'm not leading this expedition into a dead end, magos,' growled General deViers. 'We've got a critical mission to complete, by Terra. Tell me what this place has to do with *The Fortress of Arrogance*. And your answer had better satisfy me.'

Sennesdiar turned his hooded head from Bergen to deViers and back again. The threat inherent in the general's words seemed not to register at all, either that or he judged it entirely beneath his attention.

'We can be sure there is a way out,' he said, 'because the machine-spirit is our guide. Even were it not so, an exit must exist, for it would be illogical not to create one. Animals of the lowest forms know better than to build a lair with only a single exit. And we are not talking about a low-born animal species here. We are talking about an intelligent, technological race that dominated Golgotha for many ages. The scant evidence we have indexed tells us that much.'

Then the magos turned to deViers and added, 'I calculate an extremely high probability, general, that this tunnel will lead us safely to the far side of the Ishawar range. For the sake of your grand quest, and for all our lives, that is exactly where we must go. You see, as my adepts and I learned from our communion with the machine-spirit, *that* is where *The Fortress of Arrogance* awaits us.'

THE COLUMN WAS moving again.

About bloody time, too, thought Wulfe. Reports from the spotters at the very rear put the ork forces almost within striking range, and the scar on his throat had begun to itch like crazy in the last few minutes. That was never a happy sign.

It was good to be moving again, but, from his position in the rearguard, it was difficult to work out exactly what was going on. As Wulfe sat high in his cupola guiding Metzger around another bend in the trail, he listened carefully to the regimental vox-channel, trying to learn as much as he could. All he could really draw from the broken chatter was that scouts had found a way forward, and that, inexplicably, a good many of the troopers didn't seem to like it much.

That doesn't make sense, he told himself. Everyone with half a brain knows we've got to keep moving if we're going to stay ahead of those bastards. What's got everyone so damned twitchy all of a sudden?

Soon enough, he found out first-hand.

'By the bloody Golden Throne,' he gasped as Metzger followed the tank in front between two eerily symmetrical columns of red stone. Beyond the weathered pillars, the ancient alcove with its kneeling gods was revealed in all its glory. 'We're going inside *that?*'

There was a crackle on the vox.

'Company Command to all tanks. Keep your pace up. I'm talking to you, Holtz. Keep your crate in line. Why have you stopped? Get moving.'

Wulfe heard Holtz growling back, 'Sorry, lieutenant. Just caught us a bit off-guard. I mean, it's alien, isn't it? I don't like it, sir. We shouldn't be going in there. Throne knows, we shouldn't. We could be walking right into a xenos trap, sir.'

The link spat a harsh burst of static in Wulfe's ear for a few seconds before he heard van Droi's answer. 'It's not exactly my first choice either, corporal, but we're out of options. If you'd rather stay here and face the orks on your own, I can petition Captain Immrich for you. Of course, the commissars have already made it very clear that they'll execute anyone who refuses to enter on charges of cowardice.'

Holtz managed to sound angry and chastised at the same time. 'I'm no frakking coward, sir. Of course, I'm going in. I just don't like xenos abominations, that's all.'

Van Droi's voice, on the other hand, had a hint of humour in it as he replied, 'That's all I thought it was, corporal. That's all I thought it was.'

As Wulfe was listening to this, he watched more and more of the vehicles in front being swallowed up by the gaping black maw of the ancient tunnel. As soon as each vehicle went in, its driver hit the headlights but, from Wulfe's vantage point, it didn't seem as though the lights were doing much to illuminate the path ahead.

Last Rites II rolled nearer and nearer the tunnel mouth. Wulfe looked from side to side at the huge stone guardians as he passed them. What in the warp were they supposed to be? He might have said ogryn, but they were too misshapen even for that. They didn't look like orks, either. In fact, they didn't match the appearance of any xenos race that Wulfe had ever encountered or read about.

All too soon, the tunnel swallowed him. Black walls cut off his view and he was plunged into darkness. The air that moved around him was immediately cooler. He noted this as a breeze played over the hairs on his forearms and on the back of his neck. He noted, too, that the featureless black floor of the tunnel was sloping downwards.

The tanks on either side lit their headlamps, and cones of light shot forward, striking the clouds of oily exhaust fumes put out by the machines in front. There didn't seem much else to see, at least for now, just featureless tunnel walls, blue-grey clouds of exhaust smoke and the backs of the machines in front.

'Metzger,' said Wulfe over the intercom, 'hit the lights.'

'Aye, sir,' said Metzger, and *Last Rites II* added her own illumination to the darkness. It didn't make much difference.

On the vox, van Droi's voice sounded again. 'Are we all in?'

Wulfe turned and looked over his shoulder at the shrinking square of red daylight behind him. Silhouetted against it were the dark hulls of the last machines in the column. 'Looks like it, sir,' he reported to van Droi. 'I see the last of the Conquerors coming in now.'

'Good,' voxed van Droi. 'Then I want all of you to move in to the sides of the tunnel, nice and slow. We don't need any accidents. There'll be a Chimera coming back through here in a couple of minutes, heading up towards the entrance.'

'What the devil for, sir?' voxed Sergeant Viess. 'We can't send men back out there.'

Wulfe noted the hesitation in van Droi's voice, and the weariness when he said at last, 'It's a demolitions team, sergeant. General deViers has ordered the entrance sealed behind us.'

CHAPTER TWENTY-SIX

THE CADIAN COLUMN moved slowly and carefully through the dark for the best part of three hours, guided by Sentinel walkers with searchlights fitted. They discovered a plethora of side tunnels as they went, smaller passageways that branched from the broad one they were following. Each of these was given a cursory inspection, but they twisted away in countless directions and were far too small to accommodate the tanks. With little choice, the expedition force found itself committed to a single path that led ever downwards, deeper into the darkness.

DeViers marked the passing of time on the antique pocket-chronometer his grandfather, for whom he had been named, had bequeathed him over eighty years before. It was an exquisite piece of Agripinaan craftsmanship, inlaid with emeralds and white diamonds, finished in platinum, and decorated across the face with a filigree of the most delicate gold. It had been with him a long, long time. Looking at its pristine face always brought feelings of peace and comfort. He had been turning to it more and more often since his arrival on this accursed planet.

Did they think he didn't know what was going on, those damned Mechanicus? Did they think he was so easily used? Warp blast and damn them, he was Mohamar Antoninus deViers, Saviour of Thessaly IX, Protector of Chedon Secundus, decorated with the Iron Star for his overwhelming victory at Rystok, awarded the Platinum Skull 1st Class for exemplary leadership at Dionysus. Then there were Modessa Prime, Phaegos II, and a host of other glories. Age hadn't addled his mind *that* much. He knew all too well that they had an agenda. He knew they were guiding him along the path that best suited their purposes, but what could he do? He needed them to help find Yarrick's tank. Their Machine-God didn't speak to normal men, even men as worthy as him.

He hadn't missed the looks his senior officers had been giving each other, either. They were losing confidence in him. That much was evident. Even Gerard Bergen seemed ready to question him these days. That stung deViers particularly sharply. Prior to that mess on Palmeros, he had started to consider the handsome officer something of a protégé.

Well, they'd all see the error of their ways in the end. This wasn't over, not by a long shot. *The Fortress of Arrogance* was still out there somewhere. It couldn't be far. Orks had taken it, and it was his job to get it back. The Imperium depended on him. Whether the Mechanicus had initiated this expedition or not, it was a Munitorum operation now, and he was in charge. Not one man, not one ounce of Guard materiel would leave this blasted world until he had his prize. There was still everything to play for. His place in the history books was still within reach. He would join the list alongside Yarrick, Macaroth and Harazahn. He would be forever remembered as one of the great men of his age.

He looked down at the chronometer's ticking hands. There was still time enough for that.

'Caffeine, sir?' asked Gruber from the other side of the Chimera's passenger compartment. 'It's hot.'

'No thank you, Gruber. I'm wound up enough already.'

Gruber looked at the chronometer in the general's hand and let out a snort of laughter. 'Good one, sir. Wound up. I get it.'

DeViers smiled weakly. He hadn't meant to make a joke at all, but fine. Let his adjutant think what he would. Laughing in the face of such desperation made him seem strong in the eyes of others. Let them think him unfazed by the frustrating turns the expedition had taken.

What lies ahead, he wondered? What obstacle will test me next?

He was about to find out.

'Vox is flashing, sir,' said Gruber, indicating a blinking green light on the wall-mounted unit above the general's left shoulder. 'Let me get that for you.'

Even though deViers was closest to the device, he let Gruber take care of the call. It was the man's job, and it didn't do to have the other officers think they could bother their general directly with every little detail. He had enough on his mind. Over the years, Gruber had learned to screen the general's incoming vox-calls with great intuition.

Absently, deViers half-listened as Gruber spoke into the vox-caster's mouthpiece. Then the adjutant turned and said, 'It's Colonel Marren-burg, sir. He says his scouts have found the end of the tunnel.'

DeViers felt his pulse quicken.

'I'll speak to him,' he said, and accepted the mouthpiece from Gruber, who immediately returned to his seat and his flask of hot caffeine.

'General deViers, here. Go ahead, colonel.'

'Yes, sir,' said Marrenburg. 'I've just had it confirmed. About three hundred metres ahead, the main tunnel levels out. It straightens there, too. I'm told it ends another two hundred metres after that.'

'I see, colonel. And just how does it end.'

'Well, sir, I'm not sure how to say–'

'Let's not play guessing games, man. I don't have the patience.'

Marrenburg's voice was suddenly brusque as he answered. 'My apologies, general. From what I understand, it opens onto some kind of city, sir. An underground city.'

Of course it does, thought deViers sarcastically. Let's see how the magos explains this one.

WHEN GERARD BERGEN'S Chimera, *Pride of Caedus*, emerged from the end of the tunnel and into the huge open space under the mountain, half of the force's vehicles were already there, the crews gaping, staring wide-eyed at what lay before them. The other half were still moving down through the last stretches of the main tunnel. The rearguard would enter within the hour.

Bergen stood in his cupola, turning his head from left to right, taking it all in. The air around him was thick with exhaust fumes, but they were less dense than they had been in the confines of the tunnel. There was more space for them to dissipate here. The air pressure had changed. He could feel it on his skin. It was cooler here, too.

With the vehicles spreading out in an ever-widening perimeter, there was plenty of light, though not nearly enough to illuminate the cavern's ceiling or the far walls. Bergen still couldn't begin to estimate the size of the excavation. What he did see, however, stole his breath away.

A city of smooth, dark metal stretched out from the mouth of the tunnel into the blackness beyond. It was a dead city, a city without movement or sound or energy of its own, but a city nonetheless.

'So this is Dar Laq,' Bergen muttered to himself.

The buildings framed in the headlights of the Cadian vehicles shone back at him. Every single surface, every corner, every wall, was made of a shimmering, iridescent metal the likes of which Bergen had never seen before. As his eyes moved from one structure to the next, the colours seemed to shift and change like sunlight on the surface of an oily pool. It was beautiful in its own way. It reminded him of a shell he had once found on the south-western shores of the Caducades Sea. He had been practically an infant back then. The memory had been lost in the recesses of his mind until this very moment. Suddenly it was as sharp as a high-resolution pictograph.

Troopers were spilling out of trucks and halftracks around his Chimera. The beams from their torches cut like sabres through the murk as their sergeants led them down alleys and avenues, each footstep kicking up little puffs of dust. 'Safeties off!' he heard one sergeant call out as he passed within a few metres of *Pride of Caedus*. 'If there *are* any bloody xenos here, we'll be ready for them.'

Bergen doubted the barking sergeant would find any xenos alive down here. This place was as dead as the desert they had ridden through to get here. He could feel it. More so, in fact, for there was life in the desert if one only knew where to look. This place had all the atmosphere of a mausoleum.

That was changing even as he watched. After the-Throne-knew how many millennia of utter silence and stillness, Dar Laq was filling with bustle and noise. It seemed an almost sacrilegious intrusion. Bergen watched the troopers march off until they were lost behind the rows of blocky alien structures.

Each of the buildings he looked at raised the same questions in his mind. Where were the doors? Where were the windows? There seemed no obvious access points to any of them.

General deViers had questions, too. Bergen heard him bark out a short order on the vox, and powerful searchlights came on one at a time, reaching out for the ceiling and the far walls with their brilliant white beams. For the first time, Bergen saw massive towers standing tall over all the other structures. He looked up in wonder at the nearest, approximately three hundred metres away. It recalled to his mind the famous Cadian pylons that protected his home world from the vicious warp storm known as the Eye of Terror. As an officer-cadet, he had once visited the base of one of the Cadian pylons, a rare privilege largely forbidden to those of the non-commissioned ranks. He remembered the aura of power he had sensed around that inexplicable monolith. He had imagined at the time that some kind of living force resided there, something of incredible energy and potency. The Cadian pylons and the towers of Dar Laq were certainly both ancient and mysterious, but the latter exuded no sense of power or presence, only an aura of death and decay, and of a splendour lost forever to the ages.

The towers looked to be constructed of the same nacreous metal as the lower structures, but there the similarities ended. They were less blocky, less angular, suggesting that they had been conceived with a sense of the artistic at least as much as the functional. A few of them

were broken, the outer shells rusting or tearing away, revealing themselves to be stuffed full of what looked like clockwork on the most
massive scale. Great black cogs sat unmoving, frozen in the glare of the
searchlights, teeth bared at the human interlopers. Bergen's natural
curiosity kept throwing up questions in his mind and it took some
effort to quash them. What feats of science or wonders of sorcery might
the creators of Dar Laq have been able to work in their day? It was dangerous to ask, more dangerous still to actively seek such knowledge.
Heresy lurked at the boundaries of such thinking. It was natural, too,
though. It was part of the human condition to revel in discovery, despite
the warnings of the Imperial Creed.

The tech-priests were guiltier than anyone of that. Bergen imagined
they would be readying their bands of slaves and servitors to go out and
search for answers. They must have planned all this from the very beginning. Had they ever intended to help find *The Fortress of Arrogance*? Or
did their real interest in Golgotha begin and end with Dar Laq?

He watched the white discs thrown out by the searchlights as they
climbed the far wall, and his jaw dropped open. He had the measure of
the cavern now, and it was vast, easily two to three kilometres across at
its widest, and a kilometre high where the cavern walls curved inwards
to meet at a single point. Every inch of the walls had been worked by
alien hands. There were alcoves within alcoves, pillared walkways,
exquisitely wrought galleries of metal and so much more, all with the
same sharp, angular aesthetic of the ground-level buildings. How many
had lived here? How had they fashioned such a place? And why had
they chosen to live down here inside the mountain, shunning the light
and the sky above?

As the searchlights reached for the ceiling of the chamber, Bergen
gaped. There above him hung the most incredible feature of all, perhaps
a score of inverted black ziggurat-type structures linked by metal
gantries and platforms. They seemed to be floating in the air.

They can't be, he told himself.

He dropped back down into his Chimera and pulled his magnoculars
from their stowage box. Returning to his cupola, he pressed the magnoculars to his eyes and looked up again. It was only when he squinted
hard through the lenses that he realised they truly were floating as they
had no right to.

'Emperor protect us,' he muttered. 'What the devil is going on here?'

A sudden burst of loud static from his vox-bead almost made him
drop his magnoculars. A sharp, familiar voice said, 'Bergen, come in. I'm
calling a session of my senior officers at once. Meet me at the rear of my
Chimera in three minutes. I'm calling on the tech-priests to account for
all this. It's about time we had some blasted answers.'

'I'd say so, sir,' said Bergen, thinking he had a few questions of his own.

WULFE DIDN'T LIKE this one damned bit, and neither did any of his crew. Tanks didn't belong underground. It wasn't right. It wasn't natural. What if there was a cave-in or something? He wasn't claustrophobic. No tanker would last very long with that particular affliction, but something about this whole place made his scar itch like crazy. No human hands had built it.

Damned xenos, he thought. Nowhere is safe from them.

Things could have been worse. Emperor protect all the footsloggers who'd gone off down those dark alleyways looking for signs of alien occupation, and he wouldn't have swapped places with the Sentinel pilots and Hornet riders that were out mapping the cavern's extents, but sitting and waiting wasn't much fun either.

He and his crew, like most of the other tankers, had got out to stretch their legs after the long journey up the mountainside and down through the tunnel. Wulfe still felt stiff, but he tried to shake it off. Metzger was sipping water from one of the jerrycans, while Beans and Siegler were standing by the front of the tank speculating about what they saw.

Wulfe heard footsteps behind him.

'Your lot doing all right, Oskar?' asked Lieutenant van Droi, stopping right in front of him.

Perhaps it was just the quality of the light, but Wulfe thought the lieutenant looked terrible. He had never seen him like this before, so gaunt and tinged with red. His concern must have shown on his face, because van Droi suddenly stood up a little straighter, fixed his cap lower on his brow and said, 'You don't look so hot yourself, you know.'

Wulfe winced. 'I'm sure I don't, lieutenant. Sorry.'

Van Droi waved the apology off.

Wulfe gestured around at the strange metal buildings. He didn't like the angles, the proportions, the lines. They didn't look like any Imperial buildings he had ever seen, and that made them *wrong*.

'What the devil's going on, sir?' he asked. 'We weren't told anything about underground cities and alien races, excepting orks, that is.'

Van Droi nodded. 'No, I wasn't told about any of this either. To be honest, Oskar, I don't think the higher-ups expected this. General deViers was furious when *The Fortress of Arrogance* wasn't where it should have been.'

'Is it supposed to be down here somewhere? Or are we just improvising?'

Van Droi frowned. 'According to the tech-priests, their little ritual in the valley was some kind of communion with the Machine-God. They claim this route will take us directly to the objective. The general's buying it. He wants us to push on, despite the circumstances.'

'You ever met a general that *didn't* want that?'

Van Droi grinned. 'Not that I remember, no.'

When Wulfe spoke again, he was suddenly serious. 'Listen, sir. I have to ask you something. I hope you won't take offence.'

'Sounds ominous.'

'It's about Palmeros.'

Van Droi looked immediately uncomfortable, but he said, 'Go on.'

'We were talking about it in the officer's mess back in Balkar. You remember, sir. The day we lost Strieber and Kohl…'

'The canyon,' said Van Droi, not meeting Wulfe's gaze. 'Lugo's Ditch.'

'Right,' said Wulfe. 'Well, sir, things happened there… Things that I couldn't come to terms with at the time. I'm afraid I omitted them from my report, sir. I'm not sure if–'

'We don't need to do this, Oskar,' van Droi interrupted. 'I've never pushed you on what exactly happened out there. If you hadn't omitted certain things, I would have done it for you. I've seen some things in my time, let me tell you, things that beggared belief. High Command doesn't thank you for reporting things like that.'

Wulfe knew van Droi was being deliberately vague, trying to offer him a nice safe exit from the topic, but he had already committed himself.

'I saw the ghost of Dolphus Borscht in Lugo's Ditch, sir. I saw him standing on the highway as real as you are right now. He told me to stop the tank. And if I hadn't listened to him, my crew and I would be dead right now.'

Finally, it was out. The words hung in the air like ghosts themselves, hovering between the two men.

'Damn it,' hissed van Droi. 'Don't ever say that out loud. You want other people to hear?'

'Did you know, sir?' Wulfe demanded.

'Of course, I knew, Oskar. I'm not a total idiot. It wasn't hard to put it all together. But for Throne's sake, you've got to keep it to yourself, man. If the commissar ever finds out…'

'Someone would have to tell him first, sir. Someone like Corporal Lenck, perhaps.'

'Lenck?' asked van Droi. 'Are you saying he knows?'

'I can't be sure,' said Wulfe. 'Just something he said to me last time we clashed.'

Van Droi actually looked hurt for a fraction of a second, but he recovered well. 'He didn't find out from me, sergeant, if that's what you're thinking.'

Wulfe shook his head. 'I wasn't thinking that, sir. Not really. But I had to ask.'

'Listen, Oskar, Lenck might be less of a problem if you hadn't started some kind of damned vendetta with him the moment he joined the regiment. If you've got something on him, something that I should know about, don't keep it to your bloody self. If you don't, you need to accept that he's a Gunhead now. We stick together. It's the only way any of us will get through this alive. For the Throne's sake, man, he saved your life.'

'Duty, sir,' said Wulfe. 'I'd have done the same under the circumstances.'

In truth, he still wasn't sure he would have.

'That doesn't change the facts, Oskar. Lenck has more than proven himself worthy of being among us. He might be a bit of a rogue, but he's done a damned fine job with that crate of his, and he manages a difficult crew. For the sake of the mission, will you put your personal differences aside and act like proper bloody soldiers?'

Wulfe grumbled to himself, but finally he said, 'I'll try, sir. Since you asked.'

Van Droi looked pleased. He straightened his jacket and said, 'Unless there's anything else…'

'Nothing, sir,' said Wulfe.

'Right. I'd better get moving,' said van Droi. 'General deViers is having a war council, and I expect Immrich will have fresh orders for the regiment when it's done. Get some rest while you can, Oskar. And some rations while you're at it. I can't say when we'll be leaving this unholy place, but Throne willing it'll be soon.'

'Yes, sir,' said Wulfe. He saluted, and received one in return before van Droi turned smartly and marched off towards a column of parked Chimeras.

And get some rest yourself, thought Wulfe with genuine concern. *You really look like you need it.*

GENERAL DEVIERS HAD ordered a cordon set up around his Chimera. He didn't want the rank-and-file getting too close to the meeting he had called. Kasrkin troopers from Colonel Stromm's 98th Regiment were positioned in a wide circle, hellguns in hand, told to keep everyone below the rank of lieutenant out.

They were Kasrkin. He knew they could be trusted.

Bergen stood with Killian and Rennkamp at the front of a small crowd mostly composed of regiment and company level officers, adjutants, executive officers and, at the very front, positioned somewhat separate from the others, the three senior representatives of the Adeptus Mechanicus.

DeViers stood atop the back of his Chimera so that all the officers could see him. He looked, to Bergen, like a vulture on a branch glaring fiercely down at the three tech-priests, who observed him impassively with lidless mechanical eyes. If the general had thought taking an elevated position would rob Magos Sennesdiar of some of his dominating presence, or would force him to acknowledge his proper place as a mere accessory to the expedition's true leader, he had been wrong. The hulking, red-robed figure of the magos still cast its powerful aura over the proceedings.

'How do you answer *that?*' deViers demanded. He had just charged the Mechanicus with conspiring to lead the expedition force here for purposes outside the primary mission objective. As one, the crowd of officers edged forward a little, eager to hear the magos's answer.

'The accusation is false, general,' boomed the magos, 'false, but understandable. Your view of matters is being coloured by frustration and, perhaps, by the loss of so many men. The Mechanicus is not offended. We guided you to the last reported location of *The Fortress of Arrogance*. It was not there. You asked us to aid you in finding its new location. We are doing so. That our path led us to the discovery of Dar Laq is coincidence, nothing more.'

'And you expect us to take you at your word?' asked deViers.

'We were attached to the 18th Army Group to provide assistance to you. We have done little else. *The Fortress of Arrogance* is a sanctified machine. It was fashioned by us. Its machine-spirit is revered by us. We seek its recovery as much as you do, but with one small difference. We of the Mechanicus do not seek any kind of glory in recovering the tank the way you men of the Imperial Guard do.'

DeViers looked to be on the verge of being personally affronted by that remark when Rennkamp stepped forward and addressed the magos. 'Then you won't object if we leave this Dar Laq place at once, magos, since further investigation of this place is irrelevant to our mission?'

The magos turned and fixed his lenses on Rennkamp, who suddenly looked a lot less confident than when he had spoken. 'It would be most regrettable to leave Dar Laq without taking the opportunity to conduct a study of its mysteries, major general. There are gravity fields affecting the upper reaches of the chamber, though no grav-generators can be detected. There is the metal all around us. It is of a composition so far unknown to the Imperium. Its potential value can barely be estimated at this time. These are only the most obvious examples of what Dar Laq might offer us. Its existence was rumoured for thousands of years. Might we not conduct an analysis while the troops are being fed and the vehicles prepared for the next stage of their deployment?'

'This is no mission of discovery, magos,' said General deViers gruffly. 'Our rations are running low. Our fuel is limited. Our numbers, I'd rather not talk about. The Mechanicus may return to this place on its own damned time. For now, the secrets of this place will have to remain just that.' He raised his eyes from the magos and searched the group of officers, quickly finding the face he sought there. 'Ah, Marrenburg. Have your scouts found a way out yet?'

Colonel Marrenburg stepped to Bergen's side, looked up at General deViers and said, 'They have, sir: a tunnel the exact size and gradient of that which we descended. The air currents suggest it leads back to the surface on the far side of the Ishawar range. I have a Sentinel unit scouting it out right now, sir.'

'Excellent, colonel. Keep me apprised.'

There was a sudden metallic screech from one of the magos's adepts, which was immediately answered by a similar screech from the magos. Sennesdiar then said to deViers, 'General, my adept, Xephous, wishes to address you. Will you hear him?'

DeViers looked impatient, but he said, 'Very well.'

The clacking, chittering form of Adept Xephous stepped forward and, in an absolute monotone, said, 'With respect, general, are we not allowing our distrust of things alien to hasten our egress from this place before time? Our back is protected by the collapse of the tunnel behind us. The orks cannot, and in all probability *would* not, follow us down here. Might we not take this chance to effect maintenance on our vehicles, to tend to our wounded, and to recover our strength for the battles that must surely lie on the other side of this mountain?'

The general's expression said he saw the validity of the adept's comments. Bergen, too, saw the sense in what Xephous had said. Looking around at the other officers, he saw them nodding.

'Fine points, adept,' said deViers at last. 'Of course, I wasn't born yesterday. Do you suggest this for the benefit of the operation, or to allow you and your Martian brothers a window of time in which to conduct some limited study?'

Xephous was on the verge of answering when Magos Sennesdiar emitted a short burst of noise. The adept bowed and stepped back. It was Sennesdiar who spoke in his place. 'My adept makes his point for both reasons, general. Our enginseers will take care of vehicular maintenance. My adepts and I will conduct what research we can while your medicae perform their duties and your troopers prepare for what lies ahead. Clearly it is in both our interests not to rush headlong from this place.'

'Do you *know* what lies ahead, magos? deViers asked sourly. 'Did your ritual offer any clues to that?'

'Only that *The Fortress of Arrogance* awaits us, general, and it is no great feat of predictive power to say that the orks will not give it up easily.'

Bergen watched deViers closely. He saw a look of resolve harden on his face. The magos had chosen his words well, hitting the general where he was weakest, telling him his prize was still within reach. Perhaps it is, thought Bergen. But I still contend that the tech-priests led us here deliberately for their own ends.

After the meeting, with the other officers dispersing to issue new orders to their troops, Bergen took his adjutant, Katz, aside.

'I haven't called on your special talents for quite a while, my friend. But I think it's about time you got some practice in.'

Katz grinned. 'You want me to follow those tech-priests, don't you, sir?'

Bergen patted Katz on the upper arm.

'Don't let them see you,' he said and turned to march back to *Pride of Caedus.*

Katz watched him go for a moment, and then turned in time to see the three red-robed Martian priests moving off into deep shadow at the edges of the Cadians' lamplight. They were moving north along the cavern wall with a definite purpose, heading deeper into the jumble of alien structures.

Katz hurried after them, looking forward to employing his Emperor-given gifts again after so long.

'Don't let them see me?' he muttered to himself. 'You're having a laugh, boss. No one sees Jarryl Katz unless he means them to.'

CHAPTER TWENTY-SEVEN

DARKNESS HELD NO fear for Lieutenant Katz, even in an alien place like this. Shadows hid few secrets from him. The tiny, sophisticated mirrors implanted at the back of his eyeballs allowed him to see perfectly well in anything but the most absolute blackness. The three tech-priests he was following didn't seem to be having any trouble either, of course. Katz guessed they could see in a variety of spectrums. He knew it would take all his expertise not to be spotted by them, but the thought of such a challenge didn't make him anxious. It excited him. It had been too long since he'd had a chance to track a worthy quarry.

Katz had served as Bergen's adjutant for over a decade, hand-picked by the man himself, and few who looked at him would have guessed he was any more than a boot-polishing, shirt-pressing lackey. It suited him and the major general both to perpetuate such an illusion. Would anyone have believed even half the things he had seen and done? Not a chance. His history was far from that of a typical Cadian soldier.

Katz had been specially selected for sniper training barely a month after he had joined the Whiteshields. He had been in his mid-teens, but already his sharp eyes, steady aim and cold composure marked him as a young man of great potential. From sniper school, he had been inducted into a special reconnaissance commando programme so classified that it didn't appear on any Munitorum listing, one of a number of black projects ordered by Cadian High Command and funded directly by the planetary government. Most of the other trainees had been drawn from the ranks of the Kasrkin, and they were anything but kind to the precocious youngster in their midst. Katz had learned his lessons the hard way and, in due course, proved himself the equal of the older men, earning their respect and, in some cases, their jealousy. It was as part of that programme that his eyes had been augmented. Throne, had it really been twenty-five years ago?

He almost snorted out loud at the speed with which those years had seemed to pass: all those missions deep behind enemy lines; all those figures, human and alien both, that he had lined up in his sights, only to watch them topple lifelessly at the next squeeze of his index finger on that little curve of metal.

Things are much different now, he thought. But I wouldn't change it even if I could. I wouldn't go back. What would the major general do without me?

Katz was fiercely loyal to Gerard Bergen. He was proud of having been chosen to guard his life, for he judged Bergen a far better man than those around him, and it wasn't easy to be a good man when you were under orders from a soulless pig like Mohamar deViers. Whatever Bergen needed, Katz would do. Right now, that meant following the tech-priests.

Up ahead, the robed and hooded trio screeched something to each other in that infernal machine language of theirs, and Katz scolded himself for allowing reminiscences into his mind while he was *en mission*. Perhaps his skills *had* dulled with time.

With the light from the Cadian vehicles well behind them, the shortest of the tech-priests, the one with a face like a metal crab, pulled a small, pulsing electronic device from the folds of his robe. Katz soon got the impression that the device was guiding them somewhere. He saw them consult it several times and alter their course through dusty alleys lined on either side with towering hulks of dark metal.

He was concentrating so hard on his quarry that he didn't have time to wonder at his surroundings. The major general said it was alien, but ancient and long abandoned. That was enough for Katz. Like his own past, it was best not to dwell on it. The moment was all that mattered.

As the tech-priests shuffled on, he followed with all the stealth at his disposal, moving deeper and deeper into the derelict underground city, getting further and further away from the Cadian camp. They were heading northwards, and Katz soon began to wonder when they would stop. Surely the chamber didn't extend much further. They had already travelled over a kilometre in the dark.

* * *

<THERE,> SAID XEPHOUS. <The base of that tower. The auspex reading is strong.>

<He is still behind us,> said Sennesdiar as he led his adepts in the direction Xephous had indicated. <That is most regrettable. He shows remarkable skill. Had you not noticed his thermal signature, Armadron, we might not have registered him at all.>

<I would have detected him by his breath, or his heartbeat, or the scrape of his boots in the dust,> insisted Xephous.

<All irrelevant now,> said Sennesdiar. <We shall proceed as planned. I will deal with our unwelcome observer when the time comes. Hurry. Let us uncover Ipharod and be done with this. The column will be preparing to leave soon and we cannot linger long.>

They stopped at the base of a great crumbling tower. Sennesdiar looked up and, in infrared, noted the ornate black cogs and carved metal beams that were visible where large curving sections of the outer shell had fallen away.

<Xephous?>

<Here, magos.>

The adept pointed at one particularly large metal plate on the ground in front of him, and together the three tech-priests moved to lift it. It would have taken a dozen men significant effort, but, to the priests of the Machine Cult, it was an easy matter. Their mechadendrites snaked forwards from their backs, and, with a casual gesture that bordered on contempt, they flipped the heavy plate of alien metal aside.

The noise of it crashing was all the louder for the depth of the silence that had preceded it. The rumble of the Cadian machines was barely detectable in this part of the chamber.

Sennesdiar crouched down, his voluminous robe spreading out around him. <Here, at last,> he said, <is Magos Ipharod.>

The others crouched, too.

<Your wait is at an end, brother,> said Sennesdiar. <And so is ours.>

KATZ USED THE crashing of the massive metal plate to cover the noise of his footsteps as he moved closer to the tech-priests. It seemed to him that they had found the thing they sought. He could see a bundle of rags on the ground between them. He crept closer and closer, ever mindful of the slightest noise that might give him away.

Damn their bloody chirping and beeping, he thought. If only I could understand what they were saying.

He saw the largest one, the magos, unfurl the rags on the ground to reveal a skull attached to metal vertebrae.

It's another one, Katz said to himself. It's a bloody tech-priest.

He could see augmetic attachments bolted to the skull. He could see a metal collar bone. Magos Sennesdiar kept uncovering more and more. There was a structure like a rib cage, but formed of steel spars and pistons. One of the arms was missing, but the other was bulky and ended in something more claw than hand. Cables and flexible tubing trailed from the midriff like the entrails of an eviscerated man.

Katz wondered how much closer he could get without risking detection. He had to know more. The major general was relying on him.

Slowly, carefully, he moved in, keeping to the wall on his right.

So far, so good, he thought. They're preoccupied. They don't have a clue I'm here.

<HOW AUDACIOUS,> SAID Armadron. <The Cadian is barely ten metres from us now.>

<I want your attention on the task at hand,> said Sennesdiar. <I have already stated that I will deal with our observer. Now raise the body into a sitting position. Lean it against the wall. I want this done quickly.>

Xephous and Armadron saw to it. With precise and careful movements, they lifted the remains of Magos Ipharod into position. He was in a poor state. With the exception of his skull and teeth, the few biological elements left over from his human form had rotted away almost completely. His missing left arm and the absence of his legs spoke of violent damage prior to his seeking refuge here in Dar Laq. What had happened to him? If the procedure was successful, Sennesdiar would soon know.

<Armadron,> said Sennesdiar, <assist me in opening the skull. I will extract the intelligence core. Xephous, prepare to accept it. The magos will speak to us through you.>

<As you command,> said Xephous, reaching up to pull back his hood. His fingers worked a panel on the side of his metal head. There was a brief whining noise as tiny motors lifted a square section and rotated it away, revealing sockets sunk into the tissue of his living brain.

Sennesdiar detected no fear in his adept's tone, but he sensed an increase in secretions from his biological systems that suggested he was less than happy. Giving one's systems over to the control of another tech-priest's intelligence core was a dangerous and highly irregular affair. Ipharod was even older than Sennesdiar, and had enough authority to demand permanent control of the adept's body. Officially, Sennesdiar would be unable to refuse, but he valued Xephous enough to resent the idea. He did not want to lose his adept just yet.

No, he decided, Ipharod's IC module will reveal the information I seek, and then I will deactivate it for eventual return to Mars. If Ipharod wishes to live again, let it be inside another body constructed for just that purpose.

<I have it, magos,> said Armadron. He lifted a small cylinder of metal, covered in traceries of gold, from a hatch in Ipharod's grinning skull. It glowed ever so slightly in the dark, still charged with the energy needed to maintain its integrity.

<Plug it into Xephous,> ordered Sennesdiar. <Be sure to limit control to sense and vocaliser subsystems. No motor control. Is that understood?>

<Of course, magos.>

<I am ready,> said Xephous, presenting the top of his head to his fellow adept.

<Do not be concerned,> said Sennesdiar. <I will restore you once I have the information we need.>

<I am beyond fear,> said Xephous. <The Omnissiah asks it of me. You ask it of me. It is my duty and my honour to serve both.>

Armadron carefully plugged the intelligence core into Xephous's brain and closed the metal hatch.

<Shut down your central operating systems and memory subsystems. Reboot now as Ipharod.>

Xephous shuddered. Green diodes on his metal face winked out. His head lolled slackly onto his shoulder.

Sennesdiar and Armadron waited. Nothing happened.

<Are you sure you connected it properly, adept?> asked Sennesdiar. <You have made no errors?>

<I do not make errors easily, magos,> said Armadron.

A faint, tinny voice issued from Xephous's vocaliser. <Pride is an emotion. It is unworthy of a place in a tech-priest's mind. No errors have been made. I can hear you, followers of the Machine-God. I am Ipharod. And I am returned to consciousness once more.>

CHAPTER TWENTY-EIGHT

IPHAROD'S RECALL WAS absolute. Had his rescuers thought to bring a hololithic projector, they could have watched a perfect record of events in three dimensions as seen though his lenses. Unfortunately, not all Martian priests were equal. Ipharod was not impressed with Sennesdiar. He had come unprepared and under-equipped. He was probably no older than four centuries, and he was incompetent like all the new breed.

For all its flaws, its inherent ambiguities, Ipharod had no recourse but to employ spoken language. The first thing he shared with the other three tech-priests, however, was nothing to do with the past.

<We are being observed,> he told them. <Behind you, Magos Sennesdiar, there lurks a man in military fatigues.>

<His presence is known to us,> said Sennesdiar. <He will be dealt with in due course. Concentrate on the information we need, magos. In your emergency transmission, you stated that you had the fragment in your possession.>

<A partial truth, Sennesdiar. A partial truth. I located the fragment as ordered and was in the process of recovering it from the wreckage of *The Fortress of Arrogance* when my skitarii were attacked by a significant ork force. My guards were slaughtered and their bodies were taken as trophies. I was hacked apart and left for dead. They took one of my arms and both of my legs as salvage. They also took the commissar's ruined Baneblade.>

<Then you never actually had the fragment in your possession.>

<I judged that the Fabricator General would not authorise a Reclamator mission to extract me if he knew the truth. I was charged with securing the fragment, but was not given adequate resources to achieve this. A computational oversight.>

<The fragment is still aboard *The Fortress of Arrogance*?> asked Armadron.

<Who are you to address me so, adept? Your superior alone may question me. Is that understood?>

<Please answer, magos, as if the question had been mine,> said Sennesdiar.

<Very well. I crawled after the ork force, following their tracks in the sand, dragging behind me a single orbital beacon with which I could broadcast my coordinates for rescue, but the orks moved fast, heading north then east. They travelled through a heavily fortified pass in the mountains. I could not follow that way and had to find an alternative route to their base. I happened across Dar Laq, and decided it would be a safe place to await rescue, but only after I had once again located the fragment and launched my beacon. Five hundred and sixteen point seven hours later, I located a significant ork settlement to the east. *The Fortress of Arrogance* was there. From a distance, I observed that the dominant ork had discovered the fragment and judged it worth possessing. The creature was wearing it around his neck. I cannot comment on the status of the fragment now, but my probability algorithms suggest that there is a high chance it remains with the dominant ork. I coded my message into the beacon, released it and crawled down here to wait.>

<And the fragment?> asked Sennesdiar. <Is it all we hoped it would be?>

<Yes,> said Ipharod. <It is a relic from before the Age of Strife. Tech-Adept Reiyon, Yarrick's former enginseer, was the first to discover its existence on Golgotha. He planned to transport it back to Mars after the war, never predicting that Yarrick's forces would fall here. He was killed during the commissar's capture. If the fragment can be recovered once more, it will allow us to significantly refine our teleportation technologies. It must be retrieved at any cost.>

<Have you any other information relevant to our mission?> asked Sennesdiar.

<Now that I have a body again, albeit one of such limited capacity, it is fitting that I take overall command of the retrieval mission. I'm certain you see the logic in this, magos,> said Ipharod. <It is the task I was charged with.>

<It is a task you have already failed to complete, brother magos,> said

Sennesdiar. <You mishandled the original recovery operation. You transmitted false information in order to secure your rescue. Since I am the only other magos present, it falls to me to judge your actions. Thus, your IC module will be returned to Mars where you will face a tribunal. That is all.>

<Upstart. I am closer to the Omnissiah than you shall ever be. You presume to pass judgement on me?>

There was a moment of silence while Ipharod tried in vain to rise, but Xephous's body would not follow his neural commands.

<Do not waste your time, magos,> said Sennesdiar. <My adept's motor control systems are locked. I will now remove your module from his brain.>

<You must not,> insisted Ipharod. <I can still be of great value to this mission.>

Sennesdiar reached forward and touched a recessed button on Xephous's head. The metal panel whined open again to reveal the adept's soft grey brain.

<Do not do this,> said Ipharod. <I can still *czzzzztk–*>

Sennesdiar yanked the tiny, lambent cylinder from its socket and closed the panel. Moments later, the diodes on Xephous's face glimmered to life again.

<It is done,> Sennesdiar told him. He raised the intelligence core in front of the adept's face.

The first thing the adept did was to pull his cowl up over his head. <Did he not demand full control of all my systems?>

<He was unworthy of that. I am certain Adept Armadron concurs.>

Armadron nodded once. <Magos Ipharod is guilty of self-interest and deceit. He will be sentenced on Mars.>

<Incorrect,> said Sennesdiar. <He has been sentenced already. I have the necessary authority.>

Without further discussion, he crushed Ipharod's intelligence core between his metal thumb and forefinger. The cylinder crumpled easily. Its dim glow went out. Then Sennesdiar threw the ruined core over his shoulder with a very deliberate and precise motion.

It hit something soft before it struck the ground.

It hit Jarryl Katz.

'YOU MAY COME forward now, Cadian,' said Sennesdiar in Low Gothic. 'We have known of your presence for quite some time.'

Katz shook his head. The game was up. He should have known better than to get too close. They were tech-priests, so of course their senses were augmented beyond his own. Had they smelled him? Or heard him? Had they sensed his body heat?

Resigned, he stepped towards them, sweat beading on his head despite the cool, dry air.

'What is your name?' asked the largest of the three.

'Schweitzer,' said Katz defiantly.

'A falsehood,' said the magos. 'The slightest fluctuation in your heartbeat gives your deceit away. Speak the truth.'

Katz couldn't help but be impressed. 'You can detect that?'

'From this distance, yes,' replied Sennesdiar. 'That and much more. No matter who you are, you could not have followed us without our knowledge. Still, it is remarkable that you moved so quickly and quietly in this darkness. You are augmented, yes?'

The magos took a sudden pace forward, and Katz found himself looking up into a face more dead than alive. It was expressionless, unreadable, and he knew he had to get away. Whatever humanity might have once existed beneath that pallid mask of ancient skin was long gone. Despite whatever vestiges of organic matter remained, it was a machine that stared back at him through black lenses – a cold, calculating, ruthlessly efficient machine.

'The expedition force will be moving out shortly,' said Katz, working to keep his voice level. 'If you're finished here, we should all be getting back. We don't want to get left behind, now, do we?'

Katz wondered if the tech-priests were reading his heartbeat now. It was galloping.

The magos said nothing more. Katz had just decided to turn away when something metallic whipped towards him from the bottom edge of his vision. Bright, flaring agony gripped him. His lungs felt filled with liquid fire. He looked down and saw that one of the magos's writhing mechadendrites had punched straight through the fabric of his tunic and into the muscles of his upper abdomen. Hot blood began to pour out over his tunic and trousers.

He grunted in pain. He tried to speak, but there was no breath behind the words. He couldn't draw any. His lungs wouldn't work. He fumbled weakly, uselessly, for the knife at his belt.

'You will not suffer long, Cadian,' said the magos. 'Your death is inconvenient, but we cannot allow you to report what you have seen. There is already enough mistrust between the expedition commanders and the Machine Cult. The relationship must not be destabilised further at this critical time.'

Katz felt a savagely painful tug inside him. The end of the blood-covered mechadendrite withdrew from his body, taking his heart with it. Blood pattered like rain on the ground. For the briefest instant, Katz saw the wet heart held up in front of him, gripped by the sharp manipulators at the steel tentacle's tip.

Then true darkness closed over him, a darkness his augmented eyes couldn't possibly pierce.

He didn't feel anything when his body hit the floor.

THE THREE TECH-PRIESTS returned to the light and noise of the Cadian vehicles just as the preparations to move out were drawing to an end. The wounded had been stitched and bandaged and gathered into trucks. Those who were beyond medical help were given the painless death of lethal injection. In a brief, hurried ceremony, their souls were commended to the Emperor's side by a hard-faced confessor from the 88th. The supplies freed up by their deaths would help the rest of the force last that little bit longer. Vehicles were refuelled and rearmed. Troops were fed and watered, and the whole expedition force awaited only the command of General deViers to leave the ruins of Dar Laq behind them and head back to the surface, to the open air and the daylight.

For the most part, the troops were eager to put this unholy place behind them.

Only Gerard Bergen prayed for a delay. His ever-faithful adjutant had not returned from his mission. When Bergen saw the three tech-priests walking towards their Chimera, he charged over to them.

'Where have you been?' he demanded.

Magos Sennesdiar turned to face him.

'Recovering samples of metal,' he said, lifting a piece he had taken from one of the derelict towers. 'I'm certain that a proper study of it will be of great benefit to the Imperium.'

Bergen squinted up into the shadows under the magos's hood.

'You haven't seen my adjutant?' he asked. 'I sent him personally to bring you back. The general will be issuing the order to move out any minute now.'

The magos bowed. 'I am grateful that you thought of us. You are a man of fine character, major general. Alas, we did not see your adjutant. We encountered no living soul during our explorations. Dar Laq is a dead place. There is much to study here. The Mechanicus may visit again once this planet is returned to Imperial control, but, for now, we must prepare for our egress. Excuse us.'

Bergen watched the trio of cloaked figures move off.

Had Katz simply got lost? No. That couldn't be it. Bergen had tried raising him on the vox, but there was no response. Damn it all, he thought, there's no way deViers will delay leading us out of here for a single missing man. If I know the old bastard half as well as I think I do, he wouldn't even wait for Major Gruber.

Bergen turned and marched back to *Pride of Caedus*, determined to plead with the general anyway. The Chimera's engine was idling noisily, like those of the vehicles around her.

Sure enough, the general told Bergen he could not, and *would* not, order everyone to stand down because of one missing man. Had it been Bergen out there, deViers insisted, it would have been another matter entirely, but a mere lieutenant?

DeViers gave the order to move out. Drivers began revving their engines, filling the air with blue clouds of exhaust. Then, one by one, they began to move off through the eerie, lifeless streets, their headlights chasing off the shadows as they headed towards the tunnel on the far side of the cavern.

Bergen stood in his cupola the entire time, eyes facing out into the darkness on the north side, heart pounding in his chest, almost sick with emotion. It was far worse than grief. It felt like betrayal.

'I'm sorry, Jarryl,' he muttered beneath his rebreather. 'I'm so sorry, my friend.'

CHAPTER TWENTY-NINE

IT WAS TWO hours after dawn when the remnants of General deViers's expedition force emerged from the cool darkness of the tunnel into the baking heat of the Golgothan morning. They were halfway up the east face of a mountainside, but the landscape beyond was largely shielded from view. Sharp fingers of rock thrust upwards on every side, forcing the Cadians to follow a single treacherous path, the only route wide and shallow enough to accommodate sixty-tonners like the Leman Russ tanks.

The clouds were low overhead, a churning mix of orange, red and brown. Gusting winds pulled curtains of dust across the slopes. By midday, however, the winds dropped to a hot breeze. Tall rocks and ridges still confounded the view. Privately, some of the Cadians almost regretted leaving Dar Laq. Alien or not, the temperature had been more to their liking. The air there hadn't seared their lungs.

The mountain trail took them down onto more manageable ground, and additional vehicles moved up from the rear to support the vanguard. The column began moving in a meandering line along a series of low rocky gullies. Sandstone hills rose on all sides, but it wasn't long before the Cadians noticed something amiss. The sky beyond the next rise was darker than it was elsewhere, stained with copious amounts of smoke.

General deViers ordered scouts to investigate further, and small groups of Sentinels lurched off, careful to keep low so that they presented no silhouettes above the hill-line. Minutes later, the scout leader called back to recommend that the general halt the column and come in person to the forward observation point. He had found the source of the smoke.

BERGEN LAY ON his belly with his magnoculars pressed to his eyes, scanning the scene before him, uncaring of the fact that his uniform was filthy with red dust. A dozen officers on either side of him lay in similar positions, muttering and cursing at the focus of their attention.

Beyond the rise the land was broad and open, gently curving upwards on either side. The Cadians were looking down into a huge crater, a volcanic caldera ten kilometres across. The volcano was long dead, but at its centre sat the source of the dark smoke.

'Millions of them,' said Killian, lying on Bergen's right. 'There must be millions of them.'

'A hundred thousand at the most,' said Rennkamp.

'Either way,' said Killian, 'we're still heavily outnumbered.'

Bergen couldn't really decide what he was looking at. Either it was the ork equivalent of a town, or it was simply the biggest collection of scrap metal he had ever seen. Finally, he decided it was both, and in equal parts. Heaps of rusting armour plate and twisted girders rose a hundred metres into the air, the most prominent feature of the scene before him. Here and there ruined vehicles poked their noses out, some recognisable as the crumpled remnants of Chimera APCs and Leman Russ tanks, others not so familiar.

Wreckage from the Golgothan War, thought Bergen. For thirty-eight years they've scavenged the old battlefields and brought it all back here. Was this the place where Thraka constructed his war machines for the assault on Armageddon? Was *The Fortress of Arrogance* brought here?

He hardly dared to hope that it was still here today. The old certainty that deViers would never find his prize was still strong. Peering hard through the lenses of his magnoculars, he struggled to find anything even approximating the profile of the famous Baneblade.

No, nothing came close.

Perhaps they took it off-world, he thought. Here we are desperately searching for her on Golgotha so that we might repair her and ship her to Armageddon, and the blasted orks have probably moved her there already!

He zoomed in on a pair of massive cylindrical structures at the southern edge of the ork base. They appeared to be some kind of greenskin foundries. They were covered in snaking pipes and valves, and were pouring smoke into the air, some of it black, some of it a noxious yellow-brown. Now and then, great plumes of fire erupted from a series of thin, teetering chimneys. He saw hundreds of beastly figures hefting scrap through massive doors. There were workshops attached where the sharp white glare of promethium blowtorches could be seen. Showers of orange sparks accompanied the harsh metallic banging sounds that rolled towards him across the floor of the caldera.

In the centre of the base, surrounded by the mountains of scrap, there were hundreds of huts and hangars, all made of corrugated steel and arranged in no particular order that Bergen could discern. Unsurprisingly, every single surface was painted red and decorated with crude glyphs, the vast majority of which seemed to be skulls or faces.

There were towers placed all around the perimeter, too, unsteady-looking frameworks of iron and steel that rose as high as any of the mountainous junk heaps. Atop each of these, Bergen saw observation posts boasting pintle-mounted heavy weapons. They were manned by members of the smaller, skinnier greenskin slave caste. They were hideous, chittering things, known to the soldiers of the Imperial Guard as gretchin – relatively weak at close quarters, but more capable of aiming a gun than their bigger kin.

'What in the name of Terra is *that* for?' asked Colonel Graves. 'There, on the north side. Is that a cage?'

Bergen panned left and saw the structure Graves was talking about. It certainly looked like a cage, but it stood well over fifty metres tall. What in the warp had it been built to contain? The bars were thicker than an average steel girder. There was no sign of life inside, but the sight of great piles of reddish-brown dung left Bergen with a distinct sinking feeling. He thought he knew the kind of creature such a cage might have been built for. If they were lucky, the empty cage meant it was already dead. If they were unlucky, it was out on patrol somewhere, perhaps on the far rim of the crater.

He saw dozens of smaller pens around the cage, filled with the vicious-looking ovoid creatures that orks were known to eat. These were called squigs. Just over a decade ago on Phaegos II, Bergen had witnessed them being fired into the midst of a Mordian infantry regiment via a kind of crude ork catapult device. It was one of the strangest tactics he had ever seen the greenskins use. Strange, but effective. The result of such voracious and aggressive creatures landing smack in the middle of tightly packed troops was absolute panic as the squigs attacked everything they could get their razor-like teeth into. His tanks, moving up in support of the Mordians, had destroyed the catapults, but not before a good many men had died.

'That's a lot of armour they've got sitting around,' said Captain

Immrich. 'And they've plenty of light vehicles, too. They'll give your infantry something extra to worry about, colonel.'

Graves grunted something by way of reply. Bergen didn't catch it.

Immrich was a few metres away on Bergen's left. He seemed to be managing well in his new position as leader of the 81st Armoured Regiment, but Bergen had been a little stunned at the physical change in him. He looked a lot less robust than Bergen could ever remember him being. Then again, they all did. Bergen had studiously avoided looking in a mirror recently. The reddish tinge of his flesh was warning enough that Golgotha was taking its dreadful toll.

As Immrich had pointed out, ork vehicles were everywhere. Bikes and buggies roared back and forth as if their drivers were engaged in some kind of game. They hooted and hollered, and their passengers lashed out with hammers and blades every time they came within a few metres of each other. Bergen saw one ork beheaded in such a pass. The others howled with laughter as its lifeless body tumbled from the back of the buggy it had been riding. Seconds later, a trio of bikes ran straight over the corpse.

Mad savages, thought Bergen, but his revulsion was nothing to the apprehension he felt as he panned his gaze over the disorganised ranks of the greenskin armour. There were literally hundreds of tanks, half-tracks, APCs, artillery pieces, dreadnought walkers and more. Each looked just as likely to fall apart as to put up any kind of fight, but Bergen wasn't fooled. Ork machinery could be deceptively effective. Whichever Eye-blasted warboss ruled here, he was certainly well equipped.

'I've seen enough,' said a sharp, clipped voice.

Bergen heard shuffling to his left and lowered his magnoculars. General deViers was moving backwards down the slope. When he was below the ridgeline, he rose to his feet and dusted himself off.

'The scouts say there is no other way forward,' he said, addressing them all at once. 'We'll have to wipe them out. We'll need time to search all those mountains of scrap for *The Fortress of Arrogance.*'

Other officers had begun shuffling backwards down the slope. Many of them stopped at his words and turned to gape at him. Judging by the look on Colonel von Holden's face the man was just about ready to explode, but Pruscht, who had always seemed such a pragmatic and level-headed officer, beat him to it.

'You can't be serious, sir,' he hissed. 'In the name of Terra, think of the numbers. It'll be a massacre and we'll be on the wrong side of it, mark you.'

DeViers looked around, eyes suddenly hard, and Bergen had the distinct impression he was searching for a commissar. Fortunately, they had been left to watch over the troopers while the senior officers moved up to observe.

'It *will* be massacre,' the general snapped. 'A massacre of orks. *The Fortress of Arrogance* must be out there. Any coward who turns from our glorious path will be shot dead. There will be no trials. Our very fingertips brush the prize. Today, we seize it.'

Emboldened by the dismayed looks of the others, Colonel Meyers of the 303rd Skellas Rifles added his voice to the protest. 'But there's no evidence that–'

The crack of a bolt pistol cut his sentence short. His skull detonated, spraying Colonels Brismund and von Holden with a fine shower of gore.

'In the name of Terra!' exclaimed Colonel Marrenburg, turning suddenly pale.

'That man was a senior officer!' gasped Major General Killian.

'Sir,' hissed Major General Rennkamp, 'are you trying to get us all killed? If the orks heard that shot…'

DeViers's voice was utterly level. He eyed each of the men before him. 'Does anyone else wish to meet the Emperor's judgement as a coward and a traitor? If so, step forward.'

No one moved.

'Our mission has but one goal,' he continued. 'All else is irrelevant. Whether we live or die, gentlemen, we will ensure that *The Fortress of Arrogance* is taken from the orks and turned over to the Adeptus Mechanicus. Yarrick *will* have his tank back, and our expedition will be forever remembered in the proud annals of the Imperial Guard. As you have just witnessed, I will kill any man who stands in the way of that, for he is an enemy of the Emperor and no true son of Cadia.'

Those last words struck out at the officers like a lash. Bergen saw von Holden physically steadying himself against their impact. They affected the speaker, however, in quite a different way. As he finished his pronouncement, the general stood noticeably taller and prouder, his chest expanding until Bergen thought the buttons of his tunic might actually fly off.

The mad old bastard had really lost it, now.

The other officers were frozen. No one else dared speak. No one, that is, except the tall, hooded figure who approached from the bottom of the slope, his fluttering robes as red as the rocks on which he trod.

As red as blood, thought Bergen, eyes narrowing.

Magos Sennesdiar's toneless voice seemed to echo from the near hillsides as he said, 'A rousing speech, general. And I believe you will soon fulfil your destiny. My adepts have just completed consultations with the spirits of our auspex scanners. We have every reason to believe that the tank you seek is indeed located in the ork base up ahead. It is time for you to earn your place in history, and the Adeptus Mechanicus stands ready to offer our support.'

His hopes confirmed, a broad grin spread across the general's face, creasing the skin around his eyes. Bergen, however, saw all too clearly that the old fool was being manipulated. His desperation, his need to leave some mark on the Imperium, had made him a willing pawn of greater forces. Perhaps it wasn't entirely his fault. He *had* been great once, before the disaster on Palmeros had unhinged him. Most men, men of the aristocracy in particular, sought to leave something behind, though in the main this was achieved by the continuation of their bloodlines. DeViers had been denied that path to immortality, so he'd found another.

The poet Michelos had said something about fools writing history in the blood of better men, but Bergen couldn't remember the exact words.

Suddenly, Magos Sennesdiar turned his head southwards. Something had caught his attention.

'We must move at once,' he said. 'Quickly. Back to the vehicles. We have to hurry.' Though his vocaliser couldn't convey a sense of urgency through tone, his words were adequate to the task.

Everyone turned to face the same direction.

'What do you hear?' demanded Rennkamp, but the magos didn't need to answer. The officers could hear it for themselves now, the roar of an engine getting louder all the time until it was almost deafening.

'Above us,' shouted Colonel von Holden over the noise.

Bergen looked up just in time to see a chunky, snub-nosed jet fighter scream past them only a few dozen metres above the ridge line. It was painted red with some kind of shark's tooth pattern around the air intake at the front. There were rocket-pods and bombs fixed to the pylons under its wings. For the very briefest instant, Bergen thought he saw the leering face of the pilot, a hideous goggled ork with slavering, tusk-filled jaws.

'Move!' shouted deViers, and everyone broke into a sliding run that carried them to the bottom of the slope in a torrent of rolling rocks and dust.

The pilot must have reported their presence over some kind of green-skin vox device because, from the ork settlement at the centre of the crater, the thunder of war drums began.

The Cadians' chance to properly plan an assault was gone. Any advantage was lost. The beasts were already spilling out to meet them.

It was time to kill or be killed.

CHAPTER THIRTY

THEY CLASHED HALFWAY towards the ork settlement with a violence that shattered iron and bone. Things descended into madness almost immediately. There was no cover. It was open ground all the way in. The Cadians dropped hundreds of the foe at range, their Basilisk artillery pieces taking a terrible toll from about five kilometres back, but the orks had numbers to spare. They were a roaring, seething storm front of blades and guns, tusks and muscle, and they had gone a long time without a fight. At last, war had returned to Golgotha. The greenskins roared and laughed as long-range fighting quickly gave way to mutual slaughter at close quarters, and the bloodletting began in earnest.

Sheet lighting began to flash regularly in the sky above, almost as if the excitement of the orks was somehow charging the atmosphere.

Leman Russ Exterminators and Conquerors, Chimera APCs and Heracles halftracks all pushed in to support the out-muscled Cadian infantry with sheets of blistering fire, opening temporary gaps that allowed the footsloggers to employ their lasguns briefly before the enemy surged forward again, trampling the bodies of the dead. Sentinels stalked the far left and right flanks charged with preventing the fast, light ork bikes and buggies from circling around the main force and striking from the rear. Their autocannon blazed, spewing brass casings on the sand. Those sections of the battlefield soon became littered with smoking machines from both sides.

In the centre the air burned and throbbed, filled with scorching las- and plasma-fire. Solid rounds whipped and whined in every direction. Streams of liquid flame turned men and orks alike into roasted black marionettes that fell as if their strings had been cut. Shelling from both sides made the floor of the crater shake as if it might give way any second and plunge everyone into a sea of orange magma.

Outside the buttoned-up turret of *Last Rites II*, the world had descended into deafening, dust-choked mayhem.

Lesser men might have lost their minds in the face of such ferocity, for nothing could match the savagery, the gleeful brutality, of the orks. Cadians, however, were *not* lesser men. They were born and bred for war. This was their duty, and Wulfe was not afraid. His years of training and experience took over from the start, moving to the fore of his consciousness. His senses felt sharper, his movements faster and more assured, and his scar was itching, a reminder of all the hate he carried within him.

Whether or not he died today, he intended to take a heavy toll on the race that had killed so many of the men he'd known.

He heard van Droi on the vox. 'Take it to them, Gunheads. Show those bastards what it means to unleash the Emperor's wrath!'

FOOM!

The sound of cannon fire cut across everything else as the Cadian tanks loosed round after round into the melee.

Beans stamped his foot trigger and added to the fusillade.

Major General Bergen had ordered all the regiment's Vanquishers, standard Leman Russ, Executioners and Destroyers to race straight forward through the xenos lines, guns blazing, with the objective of knocking out the enemy armour and artillery pieces lined up on the settlement's western edge. From there, they could wheel around and strike at the orks' rear.

It wouldn't be easy. They were already drawing massive amounts of fire. Ploughing straight through the ork horde would put them at even greater risk, but the long-guns had to be taken out if the infantry were to push forward. There was simply no other way.

BERGEN THUMBED THE trigger of his autocannon, strafing the orks from the turret of *Pride of Caedus*, sending a row of them to the ground as lifeless heaps. All around him, the men of the 71st Caedus Infantry fought like rabid dogs. They were inspiring, even as their numbers dropped lower and lower. They made him proud. He was doing his best to support them, as was their commander, Colonel Graves, but if Immrich's tanks couldn't gain the advantage soon, all would be lost. General deViers's holy quest would end here.

The general was raging over the vox at anyone and everyone who was listening, demanding that they gain ground and break the ork charge. Bergen might normally have cursed him or ignored him, but not this time. This time, the old man was right in among them, in the eye of the storm, pouring out a hailstorm of multilaser fire from the turret of his own Chimera. No one, he had insisted, could sit this one out. The odds were too great, and too much was riding on victory.

That suited Bergen. He figured it was about time the mad old bastard got his hands dirty.

FROM LEFT TO right, the battlefield was a sea of monstrous brown bodies clad in black iron plate. Gaudily painted dreadnoughts waddled along-side them, almost comical in their clumsy movements. There was nothing comical, though, in the torrents of death they spewed from hip-mounted stubbers and flame-throwers. Cadians went down in great screaming lines, their bodies cooked or ripped to pieces by sprays of heavy enfilading fire.

The 8th Mechanised Division and 12th Heavy Infantry Divisions were pressing the enemy from the north-west and south-west quarters, hem-ming them in and forcing them to fight on three fronts. The 10th Armoured Division had the middle ground. In terms of strategy, it was hardly elegant, but there hadn't been time for much else.

Van Droi heard Captain Immrich cutting across the 10th Company command channel with a priority message. 'Immrich to spearhead. Drive straight over their infantry. Crush them under you. Once you're through, I want you to light up that damned artillery. Destroyers, focus on their tanks. Everyone else, targets of opportunity. We can make all the difference here. Do it for Vinnemann!'

For Vinnemann, thought van Droi resolutely. Throne, yes!

Foe-Breaker bounced and shook as she rolled over scores of screaming greenskins, pulping their meaty bodies under her treads. They turned on each other to get out of her way, hacking in fevered panic at the backs of their kin, but they were too slow. More fell with every metre she gained. In her wake, the sand became a blood-sodden bog.

Something slapped the turret hard, ringing the tank like a bell. The loader, Waller, cried out, 'We're hit.'

'Damage report,' van Droi called back.

'No breach, no breach,' reported Bullseye Dietz. 'Anybody hurt? Any spalling?'

They had been lucky. Looking through the vision blocks, van Droi saw a spiral trail of smoke hanging in the air between his tank and a rusty-looking dreadnought that was clanking its way towards him kicking ork infantry from its path. A rocket had struck *Foe-Breaker's* gun mantlet, detonating with enough power to give the crew a nasty headache, but little else. Without needing to be told, Dietz traversed the turret and lined her up.

'Brace!' he shouted.

Foe-Breaker rocked. Her turret basket filled with stinking smoke. The dreadnought seemed frozen in time for a split second. A melon-sized black hole had appeared in its armour, transfixing it. Then it exploded outwards in a burst of white fire, raining debris on the howling orks around its feet.

'Keep pushing her, Nails,' said van Droi to his driver. 'If we let them slow us down, we're done for.'

Orks were clamouring at her hull as she rolled on, hacking futilely at her armoured sides with their big chipped blades. Another rocket arced in and smacked the hull. Van Droi saw a different dreadnought, this one almost twice as big as the last.

'Damn it, Bullseye,' he called to his gunner. 'Take that bastard out.'

'I can only shoot one at a time, sir,' snapped Dietz, but he stamped on the floor trigger a second later. The breech slid back, dumping an empty brass shell casing. The dreadnought had its right leg blown off. It fell forward and landed on its face, bladed arms wheeling frantically, dicing ork foot soldiers on either side.

'Nice shot,' said van Droi. He scanned the battlefield for the rest of his company. It was hard to see anything. Dark, billowing smoke rose everywhere and the horde was still pressing towards him on every side. Blades clanged relentlessly on the hull.

'*Foe-Breaker* to all Gunheads,' voxed van Droi. 'Call in.'

Three of his tank commanders responded. One did not.

'Van Droi to Holtz, respond.'

Still nothing.

'*Old Smashbones*, respond.'

Van Droi knew Wulfe would be listening. They all knew what that silence would mean: another veteran dead. If van Droi had just let him stay on Wulfe's crew...

No, there was no use in thinking like that. A man could go mad on what ifs.

Go with the Emperor, corporal, van Droi thought. From the looks of it, the rest of us will be following you soon. I don't think anyone will be left to grieve, but we'll hurt the bastards on the way out. I promise you that.

'Nails,' he yelled over the intercom. 'We need more speed, damn it. Give her all she's got. Let's get our treads bloody!'

* * *

PRESSING IN ON the orks from the south, the infantrymen of the 303rd Skellas Rifles fought valiantly without Colonel Meyers. The word was that he had been shot for cowardice. The remains of his regiment – some four hundred and sixty men – set out to prove that they were made of sterner stuff. They achieved exactly that, though there was little opportunity for anyone near them to truly notice in the dust-choked maelstrom of battle.

Under their newly appointed commander, Major Gehrer, who led from the very front, waving the regimental banner in one hand and brandishing a bloodstained chainsword in the other, the 303rd railed hard against the ork infantry and momentarily managed to drive them back. It didn't last long. At such close quarters and without adequate armour support, the Cadian troopers were simply out-muscled, and, all too soon, the orks closed around them and butchered them with heavy, rusting blades.

Gehrer was the last to fall, protected to the bitter end by a swiftly shrinking circle of his strongest men. Even as the orks hacked him down and chopped at his fallen body, he fought to keep the banner upright, to stop its sacred cloth from touching the ground.

Seconds later, greenskin feet trampled it into the dust.

'SHORE UP THE southern flank,' screamed General deViers. 'Where the devil are the 303rd? And what's wrong with our artillery? Gruber! Tell them to increase their rate of fire. That's the worst excuse for a sustained barrage I've ever seen. Our men are getting slaughtered out there!'

He sat high in the turret of his Chimera, hatch locked above his head, firing rapid multilaser bursts at anything and everything that came into range. It had been too long, decades in fact, since he had led from the front. The sight of hideous greenskins being cut into smoking chunks by his own hand brought a murderous satisfaction that he had forgotten was possible. He revelled in it.

There was no leading from the rear this time. He had known it the moment he had first laid eyes on the ork base. Every man, every machine, every bead of sweat and drop of blood would be needed to win this day. The only individuals not engaging in combat were those damned Martian priests.

'We are not a combat unit,' Sennesdiar had said, as if it weren't already obvious. 'And we are not under the command of the Departmento Munitorum. We shall stay back with the artillery and offer technical assistance. Our servitor bodyguards will help to protect the Basilisks in the event that orks outflank your forces, general.'

Outflank my forces, thought deViers? That Eye-blasted cogboy!

The orks would *not* get through. To hell with the odds. Only in a crucible such as this could true legends be forged. The blessing of the Emperor had given him this chance, this shot at genuine glory. Every last one of his senior officers felt it, too, he was sure. They were out there now, Bergen, Killian and Rennkamp, leading their divisions from the front, turret guns blazing as their Chimeras pressed forward inch by inch.

It was hard to see much, what with the clouds of dust and smoke that cloaked everything, but up ahead, just a little to his left, he glimpsed the tanks of the 81st Armoured Regiment roaring straight across the thick press of enemy infantry. Big alien bodies were being mashed into the sand, pulped by the rolling, grinding iron treads.

Stubber-fire danced and sparked across hulls. Huge hand-held blades clattered uselessly against armour plates. As he watched, two were struck with anti-tank rockets or perhaps some kind of limpet charge. DeViers couldn't tell which. They stopped dead in their tracks, turned into blazing cauldrons, the men inside cooking to death.

DeViers thanked the Throne that he couldn't hear their screams.

The other Cadian tanks were almost through. Their guns coughed. He could just make out the first of the enemy armour starting to burn up.

'Gruber,' deViers yelled again, 'what about my artillery fire?'

'I've told them, sir,' replied the adjutant from the troop compartment at the back of the vehicle. 'They say they're firing at full capacity. And they're worried about hitting our own troops now.'

'Damn it,' deViers called back. 'Get in touch with their commissar. Tell him to make an example of someone. Then we'll see what full capacity is!'

He saw a massive black ork kick two others from its path and race towards the troopers in front of his Chimera with a chilling war cry. It was wielding a massive, whirring chainsword with both hands.

'No you don't,' said deViers.

With a grin, he thumbed his butterfly-trigger and gunned the monster down.

HOLTZ, THOUGHT WULFE, by the blasted Eye!

He kept repeating the name in his head, like a mantra against the truth of what he had just heard. He couldn't believe he was gone. It hurt like a hot knife in his chest. He kept seeing Holtz's face behind his eyelids when he blinked – not the disfigured face he had worn in recent years, but Holtz as he had been in the years before Modessa Prime. The man had changed a lot after that, everything but those ice-blue eyes.

He had been a good friend. Wulfe promised to let the real pain in, to stop holding it at bay, if he lived through this. For now, though, he had to fight it off. There was no time to miss anyone out here in all this madness.

'Incoming,' shouted Metzger over the intercom.

Something hit the tank's glacis plate with so much force that the back end lifted clear of the sand. Half a second later, it crashed down again. The treads bit into the dirt, and *Last Rites II* leapt forward, pulling more orks underneath her.

Through his vision blocks, Wulfe saw a black shadow peel away in the sky above.

'Damn and blast! Don't we have anything that can take out their air support? How are we supposed to clear their artillery out if we keep getting bombed from the air?'

Just as he finished his sentence, something small and bright screamed towards the jet and clipped its tail section. There was a burst of red flame and a puff of black smoke that quickly became an elegant curving trail. The ork fighter rolled slowly onto its back, and then slammed down into the horde. There was a mighty boom and a mushroom of dirt and fire. Wulfe judged that hundreds of orks must have been maimed or killed.

'By Terra, yes!' he shouted. He couldn't see the heavy weapons team that had fired the missile, but he saluted them anyway.

He had enough to worry about without the damned greenskin fliers trying to blow up his crate. In trying to crush their way through the thickest press of orks, the Cadian tanks had been forced to slow down. That made them easier targets for the ork tanks that spluttered and rumbled at the rear of the horde. They were massive, lumbering junk heaps with far too much armour bolted on at all angles. They crawled forward on rusting treads, traversing their turrets almost in slow motion, trying to draw a bead on their faster Imperial counterparts. Every few seconds, they would fire a volley. Some of them had already exploded due to misfires, while others had killed scores of their own infantry, but the closer Wulfe got, the more he knew that, sooner or later, they would make a lucky shot.

Captain Immrich must have thought so too, because, in addition to 6th Company's Destroyers, he ordered his first and second companies to break off and attack the tanks while the others dealt with artillery and static defences. As soon as the 1st and 2nd Companies broke through, they roared straight past the enemy armour, turned their turrets one hundred and eighty degrees, and began blasting them to pieces from the rear.

The Destroyers joined the attack from the front, the raw destructive power of their lethal beams cutting straight through hulls and turrets irrespective of armour thickness or density. They were a fearsome sight. Soon, most of the ork tanks were reduced to blazing metal heaps.

With the exception of Lenck, who had been ordered to support

Marrenburg's mechanised infantry, Wulfe and the remaining Gunheads broke through the rear ork ranks just seconds later. The artillery pieces were only a few hundred metres away: rows of massive, thundering howitzers crewed by skinny gretchin. They struggled to lift shells the size of fuel drums into the breech of each monstrous weapon.

From his left, there was a flash and a boom, and Wulfe saw that van Droi had opened up with *Foe-Breaker's* main gun. *Steelhearted II's* battle cannon coughed half a second later. Two of the ork artillery pieces came apart in great balls of orange flame.

'Beans,' Wulfe called over the intercom, 'light those bastards up. Don't stop until there are none left.'

'You've got it, sarge,' replied the gunner.

Traverse motors hummed, and then stopped. The gun kicked hard. Extractors whined and sucked out all the smoke from the turret basket. *Last Rites II* had notched up another kill.

COLONEL VON HOLDEN's 259th Mechanised Infantry Regiment held its section of the line with a mix of Chimeras, halftracks and troopers on foot. The vehicle gunners were charged with supporting the footsloggers by knocking out any ork vehicle that pushed in their direction. This they did with great success, pouring las and autocannon fire on them, turning a number of light, fast enemy buggies into spinning metal junk that scattered burning debris and dead bodies in all directions.

Their weapons were far less effective, however, on the heavily armed and armoured trucks that the orks were using as front-line APCs and light tanks. Some of these machines mounted fearsome customised weapons that really belonged on a more stable firing platform. The orks didn't care. Each time the trucks fired, they came dangerously close to toppling over, but the effect on the Cadians was devastating. The shots that missed the Chimeras hit the men behind them, killing dozens outright and fatally maiming scores nearby. The shots that struck managed to shred tracks and cause spalling, killing many of the men inside.

Von Holden saw it all. It happened to a Chimera just ten metres away from him, and he ordered his driver to pull back immediately.

'But we'll crush the men behind us!' protested his driver.

'Do it at once!' von Holden snapped. 'Or I'll have you shot for insubordination.'

With a prayer for the Emperor's forgiveness, the reluctant driver shifted the Chimera into reverse and began accelerating away from the oncoming ork trucks. Shots landed to the left and right, and the men that didn't die instantly went down screaming for the Emperor and their home world.

'Faster!' shouted von Holden, ignoring voxed demands from Major General Rennkamp that he explain his impromptu retreat.

One of the ork trucks spat a great gout of flame, and von Holden's Chimera was knocked sideways, slewing to a halt. The high-explosive round had shredded her right tread.

Von Holden checked himself for injuries.

'I'm all right,' he gasped. 'By the Throne, I'm all right!'

He didn't see the dark shadow in the sky above him. It dropped something small and oval. Seconds later, the burning debris of his Chimera rained back to the ground.

Janz von Holden was dead.

WITHOUT KATZ, BERGEN was having a hard time monitoring all the vox traffic from his regimental commanders. He had taken on a temporary aide by the name of Simms, a youngster from one of Captain Immrich's support crews. All things considered, Simms wasn't doing a bad job.

Over the noise of stubber fire rattling off his Chimera's armour, Bergen heard Captain Immrich's voice in his right ear. Simms had patched him straight through. At least the boy was a quick learner.

'We've practically wiped out their tanks, sir,' said Immrich. 'They looked tough, but they were a bunch of junkers. Half of them blew themselves up. Just a few left now. Companies one through four are tackling the static defences. I've ordered them to ram the gun-towers rather than waste ammunition. Those things look ready to fall over in the next breeze anyway. There are other garrisoned structures here, so I'm hitting them with high-ex shells. Companies five to ten are already mopping up the last of the artillery pieces. However, six and seven took heavy losses on the way through the horde. The orks are employing short-range RPGs and magnetic mines. Warn the Armoured Fist units not to get as close as we did. I'm ordering my Exterminators and Executioners to push through and join us. With my armour on this side and the infantry on the other, we can really start to punish them.'

Bergen was about to respond when a terrifying sound, halfway between a scream and a roar, cut across the noise of the battle.

Captain Immrich had heard it, too. Then, apparently, he saw it.

'Holy frak!' he voxed. 'That's big.'

By the Golden Throne, thought Bergen. Don't let it be what I think it is.

'What can you see, captain?' he demanded. 'What the hell is it?'

CHAPTER THIRTY-ONE

IMMRICH WAS ABSOLUTELY frozen in his seat.

An armoured behemoth lumbered into view around a towering mountain of rusting scrap metal. It was easily twenty metres tall at the shoulder, almost thirty with its heavily armed howdah.

This was no rickety ork contraption. It was a living thing, a member of the ork race, but so gigantic, so utterly different in physical form from its smaller kin that it seemed a different species altogether, unrelated in anything other than skin colour and temperament.

'Squiggoth!' Immrich gasped.

'Damn,' voxed Bergen. 'Did you just say *squiggoth*?'

'I did, sir. But I've never… It's *gargantuan*, sir! And it's not happy to see us.'

With a calmness Immrich did not feel, he added, 'You'll have to excuse me, sir. I think my tankers and I are about to be very, very busy.'

WULFE'S MOUTH HUNG open as the biggest living thing he had ever seen filled his forward vision blocks. It was a nightmare of armour-plated muscle and teeth. Its scaly skin looked as tough as rock. Each of the jutting lower tusks was easily as long as a Vanquisher cannon barrel and many times thicker, and its eyes, those giant glistening red orbs, burned with all the rage and insane bloodlust of its kind. The squiggoth shook its massive head and bellowed a challenge at the Cadian tanks. Wulfe felt his whole turret vibrating.

'By the bloody Throne!' exclaimed Beans.

'You can say that again,' Metzger replied.

'Siegler,' said Wulfe, still unable to blink. 'High-explosive. Load her up. Beans, draw a bead on that thing and make it fast. You can't miss.'

To the left and right, other turrets were already turning. Surely together, thought Wulfe, with all our firepower combined, we'll be able to put the bastard down.

It was Lieutenant Keissler, recently appointed second-in-command of the regiment, who was the first to issue the fire command. Flame licked out from the muzzle of his tank, *The Damascine*. The first shell struck the beast's armour-plated shoulder with a burst of fire and smoke. The squiggoth made an angry rumbling noise deep in its throat and turned to face Keissler's tank full on. It wasn't even scratched.

'Frak,' muttered Wulfe. 'That's just made it angry.'

Over the intercom, he said, 'Metzger, get ready to run. You understand?'

'Already ahead of you, sarge,' replied the driver. He began rotating the hull away from the squiggoth, rolling one tread forward, the other one back.

'Beans,' said Wulfe. 'Hit it somewhere soft.'

'Belly shot,' said Beans. 'I think I can get one under the skirts of the howdah.'

Other tanks began blasting away. Most of the shells struck the how-dah, and the orks onboard began firing back with rockets and heavy stubbers. Their aim was terrible. Bullets stitched the dirt. The rockets corkscrewed and exploded harmlessly in the air.

Then the howdah's gigantic main gun fired.

The sound made the squiggoth buck and rear, throwing off most of its passengers. They plummeted, hit the sand hard, and lay there, twisted and unmoving.

A Destroyer on Wulfe's left was suddenly swallowed in a great ball of fire. Tiny metal pieces rained down on *Last Rites II*.

'Frak,' exclaimed Metzger over the intercom. 'We have to move.'

The other tanks were pounding it, but the squiggoth wasn't even bleeding.

It clawed at the dirt, preparing to charge.

'What are you waiting for, Beans?' Wulfe demanded. 'Fire!'

'Brace!' shouted Beans.

Last Rites II kicked and sent a glowing round towards the squiggoth's belly.

There was a burst of fire. The monster brayed. When the smoke cleared, its belly scales were blackened, but undamaged.

That damned thing's skin must be thicker than our bloody hull, thought Wulfe.

The squiggoth had had more than enough of the tanks. With another deep bellow, it lumbered towards them, kicking ork huts and squig pens out of its way, trampling everything unlucky enough to get in its path. For the most part, this meant squigs, orks and gretchin, but one of the tanks from Lieutenant Czurloch's 3rd Company wasn't quick enough.

It had stalled.

As *Last Rites II* accelerated away, Wulfe looked back to see the unlucky tank and its crew crushed almost flat by a massive clawed foot.

'That thing must weigh a thousand tonnes!' he exclaimed.

Tanks were scattering in every direction, and officers started shouting over the vox, trying to keep their companies together, to maintain some kind of discipline. Turrets turned to fire back at the enraged beast, but shot after shot burst on its armour, only serving to enrage it further.

Immrich's urgent voice cut across all the panicked chatter. 'Listen up, tankers. Switch to armour-piercing. High-ex isn't doing a damned thing. And try to draw it onto the rear ork lines. It's mad as hell. We can use that to our advantage.'

Wulfe took half a second to survey the rest of the battlefield. Much of it was obscured by dust and smoke, but what he could see was an absolute maelstrom, the fighting insanely fierce in every quarter.

Once Immrich had dropped the link, van Droi's voice came through. 'You heard the captain, Gunheads,' he voxed. 'Stick together. Follow 1st Company's lead. And keep firing, for Throne's sake.'

'That idiot captain is going to get us all killed, lieutenant,' said a voice that made Wulfe scowl. 'We should scatter. Think about it. The minute we crash back into the rear ork lines, our speed'll drop by half. That big beast will stomp us.'

'Do as you're bloody told, Lenck,' van Droi barked back. 'That's an order!'

Wulfe cursed. He could picture Lenck's snide face. That piece of crap! He would put his own survival first every damned time. Maybe van Droi would see that now.

Wulfe looked out and saw that the giant squiggoth was giving chase. The ground shook. Every footfall was like a miniature earthquake.

Last Rites II bounced and swayed as she crashed over the orks' backs, Metzger keeping her speed as high as he could.

'Armour-piercing up the spout, sarge,' reported Siegler. 'Locked and lit.'

'Line her up, Beans,' said Wulfe. 'You'll have to fire on the move. Just do your best.'

Beans didn't answer. He was concentrating hard.

'Brace!' he shouted.

The tank kicked. The turret basket filled with smoke.

'WHAT ARE THEY playing at?' demanded General deViers. 'I want that damned thing killed this instant!'

A wind had picked up, dragging the smoke and dust away from the battlefield, improving visibility with each passing moment.

Brave men were fighting for their lives all around his Chimera, but it was the squiggoth that held the general's eye. It was the biggest threat on the battlefield, and that made it the biggest threat to his success. He saw his chances for victory thinning. Already the beast had crushed or kicked apart eight of the Imperial machines, and Captain Immrich was leading the damned thing back towards the Cadian lines. What in blazes was he thinking?

'Gruber,' he yelled at his adjutant, 'get me Bergen on the vox, right now!'

Something explosive hit the side of his Chimera and set her rocking on her suspension. He heard the rattle of stubber-fire as it struck her glacis plate like a hard rain.

'Nothing to worry about, general,' his driver shouted. 'No breach. No warnings lights on the board.'

'Bergen here,' said a crackling voice in deViers's ear. 'Go ahead.'

'What the devil are your tankers playing at, Gerard? If they lead that monster back towards us, it'll run rampage through our infantry. We'll be slaughtered wholesale.'

'Captain Immrich knows what he's doing, sir,' replied Bergen icily. 'Right now, the beast is out of control. They're baiting it. They've got it charging straight over the orks. It's killing hundreds of them, as I'm sure you can see for yourself.'

'I've seen eight of our tanks get crushed by the bloody thing. Tell me again that your damned Captain Immrich knows what he's doing. I want it killed right now. We've already knocked out most of their vehicles. Let's turn the infantry battle around and win this. What about their air support?'

'Dealt with, sir. Killian moved his missile teams forward with the Tyrok Fusiliers and took them out. All hostile birds are down. Is there anything else, sir?'

DeViers didn't like Bergen's tone. It was dismissive. Did he think *he* was leading this offensive? If the man lived through today, deViers planned to give him one hell of a dressing down. He had been too easy on Gerard Bergen up to now, too eager to believe they were on the same page.

It was increasingly clear to him that they were not.

'Just tell Immrich to kill that damned monster,' he said, and shut off the link. 'Gruber, get me Sennesdiar. I have to speak with him immediately.'

Seconds later, the voice of the magos said, 'I am listening, general.'

'Make sure you are,' said deViers. 'I want you to send that damned beacon of yours up. Code in our coordinates. Get that Mechanicus lifter down here, and tell your people to load her up with fighters, bombers, tanks… anything they can send us. Anything at all. We can win this fight if we just get some kind of edge.'

'Negative,' Sennesdiar replied.

DeViers exploded. 'Negative? What the hell do you mean by that? Do as I say.'

'General, as I have already stated, I am not part of the Departmento Munitorum command structure. I alone have the authority to decide when the beacon will be released. I will not call down a Mechanicus craft while there is still a significant threat to its safety. This battle is not yet won.'

'Don't you have eyes, you fool?' said deViers. 'My men are fighting for their lives. Now send the damned beacon up or I'll have you shot for obstructing an Imperial operation.'

'Eliminate the squiggoth and all static defences, general,' said Sennesdiar plainly. 'Purge any remaining forces from the settlement up ahead. Find the warboss. When you have achieved these things, the beacon shall be launched. Not before.'

DeViers heard the tell-tale click of the vox-link being cut from the other end.

'Gruber,' he yelled, 'get me Gerard Bergen again.'

FOUR TANKS. THEY were all that remained of Gossefried van Droi's 10th Company: his own *Foe-Breaker*, Wulfe's *Last Rites II*, Viess's *Steelhearted II*, and Lenck's Exterminator, *New Champion of Cerbera*.

Of these, only Lenck's was firing on anything other than the giant squiggoth. His crate's twin-linked heavy bolters were outstanding anti-infantry weapons, and they had helped cut a bloody path of carnage through the ork ranks, but they were little use against something like the insane behemoth that was chasing him. Instead, Lenck ordered Riesmann to concentrate on keeping the way clear with a torrent of fire. There was no way he was getting trampled to death like those other idiots.

Damn that stupid Immrich for ordering them back into the middle of the horde. Not only was it slowing them down, putting them in reach of the squiggoth's tusks and feet, but six tanks from the 2nd, 4th and 7th

Companies had been slapped with magnetic mines that blew them to tiny, spinning pieces. Other tanks were struggling through the press of bodies with dozens of orks on top of them, all yanking hard at the hatches and hammering at the vision blocks with the butts of their blades. All the weight of those hangers-on slowed the tanks to a crawl. As Lenck watched, the squiggoth thundered forward, crushing one and knocking two others onto their backs. Broken ork bodies flew in every direction. In the wake of the beast's rampage, however, more orks immediately moved in on the upturned machines. They began trying to cut their way through belly armour with chainaxes and blowtorches, desperate to get at the helpless men inside.

Lenck grimaced. It wasn't that he cared for his fellow tankers per se, but he imagined that it might not be long until *New Champion* was on her back like that. He definitely wasn't ready to die. Most of the dolts around him thought it was an honour to die for a so-called God-Emperor they had never even seen, or to die for a planet that had sacrificed them to a life of war in that same Emperor's name. Not Lenck. He still had scores to settle. He enjoyed being Voeder Lenck far too much to give it up on some foolish notion of honour and duty.

It wasn't his destiny to die here. He knew he would make it through.

Part of him hoped Wulfe would make it, too.

WULFE WATCHED TWO massive, ugly, scar-faced orks climb up onto the outside of his turret and start hacking at it with their axes. Futile, of course, but he knew how lucky he was that neither of them appeared to be carrying explosives or a burner. All he could do was tell Metzger to keep the old girl moving and pray they wouldn't get tagged with something nasty.

Beans was firing back at the squiggoth, but it was hard to aim with all the jouncing around. With armour-piercing rounds, he had managed to wound the beast twice, hitting it both times in the thick muscles of its front right leg.

Now a third round punched through its skin and buried deep, causing the creature to scream and rear up on its hind legs, towering like a Titan over the battlefield. Even the orks turned and gaped.

It was at that very moment, with the monster's belly exposed to the tanks below, that a long yellow muzzle flame erupted from the end of *Foe-Breaker's* Vanquisher cannon. The special high-velocity armour-piercing shell lanced straight into the monster's heart.

With a scream that hurt Wulfe's ears even through his baffles, the squiggoth collapsed sideways, tumbling heavily to the ground, crushing hundreds of orks and throwing out a great ring-shaped cloud of dust. The impact shook the entire crater, knocking foot soldiers on both sides from their feet.

Wulfe's tank was filled with cheering and whooping. The vox erupted with similar noises.

'Hell of a shot, sir!' Wulfe voxed. 'Give old Bullseye a slap on the back from me.'

The squiggoth was not dead yet. Few things smaller than a Titan could have killed such a beast outright, certainly not a Vanquisher tank. As the dust cleared, Wulfe could see the slow rise and fall of its belly. It was still breathing, but it was desperately weakened and pinned to the ground by the weight of the massive howdah on its back.

It wouldn't be getting back to its feet. Ever.

Its death would be long and slow.

IT WAS TOO much for the orks.

Bad enough that the squiggoth had rampaged through their ranks, leaving so many of them as little more than red smears on the battle-field; now they saw the Cadian tanks put it out of the fight, and their morale shattered like glass. Those at the rear broke ranks first, fleeing back towards the settlement, dropping heavy guns and blades on the blood-soaked sand.

The Cadian officers recognised this for exactly what it was: the shift that signalled victory. They rallied their troops, pressed their advantage, and surged forward. Those orks that did not flee suddenly found them-selves facing a resurgent foe. Without the overwhelming numbers at their back, they were lost. Their charred bodies fell to the sand, and the Cadians charged over them.

General deViers felt that the Emperor must surely be watching him at that moment. His destiny had not abandoned him. His legacy, his immortality, was within reach.

'Forward, Cadians,' he voxed, 'in the name of the Emperor. This day is ours!'

CHAPTER THIRTY-TWO

THE CADIAN ARTILLERY moved up to join the rest of the expedition force, and began pounding the ork settlement to rusting rubble. This was something for which the orks no longer had an answer. Thousands died taking shelter in their pathetic corrugated huts and barracks. Thousands more were crushed and killed when the Basilisks turned their muzzles towards the ork foundries and levelled them. It was only when General deViers received an emergency vox-call from Magos Sennesdiar that the shelling abruptly stopped.

'What the devil are you doing, sir?' asked Major General Rennkamp on the vox. 'We've got them right where we want them. Keep shelling.'

'Damn it, no!' snapped deViers. 'I want our tanks and Chimeras to move in. Each vehicle is to have infantry support. I want them to sweep each street, each building, and converge on the far side. That's how we're going to do this.'

'With respect, sir,' voxed Major General Killian, 'that's bloody non-sense. The orks will have retreated to their fall-back positions. They'll be dug-in. You're sending our boys straight into a death trap. I agree with Aaron. We have to pound them to nothing with the Basilisks and *then* send the infantry in to mop up. Anything else is just–'

'Enough!' snapped deViers. 'I've already executed one officer today. Will I have to repeat that action? I will not risk destroying *The Fortress of*

Arrogance. We go in with tanks and troops. We've already beaten them, by Throne. They won't put up much more of a fight. I want our tanks up front, is that clear? Bergen?'

'Clear, sir,' voxed Bergen. There was no mistaking the tone of exhausted resignation in his voice. His armour had just won a great victory. The Basilisks could have made it complete. However, if the damned tech-priests weren't lying for once, the most famous and sacred Baneblade battle tank in the entire Imperium was somewhere up ahead. It might be buried under a frak-load of rusting junk, but the general clearly believed it was there, and not one man present would be leaving Golgotha until it was retrieved.

FROM A PRE-EXPEDITION total of over one hundred, only twenty-six tanks remained in the ranks of the 81st Armoured Regiment. They moved slowly and deliberately through the twisting, junk-filled streets of the ork camp, halting frequently to blast apart ramshackle towers and barracks buildings from which ork rockets and stubber-fire stabbed out. Vox-chatter was terse, betraying the Cadians' anxiety. No one liked moving through the narrow lanes. The shaky metal buildings on either side looked ready to topple at any second. Their construction was almost laughable. Beams and girders stuck out at every angle. Most of the corrugated metal walls looked set to tear away on the next wind. It was a wonder any of them stood at all.

Again and again, the Cadians found themselves boxed in. Huge armoured orks, some of them almost three metres tall, poured out from shadowed corners in a frenzy, screaming oaths in their foul xenos tongue, bloodstained blades and hammers held high above their heads. The tallest were so dark-skinned they were almost black, and they fought with ferocity of a different magnitude altogether. It took twice as much fire to put them down as it did to slay the other members of the squads they led.

If not for the tanks and their crews providing hard cover and fire support to the footsloggers, any progress at all through the settlement would have been impossible. There were too many damned bottlenecks. The Cadian armour made all the difference, but it wasn't long before van Droi started hearing voxed reports of tanks being lost.

The fourth such loss was *Steelhearted II*.

Captain Immrich had assigned Viess and his crate as armour support to a company of Colonel Pruscht's 116th Lasgunners. They were purging an avenue half a kilometre north of van Droi's position when rockets had shredded the tank's left tread, rooting her to the spot. The infantry had immediately moved forward to return fire, only to be cut down by ork heavy weapon teams perched on the nearby roofs. Then the ork foot soldiers had poured in, dragging Viess and his crew out of their hatches and hacking them to pieces on the street.

A few of the lasgunners had managed to break away from the fighting and report what had happened. The commissars would probably execute them later on charges of cowardice.

The Gunheads were down to three tanks. Van Droi could hardly believe it. Soul-sapping misery hovered over him, threatening to descend and engulf him at any second, but he fought hard to keep it at bay. Other men were depending on him, now, a platoon of Colonel Stromm's Kasrkin troopers. They followed just behind his crate, hellgun stocks raised to their armoured shoulders.

He couldn't afford to lose focus.

Van Droi looked out from his cupola, fists tight around the grips of his pintle-mounted heavy bolter. His Vanquisher had already been stung twice – once on the glacis and once on the mantlet – by rockets fired from blind corners. She had soaked up both hits, but how much more could she take? Her hide was scarred silver by all the stubber-fire she had drawn, and stained black where the rockets had struck.

Thinking that his remaining Gunheads deserved to know of the company's latest loss, he hit the vox-link button on his headset and said, 'This is 10th Company Command. Listen up, Gunheads. I've just heard from Colonel Pruscht that *Steelhearted II* is dead. Viess and his crew are gone. So, keep your damned eyes open, both of you. If Yarrick's tank *is* here, this will all be over soon. You have to keep it tight until then.'

Two brief acknowledgements came back to him. One from Wulfe, one from Lenck. Van Droi knew they utterly detested each other. They were just about as different as two men could be, but they were both survivors. They had that much in common.

What was it about the character of each man, he wondered, that had got him this far when so many others had fallen along the way? Was it Lenck's self-serving ruthlessness? Wulfe's rigid honour code? Or his almost paternal concern for the lives of his crew?

If they both survived this, maybe van Droi could find a way to bridge the gap between them. Troopers who disliked each other at first were often bonded by the trials they shared. He had seen it before.

Then again, he thought, maybe not.

Up ahead, he noticed that the avenue was quickly widening. The ork structures were bigger and more widely spaced apart. From some of the roofs, great crooked armatures reached up towards the sky. They looked like construction cranes. Their heavy steel cables swung in the wind.

'Take it slow, Nails,' van Droi told his driver over the intercom. 'It looks like we're approaching the eastern edge of the settlement. I can't believe we've seen everything the orks have left.'

Nails shifted down a gear, prompting a question from the Kasrkin lieutenant at the rear.

'Trouble up ahead?' he voxed.

'Can't be sure,' replied van Droi. 'Come up and take a look.'

The Kasrkin officer, a rough-spoken man by the name of Gradz, clambered up the back of *Foe-Breaker* and stopped close to van Droi. Despite their proximity, they spoke over the vox. The noise of the engine was too loud for anything else.

'What do you think?' asked van Droi.

The Kasrkin took a moment to answer. 'I think we've just found our warboss, armour. That hangar dead ahead is the biggest structure I've seen so far. Twice the size of those ones to the side. I'll bet you ten bottles of *joi* the bastard is in there right now. The minute our lads move into that open square, the orks'll launch their last stand. The warboss will lead it.'

Van Droi nodded in silent agreement.

'Well?' asked Gradz. 'You gonna take the bet?'

Something large moved in the shadowed mouth of the hangar. The muzzle brake of a massive battle cannon poked out into the daylight. Van Droi and Gradz both saw it at the same time, but it was too late to do anything. The gun belched fire and smoke. There was a clap of thunder.

They didn't see the shell that killed them. It happened too fast for that.

Foe-Breaker was flipped onto her back by the power of the explosion, crushing eight of the men behind her. Then her magazine ignited, and her armour blew outwards as a million spinning shrapnel shards.

No one within ten metres of her survived.

CHAPTER THIRTY-THREE

ORKS WERE SPEWING out from buildings on all sides.

'We need to fall back right now,' Lieutenant Keissler voxed to Captain Immrich. 'Draw them back into the narrower streets.'

'No,' snapped Immrich. 'I will not disobey the general's orders. We are to stand firm and engage. There will be no retreat. This is their last stand, and it is ours as well.'

'You're a bloody fool, Immrich,' hissed Keissler. 'I always thought so. Death or glory, is it?'

'What else is there?' Immrich replied and took aim.

GENERAL DEVIERS COULD barely hear himself think over all the noise on the vox.

Killian was yelling for permission to pull his men *out* of the ork settlement. Rennkamp was calling on him to send everything they had *in* to support the Cadian tanks, and Bergen was raving about some monstrous ork battle tank five times the size of a Leman Russ that was ripping the forward elements of his armoured division apart.

In the general's mind, there was only one pertinent fact. His prize was in there somewhere. The path was clear.

'Army Group Command to all units. This is General Mohamar deViers. In the name of the Emperor, I order you to move in. Converge on the east side of the settlement. Give your lives if necessary, but sell them dear. Our victory must be absolute. *The Fortress of Arrogance* is within reach. For Cadia and for the glory of all mankind, we will recover her this day. Fight hard, brave Cadians. The Emperor protects!'

THE EMPEROR WASN'T doing a very good job of protecting the men of the 88th Mobile Infantry.

Wulfe had been attached to one of their platoons for the sweep eastwards, but the men were dropping like flies, hemmed in on all sides by savage aliens of simply breathtaking bulk and power. Lasgun blasts hardly seemed to affect the orks at all.

Wulfe's stubber-fire was only marginally more effective. He did his best to keep the orks off the men around him, gunning them down mercilessly with enfilading fire from his cupola, but there were simply too many. They weren't the worst of it, either, not by far.

Between them, the Cadian armour and infantry would have found a way to overcome the unmounted troops. It would have needed time, coordination, and a healthy serving of old-fashioned Cadian courage, but the orks had armour support of their own – a single lethal machine that nothing on the Cadian side seemed capable of damaging – and it was picking the 18th Army Group tanks off one by one.

Beans had fired on that clanking, rumbling, smoke-spewing monstrosity three times already, switching from high-explosive to armour-piercing when it was clear the former was utterly ineffective, but the armour-piercing shot hadn't done much in the way of damage either. The other tanks had discovered this too. Their rounds either exploded without effect or lodged in metre-thick slabs of iron skin.

Some of the remaining Executioners and Destroyers had enjoyed slightly more success, managing to blast a few pieces off here and there, but the oversized lump of metal was still rolling forward, emerging into the daylight with aching slowness.

This was the monstrosity that had brewed up *Foe-Breaker*. Wulfe had heard it all over the vox, his gut knotting until it caused him actual physical pain. Seconds after the vox report, he and the other mixed units had arrived on the open ground before the big hangar. That was when the orks had poured out to surround them.

What in the blasted warp is it? Wulfe wondered, glancing in the direction of the ork machine.

Only half of it was visible so far, but Wulfe guessed its speed had nothing at all to do with an underpowered engine. It had been built by orks. Already its armour had proved superior to the Cadian weapons. It was most likely fitted with an insane excess of weaponry, too.

As he thought this, the machine's main gun fired again, its thunderous roar shaking the hangar walls and the buildings on either side. The air trembled. A Leman Russ Conqueror belonging to 2nd Company spun on a pillar of flame and crashed to the ground on its side.

Wulfe wondered darkly if *Foe-Breaker* had landed the same way.

The report of van Droi's death had hit him with all the force of an Earthshaker round, harder, if he was honest, than the death of Holtz or Viess. He had known van Droi longer. The man had seemed immortal to a young Wulfe when he had first joined the regiment. He had been somewhat like Colonel Vinnemann in that regard. For Wulfe, Gossefried van Droi had embodied everything that was strong and true and noble about the Imperial Guard. He was a symbol. Gossefried's Gunheads had been named for him. Symbols weren't supposed to die. Only people died. People and orks.

Hungry for revenge, he loosed a battle cry and thumbed the trigger of his heavy stubber, sending another lethal torrent straight into a pack of orks that were hacking the arms and legs from an infantryman on the left. Wulfe couldn't save him – it was too late for that – but he punished the soldier's killers. Their grotesquely muscled bodies crumpled to the ground, torsos almost cut in half by the stubber's high rate of fire. Their thick red blood mixed with that of the man they had just killed.

Wulfe heard Beans calling 'Brace!' on the intercom just before a tongue of fire flickered at the end of *Last Rites II's* battle cannon. The sharp boom it made set his ears ringing.

The round went curving in towards the massive ork machine, striking a plate of red-painted iron bolted to the front. White sparks showered out as the round ricocheted and punched a hole in the corrugated surface of the hangar wall. After a second, the plate fell off and was pulled under a set of massive iron treads.

'Damn it!' cursed Beans over the intercom, but Wulfe wasn't listening to him. He was listening to the divisional vox channel. The chatter there had suddenly intensified, for Beans's shot had uncovered the forward edge of a massive black track-guard, on top of which sat an icon cast in bright, shining gold.

Every man on the battlefield recognised it. It hung from their necks, imprinted on one side of the dog-tags they all wore. Many had paid to have it tattooed on their bodies.

It was the holy aquila, two-headed eagle, icon of the Imperium of Man.

CHAPTER THIRTY-FOUR

GENERAL DEVIERS FELT his heart hammering in his chest as his Chimera raced in towards the battle. He ordered his driver to crash straight through the orks that filled the street up ahead. Beyond them, he could already see the ground where his forces were fighting for their lives. There was the massive hangar he had heard about on the vox, and, there she was: *The Fortress of Arrogance.*

There was no doubt it was her. Some tanker in the 10th Armoured Division had knocked off a piece of her disguise, and now everyone knew. They had found her. They had tracked her down at last, but what in blazes had the greenskins done to her? In all the general's dreams of how this moment would unfold, he had never imagined this. In the ultimate act of sacrilege, the orks were using her to slaughter Imperial forces. *His* forces.

Even so, he had no choice but to give the order.

Through gritted teeth, he voxed, 'This is Army Group Command to all units. Cease fire on the enemy super-heavy at once. I repeat, do not fire on the ork super-heavy under any circumstances. Concentrate on the enemy infantry.'

Gerard Bergen wasn't slow to respond. He didn't bother with propriety, either.

'You're out of your frakking mind, general,' he hissed. 'Whether that abomination is Yarrick's Baneblade or not, it's devastating my armour. We have to take it out right now. Reverse that order!'

'Mind your damned tone, major general,' deViers barked back. 'I will do no such thing. Ask Magos Sennesdiar; if a round pierces the onboard fuel or ammunition supplies, she'll be beyond all hope of repair.'

'And if we don't put her out of commission, there won't be anyone left to claim her. Have you lost your mind, you old fool? You're acting like a damned Mechanicus puppet. You know that?'

DeViers felt his face grow hot.

'I hope you live through this, Gerard,' he growled, 'I really do, because if you ever speak like that to me again, I'll see you swing from the gallows. Is that clear? The order stands. Anyone who fires on *The Fortress of Arrogance* will answer to me.'

'Fine,' said Bergen bitterly, 'and may you answer to the souls of the men you've just condemned. Bergen out.'

'YOU HAVE GOT to be bloody joking!' exclaimed Beans.

'I wish I was,' answered Wulfe. He turned to his left and fired on an ork wielding a bulky heavy flamer as if it were little more than a pistol. It had just finished roasting three Guardsmen to death at close range. When Wulfe's stubber-rounds punched into its body, the ork threw up its hands. One of the rounds punctured the fuel tanks on its back, and it exploded in a fountain of bright fire and burning meat.

The bastardised Baneblade was almost fully out of the hangar. Wulfe could see an absolutely massive ork standing on top of it. It had to be the warboss. It wasn't just the size of the creature, though it certainly made even the biggest of the black-skinned veterans look almost small. It was the massive suit of power armour that it wore. Energy crackled in blue arcs along its arms. It flexed huge blade-like claws and bellowed its war cry through some kind of amplifier attached to its shoulder.

The bestial roar swept over the battlefield, and the orks all around began fighting with fresh reserves of energy and zeal.

'Look,' said Beans, 'I might just be a gunner, but I know that order is utter bloody ball-rot, sarge. If we can't fire on it, we're dead men.'

As if to prove his point, the Baneblade's main gun fired again. The last surviving Leman Russ Executioner detonated in a spectacular burst of orange fire and glowing blue plasma.

'Throne damn it,' cursed Wulfe. 'Listen, Beans, do you think you can hit the warboss without hitting the tank?'

About twenty metres behind *Last Rites II*, a Chimera exploded. Wulfe felt the intense heat of the blast on the back of his neck and turned.

A slavering black ork was hauling its way up the back of his tank with

an axe in one hand and a rusty metal hook in the other. A string of des-
iccated human heads bobbed around its waist.

Wulfe dropped down into the turret basket just in time. The beast's
axe clanged on the rim just as his head disappeared inside.

'By the Throne!' shouted Siegler. He began scrambling to unhook one
of the lasguns from the fixings by his station. In the meantime, the ork
had thrust its metal hook into the turret basket and was slashing backwards and forwards, trying to snag the crewmen it knew were inside.

Wulfe threw both his arms around the ork's massive wrist, but the
damned thing was so powerful it began battering him off the turret
walls. In desperation, Wulfe let go with one hand and scrambled for his
knife. He grasped the handle, drew it from its sheath, and stabbed it
hard into the ork's forearm.

With a roar of pain, the ork withdrew its arm, taking the knife with it,
but the reprieve was only temporary. Seconds later, it thrust its massive
head down into the turret and began snapping at Wulfe with its razor-
toothed jaws. The stink of its foul breath filled the compartment.

'Down,' shouted Siegler, and Wulfe dropped his weight to the floor
just in time. Tusks clashed an inch above his head. Then the ork turned
to face the loader, drawn by his shout.

Siegler rammed the barrel of a lasgun into the creature's mouth and
yanked back hard on the trigger. The blast blew out the back of the ork's
head, spattering the wall of the turret basket and two of its occupants
with blood and brain matter.

'By the bloody Eye of Terror,' shouted Beans. The back of his head was
drenched in foul-smelling gore.

'Good work, Sig,' said Wulfe. He immediately set about trying to clear
the cupola, but it wasn't easy. Shifting the heavy corpse took all his
strength.

When the hatch was free, he poked his head out to check for any other
orks waiting to lop his head off. There were none. He stood and gripped
the handles of his heavy stubber again. In the few seconds it had taken
to deal with the hook-wielding ork, yet another Cadian tank had been
reduced to a flaming black skeleton.

Something else had changed, too. There were more Cadians than
before. The reinforcements from the rear had arrived. Chimeras were
pouring laser and autocannon fire in every direction but that of *The
Fortress of Arrogance*, and the foot soldiers were tapping in to some kind
of hidden reserves. They fought back with a renewed sense of purpose.
Wulfe decided it must be the sight, or perhaps the proximity, of the holy
tank that had inspired them. If they could only stop it knocking out
their damned armour...

Just as he was thinking this, the disfigured Baneblade fired again.

This time, the victim was Hal Keissler and *The Damascine*. The 2nd Company leader died instantly, blown apart with the rest of his crew. Wulfe swore, realising that he could count the number of surviving tanks on the fingers of two hands. To the right he saw *New Champion of Cerbera* and was amazed that she had stayed in the fight for this long.

Perhaps he had underestimated Lenck's skill as a commander.

It hardly mattered. If *The Fortress of Arrogance* kept picking them off like this, none of it would mean a damned thing.

'Beans, you never answered my question.'

Having been denied the only armoured target on the field, Beans was strafing ork infantry with the co-ax. 'What question?'

'Do you think you can hit the damned warboss?'

'I can try,' said Beans, 'but if I hit his ride instead, the general will have me shot!'

'Do it anyway,' barked Wulfe. 'I'll answer for it, but you have to take the shot. That damned thing is getting ready to fire again, and we might just be the next target. Siegler? Load her up. High-explosive. Let's blow that greenskin bastard into the next life.'

'We're out of high-ex, sarge,' replied Siegler. 'Only armour-piercing left, and not many of 'em.'

'Damn it,' spat Wulfe. 'AP it is. Load her up. Aim well, Beans.'

'Locked and lit,' shouted Siegler.

'Do it,' said Wulfe, 'and may the Emperor guide your shot!'

Beans stamped on the floor trigger.

Last Rites II shuddered as exploding propellant burst from her muzzle brake. The shot zipped straight in towards *The Fortress of Arrogance*. Wulfe held his breath, praying that the ork leader would disintegrate in a shower of blood and bone shards.

The shot curved low and smacked straight into the Baneblade's turret instead.

Another massive armoured plate fell away, revealing more of the black and gold that lay underneath.

The reaction on the vox was immediate. Wulfe heard General deViers screeching at the top of his voice. 'Who fired that shot? Identify yourself at once. You are disobeying a direct order from your general!'

Wulfe was about to respond when another voice cut in. It was Major General Bergen.

'Frak it!' said Bergen. 'This is a direct order from 10th Division Command. All tanks, open up on that monstrosity with everything you have. We won't lose anyone else to it. You hear me? Fire at will.'

Wulfe knew that the general's orders overrode Bergen's, but he wasn't about to let that stop him. 'Siegler, load. Beans, do what you do best, son!'

Thunderclaps echoed from the rusting metal walls all around as the surviving tanks of the 10th Armoured Division blasted the bastardised Baneblade with everything they had. Fire blossomed all over it and heavy pieces of armour spun away in all directions.

'Stop!' yelled deViers over the vox, but nobody was listening. 'I command you to stop!'

The Adeptus Mechanicus also added their protestations, overriding the Cadian vox-comms to issue warnings of their own, but to no avail.

Again and again, the tanks fired. More and more of the true shape of *The Fortress of Arrogance* was revealed. Then one shot struck the raging warboss that stood atop the turret. There was a sudden burst of bright blue light and a loud cracking sound as the energy field generated by the warboss's armour struggled to absorb the blast. Against lesser weapons like lascannons, it might have held indefinitely, but it simply wasn't powerful enough to repel the sheer force of a tank round impacting at full velocity. The field collapsed and the beast's right arm vanished completely in a fine red mist.

The warboss staggered and looked sideways at the ragged, bleeding stump of flesh with an expression of slack-jawed disbelief. That was when a second round, an armour-piercing shell from Captain Immrich's Vanquisher, *Firemane*, struck it dead centre in the torso. The round punched straight through the ork's power armour, blew its guts out its back, and blasted it from its feet.

A great cheer went up from the Cadian soldiers, and they rallied for the third time that day. Wulfe marvelled at them. He knew how tired they were, but they were Cadians, all of them. They would rather die of exhaustion than give up the fight. It was their planetary heritage, this discipline and strength.

'Cease fire,' shouted deViers again. 'Cease fire, at once!'

The tankers stopped firing. The Baneblade still rumbled forward, but without their commander, the crew were confused and lost. The ork foot soldiers were distracted by the sound of the Cadian cheer and turned to find that their warboss had been slain. Without his overwhelming strength and dominance, the unity of the ork force collapsed. Old factions that had once been rivals were suddenly free to wage war against each other again, and the entire force fell into absolute and immediate disarray. Greenskins began hacking and firing at other greenskins just as fiercely as they were fighting with the Cadians. It didn't take the Guardsmen long to capitalise on this.

The clashing of heavy blades and the barking of large calibre stubbers and pistols gradually gave way to the ordered crack of las and hellgun volleys.

Within the hour, the sounds of fighting died off altogether.

CHAPTER THIRTY-FIVE

'GET THOSE MEN down from there,' deViers stormed. 'Get back all of you. Damn your eyes, I'd have some of you shot but for the fact that we have our prize at last. Gruber, give me that vox-amp unit. And you there! Yes, you. Help me up at once.'

A young trooper bearing the insignia of the 110th Mechanised Regiment gave General deViers a boost up onto the track-guards of *The Fortress of Arrogance*.

Kasrkin storm troopers had already popped her hatches and slaughtered her greenskin crew, and her engines had stopped rumbling. She stood still and silent as the general climbed up to stand on the top of the turret. It had been a pulpit once, a place from which Commissar Yarrick had given his rousing speeches to Imperial troops before leading them into battle. DeViers could feel it now, all that glory settling on his shoulders like a fine heavy cloak. He glanced down at the body of the warboss where it lay on its back.

Disgusting beast, he thought.

The stench from its innards made his nose crinkle, but it would take much more than that to ruin the moment. He turned and faced out towards the ordered ranks of troopers. There were so damned few of them. Had he really started all this with over twenty thousand men? The losses seemed incredible, but Yarrick had demanded victory at any cost. DeViers had held to that remark, and now he had his victory.

He saw Magos Sennesdiar and his tech-adepts moving towards the front, their robes stained dark at the hem by all the blood that soaked the ground.

DeViers lifted the microphone of his vox-amp unit and began, 'Men of Exolon and of the Adeptus Mechanicus, let us always remember this day. It has taken time, resources and the sacrifice of many of our Cadian brothers to make this dream a reality. But here we stand, victorious, and the greatest prize in all the Imperium of Man is finally in our hands. I stand upon it, and I feel its holy spirit all around me: *The Fortress of Arrogance*, a holy relic the likes of which few men could ever hope to see. Come forward if you wish. Lay your hands on it. Feel its holy spirit wash over you and inspire you. Even in this wretched state, desecrated by our enemies, robbed of its true glory, it still exudes a power that surely embodies something of the Emperor Himself.'

On he went, talking of a glory that would never be forgotten. He believed every word that came out of his mouth, and the strength of his conviction convinced many of the men who listened.

Caught up in the moment with all those eyes fixed on him, all those ears hanging on his every word, General deViers didn't hear the scrape of metal on metal.

He didn't know anything was wrong until he felt hot, stinking breath on the back of his neck.

His blood ran cold as ice and he moved to turn, but it was a motion he never finished. The ork warboss was barely alive, able to stand only by virtue of a central nervous system that had been developed to work through indescribable levels of physical pain; that, and the all-consuming hatred it felt for weak, pathetic humans.

It closed its remaining power claw around the general's middle and, with the briefest twitch of its fingers, cut the man in half.

Colonel Stromm of The Fighting 98th was in the front row, standing just a few metres in front of the Baneblade's hull. He was moving before the general's upper body tumbled sideways from the turret.

'Kasrkin!' he yelled to his men as he tore his hellpistol from its holster. Together, he and his storm troopers began blazing away at the giant swaying ork.

It shuddered as it was peppered with searing shots. Then it fell backwards again.

The firing stopped.

Magos Sennesdiar wasted no time. He surged forward, leaping onto the front of the Baneblade with an agility that was totally at odds with his bulk. His adepts immediately climbed up after him. As they hurried onto the top of the turret, Armadron said, <They may have damaged the fragment, magos.>

<Or destroyed it completely,> said Xephous. <The fools.>

Sennesdiar was the first to reach the body of the ork. The creature was breathing no more. There, around its tree-trunk neck, he saw a glimmer of green and gold.

<The fragment,> he told his adepts. <It is intact. We have it at last.>

<Praise the Omnissiah,> his adepts intoned together.

'Is the damned thing dead?' asked a gruff voice.

Sennesdiar quickly tugged the fragment from around the warboss's neck, breaking the leather cord that held it there, and hid it within the deep folds of his robe. Then he rose and turned to face the speaker.

'Colonel Stromm. The ork leader no longer lives. Adepts,' he said, addressing his subordinates in Low Gothic, 'it is time we launched our beacon.'

Together, the three Martian priests climbed down from *The Fortress of Arrogance*, and strode towards their Chimera, passing Major Generals Bergen, Killian and Rennkamp on the way. All three men looked drawn and exhausted, and they were speechless as the tech-priests passed.

When Sennesdiar was within a few metres of them, he said, 'One of our lifters can be expected to arrive within the hour, major generals. My servitors will tend to the Baneblade, but I suggest we all make haste in our preparations to leave. Golgotha is still home to a vast population of orks. Tarrying too long could prove to be a grave mistake.'

The magos moved off, but he had only gone about ten metres when Bergen called out to him.

'Sennesdiar,' he said. 'Tell me, will you answer a question?'

Sennesdiar turned. 'Ask it.'

Bergen's eyes were hard. 'Did you get what you were looking for?'

The magos paused for the briefest instant, and Bergen found himself imagining that, had Sennesdiar still possessed a face capable of it, he would be wearing a smile.

'Didn't we all?' said the magos. Then he turned and moved off again.

CHAPTER THIRTY-SIX

THE SKY WAS turning from red to murky brown. It would be night soon, but Wulfe and the others wouldn't be here to see it. They were leaving. What remained of the 18th Army Group's vehicles had already been rolled or towed up the ramps and into the gaping holds of the Mechanicus lifter. On the battlefield, the fires had gone out in most of the wrecks. Men moved among the dead, collecting dog tags from the necks of their fallen brothers, and retrieving lasguns, pistols, grenades and anything else that Munitorum procedure said was too valuable to leave behind.

Wulfe's crew was already onboard the lifter, tying *Last Rites II* down in preparation for the flight. Wulfe had asked Siegler to come and fetch him when the last call to board went out. Then he had come, alone, to the place where Gossefried van Droi had died.

He stood looking at the twisted, burnt-out wreck that had once been the man's pride and joy: *Foe-Breaker*. The bodies of her brave crew were still inside her. There was no Confessor Friedrich here to take care of them. The confessor had almost certainly died in the ork siege at Balkar, another good man lost.

Wulfe's heart felt like it was made of lead. He had known van Droi for almost all of his fighting life. He trusted few people as much as he had trusted the lieutenant. That he was suddenly gone, after so many years of beating the odds, just didn't seem real, neither did the loss of Holtz or Viess. These were men he had respected, men he had liked, not just fellow troopers, but friends.

That thought threw up another name, and a shiver ran the length of his spine, despite the heat. He remembered a whispering voice he had heard on his intercom once, and a hollow-eyed face that looked anything but peaceful: *Corporal Borscht.*

Wulfe prayed that van Droi and the others would not appear to him inexplicably like his former driver had. Surely the Emperor had already welcomed them to his side. They had more than earned it.

Footsteps sounded on the sand behind him.

'Time to ship out, right Sig?' asked Wulfe without turning.

'In a hurry to leave?' replied Voeder Lenck.

Wulfe turned, his brows drawing down into a scowl. 'What are you doing here?'

Lenck grinned, but his eyes were dark and cold as he said, 'Came to pay my respects, didn't I? Think you've got a monopoly on that?'

Wulfe's eyes narrowed. There was something about Lenck's stance that he didn't like. The wiry corporal looked loose and relaxed, but it seemed forced somehow.

Silence hung between them on the warm, still air.

'What are you really doing out here, corporal?'

Lenck shifted, stepping forward, bringing his hands around from behind his back. Wulfe saw a glimmer of metal in the corporal's right hand. 'I'm doing what your mother should have done at birth, you grox-rutter.'

Lenck settled into a fighting stance, well balanced on the balls of his feet, blade ready in his lead hand.

Wulfe immediately reached for his own knife, but it wasn't there. It was lodged in the forearm of a dead ork.

'You're frakking insane,' he spat. 'Put that blade away, corporal. You're making one hell of a mistake.'

Lenck laughed. 'The way I hear it, Wulfe, you've quite a thing for ghosts. Well, guess what. Now you get to be one. You've had it in for me since the day we met, you self-righteous prick. But you didn't know who you were messing with. Time to show you.'

Lenck lunged at Wulfe in a blur, thrusting the knife out towards his belly. Wulfe barely managed to twist away in time. He heard the ripping of fabric and looked down to see a wide cut in his tunic.

Lenck reset his stance, and then lunged again, this time with a high-to-low backhand slash that caught Wulfe on the right forearm. The blade bit into his flesh and sent a flare of pain along his nerves.

'Damn you, Lenck. Are you insane? How do you expect to get away with this?'

Lenck laughed. 'You were out here grieving for van Droi when a wounded ork stumbled out of the shadows, surprised you and cut you down. Siegler will find your body.'

Lenck stepped in with another vicious slash, but Wulfe saw it coming and kicked out at the corporal's knife-hand.

He missed.

The knife sliced deep into the meat of his left shoulder.

Wulfe gritted his teeth and grasped Lenck's wrist, but the corporal punched him in the face with his free hand and sent him reeling backwards.

'You're a relic, Wulfe, like Yarrick's tank. You've had your day.'

Wulfe knew he couldn't beat Lenck's speed. Lenck had proved that already, but Wulfe was bigger and stronger. His only chance lay in clinching, but it was a huge gamble. At close range, the knife would slash him to pieces. If he could just wrestle it free.

With a sneer of triumph, Lenck said, 'I can see the fear in–'

Wulfe didn't let him finish. He bull-rushed him, ramming his wounded shoulder hard into Lenck's abdomen. Pain exploded throughout Wulfe's body, but it was worth it. Lenck hit the ground hard with Wulfe on top of him, the air rushing out of his lungs.

'Bastard,' he hissed and immediately slashed at Wulfe's face. Wulfe blocked with his forearm again and took another painful cut for his troubles.

Wulfe roared at the pain through gritted teeth, but he noticed something, too. On the ground next to Lenck lay something long and white and familiar. It had fallen from Wulfe's pocket when they had landed on the ground.

Still straddling his enemy, Wulfe snatched it up desperately.

Lenck saw Wulfe grab for something and lashed out again at his face, but this time, Wulfe caught his wrist firmly in one hand and stabbed the ork tusk straight down into Lenck's biceps with the other. The corporal howled as Wulfe yanked the tusk left and right, doing as much tissue damage as possible.

Lenck's fingers went weak. The blade dropped.

'All right, enough,' he whined, grasping at his wounded arm. 'You win, sergeant. You win. Just don't kill me. I wasn't gonna kill you, I swear. I just wanted to teach you a lesson.'

Wulfe loomed over him, growling, baring his teeth. It would be so easy to murder this worthless wretch. So many problems would be solved in an instant. So why did he hesitate? He wasn't sure what it was at first. For a brief moment, he thought it might be that there were so few Gunheads left, and Lenck had been through the same hell as he had, but it wasn't that. It was simply duty. Lenck was an Imperial

Guardsman, whether he liked it or not. His life belonged to the Emperor. It wasn't Wulfe's to take.

'Listen carefully, you piece of groxshit,' he rumbled. 'You walk around like some kind of hive-ganger boss and think it counts for something. It counts for *nothing* out here. You got that? I saw through you from the start, you little punker. You'll never have another chance like you did just now. Do you hear me? This will never happen again. I know you, Lenck. And, whether I'm dead or alive, I'm going to haunt you for the rest of your worthless frakking life.'

Having said his piece, Wulfe threw his whole body weight forward into a crushing elbow strike that smashed Lenck's nose and split both his lips wide open. The back of his head bounced hard off the ground. He was out cold.

Wulfe looked down at the corporal's ruined face.

'That one's for you, Holtz,' he muttered.

WULFE CARRIED LENCK'S limp form back to the Mechanicus lifter, the corporal draped over one shoulder like a sack of grain, and was climbing the boarding ramp just as Siegler appeared at the top.

'I was coming to fetch you,' said the loader. 'Six minutes till take-off.'

Wulfe nodded and walked past him, and Siegler fell into step behind. 'What happened to Lenck?' he asked without a trace of concern.

'He was born stupid,' replied Wulfe.

The Fortress of Arrogance sat in the middle of the hold, tied down with dozens of thick steel cables. She was swarming with tech-servitors and enginseers hell-bent on removing the ork modifications as soon as possible. On the far left, between a pair of half-tracks, Wulfe spotted the *New Champion of Cerbera* and its shifty, no-good crew. They looked anxious, and stood up nervously when Wulfe began striding towards them with their unconscious leader.

None of them seemed inclined to speak.

Wulfe threw the sleeping corporal down hard on the metal deck, and then eyeballed each of the three crewmen in turn. 'Your corporal got himself in a bit of trouble. He came off the worse for it. If any of you stupid sons-of-bitches think you'd like to find out what *kind* of trouble, make a move. Now.'

No one, not even the bully boy, Varnuss, so much as twitched.

'Is he… is he dead?' asked Hobbs finally.

Without looking down, Wulfe kicked Lenck in the ribs and was rewarded with a feeble groan. It was answer enough. Then he gestured to Siegler and together they walked off between the tanks and halftracks in the direction of *Last Rites II*.

The loading ramp was being raised, crowding out a shrinking slice of ruddy Golgothan sky. Klaxons blared, announcing imminent take-off. Orange warning lights began to spin. From scores of loudspeakers, the rhythmic, atonal chanting of the Mechanicus tech-crew began, reciting litanies for the safe, efficient operation of the lifter's ancient engines.

Onboard gravitational fields kicked in. The hull shook with the power of the ship's massive thrusters as they heaved its metal bulk up into the air. Within minutes, it had risen beyond the churning clouds of Golgotha and was making for high orbit.

There, *The Scion of Tharsis* waited.

Operation Thunderstorm was over.

EPILOGUE

THE MIDDAY SKY was a brilliant blue laced with the shimmering white trails of Lightning fighter squadrons and formations of Marauder bombers out of the Tethys-Alpha airbase in the north. Standing in his pulpit atop *The Fortress of Arrogance*, Yarrick looked out across the open plains. The Palidus Mountains sat like patient giants on the far side, waiting for the grand spectacle to begin. The ground was hard, good footing, excellent for tanks and infantry alike. In a few hours, it would be a stinking, blood-sodden marshland littered with the dead.

With the Emperor's blessing, most of the bodies would be alien.

The far foothills were already dark with the shadows of the descending xenos horde: such incredible numbers. Good, it would be a worthy fight, a fitting end to a lifetime of vendetta. There was no fear in him. Decades of constant war had desensitised him to it. All that time spent in the forge of battle had made his soul as hard as ceramite. His mind was tougher than folded steel. Victory alone was what mattered, and today he would have it, whatever the cost. Damn his detractors. They were blind to the bigger picture. They squabbled like children over body counts and budgets when it was *this*, life or death on the battlefield, that truly mattered.

It was *here* the future would be decided, *here* that he would meet Ghazghkull Mag Uruk Thraka for the very last time. The ork warlord would die today, or they both would. Either way was fine with Yarrick,

357

so long as his life's work, the mission that had made him a legend among men, was complete.

Looking left and right, Yarrick cast his eyes over the forces that Segmentum Command had amassed and placed at his disposal. Millions of men and women stood ready to do their duty. Their ranks stretched away to the north and south as far as the eye could see, and there were more to the rear.

Yarrick could sense their determination and resolve. They were here to win. He could smell it on the air. They had come from all across the Imperium, from worlds as different as night and day, but they were utterly unified in purpose. They would turn back the greenskin threat. They would protect Holy Terra. They would safeguard the destiny of mankind as the supreme race in the galaxy.

It was a rousing sight, a force greater than he had ever commanded before. Entire divisions of tanks and artillery pieces sat idling, coughing smoke out onto the breeze. Sentinel scouts prowled the forward lines like anxious predators, alert to any signs of change on the wind. There were trucks and halftracks by the thousand, all filled with devoted infantrymen, and almost as many Chimera APCs loaded with battle-hardened storm troopers.

Mightiest of all were the god-like Emperor-class Titans that towered over everything, arms raised parallel to the ground, vast guns ready to unleash death on a planet-shaking scale. They looked like gods of war cast in metal and ceramite. Surely no other creation embodied the strength of humanity so absolutely.

Well, perhaps just one.

From the railing of his turret-mounted pulpit, Yarrick looked down at her glacis plate: *The Fortress of Arrogance.*

It still astounded him that she was the same tank, the very same damned tank that he had lost on Golgotha all those years ago. From her black armour plates to her massive main battle cannon, from her fine gold detailing to the Mechanicus shrine that graced her rear, she looked exactly as she had on the day he had first laid eyes on her. To him, she was the spirit of the Imperial Guard made manifest.

He had thought her lost forever until a Mechanicus transmission received over two years ago mentioned her location. Now he knew he had been right to push for a recovery mission. Yes, men had died to get her here. By all accounts, the blood-price had been horribly high, but the effect of her presence on Armageddon was far beyond such a price. Her spirit charged the air. Men reached out to touch her cold, hard flanks, muttering prayers for strength and glory. Even now, he felt their eyes on her. She was as much a legend as he was.

A tinny voice sounded in his ear. It was his comms-officer speaking over the intercom. 'The lord generals wish to inform you that their armies are ready to march, sir. They await your order to advance.'

'Good,' said Yarrick. He looked again at the far foothills. More and more orks were swarming over them, far more than he had ever faced before. Their ugly machines filled the air above with thick black smoke. Numerous weapon misfires sent rockets screaming into the air.

Yarrick activated the vox-speakers that protruded from the Baneblade's turret. Then he raised his oversized power claw high above his head.

'All troops…' he bellowed.

His amplified words rolled out over the battlefield like thunder.

He swung his power claw downwards with a chopping motion.

'Forward!'

Engines roared. Treads turned. Boot-heels struck the ground in perfect rhythm.

The Fortress of Arrogance rumbled into battle, and the land trembled.

For ever after, men would remember this day.

ICE GUARD

Steve Lyons

CHAPTER ONE

Time to Destruction of Cressida: 48.00.00

THIS WAS THE way a world died.

Chaos forces, the Lost and the Damned, had penetrated Alpha Hive, breaking down its walls. Hundreds of thousands of Guardsmen had given their lives to hold them back, to contain them in the outer zones at least, but the advance was relentless.

It was when the generators had blown, when production had ground to a halt, that the evacuation order had been signed. The civilians had been lifted out first, those few who could still be reached and who hadn't been slaughtered or turned traitor. Now it was the turn of the Imperial Guardsmen on the ground.

Cressida had been a proud world once. Its mines had been bountiful, and its refineries and factories the most efficient in the sector. Its standard of living, on the highest hive levels, had been good, and even the underhives had enjoyed a far lower than normal attrition rate. Cressida's subjects had been loyal and happy, with a consequently high rate of population growth. They had been in the process of building their thirteenth hive, and Imperial Guard Command had advanced plans to raise another Guard regiment from their numbers within ten years.

It had taken less than half that time for Cressida to be invaded, overrun, lost, and finally abandoned.

* * *

COLONEL STANISLEV STEELE stood in what had been a mine overseer's office on Alpha Hive's eighty-third level. An explosion had ripped through the room recently, and two of its walls had been torn out. Its ceiling hung precariously over him, and every few seconds the vibrations from a fresh blast below travelled far enough to make it tremble and threaten to give way.

From this uncertain vantage point he could look out over what remained of the outer zones – at the ebb and flow of battle, at fire and smoke and metal, and the bottle-green lines of his regiment, the Valhallan 319th, marking the extent of the enemy's progress through the ruins.

It made sense, of course, that a Valhallan regiment should remain on the front lines, fighting a rearguard action to buy time for the evacuees. Cressida's temperature had been dropping steadily for the past few years – some side effect of the Chaos incursion, although no one had been quite able to explain it – but the men of Steele's world were well used to the freezing cold.

The Ice Warriors, as they called themselves, were also renowned for their tenacity in defence. Fighting in close formation, they held their ground long after the men of most other worlds would have given way.

They found themselves driven back, all the same. Again and again, blossoms of fire erupted within their ranks, and their green lines were broken and then erased, to be redrawn, a little shorter than before and a little further back, but as firmly as ever.

Steele drew his armoured greatcoat tighter around his body, tucking his gloved hands into its loose sleeves. He could have sworn that the temperature had dropped another two degrees in the past day. He checked his augmetics, but they didn't respond. So, he chose to believe his own instincts.

Streaks of light scarred the overcast grey sky: the trails of spacecraft carrying more troops clear of Cressida. They, at least, would live to fight another day, albeit in a different theatre of war, one in which they might stand a chance of winning.

Steele could hear footsteps approaching. His augmented ears filtered the soft sound from the clamour of war cries and the crump of mortars. He turned to greet Sergeant Ivon Gavotski, a tall, thoughtful man, approaching middle age, unflappable.

Gavotski threw up a crisp salute, and announced, 'All done, sir. Orders have been sent to the eight men on our list, and to four more, in case some of the first eight are already dead or can't be located. I filed a requisition order for a Termite with the Departmento Munitorum, and I mentioned the cardinal's name as you suggested. I think I impressed upon the quartermaster the importance of this particular request.'

Steele nodded, and said, 'I just hope the men we have chosen are as good as their records suggest they are. This could be the most important mission the 319th has ever undertaken, the one that will decide how we are remembered.'

He turned back to the battlefield, on which an array of Chaos-controlled tanks – Leman Russ Demolishers – had managed to gain some purchase in the rubble to advance. The Ice Warriors' tanks were responding, moving cumbersomely into position, trying to draw a fresh defensive line across this new, unexpected front.

'At any rate,' sighed Steele, 'it appears it may be the last.'

He wasn't exaggerating. The war on Cressida had been long and hard, and his men, their ranks already depleted after campaigns on Dellenos IV and Tempest, had suffered heavy casualties. He had heard the whispers, heard that when all this was over the survivors of the Valhallan 319th would be absorbed into other regiments, that their glorious history would come to an end.

It was starting to snow – but in contrast to the pure white, cleansing falls of his home world, these snowflakes were a dirty grey in colour.

TROOPER POZHAR SQUINTED down the sights of his lasgun, and scowled as a bone-biting wind whipped up a flurry of grey snow, obscuring his view of the enemy.

His trigger finger itched with the enforced delay. On the front line a man could be dead in a second, without even seeing what had hit him. Pozhar was determined to make each second count. Even so, he didn't want to waste power – not just because that would be a sin against the Emperor, but because he was down to his last pack. He had just clicked it into his gun, reciting the Litany of Loading as he did so in deference to the machine-spirits.

So, Pozhar held his fire until dark shapes began to loom through the haze, and then he thumbed his power pack setting to full auto and squeezed off fully a quarter of its charge in a deadly, low-level barrage across the rubble.

Many of the shapes crumpled, but as always there were more out there, many more. They clambered over the bodies of the fallen, bearing down on him. They were greeted by the percussion cracks of a hundred more lasguns, Pozhar's comrades following his lead, and a score of frag grenades burst and filled the air with a cloud of blood and dismembered limbs, but still they came.

Pozhar could see them now, and he felt a surge of rage at the sight of their tattered uniforms. They were the worst kind of foe: Traitor Guard. He didn't recognise their colours. So many regiments had turned on Cressida in the past few years that he had lost track of them all.

They were close enough for the Valhallans' cover to mean very little. The traitors raised their guns, and Pozhar's ears popped with the retorts of las-fire from both fronts. He had been crouching behind a half-demolished wall, but it had been all but chipped away by las-beams. A lucky shot penetrated the fur hat, and the head, of the trooper beside him, and Pozhar was left exposed.

It could only be a matter of minutes now. Soon, the order would come to fall back again, to surrender a little more ground to the enemy. But Pozhar was a Valhallan Ice Warrior, and until that order came, he would not give a centimetre.

The traitors swept over him, hardly seeming to notice that he was alive and still standing. Perhaps they expected him to fall and be trampled, but instead he cannoned into the stomach of the nearest of them, disarming him, sending him to the ground. Two more traitors rounded on Pozhar, but he dropped beneath their lunges and swung his gun like a club, scoring a pair of palpable hits to a chin and a forehead. Then his micro-bead earpiece crackled into life, and he heard the urgent voice of a vox-operator, instructing him to fall back and report to the platoon commander.

He could almost have laughed at the timing of it. The traitors were pressing in all around him, and he could measure the rest of his life in seconds. It didn't matter. A red mist had settled over Pozhar, and he felt as if he was standing outside of his body as instinct took over and he punched and kicked and swiped, and jammed the muzzle of his lasgun into one traitor's stomach and blew out his guts.

It was over too soon, of course. He was borne to the ground by sheer weight of numbers. He reached into his greatcoat for a frag grenade and prepared to go out in a ball of fire that would consume ten or more alongside him.

'*Do you hear me, Pozhar? Get your sorry carcass back here fast. Word is, you're being reassigned, by order of Colonel Steele himself.*'

The explosion deadened his ears, heat searing his skin, and he thought for a moment that his senses were deceiving him, because he hadn't yet pulled out the pin.

The grenade that had gone off had not been his. It had been thrown by a comrade, evidently unaware of Pozhar's position. Friendly fire – and friendly indeed, because, by the Emperor's will, Pozhar had been protected from the force of the blast by the press of bodies around him. He lay on his back, drained by his unexpected escape, almost smothered by a pile of corpses. And he had been doubly blessed, because for now he was hidden from the rest of the traitors.

They were advancing past him, booted feet striking the ground near his head, more bodies falling – adding to the pile – as his Valhallan comrades retrenched and a fresh burst of las-fire scythed into their foes. The voice was still squawking in Pozhar's ear, and he did laugh then, a near-hysterical outburst of relief and fear and defiance all mingled together.

It took him a minute to calm down, to be able to assess the situation in which he found himself. He was alone, behind the enemy's front line, and the only way to survive in such a position was to stay where he was, to play dead. Which was out of the question – because not only would it have been a dereliction of duty, but there was also the matter of his unexpected summons to consider, and the tantalising prospect that he had been chosen to receive some great honour.

If Colonel Steele had asked for him by name, if he had a mission that he felt only Pozhar could undertake, then Pozhar would be there. Whatever it took.

THEY HAD TAKEN the enemy by surprise.

The Chaos forces had pulled their artillery from this flank, believing it shielded by the heaped wreckage of a city street, thinking it impossible for the Imperial tanks to break through here. They had reckoned without an Ice Warrior named Grayle.

Grayle knew vehicles – not like a tech-priest knew them, from the inside out, but he had an instinct about them. It was almost as if he could bond with their spirits, and push them to incredible new heights of performance. And right now, he was at the controls of a Leman Russ Annihilator battle tank, and its sixty-tonne chassis was heaving, juddering fit to tear itself apart, and yet it was finding traction, finding a path somehow across the ruins.

Trooper Barreski, up in the turret, was able to look down on the battlefield – and as a knife-sharp blast of wind parted the snow curtain for a second, he fancied he could see the expressions of surprise and horror on the masses of the traitors, cultists and mutants as they saw what was coming their way.

Then the debris shifted, and it felt as if the tank had dropped out from beneath him, taking his stomach with it.

'Hey, Grayle,' he yelled out over the engine's near-deafening roar, 'steady on down there. You keep driving like that, you'll get this crate decorated in a nice shade of this morning's rations!'

As he spoke, the tank tore through the fragile remains of a building, its dozer blade collapsing the walls with ease. A stone beam bounced across Barreski's turret, and he ducked, avoiding decapitation by a centimetre. He picked himself up, filled his cheeks with air and expelled it slowly. He was less concerned with himself, and more with his guns: twin lascannons, objects of great beauty to him. It would have been a shame to have brought them this far and not put them to their intended use.

By the Emperor's grace, however, there was no real damage done. The beam had glanced off the left cannon, put a dent in its barrel, and the calibration had been thrown off a little, but he could compensate for that.

Then, with another great bump and a dip, they were on even ground, picking up speed, and the enemy was in Barreski's field of vision again, on a level with the tank. No obstructions remained between them.

The Chaos forces were undisciplined, some paralysed in the face of the approaching juggernaut, while some tried to fight and others simply turned and fled. They were getting in each other's way, falling over each other, their resistance collapsing before Barreski had loosed off a single shot.

The sponson gunners beat him to it, unleashing heavy bolter fire. Barreski bided his time, using his vantage point to survey the scene, seeking his optimum targets and taking aim, knowing that the lascannons' slow recharging cycle meant that he had to make every shot count.

He aimed for a giant of a man, towering over the rank and file, his face an eruption of pustules, his hair clinging to his head in clumps. Barreski could almost smell the Chaos stink on the mutant. He gave it both lascannons and let their recoil reverberate through him, through his bones, invigorating him with their power. The twin beams seemed to dissect the sky with their thunderous cracks, and when one of them struck true, the mutant was vaporised.

The Leman Russ ploughed into the Chaos army, pushing its soldiers back with its blade, mowing down those who couldn't get out of its way, powdering their bones and pulping their flesh.

Inevitably a few heretics survived – the lucky ones. And those that did found themselves behind the tank, in the sponson guns' blind spots – and, knowing their hand-held weapons were useless against its plasteel hull, they concentrated their fire on the one vulnerable spot they could see: Barreski's head.

He dropped down into the turret, abandoning his lascannons reluctantly; like the sponson guns, they only had a forty-five degree arc of fire. He swung the pintle-mounted heavy stubber, and laid down a discouraging hail of bullets in the tank's wake even though he couldn't see to aim it properly.

He was alarmed when a head appeared over the turret's rim.

The cultist must have just missed being crushed, found himself alongside the tank, behind the sponson guns, and seized the opportunity to leap on board, to climb. He was ill-equipped, his body armour salvaged from many sources, some too small for him, some too large, and his only weapon appeared to be a knife. Still, the element of surprise made him a threat.

Barreski managed to shoulder his lasgun in time. The cultist was leaping for him with a snarl when a beam stabbed through his heart. His momentum kept him going, but by the time he hit the Ice Warrior he was already dead. Barreski risked raising his head, peering over the side of the turret, to see a second cultist climbing towards him. A single lasbeam was enough to shake the man's grip and send him falling, screaming, beneath the tank's heavy tracks.

The Chaos army was reacting, slowly, to the incursion of this lone Imperial vehicle into its midst, starting to turn its war machines around. This was what the Ice Warriors had wanted, of course. Their attack had been calculated to distract, to take the pressure off their front lines, and to give their comrades time to regroup, to renew their defence of a stretch of land that would otherwise have been lost.

There were hundreds of foot soldiers in the path of the Chaos tanks, but their operators seemed no more concerned than Grayle had been about who they might crush beneath their treads. Explosive rounds burst against the Leman Russ's armoured hide, but this was where its lascannons, with their superior range and firepower, came into their own. It was not for nothing that they were known as tank-killers.

Barreski was in his element as his cannons roared. He concentrated his fire on a Chaos-held Imperial Salamander, its slight form surging ahead of its fellows, its autocannon spitting furiously. He scored one direct hit, two, three, four, until he had blown it apart. In the heat of the moment, he could almost have forgotten where he was, seeing only his targets lined up in front of him as if on a range.

And then those targets were close enough to start to hit back, for their own guns to do some real damage, and Grayle had slammed the battle tank into reverse, but Barreski knew he couldn't go far with the ruins still piled up behind him.

The cannons were out of power. Barreski yelled down at the loader below to work faster, to chug the heavy, new cell into place, to give him more shots while he could. The Chaos tanks had formed an arc in front of them, closing in; the port sponson gun was lost, and of course there was no hope of back-up out here.

He couldn't complain. The whole crew had known what they were getting into when Barreski had suggested this, when Grayle had confirmed that he could drive them into position, when the tank commander had approved their plan.

They had achieved their goal, delivered a good, solid blow to the enemy and slowed their advance, and that was all they could have hoped for.

This had always been a suicide run.

* * *

THE WAR ON Cressida was lost.

Trooper Mikhaelev had seen it weeks ago. There was something about the scent, the feel, of the air, as if the planet itself had given up. He had heard that whole continents had been transformed in days, verdant fields devolving into arctic tundra – and even here, where the walls of civilisation had only just begun to come down, there were patches of a freezing purple fungus sprouting amid the wreckage.

Mikhaelev knelt on the plinth of a statue – of whom he couldn't tell, as a frag blast had cut it off at the knees – and steadied his missile launcher against his shoulder. He saw the shape of an enemy tank, and he sent a krak missile whistling over the heads of his squad, and of nine more ranks of Ice Warriors. He didn't wait to see if he had struck the tank, too busy with the cumbersome task of reloading. He should have had a comrade to assist him, but the last one had been cut down in the enemy's last push and hadn't yet been replaced.

When he tried to fire again, the launcher clicked and jammed, and Mikhaelev let out a resigned sigh and reached for his lasgun. At the rate at which his comrades were falling, he would be on the front line soon, anyhow.

It was all right for the clerks at Naval Command, he thought. They could afford to dither, so reluctant to lose a productive world that they had hung on to hope long after hope had died. They should have ordered this withdrawal long ago. They could have spared millions of Guardsmen to fight again – but to them, those Guardsmen's lives were only numbers on a data-slate, so what did they care?

It didn't especially bother Mikhaelev that he was going to die today. It just rankled with him that it would be for nothing.

Then a voice crackled over his earpiece, and rewrote his destiny.

He slipped down from the plinth and made his way deeper into the hive, still lugging the useless, heavy missile launcher along with him in case a tech-priest could salvage it. He thought about the summons he had received, and it cheered him up a little to think how irritated his commander would be to let him go.

So, Colonel Stanislev Steele was putting together a special mission, and he wanted Mikhaelev on board. The only question Mikhaelev had was... why me?

CHAPTER TWO

Time to Destruction of Cressida: 47.04.33

THE SENTINEL WALKERS were equipped as power lifters, not intended for combat use. The lost and the damned had got hold of a pair somehow – either they had captured them or their pilots had simply defected, as so many Guardsmen had done during this war – and their Imperial markings had been defaced.

The Sentinels were being used to deal death now. They were marching amid a legion of Chaos spawn and other mutant creatures, sweeping and gouging at the defenders of Alpha Hive with their single metal claws.

Trooper Borscz's Ice Warrior platoon was ranged along the edge of an empty residential sector. So far, they had been holding the tide back, but the Sentinels' appearance threatened to change that.

It had fallen to Borscz's squad to deal with that threat. His sergeant, Romanov, was bellowing orders, instructing his nine troopers to aim their fire at the leftmost of the two leviathans. Borscz's first beams went hopelessly wide, and he cursed the unreliable sights of his lasgun under his breath. Many of his comrades struck true, but their las-beams seemed to do little damage, at least to begin with.

At last, their sustained barrage began to bear fruit, and Borscz saw sparks flying from the left knee joint of the bipedal machine. Without needing to be told, the Ice Warriors refocussed their fire on that spot – and a long, agonising minute later, the Sentinel collapsed, and flattened a number of luckless spawn beneath its mass.

It had taken too long.

Sergeant Romanov shouted again, and his squad turned its fire on the second Sentinel. Before it could be felled, though, the spawn would be upon them.

Borscz weighed up his options, and then lowered his gun. He caught Romanov's suspicious glare, and he shrugged his broad, muscular shoulders.

'Sorry, sergeant,' he yelled, 'the machine is kaput, it jams up in the cold. What is a trooper to do?' Then he drew his long-bladed knife, lowered his head and took a single giant step forward to meet the first of the charging mutants.

It cannoned into him, rebounding from his bulk, and Borscz thought he could read surprise in its twisted face. While it was still reeling, he seized it, kicked its legs from beneath it, and sent it sprawling against two more mutants behind it. Two more came up alongside him, and he dodged their clumsy swings, and threw one of them over his shoulder into the other.

Borscz knew that the mutants were stronger than he was. He was using their unwieldiness against them, keeping them off-balance, but he couldn't keep it up.

He didn't have to.

The second Sentinel was upon him, towering over him, more than three times his height. It had raised its foot to stamp on him, to crush him, and the mutants were trying to hold him still, wrapping their disgusting tentacles around him.

Borscz loosed a great roar from his powerful lungs, and hacked at the tentacles with his blade. He slashed and tore them, ploughing forward as one great foot slammed down in the spot where he had just been. Then he whipped a krak grenade from his belt, and with a grim flourish, he slapped it against the armoured stanchion of the Sentinel's leg.

The mutants saw what he had done, and even their tiny minds told them to run from the predictable explosion. This gave Borscz the chance to run too, back towards the rest of his squad, who were watching in astonishment and backing him up as best they could with las-fire.

A second later, there came a tremendous bang, and the shadow of the teetering Sentinel fell across him. Borscz twisted out of its way as it crashed to the ground, its cockpit beside him now. He could see his reflection in its cracked front shield, his wild black beard split by a white maniacal grin – and behind that shield, the pilot, the cockpit's lone occupant, his face white with terror as he realised that his unexpected plunge had taken him right to his enemy.

He was operating his controls feverishly, employing the only weapon he still had. The Sentinel's giant claw pivoted back on itself, and came snapping, grasping for the Ice Warrior. Borscz ducked underneath it, and drove his meaty fists through the plexiglas shield. He grabbed the pilot by the scruff of his tunic, tore him from his seat and drove him headfirst into the unyielding ground, breaking his neck.

Robbed of their advantage, the mutants and spawn were being driven back once more. His cheeks flushed, Borscz took his place among his comrades and drew his gun. He was alarmed to feel a firm hand on his shoulder, and, turning, he found himself fixed by the glowering eyes of an Imperial commissar.

For a moment, Borscz feared he was to be disciplined for disregarding orders. He and his sergeant had an understanding born of long service together – Romanov knew that, unconventional though his methods were, Borscz got results – but he knew that an outside observer might see things differently.

To his surprise, the commissar didn't want to talk about his behaviour. He had a message for Borscz, although, to judge by his scowl as he delivered it, he wasn't at all happy about it. It was a summons from Colonel Steele.

TROOPER ANAKORA HEARD the Chaos hounds before she saw them, the scampering of their clawed feet in the tunnels and their ravening howls as they scented fresh meat even over the underhive's stink.

She whirled around and saw the first of them, its twisted black bulk, in the light of the beam from her lamp pack as it leapt on Petrovski and tore out his throat.

There were three more behind it. Anakora swore and abandoned the limpet mine she had been struggling to adhere to the crumbling wall of a slum building.

Her squad of eight had been sent down here on a demolition mission. Their commanders were concerned that as the Imperial Guard withdrew from Cressida, there weren't enough men left to hold all fronts in the ongoing war. By collapsing strategic sections of these underground levels, they could at least close off one route to the heart of Alpha Hive, preventing the Chaos forces from coming up beneath them.

Their enemies, it transpired, were a step ahead of them. They had penetrated deeper into the underhive than anyone had known. Anakora and her comrades hadn't planted even half their mines yet.

One of the hounds came for her, but with remarkable precision she fired a las-beam through its left eye and killed it. The momentum of its pounce kept it coming, and it hit with enough force to knock her from her feet. She crashed to the ground with the hound's slavering tusks in her face, and gagged on its last gasp of rancid breath as she hauled herself out from beneath it.

She had dropped her lamp pack, breaking it, but the tunnel was lit by the crisscrossed beams of her surviving six comrades and the staccato flashes of their lasguns. The latter created an eerie kind of stop-motion effect in which Anakora saw the remaining two Chaos hounds closing with their chosen prey.

She shouldered her weapon again, looking for a clear shot. When a second comrade fell, his broken body tossed in the air to be caught in the mantrap jaws of his feral killer, she let out a strangulated cry and pulled on the trigger for all she was worth, furious with herself for her well-meaning hesitation.

Two more squad members had the same thought, and the hound was struck from three angles at once, twisting and melting in the sizzling lasbeams, slumping dead at last with a Valhallan leg still clamped in its mouth.

The third hound got past Sergeant Kubrikov's defences. It bore him down, and its claws pinned his shoulders before he could stand. Once again, Anakora couldn't fire without endangering her comrade, but this time she didn't waste a second. She leapt onto the creature's back, and felt its jagged spines digging into her thighs. She turned her lasgun around and slipped it over the Chaos hound's head so that the barrel was resting across its throat. She clenched her teeth and pulled for all she was worth. She could feel thick, knotted neck muscles resisting her, but she was determined not to fail, not to show herself to be weak again. At last, she felt bone snap. The monstrous black body sagged beneath her, and a grateful Kubrikov tore himself free from its dying grip.

In the time this had taken, Anakora's comrades had dealt with the final hound, although two more of them had been eviscerated in the process. The danger was not over, however. New shadows were looming, growing on the tunnel walls: dark, ominous shadows. A scant moment later, the first of their owners came marching around the bend, and Anakora's breath caught at the sight of them.

Clad in baroque armour and hailing from the Eye of Terror, the giant warriors exuded a palpable air of menace and power that turned men's blood to ice. They raised and fired bolt pistols, and Anakora flung herself against the wall, using the tunnel's slight curvature to shield her body. She returned fire, knowing that it was hopeless. The Ice Warriors were outgunned – outmatched not just by a little, but ludicrously, almost laughably so.

Sergeant Kubrikov knew it too, and he was screaming at his three remaining troopers to fall back. There was something else too: another sound, an insistent buzz in Anakora's earpiece. A voice, its tone urgent but its words drowned in a sea of static.

She didn't have time to worry about it. She was pinned down by the bolt pistols, but the glimmer of an idea formed in her head, and she screamed at Kubrikov, 'The mines, sergeant! Blow the mines!'

Kubrikov was ahead of her, already fumbling with the detonator. The buildings to each side of the Chaos Space Marines blew out, and a cloud of dust billowed towards Anakora. She was already running when it caught up to her, engulfed her. She could hear the throaty growls of chainswords starting up behind her, and she knew that the explosion hadn't been enough, not nearly enough – that their pursuers were still standing, still ploughing forwards, and that all the Ice Warriors had gained was to slow them a fraction and to make themselves a harder target for their ranged weapons.

She almost wished that wasn't the case.

There were just two of them left, her and Kubrikov. Anakora reached the ladder first, glanced back, and saw her sergeant's eyes glazing over. Blood poured from his mouth, and then his body separated into two pieces along a horizontal line. The dust parted for a second to show the dead face of a Chaos Space Marine behind him, jerking his sword free of his victim's remains.

Then she was climbing, hand over hand, foot over foot, expecting at any moment to feel cold fingers closing around her ankle, dragging her back. Bolts pinged off the ladder, and she dropped a frag grenade to discourage another burst. Then she could see the open manhole above her, and she knew that she could make it. She ought to have been relieved – because now at least her comrades could be forewarned that the Chaos Space Marines were about to emerge into their midst – but her stomach sank instead, because she knew that her mission had failed. Her squad was dead. And the worst of it all, the hardest thing for Anakora to accept, was that she had survived... again.

TROOPER GRAYLE STUMBLED over the rubble, hacking and coughing from the smoke in his throat, his arm gushing blood from a stray piece of shrapnel. His eyes and ears had been deadened, but he fired his lasgun blindly over his shoulder as he staggered on, just hoping and waiting – waiting for Barreski to let go of him, to stop dragging him along, so that he could fall over.

He didn't know how they had got this far. His recent past was a blur of bangs and flashes, the only clear impression being of the searing, agonising pain he had felt when the controls of the Leman Russ had blown up in his face.

Then he was on the ground, staring up at Cressida's grey sky, the last flakes of the sputtering snowstorm wetting his cheeks and soothing his burns. His chest was heaving and his arm was throbbing, and he wondered for a moment if this was it, if Barreski had been gunned down and if he was to be next.

Then he saw his comrade's concerned face looming over him, his skin a livid pink too, the stubble on his chin singed and even more ragged than usual.

'Did… did we get the last of them?' stammered Grayle.

'I reckon so, yeah,' said Barreski. Then something made him tense up, turn, and fire a burst from his lasgun at something Grayle couldn't see – though he did hear the scream that followed the blast, a scream abruptly curtailed. 'Yeah,' repeated Barreski, turning back to him, 'yeah, we got the last of them, now.'

Not many cultists had followed them back into the ruins. Those that had survived were mostly licking their wounds, shell-shocked from the fury that had just erupted around them. The Ice Warriors were safe from the enemy tanks – assuming that none of their drivers had Grayle's skill, which was a pretty safe bet.

'I think the captain made it,' said Grayle, chasing a confused memory. 'I think I saw him with… with someone else, I couldn't make out who.'

'Kampanov, probably. As soon as he heard the evacuation order, he was out of that hatch like a snow leopard with a frag grenade up its backside.'

Grayle pulled himself up onto his elbows, catching his second wind, and said, 'They took out the turret guns, I'm assuming?'

'Cold got the first, shrapnel the second. Think I'd be here if I still had a lascannon to fire? They were works of art, they were. Another minute with them, I could have polished off two more tanks, no problem.'

'Never mind, eh, Barreski. I'm sure we can find you a new toy to play with soon, maybe an even bigger one.'

'You think they'll let us have another vehicle?' asked Barreski. 'We didn't take such good care of the last one. Of the last three, in fact.'

Grayle smiled at his fellow tanker with the smug air of one who knew an important secret. 'Oh yeah,' he said, 'I think we'll get another vehicle. I expect we'll be back in action before you know it.'

Then he told Barreski about the message. The one that had come in through the Leman Russ's vox system, just before it had exploded. Grayle had never had the chance to acknowledge the message, nor to relay it to its intended recipient, the battle tank's captain – but it had now been heard by both of the Ice Warriors name-checked therein.

'Better get yourself back on your feet then, my friend,' said Barreski, 'because if we want to report to Colonel Stanislev Steele on time, I'd say we've got a long, dangerous walk ahead of us.'

* * *

CALCHAS SPACEPORT WAS teeming with Guardsmen, many of them lost, unable to hear their orders over the roar of an incoming lander. The ship was trying to squeeze its bristling form into a tight spot between a near-identical vessel and an older, scarred Ironclad. The Navy had assigned all the craft it could spare, all that could reach Cressida in time, to the evacuation effort, whatever their usual function.

The lander set down, at last, and its engines cut out, but those of another, departing ship had already fired up. Sergeants yelled themselves hoarse to be heard over the continuing racket, marshalling their troopers to the loading ramps. From the window beside Trooper Blonsky's head, the Guardsmen looked like coloured ants, streaming across a concrete bowl into the bellies of the great metal behemoths.

His interrogator delivered a backhanded slap to his face, drawing a little blood and snapping his attention back to the small, grey room in which he was seated.

'I asked you a question, Blonsky.' The lieutenant was from a Validian regiment. *Royal* Validians, they called themselves. His uniform was red with highlights in polished gold, and he displayed the same superior attitude that Blonsky had seen in so many of his breed. He was probably also one of the most senior officers on Cressida. Most of the rest had been aboard the first ships to leave – Blonsky's Valhallan commanders excepted, of course.

He glanced down at his cuffed wrists, resting in his lap. Then he looked up to meet his interrogator's glare, and he said calmly, 'With all due respect, sir, I think I have answered it. I have given you a full account of my actions this morning. I executed Sergeant Arkadin–'

'You killed him,' the Validian spat, 'killed him in cold blood!'

'I executed him,' restated Blonsky, 'because he was a deserter.'

The lieutenant's nostrils flared. 'Arkadin was a good friend of mine. If you had reason to doubt his courage, you should have come to me or to one of his other commanders. What evidence do you have, what evidence *could* you have, to support this claim?'

'I have the evidence of my own senses, sir. My platoon was fighting a horde of mutants when I was separated from them by an explosion. I took cover in an old storage depot. That's where I encountered Sergeant Arkadin. I believe he had been hiding in there for some time.'

'Did he tell you that?' asked the lieutenant sharply.

'No sir,' said Blonsky, 'but it was evident from his body language that–'

'I don't want to hear about his body language.'

'Very well. The mutants must have seen me entering the building. I had barricaded the door as best I could, but they were starting to batter it down. I was prepared to meet them with las-fire, but Sergeant Arkadin threw down his gun and tried to climb through the window.'

'I won't accept that!' The lieutenant drove a frustrated fist into the table between them. 'You made a mistake, Trooper Blonsky. Sergeant Arkadin is – was – an excellent tactician. No doubt he thought that, if he could escape from the depot, he could circle behind your attackers and–'

'He had thrown down his gun, sir!'

'What right do you have to judge one of us?' the Validian hissed.

'May I ask again, sir,' said Blonsky, 'if my commanders have been informed of my detention. By rights, one of them ought to be here.' He could tell from the lieutenant's stony silence that the answer to his question was no.

He sighed, and restated for what seemed like the hundredth time, 'Sergeant Arkadin was a deserter. I shot him, in accordance with standing orders, before he could–'

'No!' the lieutenant bellowed.

Blonsky stopped talking. No one was listening anyway.

A long silence followed, during which his interrogator stared out of another window at the activity in the spaceport below. Perhaps he was worrying about his own place on one of those ships, wondering how much longer he could afford to wait behind.

'You were lucky,' said the lieutenant at last, in a somewhat quieter voice, 'that my platoon was in the area, that those mutants died before they could break down the door and reach you. I only wish they could have been in time to save my sergeant.'

'I wish that too, sir.'

'As far as I am concerned, Trooper Blonsky, you killed Sergeant Arkadin without reason. I don't know why. Perhaps you were the would-be deserter, and he was standing in your way. The only way to be sure would be to convene a formal tribunal with, as you say, your commanders present. Under the circumstances, that would take some time. It would also mean blackening a good man's name, by airing these scurrilous accusations against him.'

'If you say so, sir.' Blonsky could see from the lieutenant's bearing, the way he could no longer quite meet his prisoner's eye, that he wanted to believe what he was saying, wanted it so much, but that he couldn't be entirely sure.

The lieutenant let out a heavy sigh, and said, 'Go on. Get out of here. It would be a mercy to keep you off the front line anyway. You belong to the Valhallan 319th, yes? The regiment that is to stay behind, that is to be sacrificed. Well, then, Trooper Blonsky, if you are so zealous, so damn loyal to the Emperor, then this is your chance to prove it, isn't it? This is your chance to make sure you die for Him!'

CHAPTER THREE

Time to Destruction of Cressida: 45.57.14

THE SIGHT OF the Termite stirred something in Sergeant Ivon Gavotski's heart.

It was just a small vehicle, its chassis almost outweighed by the great cylindrical borer it supported – but it had been given a distinctively Valhallan make-over, painted with white and green snow camouflage patterns. Six flamer emplacements had been added to its sides and four more flamers mounted on the borer itself.

Gavotski had heard the story many times, of course – about how, after his home world had been hit by an asteroid, after its lush fields had become frozen wastelands, his distant ancestors had struggled to survive. An ork invasion must have seemed like one misfortune too many, back then – but it had given the Valhallans a reason to fight back, a tangible goal to achieve.

The precise schematics of the ice-boring vehicle they had developed had been lost to history. But this Termite was the nearest thing, in the modern world, to the vehicle that had won the Valhallans their war – the nearest thing to the vehicle that had given them mastery of their changed environment, allowing them to tunnel through the hearts of the glaciers and to strike at the ork mobs where they least expected.

A single Termite wouldn't win *this* war – but with Cressida becoming more and more like Valhalla each day, it could at least carry one squad of Ice Warriors to where they needed to be. That was, if Gavotski could find it a squad to carry.

He had sent out the orders over two hours ago. Trooper Mikhaelev had been the first to report in: a quiet, lean, thin-faced man, not at all what Gavotski had been expecting from a heavy weapons expert. Anakora had arrived next, her face impassive, her eyes dead even as she had told Gavotski what an honour it was to be assigned to him. Then Blonsky had come in, his narrow, black eyes forever darting about him, alert like a hawk.

That, so far, had been it, apart from a few garbled vox messages. Two of Gavotski's draftees were listed as dead, three as missing in action, although efforts were ongoing to locate them. Of the remaining four, including his reserve choices, he had heard and seen nothing. It was with some relief, then, that he greeted the approach of a Chimera, although even the jaded sergeant couldn't help but raise an eyebrow at the sight of a squat, muscular trooper hanging from its side.

The hitchhiker didn't wait for the vehicle to stop. He hopped down and ambled up to Gavotski, his broad, toothy grin a bright white behind his black beard.

'Trooper Borscz, sergeant,' he introduced himself. 'Apologies for my late arrival, but your first message did not get through. Machines, you know.'

Gavotski introduced himself in turn, held up a hand to stem Borscz's eager questions, and indicated that he should wait beside the Termite with the others. As the newcomer moved to obey, the sergeant noted that his eyes flickered, as all their eyes had, towards the brooding figure of Colonel Stanislev Steele.

Steele stood a few metres away, his power sword at his hip, observing all with a cool but shrewd gaze. His bionic right eye glinted in the light of a flaring explosion in the sky, but there were no other outward signs of his internal augmetics.

It was said by some that Steele's emotions had been neutered by his cybernetic grafts, that he had become cold, unfeeling. Gavotski could see how that myth had been born. He counted himself privileged, however, to be one of the few who knew the truth.

The Chimera had come to a halt, and another two Ice Warriors emerged, exchanging amiable banter. They introduced themselves as Troopers Barreski and Grayle. That made six – eight, including the sergeant and the colonel. It was enough to make do, but two short of the full squad for which Gavotski had hoped. He glanced at Steele for instructions, but could see that, as always, he was happy to trust his sergeant's judgement.

He decided to wait another ten minutes. With luck, Palinev might still make it, and bring the count up to nine. Beyond that...

Gavotski had had high hopes for one more Ice Warrior. He had added Pozhar's name to his list, despite his chequered service record, despite Steele's concerns, because he had worked with the lad before and judged him to have potential. Pozhar was one of the three MIAs – which meant that Gavotski was now praying for a miracle.

Or, to put it another way, he was about to find out if his faith had been justified.

POZHAR HAD LOST all track of time.

He was so close to his goal, so close to getting back to his comrades, the returning hero. It seemed like days since he had been separated from them, days since he had lain on the battlefield, almost gagging on the stench of the fallen Chaos worshippers whose bodies had protected him. Now, he was just a few metres away.

A few metres – but it may as well have been a few thousand.

It was not in the young trooper's nature to lie still for long. Anyway, the grumbling of approaching engines had alerted him to a new danger. The Chaos army had pressed forward, most of its foot soldiers passing him by without seeing him, but behind them had come the heavy artillery, the tanks and the battle cannons, and he had had to act fast to avoid being crushed beneath their wheels.

Pozhar had scrambled to his feet, feeling the sting of cold air on his face, expecting to be shot down as soon as he was seen. Instead, surrounded by the enemy, he went unnoticed. He had realised that his uniform was dishevelled and torn, coated in grime and blood, and thus there was no real visible difference between him and any number of Traitor Guardsmen on the battlefield. Thinking quickly, he had ripped off his unit badge to further this illusion, and had considered taking a coat from one of the fallen traitors, one daubed in Chaos sigils, but the thought of wearing such a thing had made his stomach turn and his skin crawl.

He couldn't just stand there, he had realised. He had to do something, make it look like he belonged here, give himself time to think, to find an escape route.

Casting around, he had seen a pair of cultists bickering over an upset cart. A purloined plasma cannon, too heavy to carry, had spilled from the rickety contraption, and Pozhar had rushed to help lift it back into place. In so doing, he had brushed against a cultist's arm and felt something shifting beneath his cloak. He had caught a glimpse of a slimy black tentacle, and had almost vomited on the spot.

Pozhar had ached – truly, physically ached – with the driving need to pull out his lasgun, to blast these freaks to whatever afterlife they believed in, and he would have done it too had it not been for the vox-message... had it not been for the fact that Colonel Stanislev Steele needed him.

He wished he knew how long it had been.

He had slipped away from the cultists at the first opportunity, leaving his last frag grenade in their cannon's barrel. When the weapon was fired, the grenade would burst and, Pozhar hoped, trigger a devastating plasma explosion. He had made his way to the edge of the battlefield, trying to remain innocuous, finding cover where he could in deserted, half-demolished buildings.

He had not counted on running into civilians. Four women and six children were huddled in a dark corner of one of those buildings, somehow overlooked by the heretics that had burnt out their homes and slaughtered their men.

At first they had been an unwelcome burden, because Pozhar would certainly have become a target as soon as he had stepped out into the open with them. But, emboldened by the appearance of an Imperial Guardsmen, their saviour, the women had told him of a way out: a hatchway into the underhive.

And so Pozhar had ended up here, in a tunnel mouth, up to his ankles in the filth of a billion departed slum-dwellers, as the women waited some way behind him and tried to keep their children quiet. And the ladder that would take them all back up to the surface, back to Pozhar's comrades, was just a few metres away... a few metres away, but guarded.

It had been a shock to find cultists in the underhive. Fortunately, the women had known their way around and, so far, they had been able to keep out of sight, though a number of diversions due to blocked tunnels had left Pozhar fretting with impatience. His greatest fear was that Colonel Steele might have given up on him by now – worse still, might have written him off as a coward or a traitor.

Four cultists. He could take them, he thought, especially as their guns were trained on the manhole above them. They were expecting trouble from above, not from below. They weren't expecting him. He *could* take them.

And they would raise the alarm, and then more cultists would come running. Would he be able to ferry the women and the children up the ladder and hold their attackers off long enough to follow them?

A more cautious man might have waited a while longer, might have looked for a better chance, or even another ladder. Not Pozhar. He had lost enough time already.

Even though he knew that the fight ahead of him would be difficult, even though he knew that his chances of survival were slim, he drew his lasgun and he ran to meet it firing. And he did so not just because he felt he had no other choice, but with a grin on his face and a mad laugh erupting from his stomach.

A STEP GAVE way beneath Trooper Palinev's foot, and he leapt for the safety rail and pulled himself up. He had started a cascade effect, which demolished the rest of the staircase beneath him, but he had attained the balcony level of the refinery as planned.

He grinned at the memory of those comrades who had thought him mad for eschewing the standard Valhallan greatcoat. His basic flak jacket might not have provided the same level of protection against the cold, but it was much lighter, more flexible, and Palinev's unencumbered agility had just saved his life.

He reached the tall, narrow window – the one towards which his sergeant had directed him from outside, below. He settled behind it and used the butt of his long-las, his sniper variant lasgun, to knock out the glass. An icy gust of wind blew away the refinery's stuffy gloom, and further reddened Palinev's already ruddy cheeks.

He rested the long, thin barrel of his weapon against the sill, and waited.

The battle had only just spread to this part of the hive, and many of the buildings were still standing. Palinev's platoon was attempting to draw the enemy into a narrow street, a bottleneck in which the defenders would have the advantage, and the strategy was working. The first wave of Chaos forces came crashing against the Ice Warriors' front lines, and were held. That made them sitting ducks for Palinev, and the nine other snipers stationed behind the surrounding windows. He squeezed off round after round, claiming kill after kill.

And then, in a second, the tide turned.

Palinev didn't know what had happened at first, only that there had been a shift in the battle, that his comrades were reacting to something he hadn't seen. Something behind them. Then he saw las-beams ripping into them, from an area that ought to have been secure, taking them by surprise. It was a massacre.

His heart in his throat, Palinev abandoned his post and raced along the circular balcony, his footsteps ringing off metal mesh. Three windows along, he found a better view, and he saw to his horror that cultists and traitors were rising from the manholes, from the underhive, outflanking their foes. The Ice Warriors on the ground were rallying, but they didn't stand a chance. Still, Palinev did what he could to help them, sniping down all the heretics he could in the time he had.

The refinery doors crashed open, somewhere beneath him, and all of a sudden the battle seemed a great deal louder, a great deal closer to him.

The intruders knew where he was. A frag grenade arced over the balcony rail and rolled up to Palinev's feet. He was already running, just ahead of the explosion, which blew out a section of the building's wall. The balcony was mangled, left partially unsupported, trembling and creaking – and, as Palinev reached the one remaining set of steps, he found four Chaos cultists ascending towards him, recognisable by their cloaks and by their obscene tattoos.

He brought up his gun, but the cultists were too fast for him, and he had to throw himself onto his stomach to avoid their las-fire. He wasn't accustomed to close combat, wasn't built for it. Palinev had spent his years in service honing his sneaking and sniping skills. This, then, was his worst nightmare: an enemy that could see him!

A section of mesh beneath him rattled and slid. Feverishly, he pried it loose and clambered down through a web of scaffolding. He dropped the six metres to the ground floor level, rolling to absorb the impact of his landing. The cultists were up on the teetering balcony, looking for him, and he decided to give them a taste of their own medicine. They saw the incoming grenade, and one of them tried to run, while the other three saw the futility of that course and jumped for it.

Palinev managed to get off a shot while they were in mid air, wounding one of the cultists, who landed awkwardly with a snap of bone. Then the grenade went off and the balcony gave way, bringing two walls down with it. All Palinev had time to do was to drop to his knees and cover his head with his hands as he was engulfed by a tidal wave of screeching, rending sound.

When it was all over, as the echoes died down, Palinev raised his head, and saw that one of the cultists had survived, and was training a lasgun on him. He closed his eyes, heard the familiar cracking retort, and expected it to be the last thing he would ever hear.

Then, he opened his eyes again to find the cultist dead on the floor.

An Ice Warrior stood over the corpse, one whose name Palinev did not know. 'You the scout, Palinev?' the man grunted, and he nodded blankly.

'Must be something up with your comms,' said the Ice Warrior. 'They've been trying to contact you for the past half hour. Steele wants you.'

THEY HAD LINED up beside the Termite, Steele and his hand-picked squad: the nine troopers to whom he would be trusting his life, and more importantly, the success of his assignment.

They stood with their heads bowed in silence, their hats and helmets removed, as a priest laid his hands upon each of them in turn, and bestowed the blessing of the God-Emperor upon them. Steele cursed his enhanced sense of smell; it took all the self-control he had not to choke on the pungent cloud that billowed from the holy man's incense burner.

The priest's arrival had been a surprise to them all. Steele had known, of course, that the Ecclesiarchy had a special interest in his mission, but this... For an entire squad to be sanctified like this was almost unheard of. Still, the ritual provided a rare moment of calm, of inner peace, despite the background sounds of gunfire and explosions, and engines and dying from the none-too-distant war. Steele had welcomed that and been re-energised by it.

He noted that Pozhar was not quite so appreciative. The young trooper had been the last of the squad to arrive, bounding up to an indulgent Gavotski full of energy, and bursting with stories about what he had been through to get here. His body was like a coiled spring, his hands twitching with the desire to get the ceremony done with and get on with the business of finding someone to kill.

When Blonsky's turn came, his chest swelled with pride and a right-eous smile pulled at his thin lips. Mikhaelev, in contrast, held himself rigid, contained, and betrayed no reaction to his blessing at all. Beside him, Anakora reacted to the priest's touch with a little shudder, and a single tear dripped from her down-turned eyes.

Then it was done – and, with a final nod and a munificent smile in Steele's direction, the priest ambled away. The colonel took a deep breath as his moment of peace ended and he prepared to get back down to business. He nodded at his sergeant, to indicate that it was time – and Gavotski stepped forward, cleared his throat and addressed the squad.

'You may have heard the name Confessor Wollkenden,' he said. 'You may have heard that he came here to Cressida a month ago, to minister to its people, to help them resist the corruption of their world. You may also have heard that the confessor is one of the finest men the Imperium has bred. It is thanks in part to his leadership that the war in the Artemis system was won.'

In fact, Steele hadn't heard Wollkenden's name before this morning, and he doubted whether Gavotski had either. He had been left in no doubt, however, of the stock placed in him by the Ecclesiarchy, that they considered him a virtual saint.

'Three days ago,' Gavotski continued, 'the confessor was en route to an outlying settlement to the north of here, intending to make contact with a group of loyalist resisters. His shuttle came under fire. A vox-message from its pilot confirmed that an emergency landing had been made, and that Confessor Wollkenden was alive. The message was interrupted. There has been no word since then.

'The area in which the confessor's ship came down was a forest, until it fell to Chaos forces three and a half years ago. Since then, of course, conditions on the ground have changed considerably. Intelligence is sparse, but we know that there has been a great deal of glacial activity in the area, which has rendered much of it almost impassable... Almost.' At this, Gavotski gave the Termite a proud pat.

'Of course, it is possible that Confessor Wollkenden is dead. Our job, comrades, is to find out for sure, and, if he is alive, to bring him back. The Imperial Guard cannot spare the resources for a full-scale search and rescue at present – and it is felt anyway that a stealthy extraction has more chance of success. That is why Colonel Steele and I are taking only one squad through the glaciers, and it is why each of you has been chosen: because your respective commanders tell us that you are the best the Valhallan 319th has to offer.'

'Pardon me, sergeant,' said Trooper Borscz, 'but are we to understand that Colonel Steele is to lead this mission?'

'That is correct, soldier,' said Gavotski. 'You have a problem with that?'

'No, sergeant.' In fact, Borscz seemed positively enthused by the idea, and he looked at Steele with admiration blazing in his deep blue eyes.

The colonel cleared his throat, and said, 'There is one thing that Sergeant Gavotski has not yet mentioned.' It was the first time the troopers had heard his voice, and each of them became visibly more attentive. 'You are aware,' said Steele, 'that Cressida is being evacuated. What you have not been told, because this information is strictly need-to-know, is that an Exterminatus order has been signed.'

Palinev gave an audible gasp, but the others absorbed the news silently, grimly.

'Naval warships are on their way,' said Steele. 'Cressida will be virus-bombed from orbit, completely sterilised. As a world still rich in mineral resources, it is hoped that some day it can be recolonised. Until that day–'

Gavotski finished the thought for him. 'The Chaos forces may have won this battle,' he said, 'but they will not live long to enjoy their spoils.'

'All of which,' said Steele, 'means that we have a deadline. I was told this morning, in no uncertain terms, that the virus bombing would take place in forty-eight hours' time, whether we, or indeed Confessor Wollkenden, were still on Cressida or not. A little over three hours has passed since then.

'Gentlemen and lady, I suggest we get the Termite loaded up. The chrono is already ticking.'

CHAPTER FOUR

Time to Destruction of Cressida: 44.49.09

'YOU SHOULD NOT have come back.'

The passenger compartment was raucous with the roar of the Termite's engine and with the chatter of ten Ice Warriors, packed together in the confined space, getting to know one another, assessing each other's strengths. Still, Blonsky's voice cut across the noise, and brought the chatter to a halt.

'You should not have come back,' he said again, and his angular face was set into a stony scowl, his dark green eyes piercing his victim.

Pozhar had been telling the tale of how he had found himself behind enemy lines, and of his heroic return – although privately, Gavotski thought he might have exaggerated some of his more remarkable feats. The young trooper was cut off in mid-flow, and he didn't know what to say, he just gaped at his accuser.

'Your chances of survival were minimal,' said Blonsky, 'and if you had been killed it would have been by a shot to the back: a senseless death, and a dishonourable one in the Emperor's eyes. He had carried you to the enemy's heart. Instead of thinking of your own survival, you should have used your chance to strike at that heart.'

'But... but I did survive,' said Pozhar. 'I survived, and I brought back some civilians, and... and some vital information about troop movements in the underhive.' He stole a sidelong glance at Steele, presumably

387

to see if he agreed with Blonsky's assessment. The colonel's expression, however, remained neutral.

'I don't think it's helpful to talk about what might have been,' Gavotski said. 'As Trooper Pozhar has proved, his situation wasn't hopeless. He was able to come back to us, to fight another day in the Emperor's service.'

Emboldened by the sergeant's support, Pozhar rounded on Blonsky, and said, 'Anyway, how long do you think I'd have lasted, surrounded by traitors, if I'd started shooting? How many do you think I'd have taken down? Five? Six? I killed three times that many before morning rations, and I'll do the same tomorrow, and the next day. That's how I serve the Emperor! How about you, Trooper Blonsky? How many kills have you claimed today? Do you really want to talk about whose life is the more valuable?'

Blonsky's stare didn't waver. 'You should not have come back,' he repeated with the unshakeable conviction of a witch hunter.

The Termite gave a judder, and Grayle, seated at the controls, called back over his shoulder, 'We've just left the hive, sir. No sighting of the enemy as yet.'

'How do we stand on that escort?' asked Gavotski.

'Looks like we can expect two Chimeras to meet us,' said Grayle. 'Still waiting for a vox from Ursa Platoon to see if we can make it three.'

'You clap eyes on the enemy, Grayle,' said Barreski, 'you just point me in their direction. I'll show them we don't need bodyguards!' He was stationed at one of the six hull-mounted flamers, squinting along its barrel, making minute adjustments to its sights. His enthusiasm was appreciated, but Gavotski knew that the Termite was not built for combat. It didn't have the firepower. That was why they had left the hive by an eastern gate, from a zone relatively untouched by the battle to the north. For the first leg of their journey, they would be travelling above ground, and they hoped to avoid the battle altogether. Due to pressure of time, however, they couldn't give it as wide a berth as they would have liked.

'If we do come under attack,' said Borscz, 'I would rather get out there and trust to the strength of my own two hands than suffocate or freeze to death in this tin can.' He did look uncomfortable, his massive frame sandwiched between Barreski and Anakora. However, as one of the first troopers into the Termite, Borscz appeared to have chosen his seat purposely to avoid having to man a flamer.

'You would agree with me, I think, my friend,' he continued, leaning forward to give Palinev an overly familiar pat on the shoulder. The force of the blow almost knocked the smaller, slighter man to the floor. 'As a scout, you must rely on your own abilities to stay silent and hidden, yes? Not much use to you inside a great clunking machine.'

'You are joking, right?' said Barreski. 'Without machines, our ancestors would never have won the Great War. It was machines like this one that turned the tide, and allowed them to drive the filthy orks from our world.'

'The machines would have been little use,' Borscz countered, 'without good, strong men inside them. It is not in the machines that our ancestors found the will to defeat the invaders, Trooper Barreski, but rather in their own beating hearts.'

ANAKORA PLAYED LITTLE part in the conversation. She had introduced herself to the others, given accurate but short answers to their questions about her war record, but that was all. She was acutely aware that they were all here because of their proven expertise in their fields. She had no right to sit among them.

Few Valhallan women served in the Imperial Guard. With so many men being marched off to war and so few returning, they had the vital and valued task of replenishing their world's population, of birthing and raising the next generation of Ice Warriors. This, then, was the life Anakora had expected to live, the life that had been shot to pieces by a few cold words from a disinterested medic.

It had taken her a few days to come to terms with the news, to accept that her life had no purpose any longer. Even one-time friends, even family, had looked at her with contempt, seeing her as a burden, a drain on their society. But far worse than that were those few who did understand, and whose looks were laced with pity.

There had been no compulsion on Anakora to join up, not ostensibly. But she had soon seen that she had no choice. The worst sin you could commit as an Imperial citizen was to serve the Emperor to less than your full ability, and there was only one way left in which she could serve.

She had expected to find basic training a struggle. She had just kept her head down and tried to get through it, her only goal not to embarrass herself beside men who had spent their lives in preparation for this. She had worked hard, steeled herself to appear as tough and as stoic as any of them, and no one could have been more surprised than Anakora when she had passed out with honours.

Still, she had felt she was faking it, bluffing her way through a world in which she did not belong, and she had known that her first battlefield would find her out. Fifteen hours, that was the average life expectancy of an Imperial Guardsman, though for an Ice Warrior it was a little more, maybe seventeen. Anakora didn't expect to last that long, but if she could claim just one kill, take one heretic down with her, then she would have balanced the scales and justified her fleeting existence.

Four years later, she was still here, and she didn't know why.

She should have died on that first battlefield. She should have died in the underhive, a couple of hours ago. She should have died so many times, on so many worlds – but most of all, she should have died two and a half years ago, on Astaroth Prime.

Astaroth Prime... A hellhole of a world, with lakes of fire and molten rivers; a world on which no Guardsman accustomed to the sub-zero temperatures of Valhalla should ever have set foot; a world to which a company of Ice Warriors had been sent anyway, to deal with an incursion by their oldest enemies, the orks; a world on which that company of Ice Warriors had been massacred.

In her brightest hours, Anakora tried to imagine that she had been spared for a reason, that the Emperor had had a higher purpose in mind for her. In her darkest, she forever relived that moment when a fellow trooper, a good comrade, had thrown himself in the path of an ork axe to save her.

Her record showed that she was a survivor, and in the Imperial Guard that ability was as highly prized as it was rare. Anakora knew the truth. She knew that she had not survived so long through her own efforts. She had survived because someone had taken pity on her, had thought her in need of protection.

So, now she had been pulled from another suicide mission and given this chance to survive again, precisely because of her record thus far. She couldn't help but wonder if this might be the time her luck ran out at last, the time that everyone would see through her.

Anakora looked forward to the release of death. Her only fear was that, when she died, she would take the rest of her new squad with her.

MIKHAELEV JOINED IN with the general chatter. He concurred with his new comrades that the Chaos forces didn't know what was about to hit them, that Confessor Wollkenden was as good as rescued. He kept his true feelings to himself.

He was worried. Behind the false bravado, he thought, they all were. Well, perhaps not Pozhar or Borscz – they both seemed like the kind of Guardsmen who lived only to die, the perfect brainwashed soldiers. It would not have occurred to them to question their orders, to wonder if their lives might have been put to better use.

Mikhaelev asked himself those questions. He stewed over the details of his briefing, the logic of staking ten lives on the faint chance of saving just one. If Confessor Wollkenden was so important, why did the Inquisition care so little about him? Why couldn't the virus bombing they had authorised be delayed a few days for his sake?

He couldn't speak out, of course. Even if some of the others, these relative strangers, agreed with him, they would not dare to confess to it. No, the floor would be held by the likes of Blonsky, spewing his accusations, insisting that to doubt one's leaders, even if they were only men, was to doubt the Emperor. Just as those same leaders would want him to think.

Not that Blonsky would hear him, of course. No, as soon as he opened his mouth, he knew that Steele or Gavotski would do their duty and shoot him dead.

So, he kept his own counsel, said what he was expected to say, and did what he was told as if he was the perfect brainwashed soldier too. And the fact that he was here, in this Termite, in this squad, was proof that he had played that part supremely well.

He did all this because he knew there was just one thing, one choice he could make, that would prove more dangerous than serving the Imperium... and that was not serving it.

THE TERMITE WAS under attack, being buffeted by shock waves. If he tuned out the deafening sound of its engines, Steele could identify the crump of explosive shells from without, of the sort fired by a Basilisk or a Bombard.

'We have a problem, sir,' Grayle yelled from the controls. 'We're in the sights of something... long-range artillery. It's decided to take a few pot shots. Thing is, it has good cover. The Chimeras can't see to return fire. The captain of one is requesting your permission to break formation, to go after it.'

'Denied,' said Steele. 'Do what you can, Grayle. Find us cover, get out of firing range. Do not, I repeat do not, engage with the enemy.'

'Aye, sir,' Grayle answered. The Termite made a sharp right turn, sharper than Steele would have thought possible. He was sure that, for an instant, its left-hand track had left the ground.

'We need a smoke launcher on this thing,' opined Barreski. 'Do we at least have smoke grenades, something we can lob out through the flamer emplacements?'

'We are sitting ducks in here,' Borscz fretted. 'If we were out in the field, ten smaller, faster-moving targets, that machine could never get a bead on us.'

At that moment, a tremendous concussive force slammed through the Termite's chassis, from its back left corner. A direct hit. It felt as if a tank had rammed them from behind, and only the fact that the Ice Warriors were so tightly wedged into their seats saved Steele from being thrown into Grayle's back.

Grayle muttered a prayer as the engine coughed, spluttered, whined, and then roared back into full throat. The Termite's suspension was shot. It felt as if it was shaking itself apart, and the passenger compartment was filled with smoke.

'Palinev, Mikhaelev,' said Gavotski, 'go through the equipment lockers, see if you can whip up a smokescreen as Barreski suggested. Barreski, I need you to check the borer, make sure it still functions. Grayle…'

'I know, sergeant,' said Grayle. '"Get us the hell out of here!"'

No one needed to say what every one of the ten Ice Warriors present was thinking: that they couldn't take a second hit like that one.

Steele watched as they jumped to their assigned tasks. He had no need to intervene, trusting Gavotski to handle the situation. So, he took the opportunity to observe how each member of his new squad responded to pressure. The more he could learn about them, the more effectively he could lead them, and official records could only tell him so much.

There was something about Mikhaelev's body language, for example – the slump of his shoulders – that said his heart wasn't truly in this mission, that perhaps he was just going through the motions. That hadn't come across at all in his records, and it was a cause for concern. Pozhar, thought Steele, would bear watching too, although, in his case, the reports of his commanders had been perfectly clear.

Pozhar was a loose cannon. He was loyal to the Emperor, fervently so, but he appeared to have no concept of his own limitations. Send him up against a tyranid army and, unless given specific instructions to the contrary, he would be the one to seek out the Hive Tyrant and to spit in its eye. On a mission like this one, that sort of overconfidence could be the death of everyone.

Pozhar was here because Gavotski had vouched for him. He had been the young trooper's squad commander once, and had averred that he was one of the most skilled close-quarter combatants he had ever seen. Gavotski had also sworn that he could handle Pozhar's rough edges and get the best out of him, and Steele had learned that his experienced sergeant was seldom wrong.

If Pozhar was overconfident, then Anakora had the opposite problem. She had come with the highest recommendations of any of them, but Steele had already seen enough to know that she lacked the faith in herself that others seemed to have in her. He felt that he, of all people, could identify with that.

Then there was Blonsky, a trooper in whom a succession of commanders had been unable to find fault, and yet they had couched their reports in terms that suggested they were more than happy to have seen the back of him.

Blonsky had summarily executed at least six comrades in combat, accusing them of heresy. He had made three similar accusations against superior officers, one of them a general no less. On the surface of it, his actions had always seemed justified – but reading between the lines, Steele had noted that his commanders considered him a liability, and a dangerous man to be around.

Blonsky had been one of Steele and Gavotski's reserve choices for their squad. Gavotski had pointed out, quite reasonably, that the Imperial Guard had suffered more than its fair share of deserters and turncoats on Cressida. With nine pairs of eyes focussed on the search for Confessor Wollkenden, it was perhaps advisable to have the tenth pair turned inwards, watching the squad itself.

THE SHELLING HAD ceased at last. Grayle, it seemed, had been right: the unseen gunner had just been taking pot-shots, and he had evidently decided to maintain his position rather than be enticed into pursuing a handful of enemy vehicles.

For the past few minutes, the only thing protecting the Termite had been the cloud kicked up by a handful of smoke bombs dropped by Palinev and Mikhaelev. By the Emperor's grace, it had been enough. A few more explosions had vibrated through the passenger compartment, but none had come close enough to cause real damage, and Barreski, who had moved up to the front seat beside Grayle, reported that the all-important borer was intact.

Grayle ploughed on, across land that had once been fertile fields but was now coated with grey slush and the ever-present purple fungus. He itched to put his foot down, to coax a little extra speed out of the grumbling engine, to make up for the time they had lost to their unplanned diversion. He didn't want to outpace the Chimeras, however.

There were four of them, each protecting one face of the Termite, and they were just starting to have trouble, struggling to find traction as the ground beneath them grew more icy and treacherous.

As the convoy proceeded, the snow became deeper until it was piled almost to the tops of their tracks. The Chimeras were equipped with dozer blades and crewed by experienced Ice Warriors, but still the going was painfully slow. With Gavotski's permission, Grayle got on the vox to the Chimera drivers and arranged to take point.

Shortly after this, Grayle got his first sight of the glaciers – and even he, who had been brought up amid the icescapes of Valhalla, let out a low whistle through his teeth. The glaciers formed an unbroken line in the middle-distance, dwarfing the paltry vehicles that approached it. He found himself nursing an unworthy thought, one of which he thought Trooper Borscz would have approved: that very little of what the Imperium of Man had ever built could compare with such natural splendour.

They were rumbling along the base of a U-shaped valley, and Gavot-ski cautioned the troopers to go easy with the flamers lest they bring an avalanche down on the Termite. There had been no signs of trouble for almost an hour, and at last Steele gave the order to release the escorts from service.

The Chimeras fell away, a couple of their drivers voxing Grayle with good luck messages. The Termite was finally alone, and Grayle pointed it at the sheer ice face that was looming before them.

Tactical maps suggested that the glaciers formed an almost unbroken ring around a great swathe of Chaos-held territory. Grayle had no doubt that the few routes in or out of the area would be under heavy guard. The last thing the Chaos forces would expect was for their enemies to strike through the great ice walls. Like the orks that had once invaded his home world, they were in for a rude surprise.

'Hey, Trooper Borscz,' Barreski called back over his shoulder, 'we're almost there. Should I start up the borer, or would you rather get out and dig your way through the ice with your bare hands and your teeth?'

'Impact with the ice face in thirty seconds,' reported Grayle. 'You ready there, Barreski?'

'Always,' Barreski said, his hands moving over the controls with prac-ticed ease, although to the best of his fellow tanker's knowledge he had never been in a vehicle like this one before. The Termite's great white borer dropped into the ready position, so that it blocked Grayle's view through his front shield. He wasn't missing much, he thought. For the past few minutes, all he had been able to see was the flat, grey surface of the approaching glacier.

He began to count down, as Barreski started the drill head turning, 'Impact in ten... nine... eight...'

'Anyone want to bet Grayle and me we can punch our way through this berg without even slowing down?'

Barreski fired off a quick burst from all four of the borer's flamer attachments, and Grayle could see the tell-tale orange halo flaring around the drill head. The great grey wall was running with rivulets, steaming a little, but still it looked like nothing more than a solid mass of rock as it rushed up to meet the Termite's front shield, and even Grayle had to fight the urge to flinch from it.

'Three... two... one...' he counted, through clenched teeth.

And he pressed down hard on the accelerator pedal, rising to Bar-reski's boastful challenge, as the countdown reached zero.

CHAPTER FIVE

Time to Destruction of Cressida: 43.15.08

THE TERMITE BUCKED, a shudder slamming through its plasteel body as its horn impacted with the great wall of ice.

But the impact was only momentary, because then the driver's front shield was pelted with jagged shards, spattered with melted water, and the engine howled in protest as it fought to make headway against a force of nature that should by rights have been immovable... and succeeded.

Barreski fired the borer-mounted flamers again, regretting only that he had to do so remotely and couldn't feel their kick to his shoulder. The Termite wheezed and shuddered, and a fresh wave of water broke over its front, but its tracks had gained purchase, and the vehicle surged forwards.

The hard part was done. They were inside the glacier and the borer had found its groove, its drill head shredding the ice in its path like paper. All they had to do now was keep up their momentum, and stay on a constant bearing.

In the absence of a clear view ahead, Grayle's gaze was fixed to the compass – while, for his part, Barreski yearned for a greater challenge than that of just keeping the drill head spinning. He was about to get his wish.

The ice had closed in around the Termite, and the walls and the roof of its self-made tunnel were pressing in on it, squeezing it. This was to be expected, of course – and at first Barreski thought little of the occasional groan from the plasteel above him, although he could feel the increased pressure as if the air itself had become denser. An especially heartfelt groan from behind him, he put down to one of his comrades back there, almost certainly Trooper Borscz.

But the groans from the hull were becoming more frequent, and louder.

And then, Grayle reported that their speed had dropped.

Barreski knew what to do. He pressed the flamers into service again, to ease their path through the ice, and the driver seemed satisfied. But no sooner had Barreski removed his hands from the trigger controls than Grayle frowned, shook his head and announced that they were slowing again.

They repeated the sequence twice more, with the same results, until Barreski was starting to worry about depleting the flamers' promethium tanks.

'Looks like we're going to lose that bet, Grayle,' he said through clenched teeth.

Then the hull emitted a particularly violent crack. Borscz leapt to his feet in alarm and banged his head on the roof.

'Are you certain the machine can take much more of this?' he moaned.

'A couple of minutes ago,' said Grayle, 'I'd have guaranteed it. Now–'

'Now what?' Colonel Steele was on his feet too. With two long strides, he was with Barreski and Grayle, leaning between them, examining the dashboard runes. 'What's happening out there, Grayle?'

'I don't know, sir. The Termite is performing at peak efficiency. Better than peak. It's the ice, it's… I know this sounds impossible, but I think it might be replenishing itself, reforming as fast as we can bore through it.'

'He could be right,' said Gavotski. 'We know that Cressida's change of climate has no natural explanation. We know the taint of Chaos is in the soil, lending it abnormal properties. Why not in the water as well?'

'I knew it,' Borscz groaned, dropping back into his seat. 'The tunnel is closing behind us. We are going to be trapped in here, in this tin coffin, forever.'

'Not if I can help it!' snarled Barreski. He fired the flamers again, and manipulated the borer, making it describe a small circle as it drilled, widening its tunnel.

'That's helping,' reported Grayle, 'but we still aren't making the progress we should.'

'And we can't keep this up for long,' Barreski added, still mindful of his dwindling fuel supplies.

'The ice!' cried Anakora. 'It is forcing itself in here!' With a glance back over his shoulder, Barreski saw that she was right. Crushed ice was squeezing through the gun emplacements in the Termite's side, as if being pushed by an external force. Six troopers leapt to the guns, doing their best to discourage the intrusion, but both Palinev and Mikhaelev immediately reported that their flamers had seized up.

'What's your assessment, Grayle?' barked Steele. 'Can we make it to the other side of this thing?'

'No, sir,' said Grayle, 'I don't think we can.'

'Well, we certainly can't back up,' said Gavotski. 'We don't have the room to swing the borer around.'

'If we changed our heading to oh-seven-nine,' said Grayle, 'we could be through the ice a lot faster. It'd take us a fair way off course, though.'

Steele pulled up a tactical map on his data-slate, nodded, and said, 'It's our best hope. Make that course correction, trooper.'

As Grayle moved to obey, another almighty crack drew ten pairs of worried eyes upwards. A hairline fracture had appeared in the hull, stretching half the length of the passenger compartment.

'You see, Trooper Borscz,' said Mikhaelev nervously, 'you didn't have to worry about our being trapped in here. The ice is going to crack this vehicle open like an eggshell and crush us all to death instead.'

'You think the ice caused that crack?' Pozhar joked, half-heartedly. 'That's from where Borscz banged his great head up there!'

'Can you bring the back end of the borer down a little?' Gavotski enquired of Barreski. 'Use it to protect the roof? I know it would slow down the drilling, but–'

'Can't do it anyway, sergeant,' said Barreski. 'I'm trying, but the ice is already packed in too tightly under there. The borer is stuck at this angle.'

'It's a race, then,' said Steele, his voice remarkably calm under the circumstances, 'between us and the ice. I'm relying on the two of you, Grayle, Barreski. Do whatever you have to do. Just keep us moving, as fast as you can manage.'

'Aye, sir,' said Grayle. Then he turned to Barreski, raising his voice to be heard. 'I can reroute some power to the borer from the engine. The harder that drill works, the less the engine has to do anyway.'

'Another flamer down,' reported Blonsky from behind them.

'I could do with one of those things up here,' Barreski shouted back. 'Rip one out of an emplacement if you have to.' He was operating the borer-mounted flamers – just three of them now, as the fourth was returning jammed signals – almost constantly, but still the front shield was being battered, not by mere shards of ice now but by great chunks of it, which hit like rocks.

The Termite's roof was beginning to bulge inwards with the increasing pressure upon it, and the Ice Warriors in the passenger compartment were up to their ankles in freezing slush. Barreski was so engrossed in his task that he hardly heard Grayle's voice, announcing that at their current speed they would be through the glacier in one more minute. It seemed like the longest minute of his life, and especially so when his flamers, only two of them working now, used up the last of their reserves and sputtered to a halt.

He turned, and found Palinev at his shoulder with a hand flamer as requested. Barreski leapt from his seat and snatched the weapon from the smaller man, even as the ice smashed through the front shield at last, coming at them like an avalanche.

Grayle had no choice. He couldn't leave his position or they were all done for. He met the oncoming ice, head down, eyes closed, breath held, hands gripping the controls for dear life. Barreski met it with a jet of flame, driving it back. Melted water gushed into the Termite's controls, angering the machine-spirits, which responded with a salvo of little explosions – but he couldn't worry about that now.

Borscz was standing on a seat, bearing the weight of the roof on his shoulders, but the walls of the passenger compartment were starting to bulge. The one to the left burst at last, even as the engine uttered its final gasp.

Then, the Termite's front end emerged, with a cough and a splutter, into the open air, and fell still.

Gavotski gave the order to abandon the vehicle, and its occupants almost fell over each other in their haste to obey. Barreski would have expected the technophobic Borscz to be the first out – but with the back half of the Termite still trapped in the ice, its roof threatening to collapse, the burly Ice Warrior chose instead to continue in his role as human prop.

Barreski was just as surprised to see the colonel, the nearest man to Grayle, delaying his escape in order to dig the driver out of the ice drift that had buried him. He went to help, and together they freed his fellow tanker's head. A half-conscious Grayle blew ice from his nose and mouth, and murmured, 'Did we make it?'

Then, something rammed the Termite from behind, and its rear end stove in, compacting the back half of the passenger compartment – fortunately cleared by now – into a tangle of plasteel.

Hauling Grayle between them, Barreski and Steele scrambled out through the hatch, found a two-metre drop beneath them, and dived into a blanket of grey snow. Steele landed on his feet, but Grayle's weight threw Barreski's balance, and he fell and rolled onto his back, just in time to hear a roar of 'Incoming!' and to see Borscz's enormous form blotting out the dull grey sky.

The impact was tough on the pair of them, but Barre
of it. He felt as if he had been kicked in the stomach
yak. For a moment, all he could see was a haze of red
in Grayle's arms, pinned down by Borscz's bulk, and h
grinding and rending of plasteel above him. He feared t... ... .
remains of the Termite were about to come crashing down on him too.
And there was another sound, too. A sound that, if anything, made Barreski even more concerned for his immediate future.

The sound of las-fire.

THE CREATURES HAD been waiting for them.

Anakora didn't know how it was possible, how they could have been
warned of the Ice Warriors' approach – but as soon as she dropped from
the Termite, as soon she planted her feet in the snow, they converged on
her, three of them.

They were much like the Chaos hounds she had fought in the underhive, all teeth and claws and spines. The most apparent difference was
that their fur was white, with patches of light green and brown: snow
camouflage. It would have done them more good if they had been able
to contain their eager growls at the prospect of a kill. Even so, it was
hard to see where the shape of each of the beasts ended and its surroundings began, almost impossible to get a bead on any of them.

Anakora loosed off three shots from her lasgun anyway, one in the
direction of each of the beasts. Then she ran – not out of cowardice, but
in the hope of drawing the creatures away from the wreckage of the Termite, and from the nine other Ice Warriors who were about to emerge
from it, dazed and confused. She would not lose another squad today.
Not if she had any say in the matter.

The first of the beasts pounced on her from behind, sinking its claws
into her shoulders. Carried by the momentum of her run, Anakora fell
face first towards the snow – but she had been prepared for this, and she
angled her descent so that she landed side-on, rolled onto her back, and
pinned the Chaos beast with her weight.

It squealed, and scrabbled at the backs of her legs with its back claws.
Anakora could feel its hot breath on her neck, and although she frantically recited the Litany of Protection under her breath, she knew that she
had only an instant before the beast sunk its teeth into the unprotected
flesh between her helmet and her greatcoat's collar.

She shifted her grip on her lasgun and thrust it, butt-first, over her
shoulder, aiming blindly, gratified to feel a crunch as she struck the
beast in its grotesquely enlarged fangs. It howled, and its grip on her
shoulders loosened. Anakora tore herself free of it, even as the second
beast caught up with the first and leapt at her.

...e got out of its way just in time. The second beast, unable to reverse ...e momentum of its lunge, landed on the first with its claws out-stretched, and virtually gutted it. That left her free, for a moment, to defend herself against the third. As it thundered towards her, she got her first good look at it. She saw its feline features and its whiskers and she realised what the beasts were, or rather what they once must have been.

They were snow leopards, much like those that roamed Valhalla's tun-dra.

She blasted at the oncoming beast, scoring three palpable hits – but it was tough, tougher than the Chaos hounds had been, and it would not fall. It leapt for her throat, and Anakora turned her lasgun sideways, using its barrel to protect herself. As soon as the snow leopard's claws hit the weapon, she hefted it over her head as if it were the bar on a set of dumbbells, simultaneously dropping to her knees. Her attacker's huge body was carried over her head, but it reacted fast, faster than she had hoped, and by the time Anakora had regained her footing and shouldered her lasgun again, the snow leopard had reined in its momentum, turned, and was coming at her again.

Her only hope was a kill shot, right through its eye, into its brain.

It was impossible.

In a fraction of a second that stretched into an eternity, Anakora realised that she didn't have the time to level her gun, to turn it to pro-tect herself, to do anything else before she was eviscerated. She faced her death with a heavy sense of resignation. She turned her head away, felt the impact of the beast with her chest, felt herself falling, felt the spray of hot, sticky blood on her face...

... and realised, to her surprise, that the blood wasn't hers.

The leopard was standing over her, black fluid gushing from its head, streaming into its eyes, one of its legs burnt off below the knee, fused into a bloody stump. It was unable to see, unable to run, thrashing in pain and confusion, and it seemed to have forgotten its erstwhile prey.

Then it was struck by three las-beams at once. More blood and offal erupted from between its ribs, and the beast toppled onto its side, quite dead.

Anakora's comrades had come to her rescue.

Steele was questioning his judgement once more.

He should have anticipated that there might be trouble outside the Termite. He *had* anticipated it. Should he, then, have left it to his troop-ers to help Grayle? Should he have taken point, been the first out there, ready to lead? There was no point in thinking like that. Gavotski and the others had things under control, for now.

Only one mutated leopard remained upright, and it was howling and twisting in the crossfire of five las-beams. It occurred to Steele to wonder if the beasts were native to this world, perhaps confined to its polar regions before the cold had spread. Or could they actually have evolved, even in the short time since a permanent winter had fallen over Cressida, to suit their altered climate?

He used his momentary respite to survey his new surroundings.

Two metres above him, the front end of his battered vehicle protruded from the glacier's sheer face. As he watched, the Termite's great horn crumpled and its wreck was dragged, screeching, back into the ice. A moment later, it had been swallowed up, and a fresh layer of ice had formed across the mouth of the tunnel it had made. No sign remained that the Termite, or indeed its passengers, had ever been up there.

Borscz, Barreski and Grayle were on the ground beside Steele, struggling to disentangle themselves from each other. Borscz was the first to break free from the scrum, and he rushed to join in the near-ended battle with gusto.

In front of Steele, there was a forest. Its near edge was almost parallel with that of the glacier, leaving only a narrow strip of land between them, eighty metres wide or less. Like the glacier, the forest stretched out far to each side of him, a great deal further than even his bionic eye could see.

It was a forest not of wood but of ice – of obscene, twisted sculptures, mockeries of the natural shapes they had presumably replaced, growing thick around the trunks but branching out into grasping, clawing talons as they reached upwards. The ice trees grew high and thick enough to blot out the already scant daylight, and the shadows between them were dark and foreboding. Their surfaces were encrusted with the ever-present purple fungus, and Steele's sensitive nose wrinkled at its overripe stench.

He could detect something else too: a movement. There was something out there.

He activated his eye's zoom function. It took the augmetics a long second to react to his thought, but then the colonel's gaze probed, searching, penetrating the ice forest's dark depths, and there...

There it was... for a moment, at least: a humanoid creature, covered in light grey fur, or maybe it was just wearing a fur coat. Steele couldn't tell – because before he could adjust his focus to see the creature more clearly, it was off again, a blur of motion despite its odd, shambling gait. It disappeared behind an especially fat tree, and he had lost it.

Unless, he thought, he acted now.

There was no time to second-guess his instincts, this time. The figure might have been a Chaos scout, in which case Steele couldn't let it go, couldn't allow it to take news of the Ice Warriors' presence in this area to its masters. So, he drew his lasgun and set off in pursuit of it, yelling to Troopers Blonsky, Palinev and Pozhar to follow him. The rest could catch up once the final snow leopard was dead.

As Steele crossed the tree line, he was plunged into an eerie gloom, and the aperture of his bionic eye widened to compensate. The recent snowfall had, for the most part, not touched the ground here. The soil was black and infertile, but the roots of many of the ice trees protruded from it like tripwires, and patches of the slippery fungus were everywhere. Steele had to slow his pace, watch his step. Even so, he almost lost his footing – and as he caught himself, he felt a sharp, slicing pain to his left shoulder.

He had brushed against a tree trunk, and it was razor sharp. Its edge had cut right through his greatcoat, through its layers of plasfibre and thermoplas, to score his skin. He turned to deliver a warning to his troopers, but saw that they had discovered the danger for themselves.

They proceeded as best they could after that. Steele used his power sword to cut away some of the more treacherous branches in his path – even without its energy field active, the well-honed blade sliced easily through the ice. Still, it was several minutes before he reached the spot in which the grey-furred figure had lurked – and, by then, he was not at all surprised to find no sign that it had ever been there.

Blonsky and Pozhar had fallen behind, but the smaller, slighter Palinev had been able to keep pace with his colonel, slipping through the forest as if its traps and snares were little impediment to him.

'There was something here, sir,' he reported. 'You can see where its breath has started to melt this tree. I could search for its tracks, but they'll be hard to follow on this ground.'

'No,' said Steele. 'Thank you, Trooper Palinev, but we don't have time for that.'

'It does look bleak, sir, if you don't mind my saying so. We've lost the Termite. Our escape route through the ice has closed behind us, so that even if we do find Confessor Wollkenden, we've no way of getting back to Alpha Hive with him. We must be at least twenty kilometres from his crash site, and it seems our enemies know we're here.'

Steele couldn't have summed up the situation more succinctly himself.

'We should get back to the others,' he said. 'We have a great deal of work to do.'

CHAPTER SIX

Time to Destruction of Cressida: 40.42.39

POZHAR WAS BEGINNING to wonder what he was doing here.

He was a front-line fighter, not a scout. Stealth was no more a virtue of his than was patience. Bad enough, he thought, that Steele had had the Termite flee from a single artillery unit; bad enough they had let the enemy have that victory. At least, he had thought, when they got to where they were going, when he was able to climb out into the open again at last, he would have the chance to flex his muscles.

The mutated snow leopards had been a welcome diversion – and Pozhar felt confident, although it was impossible to know for sure, that his las-beams had finished off two of them. But then Steele had directed his squad into the ice forest and warned them of the overriding need for caution.

And Pozhar had come to realise that the ice forest was almost as constricting, almost as claustrophobic, as the inside of the Termite had been.

The further they had ventured between its vile, warped trees, the more densely those trees had become packed. Already Pozhar had been scratched three times by their sharp edges, and he was starting to ache with the effort of walking with his elbows clamped to his sides, his head bowed, checking the ground for the treacherous purple fungus before he dared to take each step.

Still, as bad as this was for him, he thought, it was far worse for

Borscz, who was visibly straining to rein in his massive form, and who let out an aggrieved yelp every few minutes. Borscz's greatcoat was so crazed with cuts by now that Pozhar was expecting great squares of its fabric to start falling away.

He longed to set eyes on another snow leopard or two, something against which he could cut loose – but the ice forest seemed sterile, devoid even of birds, an entire area scoured of life, given over to the creeping rot that was destroying this world.

Pozhar shivered at the thought, and decided that on reflection this was far worse than being cooped up in any vehicle. Out here, he could feel the Chaos corruption in the air, pressing in on him like a physical force, battering him. He wanted to yell defiance at it, to fight back. He wanted to hack, slash and burn this accursed place down.

'Just give me a couple of flamers,' seethed Barreski, who had obviously had the same thought, 'and I guarantee you there'll be nothing left standing here in ten minutes. We'd be wading through water the rest of the way to the crash site.'

'And the Chaos forces would hear us coming ten kilometres away,' said Borscz.

'Just making a point, that's all,' said Barreski. 'I'd put my faith in Imperial firepower over anything Chaos can muster any day, no contest.'

'Forgetting what happened to the Termite, are we?' asked Mikhaelev wryly.

Anyway, there were no flamers – only the one that Barreski had been carrying, and it was out of fuel. There had been no time for the Ice Warriors to salvage anything more than their standard kit, worn or carried in their rucksacks, from the stricken Termite. Mikhaelev in particular was mourning the loss of his missile launcher, being now a heavy weapons expert with no heavy weapons.

Pozhar heard a noise ahead of him, glimpsed a moving shape and reacted with lightning speed. By the time he recognised Trooper Palinev, he was already staring at his comrade's slender form through his lasgun sights. An instant later, and Pozhar would have pulled the trigger. He chafed at having to hold himself back.

Palinev had adapted to his surroundings with enviable ease. He moved between the ice trees like a ghost, seeming to know instinctively where to step, and when he had to twist or hop to avoid a grasping branch or a protruding root. 'I've scouted two kilometres ahead, sir,' he reported to Steele, 'but there's nothing, nothing at all. The ice forest stretches as far as I've seen.'

Gavotski's lips tightened with disappointment. 'Maybe we should have tried to go around it after all. If it gets any thicker–'

Steele interrupted him. 'We'll cross that bridge when we come to it, sergeant. In the meantime, assuming that the forest does reach all the way to our destination, if we maintain our current bearing and speed and encounter no further hostile life... assuming all that, we should be able to reach the crash site in...'

He hesitated for a second, and his eyes – both the real one and the augmetic – glazed over. Pozhar stared at his commander in fascination – but then Steele's eyes cleared and he concluded, 'Approximately four hours and forty-seven minutes' time.'

And Pozhar wanted to scream.

PALINEV WAS ALONE again.

He didn't mind that. He had become used to solitude, welcomed it even. It was a long time since he had been in an environment as quiet as the ice forest was, far from the sounds of battle or even from the thrum of an engine. He knew he had to be careful not to let the quiet fool him. Likewise, he was sure to examine every ice tree that came into his view, even though the aberrant shapes had long since lost the power to fascinate or even to repel him, had begun to take on a monotonous quality.

Palinev couldn't take anything for granted, couldn't drop his guard for a second. The others were depending on him. The information he could gather, alone and unseen, could prove vital to them. But it came with a risk attached. If he were to walk into an ambush, if he were to be captured, then the enemy would know that his comrades were behind him, and they would be prepared.

One mistake, and Palinev knew he could take his entire squad down with him.

He had left them almost an hour ago. It was time to drop back, he thought, and report in to Steele again, just to reassure the colonel that he hadn't run into trouble, that the way ahead was still safe. Cradling his Guard-issue compass in his palm, Palinev reoriented himself. He was confident that he could retrace his steps by memory, but there was no harm in a double-check. If he strayed off course by even one half of a degree, he was likely to miss his comrades altogether.

He was about to set off when a sound made him freeze.

It had been almost nothing – the tiniest of scrapes, perhaps a rustle of fabric – and yet, it had not been a natural sound. Palinev knew this because he had taken the time to attune himself to the natural sounds of the forest, such as they were: the faintest warbling of the wind between the trees, the occasional pops and cracks as a newly frozen shape settled, or perhaps even grew?

As quickly and as quietly as he could, taking only one careful step, Palinev tucked himself in behind the nearest ice tree, and dropped to his haunches. He drew his combat knife from his boot, recited the Litany of Stealth, made sure that his breathing was as soft as the breeze, and waited.

As he had expected, a figure came into view. It was a man, as slight of stature as Palinev was. He was wearing an armoured helmet and a tight-fitting flak jacket, also like Palinev's, except that where his was a bottle green in colour, the stranger's was a bold red with gold highlights. It was hardly good camouflage material.

Palinev thought that he recognised the colours, though he couldn't name the regiment to which they belonged. Evidently, though, this man was an Imperial soldier – or at least, he had been once. He was holding a lasgun, keeping it ready as he crept from one tree to another: a scout. The question was, for whom was he scouting? There were no visible signs of Chaos mutation on the stranger, but that didn't prove anything.

Palinev waited until the man had drawn almost level with him, waited for his questing eyes to turn away from him. Then he slipped out from behind his tree, and into the shade of another. He repeated this manoeuvre twice more, each time drawing closer to his unsuspecting prey, and moving further around behind him.

When at last he was close, almost close enough to reach out and touch the nape of the other scout's neck, then Palinev pounced. His prey heard him coming, too late, didn't even have time to spin around. Palinev was on the man's back, his left arm locked around his shoulders, his right hand holding his knife to the man's throat.

'A friendly warning,' he hissed. 'If you try to shout to your people, if you speak at all other than to answer my questions, I will slit your vocal cords.' He would have done it by now if only he had been sure, if he had seen any proof that this man was a traitor. 'Who are you?' he asked. 'Answer me!'

'Trooper Garroway,' the other scout spat defiantly, 'of the 14th Royal Validian regiment of the Imperial Guard. Kill me if you like. Kill us all, but it won't save you. They will send a hundred thousand more like me – a million more – and they won't rest until this world is scoured clean of your filth, reclaimed for the Golden Throne!'

'You're Imperial Guard?' queried Palinev. 'What are you doing out here? This is Chaos-held territory.'

His prisoner relaxed a little in his grip, and this told Palinev more than words could have said. Garroway was relieved, not afraid, to have found himself in the hands of a fellow Guardsman. He was telling the truth.

'There are just under four hundred of our company left,' said Garroway. 'We were helping civilians out of Iota Hive to the north-west of here. When it fell, we were ordered back to Alpha, but the glaciers closed

Hammer of the Emperor

In front of us, blocking our path. We don't have a vox-caster any more, so we couldn't call for assistance. We have no maps. We've just been trying to find a way through, but the Chaos army is behind us. We were forced to take cover in this... this forest, whatever it is.'

Palinev let go of him. 'Palinev,' he introduced himself, 'Valhallan 319th.'

Garroway turned to face him, and his eyes narrowed. 'You're an Ice Warrior?'

'Don't let the lack of a greatcoat fool you. I move a lot better without it.'

'Yeah? I can't say I'd turn down the chance of a little protection. When my regiment first came to Cressida, sure it was cold, but not like this. Maybe it's different for you, coming from an ice world, but we're losing men by the hour. But... but you've found us now, they sent someone for us at last!'

'Ah,' said Palinev, 'no, I'm afraid they didn't. We're on a mission of our own.' He frowned. 'And if the enemy is behind you, that's going to mean trouble for us.'

'You can guide us out of here, at least,' said Garroway. 'You found your way past the glaciers, you can tell us how to get out... can't you?'

'We should report back to our commanders,' said Palinev. 'I should think they'll want to talk.'

THEY CAME TOGETHER not long after that: the Valhallans in green, the Validians in red, their paths converging in the heart of the white forest.

They had been expecting each other, of course, thanks to their respective scouts. A few of the troopers exchanged strained pleasantries, and Colonel Steele and the Validian commander, a fresh-faced young captain, sought each other out and moved to one side for a private conference.

The rest of the Guardsmen took this as a cue to relax, to recharge themselves as best they could. Their surroundings, however, offered them scant comfort. It was almost impossible for a man to sit down without touching the deadly tree trunks or roots – and after trying for a time, holding themselves in unnatural positions until their muscles ached, many of them gave up and stood again.

Few of the Validians could sit still anyway. They stamped their feet, rubbed their arms, did all they could to stave off the biting cold. Mikhaelev watched them, their bright colours spread through the forest as far as he could see, and he shook his head and sighed. Here they were, these brave men, doing the Emperor's work, and their leaders couldn't even equip them with the right clothing for the job.

In a perfect Imperium, of course, the Validians wouldn't have been assigned to this frozen world at all, unused as they were to such conditions. Somewhere, no doubt, a low-level clerk had looked at his slate, seen how many Guardsmen were dying from hypothermia on Cressida, weighed this against the cost of a few million armoured greatcoats and chosen to do nothing.

Mikhaelev was standing with three of his comrades, Anakora, Borscz and Pozhar.

'What do you think they are saying?' Borscz asked, inclining his head towards Steele and the captain.

'They'll be making plans to fight,' said Pozhar with more hope than certainty. 'According to Trooper Palinev, the Chaos army is on the Validians' heels. That puts them in our path. We'll have to shoot our way through them.'

Anakora shook her head. 'This is meant to be a stealth mission. If we start a full-scale battle here, it will lead every heretic in the area to us. Even with the Validians' help, we would be hopelessly outnumbered.'

'I'm talking about a lightning strike,' said Pozhar. 'Take the Chaos scum by surprise, and be long gone before the reinforcements arrive. The heretics think they're safe here, cowering behind their walls of ice. We can teach them different.'

Borscz grinned at that. 'We can be like our ancestors, no? We can strike at our enemies' very heart, as those mighty heroes did against the invading orks.'

'We can teach them to fear us!' said Pozhar, his eyes gleaming at the prospect.

'Yeah,' said Mikhaelev dryly, 'a lesson that will stay with them for all of about a day and a half before they're virus-bombed out of existence.'

'Trooper Mikhaelev is correct,' said Anakora. 'There is no purpose in our fighting and perhaps dying when it would not advance our cause.'

'Then what do you suggest?' asked Pozhar. 'That we turn tail and run?'

'Colonel Steele will find a way,' asserted Borscz loyally. 'He has not brought us this far to give up on our mission just yet.'

'No,' said Mikhaelev, with a tight smile, 'I should think not.'

Anakora was starting to see it too, he thought. She was looking at the knots of red and gold Guardsmen around them, at the hope in their faces that, having been lost for so long, they might have been found again.

'They've been out of vox contact for weeks,' she said. 'They cannot know about the withdrawal, about the... about what is to come next. They don't know that it's already too late for them, that without air transport they have no hope of reaching Alpha Hive in time to evacuate.'

'So, they're already dead,' said Pozhar with a shrug. 'All the more reason why they should die like soldiers, with their guns blazing.'

'Anyone want to bet the Validians do just that?' asked Mikhaelev quietly.

The other three troopers turned to look at him.

'Anakora was right,' he said. 'These men are dead anyway. Frankly, even if that weren't the case, the Imperium sees them, sees us all, as expendable. The only person on this world who really matters is Wollkenden, and we are the only people who can save Wollkenden. So, if it costs the Imperium four hundred lives to preserve our ten... well, it's just numbers, right?'

'And how, my friend, might the sacrifice of those four hundred lives help us?' asked Borscz.

'Think about it,' said Mikhaelev. 'We can't go forward, can't go back. There is one other option. We can't fight our way through the Chaos forces, but perhaps we can go around them. If we are to do that, though, we will need a diversion... a big one.'

Anakora looked pale, shaken. Her gaze was pulled again to the surrounding Validians, but she turned away quickly as one of them caught her eye. She seemed almost ashamed. Pozhar, in contrast, closed his eyes and let out a groan of dismay. Mikhaelev guessed that he would have swapped regiments in a second for a chance to get back into combat.

'You want to know what our leaders are talking about over there, Borscz?' he said grimly. 'I'll lay you another bet if you like. I'll bet you a day's worth of dry rations that Steele is asking the Validians to die for us.'

MIKHAELEV WAS RIGHT, of course.

Anakora prayed he wouldn't be, that Colonel Steele and the Validian captain might have found another way between them. But the more she thought about it, the more she knew that Mikhaelev's way was the only way that made sense.

The officers parted company, and Steele called his squad to him for a short briefing. Anakora hardly listened to his quiet words. She knew what he was going to say, anyway. Her eyes wandered instead to the captain, who was chairing a similar meeting with his sergeants, fourteen or fifteen of them. She watched as they received the news: that their trials of the past few weeks had been for nothing, that they wouldn't make it home after all, that the Emperor required only one final service from them. They bore it stoically, of course, but Anakora detected a few wistful expressions and a few slumped shoulders, as the sergeants moved out to spread the word to their troopers.

Logically, she knew she had no reason to feel guilty. The Validians weren't really sacrificing themselves for her sake, nor for that of her squad. They were doing it for Confessor Wollkenden, for the Ecclesiarchy, for the Emperor. Still, she couldn't help but ask herself why, of all the good soldiers here, she should be among the few, the very few, to be spared – why this was starting to become a familiar pattern for her.

If the Emperor had a plan for her – and it seemed that He must – if He was keeping her alive for some reason, then Anakora just wished she could imagine what that reason might be.

WITH NO MORE words left to say, the regiments went their separate ways.

The depleted company of Validians turned back the way they had come, and marched to meet the pursuers from whom they had fought so hard to escape. The squad of Valhallans headed off to the north-east, planning to skirt around the inevitable battlefield as they had back at Alpha Hive. The difference was, they were on foot this time, but at least this battlefield would be smaller.

Steele led the way. He had an unerring sense of direction, another gift of his augmetics, but still he paused frequently to check his bearings with Palinev. Gavotski knew that the colonel would be watching the chrono, calculating the cost of yet another diversion from their planned course. Steele had been tight-lipped since his talk with the captain – but then, this was hardly unusual for him.

It couldn't have been easy for him, to have been the bearer of such bad news, to have had to ask a fellow commander to order his men to their deaths. It had still been just a few days, after all, since the same had been asked of him.

Gavotski's thoughts drifted back to Alpha Hive, to the many good comrades he had left behind there, the scores of men alongside whom he had been proud to fight at one time or another. He wondered how many of them were still fighting, how many might yet make it onto the last of the exodus ships. He doubted he would see any of them again.

Barreski, at least, seemed happy. Somehow, he had talked one of the Validians into giving him another hand flamer – and with Grayle's help, he was stripping it down on the move, lovingly cleaning and lubricating its components.

Presently, the squad bore north and then around to the north-west again, until they had completed a quarter-circle and were on a path parallel to the one they had been on before. They had seen and heard nothing of the Validians in an hour, but now the quiet of the ice forest was interrupted by a series of distant sounds: the usual sounds, the ones that could have been the soundtrack to Gavotski's life, to all of their lives.

Gunfire, explosions, screaming. The sounds of war.

The sounds of four hundred good men, dying.

CHAPTER SEVEN

Time to Destruction of Cressida: 38.24.44

IT SEEMED LIKE a long time before the forest fell silent again.

For Steele, of course, with his enhanced hearing, it felt like even longer. This was a good thing, he told himself. It meant the Validian company had bought him more time than he could have expected from them. It meant they had died as they had lived, as heroes, and no Guardsman could want any more from his life than that.

It meant that he had done the right thing by sacrificing them.

Not that he had doubted this, not any longer. Steele had reviewed his decision six times, and was satisfied that he had overlooked nothing. Anyway, he had Sergeant Gavotski's support, which was always a reliable indicator.

The Ice Warriors had completed their half-circuit of the battlefield. They were behind the Chaos forces, whatever remained of them, back on course for the confessor's crash site. Steele just prayed that their enemies would take some time to lick their wounds, before turning to head homeward. Just time enough for his squad to gain a safe distance from them.

He heard the approaching mutants a full six seconds before he saw them.

They were making no attempt to be quiet, crashing through the ice forest at speed, whimpering and howling. They must have fled from the heat of the battle, thought Steele. They couldn't have known that the Ice Warriors were here – and yet, by some perverse chance, they were about to run right into them.

He hissed a warning to the others, telling them to take cover. Although they couldn't have seen anything themselves yet, they didn't

411

stop to ask questions. They obeyed their colonel's order with varying degrees of success. Only a blind man could have failed to see Borscz, who was twice as broad as the ice tree behind which he attempted to hide. Still, thought Steele, if the mutants were in the throes of panic, and obviously feeble-minded, then they might not see the trap before it was sprung.

And suddenly, there was over a score of them, appearing in the gaps between the trees, their manifest and varied deformities an assault to Steele's eyes. He waited until they got closer, even closer… and then one of the mutants came scrambling to a halt, and its huge, pink eyes widened, staring at Borscz's protruding stomach. It opened its mouth to squeal a warning…

…and that was when Steele stepped out of hiding with his laspistol levelled, and before the mutant could let out a sound, he calmly blew a hole through its head.

The rest of his squad were quick to follow his lead. Pozhar, not surprisingly, was the first, his face lit up by a broad grin as he pumped las-beam after las-beam into his confused and terrified targets. Barreski took his time, waiting for the opportune moment to wreak maximum damage with one shot from his new flamer. Three mutants were engulfed in fire, filling the air with the stink of their burning flesh and the sounds of their screams.

'Don't let any of them get away!' Steele yelled.

He counted four mutants on the periphery of the group, making to turn back, deciding that the lesser of two perils was the one that lay behind them after all. He brought down a hunchbacked, tentacled horror with a shot to the back.

The other three mutants fled, and were out of sight before Steele could stop them – but an instant later a tremendous bang rent the air and a cloud of shrapnel billowed out from the trees where they had vanished. Barreski had tossed a frag grenade after the mutants – and, although Steele winced at the sound that had almost overloaded the acoustic enhancers in his right ear, he couldn't deny that it had been an effective tactic.

Was there any hope, he wondered, that no one in the main body of the Chaos force had heard the explosion, that the ice trees might have deadened its sound before it could reach them? Perhaps, at least, it might be dismissed as the work of a lone Validian kamikaze, or even a dispute between undisciplined mutant stragglers.

So long, that was, as none of the mutants lived to tell a different tale.

In focussing on the would-be deserters, Steele had let down his guard against the more immediate threats to his wellbeing. He heard the cocking of a pistol, and turned to find its barrel aimed at his head by a creature that looked as if its face had melted, its eyes and its nose running towards its chin.

Before the mutant could fire, Borscz barrelled into its side and threw off its aim. It responded by swinging its gun butt at the burly Ice Warrior's jaw. It hit with a resounding crack, but Borscz barely seemed to feel the blow. He gripped his hapless opponent by its shoulders, thrust it back against a razor-edged ice tree. The mutant screamed and thrashed as blood gushed out of its back, but with a deep-throated chuckle and a flash of his brilliant white teeth, Borscz pushed its chin up and back with the heel of his hand. The tree cut through the mutant's misshapen head, bisecting it down the middle.

Three more of its kin made a break for it, but two ran into a crossfire of las-beams set up by Gavotski and Anakora. Palinev went racing after the third, with his knife drawn. Barreski pressed his flamer into service again, and Borscz, who had been about to pounce on another mutant when it combusted in his face, gave a yelp of protest and threw his hands up to his singed beard.

Surprise and discipline were the Ice Warriors' greatest assets, and many of their foes were cut down before they could do much more than gibber. Mikhaelev in particular proved to be an expert shot, choosing his angles well so that a single one of his las-beams often sliced through two bodies.

The closest the mutants came to exhibiting teamwork was when four of them tried to swarm Blonsky. Steele's pistol finished off one before it could reach its target, but the others fell upon the trooper. Most of the Ice Warriors held their fire for fear of hitting a comrade, although Steele noted that Pozhar was the exception. He drew his power sword and activated a control in its hilt, causing the blade to flare with a crackling blue energy. He stepped up behind one of the mutants and struck with all the strength in his augmented muscles, severing its head from its spinal column.

Borscz wrenched a third mutant from its victim, while Grayle attempted a similar manoeuvre with the fourth, but found that it was stronger than he was. Nevertheless, he kept it occupied long enough for Blonsky to stand and to thrust his bayonet into the struggling creature's guts.

And then the fight was over, there were no more mutants standing, and Palinev returned, wiping his blade with a cloth, to report that the one he had chased was also dead. The Ice Warriors were left in a self-made clearing, but the ice trees that Barreski's flamer had melted were already beginning to grow again. Pozhar leapt as a new shoot sprouted with impossible speed beneath him, almost impaling his foot.

Before they moved on, Steele counted the bodies to confirm that all the mutants he had seen were accounted for. Then he took another second to rerun that calculation, four more times, to be sure.

It had become second nature for him to do this, and he did it for a good reason. He did it because he could not trust his own mind.

SOME THINGS, HE remembered too well.

He remembered every detail of his time in the hospital, everything they had done to him there. The medics had rebuilt one side of Steele's head, inserted plates into his skull, and grafted foreign objects onto his brain. They had replaced the shattered bones in his right shoulder and upper arm with plasteel, the muscles with hydraulic systems.

He remembered their assurances that the pain would be worthwhile, that they were doing the best they could for him. He hadn't believed them. He had thought it more likely that the medics were just pushing, testing, seeing how far they could go.

Steele could remember all that, but he couldn't remember what had landed him in that Emperor-forsaken place to begin with. He had no memory of Karnak, the world to which his service records told him he had been posted for more than two years. He did not know who his comrades had been on that world, in that campaign, which of the Imperium's many enemies they had been fighting, or what his orders had been on that fateful day.

He had no idea what had caused the explosion that had gone off in his face.

He couldn't remember his father's eyes, nor the touch of the woman he had left behind on Valhalla when his draft papers had arrived.

Sometimes, in the weeks that had followed his discharge, Steele had wished that the medics had just left him to die.

He was aware that people saw him as a quiet man, a deep thinker. As a cold man. Some were jealous of his augmetics, of the feats they enabled him to achieve. Those people didn't know the real Colonel Stanislev Steele. They didn't know the abiding frustration that burned at the core of his being.

He could hear the flapping of a moth's wings from forty paces now, detect its body heat from a hundred. He could perform complex calculations at lightning speed – or rather, a small part of his brain to which he felt little connection could perform them and offer up the results to him. He had near-perfect recall, and could store tactical maps and troop movements in that same small alien corner of his head.

Steele had heard it said that he could count the snowflakes in a storm, although he had never been quite bored enough to try.

And of course he had the strength of three men in his right arm –

enough, he had been told, to slice through two armoured heretics with one swing of his power sword.

It must have sounded amazing, in theory, and Steele's new-found abilities had certainly helped him to rise through the ranks. But, as Trooper Borscz would no doubt have reminded him, Imperial technology wasn't always reliable – and far less so in conditions like these, on ice worlds such as Valhalla and the world that Cressida had become. Steele's eye, his acoustic enhancers, the olfactory sensors in his nose, even his right shoulder, they were all prone to intermittent failures. They could let him down at any moment.

And so, nine years after he had been reborn, he was still trying to work out what the medics hadn't been able to tell him. He still didn't know which of his thoughts were entirely his own, and which had been influenced by the augmetics that had oh-so-subtly insinuated themselves into his consciousness. He had to second-guess his every instinct, in case it was based on flawed information.

He couldn't tell where the real Stanislev Steele ended and the augmetics began.

THEY WERE NEARING the edge of the ice forest, at last.

Steele knew this because his augmetics had calculated that the mean distance between the ice trees was a little greater than it had been a few minutes ago. He quickened his pace, knowing that his squad would fall into step beside him without being ordered to do so. There had been no signs that anyone was on their tail, but still he couldn't dismiss that possibility.

At last they emerged into the open, and Steele could see that the others were as happy about it as he was. Borscz let out a deep groan of relief, and took the opportunity to stretch his arms and legs and work out the cricks in his neck.

A great, snow-blanketed field stretched ahead of them – and in the distance Steele could see the spires and towers of Iota Hive. They had made good time, all things considered. The crash site was only a few more kilometres away, and the going looked set to be a lot easier from now on. The open terrain would bring its own problems, however. The Ice Warriors' bottle-green greatcoats would stand out like beacons to anyone who overlooked the field from any number of surrounding hills. And they would leave tracks in the grey snow, but there was no way around that.

Fortunately, the sky was beginning to darken. Steele considered waiting for a while, until the night had drawn in completely, but he concluded that the risks of so doing outweighed the advantages. His internal chrono was ticking away, impossible to ignore. It was counting down the seconds to the end of this world, making him acutely aware of the passing of each one.

It was only when Gavotski had a quiet word in his ear that he realised how hard he had been pushing his squad, how exhausting the ice forest had been for them. He conceded that they should take a short rest, while they had some cover. The Ice Warriors set themselves down on the ground, broke out their rations and their water bags, and relaxed for the first time in a good few hours.

The break buoyed their spirits, and Mikhaelev and Grayle were soon engrossed in a conversation about the relative merits of Lightning and Thunderbolt fighters. Grayle was enthusing about the time he had got his hands on the controls of one of the latter, during a short secondment to the Imperial Navy.

Gavotski, in the meantime, was reciting old war stories to an attentive Pozhar and Palinev, while Barreski and Borscz had resumed their good-natured bickering.

'I'll make you a deal,' said Barreski. 'When this mission is over, we will have a contest: my flamer against your hands, and we will see which is the more deadly.'

'Then you had best hope your flamer does not jam,' said Borscz cheerfully, 'or run out fuel, and that you do not miss with your first shot, because one is all you will get. After that, my hands will be around your throat, and there will be no doubt about the outcome then – because my hands, I can rely upon.'

'Oh, I never miss,' Barreski assured him, 'you can count on that.'

THE VALIDIAN CAPTAIN had warned Steele about the lake.

He had led his company around it – but it had taken him the better part of a day to do so, and they had run into more than one small Chaos encampment in the process. Steele had decided that, if it was at all possible, he would take his squad across; the lake, according to the Validian, was far narrower than it was long.

And so it was that, after a short, uneventful trek from the forest, the Ice Warriors came to the nearest bank of the lake and stumbled to a halt. Steele dropped to one knee, drew a long-bladed knife and held it so that its tip rested on the frozen surface. He pushed it down slowly, measuring the resistance it encountered, feeling when that resistance ended, when the knife tip had penetrated the ice and emerged into the water beneath it. By the time it did, he was pleased to note that the knife was buried almost to its hilt. The ice, he judged, was more than thick enough to support ten men.

Even so, the heavy Borscz was understandably apprehensive. He let the others get a short way ahead of him before he gingerly placed one foot on the ice, and then slowly, carefully eased his great bulk onto it. By the time he had taken four or five steps in this manner, however, he was beginning to grow in confidence, and he soon caught up with his comrades.

The Ice Warriors had fanned out so as not to concentrate their weight in any one spot. They moved slowly, focussing on their feet, mindful of the likely consequences should any of them slip and fall. Steele kept his ear attuned to the cracking, creaking sounds of the ice under pressure, hoping that those sounds would warn him in time if the pressure became too great.

The lake, he had been told, was a kilometre across, but it took his squad almost half an hour to reach the halfway point. By then, he could see the far bank, a black mass in the gathering gloom.

And it was shortly after that, when the Ice Warriors were at their most exposed, their most vulnerable, that the first shot rang out.

'Sniper!' yelled Palinev as a section of the ice exploded a few metres to his right.

Steele replayed the last second in his mind, and found that his bionic eye had picked up something that he hadn't noticed at the time: a muzzle flash, coming from the dark, rounded shape of a hill to the north-east. He relayed this information to the others, and tried to zoom in on the spot in question.

His eye's Heads-Up Display flagged up the outline of a man's head and shoulders, and identified the weapon he was holding: a long-las.

Fortunately, the sniper wasn't a very good shot, at least not at this range. Unfortunately, he didn't have to hit the Ice Warriors, not when he could shoot the ground out from beneath them. Two more beams punched through the ice, and blew up jets of water. The Ice Warriors returned fire, dropping into defensive crouches in the absence of cover to minimise their profiles. Their own lasguns, Palinev's excepted, didn't have the range of the long-las – even if they hit their target, it would be with half-strength beams. Still, they could encourage the sniper to keep his head down.

Palinev looked surprised when Steele came up behind him and snatched his long-las from his hands. 'No offence, trooper,' he muttered, 'I just think my aim might be a little better than yours.' Gavotski saw what Steele was doing, and ordered the rest of the squad to withdraw, to keep up the covering fire but to make for the far side of the lake as they did so – and to sacrifice caution now for speed.

Steele was trying to focus on the sniper again when another beam hit the ice directly in front of him, and the ensuing eruption threw him off his feet.

He landed heavily on his back and was winded, almost dropping his

418   *Hammer of the Emperor*

weapon. The frozen surface beneath him cracked, and for an instant Steele thought he might crash right through it. His relief when this didn't happen was short-lived. The twin impacts of las-beam and Ice Warrior had begun a chain reaction in the ice, and he could hear the fault lines widening and spreading.

And then the rest of his squad saw it too, as great fissures began to appear around Steele, and met to carve out little floating ice islands.

He couldn't stand. His weight was only supported because it was evenly distributed, and this wouldn't help him for much longer. His comrades couldn't reach him without sharing his fate, and they had their own problems anyway.

Unable to save himself, Steele did the only thing he could to save them.

He shouldered the long-las, lifted his head, and willed his bionic eye to work for him. He smiled as his HUD locked onto the distant sniper, and he squeezed the trigger and felt the recoil of his weapon driving him down, down, down...

THERE WERE SOME things in life, Steele thought, that it was best not to know.

He didn't need to know the exact temperature of the freezing water into which he had been plunged, nor the combined weight of the armoured greatcoat and the packed rucksack that were dragging him towards the lake bed. He would rather not have been able to hear the ice re-forming above him, sealing him in this flooded tomb.

And yet still his augmetics insisted on seeking out such information, presenting it to him as if he might draw some useful conclusion from it, as if he didn't already know what the only conclusion could be.

Any other man would have been blissfully insensate by now, his brain numbed by the cold. Any other man would have been at peace. Not Steele.

His head was awhirl with numbers. They filled it to bursting point, demanded his attention, demanded that he must know everything, every tiny detail of his impending fate. And, above it all, that damned internal chrono was pounding at his temples, counting down to a new, more imminent, deadline now...

...ticking off the few remaining seconds of Colonel Steele's life...

CHAPTER EIGHT

Time to Destruction of Cressida: 35.14.56

GAVOTSKI'S FIRST IMPULSE, as Steele fell through the ice, was to dive in after him. Holding himself back was the hardest thing he had ever had to do, but he could not have survived immersion in the freezing lake. The only thing he could do for the colonel now was to lead his squad for him, and bring honour to Steele's name by ensuring the completion of his final mission.

After all the noise and the frenzy of the past few seconds, the silence that fell now felt unnatural, dreadful. It seemed that Steele's dying shot had struck true, because the sniper fire from the hill had ceased – but no one was thinking about that now. The Ice Warriors were standing, gaping at the jagged ice hole that had swallowed their leader. A hole that was rapidly frosting over again, resealing, until there was no trace that it, or Steele, had ever been there.

They were well used to death, these soldiers. They had lived in its shadow all their lives, knew it could strike at any moment and from any quarter. But Colonel Steele had seemed like the strongest of them, somehow the least mortal, and his passing was a shock to them all.

'Everyone, get back!' growled Barreski – and his flamer flared, and melted a fresh hole in the ice, making the water beneath it steam. If Steele was somehow still conscious down there, trying to surface, then he had another chance, a few more seconds, in which he could do so –

and as unlikely as it seemed, the Ice Warriors clung to that hope, staring, waiting, hoping...

...until, to Gavotski's astonishment, a gloved hand broke the surface, fumbling, reaching, flailing, finding purchase – and Colonel Stanislev Steele hauled himself up, losing strength halfway, collapsing face down with his legs still dangling in the water. Everyone started forward at once, but Gavotski threw up a warning hand, and beckoned only Palinev to follow him onto the weakened ice where the colonel lay. They gripped Steele under his shoulders, dragged him clear of the danger area, and brought him back to the others. His skin had a pale blue tint.

It was Anakora who noticed that he wasn't breathing.

Gavotski knelt by Steele's side, blew air into his lungs and gave him chest compressions until he jerked back to life. Steele sat bolt upright, so suddenly that it made everyone jump, and he spat water from his mouth. His head turned as he surveyed the concerned faces of the comrades gathered around him. This close up, Gavotski could see the lenses tilting and turning in Steele's bionic right eye. The left eye, Steele's real eye, was open but dead, staring blankly.

'How is he alive?' breathed Blonsky.

'He shouldn't be,' said Gavotski. 'His brain should have shut down in that water. I think some parts of it did, but... but the colonel's brain isn't entirely organic.'

Barreski grinned, and nudged Borscz in the ribs 'You see? His augmetics, the machines in his head, they have saved his life!'

Steele's eyes, both of them, rolled back into their sockets. Gavotski caught his head before it could fall, and lowered him down gently. 'We must dry him off,' said Anakora, 'and take him someplace warm.'

'Look around you,' said Mikhaelev. 'There is no such place.' However, he joined the other Ice Warriors in searching his rucksack, finding spare items of clothing. In fact, as the trooper with the closest build to Steele's, he donated his greatcoat, swapping it for the colonel's sodden one.

Other than that, there was little anyone could do.

'The colonel will be OK,' said Gavotski, as much to convince himself as to raise the troopers' morale. 'He was only in the water for a couple of minutes, and I've seen people survive after ten times that long. He'll wake up when he's ready.'

THERE WERE VOICES coming from the far side of the rise.

Palinev dropped onto his stomach, scrambling the rest of the way up on his elbows. Cautiously, he raised his head – and his heart leapt into his throat.

The night had well and truly fallen, over an hour ago. There was no moon in the sky, and few stars. Even Palinev could barely see his hand in front of his face. Still, Gavotski had insisted they press on. It was what Steele would have wanted.

Gavotski had asked his troopers to carry the colonel two at a time, in shifts. Instead, Borscz had volunteered to do the job alone. He had slung Steele's unconscious body across his shoulders and hefted him with apparent ease.

And now they had reached their goal at last.

At least, their scout had reached it. The ship lay beneath him: an Aquila lander, its red wings proudly unfurled like those of the two-headed Imperial eagle after which it had been designed and named. But this eagle's back was broken, its legs buckled. It sagged in the middle, listing to one side, and it took Palinev a minute to locate its detached and half-buried tail fin through his field goggles.

This, then, was the ship in which Confessor Wollkenden had been travelling, the ship that had been shot down, the ship that Colonel Steele and his squad of Ice Warriors had been dispatched to find. And, in confirmation of their paymasters' worst fears, there had been a battle here. A battle that the Imperium had lost.

The ground was strewn with burnt and broken bodies. Bodies in red and gold. Palinev swept the goggles over them, searching for a hint of Ecclesiarchal robes among them. There was still a chance that Wollkenden had escaped the carnage, and let his willing guards lay down their lives for him. Without a closer inspection, though, it was impossible to tell for sure.

And for now, Palinev was more concerned with the living.

Chaos cultists. The area in front of the lander teemed with them: ordinary men and women, once, most likely born on Cressida itself. They had probably worked in its mines, served the Emperor in exchange for His shelter and His succour. Until their minds had snapped. Until they had succumbed to the infection of their world. Now, they dressed in robes of black and prayed to a different pantheon. Some had even had their faces tattooed with the obscene eight-pointed star of the Chaos gods.

The cultists had built a fire, and gathered around it to warm themselves. Its bright orange flames ruined Palinev's night vision, but on the plus side they cast a spotlight on his enemies while deepening the darkness around him.

The cultists had been looting the stricken lander – or rather, they had been directing a number of grovelling mutant slaves to do the job for them. Two especially deformed specimens appeared in the hatchway, struggling with a bashed equipment locker. It got out of their control and hit the ground with a crash, and an enraged cultist yelled in the mutants' faces and assaulted one of them with a lasgun butt.

One thing was clear in Palinev's mind: if Confessor Wollkenden was indeed alive, then he was a long way from here.

GAVOTSKI CONCURRED WITH that assessment.

'We need to capture a few of those men alive,' he considered, 'make one of them talk. Have they seen the confessor? Are they holding him?' He spoke in a low voice, because the enemy camp was only a few hundred metres away.

'How many did you see, Palinev?' Pozhar asked eagerly.

'It was hard to tell,' said the scout, 'in the dark and with all the activity. At least ten cultists, maybe four or five mutants, although there could have been more inside the lander. They didn't seem too well-equipped.'

'From the way you describe it,' said Mikhaelev, 'we have the terrain on our side this time. We can take cover at the top of that rise, start shooting and have half of them down before they know where we are.'

Palinev nodded. 'There's nowhere for them to run.'

Gavotski had been worried about leading the squad into combat again today. They were clearly exhausted, although none of them would have admitted to it. He was feeling the effects of his exertions himself. But Mikhaelev was right, this seemed like it would be an easy victory for them – and maybe they needed that right now.

And then there was the ship, of course. If the Ice Warriors could recapture it, then it could provide them with shelter and some warmth for the night. They would all benefit from that, Steele in particular. Borscz had set the colonel down while they talked. He had settled into what seemed like a comfortable sleep, his breathing deep and regular, and his colour was improving.

'OK,' said Gavotski at length, 'let's do this. Barreski, Mikhaelev, take point. Palinev, if you can sneak around to the other side of the camp, or as near as you can manage, you can pin the cultists down if they start to run. Everyone try to avoid hitting the lander; I don't want it damaged any more than it is already. That means no explosives, Barreski. There's a small chance that the engines are still–'

He didn't get any further.

Steele's eyes snapped open, and he opened his mouth and let out a long, full-throated scream. A scream that the cultists couldn't have failed to hear.

Pozhar didn't wait for orders, didn't even wait for the echoes of the scream to die down. The enemy knew where they were. Any second now they would appear at the top of the rise that separated them, start picking off the Ice Warriors like targets on a range. Unless the Ice Warriors could gain and secure that vantage point first.

Pozhar raced as fast as he could, threw himself onto his stomach at the top of the slope, and started firing before he knew what he was firing at. He was rewarded by the sounds of growls and squeals. The cultists had sent the mutants ahead, and before Pozhar knew what was happening one of them had crested the rise, between his las-beams, and leapt upon him.

It was a huge, shambling creature, covered in grey fur. It hit Pozhar like a brick, and tried to wrest his lasgun from him. He fought it, and they rolled down the slope together. As they reached its foot, Borscz leapt into the melee, and seized the mutant's head between his hands as if he thought he could crack its skull open – but it was too strong, even for him. With an animal roar, it broke his hold and rounded on him.

The mutant lashed out with a gnarled talon, and Borscz wasn't fast enough to back out of its way. Three parallel tears opened across his chest, and the burly Ice Warrior went down.

The mutant turned to Pozhar again as he was still scrambling to his feet, still fumbling with his weapon. It leapt at him, and he delivered four rapid-fire bursts to its stomach, but they weren't enough to stop it. He went down for a second time, with the creature on top of him, bleeding onto him. Its brow was low, pronounced, and its narrow, crazed eyes bored into Pozhar's skull as he fought to keep its blood-dripping talons at bay with the stock of his lasgun.

It was Borscz who came to his rescue again – Borscz who, incredibly, must have kept himself awake, lifted his massive body from the ground by sheer force of will and the strength of his own two arms. He landed heavily on the mutant from behind, gripped its ribs between his knees, and drove his meaty fists again and again into its head until it was insensate. Pozhar slipped out from beneath its bulk as the mutant rallied, as it tried to throw Borscz from its back but found that, this time, his grip was unbreakable: he was literally holding on for his life.

Pozhar fired again, aiming three more point-blank beams at the gaping wound in the mutant's stomach. He must have struck something vital, because the mutant fell at last – but it fell backwards, and it landed hard on top of the still-clinging Borscz. It was the final straw for the Ice Warrior: his eyelids fluttered and closed. Pozhar saw that his comrade was still breathing, shallowly, but he was bleeding from his chest. Borscz needed synth-skin, needed someone to close his wounds for him, and he needed it soon. Pozhar could have helped him, but it would have cost him precious seconds, rummaging through his field rucksack for his Guard issue medi-pack.

He surveyed the scene around him. Another four mutants had

appeared over the rise, all of them with the same grey fur, and each of them appeared to be as tough as the first one had been. Two of them were on fire, no doubt the work of Barreski and his flamer, but still they fought on. One of them had Gavotski in a bear hug, no doubt hoping he would burn with it. Having seen how resistant the creatures were to las-fire, Anakora and Blonsky were attacking it with bayonets, trying to loosen its grip on their sergeant. Another mutant was attempting to get Palinev in a similar hold, but for now his agility was keeping him out of its clutches.

As Pozhar watched, another creature staggered under a barrage of las-beams from Grayle and Mikhaelev – staggered, but did not fall. The mutants were doing their job well, keeping their foes occupied. The Ice Warriors had given up all hope of securing the rise as the first robed cultist appeared at its top, and levelled a lasgun, able to take his time and choose his target.

It was all the excuse Pozhar needed. He abandoned the fallen, bleeding, dying Borscz and charged back into the fray.

THE BURNING MUTANT could ignore Blonsky and Anakora no longer.

It let go of Gavotski, who dropped and rolled in the snow to extinguish the flamer chemicals that had stuck to his greatcoat. The mutant lashed out at Anakora, but she parried its talon with her lasgun. For an instant, the creature was wide open to Blonsky, and he took great pleasure in driving his bayonet through one of its narrow eyes. It howled and recoiled, but he stayed with it, driving the spike further into its head like a corkscrew, simultaneously blasting at its simian face with las-fire.

The merest touch of this aberration, the brush of its fur against his elbow, the spatter of its blood on his skin, made him feel unclean. Like the cultists on the other side of the rise, like all of the insane devotees of Chaos, it must have been human once. It must have known, back then, that this was what the future held for it, must have seen what lay at the end of its chosen path.

Blonsky had no sympathy for it. It deserved what its gods had done to it.

The mutant died at last, as did one of its fellows, succumbing to a second flamer burst. That left just two. One was being kept occupied by the nimble Palinev, while the other had just lost a claw to Grayle and Mikhaelev's beams and had dropped to its knees. Blonsky set his sights on Palinev's opponent, but was suddenly tackled by Anakora. For a second, as they fell, he wondered if her mind had snapped as well, if she had chosen this moment to turn traitor – but then, a las-beam rent the air above his head, and he realised that she had just saved his life.

A cultist had attained the top of the rise, a perfect sniping position –

and, had he fired again, with both Blonsky and Anakora on the ground, he could have killed one of them. Instead, he saw Pozhar charging him, gun blazing, and he turned his fire upon the young trooper – and Pozhar was hit, a glancing blow to the shoulder. The force of the blast knocked him head over heels, and for the second time in as many minutes he came rolling back down the slope.

Emboldened by his success, the cultist became careless. He lifted himself up to get a better angle on his fallen foe, to finish him off – and two las-beams ripped through him. As the sniper fell, his killers, Blonsky and Anakora, started forward, joined again now by Gavotski. The other cultists had mistimed their advance, must have hung back too long behind their mutant cannon fodder, because the opposing factions met at the top of the rise. The Ice Warriors were the first to react, and three of their foes were dead before they could return fire.

The cultists, despite their greater numbers, were outmatched. They were untrained, unarmoured and, in some cases, even unarmed. The outcome of the battle was already beyond doubt when Pozhar waded back into it. He wielded his lasgun in his left hand, his right hanging uselessly by his side, and most of his shots went wild.

A cultist slipped in beneath the Ice Warriors' beams, and was suddenly in Blonsky's face, trying to push a knife through the layers of his greatcoat.

'You're too late, Guardsman,' the foul heretic hissed. 'Mangellan has the power on this world, and if you wish to live you will renounce your decadent Emperor and turn to–'

The threat was never completed. Blonsky seized his attacker's wrist and twisted it until it broke. The cultist screamed, and the blade dropped from his numbed fingers.

Blonsky raised his bayonet to the wretch's throat, but remembered that Gavotski had wanted a hostage. So, as much as it went against his instincts to do so, he turned his lasgun around and drove its butt into the cultist's skull, knocking him cold.

BARRESKI SKIRTED THE final mutant, trying to find an angle from which he could torch it without setting light to Palinev too. The scout was still keeping clear of the mutant's raking talons, ducking and weaving, twisting and turning – but the mutant was relentless, starting to wear him down.

Barreski ventured a little closer to it. He thought it was too busy with Palinev to notice him. He was wrong. The mutant swung around, and suddenly he was the focus of all its attention. With a powerful swipe, it knocked the flamer from his hands. Barreski recovered his wits only just in time to avoid a second talon, which would have ripped out his throat.

He had no way of fighting back, didn't have time to draw his lasgun – and he knew that he was far less agile than Palinev, and couldn't evade many more attacks like that one.

Mikhaelev and Grayle came to his assistance. They had finished with their opponent, and turned their las-fire upon his. The mutant shuddered with the impacts of the beams to its back – but, to Barreski's horror, its red eyes never flickered from him. Somewhere in its disturbed little mind, the mutant must have known it was finished, and it was determined not to be distracted from its prey, determined to take at least one of its foes down with it.

Palinev saw what was happening and flung himself at the mutant, heedless of the danger of incoming las-beams. He bought Barreski a second, but no more than that, before the mutant flung him aside with an almost casual shrug.

And then it pounced on Barreski, and although he was prepared for its weight he was still driven down onto one knee, struggling to push the rancid creature away from him. It raised its talon and he knew that this would be the killing blow.

And then the air itself exploded. The mutant stiffened and crumpled and Barreski was left gaping at its blackened corpse, wondering what had just happened.

His nostrils were filled with the stink of burnt ozone, and he glanced to the sky and wondered if somehow, through some incredible twist of fate or perhaps even through divine intervention, he had been saved by a thunderbolt from on high.

Then he saw Steele, standing unaided, looking down at the dead mutant with an expression of grim satisfaction – and Barreski saw that the colonel's right eye was black, smouldering a little.

'A small enhancement I had made on Pyrites a few years back,' explained Steele gruffly, seeing that Barreski, Mikhaelev and Grayle were all staring at him. 'A one-shot electrical weapon of last resort. It will take about twenty hours to recharge now, and my right eye will be useless until it does.'

He looked down at the mutant again, and smiled. 'Still, some things are worth a little inconvenience.'

CHAPTER NINE

Time to Destruction of Cressida: 33.16.04

BORSCZ WAS DEAD.

It wasn't easy to tell, at first. He was covered in blood, but much of it was from the mutant that he and Pozhar had slain. The Ice Warriors had to shift its carcass before they could get close to him, close enough to tell that he was no longer breathing.

Anakora wanted to bury him, but Gavotski pointed out that they lacked the tools to dig in the frozen ground. They could do it, but it would take them most of the night.

'And it's not as if a normal-sized hole would do,' Grayle muttered.

Anyway, they all agreed that it would make little difference at this point. Below ground or above it, Borscz's body would be liquefied by the imminent virus bombs, reduced to a protoplasmic slime. And after all, the last thing any Guardsman expected when he went to war was a decent burial; his remains, he knew, were far more likely to be trampled into the mud of the battlefield.

So, in the end, they gathered around their fallen comrade and Gavotski said a short prayer for his soul, and that was that – although Anakora still insisted they take Borscz onto the Aquila with them, and seal him into its hold, sparing him at least the attention of passing predators.

'If only he'd been a better shot,' said Barreski with a shake of the head. 'If he hadn't been so keen to go toe to toe with that thing...'

'Then it would have been Pozhar lying there instead of him,' Anakora

427

pointed out crisply. 'You saw how resistant the mutants were to our las-fire.'

Apart from the loss of Borscz, casualties were mercifully light. Palinev had a mild concussion from where the last mutant had backhanded him, and Gavotski had a couple of second-degree burns, which he had dressed. And Pozhar's firing arm was in a sling, which aggrieved the young trooper no end.

Steele was back on his feet, but he seemed deeply tired – and, although no one would have said it to his face, even a little shell-shocked. Gavotski covered for him by taking charge again. He sent Anakora, Barreski and Grayle onto the lander to ensure that no one was hiding inside. Grayle was also to report back on the state of the engines. Two cultists remained alive, and so Blonsky and Mikhaelev were detailed to bind them with tent ropes from their rucksacks.

Steele examined one of the mutants' corpses.

'It looked like this,' he said to Gavotski. When the sergeant looked puzzled, Steele expounded, 'The creature I saw in the forest. It had grey fur, like this one does. Some sort of adaptation to the cold, I expect. But if it was a mutant I saw, then where did it go? The cultists didn't know we were coming until I… until they heard us.'

'So, who did it report to?' Gavotski concluded the thought. 'Who knows we're here? And how many more mutants like this one are still out there?'

STEELE DIDN'T NEED to ask what had happened while he had been uncon-scious, since he had plunged into the lake. His bionic eye had recorded all the details – every visual detail, at least – and stored them for his later inspection.

The whole episode had left him feeling deeply uneasy. The organic parts – the real parts – of his brain had shut down in the water, but the mechanical parts had kept him going. He was grateful to be alive, of course – but the thought that his augmetics could function without him, even in a limited capacity, chilled him to the marrow.

The two prisoners had started to come round. Mikhaelev and Blonsky had carried them to the campfire, and were standing guard over them. Despite his weariness, Steele had chosen to conduct the interrogation. He deliberately started with the toughest-looking of the pair, the one least likely to break. He was a heavy-set man with a tattooed face and a broken wrist – this latter courtesy of Blonsky – who returned the colonel's glare with mute defiance.

'I know what you're thinking,' said Steele. 'You think you have noth-ing to gain by answering my questions because I won't let you live anyway. You're right. But you can die quickly, and as easily as possible, or I can make you suffer.'

The cultist spat in his face.

Steele nodded at Blonsky, who took the man's wrist and manipulated it, grinding the shattered bones into each other. The cultist suppressed his screams for almost a full second. By the time the Ice Warrior had finished with him, there were tears in his eyes. Still, he hadn't said a word.

Nevertheless, the technique was having an effect – not on this cultist, maybe, but on his fellow. The other man was smaller, younger than the first, and abjectly horrified by what he had just seen.

'Very well,' said Steele calmly, 'it looks like this one has made his choice. You may as well dispose of him, Blonsky. We'll talk to his friend instead.'

Blonsky knew what was required of him. He planted his boot in the larger cultist's back, and propelled him face first onto the fire. He started to scream again, and struggled to stand – but whenever he came close to so doing, Blonsky's foot was ready to kick him back into the flames.

It took the cultist a long time to die, and by the time he did the air was rank with the smell of his burning flesh. His smaller comrade was so afraid that he was shaking, and he had vomited into his lap. He looked like he might be about to do this again, as Steele turned to him with the smile of a wolf.

'I... I didn't want to join them,' the cultist bleated, 'I swear. It's just that, once it started, it spread within days, and soon...'

'Mangellan?' prompted Blonsky.

The cultist nodded, seeming glad that the Ice Warrior knew the name, that he hadn't had to reveal it himself. 'No one knew where he'd come from, he was just... suddenly, his followers were everywhere, in the streets, and no one seemed able to stop them, and my family, my friends, they were saying that Mangellan was right, that we owed the Emperor nothing, that He couldn't protect us. Then they were banging on our doors, dragging us outside, putting guns to our heads and making us swear allegiance to them, and we had no choice.'

'There is always a choice,' growled Blonsky.

'When this ship landed here,' said Steele, indicating the Aquila behind him, 'it was carrying an important member of the Adeptus Ministorum. He could have helped your people, could have guided them back to the path of righteousness.'

The cultist nodded eagerly. 'I did hear something, that they'd found someone... a religious man. Is that why you're here? Are you looking for him?'

'Do you know where he is?' asked Steele.

'He... he's dead,' said the cultist.

Steele saw the look that passed between Blonsky and Mikhaelev, but he kept his own gaze fixed on the prisoner. Normally, his bionic eye would have enabled him to count the beads of sweat on the cultist's face and hands, his acoustic enhancers would have tuned in to the skip of the man's heartbeat, and Steele would have been able to tell if he was lying or not. With his eye out of action and only the heartbeat to go on, it was harder to make that judgement. Despite the inconvenience, he felt oddly liberated.

'You saw him die?' Steele asked.

'I just thought,' said the cultist, 'I mean, he must be by now. The confessor was brought into the hive, Iota Hive, three days ago. I saw him being marched up the steps of the Ice Palace. Mangellan has him.'

'Where is it,' asked Steele, 'this Ice Palace? Can you take us there?'

The prisoner blanched at the prospect.

'Please,' he stammered, 'I've told you all I know. Don't make me... I can't go up against him, he's too... he's too strong. You can't beat him. It took Mangellan less than a month to drive the Imperial Guard out of Iota Hive, hundreds of thousands of them. Hundreds of thousands of men dead, and you... There are only a handful of you.'

Steele had made up his mind about the cultist now, but still he glanced up at Blonsky and Mikhaelev for a second and third opinion.

'Do you believe him?' he asked, and the troopers confirmed that they did. 'Good,' said Steele. 'I do, too.'

He drew his laspistol, and shot the young cultist through the head.

THE AQUILA HAD been gutted. Even its seats, once luxuriously appointed for the carriage of dignitaries, had been torn out, and the mutants had left their slobber everywhere. Still, once the passenger compartment had been cleaned up a little and blankets laid out, it made an adequate shelter for nine dog-tired soldiers.

Much more than that, the ship could not offer. Grayle had been unable to start the engines, to no one's surprise, and the comms were fried. Barreski, however, had found a portable vox-caster, not too badly damaged. The only thing it lacked was power – and a few hours of sunlight, even through Cressida's grey clouds, would provide that. He thought he could have it working by mid-morning. Steele could then contact a naval vessel, report the loss of the Termite and arrange an airlift for after they had found Wollkenden.

For the first time in half a day, Grayle could see a way off this world, and the prospect cheered him – almost enough for him to overlook the small fact that an army of Chaos worshippers stood between the Ice Warriors and their goal.

He and Barreski had taken the first shift of the night watch, being in better condition than most. Grayle sat in the Aquila's hatchway, alert for any sign of an approaching foe, hearing only the deep breathing of the sleeping men behind him. Barreski was over by the embers of the camp-fire, laying out a number of broken machine parts in the scant light. It was unlikely he'd be able to salvage anything more of use, but he wanted to be sure.

It was Grayle, then, who saw it: a movement, behind the rise on which the Ice Warriors and the cultists had fought. He had only glimpsed it out of the corner of his eye, couldn't be sure that there had been anything at all. But Barreski had picked up on his body language, and ceased his tinkering.

They watched the dark shape of the rise for a while, but saw nothing, heard nothing. At last, Grayle signalled to his fellow tanker that he was going to take a closer look.

While Barreski covered him with his lasgun, Grayle crept forward, keeping low. As he climbed the rise, he lowered himself onto his stomach and crawled the final few metres. He lay there for a few minutes, overlooking the field through which his squad had so recently marched, feeling the wet snow seeping into his greatcoat, letting his eyes adjust to every shadow in the darkness until he was sure it was no threat.

There it was again!

It had just disappeared behind another natural contour: a grey-furred figure with an odd shambling gait. Quickly, Grayle weighed up his options. If this was indeed a mutant, and it was alone, then he and Barreski could handle it. They had no need to wake the others – and anyway, by the time they had done so, it might have escaped, might have gone to fetch more like itself. But then, what if it was not alone? What if it had been sent to lead him into an ambush?

He didn't think that was likely. It was trying too hard not to be seen.

With a quick warning gesture to Barreski to stay where he was, Grayle plunged down the rise and went after the creature.

'COLONEL STEELE. COLONEL Steele, sir.'

Steele was sitting up before he had opened his eyes, some inbuilt danger sense putting him on the alert. Immediately, he checked his internal chrono, which told him that he had been asleep for just under three hours. He was still blind in his right eye. Palinev was beside him, had just shaken him awake, and around them five more Ice Warriors were beginning to stir.

Something was burning, but Steele couldn't pinpoint the source of the smell.

'I heard a shot,' reported Palinev, and Steele could tell from his comrades' body language that Gavotski, Blonsky and Anakora had been woken by it too. It irked him that he had not, that his acoustic enhancers had apparently failed him again.

'It sounded close,' said Anakora, 'maybe just outside.'

'And I don't see any sign of Barreski or Grayle,' added Palinev.

Gavotski and Pozhar had drawn their lasguns and were making for the open, empty hatchway. They peered around its frame, and Pozhar reported that there was nothing out there. A second later, he added, 'No, no, wait, I can see someone, running towards us. It looks like... It's Barreski, and here comes Grayle. It looks like they're okay.'

'Maybe they were just taking pot-shots at rats,' said Mikhaelev.

'I don't think so,' said Blonsky. 'I think Trooper Anakora was wrong. I don't think that gunshot came from outside the ship at all.'

Everyone turned to look at him, and Steele saw that he was holding the vox-caster, now a smouldering wreck, its components fused together, the source of the burning smell.

'You think...?' began Palinev, in disbelief.

'I think,' said Blonsky, 'that a single las-beam was fired at this machine – and it must have been fired from inside this compartment.'

Barreski appeared in the hatchway to find seven pairs of eyes staring at him. 'What the hell happened here?' he asked. 'Did someone fire a lasgun?'

'We were about to ask you the same question,' said Steele.

'You're the one who's supposed to be on watch,' said Pozhar. 'You and Grayle.'

'You didn't see anyone?' asked Anakora.

Grayle had appeared at Barreski's shoulder. 'There was something,' he reported. 'Another mutant, I think. I tried to follow it, but I lost it. I don't know how it got away, it must have moved like lightning.'

'So, you let this mutant lure you away from the ship?' asked Steele.

Barreski shook his head firmly. 'Grayle went after the mutant. I went as far as the top of the rise, to keep an eye on him, but I never left sight of the lander. There's no way anything could have got near this hatchway without my seeing it.'

'Are you certain about that?' asked Steele. He indicated the remains of the vox-caster, still in Blonsky's hands, and Barreski's face fell as he saw the damage for the first time. 'Because if this was not the work of an intruder...'

'Then one of us is a traitor,' said Blonsky.

'Now steady on,' said Gavotski. 'Let's not jump to conclusions, shall we?'

But Blonsky insisted, 'The evidence speaks for itself. One of us must have woken, found himself unobserved and taken the opportunity to destroy the vox-caster, our best hope of being able to complete this mission.'

'Why are you looking at me?' cried Pozhar. 'I saw you, you were looking at me as you said that. You've done nothing but criticise me, and question my loyalty, since we climbed into the Termite.'

'I think you are more concerned with your personal glory,' said Blonsky, 'than with serving the Emperor. I consider that a dangerous attitude.'

'Even if that were true,' said Gavotski, 'it doesn't make Pozhar the guilty party.'

'You're just accusing me,' said Pozhar hotly, 'because you have something to hide. Well, how about it, Blonsky? I didn't see you when that mutant attacked me. What were you doing when Borscz died?'

'He was fighting alongside me,' said Anakora. 'He played his part.'

'Yeah?' said Pozhar. 'So, maybe we should look at you then. Maybe we should ask how you managed to survive Astaroth Prime when no one else in your company did. Oh yeah, I know all about that, Anakora. I remember your name.'

'Sergeant Gavotski is right,' Steele broke in. 'None of us is above suspicion.'

'Well, Grayle and I can vouch for each other,' said Barreski.

'Can you?' asked Palinev. 'I... I don't meant to imply anything, it's just... well, you know that Grayle couldn't have snuck in here, but can he say the same for you? He must have taken his eyes off you to search for that mutant.'

'I've known Barreski since basic training,' said Grayle, 'and apart from anything else, the last thing he'd do is harm one of his precious machines. It was him who found the vox-caster in the first place, remember?'

'Then there is our comrade Mikhaelev,' said Blonsky, 'who has had nothing to say for himself so far. In fact, it is rare that he voices his thoughts – but when he does speak, he says more than he thinks he does.'

Mikhaelev turned purple, and spluttered, 'I have always followed orders.'

'But you have not always agreed with them, have you? Tell me, Mikhaelev, how greatly does it bother you that the Emperor considers your life less valuable than that of a man like Confessor Wollkenden?'

'There's one possibility none of you has considered,' said Steele. 'The traitor could be me.' His quiet words brought down a heavy silence, as he had known they would.

'You all know about the augmetics in my brain,' he continued. 'My heart may not have been corrupted by Chaos, but what if my head has been?'

Their initial shock dispelled, the Ice Warriors rushed to assure their commander that they couldn't believe it, that the Emperor would allow no such thing to happen. He raised his hand to stem their protests.

'I'm just making a point,' he said. 'We know nothing for sure – and until we do, we can gain nothing by hurling accusations.'

'Colonel Steele is right,' said Gavotski. 'I am pleased with the way this squad has bonded so far. We must not jeopardise that. We will fight again tomorrow, as comrades, and we need to be able to trust each other.'

'Nevertheless,' said Blonsky, 'I would request that the colonel search each of us for signs of mutation – and that, for the rest of the night, we have one man standing sentry outside this ship, and two inside.'

POZHAR PRETENDED TO be asleep.

Anakora and Mikhaelev were sitting nearby, Steele having agreed to Blonsky's suggestion that the guard be increased. Pozhar didn't want them to see that he was awake, couldn't let them suspect that his conscience was troubling him. The back of his right hand itched, but he didn't dare scratch it.

He didn't know why he had done it.

He had woken from a vivid and troubling dream, had perhaps been half-dreaming still. It had taken him a minute to work out where he was, to identify the shapes around him as those of his comrades, to see the vox-caster on the floor beside the hatchway, to remember...

In the dream, Steele had contacted the Imperial Navy on that caster. They had told him that the search for the confessor had become too dangerous, that they were sending another lander for his squad, that Cressida was to be left to its new masters. The details were hazy, but Pozhar thought he remembered an army of cultists and mutants, laughing. Laughing at the Ice Warriors as they turned their backs on their mission, as they turned and ran.

He had acted on instinct. He had seen that Grayle had abandoned his post. No one was watching him. It had all been exactly as Blonsky had said: one las-beam, one squeeze of his trigger. He hadn't even thought about the sound it would make. As the other Ice Warriors had woken, Pozhar had dropped back onto his blanket and pretended to be waking too, although his heart had been hammering in his chest and he had felt a cold flush down his back.

His right hand was itching like crazy now. He shifted his position, carefully, until he could reach it with his left. Steele and Gavotski had searched everyone, again as Blonsky had suggested. Pozhar had been certain he would pass their inspection, but still he had felt relieved to be given the all-clear. The verdict had reaffirmed his belief in himself, reassured him that although he couldn't explain what he had done, he had done it for the right reasons. For the Emperor.

His questing fingers found the back of his right hand, and Pozhar froze in horror as he felt something unfamiliar, something strange, something that had not been there an hour ago: a tuft of fur.

CHAPTER TEN

Time to Destruction of Cressida: 23.53.42

THE FIRST AVALANCHE was a small one.

The Ice Warriors had been expecting it. Still, all they could do was brace themselves as the snow shifted beneath their feet – and hope, of course, that this small slide would not trigger a bigger one.

They had faced a choice this morning: take the well-trodden roads to Mangellan's stronghold, the erstwhile Iota Hive, facing the likelihood of more encounters with the enemy en route, or attempt to approach through treacherous, snow-laden hills. Steele, being unlike many other commanders, had opened the question to debate. It had been the only time so far today that his troopers had spoken more than two words to each other.

The accusations of the previous night hung like a dark cloud over them. Even Palinev, although still scouting ahead, reported back more frequently than he had done yesterday, as if thinking that too long an absence might arouse the suspicions of his comrades. He might have been right. Everyone was watching each other, and Steele could hardly blame them. He was watching too.

They waited for the snow to settle, and then they moved on in silence.

As they rounded the edge of a hill, the contours of the land brought the hive back into view, just a few kilometres ahead of them. The sight made Steele's stomach turn. Every horizontal surface of the city was thick with snow, every vertical plane iced over. It looked unreal, like a life-sized model sculpted from the ice. There was no doubt at all that the Chaos infection of Cressida had Iota Hive in the firmest of grips, had corrupted it beyond all hope of reclamation.

This morning, Steele's squad had agreed that they stood a better chance against the perils of their environment than they did against more of Mangellan's followers. Even Pozhar had not argued too strongly for a full-frontal approach to the hive. In fact, he seemed unusually subdued, although whether this was due to the events of last night or to his damaged gun arm, Steele could not say.

He was starting to wonder if they had made the wrong choice.

His men had all been brought up on Valhalla; these surroundings looked almost familiar to them. They thought they knew all the perils that the snow and the ice could bring, were alert for the warning signs – and if the worst should happen, as it had on the frozen lake, then they thought they knew how to minimise the consequences. A squad from any other world would have been dead by now; for the Ice Warriors of Valhalla, this was just a morning stroll.

But as Gavotski had pointed out inside the glacier, the water on this world had been infected too. And the snow and the ice didn't always behave as it should.

THE SECOND AVALANCHE was bigger. Much bigger.

Steele couldn't blame anyone in his squad for setting it off. It started high above them, and came crashing down at them like a tidal wave. It might have been a natural consequence of recent snowfall upon hard-packed ice – but the timing of it, at least, was suspicious.

The Ice Warriors, minus Palinev, were spread out across a hillside, keeping a short distance between each of them in case of just such an occurrence – but the avalanche was in the perfect spot, and exactly wide enough, to threaten all eight of them.

Barreski and Grayle were at the greatest risk. They were closest to the centre of the flow, the point at which the snow would be moving its fastest. They knew they couldn't outrun it – an avalanche of this size could reach a speed of two hundred kilometres per hour – but they used the few seconds they had before it hit to make a sprint for its edge, as did their comrades.

Gavotski and Steele, who had been respectively leading the procession and following at its rear, had the least far to go. Steele ran for all he was worth, but still it wasn't enough. It could never have been enough. He turned his back to the avalanche as it reached him, and prepared for the impact.

It felt as if a rug had been pulled out from under him. He maintained his balance for as long as he could, but he was soon swept away. He pedalled with his arms and legs, as if swimming, knowing that to resist the tide would be futile, attempting to ride it instead. The landscape flashed by to each side of him, and Steele could only hope that he wouldn't be dashed against something solid.

He was aware of Blonsky being carried alongside him – and of Anakora, who had managed to grab a sturdy tree before the snow hit and was clinging to it for dear life, being left behind. He did the best he could to keep track of them both, as he knew they would be doing for the comrades to each side of them.

Steele went under several times, and his mind flashed back to the frozen lake. He was determined not to be buried, not to lose consciousness again – and so, each time he was engulfed, he kicked and he thrashed, and he put all the strength he had into his swimming stroke, and he resurfaced.

After what seemed like an age, it was over. Steele was half-buried, breathless, but still able to dig himself free and climb to his feet. He had only been carried a short distance, but his surroundings looked very different to him now. The shifting snow had formed new contours, and covered old landmarks. Closing his one good eye, the colonel reoriented himself by his internal compass.

He found Anakora first, three hundred metres up the slope behind him, still holding onto her tree, although she had been buried up to the chest. She was stronger than she looked, he thought. She was also safe.

He couldn't say the same for Blonsky. There was no sign of him. He had to have gone under. Steele hurried to the spot at which he had last seen him, and soon found a single gloved hand protruding from the snow, its fingers waggling in a feeble attempt to summon help. Fortunately, the snow hadn't set too hard yet, and Steele was able to scoop handfuls of it away, to reveal Blonsky's head. A minute later, he had freed an arm too, and he knew his trooper could do the rest for himself.

'G-Grayle,' gasped Blonsky, raising a hand to point – and, joined by Anakora, who had managed to free herself, Steele repeated the whole process again, until a fourth Ice Warrior was dragged spluttering to the surface. Fortunately, Grayle had been able to make an air hole for himself as the snow had settled around him, otherwise he would have suffocated.

WHEN THE AVALANCHE had started, Pozhar had been a few metres behind Sergeant Gavotski. However, he was young and he was fast, and he had easily overtaken the older man. Relatively safe on the edge of the flow, he had surfed the snow with consummate skill and exulted in the head rush it gave him. In so doing – he had realised too late – he had quite lost track of his sergeant.

He had clambered over the freshly turned snow, yelling for Gavotski, his stomach churning with the thought that he had failed this man of all men, his mentor, his sponsor. His hand had started to itch again, beneath his glove, and Pozhar would have sworn that at that moment he could feel the grey fur spreading across it.

He had located Gavotski at last, worried that he might have left him buried too long. He had tried to dig down to him, but his bad arm had slowed him too much. Fortunately, Palinev had seen the avalanche from ahead, and returned to assist him.

Gavotski had not questioned the delay in his rescue, doubtless assuming that Pozhar had had his own problems. He had led the way to the next Ice Warrior instead, and now he and Palinev were digging for Mikhaelev. Pozhar hung back for fear of getting in their way. He felt useless. Useless and ashamed. And for the first time, he wondered if he might deserve what was happening to him after all, if the fur on his hand was a warning that he could do better, that he wasn't serving the Emperor to the fullest of his ability. That he could have saved Borscz.

He vowed that, from this moment on, he would try even harder, become even more fierce in the execution of his duty. He would cleanse Iota Hive of the Chaos filth single-handedly if he had to, or die in the attempt.

Then Pozhar heard a sound behind him – the soft crunch of a footstep in the snow – and he whirled around, and caught a glimpse of a grey-furred mutant as it ducked out of sight. He grinned and offered up a grateful prayer to the Emperor for giving him this chance to prove himself so soon.

His comrades were still occupied, hadn't seen anything – and something stopped Pozhar from calling to them. This was his test, not theirs. He crept away from them, and only built up speed once he knew they could no longer see him, as he rounded the side of the hill down which the avalanche had come.

This was probably the same mutant that had stalked the Ice Warriors outside the Aquila, and before that in the ice forest. Barreski and Grayle had already failed to kill it, as had Steele himself. Pozhar would not fail.

His enemy had made a mistake. Post-avalanche, the snow was deep and smooth and undisturbed, like a virgin fall. The mutant was trying to hide from him, but it had left a clear trail. It would not escape this time.

ALL BUT ONE of the Ice Warriors had been found.

They converged on the spot where Mikhaelev and Grayle had last seen Barreski. He could have ended up anywhere within a hundred metre radius, but a quick search turned up no sign of him. That was bad, thought Steele. It meant that the trooper had been completely buried, and would be running out of air.

'Start digging,' he instructed. 'Centre on this spot here. Take a five-metre square each to begin with.' His augmetics had already analysed the speed of the avalanche's flow as he had experienced it, extrapolated its likely speed this much closer to its centre, and correlated Barreski's reported trajectory and last known distance from his starting point – to conclude that they couldn't narrow the search area much more than his comrades' instincts already had.

Then Steele picked up a sound from beneath his feet, a sound that he identified a moment later as the muffled cough of a misfiring flamer.

He grabbed Anakora by her greatcoat collar and yanked her backwards as a boiling geyser erupted from the ground where she had been standing. The Ice Warriors were showered with cooling water. When the deluge had ended, they crowded forward to find a large, round hole in the snow – and, at its bottom, the top half of a red-faced, spluttering Barreski.

'S-sorry, sir,' he addressed Steele breathlessly. 'Couldn't breathe down there, couldn't wait any longer. I knew it was risky, but…'

He was cradling his flamer across his chest.

That was when they all heard las-fire, coming from behind the hill – and Steele realised, in that selfsame moment, that one of his troopers was missing.

POZHAR RAN AT the mutant, firing. It had been fleeing from him – but as fast as it was, he was faster. As his first las-beam hit, the mutant gave a roar of pain and spun around to face him, throwing up its arms. It looked as if it was trying to surrender – although Pozhar doubted this, and it would have made no difference to him anyway.

'Not… what you… think…'

It took Pozhar by surprise, to be addressed by something he had thought of as an animal, dumb in both senses of the word. The mutant's voice was hoarse and rough, like gravel across a rock surface, and the words came out slowly as if speaking was an effort for it.

'I can see what you are,' spat Pozhar, and he fired again.

His next two beams missed their target. He still wasn't used to shooting left-handed, and that gave the mutant its chance. Having seen that it couldn't fool him, it reverted to type – at least, that was how Pozhar chose to see it.

It came in low, its talons outstretched, and Pozhar slid to a halt and braced himself to meet it. As it thundered towards him, growing larger in his sights, he was able to zero in on it, and two beams sizzled through the mutant's chest fur and created livid red sores. Then it cannoned into him, clawing at his throat – but Pozhar wasn't about to be knocked down by another of these things, and although he was forced onto his back foot, he remained upright and jabbed at the creature's stomach with his bayonet.

'Listen,' it rasped, switching its grip to Pozhar's lasgun, twisting it so that it pointed away from them both, 'Trying to… help. I know where Confessor… Confessor Wollkenden! Can take you.'

The mutant's breath was hot and fetid in his face, and he recoiled from it, lost hold of his gun, panicked as he began to fear that he wasn't strong enough to pass this test after all.

'You expect me to trust you?' he yelled. 'You're a filthy stinking mutant, and I won't listen to you, I won't be corrupted, I won't!'

Somehow, he found the strength to hurl his foe away from him, and he leapt for his gun, lying in the snow. The mutant leapt for it too, but Pozhar got there first. He grabbed the gun, rolled onto his back, and he fired, striking the mutant again in the chest, and then in the stomach, widening its bayonet wound.

It was losing too much blood, It couldn't survive. But it was still fighting. It came at Pozhar with a roar of rage, its eyes a blazing red, and he knew that he couldn't fend it off again. He knew it would kill him, but that was all right because he had killed it first and would die a pure man. The mutant was on top of him, pinning his good arm, and it brought up its talons to strike, to tear out his throat.

Then it hesitated, and the fire in its eyes died out, and when it next spoke its words were more lucid than they had been.

'A few months ago,' said the mutant sadly, 'I would have tried to kill me too.'

'Don't you dare say that!' hissed Pozhar. 'Don't you dare try to say that I'm anything like you. And don't stay your hand, I don't want your… your pity. Kill me!'

But instead, the mutant died, and Pozhar let out a howl of frustration. He punched and kicked at it until it rolled off him, and then stood and drove his lasgun butt into the creature's corpse again and again, shattering its bones.

He only stopped when he was exhausted. He looked down at the mutant's staring red eyes seeming to accuse him even now, and he felt the itch on his right hand spreading, crawling up his arm. His right glove had come adrift from his greatcoat sleeve, and he was sickened by the sight of grey fur bristling in the gap. He pulled up the glove quickly, and buried the hand in its sling to conceal it more fully. He could almost have cried. Hadn't he done what the Emperor had asked of him? It wasn't his fault that the mutant had stopped fighting, hadn't challenged him fully. Pozhar had expected redemption, but instead he felt empty.

And that was how Steele and the others found him, a short time later: standing over the fallen mutant, staring down at it, unable to tear his gaze away from it, unable to answer the one burning question, the unthinkable question, in his thoughts.

Is that my future?

IOTA HIVE WAS a little smaller than Alpha, and yet still it dwarfed the Ice Warriors as they emerged from the hills into its shadow. Its size fooled Mikhaelev, making him think that the hive was closer than it was. And the closer they got to it, the larger – and the further away – it seemed to grow. Even so, he could already smell the rank purple fungus that encrusted its iced-over surfaces.

It looked as if the hive had been abandoned a long time ago to the uncaring elements. If only, Mikhaelev thought, that could have been the case.

There was a breach in the hive's blackstone outer wall, but Steele steered his squad well clear of this after Palinev sighted through his field goggles and reported that he saw figures moving amid the wreckage.

The hive stopped growing at last, and the great wall filled Mikhaelev's field of vision. The Ice Warriors tucked themselves in against it, careful not to touch the reeking ice, and Steele led the way along the sheer black face. It soon became evident to Mikhaelev that they were making for the breach after all.

Not long after that, the colonel motioned to his squad to be silent and still. They were nearing their goal, he said, although Mikhaelev had no way of seeing this for himself. Presumably, Steele's augmetics had helped him calculate the distance to the breach.

'We don't know how many guards there might be in there,' said the colonel, 'but as always it only takes one to raise the alarm.'

'Fortunately,' said Gavotski, 'we still have surprise on our side. If anyone had seen us coming, I'm sure we would know about it by now.'

'We're a long way behind enemy lines,' said Blonsky. 'Those guards have every reason to be complacent, to have let their attention wonder. We all know that the followers of Chaos lack self-discipline.' A couple of the others murmured their agreement, and Mikhaelev joined in belatedly. After what Blonsky had said about him last night, after the number of suspicious glares he had drawn today, he thought it wise to display his enthusiasm for their cause.

'What we need,' said Gavotski, 'is for a couple of troopers to scout ahead, to take out the sentries without being seen if they can. Palinev should be one.'

'I can do that!' Pozhar chirped up. Seeing Gavotski's doubtful look, he said, 'It makes sense, sergeant. After Palinev, I'm the lightest on his feet

– and I know what you're thinking, you're thinking this sling will slow me down, but I'm getting used to it. I know I'm having trouble shooting with my left hand, but I can handle a knife with it, just let me show you.'

The look on his face was imploring, almost desperate – and Gavotski gave Pozhar a long, appraising stare, and then glanced at Steele, before he made his decision and announced it with a curt nod of his head.

Mikhaelev thought that he had made a mistake. Pozhar was too impatient for a job like this one. He had volunteered for no other reason than that he wanted some action, and nothing would get in the way of that for him. But then this wasn't the first time Gavotski had shown a soft spot for the young trooper – and the last thing Mikhaelev could afford to do right now was question that.

In the event, his pessimism was proved ill-founded. Only a few minutes after Palinev and Pozhar had slipped away, the latter returned beaming from ear to ear, to report that there had been four cultists on sentry duty and that they had all been despatched. Steele motioned the squad forwards again, and soon the black wall beside them fell away, and they were climbing over rubble.

There were, indeed, four robed corpses at the entrance. It looked as if the cultists had been playing cards when Palinev and Pozhar had got the drop on them and slashed two of their throats. A third cultist had struggled, and had had his neck broken. The fourth had evidently tried to run, and had been brought down by a knife to the back.

'We should try to hide the bodies,' said Anakora. 'Then, if anyone comes by, they might assume that these guards have just deserted their post.'

They were inside the hive at last – Mangellan's hive, as it was now.

From now on, thought Mikhaelev gloomily, things could only get a great deal more dangerous.

CHAPTER ELEVEN

Time to Destruction of Cressida: 20.32.13

FROM THE OUTSIDE, Iota Hive had seemed relatively intact.

Inside, it was a different story. Hardly a structure had been left untouched by the war that had raged within. Bridges had been blown out, gantries collapsed, water tanks exploded. A burnt-out Chimera lay on its roof, the corpses of a driver and two gunners rotting inside. There were many more bodies, and parts thereof, strewn about the streets or half buried in the wreckage of demolished walls. Barricades had been built up from whatever materials were available, to be broken down again.

No natural light could penetrate this deeply into the hive – and the electric lights were intermittent, unreliable, allowing black pools to congregate between them. Grayle drove through it all, along narrow streets that had once teemed with people. Those streets were empty now, most of the people dead – and of those who had survived, most would have joined their attackers and left with them, marching on to wage their next bloody battle.

Even so, the sounds of other vehicles and of pounding machinery still thrummed through the hive, and occasionally a voice could be heard raised in maniacal laughter or a tortured scream.

All in all, it was a sobering scene – especially for these nine soldiers who had, only yesterday, been fighting to defend a hive much like this one. The difference was, thought Grayle, that Alpha Hive had been attacked from without, its walls beaten down. The reason that Iota's walls were still, for the most part, standing was that it had suffered a far worse fate. Iota had been attacked from within.

When he had started the truck's engine, it had roared like an asthmatic lion. The unnatural sound had reverberated from the roof and the walls until it had seemed loud enough to bring them all crashing down. Gavotski had handed him a tattered robe, torn from a dead cultist, and offered the same to Barreski who was seated beside Grayle now in the cab. Neither of them had been happy about touching the foul cloth, wrapping it about their shoulders, but it had had to be done.

'The cultist I questioned talked about an Ice Palace,' Steele had said, 'the stronghold of the Chaos leader in these parts. He didn't exactly provide a map, but there's no doubt that it will be the most defensible and defended building in the city. That means it will be as near as damn it to the centre, and most likely on one of the higher levels. We'll have to make our way inwards and upwards, get as close as we can to our goal before the enemy knows we're here.'

So far, Grayle had seen precious little of the enemy – just a few shapes flitting across high walkways, and at one point a cloaked figure slumped in the gutter, singing to herself. That changed as he guided his truck around a tight corner and was confronted by at least twenty of them.

It looked like they had been celebrating here, among the ruins. There were bottles everywhere. The revelry had died down now, though, and most of the cultists were lying around listlessly. That was, until they clapped eyes on the new arrivals. A half-hearted cheer went up at the sight of what the drunken cultists took to be friends, partners in their recent victory – and they rushed to surround the truck, banging on its sides and rocking it on its suspension.

Grayle fought down his natural disgust, forced a tight smile onto his lips and gave a thumbs-up sign through the window. Beside him, Barreski tried to do likewise, but his smile didn't quite reach his eyes. The cultists were probably too far gone to notice anyway, thought Grayle. The real problems would arise if they were to open the truck's back door and find a squad of Valhallan Ice Warriors seated inside.

He had to get away from here – but the cultists were in front of him too, slowing him to a crawl lest he crush three or four of them beneath his wheels. The temptation to do just that was almost irresistible. However, he kept his cool, and was soon through the crowd, able to pull away from them.

A moment later, Barreski sat bolt upright and cried, 'Stop! Stop here!' And Grayle stepped hard on the brakes, although he couldn't see the reason for the urgency.

Barreski hopped out of the cab, and scurried over to the corpse of an

Imperial Guard officer. Grayle almost laughed with relief. There was no danger, his fellow tanker had just noticed a salvageable piece of kit and hadn't been able to resist it. He peeled a metal gauntlet from the dead Guardsman's hand, and his face was alight with enthusiasm as he climbed back into his seat with it.

'Nice glove,' said Grayle. 'What's it supposed to be?'

'A power fist, of course,' said Barreski, sounding surprised that his comrade didn't know. 'You put this on your arm, and it generates an energy field, lets you punch with the strength of ten men. It doesn't seem too badly damaged, either. The casing is a little scorched, that's all. Never used one before, but I've seen them in action. I'm pretty sure I can work out how to activate it.'

'Activate it?' said Grayle. 'You can barely even lift it!'

'Once this thing is working,' said Barreski, 'it'll lift itself.'

At that moment, knuckles rapped on the partition behind them, a reminder from their colonel that they had a deadline. Grayle started up the truck again, and guided it into an area of relatively untouched streets, where the going was a little easier and cover more plentiful. The habitats of the lower-level hive-dwellers rose up around them, rows of tiny windows stretching to the roof.

They made good progress for a couple of hours – but eventually, inevitably, they ran into more cultists. The further they went, the more they saw, no matter how many detours Grayle took to avoid them. Their comings and goings appeared to be centred around a large, black building. It was obviously a manufactorum, and its great steaming chimneys signified that it was in use.

He performed a U-turn, heading back into the dark residential sector. He pulled up in the shadows just out of range of a sputtering light, and when Barreski asked him why, he explained, 'There are just a few too many heretics out there for my liking. Someone's bound to notice us soon, and start asking questions.'

He had been intending to consult Colonel Steele, to ask his permission to abandon the truck. He was surprised to find his comrades already disembarking onto the street.

'I think you're right, Grayle,' Steele said – and Grayle realised that, thanks to his augmented senses, he had been well aware of everything that was happening outside the vehicle, had probably heard its driver's every word. 'It's far too much of a risk to go through that crowd. It's time we headed upwards.'

IT WAS PALINEV who found the lifter.

On Gavotski's orders, the Ice Warriors had spread out in search of a way up to the hive's higher levels. Creeping down an unlit street, Palinev had found himself uncomfortably close to the manufactorum that Grayle had described. He had seen cultists thronging in the lit area before it, but so long as he kept close to the wall they couldn't see him – and there had been a ladder in front of him.

He had climbed it carefully, disappointed to find that it led only to a high bridge. He had decided to scout along it anyway – but before he could do so, his attention had been drawn to the scene laid out beneath him.

The manufactorum had no roof. This appeared to be by design rather than the result of battle damage, as all six of its walls were whole. Palinev was looking down into an enormous, round vat filled with what he could only describe as liquid fire. Suspended above this were a number of thick chains, attached to pulley systems, many of them trailing into the vat itself –and surrounding the vat were hundreds of cultists, cheering and chanting while some of their number operated the levers of squat grey machines in precise, arcane sequences.

Palinev could feel the heat of the fire, but that wasn't the only thing that made his throat dry.

This, then, was the Chaos war machine at work, extracting iron from Cressida's fertile ore as the Imperium had done before it, using foul practices to fashion that iron into weapons, armour, vehicles of destruction. Cressida had fallen, but its occupiers were already equipping themselves for the next conquest.

The lifter doors were tucked around the corner of a narrow walkway, out of sight of the evil below. The summoning rune was lit, so Palinev pressed it and took cover as, with a grinding and a screeching of gears, the cab rose from what sounded like it must have been the lowest level of the underhive. The lifter was functional, and empty, so Palinev returned to the others to report his discovery, being sure to keep low as he crossed the bridge again.

A few minutes later, the nine Ice Warriors packed themselves into the cramped cab, and Steele activated one of the highest runes on its wall.

The journey upward took an age. The wall runes lit in sequence as they passed each of the hive's hundred-plus levels. Palinev was uncomfortably aware, as he was sure the others were, that were anyone to hear their noisy approach, were they to stop the lifter for any reason, then its occupants would be sitting ducks.

His heart sank as they bumped to a halt and, although the doors failed to open, the cab was filled with a soft but insistent chime.

Gavotski sighed. 'I was afraid of this. We can't go any higher without an access code. It's to keep the underhive dwellers from the higher levels.'

'Let me,' said Barreski. He produced a knife, and inserted its blade into a vertical seam beside the runes. With some expert manipulation, he was able to flip open a section of the wall to reveal a jumble of wires. Palinev gasped as his comrade cavalierly plunged his hands into them.

Barreski pulled on several wires, tearing them from their mountings, seeming not to care as the machine–spirits spat their disapproval. He grinned as the chiming sound cut out and the lifter began to rise again.

'A little trick I picked up as a boy,' he said.

THEY REACHED THEIR destination at last, and the doors rumbled open, allowing nine grateful soldiers to spill out onto a wide, empty street.

The contrast with the ground floor was extreme. Although the Ice Warriors were still surrounded by buildings, there were open walkways and squares inbetween, into which some natural light fell from translucent panels in the hive's roof some ten levels above them. Below, the architecture had been strictly utilitarian, but up here there were statues and fluted columns and fountains and gargoyles.

Many of the buildings sported eagle crests over their doorways – administrative offices – but Barreski could also see an apartment block with wide windows opening onto balconies.

Not that Chaos hadn't left its mark here too. Many of the walls had been defaced with hateful sigils, most of the buildings looted and some burned out. And the air was cold, far colder than it had been below – almost as cold as it had been outside.

Steele had found something: a rectangular, white-framed data panel, mounted on a free-standing, pivoting base. He motioned Barreski to join him at it, and had him confirm that it was a public terminal. The interface was designed to be accessible, the inlaid runes simple to interpret, and Barreski was soon able to punch up a plan of the hive, and to show Steele how to select more detailed views of each of its levels and sectors. Then he watched in fascination as the colonel scrolled through map after map, hardly pausing at some long enough to read their labels, but – Barreski felt sure – somehow committing the details of each one to his augmented memory.

'Spaceport,' Steele muttered, as he lingered briefly over one map. 'That's good to know. Could be a way out of here for us, if we're lucky.'

'No mention of an Ice Palace though, sir?' asked Barreski.

'I wouldn't have expected one. I should think the Ice Palace is a recent addition, something Mangellan has had built for himself.'

It was Gavotski who suggested sending someone further upwards, to the roof of one of the taller buildings. 'We must be close to the centre of the hive,' he said. 'If the palace is on this level, it should be visible from up there. If not, then we'll know we're wasting our time here.'

Palinev volunteered to be the scout, of course. Everyone was surprised when Steele sent Grayle instead.

'Get up there,' he instructed, 'take a quick sighting and come straight down again. You still have your cloak, so if any heretic does spot you he should think you're an ally. Still, I'd rather not take that chance.'

Grayle disappeared into the apartment building, emerged a few minutes later onto one of its topmost balconies, and began to find handholds in the brickwork, hauling himself all the way up to the roof. It was only then that Barreski realised why it was that his fellow tanker had been assigned to the task. Grayle was the only one of them who had a solid alibi for when the vox-caster was destroyed, an alibi that Barreski had provided. He was the only one Steele trusted to stray so far from the squad on his own.

A few minutes later, Grayle was back, flushed and breathless.

'It's on this level, all right,' he reported, 'the Ice Palace. It's on *all* the levels, all the ones up here. Its foundations are a couple of floors down, but it reaches all the way up to the roof. It looks like… like it's almost organic, like it wasn't built or carved or whatever, like it must have… grown.'

'Like the so-called trees in the forest,' said Mikhaelev.

'Like them, yes,' said Grayle. 'It's huge, at least a kilometre square, and the area around it is in ruins, as if the palace just… as if it burst through from below, destroying everything in its path as it sprouted upwards. I could see bridges, great bridges of ice, leading across to it from the streets.'

'How far?' asked Steele.

'It was hard to tell,' said Grayle, 'with the sheer scale of the thing. Another three or four hours, I'd say, on foot. But there are patrols in the streets: Traitor Guard, lots of them, between the Ice Palace and here. I don't think it's safe to take a vehicle.'

'Mangellan is well protected,' said Steele. 'I'd expect no less. The sound of an engine won't go unnoticed up here, and I can't see a couple of cultists' robes fooling anyone either.' This was good news for Barreski, whose borrowed cloak had been making his skin crawl where it touched his bare neck. He ripped it from his shoulders, bundled it into a ball and flung it into a nearby gutter.

'We have to face the fact,' said Gavotski, 'that we have come almost as far as we can on stealth alone. I think we all knew from the start that our chances of surviving this mission were slim. Once we learned that Confessor Wollkenden had been brought here, to this hive… well, that's when this turned into a suicide run. Most of us will die here today, but remember: if just one of us can beat the odds, if one us can escape with the confessor, then we will have won the kind of victory that men sing about. We will have secured the memory of the Valhallan 319th for a thousand years, and I think that's a cause well worth fighting for.'

THE FIRST PATROL, they heard coming.

They took cover on the portico of a great librarium, crouching behind its pillars as the well-drilled ranks of a traitor platoon marched through the bordering public square. While the other Ice Warriors were watching the traitors, Blonsky watched his comrades. Would this be the moment, he wondered, when one of them would make his move, give them away? Or just lose his nerve and run?

And then the traitors had passed them by, and the Ice Warriors let out a collective sigh of relief – all except for Pozhar, who was itching for a fight as always – and they moved on.

It seemed to Blonsky that the further they went – the deeper into the hive – the colder it became, in defiance of all logic. It had already been a long, tiring day, but Steele set his usual brusque pace – and Gavotski, in particular, was starting to flag, although he tried not to show it.

And then it came, at last. The moment they had all been dreading.

Steele must have heard something, seen something, sensed something, because he threw himself at Palinev an instant before they all heard the crack of a lasgun, and knocked him out of the path of its beam. The sniper had to have been on a nearby roof, but Blonsky didn't have time to locate him. Steele was running, yelling at the others to follow him. Two more las-beams stabbed into the street like lightning bolts, but then they were around a corner, out of the firing line.

'We can't just let them get away with that,' protested Pozhar, 'with firing at the Emperor's troops. We have to–'

Gavotski interrupted him firmly, saying, 'We can't kill every heretic in this place, much as we'd like to. We have to concentrate on reaching the Ice Palace – which means getting out of this area before that sniper calls in reinforcements.'

They ran across another public square, through an ornate archway, and down another wide street. Steele was leading the way, but he suddenly came to a halt, listened for a moment, reversed direction. They rounded the corner of a generatorium relay station – and this time, even Blonsky could hear the footsteps tramping towards them, forcing them to revise their course again.

They made for a wide flight of steps leading up to the next hive level. But four Traitor Guardsmen appeared before them, dropped to their knees and fired. The Ice Warriors plunged into a network of side streets, making so many twists and turns that Blonsky had soon lost all sense of direction. Then Steele stopped again, listened for a second, and growled, 'This way!' He ushered his squad through the gaping doorway of a residential block as Blonsky too heard the whine of a vectored thrust engine and saw a thin grey shadow flitting across the ground behind him.

He suppressed a shiver. Someone... something out there was using a jump pack to search for them. And they all knew that no mere Imperial Guardsman, traitor or otherwise, had the strength to bear such a device.

They raced along a carpeted corridor. To each side of them, the doors of once-luxurious rooms had been smashed open. The furniture in those rooms had been trashed, and more than a few dead bodies had been left behind. Imperial citizens, thought Blonsky, who had tried to hide in their homes once the fighting had started, who had died in them. Cowards, all of them. They had got what they deserved.

They emerged into the street again, but the sounds of footsteps were all around them.

'They're everywhere!' breathed Anakora.

'Not quite,' said Steele. 'We're dealing with a single traitor platoon – perhaps forty men, fifty at most – but they know this ground and they know where we're heading. They're cutting off all our routes to the Ice Palace – and at the same time, they're closing in behind us, making sure we can't turn back.'

'Then we have to go through them!' Pozhar declared.

Steele looked at him, then sighed and nodded.

'The palace is in that direction,' he said, pointing. 'Just remember, all of you, that to reach that palace, to find Confessor Wollkenden, is our only objective. If that means leaving heretics alive behind us, then so be it. Let the virus bombs take care of them.'

'Yes sir,' chorused the Ice Warriors.

'We hit the traitors hard and we hit them fast,' said Gavotski. 'We break through their circle, and we keep on running. We don't stop for anything.'

'Comrades,' said Steele, 'prepare for the fight of your lives.'

Blonsky was just close enough to Pozhar to hear the young trooper's murmured exclamation of, 'About damn time!'

CHAPTER TWELVE

Time to Destruction of Cressida: 17.12.41

THEY TOOK THEIR foes by surprise.

The traitors had probably expected the Ice Warriors to go to ground, to find a defensible position – a secure building, maybe – from which they could sell their lives dearly. The last thing they had considered was that they might come out fighting.

Several of them died in that first barrage of las-fire, some marching right into the beams before they could stop. A few turned and fled – which made sense, thought Anakora, as these one-time Guardsmen wouldn't have defected in the first place had they possessed any real moral fibre.

The rest of them rallied and returned fire even as they looked for cover. A frag grenade hurled into their midst by Steele shredded two more bodies and left the rest reeling, more disoriented than ever. And then, before the debris from the blast could settle, the Ice Warriors surged forwards, knowing that to do so was to leave themselves wide open, but also knowing that to stay still was to invite certain death at the hands of the rest of the traitors, who were still closing in around them.

They kept their heads down, relying on speed and surprise – and the las-beams they were pumping out to each side of them – to carry them through. Anakora trampled over traitor corpses, and was alarmed to find one of them still alive, a gloved hand lashing out to seize her by the ankle. She stumbled, putting out her hands to arrest her fall. She kicked at the traitor's fingers with her free foot, and luckily he was injured, his strength drained, because he let out a groan and let go of her.

She saw that Palinev had stopped, half-turning, to come to her aid. She shook her head firmly, didn't need his help, didn't want him to risk his life for her. This was what she had feared, after Pozhar had revealed her secret to the others: not that they would suspect her motives, but that they would think her weak.

Palinev seemed to get the message, though, and he ran on, pausing for a second to snatch a lasgun from a fallen traitor. Anakora realised that he wanted its power pack, and this seemed like a good idea – so she saw to it that, by the time she caught up with her comrades, she was carrying two extra guns. She detached the pack from one of them and tossed it to Pozhar, who seemed like the trooper most likely to need it soon.

And then the second wave of traitors was upon them, moving in from either side, threatening to trap them in a pincer movement.

Pozhar was the first to react, running left, ploughing into the oncoming ranks, swinging his lasgun wildly, one-handed – but most of the others were right behind him. Anakora found herself plunged into the chaos of the melee, looking for her nearest comrade – Mikhaelev – and she stood back to back with him, as they fought with knives, bayonets and even fists against odds that were swelling by the moment, becoming almost overwhelming.

Only Palinev held back. Palinev, who had slipped into a deep doorway before he could be seen by the newcomers. Palinev, who now raised his long-las.

He took his time, choosing his targets well. His eight comrades were under attack by over twenty traitors, but they had formed into a tight knot so that only one or two men could attack any of them at once. Their more numerous enemies were also providing them with cover, and more than one traitor fired into the skirmish, aiming for an Ice Warrior but striking an ally instead. Palinev didn't share that problem.

A traitor landed a punch to Gavotski's chin, sending him reeling, so Palinev blew a hole in his head before he could press his advantage. He picked off another figure on the periphery of the battle before anyone knew he was there, and another two while they were trying to find him in the confusion. And then, when the traitors did start to fire back at him, las-beams blasting chunks from the stonework by his head, at least he knew that four or five of them were no longer focussed upon his comrades.

He shouldered open the door beside him, and leapt into another apartment complex, even as a frag grenade rolled into the space he had just vacated. The explosion tore the door from its hinges, followed him down the corridor, and almost lifted him off his feet.

He paused at a window, fired six more shots from a fresh angle, claimed another kill. Then Palinev was running again before he could be pinned down.

From the next window, he saw that the melee was thinning out, the odds becoming more even. Some of the traitors were starting to disengage, to realise that they would be better off gaining some distance and using their guns.

Barreski charged two of them. They set their bayonets to greet him – but the gauntlet he was wearing on his right arm crackled with energy, and with one well-timed swipe he knocked the weapons right out of their hands.

He drove his gauntlet into a traitor's stomach, doubling him up with pain, causing him to cough up blood as he crumpled. The other traitor grappled with him, tried to wrest the gauntlet from him, but Barreski gripped him by the front of his flak jacket and tossed him almost casually over his shoulder. The traitor described a graceless arc, his arms and legs flailing, and slammed into the side of a building.

Pozhar was dragged clear of the others, thrown against a balcony rail, a ten-storey drop behind him. With his injured arm, he couldn't draw his lasgun in time. Two traitors shoulder-charged him, trying to force him over. Palinev fired at them, and managed to strike one between the shoulder blades, taking him down.

His heart leapt into his mouth as Pozhar toppled backwards, flipping over the railing, but somehow managing to take his remaining attacker with him. Palinev leapt out of his window, and raced across the street, fearing that he was already too late, only too well aware that he had no cover out here, but knowing that the rest of his squad were tied up with their own problems. He was Pozhar's only hope.

His sudden appearance took the traitors by surprise – and like Palinev's comrades, most of them had their hands full. He reached the railing, and found Pozhar clinging one-handed to the edge of the road beneath it, the traitor hanging from his waist, still trying to drag him down.

It would be a tough shot. Palinev took the time to steady his aim, tried to forget the imminent danger to himself. His las-beam struck the Traitor Guardsman in the face, and he lost his hold on Pozhar and fell with a bloodcurdling scream.

And Palinev turned to find a knife-wielding traitor barrelling towards him, just in time to sidestep and to fling the man over his shoulder, to join his comrade below.

* * *

FOR THE LONGEST time, Gavotski hadn't known where he was, hadn't seen any comrades beyond Colonel Steele to his immediate left and Blonsky to his right, hadn't known how many Traitor Guardsmen were still standing, hadn't been able to see a way out of this for himself or for any of them.

All he could do was keep fighting, keep swinging his lasgun, keep slashing with his knife, keep dodging the blows that were aimed at him in return. Gavotski prided himself that he was still a strong man, almost as strong as he had been in his youth, and the reactions of his opponents as he struck at them confirmed this in the most satisfying way. With every traitor that fell, landing in a growing pile at the sergeant's feet, it became harder for the next one to reach him.

And then, to his surprise, there was nobody left. He regained his bearings, and saw that they had done it, they had broken through the cordon – that, although there would certainly be yet more foes searching for the Ice Warriors, perhaps already coming up behind them, the way ahead was clear for the moment, and Gavotski yelled out for the others to follow him as he took it.

Once again, they sprinted through the streets, and Gavotski prickled with fresh hope, knowing that each step was taking them closer to their goal.

It couldn't last. He knew that. But it ended sooner than he had hoped.

As before, it was Steele who heard the incoming platoon first, who tried to find a way around it. This time, however, his options were more limited by the Traitor Guardsmen, the remnants of the first platoon, still pursuing them.

They found themselves outside a censorium, and Gavotski was disheartened when Steele turned and led his squad inside the building. They clambered over upturned filing cabinets, and kicked up the ashes that were all that remained of hundreds of thousands of Imperial documents. A few of the Ice Warriors took up sniping positions in the frames of the shattered ground floor windows, but Gavotski followed Palinev and Blonsky up a flight of stairs in search of a better vantage point above.

He looked out onto the street again, and saw that two squads of traitors had just turned into it, one from each end. Steele's senses had saved the Ice Warriors again, warning them that they were surrounded.

It took the traitors a moment to work out where their prey had disappeared to. By the time they had, almost half of them were dead. Gavotski leaned out of his window, pumping out las-beam after las-beam on full auto as the remaining traitors scattered, feeling a momentary catharsis with each one that fell. It was not enough, though, to quell the searing frustration inside him.

The last thing the Ice Warriors had wanted was a siege situation. The last thing they could afford was to be trapped.

A traitor ventured into view with a frag grenade in his hand. Gavotski fired at him before he could hurl it, and his beam was joined by two more from the windows below him. A second later, another traitor tried the same stunt, but Palinev and Blonsky made just as short work of him.

This was getting them nowhere. The traitors had time on their side. Word of the Ice Warriors' presence would have spread, and for every traitor they felled there could be no doubt that ten more were on their way to replace him. They needed a way out, and they needed it fast.

No sooner had Gavotski formed that thought than the whole of the censorium trembled with a powerful explosion, showering him with mortar from the ceiling, almost knocking him off his feet. For a second, he feared that a traitor had somehow, unseen by him, run the gauntlet of the Ice Warriors' las-fire and managed to lob a frag grenade into the building. But then Steele's voice drifted up to him:

'Everybody,' yelled the colonel, 'down here!'

THEY RACED DOWN ten flights of a winding metal staircase, which rang and shook with the impacts of eight pairs of boots.

It had been Mikhaelev who had offered up the demolition charge. Barreski had helped him set it up in the censorium's basement, standing the cylindrical shell on its end to focus its explosive power downwards. Grayle's ears still rang with the force of the blast, but it had achieved the desired results.

A hole had been blown through the building's foundations – and, peering into it, Grayle had been pleased to see the remains of a top-floor apartment. The Ice Warriors had dropped into the room one by one, looking for a way down, and now at last they burst out onto the street of the hive level below.

They were greeted by las-fire. The traitors, having just worked out where their foes had gone, were crowding the balconies above them. Steele kept his squad moving, steering clear of open squares, hugging the walls of buildings, making sharp turns beneath archways and bridges.

The strategy proved successful. The fire from above dropped off, the traitors finding it hard to track the fugitives below them, impossible to target them when they did. Some of them, frustrated, were swarming down ladders, just trying to get closer, but making themselves easy pickings for the Ice Warriors' guns.

They were gaining ground, putting their foes behind them, closing in on the Ice Palace, and for a moment Grayle thought they might actually make it. But then, the deep-throated roar of an engine heralded the onset of a new peril.

Steele must have heard the bike coming – but it was too fast, there had been no chance of avoiding it. It shot out from a narrow alleyway, squat and black, its twin-linked bolters spitting out death metal.

Even ridden by a cultist or a traitor, it would have presented a significant threat to the Ice Warriors. But the rider of this bike was no mere traitor. His eyes were dead, his face crisscrossed with badly stitched scars, and his features warped so that his lips were forever twisted into a disdainful leer. The rider's muscular frame was made even bulkier, more imposing, by a suit of jet-black power armour – and that armour had been daubed with red Chaos sigils, and bristled with spikes on which had been impaled a number of cracked, blank-eyed skulls.

A Chaos Space Marine!

He was standing in his broad saddle, leaning eagerly over his handle-bars, slashing at the air with a chattering chainsword. Grayle found himself running at full pelt, almost before Steele had given the order to do so, with Gavotski, Blonsky and Pozhar beside him.

He hesitated as he reached the nearest corner, glanced back, and saw that Palinev had actually run at the oncoming monster. The Chaos Space Marine swiped at the scout with his chainsword. Palinev twisted nimbly and avoided the blow by a hair's breadth. It was one of the bravest things Grayle had seen, albeit somewhat undermined by the terrified expression on Palinev's face. It seemed he had put a little too much trust in own his speed and agility, hadn't expected the sword to cut quite as close as it had.

He slipped around behind the bike and was gone, haring up the alleyway from which it had emerged. The Chaos Space Marine tried to wrestle his vehicle around on its axis, to follow, but only succeeded in unseating himself – as Palinev had no doubt hoped he would. He fell hard on his shoulder, and the bike veered off into a wall, but its rider was back on his feet in a second.

Grayle didn't wait to see what he did next, who he would go after. Whichever of the Ice Warriors drew the short straw, he would probably end up dead – and the only chance the rest of them had was to be long gone before that happened. So, Grayle and Pozhar ran one way, Gavotski and Blonsky the other, and Grayle was so worried about what might be closing behind him that he almost didn't see what was waiting ahead.

He was rushed by two traitors, one from each side. He sidestepped the first, and greeted the second with his lasgun butt, striking his jaw. As the traitor reeled, Grayle grabbed him by the shoulder, and spun him into his comrade. While both were off balance, he stepped back, brought up his gun, then thought about the noise it would make, the attention it would draw, and thrust his bayonet instead through the first traitor's kidney until he choked on his own blood.

The second traitor made to run, but Pozhar – following Grayle's lead in not firing his gun – brought him down with a low tackle. The traitor opened his mouth to yell out, but Pozhar filled it with his fist. Then he drove his gun butt repeatedly into the traitor's head until he was quite certain that he was dead.

'Quickly, in here!'

Grayle whirled around, brought up his gun, and saw a slim, fair-haired young man in its sights. The man was wearing a basic blue worker's smock; he certainly didn't look like a traitor or a cultist. Still, Grayle wasn't the only Ice Warrior to be suspicious, and the new arrival blanched as he found himself staring down two lasgun barrels.

The man threw up his hands to show that he was unarmed.

'I can help you,' he said, 'but you have to come now. We don't have long.'

'How do we know this isn't some trick?' demanded Pozhar.

'I don't know how to convince you,' said the man, 'but I am loyal to the Emperor, praise His name. I am one of the few men left in this city who is. And the Traitor Guardsmen are moving to surround you again. If you stay out here, you're dead for sure – you may as well take your chances with me.'

Grayle looked at Pozhar, and could see that they were both thinking the same thing: that the stranger was right. He was their best hope. So, Grayle turned to him with a nod, and said, 'Okay, lead the way.'

'But if you are lying to us,' Pozhar hissed, 'it won't matter how many friends you have waiting back there, what sort of a trap you might be leading us into, I will fight my way to you and I will cut your throat – with my dying breath if I have to.'

STEELE WAS RUNNING with Anakora, Barreski and Mikhaelev when he heard the bike roaring up behind them. It came screaming past the Ice Warriors, skidded to a halt in their path, and its rider was already in mid-leap towards them.

They greeted him with las-fire, but they may as well have been shining flashlights in his face for all the effect it had. Steele ducked beneath the Chaos Space Marine's chainsword, while Anakora drove her bayonet at him. She was aiming for an armour joint but missed, and the tip of her blade snapped off. The Chaos Space Marine grabbed her by the greatcoat, lifted her and flung her away like a piece of trash.

Barreski took the opportunity, while his foe was distracted, to attempt to drive his power fist into his stomach. The Chaos Space Marine caught Barreski's hand and squeezed, and the gauntlet broke with a shower of sparks. Barreski was barely able to pull out his hand in time to spare it the same fate.

Steele was aiming his laspistol, looking for an opening, when the chainsword lashed out at him again. He could smell the engine oil on its whirring teeth as he stumbled backwards away from it.

The Chaos Space Marine was focussing his attacks upon him. He must have seen the rank insignias on Steele's coat, identified him as the leader. He had chosen his victim; the other three Ice Warriors were just an inconvenience, a minor one at that. Steele offered up a prayer to the Emperor – not for his own life, because he knew this was lost, but that he could occupy this monster long enough for his comrades to get clear.

He ran, knowing he would not get far, hoping that he could get just far enough. He could hear the jackhammer footsteps of the Chaos Space Marine behind him – it had taken him less than a second to cast Barreski and Mikhaelev aside, to set off in pursuit of his true prey – and then he heard the whine of a jump pack.

Steele threw himself onto his stomach, and the Chaos Space Marine hurtled over him, having not expected such quick reflexes from a Guardsman. Scrambling to his feet, Steele raced for a litter-strewn alleyway, slipped through a gateway, hauled himself into a burned-out building through an open window, and ran out through the main door.

He ducked behind a statue of a great Imperial general, and tried to control his breathing, not to make the slightest sound.

And the statue exploded, shredded by the explosive payload of a bolt pistol.

The Chaos Space Marine was upon Steele again, marching through a cloud of dust and debris, and for the third time Steele only just avoided being sliced in two by his chainsword. There was no running now, no one to get between him and his attacker, and no hope of matching him for sheer strength.

He drew his power sword anyway, and triggered its energy field.

He was in this fight to the death, and he had no doubt that he would be the one to die. But by the time Colonel Stanislev Steele went down, his killer would be left in no doubt that he had just gone toe to toe with an Ice Warrior.

CHAPTER THIRTEEN

Time to Destruction of Cressida: 16.24.39

'THE CHAOS WORSHIPPERS don't come down here,' said the man in the worker's smock.

'I can see why not,' muttered Grayle.

They were picking their way along a dark, dank tunnel, lit only by the yellow glow of their lamp packs. Their guide, who had introduced himself as Tollenberg, had led Grayle and Pozhar through a concealed manhole in the basement of an office building. The foul smell had been the first thing to hit Grayle. He had been wading ankle-deep in cold, rank water before he realised what this was: a sewer pipe.

'Oh, they've tried a time or two,' Tollenberg went on. 'Mangellan knows we're here, even if he underestimates our numbers and our fortitude. He's sent cultists to find us. I don't think he knows how extensive these tunnels are, doesn't realise it's a maze down here. It's all too easy to get lost, easier still to walk into an ambush.'

They climbed up onto a crumbling ledge, and slipped through an iron door that had been left rusted, half open. Then Tollenberg led them down a long ladder, its rungs made slippery by a continual dribble of the foul water. At its base, they found another tunnel, apparently identical to the one above.

'We've had time, you see – those of us still loyal to the Emperor, still free. We've had time to find our way around, draw up maps, scope out the best hiding places. We can get from one side of the hive to the other now, from its top to its bottom, without leaving these pipes for more than a few strides. We can–'

Tollenberg came to an abrupt halt, fell silent, and held up a hand for the Ice Warriors to do likewise. They switched off their lights and stood waiting in the darkness, in the quiet, and they could all hear it: footsteps, sloshing towards them from behind another opening in the brick wall. Footsteps that now fell silent, as if the people making them had also realised that they weren't alone, were also standing and waiting.

Cautiously, Tollenberg tapped his lamp pack against the wall, three times, paused, then tapped twice more, each knock echoing along the tunnel behind and ahead of them. A moment later, answering knocks came, four in quick succession, and Tollenberg relit his pack.

'It's OK,' he said. 'They're friends.'

They met at the tunnel junction, Tollenberg embracing a middle-aged woman with tied-back red hair, who wore a blue smock like his, while Grayle and Pozhar were delighted to find her accompanied by two comrades: Gavotski and Blonsky.

'We have people searching the whole of this sector,' explained Tollenberg. 'With luck, they'll find a few more of your fellows yet.'

'But why?' asked Pozhar impatiently. 'What do you want with us?'

'Where are you taking us?' asked Blonsky.

'Somewhere safe,' said Tollenberg.

ANAKORA WAS ALIVE.

Her encounter with the Chaos Space Marine had lasted all of about three seconds, and was a blur in her memory. She only knew that she had hit the ground hard, been winded, and now she could hear the growling of a chainsword blade. It filled her ears, seeming to come from right beside her – but as she picked herself up, as she made herself look, she saw that she was alone in the gutter.

She could hear the retort of las-fire, too – from a pistol, if she was not mistaken. Colonel Steele!

She didn't stop to think. She pounded down the street, heedless of the risk to herself, of the possibility that more traitors might be lurking between the buildings. And she wasn't running away from the sounds of battle, as would have been the sensible thing to do, the right thing, as Barreski and Mikhaelev must have done already. No, Anakora ran towards them – and she realised as she did so that those sounds ought to have ceased by now, that no human opponent of a Chaos Space Marine could have survived this long. It just wasn't possible.

Rounding the next corner, she saw that the impossible was happening.

Beside the Chaos Space Marine in his black power armour, Steele looked small and helpless. Still, somehow he was managing to go toe to toe with him. He ducked each blow almost before it was thrown, or parried it with his blue-flaring power sword, making his foe look clumsy. He aimed the majority of his thrusts at the Chaos Space Marine's face, and some of them had got through. Even as Anakora watched, Steele drew blood again, scoring a red line across the bridge of his opponent's nose, a fresh scar to add to his collection.

The Chaos Space Marine didn't flinch, hardly seemed to register the shallow cut, his system no doubt flooded with painkilling drugs. Anakora knew that, in contrast, one punch from him would be enough to break Steele's neck, one hit from his chainsword enough to decapitate him. Steele's reflexes, or his augmetics, only had to let him down once and he would be dead.

Her first las-beam glanced off the Chaos Space Marine's armour. She had been trying to find a joint, hoping to blow it open, but with Steele in her line of fire she had to err on the side of caution. The Chaos Space Marine didn't even look, never took his eyes off Steele. He simply drew his bolt pistol with his left hand and loosed off a short burst in Anakora's direction. For a blind shot, it was horribly accurate, and she was barely able to leap back around her corner as a chunk of the wall was blown out behind her head.

She tried two more beams, each provoking an answering burst of bolts, before she decided that she needed something bigger.

A big green truck was parked on the street, a few metres away. The door to the cab hung loose, and Anakora yanked it open so hard that she wrenched it from its hinges. She hadn't driven a vehicle since her training, she was hardly a specialist, but she could remember the basics and she had seen Grayle at work.

She hauled herself up into the driver's seat, closed her eyes, muttered a fervent prayer to the engine's machine-spirits and almost brimmed over with gratitude towards them when they came alive for her.

The frame of the truck juddered as she pulled away, and the vehicle proceeded in fits and starts, and almost stalled. But Anakora was getting a feel for its workings, and she picked up speed as she pulled the steering wheel around hard. And now Steele and the Chaos Space Marine were dead ahead of her.

They heard her coming, of course. She had been counting on that, counting on Steele being able to get out of her way somehow. As the chainsword lashed out again, he feinted and, instead of ducking beneath its teeth, he darted inwards, caught the Chaos Space Marine's elbow, and twisted and pushed for all he was worth.

He couldn't overbalance his opponent – he was too strong, too heavy – but he did make him shift his footing, and that gave Steele the tiniest of openings. It gave him time enough to disengage from the battle, and to throw himself backwards. Seeing what he was doing, the Chaos Space Marine made a grab for him, tried to make a human shield out of him, but Steele was just a fraction too fast for him – and Anakora had a clear run at her target. She floored the accelerator pedal.

The Chaos Space Marine whirled to face her, flexing his powerful leg muscles, making to jump. For a moment, Anakora thought he was actually going to make it, thought he was going to leap up onto the bonnet, thrust his hands through the windscreen and find her throat. But then the truck smacked into him, and carried him ten metres or more, before, with a rending and a screeching of metal and plasteel, it slammed him hard into, and almost through, a solid stone wall.

Anakora was flung forward, and her head hit the windscreen, shattering the plexiglas. Her helmet protected her, but she was dazed. She thought the sensation she could feel in her stomach, the feeling that the world was tilting, was a symptom of nausea, until firm hands took her shoulders, and she was distantly aware that Steele had reached into the cab, grabbed her, and was dragging her out of there.

Even so, the sword was inching its way towards the colonel's heart, howling as if in anticipation of the moment when it would sink its teeth into his flimsy armour.

Anakora raised her gun, but Steele yelled, 'No! Leave me! Find the others! Complete the mission! I'll hold this thing off for as long as I can!'

She was rooted to the spot, still unsure, still thinking, *If only I could find some way to die instead of him.* She couldn't be the one to report to the others that he'd fallen, that she had done nothing to stop it, nothing but run. She couldn't do that again.

She moved around behind the Chaos Space Marine, putting his great bulk between her and Steele. She set her gun to full auto and pounded him with las-fire until her power pack was exhausted – by which time she had burned through his armour and dislodged a shoulder plate, but Steele was on his knees, unable to keep his attacker at bay for much longer, and through clenched teeth, in a hoarse voice, he yelled, 'Get out of here. That's an order, Trooper Anakora. Go!'

She had no choice now. Anakora ran – because, if there was one thing the Imperial Guard instilled in its troopers, one mantra by which they lived, it was that an order was always to be obeyed, immediately and without question.

That, and because Steele was right, because she couldn't achieve anything by staying, because the Emperor would have disapproved of her giving her life in a lost cause, taking the easy way out.

Anakora ran, with the ghosts of Astaroth Prime howling in her ears.

And the teeth of the chainsword gave one final, piercing scream behind her, and then silence fell.

THAT DAMNED ITCH had spread to Pozhar's shoulder.

He almost wished the Chaos Space Marine had come after him instead of choosing another target. He longed to be discovered by more Traitor Guardsmen.

It was no longer just that he wished to serve the Emperor through combat. It had become much more than that. When Pozhar was fighting, he couldn't feel what was happening to him. He could believe that, when the fighting stopped, everything would be all right – that, through the practice of exercising his muscles in a righteous cause, he could somehow cleanse his system, force a reversal of the… the…

He couldn't even think the word, couldn't form it in his mind.

He would have hacked off his own arm to keep the grey fur from spreading, had there been a way to do that without betraying his shame to everyone.

He tried not to think about it, tried to concentrate on the gloomy surroundings of the sewer tunnel and on his comrades. Sergeant Gavotski was walking at the head of the six-strong group with Tollenberg. The rest of the Ice Warriors were behind them, with the red-headed woman bringing up the rear.

'How many of you are there?' asked Gavotski.

'A couple of hundred,' said their guide. 'We were civilians before the war: miners, administrators, teachers. When Chaos came to our doorsteps, we gathered in the chapels to pray for His guidance. When the chapels fell, He led us into these tunnels.'

'You should have stayed and fought,' grumbled Blonsky.

'We're fighting now,' Tollenberg assured him, 'fighting to keep our minds pure, learning how to use what weapons we can scavenge, preparing for the day when the Imperial army arrives to retake our home. On that day, we will emerge into our streets again, into the traitors' midst, and we will die for that glorious cause.'

His words swelled something in Pozhar's heart. He wished he could tell this eager young man that salvation was on its way, that the Ice Warriors were merely the vanguard for a far larger force, and that the loyalists of Cressida had not been abandoned. He wished he could join them in their fight, a glorious cause indeed.

'We have a mission,' said Gavotski, skirting the issue, 'a very specific mission. We have come here to rescue one man.'

'Confessor Wollkenden, yes.' Tollenberg nodded. 'We know about him.'

'Then you know we have to get to the Ice Palace.'

'And you're leading us away from it,' said Grayle, suddenly. He had been inspecting his compass in the yellow lamplight, but he was not as adept with it as Palinev would have been, and it had taken him some time to confirm his suspicions.

They had been walking along a narrow ledge, in single file, but now the brickwork tapered away and they were forced back into the water. Pozhar thought he felt something – a cold, wriggling something – brushing against his foot.

'The direct approach is dangerous,' said Tollenberg. 'Mangellan may not have men down here, but there are other things, dreadful things, in the dark – and the closer you get to the Ice Palace, the worse the corruption becomes.'

'We're not afraid of any stinking mutants!' grumbled Pozhar.

Tollenberg fixed him with a long, narrow-eyed look that the young trooper couldn't quite read. Then, quietly, he said, 'No, I am sure you're not. Still, we can help you avoid the worst of the dangers – if you trust us.'

THERE WAS SOMETHING wrong.

Blonsky knew it as soon he emerged into the candlelit chapel, as soon as he was able to stand upright, and his hand went to his lasgun.

They had climbed another ladder – a short one, this time – and Tollenberg had rapped on the underside of a manhole cover at its top: the same signal as before, three taps, then a pause, then two more. The cover had been scraped aside, and the silhouette of another smock-clad man had loomed over them, against a circular background of flaring light. The man had reached down a hand towards them.

Blonsky had been the second of the Ice Warriors to be hauled up out of the hole, behind Pozhar – and immediately, he had detected the stench of Chaos. But reeking as he was, as they all were, from the sewer water, he couldn't pinpoint its source – and, casting around, he could see no immediate threat.

Perhaps, he thought, his senses were reacting to the desecration of this once-holy place. Some effort had been made by the loyalists to reclaim the building, to reconstruct the altar and to scrub the disgusting Chaos sigils from the walls – but still, he couldn't help but feel that the spirit of the God-Emperor had withdrawn from here and that no amount of restitution could induce its return.

At one end of the chapel, two ornate pillars had been shattered, bringing about a partial collapse of the vaulted ceiling. A little daylight spilled in through a broken window frame, and glinted off fragments of coloured glass amid the rubble. Wall hangings had been torn down and burnt.

There were more figures here, thirty or forty of them, their blue worker's smocks beginning to look like a kind of uniform. They were scrubbing the floors or trying to piece together the remnants of broken treasures, or just kneeling at the altar in silent prayer. All of them started to react to the arrival of four strangers, to clamber to their feet, to stare in both awe and hope.

They began to close in around the Ice Warriors.

And that was when Blonsky realised what was happening: when he saw the figures' odd, shambling gaits and glimpsed a tuft of grey fur protruding from a blue sleeve. And he drew his lasgun, and spun around and shot the red-headed woman through the head as she was helping Gavotski up from the ladder. She fell, a look of wounded surprise on her face, and Blonsky turned to deal with Tollenberg.

He had been beaten to it. Their fair-haired young guide was lying at Pozhar's feet, his hands clutched to his throat, blood welling between his fingers.

'I warned you,' Pozhar snarled. 'I told you what I'd do to you.' And as Tollenberg died, his smock slipped from his left shoulder, and Blonsky saw a bright green mole on his skin, proof that he had been right.

By now, Grayle was reaching for his weapon too. Gavotski scrambled to his feet, looking as surprised as the woman had been, and Blonsky spelled it out to him:

'It's an ambush, sergeant. They're mutants, all of them. They're stinking mutants!'

THIS WAS GETTING to be a habit, thought Steele: facing his own death, making peace with it, only to be given a very rude awakening.

This time, even the mechanical parts of his brain had shut down. His memories ended with the battle, with the chainsword that had shredded his armoured greatcoat, and the flesh beneath it. Bleeding from the chest, Steele had fallen onto his face, and blacked out. The Chaos Space Marine could have, should have, finished him off there and then. He didn't know why he hadn't.

He couldn't feel his legs. He was surrounded by Traitor Guardsmen. They were pressed up against him, holding his arms, half-carrying him so that his feet dragged along the street behind him. His greatcoat hung open, no more than a few ragged strips of plasfibre now. His chest and his stomach were stiff with synth-skin.

'He's awake!' a voice grunted, somewhere near his ear.

'Yeah? Then why are we still carrying him?' He felt the muzzle of a lasgun in his back, and the second voice snarled, 'Get walking, Emperor-lover!'

Steele's response to this was short and succinct, but it effectively conveyed his thoughts on the question of taking orders from a heretic.

The heretic in question made to lash out with his gun butt, but one of his fellows stayed his hand.

'You can't risk it,' he said. 'He's already damaged goods. You could break his skull, spill his brains out onto the street, and what would *he* say then?'

Steele smiled tightly to himself. The traitors had confirmed what he had already guessed, that their leader in Iota Hive wanted him alive. Most likely, Mangellan intended to question him about his comrades: their numbers, their plans and their current whereabouts. Not that it would do him any good.

They had taken Steele's weapons, his field rucksack, even his fur hat. They had turned out his pockets. They thought he was helpless. They were wrong.

Steele's greatest weapons were inside him. His mechanical shoulder was still in working order, and his bionic eye had almost completed its repair cycle. He could see with it now, albeit through a faint blur. He could call up its HUD, which told him that the eye would be fully functional in just fifty-eight minutes' time.

In the meantime, the traitors were doing him a favour. A prisoner he may have been, for now – but they were taking him just where he wanted to go.

They were taking him to the Ice Palace... to Confessor Wollkenden.

CHAPTER FOURTEEN

Time to Destruction of Cressida: 14.33.04

THEY WERE SITTING ducks.

Gavotski cursed himself for having trusted the red-headed woman when she had called to him and Blonsky out in the street. He had followed his instincts about her, not stopping to interrogate her further despite his comrade's misgivings. But then the Traitor Guard had been so close on their heels, and his instincts had never steered him wrong before.

His instincts were telling him something now.

The chapel was filled with the retorts of lasguns. They echoed from the vaulted ceiling to return to their wielders' ears with deafening force. But the only guns being fired belonged to the Ice Warriors. The mutants were not fighting back; few of them were even armed. They were cowering, whimpering behind stone columns and the remains of splintered pews, behind the altar itself.

'Cease fire!' yelled Gavotski over the clamour. 'I said cease fire, that's an order!'

Grayle was the first to obey, although he turned to his sergeant with a puzzled frown. Pozhar looked like he was a second away from mutiny, while Blonsky...

Blonsky didn't exactly aim his gun at Gavotski – he held it at a downward angle, pointed at the floor between them – but the muscles in his arms were tensed, ready, as his black eyes searched and probed.

'With respect, sergeant,' he said, 'may I ask the reason for that order?'

'Look at them!' said Gavotski. 'Does this look like an ambush to you? No one has attacked us. They've done nothing but defend themselves.'

'They are mutants,' spat Blonsky. 'Their existence is offence enough!'

Gavotski returned his glare evenly. He wasn't about to be intimidated. 'Ordinarily, yes,' he said, 'but these are extraordinary circumstances. I don't think our guides lied to us. These... these "people" have information we can use. They have ways into the Ice Palace and knowledge of Mangellan's capabilities.'

'In the circumstances, sergeant,' said Blonsky, 'I think it is my duty to ask if you're protecting these abominations because of some misguided sympathy with them? Can you swear that you are still loyal to the God-Emperor?'

Gavotski hit him with the butt of his lasgun. He hit him so hard and so fast that, even though Blonsky had been watching for such a move, he was taken by surprise and floored.

'When you can prove an accusation like that,' growled Gavotski, standing over him, 'then I expect you to shoot me dead. Until then, you will keep your mouth shut and do as I tell you. Is that understood, trooper?'

'They were praying,' said Pozhar in a small voice. 'They were praying to the Emperor.' The resentment had drained from him, and he looked confused, even afraid. Gavotski hadn't expected that. He had expected Pozhar to disapprove of his decision as vociferously as Blonsky had.

And the mutants – the human-looking mutants – were picking themselves up, re-emerging from their hiding places, and closing in around the Ice Warriors, emboldened by their inaction. Gavotski brought up his gun, and focussed it on the nearest of them.

'That's far enough!' he snapped, and the mutant came to a halt, raised its hands.

'We understand your... suspicions, don't blame you for being... repulsed.' The voice was a lumbering baritone, and it came from behind Gavotski. He turned, and felt his throat tightening. The speaker stepped out of the shadows: a shambling monster with grey fur, its fingers twisted into claws, its eyes a burning red, its brow unnaturally pronounced. 'We repulse ourselves,' it said, 'but none of us... chose this. Didn't want to be this way. Chaos, so... so strong... in the water, the air... It has taken a hold of... our bodies.' He swallowed painfully.

Gavotski remembered what Tollenberg had said.

'But you're fighting it, fighting to keep your minds pure.'

'If you are so loyal,' grumbled Blonsky, massaging his jaw as he climbed to his feet, 'then you know your duty. The Emperor's edict on impurities is clear. There is only one way you can be purged.'

'And we know we must... die,' the mutant said, 'but want it to be for a… purpose. We want to… want to strike against the heretics. They did this to us. They did this to our… world, to Cressida.' It was having trouble breathing, and it broke off its speech as it groaned and wheezed, sucking air into its lungs.

'You knew we were coming!' Grayle realised. 'You sent out spies, into the mountains and the forest. I saw one of them. You've been watching us!'

'Just… sorry,' said the mutant, 'we could not approach sooner… before the sniper on the lake, before you lost your… comrade at the landing site… before the Traitor Guardsmen… Had to choose our moment carefully, as you will… as you will appreciate. So hard, these days, to know who can be… trusted.'

Gavotski followed the mutant's sorrowful gaze, down to the floor, to the body of the Ice Warriors' erstwhile guides, and to the others – six of them – cut down before he had called for his ceasefire.

'We can't save your world,' he said quietly. 'That's not what we're here for. But with your help, we can save one man. An important man.'

'Then we will give… what help we can,' the mutant promised. 'We will fight in the Emperor's… service, and pray that, when we reach the afterlife, He will… look upon our tainted souls with… with understanding.'

THE ICE PALACE was as huge as Grayle had described. It rose up high above Steele – higher than he could see, held as he was.

He was starting to get his strength back, though he was concealing this fact from his captors, letting them half-carry him, letting them think him still weak.

The traitors bustled him down a stone staircase, flight after flight – all the way down, he guessed, to the next hive level. As they stepped out into another street, as the traitors repositioned their grips on him, Steele was let go for a second and he feigned a collapse, taking the chance to steal a glance upwards.

He saw grand towers and turrets, and the broad undersides of bridges of ice.

The air was more than cold, it was like invisible daggers were being driven through his bones. Steele rued the damage done to his greatcoat, though he suspected that even it would not have afforded him a great deal of protection. He knew cold, natural cold, and he knew that this was something different. The traitors, in contrast, seemed perfectly comfortable in their flak jackets.

They were taking him to an archway in the base of the palace's front wall. As they drew closer to it, the white surface took on a translucent quality, and Steele could see faint veins of the familiar purple fungus crazing through it.

The archway was protected by four Traitor Guardsmen – and by a heavy portcullis, this too formed from the ice. Steele remembered Barreski's confident words in the forest: 'Just give me a couple of flamers, and I guarantee you there'll be nothing left standing here in ten minutes.' If only it could be so easy.

On his way here, Steele had seen at least two hundred more traitors, many of them attaching themselves to his entourage as it passed, basking in their fellows' victory. His comrades, he accepted now, hadn't a hope of beating those odds, of making it here. At best, they could keep some of the traitors occupied outside the palace.

The rest, he feared, was up to him.

POZHAR HAD NEVER felt less comfortable.

The mutants had offered him and his three comrades seats, which they had accepted, and food, which they hadn't. Gavotski had suggested that Grayle and Pozhar get some sleep while they could, while he and Blonsky kept watch. Grayle had nodded off with his chin on his chest, but Pozhar couldn't rest.

Most of the mutants stayed well away from their guests, in deference to their sensibilities, or perhaps just in fear of arousing their wrath again. However, the most mutated of them, the one that had spoken to them earlier, now shuffled over to them, and announced that it had bad news.

'Your commander has been… captured,' it wheezed. 'He fought… well, but was outclassed by a… a Traitor Space Marine. However, we have found your… remaining four comrades… bringing them here.'

Since Tollenberg, none of the mutants had introduced themselves by name. Pozhar wondered if they had names any more. Perhaps they considered themselves unworthy, had come to think of themselves, as he would once have thought of them – *as he still thought of them* – as mere monsters.

'Colonel Steele isn't dead?' asked Gavotski.

'They are taking him to… the Ice Palace,' said the mutant, 'to Mangellan.'

'Then we can still save him,' said Gavotski. 'If you can do as you said, if you can get us into the palace, we can rescue the colonel and Confessor Wollkenden. But we have to make our plans soon. We have less than fourteen hours.'

The mutant inclined its shaggy head, graciously, and withdrew.

Blonsky watched it go with a shudder.

'They're fooling themselves,' he muttered, 'or lying to us. If a man's faith is strong, he can resist the corruption of Chaos, the Emperor has taught us that. To have been mutated as these wretches have–'

'But they're fighting it!' said Pozhar.

'Too late.' Blonsky turned to Gavotski. 'We can't trust them, sergeant. We don't know what they did to deserve this, don't know if they are cowards or traitors or just weak – but whichever it is, they are already lost. Even if they are sincere in their intentions, they cannot be cleansed of their sins. Sooner or later, Chaos will take their minds – and when that happens, they will turn on us.'

Gavotski just nodded. 'I know,' he said.

And his words were like a knife blow to Pozhar's heart.

THE INTERIOR OF the Ice Palace was no less impressive than its exterior – and no less well-guarded. Steele was guided through what seemed like legions of Traitor Guardsmen, across an enormous hallway – formed from the ice, of course, but lushly appointed with velvet rugs and wall hangings.

The hall was festooned with elaborate ice sculptures, lent a certain beauty by soft and perhaps sorcerous inner lights – until Steele drew close enough to make out their twisted, daemonic shapes. A frozen staircase swept in an elegant curve upwards to the balconies and balustrades of the next floor. He was dragged past this, into a small, dark corner, and bundled through a nondescript doorway.

Behind this, steps – stone steps – stretched downwards into an oppressive gloom. There was scarcely room to descend in single file, so Steele was set on his feet and prodded in the back with a lasgun muzzle, forced to walk with a traitor close in front of him and another close behind.

Rough-hewn stone walls opened up around them, lit only by the glows of the traitors' lamp packs. Steele could hear an insistent drip, echoing and re-echoing until even he could not have pinpointed its source. He felt as if he was sinking into the depths of the underhive, except that he knew he was still high above ground level. The cavern appeared natural enough – but Steele suspected that, if he could have looked with his bionic eye, he would have found tell-tale signs that it was man-made.

Mangellan had decided, it seemed, to complement the splendour of his castle above with the traditional dungeons below.

The steps were streaked with ice fungus, some of them treacherously so. Steele contrived to slip, and to fall backwards, toppling the unprepared traitors that followed him like a row of dominoes. Three of them fell, screaming, over the side, and were broken on the rock floor below. It didn't ease the colonel's predicament at all – the casualties were immediately replaced, new hands grasping for him, forcing him to walk onwards – but it did make him smile.

Thick iron doors had been punched into the cavern walls. They nestled in nooks, listing at odd angles. Steele felt his heart beating a little faster at the thought that Confessor Wollkenden might have been behind one of them. He resisted the urge to call out to him. He didn't want to tip his hand just yet, thought it best to bide his time, to continue the pretence that he was a broken prisoner. Not that it was so hard to pretend.

A door was heaved open, and Steele was thrust through it. His new quarters consisted of a windowless stone box, extending no more than a metre and a half in any direction. He had to stoop to avoid knocking his head on the ceiling, nor was there enough space for him to lie comfortably.

A solid metal ring was set into one wall, a heap of chains draped across it. Two of the traitors placed their hands on Steele's shoulders, pushed him down to the ground and wrapped him, quickly and efficiently, in the chains, passing them four or five times through the ring and securing them at last with a heavy padlock. By the time they had finished, he was so tightly trussed that he could neither sit nor stand, his body forced instead into an unnatural, painful hunch: the traitors' revenge, he supposed, for his trick on the steps.

They withdrew, and took their lamp packs with them. The slam of the cell door plunged Steele into an impenetrable darkness. He tried to switch to infrared vision, but his bionic eye still wasn't responding. Its HUD reported that the self-repair cycle would be completed in thirty-five seconds' time.

Ten minutes later, that countdown still stood at thirty-five seconds.

THE ICE WARRIORS were back on the move, back in the sewers – and despite their odorous surroundings, Pozhar was just grateful to be out of that chapel. He had felt no trace of the Emperor's presence in there, not for him. He had felt like an intruder.

His squad was eight-strong again. Barreski, Mikhaelev and Palinev had been brought up through the manhole together, and Gavotski had greeted them and explained the situation, explaining the details of their unlikely alliance with the mutants.

Barreski had looked appalled, but he had kept his own counsel. Mikhaelev, however, had been surprisingly supportive.

'They can help us,' he had said to the others, when Blonsky was safely out of earshot, 'or we can kill them, and throw away any hope of succeeding in our mission for the sake of Imperial dogma, rules written by men who have never set foot on a battlefield. I ask you, why shouldn't we do this?'

Pozhar had wanted to answer that question. He had itched to tear open his greatcoat, to expose the fur that was crawling across his chest, to yell out, 'Because you don't want to end up like me!' But he had no wish to die like that.

'Once we have the confessor,' Barreski had said sullenly, 'we can pump these abominations full of las-fire. We can do that, right?'

The sounds of combat from below had heralded Anakora's approach. She had been collected by one of the more human-looking mutants, as had the others – but evidently she had seen through its disguise. Gavotski had sent Palinev down into the tunnels, to find her before she could flee, to convince her that there was no threat here.

They had all listened with heavy hearts as Anakora had related the details of Steele's last stand.

'I shouldn't have left him,' she had sighed – to which Blonsky had retorted that of course she should, she had been following orders.

They had all felt as uneasy as Pozhar had in the chapel – and so, although it might have been safer to sleep there and set out for the Ice Palace in the morning, Gavotski had declined this offer. He had also stipulated that no more than two mutant guides should accompany the Ice Warriors – and so, two had been detailed to the task, chosen once more it seemed for their near-human looks and ease of speech.

Pozhar was wading behind one of them, wondering how misshapen it was beneath its blue worker's smock. He would almost have preferred the company of an obvious monster. At least that would have been concealing nothing.

Not like me, he thought.

The mutants had built a fire on the chapel floor, in which all of the Ice Warriors had recharged their lasguns' power packs. They had also provided a few scavenged frag grenades and knives, but nothing more useful than that.

Pozhar was concerned that they seemed to have climbed a long way down, via various ladders and sometimes short drops into underlying tunnels – but their guides had assured them that they knew where they were going, that the best way to reach the Ice Palace was to come up from below it.

They were sloshing their way along another stinking tunnel when Palinev brought them to a halt.

'Does anyone else hear that?' he asked. 'Something up ahead.'

They fell silent, still, listening, and they could all hear it now, could feel as well, the flow of the usually stagnant sewer water about their shins.

Something was coming this way, *swimming* this way.

The mutants were the first to react, to turn, to look at each other in pale-faced horror... and to run. One of them slipped through Grayle's fingers, but the other was caught by Barreski and pinned against the wall.

'What is it?' the Ice Warrior yelled in the mutant's face. 'What are you afraid of?'

'And did you bring us down here on purpose?' spat Blonsky. 'Were you leading us to it?' The mutant couldn't answer, could only stare and babble and whimper and kick in a futile attempt to shake off Barreski's grip.

And then a miniature tidal wave slapped out from the opening of a nearby side tunnel, to be followed an instant later by a body: green, scaly, sinewy, bristling with eyes and teeth. It leapt into the tunnel, almost bounced off the wall, landed on its feet, and oriented itself with incredible speed as it sighted its prey.

And then the monster was upon them.

STEELE HAD BEEN alone for almost an hour.

He knew this because his internal chrono told him so; it had kept him horribly aware of every second that had passed. And because of that drip, that infernal drip, marking off the slow passage of time, one beat every two point four seconds, a total of fourteen hundred and sixteen drips so far.

He half-stood, stooped, in his heavy chains, his spine aching fit to break, and he prayed to the Emperor, and silently cajoled the machine-spirits in his bionic eye, but they were deaf to his pleas, those same two digits frozen in the HUD:

Thirty-five seconds...

He heard footsteps on the steps outside, and he knew that his time was up.

A small, square panel in his cell door slid open, and light spilled in, almost blinding Steele after so long in the dark. A cultist peered in through the hole, satisfied himself that the prisoner was still bound, and opened a heavy lock.

The door creaked open to reveal a tall, thin figure standing on the threshold. Like Steele before him, this new arrival had to stoop to enter the cell; there was hardly any space between the two of them as he perched on a narrow ledge in the wall opposite the colonel, arms folded casually, a smug smile twisting his lips.

He was no longer backlit now, and Steele saw him properly for the first time, could make out his pinched features. The newcomer's eyes were like deep black holes, into which Steele felt he could almost have fallen. He sported no visible mutations, but he wore the black robes of a cultist. His hood was folded back, to show off an elaborate tattoo that spread like a spider's web across his face, over his shaved head, behind his ears and down his neck. He also wore a golden sash, and a general's shoulder flash on his right shoulder only – and he carried an ornate sceptre with the most vile obscenities carved into it: purloined and makeshift symbols of rank for a leader whose army barely acknowledged the concept.

'Let me introduce myself,' he said in a voice as smooth as silk. 'I am the ruler of this hive by right of conquest. I am the favoured of the Chaos gods, a high priest in their service. I am your jailer, your interrogator, and perhaps in time your executioner. I am all of these things and more – but the one thing you need to know about me, the most important fact in your life right now, is that I am your new, your only, master.'

'Oh, I know who you are,' said Steele, not bothering to disguise the contempt in his voice. 'You're Mangellan.'

CHAPTER FIFTEEN

Time to Destruction of Cressida: 12.12.08

THE CREATURE WAS moving so fast they barely had time to react.

It came surfing towards them on the shallow sewer water. Then it flexed its stumpy legs and its prehensile tail, and sprang into their midst, shrugging off Pozhar and Anakora's las-fire. The Ice Warriors scattered as best they could, but the tunnel was narrow, confining. The creature lashed out at them with claws and fangs; its mouth was wide, incredibly wide, its teeth like chainsword blades. It almost caught Gavotski's arm in its jaws, but he pulled away in time.

The creature smacked back into the water on its stomach – its natural orientation, Barreski realised. It was like an alligator, its body elongated and scaled, but its back was a mess of spines, and its head a splatter of misshapen, rheumy eyes.

It reared up again. He felt its hot, fetid breath and its spittle on his face, and he grabbed the mutant he had been holding, swung it around and gave it a push.

The mutant screamed as it stumbled into the sewer creature – which, not questioning its good fortune, immediately sank its claws into the mutant's shoulders, clamped its jaws over its head and dived back down into the water with it.

This gave the Ice Warriors time to regroup, to start firing in earnest. The creature hardly seemed to notice. It tore the mutant's head from its shoulders, and threw back its own head with a triumphant roar, showering the walls with blood.

But if the Ice Warriors had hoped that one kill might satisfy its appetite, they were about to be sorely disappointed.

'COLONEL STANISLEV STEELE,' recited Steele, 'officer in command of the Valhallan 319th regiment of the Imperial Guard – and that's all you're going to get from me.'

'A regimental commander, hmm?' said Mangellan, the smirk still on his lips. 'Should I be honoured that they sent you to fight me? Or should I feel slighted that, apparently, you only brought a handful of men with you?'

Steele snarled back at his captor, baring his teeth. 'You should feel afraid! When I get out of these chains–'

'Oh yes,' said Mangellan, 'you would like to be free, wouldn't you? Isn't that what we all want, ultimately? To be free of the chains that bind us?'

'All I want,' growled Steele, 'is to do my duty to the Emperor.'

'And you serve him well. You have done your best. You made it a lot further into my hive than I would have thought possible. You are evidently a skilled combatant, and a great leader. How, then, does your god repay your devotion?'

'The Emperor provides all we need.'

'How does it feel, Colonel Steele, to know that he thinks so little of your life as to waste it on a fool's errand?'

'It is never a waste to fight for order, to strike a blow against your philosophy.'

'Oh, I know why you're here. It seems that Confessor Wollkenden's opinion of his own importance is not quite as inflated as I had believed.'

Steele tightened at the mention of the confessor's name. He couldn't help himself.

'Oh yes,' said Mangellan, basking in the reaction, 'I thought that might get your attention. Wollkenden is here. He is alive. We have spoken many times, he and I. You can see for yourself soon. I will bring you face to face with the man for whom you were prepared to sacrifice yourself. It should prove an interesting meeting.'

'Shall I cut him, master? Shall I make him talk?'

Steele's glare had been fixed on Mangellan; he hadn't noticed another arrival. It had pushed its way through the traitors outside, and stood now in the doorway to the cell: a black-robed mutant, short and stooped, with lank black hair hanging over its sloping brow, tufts of grey fur sprouting from its ears, its eyebrows, its neck. It was carrying a long-bladed, blood-caked knife, fingering its edges almost lovingly.

'There will be no need for that, Furst,' said Mangellan. 'Colonel Steele is not our prisoner, he is our guest.'

'Then unchain me,' suggested Steele, 'and let me show you how a Valhallan Ice Warrior repays your hospitality.'

'And I have no questions to ask him,' Mangellan continued as if the colonel had not spoken. 'I know why he came here, and I suspect that I know as well as he does the whereabouts of his troopers. They will be cowering out there in the city somewhere, plucking up the courage to attempt to approach my Ice Palace again.'

Had Steele's bionic eye been working, he would have discharged it into Mangellan's face right then. It was a good thing, then, that it wasn't. He might have maimed his foe, gained some satisfaction, but it wouldn't have helped him in the long term. He had to keep Mangellan talking, await his moment – and hope that, when that moment came, he would be ready. Thirty-five seconds...

'Then why am I alive?' he asked. 'If you don't want anything from me...'

'You do not question the high priest!' spat the stunted mutant, Furst, hopping from foot to foot as he became agitated, panting with the effort.

'It's all right, Furst,' said Mangellan, sounding a little weary at the interruption. 'I am quite happy to tell Colonel Steele all he wishes to know. That is why I came here, after all: to talk with him, to reassure him.'

He looked directly at Steele, and something glinted in the black depths of his eyes as he concluded, 'To invite him to join our cause.'

'CONCENTRATE YOUR FIRE,' yelled Gavotski. 'Try to burn through its hide!'

The sewer creature had reared up again, its broad mouth stretched into a great, keening howl – of defiance or of pain, it was impossible to tell.

It was caught, dazed, confused, swaying for an instant in a crisscross of las-beams, and Mikhaelev dared hope that it might succumb, might fall, might at least err on the side of caution and flee – but then it chose its target, and it lashed out.

Palinev dived out of the creature's way. Its snout smacked hard into the tunnel wall, so hard that it seemed like its neck must have broken. No such luck, though. It hit the water on its stomach, and the head of its previous victim, the luckless mutant, was tossed on a wave born of the impact.

The creature was stunned, immobile, its back crowning the water like a miniature island, covered in thorns. The Ice Warriors pressed their advantage, and the scales at the base of the creature's spines began to bubble and blacken in their beams. Its tail thrashed helplessly, and Anakora moved in, thrusting her bayonet downwards at it, attempting to pin it. Her aim was true, but her broken blade too weak for the task.

The creature was recovering, raising its head so that its scalp formed another little island, its many eyes glaring in all directions so that it was impossible to work out which way it would go, who it would target next.

Suddenly, Anakora was yanked off her feet. As she landed heavily, Mikhaelev, behind her, caught a glimpse of the great tail looped round her ankles. The creature was twisting back on itself, with incredible agility and litheness, bending double to reach its ensnared, floundering victim.

Mikhaelev was about to fire again when his line of sight was blocked by Pozhar, who threw himself onto the sewer creature's back with a zeal of which the late Trooper Borscz would surely have approved. He found an eye with his knife, and punctured it with a jab, eliciting another howl – and the creature relaxed its grip on Anakora to deal with the more immediate threat.

It bucked and squirmed beneath the young trooper's weight; Pozhar let out a groan as a spine slipped through his greatcoat and into his stomach. Then he slid into the water, winded, and Anakora was trying to pull him clear, to return the favour he had done for her, but the creature had reared up again, was looming over the pair of them.

Mikhaelev's hand was in the pocket of his greatcoat, fingering a hard, cylindrical object, one he had kept ready for just such an occasion. It would be risky to use it in this confined space – especially for Anakora and Pozhar – but, unless he did something, his two comrades were dead anyway, and he had a perfect shot.

'Demolition charge!' he yelled as he lobbed the device. His aim and his timing could not have been better. The charge disappeared between the creature's teeth, bounced off its tongue... and Mikhaelev was running, as were the other Ice Warriors – six of them, at least. The remaining two were still cornered, helpless.

The blast, when it came, filled Mikhaelev's ears, shook the tunnel around him and splattered his back with chunks of something soft and moist. But it didn't lift him from his feet, and it didn't bring down the roof – and when he stopped, when he turned, when he looked, Anakora and Pozhar were still alive, covered in the blood and the guts and the sizzling flesh of the monster that had menaced them...

...the monster that, if it hadn't swallowed his charge outright, or found it lodged in its throat, must have closed its mouth reflexively around it, and contained the brunt of the explosion, as Mikhaelev had prayed it might, within itself.

Barreski punched the air, let out a whoop of delight, and clapped Mikhaelev on the back.

'Well, I hope you're pleased with yourself,' said Grayle with a mock frown, as he brushed clinging, rancid lumps of meat from his hat and his coat. 'You know, after sloshing my way through this hive's sewer system for about an hour and a half, I didn't think it was possible to smell any worse. Obviously, my mistake.'

'Unfortunately,' said Gavotski grimly, 'we do have a more pressing problem than your personal hygiene, Grayle.'

Blonsky spelled it out, 'We've lost our guides, both of them.'

'And with them,' sighed Mikhaelev, 'our way into the Ice Palace.'

STEELE LAUGHED IN Mangellan's face. It seemed the only rational thing to do.

'You're insane!' he accused the high priest. 'Well, of course you are, that goes with the territory – but do you really expect an officer of the Imperium to just... to...?'

Mangellan was unfazed. 'Many of us here were once officers in your Imperium,' he reminded his prisoner. 'You know that. Of course, the idea of joining me is abhorrent to you. You have been brought up, conditioned, to look at the universe in one way, and one way only: the Imperium's way.'

'There is no other way,' Steele growled. 'At least, none that bear thinking about.'

'Ah yes,' said Mangellan, 'that is what they tell you, isn't it? That you mustn't think about it, that the knowledge itself is forbidden. Don't you wonder why they tell you that, Colonel Steele? Don't you wonder if there could be more to life than following orders, being shipped from one war zone to another? Have you asked yourself what they are keeping from you, what they are so afraid you might learn?'

'Let me cut him, master,' whined Furst, his knife trembling in his hand as if it were all he could do to keep from thrusting it between Steele's ribs. 'Let me punish him for his insolence.'

'All I need to know,' said Steele, 'is right here in this cell with us.' He jerked his head towards the mutant. 'That is the price of your knowledge, Mangellan. That is what happens when we stop fighting it, when we start to question.'

Mangellan snorted with derision. 'Furst is a pawn, no more. Our gods have gifted him with physical strength, so I use him to fetch and carry for me. Look at me! I have worshipped Chaos all my life. Do you see the mark of the mutant on me?'

'Perhaps,' growled Steele, 'your mark is inside you.'

'I used to think I had been overlooked. I used to pray to feel the touch of my gods. But now I know the truth. They have recognised my intellect, my vision, my strength of will. They do not need to make me over in their image, because I am already their perfect servant. The gods have favoured me over all.'

'You know,' said Steele, 'when I first heard about you, when I heard your name, I feared you might be a challenge. But you're just a small man, after all.'

Mangellan's smile faded for the first time. Steele had touched a nerve.

'And yet,' the high priest growled, 'I am in control of my destiny. That is more than anyone can say of you. You could wield power in this world, Colonel Steele – the power to build an Ice Palace like this one, to have men grovel at your feet.'

'I'd rather bare my backside to a Valhallan tusked mammoth,' snapped Steele, 'because your gods will betray you. That is what Chaos does. That is what Chaos is. It is treachery and deceit. How many men did you betray to get here, Mangellan? You didn't lead the invasion of Iota Hive, did you? No, you let others do that, and waited for them to die so that you could seize power. Did you even fight with them?'

'That is where we differ, my friend. While you foolishly risk your life on the front lines, I stand back, taking an overview, waiting for my chances.'

'Like finding a Chaos Space Marine that will throw in his lot with you? That would buy you a bit of respect around here, I suppose – for as long as it lasts. As long as it takes him to realise that, whatever you promised him, you can't deliver on it.'

'You will serve me too, Colonel Steele – if not as an ally, then as a sacrifice, an offering to my gods. They will be only too pleased to receive your soul, and will reward me for conveying it to them.'

'Is that what you have planned for Wollkenden?'

It was a bold question, and Steele didn't expect Mangellan to answer it, to give anything away. To his surprise, however, the high priest smiled and said, 'Such a pious man, your confessor; an important man, as your presence here proves. A man who, to hear him tell it, saved an entire star system for your Emperor. For him to fall from the sky as he did, into my grasp... well, my gods were smiling upon me again that day. And then, along *you* came.'

Mangellan pushed himself up from his stone ledge, leaned over Steele so that his lips almost touched the colonel's ear. Steele tried to flinch from him, but his chains held him too tightly. A feeling of revulsion shuddered through his body. He called up his bionic eye's HUD again, but still it gave only the same discouraging report: thirty-five seconds... thirty-five seconds...

'The irony of it,' Mangellan crooned, 'is that your masters do not value you. They would snuff out your life in a second for the chance, the merest chance, of getting their important, pious man back. But I have met the both of you, spoken with you, and I know the truth of it. I know that you, Colonel Stanislev Steele, are a far better man, a far stronger man, than Wollkenden will ever be.'

'THIS IS IT,' said Palinev, staring at his compass. 'This must be it!' Then he looked at the walls of yet another nondescript tunnel, and he felt a lot less confident. 'At least, I think... If the colonel were here...'

'You haven't let us down yet, Trooper Palinev,' said Gavotski. 'If you say we're underneath the Ice Palace, then that is where we are.'

Grayle reached up to touch the tunnel roof, and snatched his hand away with a wince.

'Ice burn!' he exclaimed. 'And it's been getting colder for the past half-hour, since before we ran into that creature. The Ice Palace is up there, all right.'

'The question is,' said Blonsky, 'where is this supposed entrance to it?'

Mikhaelev shrugged. 'Hardly likely to be in plain sight, is it? Maybe we should have turned back after all.'

'We discussed this,' said Gavotski firmly. 'It would have wasted too much time. No, our guides have brought us most of the way, and they assured us that there is a way into the palace from down here. We just have to find it.'

'If we can't,' offered Palinev, 'I could go back to the chapel. I can find my way... at least, I think I can. I could fetch us another guide.'

'Maybe,' said Gavotski, 'but only as a last resort. We've all seen what's out there. I don't want anyone wandering about down here alone. For now, I suggest we search the tunnels from roof to floor. And remember what Grayle told us: the Ice Palace is at least a kilometre square. The entrance could be anywhere in that area. Remember this too: Confessor Wollkenden is in that palace, as is Colonel Steele. All that stands between us is a thin layer of masonry – and we aren't going to let that stop the Ice Warriors of Valhalla, now are we?'

MANGELLAN'S WORDS STILL echoed in Steele's head, making him feel sick.

He imagined he could still feel the condensation from the high priest's rancid breath on his ear, and he itched to be able to move his hand, to wipe it away.

'I think it's time,' Mangellan had whispered to him. 'Time for Wollkenden to leave this mortal plane, to take his place as the plaything of Khorne, of Slaanesh, of Tzeentch, of Nurgle. The ceremony will take place at dawn. That is the usual time, I believe, for rituals of this kind. If you wish, Colonel Steele, I might let you watch. It may help to concentrate your thoughts.'

Alone again, he had released a primal scream from the depths of his stomach, and had struggled against his chains, although he knew he had no hope of breaking them.

There was nothing he could do.

So, he had tried to sleep instead, so that when his chance did come he would be ready to take it. He had succeeded only in dozing fitfully, woken each time by the pain in his muscles and along his spine, and by the urgent ticking of his internal chrono, and the ever-present drip-drip-dripping from somewhere outside.

And this time, by the creaking, squealing, scraping of his cell door.

Again, the light of a lamp pack spilled over him. This time, Steele didn't flinch. His left eye closed to protect itself, but his right eye adjusted instantly to the glare. He didn't question this at first, didn't see anything unusual in it. It took a moment for him to realise what it meant. By the time he had, he was focussed on the short, stooped figure that had come shuffling into the cell, glancing back over its shoulder, moving with what appeared to be a clumsy attempt at stealth.

'Well, well,' said Steele, 'so Mangellan's dog has slipped its leash.'

Furst snarled up at him; even with Steele hunched over as he was, the mutant's head barely came up to his chin. 'You can insult me all you like, but you will regret your slurs against my master. I will make you scream for the mercy of death.' The mutant produced his knife again, brandishing it before his prisoner's eyes – but Steele was more concerned with what he was holding in his other hand.

'Mangellan doesn't know you're here, does he?' he said. 'So much for loyalty among heretics.'

'The master will be grateful that I have dealt with his enemy. He will see that I can take the initiative too.'

'Will he? I know you're only trying to be like him, Furst – a traitor like him – but the last thing a traitor can afford to tolerate when he gains power is the treachery of others. He will squash you, Furst, like the loathsome bug you are.'

Steele's goading was working. Furst was pressed right up against him, reaching up with the tip of his knife, tracing faint lines across the colonel's face. The mutant's breathing was excited, ragged, and Steele could see flecks of drool on his chin and feel the shape of a bunch of keys against his stomach.

'Join us or die,' gurgled Furst, 'that is the choice you were given by the master. Well, I can make that choice easy for you. I can use this blade to carve the mark of Chaos Undivided into your face.'

'Do your worst,' said Steele calmly, 'but do this one thing for me, would you, Furst? Have the courage to look me in the eye as you do it.'

CHAPTER SIXTEEN

Time to Destruction of Cressida: 09.53.21

THE MUTANT FURST didn't have time to scream.

The energy discharge from Steele's bionic eye hit him square in the face, scorched his skin, made his hair stand on end, froze the open-mouthed leer on his lips. It also propelled him backwards into the stone wall of the cell, which he hit with the back of his skull. He slumped to the floor, leaving a smear of blood, his eyes rolling into his head, his tongue hanging out.

And Steele had the keys. He had managed to wrap two fingers around them before he had struck, had almost lost them as Furst had been wrenched away from him but had kept his hold, pulling them out of the mutant's hand. He gathered them carefully into his palm, securing his grip, trying not to be impatient, to rush.

There were nine keys in the bundle, and Furst's lamp pack had been extinguished when he'd fallen. Steele worked by touch alone, analysing the shape of each key until he found the one that matched the padlock on his chains. If he hunched his left shoulder, thrust his elbow back, twisted his wrist, he could just about reach it. After a couple of false starts, scrabbling and scratching in the dark, the teeth of the key clicked into place in the hole. It was the sweetest sound he had heard all day.

As the chains fell away, Steele's legs almost buckled beneath him. It took all the will-power he had not to fall, to crouch beside Furst, to take his knife and his lamp pack, and then to half-stagger, half-fall out through the door that the mutant had left open, out into the cavern. Steele's right eye was blind again, but his augmented ear told him that he was alone down here. Fortunately for him.

He found a damp, uneven wall to lean against, to cool his forehead – for he was burning up, despite the freezing temperature. He gave his muscles time to adjust to being able to stretch again. His throat was parched, and there was condensation on the wall – but it was stained purple by the clinging fungus, and Steele didn't dare drink it.

When he felt able, he pushed himself up, took his own weight, lit his purloined lamp pack and inspected his surroundings. He could see six cell doors, but the cavern meandered off into passageways and alcoves that were hidden from him. If he upped the gain on his acoustic enhancers, he could hear the soft breathing of people behind some of those doors. Some were asleep, letting out the occasional snore, while others stirred, clanking their chains, and someone was sobbing to himself.

Each door had a small inspection hatch, secured by a metal bar. Steele opened the nearest and raised his lamp, letting just enough light fall into the cell for him to make out its occupant. It was an Imperial Guardsman, in the tattered remains of a red and gold Validian flak jacket, chained as Steele had been – and to judge by the smell of him, he had been there for some time. He looked up at the colonel with a wretched expression, and gasped, 'Help… help me… for the love of the Emperor, help…'

It was with some regret that Steele closed the panel, leaving the man to his fate. He would have been dead weight, more hindrance than help. And his suffering would be over soon, Steele told himself. As soon as the virus bombs fell.

He opened another hatch, and something heavy threw itself at the door. Steele leapt back by reflex, and narrowly avoided a clawed hand that swiped at him through the aperture. He discouraged it with a blow from the hatch's locking bar, and its owner – another grey-furred mutant – howled and recoiled.

The vile creature was still howling a minute later, and Steele cursed it under his breath. He had taken cover as best he could behind a rocky outcrop, and was wondering if he dared make a sprint back to his cell, to hide in there.

He kept his good eye fixed on the steps, expecting Traitor Guardsmen to appear at their head. He cast around for a weapon with which to greet them if they did, but could see only rocks. He collected a few anyway, but was relieved not to have to use them. The mutant's howls subsided into a quiet whimpering, and Steele assumed that the traitors were more than used to hearing sounds of anguish from down here and so had not bothered to investigate.

He recognised the prisoner in the third cell at once.

He had seen him only once before, and then only in holographic effigy – but he had studied the image, committed it to his enhanced memory.

Confessor Wollkenden looked thinner than he had in his hologram. He was also dehydrated, his skin stretched like parchment, but his bone structure was unaltered. His prominent jaw was unmistakeable. The hologram, Steve saw now, had also been an old one, showing the confessor in his prime.

To his surprise, Wollkenden was not chained, but instead lay curled on a filthy mattress, asleep, wisps of white hair splayed about the oval crown of his head. Steele fumbled with Furst's keys, almost dropping them as his hands trembled in anticipation. He opened the cell door, stepped inside, leaned over the prone form of its occupant and tried to shake him awake. Wollkenden didn't respond at first, and for a moment Steele feared that he might already be dead, that he might have come all this way for nothing. Then, as he tapped the confessor lightly on his pale cheeks, he rolled over onto his back, let out a soft groan, and his eyelids fluttered.

'Confessor Wollkenden. Confessor. It's OK, I'm going to get you out of here. Can you hear me? Confessor?'

Steele glanced over his shoulder anxiously. He didn't know how much time he had. Somebody had to know that Furst had come down here – and, if not, they might yet find a set of keys missing and come to investigate.

He took Wollkenden's right arm, draped it around his shoulders, put his arm around the confessor's waist and hauled him to his feet.

'We need to find you some water,' he muttered. 'We need to find us both some water.'

He carried Wollkenden out into the cavern, walked him up and down. He was gratified to feel the confessor responding, finding his strength again – but worried, at the same time, that he wouldn't find enough.

'Who… who are you?' the confessor asked hoarsely.

'Colonel Stanislev Steele, sir, of the Valhallan 319th.'

'They… sent a regiment to rescue me?' Wollkenden seemed to find the idea amusing, although Steele had no idea why. Perhaps it was just relief, or a mild form of hunger-induced hysteria that choked a spluttering laugh out of him. 'I told Mangellan. I told him they wouldn't leave Helmat Wollkenden to rot in these dungeons, he is too important… too, too important.'

'The Ecclesiarchy is keen to get you back, confessor,' said Steele. He thought it best not to mention, for now, that he hadn't exactly brought a whole regiment with him.

And then Wollkenden was struggling in his grip, trying to stand by himself although he evidently wasn't able.

'Where are they?' he babbled. 'Where are your men? I wish to address them. They need to know what is expected of them, and they will listen to me. I can inspire them, turn them into heroes.'

'I know, confessor, but–'

Wollkenden squirmed around, gripped the front of Steele's ragged coat, and stared intensely into his eyes. 'That's the worst thing, you know, the hardest thing about imprisonment. So much time to think, and yet... Did they tell you about the Artemis System? They say that, without my words, we would have lost a score of worlds to the Chaos blight there.'

'I know you have had a distinguished career,' said Steele, 'but we ought to–'

'What am I, then, without an audience? What am I without my voice?'

'We'll find you an audience,' Steele promised, 'but not here. Mangellan is–'

'How did he die? Las-beam? Grenade? Did he live to see his Ice Palace fall? I imagine that was some sight, yes? Did you break down the walls, or just melt through them? Water running through the streets, washing away the blood... Oh, I knew you'd come, I knew you'd kill Mangellan for taking me, I told him so.'

Wollkenden's voice was getting louder, more strident, and Steele couldn't interrupt him. He pressed his hand over the confessor's mouth, stifling the flow, and prayed that the Emperor would forgive his discourtesy.

'With respect, sir,' he hissed, 'Mangellan's palace has not fallen, and if we make too much noise his men will be down here in a second. We have to get out of here, and we have to do it quietly. Do you understand?'

Wollkenden nodded frantically. He looked almost afraid of his rescuer now; still, the message appeared to have got through to him. Steele removed his hand, and guided the confessor to the steps. It became apparent, as they tried to climb them, just how weak Wollkenden truly was. He slipped on the purple fungus, and would have fallen on his face had Steele not caught him. With each subsequent step they took, he threatened to overbalance the pair of them, send them over the side.

Somehow, though, they made it to the top. Steele lowered his charge into a sitting position, cautioned him to be silent and still. He put out his lamp, flattened himself beside the doorway through which he had been dragged almost four hours before, and peered out into the Ice Palace's grand hallway.

A part of him had hoped to find the hall empty, its sentries off-duty for the night. He had known, however, that this was unlikely. Almost immediately, he heard the footsteps of a pair of Traitor Guardsmen, and he shrank back into the shadows. The traitors had hardly gone by when another pair approached from the opposite direction.

Mangellan had set regular patrols. Funny, thought Steele, how men like that preached Chaos and yet were so quick to dispense orders. That said, there was no point in his trying to time the traitors, to deduce when there might be a gap between their patrols – they would hardly be so disciplined.

There was no hope of crossing the hallway unseen, and the portcullis would be guarded anyway. But Steele remembered the ice bridges spanning the expanses between the palace's upper levels and the hive streets around them. And closing his eyes, concentrating, he also remembered something else, something to which he had paid scant attention as he had passed it earlier. He remembered a door, standing half-open – and behind that door, the base of a winding staircase.

He would have to rely on his enhanced ear to alert him to approaching patrols – and on the Emperor's grace, to ensure that the guards at the entrance wouldn't turn and see him and Wollkenden while they were exposed. But Steele thought that they could reach that door. And from there...

The palace was an enormous building. There had to be places in which they could hide. And maybe they could find weapons, and robes to disguise themselves. Maybe they could find an unguarded bridge. Anything was possible... if they could just reach that door.

Steele crouched beside Wollkenden, told him what he had planned, asked him if he felt up to it. Wollkenden stared through him, and he said, 'It looks majestic out there, doesn't it? All that ice... It reminds me of the victory celebrations on Artemis Major, of the crystal statues they erected in Imperial Square.'

Steele explained the plan again, patiently. Then he helped Wollkenden up to the doorway and waited.

They crept out behind the next two-man patrol, Steele praying that neither of the traitors would look over their shoulders. He could already hear the next pair, tramping towards them. They had... his processors quickly worked out the figure... eleven seconds before they came into view around the grand staircase. He tried to pick up the pace, but Wollkenden chose that moment to apparently lose all strength in his legs. He let out a grunt as Steele caught him, and the colonel felt his heart freeze, expecting the sound to reveal them.

Five seconds... and the door, that inviting door, was still an unattainable four metres away.

Wollkenden's chin sagged onto his chest. He was losing

consciousness, but they had come too far to turn back now. Steele bundled the confessor's limp body into his arms, almost staggered by the weight. He would have to run, have to sacrifice silence for speed.

He had made it all of three paces when Wollkenden began to struggle violently. 'No!' he yelled. 'No, you won't take me through that door, you won't put me in chains again!'

Steele tried to hush him, made to put his hand over the confessor's mouth again, but it was already far, far too late.

Wollkenden wriggled out of his grip, tried to stand, but fell to his knees, and crawled up to an ice statue of a leering, gargoyle-like figure. 'Help me,' he beseeched it, extending his clasped hands towards as it as if in prayer. 'It is your duty to help me, for the Emperor, for the score of worlds I liberated from-'

There was more, much more. But Steele heard none of it – because Traitor Guardsmen were streaming in from all directions, even through the door that he had hoped would be his escape route. And even if he had been in any condition to fight them, he could never have won. Even if he could have run, there was nowhere he could have run to.

THEY WERE DRAGGED along endless passageways, Steele and Wollkenden, by cultists and traitors – their numbers growing as more of their kind rushed out of their rooms or abandoned patrols to join the throng, until the two prisoners were all but borne aloft on a fast-moving river of bodies.

Steele said nothing, bearing his fate stoically, but Wollkenden was delirious. He was waving to the crowd, thanking them, assuring them that a parade was not necessary, that he had only done what any man of his considerable talents would do.

They emerged, at last, into a large courtyard, bordered by four sheer walls, overlooked by hundreds of windows. Ice trees grew around its edges, reaching sizes of a hundred storeys tall, their branches spreading across the yard to intertwine with each other. Moonlight streamed in through this intricate frozen web, and bathed the courtyard in a cool shade of blue.

Overlooked amid the crowd, one cultist watched all this, and tried his best not to rub shoulders with those around him. He kept his hood pulled over his head, concealing his face, and was careful not to catch anybody's eye. When the crowd yelled out anti-Imperium slogans, he pretended to join in, although he couldn't bring himself to give voice to the words.

A huge stone dais stood in the centre of the courtyard – and from this, there rose an ice column, eight-pointed like the Chaos star, its sides engraved with sigils that hurt the naked eye to look at them. Steele and

Wollkenden were thrust against two of the column's points, secured to them with chains.

That was when Mangellan appeared, with an imposing figure marching at his shoulder. The lone cultist recognised the Chaos Space Marine, and could tell that he had been in a fight since last he had seen him. His black power armour was damaged, his face bloodied. Still, the crowd parted as he moved through it, even the heretics keen to give this abomination a wide berth.

Shuffling at Mangellan's heels was his disgusting, mutated little servant, his head bandaged. The lone cultist had heard that his name was Furst, that he was a man of scant intellect – but favoured by Mangellan, perhaps for that very reason. The rumours had been rife since the attempted escape of Steele and Wollkenden that it was Furst who had let them go. It seemed that Mangellan either didn't believe those rumours or did not care.

As the high priest mounted the dais, Wollkenden seemed to recognise him, to realise where he was at last, and he started to yell out, to struggle. Mangellan ignored him, turning to his audience, raising his hands for silence. It took a moment for the clamour to subside, and then Mangellan assembled a squad of Traitor Guardsmen and instructed them to patrol the courtyard for the rest of the night, to keep a close eye on the prisoners. The Chaos Space Marine had taken up a position at a back corner of the dais, and it looked like he intended to stay put too.

'Our guests will not trouble us much longer,' Mangellan assured his flock. 'Our plans remain as they were. In four hours' time, we will meet here to begin the ceremony. As the first light of dawn touches the courtyard, we will deliver not one but two noble souls to our gods.'

The lone cultist had heard enough.

The crowd was shouting, roaring its approval of Mangellan's plan. The cultist slipped with surprising ease through the crush of bodies, heading for the archway through which most of them had entered. He didn't want to be the first to leave, so he waited nervously for the crowd to begin to disperse, to return to their rooms or their duties in twos and threes, chattering about the undoubted spectacle to come.

He retraced his steps through the Ice Palace, trying not to appear too hurried. As the other cultists peeled off around him, streaming up staircases, he was left on his own for a moment. He ducked into a side passageway, narrow, dark, uncarpeted, its floor smooth and slippery in contrast to the well-trodden paths elsewhere.

An iron door caught in its ice frame, and it took all the cultist's strength to wrench it free. He stepped through onto a flight of stone steps, and produced a lamp pack from beneath his robes to light the way down into a dank cave.

This unnatural system extended, as far as he had been able to tell, beneath the whole of the Ice Palace. The dungeons, he had learned, were housed in a part of it – a part that, after much searching, he had reluctantly accepted could not be reached except through the palace itself – as were various wine cellars and treasure troves housing the spoils of the Chaos army's recent victory. This cave, however, had not found a use yet. Indeed, the cultist had seen no sign that anyone had passed this way before him.

It was with some relief, then, that he shucked off his purloined robes, and became Trooper Palinev of the Imperial Guard again.

He squeezed through a niche in the rock wall into a tiny antechamber. Lying there, where he could not be seen from the steps, was the corpse of a defrocked cultist, his throat slit. The man had made the fatal error of passing the wrong door at the wrong moment. And of being about Palinev's size.

A hole had been knocked through the wall of the small cave. Palinev had to lie on his stomach in order to squeeze through it. He lowered himself feet first, and dropped the last half-metre into the tunnel below. He landed on a precarious ledge, its brickwork slimy with sewer water – and immediately, dark shapes rose around him.

Raising his lamp pack, he identified those shapes as his comrades. Anakora and Mikhaelev greeted the scout's return with relief, and quickly woke Sergeant Gavotski as they had been instructed. The Ice Warriors had been taking the opportunity to catch up on their sleep, spread out across the ledge, while they awaited the outcome of Palinev's scouting mission – although of course they had left two troopers on watch.

Everyone was cheered by the news that both Wollkenden and Steele were alive. Beside that, the matter of rescuing them seemed almost inconsequential. Palinev had to remind himself that they still had much to do.

'We could go in there now,' said Gavotski, 'but it sounds as if the colonel and the confessor are well-guarded, and we're dog-tired. We can't take out two squads of traitors, not before they can raise the alarm and surround us. I suggest we wait until this ceremony of theirs has started. At least then we'll know where most of the heretics are, and that they'll be distracted. We should have the run of the palace.'

'Until we reach that courtyard,' said Mikhaelev, as always sounding the first note of caution. 'Then we'll have to fight our way through the heretics, and they'll outnumber us by hundreds to one.'

'You're right,' said Gavotski, with a quiet smile. 'They won't know what's hit them.'

CHAPTER SEVENTEEN

Time to Destruction of Cressida: 04.22.14

STEELE WISHED HE could close his senses to it all.

He wished he couldn't hear the baying of the heretics – hundreds of them were packed into the courtyard, standing in the arched doorways, even hanging out of the surrounding windows. He wished he couldn't feel the touch of the cultists that had gathered around him, preparing him, painting their vile symbols on his face and his exposed chest. He wished he couldn't smell the stink of the incense burner that Furst carried, waving it under Steele's nose as if it were some kind of a trophy, or feel the evil presence of the Chaos Space Marine lurking behind his right shoulder.

And he wished he couldn't hear Wollkenden, to his left, still chained to the eight-pointed ice pillar as was Steele, but whimpering and pleading for mercy. The so-called saviour of the Artemis system, his demeanour shaming his legend.

Steele wasn't afraid to die. Even now, he would have given his life gladly in exchange for the confessor's freedom. But he could think of nothing worse than this: to die a failure.

He closed his good eye, tried to blot it all out, tried to cast his mind back to a happier time, a more serene time, a more welcome ceremony. It seemed like months – although, in fact, little more than a day and a half had passed – since he had stood beside the Termite borer, his head bowed, to receive the blessing of an Imperial priest.

Had the Ecclesiarchy known, then, that this was to be his fate? Had they sanctified his soul to deny it to the Chaos gods? He prayed that this might be the case. He prayed as hard and as loud as he could, tried to fill his own head with the uplifting sound.

'Your Emperor can't save you now,' Furst hissed spitefully in Steele's ear.

The mutant's master, Mangellan, was on the dais too, strutting around, circling his captives, waving his sceptre, playing to the crowd. His voice rose and fell as he half-chanted, half-sang words in some ancient, evil language – words that Steele didn't understand, didn't want to understand. He knew that his augmented brain wouldn't let him forget those words; he couldn't bear that they would be captured inside him, a part of him. They were dark words, cold words. Words that seemed to distort space itself, to punch open a channel to a more malignant realm.

But the words were, he sensed, coming to an end. Mangellan had whipped his audience into a frenzy. He was gesturing at the pillar, at the readied sacrifices – the colonel and the confessor – with the sceptre in one hand and a large, ornamental dagger clutched by the jewelled hilt in the other.

And now he turned to Steele, rested the dagger's point on his chest, traced the outlines of the symbols that had been daubed onto his skin – and Mangellan sighed, and in his calm, honeyed voice, he said, 'You should have joined us when I gave you the chance. A shame that such a spirit, such an intellect, as yours should have been wasted on a lifetime of servitude to an ungrateful master. You could have been anything you wanted to be, Colonel Steele.'

Steele looked him in the eye, and he said, 'I was.'

And at that moment, a ray of sunlight streamed into the courtyard, through the network of ice-formed branches above their heads, and glinted off the dagger as Mangellan drew it back, let the crowd see its blade for a final time as he prepared to plunge it into its first victim.

'Do it, master,' breathed Furst eagerly. 'Do it now! Cut out their hearts!'

That was when the first bomb went off.

GRAYLE AND PALINEV had timed their ascent to the dais perfectly.

Cloaked in their purloined robes, they had given themselves enough time to reach Wollkenden and Steele respectively – but not quite enough for the cultists to realise that their numbers had been swelled by two, to start asking questions.

The explosion ripped through the courtyard, incinerating heretics by the score in a great blossom of fire. They hadn't seen it coming, hadn't spotted that their enemies were walking among them in disguise. And

Mikhaelev had placed his demolition charge well. It collapsed two huge ice trees, their razor branches falling clear of the dais and into the crowd, where they sliced, dismembered and decapitated. Grayle just hoped that his comrade was not among the casualties, that he had had time to get clear. He concentrated on his own task, concealing his lasgun as best he could with his body as he placed its muzzle to Wollkenden's chains.

The heretics were screaming, surging away from the site of the first blast... to where the second was waiting.

The courtyard became a seething mass of panic. None of the heretics knew which way to run, but they trampled each other in their haste to run somewhere.

A hand came down on Grayle's shoulder; he was spun around to face a suspicious cultist, whose eyes widened at the sight of a stranger's features beneath the hood. The cultist opened his mouth to yell a warning that might have been heard by the augmented ears of the Chaos Space Marine even over all the noise. Two las-beams struck him in the head, one more in the shoulder, and he went down.

More beams flashed from the surrounding windows, and the cultists on the dais cried out, scattered, leapt into the turmoil around them rather than remain sitting ducks. Grayle prayed that his comrades knew who they were shooting at, that they wouldn't mistake him and Palinev for their targets.

Most of their fire, in fact, was directed at Mangellan – but he was well-protected, by the Traitor Guardsmen around him, bustling him away down the dais steps. Furst scurried along behind them, keeping close, benefiting from their armour, although Grayle couldn't tell if the traitors had even seen him in their wake.

And then there was the Chaos Space Marine.

He leapt from the dais, reaching the edge of the courtyard with one powerful spring. He smacked into the palace wall, punching through the ice to make handholds for himself, started to haul himself upwards. Grayle saw Blonsky's face in a window, paling as a gauntleted hand clamped onto the sill in front of him. He drove his gun butt into the Chaos Space Marine's fingers, but couldn't dislodge them. He turned and ran, disappearing from Grayle's view as his pursuer squeezed his massive form through the small window after him.

In the confusion, no one had thought to secure the would-be sacrifices. Perhaps Mangellan thought them secure enough, hadn't realised that his enemies had already got to them. Grayle's lasgun burned through Wollkenden's chains at last, and the confessor fell into his arms.

'Is it my turn to speak?' he asked weakly. 'I must say, I expected a little more discipline from the troops. Obviously, I've been gone too long. That's the trouble these days, no leadership.'

'Please, confessor,' said Grayle, 'I'm trying to rescue you. Just... just hold still... sir, please... I need to get this cloak over your head.'

'Take your hands off me!' bellowed Wollkenden – and he pushed Grayle aside, took his own weight unsteadily, and looked around like a startled rabbit about to bolt...

...as Steele, having been freed and disguised by Palinev, strode up beside him and, without breaking his step, threw a punch to Wollkenden's head that knocked him spark out. Grayle and Palinev watched in abject astonishment as the colonel hoisted the confessor's limp body over his shoulders.

'Well?' he barked at them. 'Are we getting out of here or what?'

BARRESKI COULD HARDLY breathe.

The explosions had kicked up twin plumes of smoke, which were settling now upon the occupants of the courtyard. The Chaos worshippers were packed too tightly around him, restricting his movement, their elbows digging into his ribs and his stomach. He braced himself against them, knowing that if he let his guard down for an instant he would be crushed between them or just overrun.

He had one advantage, though, over the heretics. He knew where the bombs were – or rather, where they had been, because Mikhaelev had only had two demolition charges left and they had both blown. Barreski had placed one himself, and was proud of his handiwork, the carnage he had caused.

A hapless cultist lost his footing and fell coughing against the disguised Ice Warrior. Barreski took the opportunity to slip his knife into the man's heart, let him slide to the floor. Another one less to worry about, he thought.

His quarter of the crowd appeared to have reached an unspoken consensus. They had chosen an archway, an escape route, through which to evacuate, had started to move together instead of fighting each other. Barreski hoisted himself onto the shoulders of a protesting cultist in front of him, and he screamed out, 'Another bomb! Look! There it is! Can't you see it? In the branches of that tree!'

No one could see the bomb, because it didn't exist. Still, Barreski's words were enough to make a significant number of the heretics turn back, to fight once more against the tide of their fellows, to spread more panic.

He glanced up at the dais, and saw that it was empty. Grayle and Palinev would be heading for their preselected exit, taking Steele and Wollkenden with them. He muttered a quick prayer for their safety.

It was time for him to get out of here himself.

Palinev had chosen a different way out for Barreski, a closer one to his position. He had scouted a route for him back to the sewer tunnel, made sure that he had memorised the directions. Barreski pressed his elbows into service, and started to force his way across the yard.

And that was when he saw Mangellan, his traitor escort clearing a path for him, using their lasguns when they had to. And he was just a few metres away...

He couldn't resist it. He knew it meant giving himself away, but he snuck his lasgun out from beneath his robes, flicked its power pack to full auto and squeezed off ten las-beams in the high priest's direction.

The traitors reacted quickly, putting themselves in the line of fire, deflecting most of it with their armour... most of it... Barreski gave a triumphant cry as one of his beams glanced across Mangellan's face, causing him to scream out, to clap his hands to his eyes. But now he had his own safety to worry about.

Already, the traitors were starting to move towards him. He had to lose himself again. He put his head down, tried to slip away amid the other black cloaks, but he was brought up short by a brawny cultist with a knife.

'Did you see him?' bluffed Barreski, pointing wildly. 'He had a bomb, and he was coming up behind the high priest. He would have killed him if I hadn't... Look, you need to defend yourself!' He thrust his lasgun into the cultist's hands while he was still gaping, trying to work out what it was he had seen.

Then Barreski was gone, leaving the brawny cultist with the weapon. Which was how the Traitor Guardsmen found him, a second later.

'SPACE MARINES! COMING up the passageway!'

Pozhar hated this.

He was stationed in one of the arched doorways into the palace proper, his job to keep it as clear as he could for Steele and Wollkenden's escape. This meant pretending to be one of the heretics – almost as bad, pretending to be afraid – but Gavotski had given him no say in the matter.

Few of the cultists were coming this way, anyway. Mikhaelev and Barreski had placed their charges carefully, herding them in the opposite direction – and of those who did try to pass Pozhar, about half were turned back by his feigned panic. Still, there were some who didn't seem to hear him, or were so eager to get out of the courtyard that they took their chances. As one of them bumped into him, it was all he could do not to draw his lasgun and start shooting.

'They... they've got chainswords!' he shouted desperately after the escapees. 'And guns! Big guns!'

'Pozhar!'

He turned at the sound of his name, couldn't see who had called it at first. In a yard full of robed figures, it was near impossible to tell which ones were his comrades. Then he recognised the slight form of Palinev – and there, beside him, that had to be Grayle. And between them…

Pozhar raced forward, dived into the crowd, helped Palinev to lift the unconscious Wollkenden. He had discarded his sling, declaring himself healed; still, this exercise of his muscles sent a lance of pain down his right arm.

'What happened?' he cried. 'What went wrong?'

'It's okay, trooper,' said Steele breathlessly, picking himself up, leaning on Palinev. 'I just… overestimated my strength, that's all. Still tired… Perhaps you and Grayle could… could look after Confessor Wollkenden for me?'

Pozhar would have accepted that burden gladly. But at that moment, he heard gunfire from somewhere close by, and he turned to see a squad of Traitor Guardsmen pushing their way towards the Ice Warriors. They were brandishing lasguns, firing into the air so that the heretics parted before them.

Pozhar drew his gun, shouting to Grayle and Palinev, 'Go! Get the confessor and the colonel out of here. I'll hold them off!'

And he started firing – not upwards, but straight into the bodies in front of him.

The cultists were taken unawares. They fell like dominoes, each hit felling three or more of them – and the ripple effect spread back to the Traitor Guardsmen, blocking their path, threatening to knock them down too. They tried to fire back, but the seething mass of people between them and Pozhar made it an impossible shot, and they only succeeded in taking out a few more of their own.

He could have gone after the others, then, could have taken the chance that he had delayed their pursuers long enough for them all to escape. Yes, he could have done that…

The cultists between Pozhar and the Traitor Guardsmen had begun to rally, identified the threat in their midst and, unable to flee, swarmed him instead. Few of them were trained fighters – half of them were women – but they had overwhelming numbers on their side. They punched the Ice Warrior, clawed at him, dragged him down. He saw the glint of a knife blade, too late to avoid its swipe, felt it breaking the synth-skin on his stomach where the sewer creature had holed him with its spines. His lasgun was snatched from him. He took blow after blow to his head. He wasn't quite sure what kept him from falling down – but as long as he was standing, he would fight.

Pozhar was a whirlwind of limbs, punching, kicking, scratching, defying any of his foes to get a firm hold on him.

And clutched in his left fist, he held his ultimate weapon: the primed frag grenade that would collapse the archway behind Steele and the others, slow down anyone who tried to follow them – and also ensure that the heretics that killed him would die by his side. Just as he had planned would happen outside Alpha Hive two mornings ago.

He wondered if this, then, was what the Emperor had spared him for on that occasion. He wanted to believe this. But the itchy grey fur was all over his chest, spreading down his back, and he could no longer open his right hand fully. His fingers had hunched over and he thought his fingernails had grown longer, and Pozhar knew in his heart that his god could have played no part in any of that.

He hadn't come into this battle with the intention of dying in it. At least, he didn't think he had. But the only thing keeping his secret now, he was sure, was the black cloak he was wearing, and he couldn't bear to see the expressions of his comrades, didn't want to have to face their judgement, when that cloak came off.

The Traitor Guardsmen were almost upon him. Another few seconds, and they would have a clear shot, would be able to finish him. He activated the grenade, on a short fuse, and he lured them back towards the archway.

It was better this way, he thought.

Better that his body be blown apart, and then liquefied by the virus bombs before any piece of him could suffer the ignominy of being flung into a Chaos burial pit. Better that no one should have the chance to inspect his remains, that his comrades, let alone his commanders, should never learn of his shame.

Better to let them all believe that Trooper Pozhar died a hero.

MANGELLAN WAS BLIND.

He hadn't seen the las-beam that had hit him, his eyes already teary with smoke. There had just been a flash, and a searing pain. He felt as if his face was on fire. He couldn't see where he was going, didn't know what was happening, he had to trust to his escorts to guide him to safety.

He stumbled into the cooling embrace of his palace, his magnificent Ice Palace, his gods' gift to him – but, for the first time, he felt unsafe within its walls.

He could hear running footsteps, cultists evacuating around him, and he yelled at the Traitor Guardsmen to keep them away from him, to trust no one.

He felt an insistent tugging at his sleeve, heard Furst's voice ask, 'Why are we running, master? What about the sacrifices? Who is guarding them?'

He brushed the irritant away.

'They are chained!' he insisted, leaning against the wall to compose himself, rubbing his eyes and blinking, praying to his gods that the blindness might only be temporary.

'But if their allies have come to free them–'

'Try to use your brains, Furst,' Mangellan snapped, 'such as they are. Steele brought only a handful of soldiers into our hive. How could they have penetrated this palace, my palace, without our knowing about it? No, this attack has come from the inside, from someone who is jealous of all I have achieved, the power I have earned, someone who wished to sully my most glorious moment.'

'I am sure you are correct, master, but–'

'I always knew it would happen. I knew the priests were always scheming and plotting, but to act so boldly... Which of them was it? What do you say, Furst?'

'I... I wouldn't know, master. I–'

Mangellan lashed out, trying to grab Furst by his robes. He felt his hand brush against the loathsome little mutant but failed to take hold of him.

'You are always sneaking about,' he growled, 'lurking in places you should not be, overhearing what you should not have heard. Tell me, Furst, who is to blame for this attack upon my person, this affront to the gods I serve?'

'Nobody, master. None of us would dare cross you in this way.'

'You saw him, didn't you! If not the traitor who planted the bombs, then certainly the wretched opportunist who shot at me, who dared take my sight! I will find him, Furst, and when I am through with him, he will wish he... he...'

Mangellan hadn't felt the knife enter his stomach, so quick and clean had been the incision. Only now, as he felt his blood spill out, as a dull pain spread through him as if he had been kicked... only now that he realised what had happened.

He was speechless, weak, dizzy. He could only listen in uncomprehending horror as Furst leaned close to his ear – Mangellan's legs must have buckled, making him slide down the wall that was supporting him, bringing him down to the mutant's level – and whispered to him, 'You are the one to blame. You presumed too much, thought too much of yourself, and now look what you have wrought. A "handful" of Emperor-lovers has humiliated us, brought you to this. I hear the gods – oh, you were so certain they would not deign to speak to one such as I, that I would not understand them – but I hear them, and they are disappointed with you. You have failed them, Mangellan.'

He was on the floor, although he didn't remember falling. He tried to lift his hands, tried to turn his head to where he imagined his protectors might be, tried to cry out to them, 'Guards! Guards, attend me!'

'They won't help you,' Furst's voice said through the deepening darkness. 'They too know that this is the gods' will. And they now serve a new master.'

CHAPTER EIGHT

CHAPTER EIGHTEEN

Time to Destruction of Cressida: 03.34.45

THE ROOM WAS small, not much bigger than the apartment blocks on the lower hive levels. It was dominated by a single bed, though there was plenty of junk piled in the narrow spaces around it: bits of furniture, clothing, broken lamps, even a couple of paintings with their corners touched by fire.

The walls were made of ice, of course. A large, eight-pointed star had been painted clumsily on one, so that black rivulets ran from it to the floor.

It didn't surprise Blonsky that, with all the power he had, all the space available in the near-emptied hive and in the Ice Palace, Mangellan still had his followers live like this. The harder they had to work to survive, the less time they had to plot against him. Not that the occupant of this room could care much any more.

He lay crumpled beneath the window to the courtyard, through which he had been leaning when Blonsky had kicked open his door. Some Ice Warriors held that it was wrong to shoot an enemy in the back, but Blonsky disagreed. All that mattered was that the heretic was vanquished. To fail to take that shot was the sin.

He only wished he had had a few more shots at Mangellan. He had been taking aim when he had seen that Grayle was in trouble, had had to help him out instead. And the high priest's guards had reacted too fast, faster than he had expected.

One of them was here now. The Chaos Space Marine. His bulk filled the window frame, casting the small room into shadow. Blonsky had backed up as far as the door, scrambling over the bed, wading through the junk, firing his lasgun, knowing it would do little damage, hoping at least to throw off the Chaos Space Marine's balance, make him lose his grip on the outside wall and fall.

He should have given up by now, should have withdrawn.

He hurled a frag grenade, but the Chaos Space Marine caught it easily, and tossed it over his shoulder to erupt in the sky above the courtyard. And then he was inside the room, and Blonsky was out of both ammunition and time.

The Chaos Space Marine raised his gun and fired, and Blonsky slammed the door between them and ran as bolts punched through the wood. Barely a second later, he heard a cracking, wrenching sound as the door was torn from its ice frame.

He raced along empty passageways, sprang down a flight of steps, but his pursuer remained doggedly on his heels. Blonsky could hear his heavy footsteps, thump, thump, thumping behind him. The only thing that kept the Chaos Space Marine from closing the gap between them was the fact that the Ice Warrior was lighter, more lithe, able to corner more efficiently on the slippery, uncarpeted floors.

He sped past two shaken cultists, refugees from the courtyard, and was away from them before they could react to his presence. Next time, he knew he might not be so lucky. He rounded two corners in quick succession, and heard a great crash behind him as the Chaos Space Marine lost control and slammed into a wall. For the first time, Blonsky had a few seconds' grace, and he knew he couldn't wait for a better chance. He chose a door at random, and found himself in a banqueting hall, decorated in rich shades of brown and red with tapestries hanging from the walls.

He had intended to find a hiding place, and hope that the Chaos Space Marine went past. He had known that this was a long shot, but it was the best he had had. He got lucky, again. There were more doors out of the room, on opposite walls at its far end. He hurried to one of them, and was turning the handle as the main door was smashed open, quivering on its hinges.

The Chaos Space Marine leapt into the room, propelling himself over the table. Blonsky didn't wait for him to land. He raced through a small kitchen and out into another passageway, worried that he was starting to lose his bearings, that he might not be able to find his way out. As if that was the worst of his problems.

He had gained some distance on the Chaos Space Marine, but it was still behind him. He could still hear its footsteps. It just kept on coming.

* * *

THERE WERE FEWER heretics on their heels than Palinev had feared.

He didn't stop to ask why, he just counted his blessings. He suspected that the explosion he had heard a moment ago, the distinctive burst of a frag grenade, might have had something to do with it. He didn't stop to wonder what had happened to Pozhar, why he hadn't followed his comrades out of the courtyard, because he guessed he would not like the answer.

Anyway, there were still some heretics out here – cultists and a few Traitor Guardsmen who had escaped before the Ice Warriors had, who were starting to regain their senses, to gather and to talk, and to look for the threat in their midst.

And they found it.

'It's him!' a cultist screamed, pointing at Steele, her finger trembling. Then her eyes turned to Confessor Wollkenden, still unconscious, slung over Grayle's shoulder. 'It's both of them. The sacrifices! They're escaping with the sacrifices! They–'

Palinev shot her through the head, but it was too late. More cultists were coming at them with knives, while others hung back, shouldering lasguns. They must have looked like easy pickings, Steele still leaning on Palinev's shoulder, Grayle encumbered by Wollkenden. But Steele was not as helpless as he seemed. He seized two incoming cultists by their robes, smashed their heads together, thrust them into the path of the first las-beams.

Taking advantage of their temporary human shields, the Ice Warriors ducked into a side passageway – but it came to a dead end, a few metres along.

Steele snatched Grayle's lasgun from him and ordered him to keep back, to keep Wollkenden out of the line of fire. Palinev was already strafing the corridor behind them, discouraging the heretics from approaching, forcing them to run for cover. As his power pack ran dry, Steele took his place and continued the barrage. Palinev reloaded and was able to relieve the colonel in turn.

'We can't keep this up,' Steele grumbled. 'The longer we're pinned down here, the more attention we'll draw. And once that Chaos Space Marine gets wind of our location…' He didn't have to complete the sentence.

'Can we burn through the walls?' asked Palinev.

'I doubt it,' said Grayle. 'We could try, but remember the glacier, remember how it re-formed around the Termite.'

Palinev was firing into an empty passageway. He eased his finger off the trigger, thinking to conserve power – and immediately, four Traitor Guardsmen rushed his position. He fired in concert with Steele, counting them down, one, two, three… but the last of them refused to fall. It just kept on advancing.

The fourth traitor had hung back, using his fellows as cover so that only when he was almost upon the Ice Warriors did they have a clear shot at him. Their beams glanced off his flak jacket, failing to score that critical hit – and Palinev could see behind the traitor the shapes of more of his kind beginning to rise, to crane forward, ready to advance as soon as he engaged the enemy.

They were to be disappointed. The traitor staggered up to the corner, raised his gun, collapsed and died at Palinev's feet.

Steele strafed the corridor for another few seconds, then turned to his two troopers. 'This is what we're going to do,' he said. 'How many frag grenades do you have left between you? We're going to pitch the whole damn lot of them out there, at the heretics, bring down the roof if we can. And then we're going to run like hell in the other direction. Palinev, you must know where we're going, you take point. Grayle, behind him, with Wollkenden. I'll bring up the rear, lay down covering fire, make sure that anyone who survives the explosion doesn't dare so much as glance after us.'

'I should take the rear, sir,' said Grayle. 'It's too dangerous for–'

'Those are my orders, trooper,' interrupted Steele.

'At least take my greatcoat. Yours is in shreds. One bull's-eye from a lasgun and–'

Steele shook his head. 'You have the most important job of any of us. I'm not strong enough yet to carry the confessor. You have to protect him. We move on my mark. Three, two, one… Palinev, do you hear that?'

Palinev did hear it, although his ears were a second behind the colonel's. 'Gunfire, sir. To the right of us. It must be the others. They had to come this way too. They must have come up behind the heretics, taken them by surprise.'

Steele considered that news for a moment, then a tight smile pulled at his lips and he hefted Grayle's lasgun. 'In that case,' he said, 'change of plan.'

ANAKORA HAD KNOWN it wouldn't be easy. No matter how much confusion, how many distractions the Ice Warriors could cause, no matter how good their disguises nor how skilled they were, she had not expected to get out of the Ice Palace without a fight.

Already they appeared to have lost Blonsky; having abandoned their sniping positions up above, she and Gavotski had planned to meet him at the base of a flight of stairs. They had waited as long as they could.

They had set off running at first, but slowed down as they had begun to run into heretics from the courtyard. They had tried to look less like they had an urgent purpose, less like they were trying to get out.

Anakora's stomach had tightened as a squad of Traitor Guardsmen had rushed out of a side passageway into their path, but they had drawn their cultists' robes around themselves, bowed their heads and kept their cool, and the traitors had hurried right on by.

Not long after that, their path had converged with those of Barreski and Mikhaelev, and Anakora was glad that two comrades at least had made it this far.

And then they had heard las-fire, and she had feared the worst.

A score of heretics had gathered at a four-way junction, and more were rushing up to join them from all directions. No one had questioned the arrival of what they took to be four more reinforcements to their cause. The heretics were laying siege to an opening in the wall a few metres away, being kept at bay only by a volley of las-fire from said opening. Anakora had guessed who was wielding the guns, even before she had caught a glimpse of Colonel Steele's face.

A dark-skinned Traitor Guardsman with narrow eyes and pinched nostrils had taken command. He was barking out orders: 'Hold your fire! Let the Emperor-lovers discharge their power packs, then they'll be defenceless.'

Gavotski moved up behind him, tapped him on the shoulder – and the traitor turned to find himself staring down a gun barrel. A las-beam stabbed into his right eye and fried his brain. The other three Ice Warriors took this as their cue to act. Anakora took another traitor by surprise and slit his throat with her knife. Barreski tried to do likewise, but his chosen victim had faster reflexes and was able to throw off his hold. And Mikhaelev was firing his lasgun on full auto, apparently indiscriminately, creating the maximum amount of panic.

As in the courtyard, the cultists were confused, terrified by this sudden threat in their midst, by the loss of their leader. Some of them fled. But others chose to fight back.

At first, the Ice Warriors had the advantage. The cultists still weren't quite sure who their enemies were, which of the robed figures around them they could trust, to whom they could turn their backs. It made them fight with one eye over their shoulders, which proved to be the downfall of many of them. Anakora bludgeoned two to the ground with her fists, and gutted a third with her blade. She smiled to herself as a disoriented cultist plunged a knife into a friend's ribs. His fellows interpreted his mistake as an act of treachery and fell upon him.

The Traitor Guardsmen, however – the few that remained – were more perceptive, zeroing in on their true foes. Anakora found herself in a knife fight with one, straining to get her blade past his defences, aware that every second he could keep her occupied was a second longer for his allies to rally.

Sure enough, she felt hands grasping at her from behind, an arm around her throat, and she was held by two cultists. If they had been armed, she would have been dead already. But the Traitor Guardsman did have a knife, and Anakora's arms were pinned so that all she could do to defend herself was to kick out at him, at the same time pushing backwards, trying to slam her captors into the wall, to make them release their grips. Out of the corner of her eye, she saw that Mikhaelev was in trouble too, forced onto his knees.

And then, once again, the tide of battle turned – as Colonel Steele and Palinev broke cover and came racing onto the scene with guns blazing.

THEY WERE RUNNING again.

Somehow they always seemed to be running – and Gavotski's lungs were burning, his legs aching, and he began to wonder if he was finally getting too old for this.

They had disengaged from the melee as soon as they were able, knowing that they couldn't win that fight, that their enemies' numbers would just keep on growing. There were Traitor Guardsmen at their heels, sending las-beams after them. The Ice Warriors were returning fire as best they could. Barreski and Grayle, both of whom seemed to have lost their guns, were carrying Wollkenden.

And as they hurried past a junction, Gavotski saw a robed figure barrelling down the connecting corridor towards them. He whirled, brought up his lasgun... and the figure skidded to a halt, threw up his hands and whipped back his hood, to reveal the flushed face of Trooper Blonsky.

'He... he's behind me!' the new arrival panted, gesturing over his shoulder.

And there he was now: the Chaos Space Marine, stumbling into view just a couple of hundred metres behind Blonsky, raising a bolt pistol. Gavotski grabbed his exhausted comrade, bundled him around the corner, and pushed him off after the others. He hurled a frag grenade at the Chaos Space Marine in the hope of at least slowing him down, and then he followed at full pelt.

They returned, at last, to the stone cellar through which they had entered the Ice Palace an hour ago. Anakora and Mikhaelev took up positions in the doorway, firing out into the corridor, as the others negotiated the slippery steps and began to squeeze themselves, one by one, through the hole in the wall. This rearguard action would buy them time, but not much. Gavotski knew that once the Chaos Space Marine caught up with them, his two comrades would have no choice but to fall back.

He helped Grayle feed Wollkenden through the hole headfirst, to

Barreski and Palinev on the far side, below. Then he wriggled through himself, and dropped down into the sewer tunnel. Colonel Steele hadn't seen this side of Iota Hive before, and he was inspecting his surroundings in the glow of his comrades' lamp packs.

Palinev set off along the narrow brick ledge, Barreski and Grayle hauling Wollkenden along after him. Steele shouted at them to wait. 'We need to head for the spaceport,' he said. 'If there's still a way off this planet, one we can reach in time, that's where it'll be. And it's in that direction.' He pointed through the wall, and Gavotski didn't doubt for a second that he knew what he was talking about.

'I don't know if we can get through that way, sir,' said Palinev. 'These tunnels are a maze. We might end up being cornered, and with that Traitor Space Marine on our tails...'

'Yeah,' Barreski muttered to Blonsky, 'thanks for leading that straight to us.'

'And the less time we spend down here,' said Gavotski, 'the better.' Catching Steele's inquisitive look, he said, 'I'll explain later. With your permission, sir, I'd like to make our way back to the mutant chapel. I'll, ah, explain about that too. We can get our bearings there, and strike out for the port above ground. We might even get some help, someone to run interference for us.'

Steele nodded, accepting that his sergeant knew the situation better than he did at the moment – and the Ice Warriors set off again. Gavotski lingered behind, to help first Mikhaelev and then Anakora down from the cellar. As Anakora's first foot touched down, Gavotski saw the muzzle of a bolt pistol poking through the entrance hole above her, and he threw himself at the startled trooper, flattening them both against the side of the tunnel.

A hail of bolts rained down at their backs, and churned up the black water below them. They waited for a lull in the firing, then they hurried after their comrades. The last of them, Mikhaelev, was just disappearing through a hole in the wall – and as Gavotski reached the hole, he heard a heavy thud behind him, and he turned to look, and found his worst fear realised.

The Chaos Space Marine had just dropped into the tunnel, and was turning to follow them. But there was something else too, something in the water.

And the water erupted, and a monster filled the tunnel, looming over the new arrival, its jaws darting for his throat: a sewer creature, perhaps attracted by the Chaos Space Marine's own bolter fire – a creature like the one the Ice Warriors had fought earlier, only Gavotski thought this one might have been even larger.

The Chaos Space Marine was trying to bat its thrusting head away from him, swiping at the creature with his chainsword, carving into its scales, drawing black blood. But Gavotski didn't wait to see the outcome of their battle.

He slipped away from there, and he kept on running.

THERE HAD BEEN rubble on top of the manhole cover.

Palinev had been unable to shift it. Blonsky had volunteered to climb the ladder instead, to put his shoulder to the task. By now, of course, they had all been worried about what they might find out there, in the chapel, on the surface. Steele had listened for a moment, and assured his squad that he could hear nobody. No foes. But no friends either.

The cover had yielded at last, and Blonsky had been the first to climb through it, to stand blinking in the unexpected light, though the others had soon joined him.

The Chaos forces had done a more thorough job, this time.

They had left no walls of the chapel standing. They had demolished its columns, brought down its roof. They had burned what was left of its pews, and smashed its altar beyond all hope of reclamation. The smell of cordite still hung heavy in the air, as did the altogether more rotten stench of death.

Blonsky jabbed at the nearest corpse with his toe, turned it over to inspect it properly. He didn't want to stoop, didn't want to get closer to it than he already was. It was a mutant, of course. Its grey fur was matted with dark blood, beneath its torn blue smock. It might have been one of the loyalists they had met, one to which they had talked. He couldn't tell. They all looked the same to him.

'What happened here?' asked Steele. Gavotski told him about the mutants, their chapel and their apparent desire to help. Steele frowned and said nothing. Blonsky guessed that he was unhappy about his men allying themselves with the impure, but he didn't want to question his sergeant's judgement, not in front of the troopers.

'Anyway,' sighed Gavotski, 'it seems they got what they wanted. They died, fighting. For the Emperor.'

'It must have happened just after we left,' said Palinev. 'Maybe just a few minutes after. Do you think any of them escaped?'

Gavotski shrugged. 'Without a full search of the rubble…'

'Either way,' said Steele, 'it looks like we are on our own after all.' With a sidelong glance at Gavotski, he added, 'And perhaps it's best that way.'

Blonsky couldn't have agreed more. 'The only good mutant,' he muttered with some satisfaction, 'is a dead mutant.'

CHAPTER NINETEEN

Time to Destruction of Cressida: 01.29.22

THE SPACEPORT LAY at the eastern edge of the hive, on one of its mid-levels. Steele knew the way, of course, thanks to his brief inspection of the city maps the day before.

And so, for the second time, he found himself in the back of a rickety old truck, pressed in against his comrades. Grayle and Barreski had taken the cab, still in their black robes – although Steele doubted whether the disguises would do them much good, not with every heretic in the hive on their trail.

They had been driving for some time when he felt the truck swerve, heard its tyres squeal, felt an impact with its front bumper. 'What's happening up there?' he yelled.

'We've been seen, sir,' Barreski's voice came back through the partition that separated them. 'A bunch of cultists. Grayle tried to run them down – got a few of them, too – but two more escaped.'

'And they'll run to the nearest vox-caster,' sighed Mikhaelev.

Steele feared that he was right. Until now, he had been banking on the hope that their enemies didn't know where they were heading, didn't know they had lost their own transport. The bulk of the Chaos forces, with luck, would be guarding the hive's exits, leaving a clear run to the Ice Warriors' real objective. Now, that hope was lost. Now, all they could do was try to reach the spaceport first.

Steele hammered on the partition, and shouted to Grayle to put his foot down.

Confessor Wollkenden had woken half an hour ago, looking

nauseous. He had stared at the faces of each of the Ice Warriors in turn, before drawing his knees up to his chest and resting his forehead on them, shutting out the world. Steele had collected dry rations and water from his troopers, and the confessor had consumed them greedily, but he hadn't moved since nor spoken a word.

He looked up now, though – and in a loud, clear voice, he said, 'Is this transport appropriate for a war hero? I will have somebody's head for this. This engine should be silent. We don't want *him* to hear, to come down here. Is it almost time to eat? They're waiting for me to address them. They need me to give them hope, and the strength to resist.'

The others were looking at each other, at the roof, anywhere but at the confessor. Steele shared their discomfort. He had been worried about Wollkenden since he had found him in the dungeons, had feared that whatever Mangellan had done to him had broken his mind. He had pushed that fear to the back of his thoughts, concentrated on the job at hand. Now he had no choice but to face it.

'You're free, confessor,' he said. 'Mangellan isn't coming. He can't hurt you any more. Do you remember me? I'm Colonel Stanislev Steele. I rescued you. I just need you to be patient, to be strong, and we'll get you out of here. We'll get you to a doctor. They can treat your… fever.'

'I still have some water left,' offered Palinev, 'if you think that might… I mean, if the confessor…'

Wollkenden looked Steele in the eye, and he said, 'I'll say a prayer for us.'

Steele smiled. 'I'm sure we would all appreciate that, sir.'

'And you will kill him for me, won't you?'

'You don't have to worry about that, confessor. In a few hours' time, there will be nobody alive on this planet. Mangellan will be–'

'I don't mean him, not the one with the words. I mean the big bruiser in the cloak, the one who punched me in the face. You will make him suffer, won't you? You will make him pay for presuming to lay his hands on a holy man.'

Steele was saved from having to answer that, as, again, something smacked into the truck and made its frame judder. 'What the hell has Grayle hit now?' complained Blonsky, who had been caught unawares and banged his head. But Steele and a couple of the others had felt that this impact was different from the first – and his enhanced hearing confirmed it.

It wasn't the front of the truck that had hit something this time, rather that something had landed on its roof… something that was moving about up there. Something with a roaring chainsword…

* * *

THE TIP OF the sword came slicing through the roof of the cab, above Grayle's head. He let out a cry, and slid down in his seat until he could only just see through the windscreen, barely see where he was going. He spun the wheel hard right, left, right again, and pumped the pedals furiously. Beside him, Barreski was tossed back and forth, and Grayle could hear muffled protests from the rear compartment.

But he could not shake his unwanted passenger.

The Chaos Space Marine clung on, and his sword cut deeper. It was rising and falling, in a sawing motion, scoring a seam across the roof. Then the sword was withdrawn, and Grayle saw gauntleted fingers scrabbling at that seam, widening it.

Barreski fired at those fingers – he had replaced his lasgun with one taken from a dead Traitor Guardsman in the street – and the hand was withdrawn, stung. A moment later, it returned, looking for and finding fresh purchase. And then, with a terrible, nerve-jangling wrench, the Chaos Space Marine peeled back the roof, and Grayle gaped up into his leering face, could smell his fetid breath.

'Everybody, brace yourselves!' he yelled, and he stamped on the brake pedal.

This time, the Chaos Space Marine was taken by surprise. He was reaching for Grayle when the truck jolted to a halt and catapulted him forwards. He hit the windscreen, shattering the plexiglas, and then slid sideways across the bonnet and disappeared from sight. Feverishly, Grayle slammed the engine into reverse. He felt his front right wheel bouncing over an obstacle in the road – the monster's head, he hoped, although whether this was the case or not it seemed to make little difference.

The Chaos Space Marine was already back on his feet, his head down, charging towards the retreating truck like an enraged bull. He looked a mess, his black armour barely clinging to his battered body. His left arm had been amputated at the elbow, presumably by the teeth of the sewer creature. One of his eyes was missing. He had dropped his chainsword, but he was wielding his bolt pistol.

Grayle couldn't outpace him, not driving backwards. He forced his back wheels around, made to set off along another street. He was too late. The Chaos Space Marine had caught up to them. He braced himself against the bumper so that no matter how hard the engine strained, or how fast the wheels spun, they couldn't gain headway against him.

And now the Chaos Space Marine stooped, took the truck by its axle, lifted it, one-handed, and Barreski was banging on the partition, yelling, 'Everybody out!' and he and Grayle kicked open their doors, and leapt as the Chaos Space Marine flexed a powerful shoulder and gave the truck one final *twist*...

* * *

BLONSKY AND MIKHAELEV had been the nearest troopers to the back doors, and thus the first two out of them. Steele had made sure that Wollkenden went next, helping him along with a push to the back when he had hesitated. The confessor had fallen awkwardly, landing face first in the street, and Steele had leapt down beside him and hoisted him to his feet.

All of which had left Anakora, Gavotski and Palinev in the back of the truck as it was flipped over.

Anakora had been in the doorway, poised to jump, when the world had spun in front of her. The next thing she knew, she was on her back, tangled up with her comrades, on a plasteel surface that had been upright a moment ago. She had bumped her head, and black spots were crowding her vision, threatening to close in, to enshroud her in their darkness. She would not give in to them.

She could hear las-fire, and the answering bark of a bolt pistol. She couldn't just lie there, letting the others down.

Palinev was the first to extricate himself and crawl away. Anakora watched as his blurry shape was swallowed by a fierce white light – streetlights, she realised, shining in from outside. The truck was on its side, and one of its back doors – the higher one – had fallen shut. The lower door had been snapped from its hinges. Its frame had crumpled a little, but there was still room to squeeze through it.

'Are you OK?' asked Gavotski, waving a hand in front of Anakora's eyes.

She gritted her teeth and gave a determined nod. Gavotski followed Palinev through the bright white square. Anakora blinked, wishing her eyes would clear, and forced herself up onto her hands and knees and made to follow him.

Then she heard a strangulated cry, and Gavotski was whipped away from her – and she caught her breath at the sight of a pair of black armoured boots through the exit hole. Gavotski had crawled right into the Chaos Space Marine's clutches.

She could see his boots too, half a metre off the ground, kicking furiously. He was pinned to the back of the truck, doubtless having the life squeezed out of him, and the desperate las-fire of the other Ice Warriors was doing little to change that situation. But from down here, up close, Anakora could make out cracks in the Chaos Space Marine's black armour. She could see the flesh beneath them.

She pulled her knife, thrust it into an exposed ankle, twisting it around and burying it deeper, hoping to sever a tendon. She couldn't tell if she had been successful in this – but she had certainly had some effect. The Chaos Space Marine gave a howl of fury and flung Gavotski aside. Then he gripped the truck's remaining door and tore it free, to expose his attacker.

It was only now that Anakora saw how damaged he was. She couldn't believe he was still standing, still fighting. But she didn't doubt that he was still more than capable of killing her in a second.

She scrambled away from him, until she was backed up against the partition to the driver's cab and was cornered there. The Chaos Space Marine dropped to his haunches, down to her level, blocking out the white light, and he screamed obscenities at her, and brought up his bolt pistol. Her head was still pounding, and she closed her eyes and yelled to her comrades, 'Go! Get out of here while you can!'

Just as Steele had yelled at her when they had last fought this monster.

But then: she heard a mechanical scream, and her would-be executioner stiffened. His eyes glazed over, blood spewed from his mouth, and he turned, he made to rise, but the effort was too much for him and he toppled and fell – and Anakora saw a chainsword embedded in his back, sputtering and sparking.

Palinev helped her out of the truck, and she stood unsteadily in what now seemed to be a rather faint light after all. And like the rest of the Ice Warriors, her eyes were drawn to her commander, his face and his chest still painted with vile symbols from the ceremony – although he had tried to scrub them off with sewer water – and his right hand held away from his body as if he considered it unclean.

It was with that hand, Anakora realised, that he must have lifted the Chaos Space Marine's own weapon, his augmented muscles giving him the strength to do so.

But there was no satisfaction in Colonel Steele's eyes at his victory. Just a look of deep-seated disgust.

THEY REMAINED ON foot after that. Steele didn't want to waste time searching for another working vehicle – and the spaceport, he said, was only just over a kilometre away. They formed up in two ranks and advanced at double time. The effort of keeping pace with each other, of maintaining formation and step, helped to spur on these soldiers, to overcome the fatigue they were all feeling. It helped them feel more in control, like they had imposed a little order of their own upon this chaotic world – and even Wollkenden responded well to this. He said nothing as he marched at Steele's side, although he stumbled now and again.

Palinev could tell they were approaching their goal, because the buildings grew a little taller, a little more proud. Eagle crests began to appear over the doorways of customs and shipping offices, and the streets grew wider and brighter, more like those on the upper levels.

Steele brought his squad to a halt and ordered them to break step, to proceed with caution. He appeared to be worried – and a minute later, Palinev learned why.

There were people ahead of them. He could hear them – they could all hear them now – talking and laughing. The Ice Warriors took cover in a narrow alleyway, and Steele sent Palinev ahead to see what they were facing.

The spaceport was a magnificent, circular building of white stone, studded with dark windows. Evidently, there had been small-arms fighting here, and the front wall was pockmarked but unholed. Laid out in front of that wall was a wide forecourt, in which broken fountains brimmed with frozen black water. Lifter tubes had been shattered, and trees – real organic trees – had withered and died. Once, this area would have been a welcoming first sight for visitors to Iota Hive, maybe to Cressida itself. Now, it gave an entirely different impression.

Palinev looked down on all of this from a gantry between two buildings. Below him, a wide flight of steps swept down from the street where the rest of his squad hid, to the forecourt and the enticing open gates beyond it.

At some point, a sleek, black grav-car had come speeding this way, its driver presumably hoping to ferry an important passenger to safety. It had lost control, had maybe come under fire, and had smacked into a pillar at the top of the steps, crumpling its front end. The car was empty now; Palinev wondered if its occupants had escaped or been dragged from the wreckage.

There were more grav-cars down on the forecourt, most of them burnt out or turned over, or both. There was also a dirty old bus – transport for the less privileged – leaning against a fountain, its windows broken, its tyres slashed.

And there were heretics: cultists, Traitor Guardsmen, mutants, even a few spawn, spread out as far as Palinev could see, almost certainly surrounding the whole building, and more of them arriving with each moment that passed. The encounter with the Chaos Space Marine had cost the Ice Warriors dearly. Their enemies had beaten them here.

Palinev slipped away from his vantage point, dispirited, and returned to the others. Steele listened to his report in grave silence, and Palinev knew that he was only confirming what the colonel had expected to hear.

'We have less than an hour before the virus bombs drop,' said Steele. 'We don't have time to find another escape route, even if we had somewhere to look. Our only hope, however small, lies in that spaceport, and the sooner we make our move the fewer enemies will be standing between us and it.'

No one could argue with that. Still, it seemed as if a dark cloud had settled upon the squad, and Palinev could feel its weight too. It seemed so unfair that they had come so far to fall at this final hurdle. They had achieved so much, pulled off feats that had seemed impossible, and no one would even know.

'I won't give you the speech again,' said Gavotski. 'You all know what to do, and you know what the odds are against us. Just remember that, last time, we bucked those odds. Nine of us went into the Ice Palace, and nine of us, including Confessor Wollkenden, came out again. If that doesn't prove that the Emperor is with us, then nothing does. I know you'll make me proud.'

THE HERETICS' VOICES were getting louder.

It wasn't just that Grayle was drawing closer to them. He could hear that the crowd was growing in size, and in confidence too. He feared that, at any moment, someone might come rushing up the steps from the spaceport to find him and Palinev sneaking along the street towards them.

Either that or, by chance, reinforcements might come up behind them.

He quickened his pace, reasoning that with all the noise down there, no one would hear the footsteps of two men up here. He was still twenty metres away from his objective, the stricken grav-car, when Palinev took his arm and brought him to a halt.

'This is as far as we can go,' said the scout, 'without being seen from down there.' Grayle nodded and dropped onto his stomach, preparing to pull himself the rest of the way on his elbows.

That was when the pitch of the crowd changed, confidence becoming fear in an instant. And then Grayle heard a series of staccato explosions. Then gunfire.

He looked at Palinev in alarm. Palinev looked back at him with a helpless shrug. Then the scout turned, made a dash for the side of the road and swung himself up onto a metal gantry. He returned a few seconds later, his cheeks flushed with excitement.

'It's the mutants!' he reported. 'The loyalist mutants. There are... I didn't know there were so many of them. More than we ever saw. More than the heretics killed at the chapel. They're everywhere, climbing up through the manholes. They've taken the heretics by surprise.'

It seemed that the Emperor was with the Ice Warriors after all.

'Can they win?' asked Grayle.

Palinev shook his head. 'There aren't enough of them. But they're providing a perfect distraction. If we move fast enough...'

Grayle nodded, stood and raced to the grav-car. He doubted that anyone would notice him now – and even if they did they would probably be too busy to do much about it. As he reached the steps, he caught a glimpse of the melee that his comrade had described, below – but his attention was reserved for the car itself.

The driver's door had jammed shut in the crash. Grayle had to brace his foot against the bodywork, had to pull at it with all his might. It came free at last, flying up with such force that it almost caught him on the chin. He leapt into the vehicle, and sent a silent appeal to its machine-spirits as he jabbed at the dashboard runes. Fortunately, as Grayle had already noticed, the twin engines were housed at the back of the vehicle, and were therefore relatively unscathed.

They caught on the third attempt, and the grav-car gave a protesting screech as its back end was raised, but its front end remained stubbornly embedded in its pillar. Grayle eased the vehicle backwards, and winced as it slowly tore itself free, as parts of it became detached and clattered to the ground. For a moment, he feared that the car might have been supporting the pillar, that it might now come crashing down across his windscreen – but, although the pillar wobbled, it held.

And the car was free now, and picking up speed, and Grayle could see in his rear-view mirror that the rest of his squad was running to meet it.

They bundled Wollkenden into the back seat first, told him to keep his head down. Steele and Gavotski squeezed in to each side of him, while Anakora and Palinev joined Grayle in the front. The car couldn't lift any more weight than that, so Barreski, Blonsky and Mikhaelev would have to advance in its wake, trust that Grayle could clear a path for them and also lay down some covering fire behind him.

'Everyone ready?' asked Grayle. 'Then hold on to something!'

And he stepped on the accelerator.

The grav-car's top speed was not exactly remarkable, but it seemed fast enough as it hurtled towards the steps and shot over the edge. The Ice Warriors were flying for a moment, but they came down with a bone-shaking jolt. The car surfed its antigravity cushion onto the spaceport forecourt, where a jostling crowd tried to part before it but some stumbled across its mangled bonnet or tumbled beneath its skirt.

A few of the heretics – those not immediately occupied by mutant attackers – saw what was happening, saw that their targets were getting away, and started to fire. Most of them were cut down in a second by the three Ice Warriors following in the car's wake.

And then they were through the spaceport gates, speeding along the main concourse, and the sounds of battle were receding behind them.

CHAPTER TWENTY

Time to Destruction of Cressida: 00.18.49

THE FIGHTING HAD spilled into the spaceport. The grav-car smacked into a smock-wearing mutant, tossed it into the air. It landed on the windshield, clung there for a second, and its red eyes seemed to be pleading with the Ice Warriors inside the vehicle: why?

Steele didn't want to think about that, didn't want to have to acknowledge that his life, Wollkenden's life, all their lives, might have been saved by such aberrations. He blinked, and the mutant was gone, fallen beneath the car to die.

And Grayle drove on. He took a sharp right turn through a vandalised waiting room, crashed through a glass door, and then they were out on the spaceport's main ramp: a vast circular floor that would once have been filled with spacecraft of all types. Right now, it was almost empty. Steele had expected that. He and his squad wouldn't have been the first to try to leave Iota Hive this way. He could only pray that the previous evacuees had left them something they could use.

'There,' he said, 'that frigate. You think you can fly that, Grayle?'

'I don't know, sir. I don't have much experience in the air. I could try.' Grayle had already brought them around so that they were circling the decrepit old vessel. They saw that its engine housings had been torn open, perhaps by an asteroid strike, perhaps by enemy fire. Steele took a cursory glance at the exposed machinery, then shook his head and instructed Grayle to keep going.

They could see the concave far wall now, lined with hatchways. Some of them gaped open, and they tantalised Steele with a view of the grey sky of Cressida beyond. He had only been in this Chaos-held cesspit for a day, but it had been too long. That way lay freedom, if they could just claim it.

'This one might be worth a look, sir.' Grayle had pulled up beside a tiny lander, similar to the one in which Wollkenden had made his forced landing – and hardly in better condition. Its surfaces were encrusted with ice, its engine pods fire-blackened, and its landing legs were crippled so that it listed to one side. It was a sorry sight, and it was easy to see why the ship had been overlooked thus far – but there was nothing to indicate that it couldn't be made to fly.

The Ice Warriors piled out of the car. Grayle and Anakora worked on the lander's frozen hatch with their knives until, with a throaty whine and a splintering of ice, it opened part-way, and Grayle was able to duck through. Steele ordered Palinev to follow him, with Wollkenden.

The Chaos forces had started to pour onto the ramp. Barreski, Blonsky and Mikhaelev came running ahead of them, firing back at them – but, as Steele watched, Blonsky was cut down in a crossfire of las-beams. He wasn't dead yet, but he had evidently been crippled. The only thing Steele could have done for him, if he could have reached him, was to put him out of his misery.

It looked like Barreski and Mikhaelev had reached the same conclusion – because, after a brief hesitation, they resumed their fighting withdrawal and left their fallen comrade behind. They joined Steele, Gavotski and Anakora, breathless and, in Mikhaelev's case, wounded, a livid burn standing out on his temple.

Gavotski was already barking out orders: 'This ship has armour plating. Use it. Find a defensible position and fire at will!'

With the Emperor's favour, thought Steele, it might work. There were less than a score of heretics in the first wave – most of them, he guessed, were still out on the forecourt, dealing with the mutated loyalists – and so far they were wielding nothing more deadly than lasguns. They couldn't damage the lander itself, so the only threat they posed to Wollkenden was if they were able to board it. He prayed that, with just five Ice Warriors including himself, he could stop them from doing that.

He crouched behind one of the ship's wings, as las-beams cracked into it and were comfortably absorbed. When it was safe to do so, he returned fire, and gritted his teeth with malicious satisfaction as he mowed down cultist after cultist.

The second wave came with barely a moment's respite. And this one was larger, and consisted primarily of mutants and spawn: a sure sign that the heretics were becoming more organised, enough to send in their cannon fodder ahead of them.

A particularly large, hairy mutant shrugged off all the las-fire aimed at it, staying on its feet long enough to reach Steele. It came around the wing, growling and clawing at him. When the colonel avoided its first swipes, the mutant shoulder-charged him instead, and slammed him into the hull.

He jammed his bayonet into its throat, fighting a gag reflex as its stinking blood spewed over him. The mutant fought on, although it could only have been kept alive now by the force of its own fury.

Steele ducked under its claws and slipped beneath the lopsided lander itself, squeezing himself into the acute angle where its belly almost touched the ground. The mutant tried to follow, but its shoulders were too broad. It strained to reach its prey, and its claws came within a hair's breadth of Steele's chest – but, at last, it shuddered and died. At almost the same moment, an enemy las-beam struck one of the few undamaged struts around Steele, and it bowed and almost broke. The ship's bulk shifted over his head and threatened to drop, to crush him. He scrambled out of there as fast as he could.

The heretics' advance had faltered. Steele's comrades were mounting a stout defence, as was the Valhallan way, giving him a moment to pause and take stock. He saw three Traitor Guardsmen darting behind a gutted lander. They were trying to circle around behind the ship, just as he would have done in their place.

Steele sent a volley of las-beams after them. He didn't manage to kill any of them before they took cover – he was starting to miss his bionic eye, still on auto-repair after its latest discharge – but he did send a message. The traitors knew he had seen them. They would proceed more slowly, more carefully, from now on – if they dared to proceed at all.

One of the lander's engines groaned, and belched smoke from its exhaust port before it fell silent again. The hull of the ship creaked and shuddered, and gave an alarming lurch as the weakened landing leg buckled a little further.

Steele concentrated on gunning down the oncoming mutants. The most important task was out of his hands. It was all down to Grayle now.

And then, to his relief, the engines started – both of them.

'Fall back,' he yelled to the others. 'Onto the ship. We're getting out of here!'

He was closest to the stubby loading ramp. He raced up it, firing a few parting shots back over his shoulder, and leapt through the hatchway that Grayle had left half-open.

He was greeted by a sight that made his heart sink into his boots.

Palinev was sprawled out on the floor of the passenger compartment, unconscious. Of Confessor Wollkenden, there was no sign.

Steele dropped by his scout's side, and shook him vigourously until his eyelids fluttered. 'The confessor,' he hissed. 'Where is the confessor?'

'He... took me by surprise,' groaned Palinev. 'Came up... behind me.

He was burbling something about… I think he thought I was Mangellan, he…'

Steele didn't need to hear any more. He turned to find Gavotski and Mikhaelev behind him, pushed his way past them and collided with Anakora and Barreski in the hatchway. Gavotski began to ask him what was happening, where he was going.

'None of you,' Steele ordered, 'are to leave this ship under any circumstances. Give me as much time as you can – but as soon as it looks as if the heretics might board, you get up to that cockpit and you tell Grayle to lift off, whether Wollkenden and I have returned or not. Is that understood, sergeant?'

He didn't wait for an answer.

He was out in the open again, cursing himself for not having foreseen this, for not having detailed more men to watch Wollkenden – for not having heard as the confessor had knocked out Palinev and escaped behind his back. It must have happened, he thought, while he was underneath the ship, occupied with the mutant.

The heretics were just realising that the lander was no longer defended, just starting to close in. They reacted to Steele's sudden reappearance – too slowly. Steele reasoned that Wollkenden would have made for the nearest cover. He saw a line of man-sized, metal-framed packing crates, and he leapt behind them as the first las-beams stabbed out behind him.

His acoustic enhancers led him straight to the confessor, who was sitting behind the crates, whimpering into his hands. He seized Wollkenden by the front of his robes, hauled him to his feet. 'I'm sorry I don't have time to show you all due respect, sir, but this is the situation: you are boarding that ship with me – and I would rather you did so willingly, because if I have to carry you it will probably get us both killed, but I will knock you out again if I have to. Which is it to be?'

Wollkenden squirmed out of his grasp and ran for it. Steele caught him before he could take two steps, and slammed him into a crate hard enough to splinter one of its wooden panels. 'Get your hands off me!' Wollkenden gasped, winded. 'You're just like the rest of them, telling me what to do. He was right all along, with his words… Let me go, I want to go to him!'

'You're confused,' said Steele. 'You don't know what you're saying. I need you to trust me, confessor. I need you to do as I say, just for a few–'

A Traitor Guardsman, bolder than Steele had expected, stepped into view. His lasgun was readied, but he didn't fire. Perhaps he was out of power, or the gun had simply jammed. Steele didn't stop to question his good fortune. He bundled Wollkenden into the narrow space between two crates and started firing himself. The traitor leapt back into cover, but Steele could hear footsteps running to join him.

He cursed under his breath. Wollkenden had delayed him too long. Their way back to the lander was blocked, and the heretics were moving to surround them. They couldn't stay where they were. But there was nowhere to run, nowhere that didn't involve breaking cover and making themselves easy targets.

If Steele had been alone, he could have hauled himself up onto one of the crates, got the drop on his foes from up there – but he doubted Wollkenden could make the climb even if he was willing to try.

Wollkenden… Suddenly, it occurred to Steele that his presence might be his greatest asset, that that traitor's gun might not have jammed after all.

He turned on the confessor, spun him around. He yanked his arm up behind his back, slipped his arm around Wollkenden's throat and pulled tight to choke his words of protest. 'Sorry about this, sir,' he muttered, 'but needs must, and this is the only way I can think of to keep you alive.'

He pushed Wollkenden ahead of him, stepped out from behind the crate, found himself facing a score of armed traitors...

...and was relieved to find that his hunch had been right. The traitors kept him covered with their guns, but didn't dare fire, couldn't risk hitting his hostage. Evidently, they had been ordered to retake Wollkenden, their offering to their gods, alive. It occurred to Steele that those same orders might apply to him too – until Wollkenden's legs gave way and he sagged in the colonel's grip, and one of the traitors fired a las-beam, tried to hit Steele over the confessor's head and only missed him by a whisker.

'I wouldn't try that again,' Steele snarled. 'Even if you could hit me, I could snap Wollkenden's neck as I went down. And I swear this by the Emperor's name, I will do it. I will see him dead, rather than let Mangellan have him.'

'Don't speak that name,' spat one of the traitors. 'Mangellan is dead. He failed our gods and has paid the price for it. Furst is our high priest now.'

'Then you're in more trouble than I thought,' said Steele.

He was inching his way around them, keeping his back to the crates so that no one could come up behind him – and he could see it now, the lander, his goal. Its engines were still ticking over, ice melting and dripping from its hull.

And it was under attack.

The ship had been rushed by mutants and spawn – and Steele could see Barreski and Anakora in the hatchway, fighting to keep it clear, to keep the creatures away from it – a losing battle.

As he watched, one muscular mutant landed a blow to Barreski's head, send him reeling back into the ship, out of sight – and then it disappeared inside after him. Anakora had to fall back as two more creatures forced their way on board. And there were more of them, jostling each other, knocking each other off the loading ramp in their haste to follow. In a few seconds' time, the Ice Warriors would be overwhelmed, the ship taken. Unless…

The pitch of the engines changed, the sound building to a deafening shriek, and the lander begin to haul itself into the air.

For a moment, all eyes were off Steele and Wollkenden, but Steele couldn't take advantage of this distraction – because he was staring too, watching as his last hope of survival, of completing his mission, rose out of his reach.

The lander rotated clumsily, orienting itself towards the exit hatches. The few mutants that had clung to its landing ramp were shaken free and dashed to the floor. Another was wedged in the open hatchway – but as Steele watched, this too was thrown clear by a volley of las-fire from inside the ship. It gave him some satisfaction to know that his squad was still fighting in there.

And then another hatchway slid open – in the belly of the lander, this time – and something was tossed out: a coiled something that rolled and unfurled as it fell, something that told Steele that his men were still fighting for more than themselves.

He raced around the still-gaping traitors, somehow finding the strength to lift Wollkenden off his feet, to carry him. He leapt for the trailing ladder, and caught it with his left hand.

That was when the firing started, the traitors no doubt reasoning that Furst would prefer Wollkenden dead than escaped. A las-beam glanced off Steele's shoulder, only part of its force absorbed by the ragged remains of his armoured greatcoat, and he clenched his teeth against the searing pain and forced himself to hold on, although he couldn't feel his fingers any longer.

The ship lined itself up with an exit hatch, shot forwards, and the sudden acceleration almost yanked Steele's numbed left arm out of its socket. His right hand was still fastened around Wollkenden's arm, the confessor reaching but unable to establish a grip on the ladder for himself. Then the lander's hull scraped the hatchway, showering them both with sparks – a sign of Grayle's piloting inexperience – and the ground dropped away beneath them, and Wollkenden fell…

Steele caught his hand, felt the augmetics in his right shoulder whirring and straining to arrest the confessor's plunge.

They were soaring above fields of snow now, above glaciers, high enough to see the burning spires of Alpha Hive towards the horizon, to trace the whole of the Ice Warriors' journey from there to here. And Wollkenden's legs were flailing, pedalling at the air, and his face was white, his eyes bulging with fear.

Five minutes. That was all the time they had, according to Steele's internal chrono. Five minutes before the virus bombs dropped. Five minutes for Grayle to reach escape velocity and leave this doomed world behind. And before he could do so, Steele and Wollkenden had to climb that ladder.

Looking up, Steele could see Gavotski peering through the aperture in the lander's belly, calling to him, his words whipped away by a howling, freezing wind.

The ladder was buffeted in that wind, and it was all Steele could do to hang on to it. He couldn't get his feet to it, couldn't do anything without letting go of Wollkenden.

Maybe, just maybe, he thought, if he could persuade his passenger to hang on to him, to free up his right arm, he could haul them both up. He screamed instructions at the confessor, but they didn't seem to get through.

And Wollkenden was screaming back at him, and Steele tuned his enhanced ear in to his voice, and he heard, '…me go, damn you. I don't want to go back to your shackles, be a slave to your Emperor. Mangellan promised me I could be free. He promised me…'

And suddenly, it all made sense: why the Ecclesiarchy had appeared so keen to retrieve their confessor, keen enough to have his would-be rescuers sanctified, and yet the virus bombing couldn't be delayed for him; why the fate of such a dignitary had been left in the hands of a mere ten men. Not that Steele had ever questioned those orders, of course, but he had wondered…

'A virtual saint.' That was what he had been told about Wollkenden. A man who, through words and faith alone, had inspired great deeds. A man who could turn the tides of war, whose name was fast becoming legend. So, the Ecclesiarchy could hardly have turned their backs on him, could they? Even if they had known…

Mangellan had known. He had delighted in telling Steele, gloating about it, only Steele had refused to listen. He had no choice now.

The legend was a lie. The man for whom he had come so far, risked so much, was just an ordinary man after all: a man touched by Chaos. Wollkenden had been tested, and he had failed that test. His mind had been forever warped.

Steele had never had a chance to succeed in his mission. He had never been meant to succeed in it. Wollkenden could not be saved.

In the end, it was easier than he had expected. He didn't even have to try. He just had to relax his fingers, just a little.

And then it was done, and Confessor Wollkenden was plunging away from him – and he felt his heart lurch at the sheer speed of it all, at the suddenness with which it had become too late to turn back, to regret.

He had done the right thing. Steele knew this with a certainty that he had seldom before experienced. He knew it not just because his enhanced brain told him it was true, but because he could feel it. He had done what the Emperor would have wanted him to do, what the Ecclesiarchy could never have asked of him.

And Wollkenden was shrinking beneath him now, dwarfed by the white expanse that awaited him below, but Steele did not wish to see that. He turned away, reached up and caught the next rung of the ladder with his right hand. And, wearily, he pulled himself up that ladder, to the lander, to his comrades, to safety.

COLONEL STANISLEV STEELE stood silently in the lander's cockpit and looked down on the bleak, white globe of Cressida through the forward screen.

It looked the same as it had when he had first been posted to it. He only knew that it wasn't because his internal chrono had completed its countdown. Cressida was a dead world now; no man would touch its soil again during his lifetime.

The rest of his squad – Gavotski, Anakora, Barreski, Mikhaelev, Grayle, Palinev – had all made it. They had survived the mutants' attack on their ship. They had contacted an Imperial Cruiser, and were waiting to be picked up. He was fiercely proud of all of them, although they did not feel that pride in themselves.

They had failed in their mission, fallen at the last hurdle – or so they thought.

He wished he could tell them the truth – tell them that, in the end, one man's life did not matter after all. What mattered was his legend – and today, the Ice Warriors had safeguarded one such legend, ensured that it would inspire more great deeds yet.

Colonel Steele's report would state that Confessor Wollkenden had died a hero.

A BLIND EYE

Steve Lyons

RED AND GREEN lights danced in the night sky. The air was a bracing minus-four degrees. Ice floes stretched to the horizon in each direction like white jigsaw pieces.

It might have been a beautiful scene – but for the Imperial drop-ship, the roar of its engines shattering the peace as it fought to remain suspended above the fragile ice.

In its shadow stood two tiny figures, one relaying instructions to his comrades above, shouting to be heard even over the vox-net. Steele wished he knew what he was doing here, on Poseidon Delta.

Oh, he understood his orders. Somewhere in the water beneath him, there was an Imperial base. An Adeptus Mechanicus facility. Transmissions from this base had ceased, some months ago, and Steele had been sent to find out why.

His only question was... why him?

They were winching down a vehicle from the belly of the ship: a Valhalla-pattern Termite. With its gun emplacements closed and sealed, it was watertight: Kellerman had spent the past few hours making sure of this.

He stood beside Steele now, ostensibly overseeing the winching operation, in fact saying little. Kellerman was a tech-priest, swathed in the red robes of the Martian Priesthood. Currently, these were but the outermost of the many layers of clothing he wore. The bulge in his back, Steele took to be a mechanical servo-arm, although he hadn't yet seen

531

this in action. Kellerman wore a scarf around the lower half of his face, and a hood pulled down over his eyes.

He was still shivering with the cold.

'ALL I AM saying is, it makes no sense to me.'

The troopship. That morning. Mikhaelev had lowered his voice, so that only his four comrades at the mess hall table could hear him. So he had thought.

Anakora had scowled at him. 'It is not for us to question the wisdom of the Departmento Munitorum,' she had said gruffly.

'But why us?' Mikhaelev had persisted. 'Why extract us from Dask and fly us halfway across the galaxy for something so trivial?'

'Perhaps there is more to this than we have been told,' Grayle had suggested.

Barreski had nodded eagerly. 'An Adeptus Mechanicus base on an ocean world.'

'A world that has never been settled,' Grayle added.

'They could be doing anything down there – studying xenos tech, perhaps, that could change the course of a thousand wars.'

'They've probably heard of the legendary Colonel Stanislev Steele,' said the young, enthusiastic Trooper Chenkov, 'and his daring exploits on Cressida.'

Mikhaelev had shot him a withering look. 'We lost almost nine thousand men on Cressida, and failed to rescue Confessor Wollkenden from the enemy.'

'That was hardly the colonel's fault!' said Anakora.

'I'm not saying it was,' said Mikhaelev, 'but Cressida is the reason why Colonel Steele no longer commands a regiment, and if you want my opinion–'

'Do we have any choice in the matter?' Grayle had said, with a grin.

'I'd say we have likely been chosen for this fool's errand,' Mikhaelev had continued, 'because our new commander would be pleased to be rid of us.'

Steele's augmetic right ear had cut out, then, but he had heard enough. Not that anything had been said that hadn't crossed his mind already. He had resumed his circuit of the troopship's main deck, deep in thought.

THE TERMITE SWAYED on creaking chains, above the ice.

Anakora and Petruski helped haul Steele and Kellerman up into the passenger compartment, to join the other six men within. Once they were shut in, Sergeant Gavotski instructed the driver, Grayle, to vox the troopship. A moment later, Steele could feel the Termite being lowered again. His augmetics picked up the sound of ice cracking beneath its tracks, then water slapped against the front shield.

The Valhallan 403rd, Steele's new regiment, had no sub-aqua vehicles. They had had no need of them before. The Adeptus Mechanicus base, however, was over two hundred metres down, too deep for even an Ice Warrior to dive to it unprotected.

They had been forced to improvise.

It seemed an eternity before the Termite set down on the seabed. Grayle reported that the winching chains had been unhooked and retracted. It took him four attempts to start the engine, and when it caught at last it proceeded to spit and to splutter asthmatically. 'It doesn't much care for the water,' murmured Palinev.

'This Termite was modified to burrow through glaciers,' said Sergeant Gavotski. 'Its engine has been drenched with melted ice a thousand times.'

'It's old, that's all,' said Grayle. 'Well, no sense in sending a newer vehicle down here when there's little hope of retrieving it later. It'll cope.'

'I hope you're right,' said Mikhaelev. 'If that engine fails before we get where we're going, there'll be little hope of anyone retrieving us either.'

He was right. Kellerman had only been able to narrow the location of the undersea base down to a few square kilometres. Grayle began to search that area, in an efficient grid pattern, but the Termite's luminators were next to useless in these murky depths. He could have driven them right past their goal without their seeing it.

And the rest of it? What Mikhaelev had said in the troopship's mess hall?

Steele had served long enough to know what it was like when one regiment was absorbed into another, how petty insecurities and grievances could grow out of hand. Not with Colonel Boiski, though; he would have staked his artificial right eye on it.

Gavan was an old friend. He had been almost embarrassed to find Steele under his command, and had bent the rules to give his fellow colonel as much autonomy as he could. He had even kept Steele's old command squad from the 319th together, though there had been a few new faces to replace those lost on Cressida.

It hadn't been Gavan who had sent Steele and his men to Poseidon Delta. That order had come from someone higher up than him.

THEY HAD BEEN searching for thirty minutes when they encountered the creature.

A giant tentacle lashed across the front shield, causing Grayle to let out an ancient Valhallan curse. A moment later, a heavy weight landed on top of the Termite, making its roof groan and bow. Barreski gave the massive borer attachment a spin, and this seemed to discourage their attacker for the present.

'You said there was no aggressive fauna in this area,' said Steele to Kellerman.

'According to our scans,' said the tech-priest, 'there wasn't.'

'Get us away from here, Grayle,' ordered Gavotski. 'If that thing comes back–'

'No,' said Kellerman sharply. 'Colonel Steele, if you please,' he added quickly, moderating his tone in the face of the colonel's glare. 'Intelligence suggests the facility is close by. The warm currents vented from it would naturally attract some life forms.'

'The drill-mounted flamers should work underwater, sir,' Barreski offered. 'I can loose off a few bursts to keep it at bay.'

'Do it,' Steele agreed.

It was soon after this that Grayle sighted something. Steele leaned forward keenly, but even he could only just make out a looming shadow ahead of them and to the left. It could have been the Adeptus Mechanicus base. It could have been a rock formation.

He was still trying to work out which it was when the creature struck again. It rammed them from behind, and almost tipped the Termite tail over nose. Barreski's hands flew over the flamer controls, but he was firing blindly, and a moment later he reported that the promethium tanks were all but empty.

'We're not making headway, sir,' Grayle cried over the rising shriek of the engine. 'It's like… It's as if we're being pulled back!'

'We've been breached!' It was Chenkov who sounded the warning, but there was scarcely need of it. The back end of the Termite was being slowly crushed. Cracks scored their way across the tortured metal, and water had begun to gush through them.

There was nothing else for it now.

'Get those hatches open,' Steele ordered. 'We're going to have to swim for it!'

STEELE WAS THE last out of the stricken Termite. By now, even the newcomers to his squad knew that such was always the way with him. He knew he could last longer than any of them in the water. Not long enough to reach the surface, though.

Kellerman had been right. The water was warmer than it should have been at this depth. Still cold enough to paralyse a less hardy man than a Valhallan soldier. Steele had shed his backpack, but he needed the protection of his armoured greatcoat. It weighted him down to the seabed, as he turned to see what he was facing.

The creature was huge, squid-like in shape, a dark purple in colour, and it held the Termite enwrapped in its ten long tentacles. As Steele watched, the hatchway through which he had just swum was crushed.

Then the squid lost interest in its catch, as it noticed ten more enticing targets.

Its tentacles lashed out like whips. Steele's comrades had struck out for the nearby base – what they hoped was the base. They were scattered by the attack, and Mikhaelev was hit. Worse, Palinev was caught and held fast by a tentacle.

Mikhaelev was sinking, apparently insensate. Anakora and Sergeant Gavotski turned back for him. In the meantime, Palinev was being reeled in towards the creature's great maw – but Barreski had a hand-held flamer.

A stream of burning promethium seethed through the water, struck the creature between its eyes. The recoil sent Barreski spinning away. He was caught by Petruski, who braced his comrade as best he could to fire again.

The creature must have had no pain centres, because it didn't flinch at all and its grip remained strong, despite a pair of angry red burns. On dry land, it would have died anyway, but the water kept the promethium flames from spreading to engulf it.

Barreski refocussed, aiming now at the tentacle that was holding Palinev, perhaps hoping to sever it, but his look of frustration told the story. He couldn't fire at the creature for fear of burning its captive too.

Palinev was still fighting. He was the smallest of the Ice Warriors, but perhaps the most tenacious. He was hacking at the tentacle that held him with a knife, unleashing tiny geysers of black blood. But the creature was crushing him, and the last of his air was bubbling out through his nose and mouth.

Steele motioned to Barreski and Petruski to disengage, head for the base, save themselves. There was nothing more they could do here.

Palinev had gone limp, his knife drifting out of his grasp. His strategy had been sound, though. He had just needed a bigger blade.

Steele drew his power sword. He didn't use the controls in its hilt – he wasn't sure what the water would do to the machine-spirits within if he did. The metal itself, along with the enhanced strength he gained from his bionic upper right arm, would have to suffice. He launched himself at the creature, kicking off from the seabed.

He drew the sword back, over his head, and brought it down two-handed. It was slowed by the water, but still bit deep. Black suckers on the sea creature's tentacle exploded like pustules. Palinev was freed, but unconscious, and Steele's sword was embedded in the creature's flesh. He lacked the leverage to pull it loose.

The tentacle thrashed, and Steele, unwilling to let go of his weapon, was carried with it, over the creature's head. It was all he could do not to exhale precious air. His lungs were starting to burn. He had no choice but to activate his sword, after all. It freed itself with a startling blue flash. Just in time. Another two tentacles were reaching for him. He discouraged them with a swipe of his still-glowing blade.

The water around him turned black; the creature had discharged some kind of ink. Steele had lost his bearings. As he settled on the seabed again, he interrogated his internal compass, but it failed to respond.

Cursing the vagaries of machines, he didn't see the next tentacle coming. He did, however, hear the whoosh of water displacement that preceded it, in time to throw up an arm to protect his head. Steele was struck in the side. His greatcoat kept his ribs from breaking, but he lost almost half his air.

On the third time of asking, Steele's compass responded to him. He headed for the base, half-swimming, half-walking. He emerged from the ink cloud, and could see it ahead of him: a dull, grey dome, strictly utilitarian in design.

He saw no sign of Palinev's body, and had no time to search for it. His internal chrono was counting down remorselessly to the moment when he would lose consciousness. His augmetics calculated that, at Steele's current speed, he wouldn't make it.

A shadow fell over him. The squid was hanging back, more cautious than it had been since its taste of Steele's blade, but reluctant to let the last of its morsels get away. Steele braced himself to fight again.

Then a jet of fire flared over his head, and burned the tips off two grasping tentacles. It was enough, finally, to make the squid creature turn and to skulk away, hungry.

Barreski was drifting in the water above Steele, his flamer to his shoulder. Ahead of them both, Steele could make out Petruski, plodding along the seabed with a slighter form that could only have been Palinev slung across his broad shoulders.

No doubt both troopers would claim not to have seen their colonel's hand signals earlier, or to have misread them. They didn't all have bionic eyes, after all. They would swear they hadn't disobeyed orders – and Steele would choose to believe them.

'WELL,' SAID GRAYLE, when he could speak again, 'that was a new experience.'

They were slumped in a musty airlock, shivering and coughing up water.

'I… I'll say,' gasped Barreski. 'You've lost a lot of Imperial vehicles in your time, Grayle, but I think you just set a new speed…' He succumbed to a choking fit.

They had been lucky. They had all survived. Kellerman, too – the tech-priest must have been tougher than he looked. It was he who had opened the door for them. Steele had been the last through, his body in convulsions, light-headed, but confounding the predictions of the machines inside his brain. His men had waited for him, of course.

There had been a tense minute, then, as the last of the draining water had sloshed around their boots, as Anakora had had to resuscitate the unconscious Palinev. She had brought him round, at last – not that Steele had doubted she would.

'The Termite served its purpose,' said Gavotski. 'Grayle too. They got us here.'

'Shouldn't someone have come to meet us by now?' asked Mikhaelev.

His luminator found a rune-pad on the wall. There had been a simi-lar one outside. When Steele judged that the Ice Warriors were ready, he nodded to Kellerman, who tapped a code into the pad. An inner door slid open with a hydraulic whoosh. The passageways beyond were as dark as the airlock, and the atmosphere as stale.

Normally, Palinev would have been sent to scout the way ahead. He was still weak, however, so the job went to an eager Chenkov.

As soon as the young trooper set foot inside the base, lasguns barked out from each side of him. He was caught in a crossfire of ten or more beams and cut down.

Seven Ice Warriors went for their own lasguns, and Barreski for his explosives. He was beaten to it. An Imperial frag grenade came clinking, skipping along the floor, and landed perfectly in front of the airlock doorway.

Steele had already pushed Kellerman aside, slapped his palm against the rune-pad. The others flattened themselves against the airlock walls as the door whooshed closed and, in that same instant, was blasted off its frame.

The door had saved the Ice Warriors' lives, taking the brunt of the explosion. There was enough smoke, too, to provide them with some cover. Grayle and Mikhaelev were the first through the doorway, firing left and right, diving into the mouth of the passageway opposite as the answering fire came. Right behind them, Barreski braved a las-beam gauntlet long enough to hurl a grenade of his own back the way the other had come. 'Easy on the explosives,' Steele cautioned through his comm-bead, as metal floor plates trembled beneath his feet. 'Remember where we are. One hole in the outer wall of this–' He broke off as a sta-tic burst threatened to deafen him.

Barreski's frag grenade had put paid to the las-fire from the left. How-ever, with the smoke clearing now, most of Steele's squad was still pinned down. Crowding into the airlock doorway, Anakora, Mikhaelev and Petruski sent a volley of las-beams to their right, as did their three comrades opposite. The battle lasted for several minutes, but slowly the enemy fire lessened, then ceased and, with his augmented hearing, Steele detected several pairs of footsteps half-running, half-shuffling away.

CHENKOV WAS DEAD. But there was no time to mourn him. They had hardly had time to get to know him, anyway. At least he had been avenged.

They found four bodies down the passageway to their right, and the remnants of seven to the left: mutants, all. One of them clung to life: it seized Grayle's foot in its gnarled claws, tried to bite his ankle through his boot. He didn't waste his ammunition on it. He speared it through one of its three eyes with his bayonet.

Steele felt a familiar rush of disgust, just looking at those twisted corpses. Even more disturbing, however, were the tattered red robes in which they were wrapped.

'Adeptus Mechanicus robes,' said Mikhaelev, with a sidelong look at Kellerman.

'They could have taken them from this base's personnel,' said Anakora.

Sergeant Gavotski shook his head. He had seen what Steele had seen. Most of the dead mutants had servo-arms, or mechadendrites of some description. From where else could they have come, anyway? Where else but here?

How long, had Kellerman said, since contact with this base had been lost? That was how long it had taken for these men, once good men presumably, to succumb to the lure of the Ruinous Powers, for their bodies to have become as ugly as their minds.

'How many?' asked Steele.

'Twenty-three,' said Kellerman quietly, seeing his implication. 'Twenty-three tech-priests were stationed here. I have faith that some of them–'

Gavotski nodded. 'Some of them would have resisted. At least three mutants remain alive, but there may be no more than that – or as many as twelve.'

Steele tested the vox-net. It was working, but intermittently. They had left the heavy caster behind in the Termite, and evidently it was damaged, unreliable.

Steele chose to divide his forces, anyway. There would be little chance, that way, of a mutant slipping past them as they fanned out across the base. They had all seen hololithic plans, which showed a large central control shrine. Gavotski and Petruski would take the most direct route to this, and take Kellerman with them; the rest of the Ice Warriors would circle around and join them there later.

Steele, Anakora and Palinev went left. Anakora had the only working luminator of the three of them, so she took point. Steele kept a close eye on Palinev, who professed to have recovered from his near-death ordeal but looked pale. They followed a curving passageway, searching bunkrooms and store cupboards as they passed them.

They found wires torn out of a wall, the machine-spirits in them spitting their annoyance. That explained the lack of lighting in the base, at least. They also came across the corpses of three tech-priests, seemingly unblemished. Kellerman had been right – some of them had resisted.

Barreski reported in. He had to repeat himself, and even then Steele heard only half his words – enough to know that his team had found a second airlock, and a four-man escape vehicle. Grayle was checking to see if it was functional.

Anakora raised a hand, bringing her comrades to a halt. 'There are mutants ahead,' she whispered. 'I can smell their stink.' Palinev agreed that he could, too.

Steele could detect nothing. However, in such matters, he had come to trust the natural instincts of others above his own.

Palinev asked to be sent ahead, reminding Steele that he was the lightest on his feet. Steele gave him a long, appraising look before nodding his assent.

Palinev removed his boots, fearing that the squelch of water in them would betray him. He screwed an infra red scope onto his long-las 'sniper's gun, and put it to his eye. Steele switched his bionic eye to infra-red, too, as Anakora extinguished her light. Then Palinev set off again, alone, hugging the passageway's inner wall, his footsteps barely audible even to Steele. He had gone less than twenty metres before he stopped, drew back a step and lowered himself onto his haunches.

He took his time, finding his unsuspecting targets through his scope. Then he fired around the curve of the wall, just twice. Then he waited again.

At last, he stood and beckoned for the others to join him. 'There were just two of them, sir,' he reported to Steele. 'Both dead.'

Steele was about to speak, when he heard more las-fire. It was distant, muffled by the base's internal walls, and it lasted only seconds.

He voxed the other two teams for status reports. Mikhaelev's voice buzzed through Steele's comm-bead, but its words were indistinguishable.

From Gavotski, Petruski and Kellerman, there was nothing.

THEY TURNED DOWN a radial corridor, making straight for the centre of the base.

Steele led the way at a run, slowing only to approach the arched doorway into the circular control shrine. He cranked his hearing up to full. He could hear a mechanical pump, and the ragged, shallow breathing of a man close to death.

He stepped inside, and almost stumbled over a corpse. A fourth tech-priest.

The shrine was crowded with big, black metal engines, streaked with soot. Most were silent and dark. One machine, however, still functioned, grinding and wheezing.

There was something atop the machine: the body of some creature, splayed out. As Anakora walked up behind Steele, as her luminator light fell on that body, Steele almost gagged. It was a foul, black thing, bigger than a man, a near-formless mass of tentacles and legs and eyes.

Steele had never seen a daemon before. He had only heard tales of those warp-spawned abominations, enough to know they came in all shapes and sizes. He had no doubt, however, that a daemon was what this malformed creature was. He made the sign of the aquila, and Palinev tried to do the same but had to turn away and vomit into a corner.

It was bound to the machine – nailed to it, in fact, its blood dried black around its wounds. Numerous wires and tubes burrowed into the daemon's flesh. Its leathery chest – what Steele took to be its chest – had been sliced open, to expose muscle and sinew. Inside, a shrivelled, black organ emitted regular spasms. The machine, it seemed, was keeping the daemon alive, so that it could be dissected, studied.

'Colonel,' said Palinev, in a small voice, sounding quite ill.

Steele followed his down-turned gaze, saw that Palinev's toe had touched another corpse. Its head had been severed and was nowhere in sight, but Steele had served long enough with Sergeant Ivon Gavotski to recognise his body.

Anakora found Petruski. He was still alive, just. She broke out a medi-pack, did what she could for him. She stayed as far from the daemon as she could. Steele was still staring down at Gavotski, his oldest friend. He had never expected to outlive him. He had thought his imperturbable sergeant a constant in his life. He had come to rely on his counsel – perhaps too much.

He hadn't heard the quiet footfall behind him. His augmetics, however, had registered the sound and shrieked a warning in the back of his brain.

Steele whirled around. He found himself facing Kellerman. He must have been hiding in the shadows. Kellerman didn't flinch, though Steele had raised his sword to strike. He lowered it again, wondering how he had not detected the tech-priest's presence earlier. He cursed himself for having been distracted.

'What happened here?' he asked brusquely.

'A mutant ambush,' said Kellerman. He was perfectly calm.

'They were wielding blades?' asked Anakora, still tending to Petruski. Steele noted the gaping wound in the fallen Ice Warrior's side.

'Maybe they hoped not to be heard,' said Palinev, 'but our people got off a few las-shots.' He looked around as if expecting to find a couple of mutant corpses to add to the human ones. There were none.

'How many?' asked Steele.

'I didn't see,' said Kellerman. 'Your sergeant had me wait outside while he and his man searched the shrine. I heard the mutants fleeing as you approached. I tried to vox a warning to you, but the machine-spirits have abandoned my comm-bead.'

Even as he was speaking, he walked past Steele, as if their conversation held no interest for him. His gaze had alighted upon the captive daemon. Barreski, Grayle and Mikhaelev arrived, then, and Steele had the three of them and Palinev guard the control shrine's four doorways as he waited patiently.

He couldn't see Kellerman's expression – he still wore his scarf and hood. His body language, however, suggested that he was more angered by the daemon's presence than repulsed by it. The tech-priest turned his back on the ghastly thing with a shudder, and recited a prayer to himself.

'What is it?' asked Steele, though he knew the answer already.

'It seems,' said Kellerman, 'that the tech-priests assigned to this base were the architects of their own downfall.'

Steele summoned Barreski forward. He came unwillingly, his eyes on the slumbering daemon. He brightened considerably when Steele gave him his orders. Anakora took his place on watch, as Barreski assembled his flamer. A single burst set the daemon's flesh alight, and melted the tubes that sustained it. Barreski fired a second, anyway.

The daemon dissipated before Steele's eyes, no spark of life remaining to anchor it to this physical realm. For a long time afterwards, nobody said a word. The daemon may have been gone, but this shrine had been tainted by its presence.

Steele had never been told the purpose of this base. He hadn't asked. He wondered if Kellerman had known – if any of the hierarchy of the Adeptus Mechanicus could have known – what was being researched down here.

He could understand the temptation. It had probably been born of the purest of motives: the desire to better comprehend the forces that beset Mankind and, in so doing, to find their weaknesses. But that knowledge was forbidden for a reason – one to which the ruined bodies in the passageways around this room well attested.

Was that why this base had been constructed down here, he wondered, so far from any pocket of civilisation? Was that why it had been submerged?

'I think we have seen enough,' said Kellerman. 'It is our duty now to destroy this facility, and bury the dark deeds that have been done here.'

'I agree,' said Steele. 'First, however, we should complete our search.'

Grayle reported that his team had found two more tech-priests – they had shut themselves in a bunkroom and taken their own lives. This left four unaccounted for, at least two of whom were now sword-wielding mutants. 'The chances of saving any of them are slight,' said Kellerman, impatiently. 'We ought to proceed with–'

'If we are to clear this base before it blows,' said Steele, 'we will need to set our explosives on a long timer. I'd rather not take the chance of leaving anything behind that could defuse them.' Kellerman bowed to his wisdom, and Steele divided his squad again. Barreski and Grayle were to head for the base's third and final airlock, in the hope of finding a second escape vehicle. Anakora and Palinev were to cover their backs as they hunted down the last of the mutants.

'Mikhaelev and I will stay here,' said Steele, 'with Kellerman. We will set the majority of our charges in this shrine, so we can be sure of blasting these machines to dust.' Palinev couldn't conceal his look of surprise at this. It must have seemed to him that his colonel had assigned himself to the detail least likely to see combat. Had this been so, it would indeed have been unusual.

Steele, however, had his reasons.

MIKHAELEV HAD SIX krak grenades. More than enough, if they were placed wisely. He attached two to the half-melted machine that the daemon had befouled with its touch. Just to be sure. 'If there's anything else,' he said to Kellerman, 'anything on this base we don't want salvaged, we should bring it here.' The tech-priest nodded.

'Set the timers for two hours,' said Steele.

'Can we not work more quickly?' said Kellerman.

'We're in no hurry,' said Steele. Kellerman's body language said otherwise – his hands were twitching impatiently – but he didn't push the point.

Petruski hadn't come round. He needed better medical care than could be provided for him in the field. Steele had hoped for a chance to question him. He didn't know Petruski well, but he had been impressed on more than one occasion by his physical strength. When this was coupled with Gavotski's natural caution and instincts honed by long experience, it seemed incredible that they could have been defeated so easily, at least without claiming a few mutant scalps first.

It was likely Petruski could have told him nothing, anyway. The angle of his wound, and the way he had fallen, suggested he had been hit from behind. He may not have seen his attacker.

Static hissed over Steele's comm-bead. He couldn't make out a word of the incoming message, nor identify the voice that had sent it. He could hear las-fire again, however, and this told its own story. Mikhaelev could hear it too, and he reached for his gun and looked to Steele expectantly.

'Stay here,' said Steele. 'Keep laying the explosives. I'll deal with it.' He drew his laspistol and power sword and marched out of the control shrine, determinedly.

As soon as he judged he was out of earshot, he came to a halt. He turned around, and crept back the way he had come.

Steele wasn't sure about this. Sometimes, the augmetic part of his brain could piece things together and came up with a conclusion a more intuitive man would dismiss out of hand. A man like Sergeant Gavotski, perhaps. A voice in his head was screaming at him to go to his men's aid, while another insisted they could take care of themselves, and that the real threat was right here behind him.

He didn't know which voice to trust. He didn't know which of them was which.

He flattened himself to the wall outside the shrine. He peered around the doorway.

Mikhaelev was crouching by the opposite entrance, setting another grenade. At first, Steele feared he must have been mistaken. In which case, it was the other members of his squad who needed him, and he had let them down.

Then, the red-cloaked figure of Kellerman swept into view. He crept up behind Mikhaelev – and, from the folds of his robes, he drew a power sword, and ignited it.

Steele had seen enough. He stepped into the doorway, levelling his pistol. He didn't shout a warning. He shot Kellerman, twice, aiming at his head.

The first beam struck true. It ought to have been fatal.

Kellerman spun around and threw up an arm, deflecting the second beam. His reflexes were incredible – and he had to be armoured beneath his layers of clothing.

He threw out his arm, and bright energy crackled from his fingers. The air was split by jagged bolts of lightning, and Steele dived for the protection of one of the machines but was struck, speared through his augmetic right shoulder.

The lightning was conducted through metal, through flesh, into his brain, where it burned like a thousand suns. Steele heard himself screaming, but turned the scream into a howl of defiance. There was a moment of blackness. Then, Mikhaelev was standing over him, helping him to his feet, and Kellerman was gone.

'I don't understand, sir. I thought Kellerman was one of us. How could he be...?'

'A mutant,' growled Steele. 'A psyker.' He didn't know the answer to Mikhaelev's question, not for sure. But he had his suspicions. 'Where...?'

'Escaped, sir.' Mikhaelev nodded towards the opposite doorway. 'He was gone before I could get off a shot at him. If you hadn't come back when you did...'

Steele felt drained, weak – not of body, but of mind. He was afraid his organic half had blacked out, for a second, his augmetics bringing him around. It had happened before. He felt as if someone had taken a scouring pad to the inside of his head.

He could no longer hear las-fire. The battle with the mutants was over. The rest of his squad were probably on their way back here: Kellerman's psychic lightning had been almost silent, but they ought to have heard Steele's own two shots. To be sure, he aimed his laspistol at the ceiling and fired three more times, a call to arms.

'Colonel Steele,' said Mikhaelev, 'there's a krak grenade missing. It was attached to the console here. Kellerman was standing right by–'

'Wait here for the others,' said Steele. He was already running.

HE FALTERED AT a junction of passageways. He swept each direction with his infra-red gaze, listened for footsteps. There was nothing.

Steele was short of breath and his legs were weak: the lingering effects of whatever it was Kellerman had done to him. Unacceptable. He refocussed his mind, and immediately felt stronger. He had allowed his augmetics to take on a few more of his brain functions, surrendered another small part of himself to them.

He didn't know where Kellerman was. But he could guess where he was going.

Steele closed his eyes for a half-second, called up the plans of the undersea base that he had seen once and memorised, plotted the most direct course to his destination.

He reached the airlock in less than a minute – the one in which his men had discovered the escape vehicle. It was still there: a grey, egg-shaped pod, slimy with seaweed and lichens, balanced on a square launching pad.

He waited in silence, in the darkness. He began to wonder if he had been wrong. Then he felt the slightest shift in the stale air, and knew he was no longer alone.

'Kellerman, I presume?' said Steele. 'Or should I say, *inquisitor*?'

Kellerman stepped out of hiding. He had discarded his red robes, along with whatever apparatus had given the illusion of the servo-arm beneath. He wore a darker-coloured cloak over armour. The lower half of his face was still covered, but his hood was gone and for the first time Steele could see that he had only one eye. An old, deep scar ran through the empty socket of the other, to disappear beneath the scarf. Steele wondered if Kellerman had been offered a replacement as he had been, and if he had refused it.

He didn't correct Steele's assumption. Not that it had been difficult to work out, once Steele had seen all the evidence. No mere impostor could have infiltrated his squad as Kellerman had. He would have needed the cooperation of the Departmento Munitorum, and most likely of the Adeptus Mechanicus too.

'Ordo Malleus?' Steele guessed.

'I have the authority of the God-Emperor of Mankind behind me, Colonel Steele.' The daemon hunter's voice was quiet but commanding.

'I recognise that, Inquisitor,' said Steele. 'But my men have fought bravely and well for the Emperor. They deserve a better fate than you intend for them.'

'None of us can escape the taint of this place, colonel.'

'The daemon is dead now,' said Steele, 'and its taint has not spread to my heart, nor, I would warrant, to any of theirs.'

'Would that we could be sure of this.'

'I am sure,' Steele countered. 'I know those men, Inquisitor Kellerman. I have fought alongside them. On Cressida, when the stench of Chaos was in the air itself...'

He didn't complete the sentence. He had seen the look in Kellerman's eyes when Cressida had been mentioned, the flicker of an expression on his face, and Steele *knew* now. He knew the truth.

Experimentally, he edged a little to his right. Kellerman's single shrewd eye followed him unerringly. The darkness was of no advantage to Steele, then. He activated his power sword, to dispel it. Kellerman did likewise. They circled each other slowly, both of them accepting, in that moment, how this had to end.

'You knew what we would find here,' said Steele, 'or suspected it at least, before we even embarked upon this mission.'

'There is a higher concern here,' said Kellerman. 'Were it to become known, this attempt by the Cult Mechanicus to truck with the Ruinous Powers, then–'

'I understand the stakes,' said Steele.

'Then you understand,' said Kellerman, 'that faith in all too many is a fragile thing, and that the unity of Man must needs be preserved.'

'I understood,' said Steele, 'that the purpose of your order was to shine the Emperor's light upon the sinner, not to hide his deeds in deeper shadow.'

'The Emperor sees all,' said Kellerman, 'and our deeds are for Him to judge.'

'You didn't need to bring us down here,' said Steele. 'You could have had this facility torpedoed from orbit, and protected its secrets that way.' He left the accusation implied: *Had you not been so keen to learn those secrets for yourself. Had you not known full well the purpose of this base, and turned a blind eye to it.*

And that was why Steele had been chosen for this mission. Cressida. He had never told a soul about what had happened there, about Confessor Wollkenden's madness. In some quarters, however, suspicion was often enough. Kellerman had required an expendable squad – and, in the eyes of some of the members of his order, there was one whose commander had already seen too much.

Steele was not an emotional man. His augmetics saw to this, swift to counter any perceived imbalances in his brain chemistry. Right now, however, there was an ice-cold ball of fury forming in his stomach.

He held it down, long enough to make one final appeal to the daemon hunter.

He had to know he had no choice, that it was kill or be killed.

'I will keep your secrets, inquisitor,' he vowed. 'What would it gain me to do otherwise? My devotion to the Emperor is beyond question. What I will not accept is the slaughter of good men, good soldiers, in His name – struck down from behind by one they took to be an ally.'

'Stand aside, Colonel Steele,' Kellerman growled. 'Stand aside and let me pass.'

And Steele could see it again, in his mind's eye – Gavotski's headless corpse, lying at his feet – and there was no going back now. He shut out the part of his brain, the logical part, that wanted to restrain him. He gave himself to the ice-cold anger.

His first sword thrust was parried easily. Steele's blade locked with Kellerman's, their energy fields clashing in a shower of blue sparks. The daemon hunter was stronger than he looked, perhaps another expression of his damnable psyker talents.

He was fast, too, or perhaps Steele was beginning to slow down. He was driven back, step by inexorable step, as Kellerman went on the offensive, slashing at his opponent again and again. An unexpected thrust to Steele's stomach threw off his footing, and Kellerman's blade struck for his neck.

It took Steele's augmetics a tenth of a second to calculate that there was too much power behind the attack for him to stand a chance of blocking it. Too long.

He let his blade take the brunt of the blow, but dropped at the same time. His sword was wrenched from his hands, but Steele rolled beneath a second strike and came up with his laspistol flaring. Kellerman winced and aborted another thrust, as he was hit in the shoulder.

The daemon hunter raised his right hand, and bright energy collected at his fingertips again. Still on his back, Steele was a sitting duck.

He smiled to himself. He had heard what his opponent had not: four pairs of booted footsteps, running to Steele's rescue.

Palinev was the first to make his presence felt. He sniped around the nearest corner, striking Kellerman between his shoulder blades. Kellerman swung around, unleashed his psychic lightning bolts at this new target, but Palinev had already ducked back out of sight. Anakora and Mikhaelev appeared next, around the curve of the passageway – and, as the Witch Hunter turned to defend himself against their las-fire, Barreski came up shooting behind him.

Kellerman was staggered, at last, then driven to his knees. His power sword slipped from his weakened grip, and Steele retrieved it, stood over his vanquished foe.

'The... the Emperor,' Kellerman gasped. 'The God-Emperor sees all, and He will... He will judge you for your deeds today, Colonel... Stanislev...'

Steele swung his borrowed blade. He repaid the murderer of Sergeant Ivon Gavotski in kind. He parted Inquisitor Kellerman's head from his shoulders.

'I DON'T UNDERSTAND, colonel,' said Anakora, as they gathered around the body. 'Was that... was that Kellerman? What happened to him?'

'He must have been infected,' said Steele, 'as the other tech-priests were. This place...' There was no need to tell them the worst of it.

Palinev's eyes widened. 'Then we must get out of here, before–'

Steele nodded. 'More urgently than you might think, trooper. Where's Grayle?'

'He took a hit to the leg, from the mutants,' said Barreski.

'He stayed with Petruski in the control shrine,' said Mikhaelev.

Steele was already trying to raise Grayle on the vox. He heard his voice, through a static hiss, and spoke slowly and loudly: 'Listen, Grayle. You have to take Petruski and make your way to...' He broke off, and asked Barreski, 'Did you reach the other airlock? Did you find an escape vehicle in there?'

'No, sir. We never reached it, I mean. We had only just slain the last of the mutant scum when we heard your–'

'Take Petruski,' Steele instructed Grayle, 'and make your way to the third airlock. Quick as you can. I'll meet you there.'

He turned to the others, and jerked his thumb towards the four-man pod in the airlock behind him. 'Go,' he said.

'But, sir!' protested Anakora. There was always a protest, though they knew by now it would make no difference.

'I'll bring the vehicle back for you, sir,' said Barreski, 'in case there are no others.'

Steele nodded. Another lie he was letting his men believe.

This time, the truth was revealed to them in the thunderclap sound of an exploding krak grenade. It made the floor at their feet tremble, and almost shook the escape vehicle off its pad.

This had been Kellerman's plan, of course – except that he would have been far from here before his bomb went off, before the base's outer wall was breached.

The explosion had been close. Before its echoes had died down, Steele heard the roar of oncoming water. He was running before the others could react, before they could try to stop him. He took the nearest radial passageway, towards the control shrine.

He had almost made it there when he was struck from behind by a tidal wave. He was swept off his feet. He tried to fight it, in vain. He could only go limp and let the water carry him. It expelled him from the passageway, and Steele was dashed against something hard and metal. One of the shrine's black engines.

He scrabbled at its pitted surface, found purchase, clung on for his life as more water lashed against him. It was cascading into the shrine from all directions, now.

It wasn't until the room was almost totally submerged that the water calmed down, and returned control of Steele's body to him. He climbed up onto the machine that had been his anchor, pushed his face above the rising surface, took one last lungful of air, then let himself sink again. He still had half the base to cross.

Progress was easier, thankfully, than it had been outside. He had the machines to push off against, and then the walls of the passageways that led to the third airlock. There had been no sign of Grayle in the control shrine. Hopefully, this meant he had received Steele's orders and acted on them. With luck, his squad would lose no more of its members today. With luck, and the Emperor's favour.

THE ICE FLOES again. The sun had risen: a distant, cold light in the violet sky.

Seven of them had made it back. Seven out of ten. The survivors had clambered out of their floating escape vehicles, soaked and exhausted.

Steele had marched them almost three kilometres across the half-frozen landscape before allowing them to rest.

They were still waiting for the drop-ship to collect them when the explosion came.

They saw the flash first, lighting up a wide area of the sea. Then, a column of seething water was thrust skyward, a hundred metres high, and even at this distance the Ice Warriors were spattered with stinging hot droplets.

When it was all over, there was a hole in the ice, four hundred metres in diameter. A hole centred on the spot where, an hour before, the seven of them had stood.

Steele removed his fur hat, bowed his head, and led his squad in a prayer for the souls of Sergeant Gavotski and Chenkov. For those courageous men, the shattered remnants of an underwater dome would be the only grave markers they had.

He made no mention of Kellerman.

He gave thanks to the Emperor, for protecting the rest of them. There had been a second escape vehicle, as Steele had prayed there would be. It had taken him all he had to reach it – and then he had found the airlock in which it had stood waterlogged, the door jammed open. Fortunately, Grayle had made it too, with Petruski. He had studied the vehicle's dashboard runes, worked out how to drain its cockpit.

There had been no sign of the squid creature, or any other hostile life forms, as they had bobbed up onto the surface of the water – another palpable blessing.

'Did we succeed in our mission?' asked Palinev.

Mikhaelev nodded. 'We left nothing alive.' Of all of them, he was the most likely to have guessed the truth. The truth that Steele couldn't tell them.

No one could prove that he had knowingly killed an inquisitor.

He did not doubt, however, that the Ordo Malleus would have their suspicions about his dealings with Kellerman, just as they had had about his dealings with Confessor Wollkenden. They would ask themselves how many dangerous secrets were stored in this upstart Ice Warrior's half-augmetic brain.

More so now than ever, Colonel Stanislev Steele was a marked man.

This was not the end.

DESERT RAIDERS

Lucien Soulban

CAST OF CHARACTERS

NEUTRALS
Commissar Torrent Rezail: Cadian native and commissar for the newly formed 892nd Tallarn Regiment.
Sergeant Tyrell Habaas: Hawadi tribesman and adjunct to Commissar Rezail.

TURENAG MEMBERS
Colonel Nisri Dakar: Regiment commander and leader of the Turenag contingent of the 892nd. Prince of the Turenag Tribal Alliance.
Major Ias'r Dashour: Commander of 1st Company.
Kamala Noore: The unit's only sanctioned psyker and female.
Captain Qal Abantu: In charge of the regiment's armored support and a D'Shouf tribesman, the largest tribe of the Turenag.
Captain Lakoom Nehari: F Platoon leader.
Sergeant Darik Ballasra: Squad sergeant and among the best trackers in the regiment. A member of the Ma'h'murra tribe within the Turenag Alliance.
Sergeant Abasra Doori: Chimera commander with armoured support.
Sergeant Saheen Raham: E Platoon's leader and Tallarn soldier of Cadian heritage; Cadians settled on Tallarn following the Iron Legion's attempts to invade the sulphur-laden world.
Duf'adar Nab'l Sarish: Regiment pack master and a member of the Sen'tach tribe, who are known for their dromad riders.
Corporal Elaph Cartouk: Squadron leader for the Burning Falcons.
Corporal Magdi Demar: E Platoon leader.
Corporal Bathras Euphrates: Hellhound commander.
Corporal Kadi Y'dar: Sentinel squadron pilot.
Private Ignar Chalfous: Pathfinder in Sergeant Ballasra's squad.
Private Dubar iban Dubar: Sentinel pilot with the Burning Falcons.
Private Darha Lumak: Hellhound flame gunner.
Private Trask Abu Manar: Hellhound cogitator.
Private Shanleel Qubak: A Sentinel squadron pilot.
Private Ibod Sarrin: Hellhound driver.
Private Apaul Wariby: Chimera driver.

BANNA MEMBERS
Battalion Commander Lieutenant Colonel Turk Iban Salid: Second-in-Command of the 892nd, Prince of the Banna Tribal Alliance and leader of the regiment's Banna contingent.
Major Wahid Anleel: Commander of 1st Company.

Major Alef Hussari: Hussari commands the 892nd's Sentinel squadrons.

Captain Lornis Anuman: Commander of B Platoon.

Captain Ural Kortan: Quartermaster of the 892nd.

Captain Ber'nam Toria: Commander of C Platoon.

Master Gunner Tembo Nubis: Nubis leads A Platoon, which handles fire support, heavy weapons and demolitions. He belongs to the Nasandi Tribe.

Sergeant Umar Hadoori: Squadron leader of the Heretic Slayers.

Sergeant Cortikas Iath: Squadron leader for the War Chasers.

Sergeant H'lal Odassa: Squadron leader of the Dust Marauders.

Sergeant A'rtar Shamas: Squadron leader of the Orakle's Apostles.

Corporal Tanis Maraibeh: Pilot in the Dust Runners.

Corporal Adwan Neshadi: Member of Nubis Platoon and demolitions expert.

Corporal Ziya Rawan: Squadron leader for the Holy Striders.

Private First Class Venakh Mousar: A scout serving under Captain Toria.

Private Amum Bak: A pilot in Major Hussari's Dust Runners Sentinel squadron.

Private Harros Damask: A Sentinel squadron pilot.

Private Lebbos Lassa: Private serving in Captain Toria's squad.

Private Deeter Mohar: Pilot in the War Chasers.

Private Damous Obasra: Pilot in the Holy Striders squadron.

Private Ahsra Sabaak: A soldier working for Quatermaster Kortan.

Private Elma Taris: Pilot in the Holy Striders squadron.

PROLOGUE

'There was, there was not…'
'All tales spoken from Tallarn fathers to their sons, and mothers to their daughters, begin in this fashion. It is a way of saying that, by the Emperor's will, this story may or may not be true.'

– *The Accounts of the Tallarn*
by Remembrancer Tremault

1

There was, there was not…

2

THE TRANSMISSION FELL like a carelessly discarded blade from the heavens, straight into his naked brain. The astropath's muscles seized into hard cords, and his teeth snapped down, cracking the enamel. His skeletal hands gripped the cradle's iron grasp-bars, cutting flesh with rust, and he bucked against the leather straps holding him fast. There wasn't enough time to mouth a litany of protection or to will a psychic bulwark into place against the buckshot rain of thoughts. From the heavens, tonight, fell death, and visions of history undone and ghosts unmade.

The warning chimes rang and the lume-tubes in the alcove washed the psyker in an infernal red light. He saw none of it; heard none of it.

The psychic images slowed and then accelerated. They toppled and turned his mind inside out. He didn't understand the visions, but they crucified his senses: faces he did not know, voices he'd never heard, yet each intimately familiar as a sort of déjà vu. In his mind, flesh unravelled and skin was spooled like string; mothers grieved over the bloodstained sand and stabbed each other in their lunatic grief; the foul miasma of discharged bowels, ozone and cordite filled the nostrils; a moon in the sky with eyes for craters drowned the stars with its black tears; an eagle caught in tar, struggled and dissolved.

The astropath screamed. He saw himself seeing himself seeing himself, ad infinitum, like two mirrors facing each other with him trapped in the middle, and within the infinite reflections. He saw himself dying between the razor-edged flashes of the transmission, strapped into the cradle, his death echoed endlessly.

A grey-robed tech-acolyte with the Adeptus Astra Telepathica ran down the narrow corridor with its exposed wiring and moisture weeping walls. He moved past the alcoves where astropaths sat in restraint bubble-cradles, up to the alcove marked 'Socket 9:12' with its flashing red alarms. He checked the green-hued monitors that hung from the ceiling as the astropath struggled and bucked. On screen, his vitals sent out jagged peaks and troughs of activity. The echo-plasm box imprinted psychic visualisations that bled into one another and sent images into the vist-immateria plate. The fusillade of visions, however, came fast and hard, fusing the already grainy images into a horrid collage of blood and static.

The tech-acolyte quickly punched the button below the wall-vox. 'This is Tech-Acolyte Resalon on Providence Watch. Father Nuvosa, we–'

'I know,' the impatient, metallic voice replied. 'It's a mortis-cry, relayed through the Torquadas Observium Array. A nasty one at that.'

'The cogitator banks cannot process most of the images,' Resalon said. 'It's interpreting them as static. We're losing the sanctity of the vision.'

'Then filter it through the other astropaths. Let them pick it clean of chaff.'

'The Emperor's Will be done,' Resalon said.

He studied the astropath. The restraints cut into the psyker's flesh, but they were necessary so the astropath didn't pull free the filaments plugged into his spine and helmet. Blood dribbled in fat droplets from under the astropath's black sens-dep helmet, however, and although Resalon could not see through its poly-fibre surface, he imagined that the man's nostrils and eyes were bleeding freely. He briefly wondered if the sens-dep helmets weren't just designed to tune the world out, but to shield others from the horrors perceived by the psykers. Indeed, the other astropaths merely rested in their cradles, unaware that one of them was dying in agony.

Resalon opened the echo-plasm's control panel and drew out the red filament and tube bundle pinched with yellow parchment. He plugged the leads into the adjoining sockets and suddenly, four astropaths in their cradles seized and bucked against the mortis-cry.

3

'WHAT DO WE have?' Tech-Father Nuvosa demanded. His winnowed frame rested at the centre of the room, his body plugged into a circular dais. The lower half of his body had been surgically amputated years ago, the metallic sacrum of his reinforced spine the platform's socket that linked thought to the surrounding techno-artefacts. Slow-moving plates orbited him, each of them pulling streams of rune-code from the etherium.

Tech-Acolyte Resalon was pale, his eyes sunken. He wavered on his feet, but he handed the flims-pic to Nuvosa. It was part image, part X-ray. 'It's the only thing the cogitators could translate,' he said. 'Three astropaths dead... one we had to put down after he–' Resalon sighed. 'The vision's too corrupted by the psyker's death.'

Nuvosa studied the flims-pic. It was grainy... a tattered, blood-caked standard half-buried in sand among a sea of torn bodies. The shot caught the standard's frayed edges in mid-flutter. Upon it, the double-eagle crest of the Imperium.

'Where did the mortis-cry originate from?' Nuvosa asked.

'A desert world in the Barrases System... Khadar. It's in the underbelly of the galactic plane of the Ultima Segmentum. The transmission was an Imperium distress cry. The cogitators couldn't identify the astropath that sent it.'

Nuvosa's eyelids fluttered briefly as he accessed the Administratum's data-scrolls. The million-plus planet names were transmitted to the cerebra-ocular implant keyed into his occipital lobe. The names appeared only to Nuvosa, as scrolling ghostly runes. The search distilled it down to a thousand, a hundred, a dozen worlds, and finally to one. After a moment, his eyes shot up and he captured Resalon in his gaze.

'That's not possible,' Nuvosa said. 'Khadar's a desert planet, yes, but there's no Imperial presence there. It's not even settled. Khadar is uninhabited.'

CHAPTER ONE

'My tribe and I against outsiders,
'My brother and I against our tribe.'
– *The Accounts of the Tallarn*
by Remembrancer Tremault

1

DAY ZERO

The fleet of small ships drifted in the pitch of stars and held formation on approach to the system's outer planet – a frozen ball of nitrogen and methane. Ribbons and spittle-threads floated around them, grey immaterium plasma ejected during the fleet's explosive birth at retranslation from Empyrean space.

Cruisers with gun-barrel bodies, frigates with flying ribbed buttresses, destroyers, transports and squadrons of patrolling Fury interceptors all orbited the heart of the fleet – the Defiant-class cruiser *Oberron's Flight* with its carbon scorched prow and eagle figurehead.

2

COMMISSAR REZAIL STOOD at the ornate lancet window of his small cabin aboard *Oberron's Flight* and soaked up the hum of the ship through his black boots. He stared out at the fleet, but could barely see the ships against the star scattered darkness. Only their blinking red and yellow beacons assured him of their presence.

'Attention.' The vox-box crackled, and a voice echoed through the ship's corridors. 'This is the officer of the watch. We're entering the Barrases System. We'll anchor in three hours. Prepare for planetfall.' The vox-box went silent.

Rezail straightened his peaked cap and the high collar of his brown coat. He turned and faced the Tallarn Guardsman standing at attention, the one in the yellow tunic, leather boots and white cotton kafiya, wrapped loosely around his neck. The Guardsman's skin was a sunbaked brown, which brought out the streaks of white in his peppered moustache. An ivory-handled dagger hung from his black leather belt. He stood in sharp contrast to Rezail's pale skin and stocky, almost soft, body.

'Sergeant Tyrell Habaas,' Rezail said. 'As my aide, one of your chief duties will be to teach me Tallarn battle-cant.'

'Yes, commissar,' Tyrell said, 'but which one do you wish to learn? Tallarn has many tribes and tribal alliances. There are four battle-cants and many–'

'High Cant... from your holy books.'

'That is a language of nobles. Not many soldiers–'

'They'll learn. Which tribal alliance do you belong to?' Rezail asked.

'The Hawadi. We number eighty-seven tribes.'

'Your people are neutral?' Rezail asked, studying the densely clustered runes of the intelligence dossier.

Tyrell wove his head a touch. 'We are teachers and scholars.'

'Yes,' Rezail said, motioning with the data-slate in his hand. 'It says here that your tribe serves the Tallarn regiments as support staff. Why is that?'

'We are respected by the others for our great learning. We arbitrate disputes. We mediate. We are trusted because we allow two sides to reach a truce without either losing face.'

'Face is very important to your people.'

'Of course. Without it we are dishonoured.'

'And you are neutral in this conflict, between the Turenag and Banna alliances?'

'Always.'

Rezail considered his steps carefully. This wasn't going to be easy. The different battle-cants were only a symptom of a larger problem facing the newly formed regiment. The Tallarn were a 'passionate people' according to one scroll in the Stratum Populace dossier prepared for him by the Administratum, but in his experience, 'passionate' was a bureaucratic cipher for 'hothead', and by that definition, orks were exceedingly passionate and exuberant.

'In that case,' Rezail said, 'I need you to teach me something... something called the promise of salt.'

3

THE OBSERVATION DECK of the light cruiser, *Blood Epoch*, offered an unparalleled view of the surrounding stars. The striated green and white marble of a gas giant drifted by the port lancet windows, the last planet before Khadar swung into view. Prince Turk Iban Salid, lost to private thought, was barely aware of proceedings.

Commissar Rezail stood on a rusting iron dais, coroneted by the system's distant blue sun in the window behind him. As Rezail spoke, Tyrell stood by a window near the stage and spoke softly into the microbead, translating Rezail's speech for those officers unfamiliar with the nuances of Gothic.

'Five weeks ago,' Rezail said, 'astropaths received a psyker distress cry... Imperial. It originated from the uninhabited desert world of Khadar.'

Turk nodded automatically and cast a sidelong glance at the other high-ranking officer in the room, the ebony-skinned Nisri Dakar. Nothing short of Turk's knife at his throat would bring Turk pleasure. Every centimetre of Nisri's two metres disgusted him: his clean-shaven head demanded to be split, his thin body broken, his wiry muscles snapped, and his dark skin deserved to glisten with his blood instead of his sweat.

'It is our glorious duty to establish a small garrison on Khadar, to investigate the source of the transmission.'

Nisri nodded, but Turk noticed that he also listened with a half-cocked smile. He was no doubt pleased with his new posting.

'Prince Iban Salid, who do you serve?'

Turk started; he almost didn't realise that Rezail was speaking directly to him in a broken Tallarn that fumbled over the guttural consonants. Turk straightened, immediately aware that all eyes were upon him. It electrified the room and set everyone on edge. He could see it in the darting glances, and in the hands that looped their thumbs on their belts, closer to their blades.

'I war for the Emperor! All that is left of the 82nd Shaytani of the Dust wars for the Emperor,' Turk said.

'Aya!' Turk's officers cried out.

'May His light bless our meagre lives,' Turk concluded.

'And whose hand does the Emperor guide?' Rezail asked, again in broken Tallarn.

'Yours,' Turk responded, but Rezail stared at him for longer than was comfortable. He gritted his teeth against the admission, but continued, 'and our Iban Mushira – Colonel Nisri Dakar – our new commander's. May his bravery lead us to victory,' *and may the saints take his eyes*, he concluded silently.

Colonel Nisri Dakar watched as Turk responded to the commissar. He watched how the commissar gestured to both men with his right hand.

He understands our customs, Nisri thought. *He isn't showing favour by using the left hand to signify a lesser.*

Nisri despised Turk, who seemed lazy and dull with his squat body, his heavy muscles and the tan-brown touch of many suns. Turk kept his beard trimmed short, but there was cold calculating mischief in his black eyes.

Although he delighted at Turk's forced conceit, Nisri took care not to display it. He was the regimental colonel; he had to lead by example.

'And you, Colonel Dakar,' Rezail asked, turning to Nisri. 'Who do you serve?'

'I serve the Aba Aba Mushira, the Emperor, in all things. I am His sword and He is my hand. All that is left of the 351st Derv'sh Blades of the Imperium submits to his will.'

'Aya!' cried the officers of Nisri's regiment.

'And who do you greet as brothers in this room?' Rezail asked.

Dakar smiled; the commissar already possessed the small tokens of Tallarn formalities, enough to tie his hands in honour and custom.

'I share my salt with you, Commissar Rezail,' Nisri said, bowing his head, 'and I share my salt with Iban Mushira, Battalion Commander Turk Iban Salid. May I prove worthy to lead him,' *and may he prove himself unworthy to be led.*

Rezail nodded to his adjutant, who rushed forward and offered the commissar a worn leather pouch. Rezail opened the drawstrings and tipped the pouch. Nisri accepted the poured salt in both palms.

'We are brothers in battle and we are both sons of the Emperor,' Nisri said, slowly spilling the salt to the ground. 'Will you offer me the wisdom of your council?'

'I will,' Turk said, accepting his share of the salt from Rezail and spilling it slowly. 'Will you offer me the wisdom of your guidance?'

'Indeed,' Nisri said.

There was a slight pause; Rezail caught the translation of the exchange with Tyrell's discreet assistance over the micro-bead. 'I'll leave you to prepare your men, then,' Rezail said with a simple nod.

* * *

4

TURK DID NOT slow his clipped pace down the ship's corridor, but Master Gunner Nubis caught up to him in a handful of long strides. Nubis glanced back at the officers following Turk, and they immediately fell back, offering them a moment alone.

Master Gunner Nubis was a large man and he took up space in every sense of the word. His skin was the kind of deep ebony that space itself envied, while across his forehead rose the patterned scars of his tribe, made from rubbing ash into tiny cuts. Each signified a campaign won, a kill of prestige made. They were but a fraction of the scars on his back, most of them trophies belonging to the regiment's lash-officer.

'Now's not the time,' Turk said, anticipating his friend's grievance.

'When then?' Nubis whispered, half-turning to address Turk. His voice was thick with the tribal dialect of the free-spirited Nasandi tribesmen. When he spoke, his accent added spice to his words. 'When Nisri sends his men to slit our throats?'

'We shared salt. Tradition is–'

'Yes,' Nubis replied, 'you shared salt while the commissar pressed a gun to your head.'

Turk grinned. Nubis's flare for the melodramatic always brought a grin to his face. 'The commissar did not press a gun to my head. He, rightly, reminded us of our duty.'

'Did we need reminding when the orks killed half our men?'

'My men,' Turk corrected.

'Your men, my friends,' Nubis said. 'May their deaths honour the Emperor; they died doing their duty. To say we need reminding is an insult to their sacrifice.'

'Yes,' Turk said, 'but that's not the point. The 82nd's record is not in question. Our feud with the Turenag is.'

'We have a right to demand blood,' Nubis said, 'and having that Turenag dog as your superior is too much to bear!'

Turk sighed, but slowed down. He motioned for other officers to join him.

'I haven't forgotten the blood feud,' Turk whispered, his voice soft against the walls, 'but I will not disgrace us as a regiment. We serve the Emperor first. Nisri and his men are insignificant in the face of that duty. But keep a vigilant eye, and protect yourselves. If you suspect anything, see me first. Spill no blood.'

Nubis smiled, but Turk fixed him with a scowl. 'Swear it, Nubis.'

'What?' Nubis replied. 'You do not trust me?'

'You are a stubborn goat–' Turk said.

'And about as ugly,' one of the officers interjected. The others laughed.

'I trust your word when you give it and I've seen you endure the lash to keep it,' Turk said. 'Give me your word.'

Nubis shook his head. 'Fine, I will not spill a drop of their watery blood unless you ask it.'

Turk nodded. 'Good. You'd better not, because if it comes to that, Nisri belongs to me.'

The men laughed and patted Turk on the back.

5

NISRI WALKED INTO the sacrarius chamber and tucked the end of the seamless white cloth into his braided waistband. The cotton cloth measured roughly four metres long and was wrapped around his body and over his shoulders in the traditional manner of the humble supplicant. Nisri's bare feet ached at the touch of the cold metal floor, but once inside the sacrarius chamber with its wood-panelled floors, his toes unclenched.

He greeted the handful of surviving officers of his 351st Derv'sh Blades with a nod and a smile. Then, he knelt at the edge of the washing pool with its white cerite tiles and the iron lock-box in the corner. The *Trumpet of the Golden Throne* was a Sword-class frigate and one of the few ships in the fleet with a Tallarn captain. As such, the good Captain Abrahim had converted part of the ship's cathedrum into a sacrarius where the Tallarn could observe worship of the Emperor in their own fashion.

The officers washed their pattern-scarred arms and faces at the edge of the pool, while the hum of regurgers filtered and recycled the water; the erratic gasps of the ship's engines sent ripples across its surface.

After several minutes of prayers for absolution, strength and victory, Nisri straightened and looked to each officer.

'This is the last time we bathe together as a regiment,' Sergeant Saheen Raham said. He was deeply tanned, but his blond hair and purple eyes betrayed his Cadian heritage, a rare gene-stock on Tallarn.

'I know,' Nisri said, simply. 'After this moment the 351st exists only in Imperial records. We are the 892nd now.'

The officers exchanged glances. Nisri knew what they were thinking, but he chose to let them voice their concerns.

Sergeant Darik Ballasra cleared his throat and waited. He was the old man of the unit and a true tribesmen with his leathery, brown skin. His hair and beard were white and thin, and his body lean with age but alive with strength. A delta of wrinkles splashed out from the corners of his dark eyes. Once everyone turned to face him, he spoke, his voice soft and silken. 'The 892nd cannot be a regiment. Its left and right hands are at war. Peace will only come when one hand severs the other.'

'Turk won't hesitate to kill you,' Raham said.

'You should not have put him at your back,' Ballasra concluded.

Nisri nodded and calmly dried his hands on the skirt of his own cloth. 'Prince Iban Salid is at my back because I know you are at his.'

'We will protect you,' Raham said, 'but–'

'But,' Nisri said, interrupting, 'Prince Iban Salid is also a cunning man, give him that due. He will not easily betray his oath to the Imperium, and he won't allow his men to do so either. He would shame his tribe after that oath he gave.'

Raham shook his head, but it was Ballasra who spoke. 'The feud continues because of the Banna Alliance. The Commissariat said our actions were righteous.'

'It is the Banna who ignore the Writ Nonculpis. They are the traitors. They deserve to be struck down!' Raham said.

'And in doing so,' Nisri replied with a languid smile, 'you ignore the same edict that proclaimed the Banna Nonculpis. It is a stalemate. The Commissariat left it for us to finish.'

'Then let us finish it,' Raham said.

'No,' Nisri replied. 'I will not allow my first command to fall under disgrace. We serve the Emperor; Commissar Rezail was right to remind us of that. Prince Iban Salid also serves the Emperor, in his limited fashion.'

'And if Turk moves against you?'

'Then I expect you to act accordingly or to let me die a martyr's death.'

'What would that serve?' Raham said, a bitter edge to his voice.

'If I die a martyr,' Nisri said, 'then Turk and his men have done nothing but impale themselves on their own blades: the commissar will put them to the slaughter. Let them be the fools, the disloyal ones. But, if you see the blade poised at my back... well, don't let it come to that, eh? I have a few more prayers left in me.'

A few smiled, but it was a hard edict for them to follow. The voice of their kinsmen was strong, and the cry for satisfaction a steady thunder overhead.

'The Emperor will reward us for our loyalty,' Nisri said. 'Our actions have remained righteous. It is the other tribes that have faltered. It is they who will fail. Nisri nodded to the iron lock-box and waited as Ballasra opened it and removed the rosewood case.

The men nodded and knelt before the sacrarius pool. Nisri entered the waters and waited with his back turned while Ballasra removed the hooked suturing needles and threads soaked in charcoal dye from the rosewood box. Ballasra gently pinched a measure of flesh along Nisri's back and pierced the skin with the needle.

Nisri inhaled softly, but refused to gasp. He would not shame himself in the eyes of his men or the Emperor. Ballasra threaded the charcoal string through Nisri's flesh, tattooing more intricate and florid patterns along his already scarred back. Occasionally, he splashed cooling water to wash away the blood, while the officers uttered the melodic cantos of submission to the God-Emperor and waited for their turn.

6

'WILL THAT BE enough?' Commissar Rezail asked as Tyrell helped him remove his jacket. 'How strongly will the promise of salt bind them to their word?'

Tyrell sighed as he thought of the answer. He strung the jacket on a wire frame and turned to face the commissar, his expression apologetic. 'The promise of salt does not make honest men of the liars. It makes honest men honour their word, and it makes dishonest men more careful.'

CHAPTER TWO

'Constant sunshine a desert makes.'
– *The Accounts of the Tallarn*
by Remembrancer Tremault

1

DAY ONE

The heavy whine of atmosphere brakes pierced the dust choked air. The artificial sandstorm was a fiery orange churned by the waves of landing crafts that roared to the surface with supplies and soldiers. The storm was spread across kilometres, a mix of displaced dust and the exhaust smoke of the transports that left fat skid marks in their climb back up.

Private Ahsra Sabaak fired a flare skyward. Vox-chatter on his headset marked another flight inbound to his location and he needed to show them where to land. 'Acknowledged,' he cried over the roar of a nearby ship. He pulled his kafiya tighter over his youthful face and adjusted the oculars protecting his eyes before fighting his way through the howling winds. He stabbed more phosphor-lume torches into the sand to mark the corners of his grid.

A moment later, the screaming whine of the protesting transport threatened to rattle his teeth loose. He barely avoided the blast of the ship's backwash, as its thrusters fought to control its descent. Sabaak was sure his uniform was singed, and muttered a curse against the pilot's mother.

The sand melted under the inferno thrust exhaust and would later rematerialise as rippled and blackened obsidian. Sabaak steered clear of the vessel's melted footprint and waited for the vice clamps to disengage with loud metal *pangs*. Rectangular bolted containers lining the ship's underbelly suddenly dropped, shaking the earth. The landing craft tore off into the dusky sky again.

Sabaak ignored the lingering heat and examined the cargo containers. He squinted at rune markings in confusion, and groaned. He pulled the vox from his belt and fumbled for the switch through his heavy gloves.

'This is grid 12-23,' he yelled into the vox. 'Tell those old whores aboard the *Trumpet* that they're sending the wrong supplies!'

Sabaak listened to the angry chatter for a moment before yelling back. 'Fine! If you can find me a river on this world, then I'll apologise. Until then, you tell me why we need two hundred rafts on a desert planet!'

2

THE SEARING WINDS rattled bones, while black-hulled troop carriers disgorged Guardsmen. The soldiers wore calf-length puttees, webbing with canteens, battle-pack bags and shelter quarter rolls. They wrapped their weapons in swaddling cloth and protected their faces in kafiyas and blast-oculars. Many soldiers scooped up a handful of sand or knelt down to kiss the earth before scrambling back into formation.

Turk watched the Guardsmen, like ghosts in the storm, file past the Chimera's armoured visors before directing his attention back to the others. The chatter inside the command Chimera was loud, partly to be heard over the thunderous din, but mostly, just to be heard. The Chimera was cramped compared to the more open HQ Salamanders, used for this exact purpose, and it was a speck's shadow in relation to the mammoth command Leviathans used during major offensives. For the Tallarn regiment, it was the best they could muster, especially since the open-topped Salamanders proved less than useful in desert campaigns.

Along the Chimera's back wall sat a bank of auspex devices, runeplates, a vox-transmitter, a small holocaster, and two operators. Nisri and Turk stood hunched over behind the operators, each accompanied by their respective and immediate subordinates. They motioned to an iron-framed brass plate mounted on the wall. The brass plate was acidetched with the soft contours of local cartography. The subordinates spoke, while Nisri and Turk remained silent and studied one another in quick glances.

'We should pitch camp here,' Major Alef Hussari said, indicating an area of rippled lines. Alef appeared as weathered as the map, his wrinkles carved into his dark brown skin. His bushy goatee hid his mouth and seemed to dance almost comically to his words. 'The dunes will shelter our tents.'

'The dunes migrate,' Sergeant Ballasra said.

'It's sand, not water,' Hussari countered. 'The dunes won't drown us.'

'They may,' Ballasra said. 'Many dunes are even on both sides. Their faces might collapse.'

'Possibly,' Nisri said, stroking his chin, 'but that's not what concerns me. We'll pitch here,' he said indicating a small plateau. 'This will protect us from this sea of sand, and that dune pressed against it will be our ramp.' He pointed to the snaking contour of an ancient riverbed at the base of the plateau. 'With the riverbed protecting our backs, we can see for kilometres in all directions.'

'On the plateau?' Turk asked, impatience skirting the edges of his temper.

'We're exposed. The tents–' Hussari began.

'We will not stay in tents,' Nisri responded. 'We will build an outpost with defensible walls and turrets.'

Hussari raised an eyebrow, but swallowed his words. By Turk's reaction, he shared Hussari's disbelief.

'An outpost?' Turk asked. 'Our strength lies in our mobility. You're talking about penning us in a cage.'

'I'm talking about protecting us,' Nisri said. 'Some enemies you cannot outrun. They are a flood that will overtake you. Your best hope is to let their tide break around the rocks of your shores.'

'Tyranids,' Turk said. 'You're talking about your fight at the Absolomay Crush.'

Nisri said nothing, but Ballasra nodded.

'With respect,' Turk said, 'by placing us on a landmark, you make it easier for rangefinders to target us with artillery.'

'What artillery?' Nisri said, shaking his head. He tapped one of the auspex operators on the shoulder. 'Have the fleet's cogitators found any sign of life yet? An army? Machines? Flint arrows? Anything?'

The operator shook his head. 'Auspex are clean so far.'

'There you have it,' Nisri said.

'And the transmission?' Turk asked. 'Someone sent the mortis-cry. Someone died here.'

'The word of the mind witches,' Nisri said. A look of displeasure eclipsed his features. 'Who knows what they saw, or why they claim to have seen it. There's no sign of life here and the dunes stretch to the horizons. Even if an army hides here, no artillery can navigate the dunes easily. We make our base on the plateau. That is my order.'

Turk bit his tongue, but it was difficult to keep it coiled in his mouth. He felt foolish; he knew the artillery argument was weak the moment he raised it, but he was eager to dissuade Nisri from his decision. An uncomfortable moment passed, long enough for everyone to exchange wary glances. 'As you wish,' Turk said finally, biting down on his words.

'Now,' Nisri said, barely acknowledging Turk's bitter acquiescence, 'on to the matter of the patrols.'

3

COMMISSAR REZAIL NAVIGATED past the crates and boxes, the soldiers, and the packs of baying dromads and muukali. Chaos had overtaken the plateau, but at least Rezail's tinted oculars and rebreather mask protected him against the dusty winds. Several kilometres away, transports and troop carriers continued to labour skyward, further agitating the storm.

Tyrell, meanwhile, pointed out the various members of the expedition. The first man to earn description was Duf'adar Nab'l Sarish, a lanky man with ropes for muscles, dark brown leather for skin, and an untamed beard and moustache. He wore a bandolier across his chest and two laspistols at his belt. Sarish pulled at the reins of a mottled dromad that complained and snapped. With its long neck and skinny legs, thick bristles of hair, humps and hooked snout, it was a creature alien to Rezail's experiences. Sarish gripped its reins tight and yanked the beast along.

'Duf'adar?' Rezail asked. 'That means sergeant, correct?'

'In a manner, but do not tell him that,' Tyrell responded. 'Duf'adar Sarish is a Sen'tach rider. They are a very proud people, very stubborn. Sergeant means servant, yes? And they are no man's servant.'

'We are all servants of the Emperor,' Rezail said. 'So the rank of Duf'adar is equal to sergeant, but nobody calls them that, correct?'

'Yes, commissar. Duf'adar Sarish tends to our riding animals and teaches us how to shoot at full gallop. He is an accomplished marksman.'

Rezail nodded. 'Excellent, but there is one thing I find confusing. Tallarn was viral bombed, yes? Sulphuric and rust deserts from the decomposing corpses of a million tanks.'

'Yes, commissar,' Tyrell responded, a faint smile on his lips. 'You are wondering why our people need pack animals? Tallarn is a wasteland, but our sheltered undergrounds are a vast network of tunnels as great as any hive-world. We also have a sister planet, two systems away, Ibanna Tallarn. The princes of the various tribes grow and train their herds there.'

'Why?'

'Livestock is the privilege of the truly wealthy, commissar. The princes have great estates on Ibanna Tallarn, and they train their riders there.'

'Is this sister world of yours free of tribal friction?'

'No, commissar,' Tyrell said as he shook his head. 'No place is free of it.'

4

TURK NODDED TO the commissar as Tyrell gave him the tour of the camp. The battalion commander arrived at a small tent and entered without knocking. The stench of fuel and pack animals seemed instantly forgotten, overtaken by the scent of oil and freshly crushed jasmine. The censers added a pleasant haze, but the cot and regulation gear were otherwise standard issue.

'This is opulent,' Turk said, half-entering, making sure the tent flap remained open to avoid any suggestion of impropriety. He locked eyes with the woman who sat on the cot. She stood slowly, uncertain, and nodded. Her black hair curled at her shoulders and her thick, black lashes swept him into her almond-shaped, black eyes. Red henna tattoos with florid curls covered the backs of her hands and the lower half of her face. She wore loose robes, and a psychic hood made from bulwark plates, haemorrhage valves, a focussing visor and sheathed cable bundles rested next to her, to help focus her powers as the unit's sanctioned mind witch.

'Colonel Nisri Dakar is a conservative man. It's best I not be around the men, battalion commander,' the woman said. 'It wouldn't be good for their morale.'

'Battalion Commander Turk Iban Salid. It is only fair you should know my name, Kamala Noore.'

She nodded. 'Of course. How may I serve a prince of the Banna?'

'Have you… sensed anything yet?'

'If a psyker died on this world, then the winds swept his cries away. I sense nothing. It's as if we're alone in the most terrible way possible.'

'I'll expect a full report later,' Turk said. He paused, saying nothing, but remaining at the door.

'Yes, battalion commander?' Kamala said, apparently uncertain how to act around Turk.

'If you were Banna, you would receive better treatment than this,' Turk said. 'You are blessed, an instrument of the Emperor.'

'And you are idol-worshippers according to the Turenag,' she whispered.

'The Orakle is the Emperor's voice. We do not worship him. He is an astropath and he guides us: a saint keeping us on the Emperor's road.'

Kamala smiled and her face seemed to blossom. Turk almost gasped at the sudden and honest beauty in her features.

'Perhaps,' she said, 'but your men fear me as much as the Turenag. I've seen them ward themselves when I pass.'

'Our fear is respect. You could have a place of honour among my people, a consort to the Orakle perhaps?'

'And the blood spilt between our two people?'

'What the sand drinks, the Banna still remember. I won't deny that.'

'As do the Turenag. Oh trust me, I know,' Kamala said. 'It's all I can see on everyone's mind.'

'How close are we?' Turk asked softly, taking a step inside, the tent flap kept open by the whisper of his fingertips. 'How close to bloodshed?'

'Very close. I can taste iron on the winds. The men would gladly spill their enemies' blood.'

'Who will start it?'

'It has started already,' Kamala said, her smile retreating. Her eyes seemed to fall away.

'What of you, then?' Turk asked. 'Where do you stand? Should I fear you?'

Kamala smiled, the question anticipated. 'You already fear me, sir,' Kamala said, each word spoken with some pain. 'But Banna or Turenag, I serve the 892nd. I serve the Emperor to my dying thoughts.'

'Thank you,' Turk replied. 'I'll expect your report in an hour.'

5

DAY ONE: HOUR NINE

The camp was only hours old and still in turmoil when the planet's whispers turned into a steady howl that drove thick drifts of sand across the dunes. The horizon was already a deep orange, a sure omen of the storm's power, and the fleet had stopped the supply drops for the night. The Guardsmen didn't have time to erect storm walls or to dig trenches; instead, they lashed down the supply containers using gas-powered nail-pumps to secure the cargo netting before running for cover. The dozen or so vehicles were already parked at the foot of the plateau, facing away from the storm, and several platoons lay sheltered behind their treads.

Colonel Dakar tightened the kafiya around his face and adjusted his blast-oculars. He stumbled towards the command Chimera, which had already extended its snort mast high into the dusty air. If the storm buried the vehicle under a lake of sand, the collapsible snorkel tube would be the only thing saving the crew from certain suffocation, and it would indicate to other Guardsmen where to dig. Nisri grimaced and entered the coffin. Being buried was the worst part of these storms, if one discounted being caught outside by the flaying winds. Nisri silently wished his own men good luck tonight, and hoped the storm would take some of Turk's soldiers.

6

MAJOR WAHID ANLEEL trudged through the maze of cargo containers, pulling at locked doors and cursing a dozen epithets against the storm. Anleel's men, 1st Company, were scattered somewhere in these stifling steel boxes. The storm, however, tore at his clothing and threw drifts of sand at his feet. He needed shelter, and he needed it now.

Anleel spotted a raised snort mast in the near distance. All Tallarn regiment containers were equipped with such devices, and functioned as emergency shelters. Unfortunately, the regiment's new quartermaster had only opened and unloaded a handful of containers before the storm had overtaken them.

Anleel stumbled towards the cargo container. Half-buried metal crates lay scattered outside its door, probably supplies thrown out to make room for more refugees inside. A black, carbonised flash mark from a laspistol marked the demise of the door's missing padlock: not the quartermaster's standard key, but Anleel was grateful for someone else's initiative. He touched the door and yelped at the nasty jolt of static electricity. His entire arm jerked and cramped. He shook his hand, freeing it of the tingling.

He opened the door, and then quickly shut it against the protest of the winds outside and the huddled men inside. With a grateful gasp, he removed his oculars and kafiya.

'You're not one of us,' a voice said.

Anleel spun around and put his back to the door. He faced two-dozen men, all unfamiliar to him, all hostile, all rival tribesmen belonging to the Turenag. Some had drawn their long scimitars.

'You're not welcome here, dog,' a voice said from the darkness. 'Leave while you have the legs for it.'

'The storm outside–' Anleel said, stammering. 'You cannot refuse a man protection from the desert – Colonel Dakar and Battalion Commander Iban Salid... they shared salt.'

'That is why we're letting you leave alive.'

Anleel studied their faces before pulling his oculars back down and yanking the kafiya over his face. He backed out of the door, pushing against the drifts piled against the container, and vanished into the howling storm. He was completely turned around, uncertain which direction offered safety. His best hope was to stay near the cargo containers. He stumbled away, one arm against the corrugated walls as a guide.

A flash of light pulsed by Anleel and was swallowed by the storm. He barely had time to turn before a second laspistol beam caught him on the shoulder and cooked the wound. Anleel tried to scream, but his kafiya slipped off his chin, and sand rushed in to choke him. Two more shots punched him in the chest, both white hot, both cooking and cauterising flesh, muscle and bone.

Anleel collapsed face first into the sand. Two Guardsmen swathed against the storm grabbed him by the armpits and pushed his body over the plateau's edge. The wind and sand took care of the rest.

7

CAPTAIN BER'NAM TORIA of C Platoon was exhausted. He was searching for Major Anleel, who'd failed to report back to his company. When Anleel was nowhere to be found among the containers, Toria ventured down to the base of the plateau to search the vehicles. Foolish of him, he knew, but the storm made vox chatter impossible, and now he was alone, lost and turned around, his compass useless.

Toria's legs were iron bundles. The fatigue settled in with a deep ache that burned at the wick of his muscles. His shins sank into the loose sand, and it was growing harder to pull them out. He'd heard something about the properties of the desert, how the sandstorm generated an electric charge. He didn't understand mechanical crafts, specifically why they affected his compass or the voxes, or even friction, but he was told they did. So there he was, in sand drifts that seemed more liquid than solid as they almost parted beneath his feet. It cost him more in energy to pull his feet out than it did for his weight to push them down.

In the distance, over the howling winds, a crack of electricity snapped and lit the murky air. Captain Toria had never seen lightning without storm clouds, and the notion that air could generate a charge from nothing frightened him. He stumbled forward, crying out for someone, anyone. More electricity bit at the air in the furthest glooms, coming from the same direction as the last two blasts of lightning.

Toria hesitated. It was hard to think; the fatigue had numbed him, and even the storm's sting was too distant to wake him. He shook his head. 'Think,' he muttered. 'Why would lightning strike the same area?' Something was attracting the electricity, something constant in the storm. It was his only landmark. Static lightning be damned, Toria didn't intend to drown in this dusty sea. He lurched forward, burning through the last rush of adrenaline, forcing his feet to make one step after another.

Too far, it was too far. Toria stumbled and fell forward. The sand swallowed his arms past the elbows. His knees sank and dragged him down to his waist. His face hovered centimetres above the sand, his strength fading, his leverage gone. He tried pushing up, but he sank further. He cried out, but the winds smothered his voice. The struggle to be free pulled him down another deep centimetre. He fought harder, panic overtaking reason, rational thought all but gone. Toria grunted and whined like an animal facing death.

Another few centimetres, and Toria would be drinking sand. His limbs quaked at the exertion, and he moaned softly.

'In or out, boy?' a voice asked, shouting over the wind. 'I can push you in if you've surrendered; make it easier for you to die.'

'Help,' Toria shouted. He could barely see the man out of the corner of his oculars, but he struggled against the sand.

'Out it is.' Someone's arm looped under Toria's armpit and struggled to pull him up. 'Work with me, boy, I'm too old to lift you.'

One arm came free, and then another. In a moment, Toria was standing again, his heart pounding and rattling his senses. His vision swam with fatigue, and the head rush almost tipped him over again. He allowed his rescuer to pull him along.

Moments later, they arrived at a full-track lorry that was buried up to its lower road wheels in sand. A faint bluish light flickered and jumped at the treads, sprockets and rollers; the static electricity was expending itself, the sand no longer as frictionless. The man pushed Toria up the access steps despite the minor jolts that shocked them both. Toria collapsed in the cabin's seat while his rescuer sat in the driver's seat. The engine was running and the air gauzers cleared away most of the interior dust.

'Thank you,' Toria managed, stripping off the kafiya and leather chamfrom wrapped around his helmet. He was olive-skinned, his nose aquiline.

His rescuer nodded. 'You're lucky I saw you,' he said tapping the night vision periscope attached to the ceiling before unwrapping his kafiya. He was old, with a full growth of frosted hair that glowed against his nutmeg dark skin and elaborate, looping tribal scars spread across his chin.

A jolt shot through Toria. His rescuer was Turenag, his markings those of one of their chief tribe, the D'Shouf.

'You're Turenag,' Toria said.

'I couldn't tell which tribe you belonged to,' the man admitted. 'But, curse my father for raising me right, I would have saved you either way.'

'I thought all Turenag blood ran hot at the thought of killing us.'

'Not mine,' the man said. He leaned in close, the glimmer of a mischievous smirk on his lips. 'My blood is ice cold, boy. Would you care for a sip?'

Toria smiled despite himself. 'No,' he said, drawing up his canteen, 'I have my own water.' He tilted the bottle towards the D'Shouf tribesman. 'Not as cold as yours, though. Have some.'

The old man shook his head. 'Thank you, no.' He revved the engine of the lorry and pushed the steering lever forward. 'I have to keep her out of the sand. Another minute and I wouldn't have seen you at all.'

'Captain Toria, 1st Company, C Platoon.'

'Captain Qal Abantu, Armoured Support.'

Toria grinned. 'We have armoured support?'

Both men started laughing.

'Barely, boy,' Abantu replied, 'barely.'

It was the last thing Toria heard before he fell fast asleep.

8

DAY TWO: HOUR TEN

The storm was a day old and still pitching its fit. The interior of the command Chimera had grown stale and humid on body sweat, and a crackling voice filled the interior. From the wash of hard static, a few words floated through the cacophony.

Immediate – Forced – Althera Beta – 892nd – Orbit – Weeks

One of the two auspex operators continued fiddling with the knobs on the vox, trying to fine tune it. The voice was heavily distorted, the bursts of static haemorrhaging through the signal.

'Can you decipher it?' Nisri asked.

Corrupted – Anchor – More – Hives – Sector Lord

The operator shook his head. 'It's the storm. She dirties the air and wreaks havoc with communications.'

'I've heard worse,' the other operator replied. 'On Canimos Prime, the static discharge was enough to kill a man. But, this is the best we can get, sir.'

The vox warbled in response.

Alert – Command – Light of – Unable to – Estimated, two –

'I've heard that before,' the fair-haired Sergeant Raham said, straightening up in his seat. 'That sentence fragment, I heard it before.'

'Confirmed, sir,' one of the operators replied. 'The transmission is looping.'

Supplies – Time –Munitorum – Location – Convine

'I heard Convine,' the second operator said. 'Isn't that a hive?'

'I heard hive mentioned before,' Raham said.

'Why would they be sending us a looped transmission?' Nisri muttered.

Expedite supplies – Weigh – Unable to – Two.

'They may have been trying to reach us for several hours, sir,' the second operator replied. 'The interference varies. This is the clearest window we've had in a few hours.'

'Fine,' Nisri said, annoyed. 'Keep listening, start piecing the transmission together. Raham, I need your ears on this.'

Nisri and Raham gathered around the vox-caster while the two operators collected message strings and transcribed them to a data-slate. The words slowly clustered together into sentences.

Alert ground forces Khadar, 892nd Command.

They switched words out...

The Convine Manufactorum Hives on Althera Beta have turned against the Light of the Emperor.

...and back in again, like a grammatical puzzle.

All Imperial forces required to respond by order of Sector Lord General Behemot.

The sentences flowed together...

Fleet immediately weighing anchor to respond to call.

...some more easily than others...

Unable to send more supplies for the time being.

...until finally, the truth stood out.

Will request Departmento Munitorum expedite supplies to your location, estimated, two months.

Nisri's eyes widened. 'When was the message sent? When?'

The operators scrambled, trying to find a time-stamp in the transmission.

'About seven hours ago,' one replied, 'probably more.'

'Transmission source confirmed to be a satellite relay,' the other responded.

'That puts them outside the system,' Raham said.

'They've already left,' Nisri said, falling back into his seat.

'But it's only two months,' Raham replied. 'They sent us enough supplies for that.'

Nisri shook his head. 'They sent us the wrong supplies, sergeant, and the storm prevented them correcting their mistake! Get me the quartermaster on vox. We need to find out how much trouble we're in.'

CHAPTER THREE

'The Greedy pray for what they do not have. The Blessed pray for what was given them.'

– *The Accounts of the Tallarn*
by Remembrancer Tremault

1

DAY THREE

The desert seemed renewed, the passage of the 892nd brushed away by the winds and new coats of sand. On and around the rocky island, Guardsmen were busy digging out vehicles and cargo containers. The rosy hued plateau rose a dozen metres from the dunes on its east side, while on the west, a large dune had pressed against it, forming a ramp for treaded vehicles to traverse. The plateau's roof was a hundred metres in diameter, and the highest one the Guardsmen could reach among the many scattered throughout the region. A tall pole already stood at its centre, the newly minted double-headed eagle banner of the 892nd.

While the men worked in groups that were exclusively Banna or Turenag, they sang songs, each trying to be louder or more insulting than the other. Naturally, they weren't vulgar or deliberately demeaning, but they said enough to hint at a slur. The Banna's songs praised the Emperor and the Transmitter of His Word, the great Orakle, while the Turenag sang of their love for the Emperor alone and of the perils of following false gods.

* * *

THE REMAINING VEHICLES were clustered around the command Chimera in the shadow of the plateau. Colonel Nisri Dakar sat with his men upon a mottled tan Hellhound, while Lieutenant-Colonel Turk Iban Salid stood with his at the treads of a tan Chimera. Commissar Rezail and Tyrell Habass stood off to the side, at the open ramp of the command Chimera.

Captain Ural Kortan, Quartermaster of the 892nd, had noticed the commissar's adjutant dropping sodium and potassium powder into the commissar's canteen earlier. Heat exhaustion, Kortan surmised, given the commissar's pale, sweaty complexion. Kortan, standing in the open circle between the vehicles, continued with his report to the command staff and ranking officers. He motioned to the data-slate for emphasis.

'We were sent supplies we didn't need,' Kortan replied, 'inflatable rafts, carbon-filtered rebreathers, five full pallets of green vehicle paint… I can continue,' Kortan said, shrugging.

'Fine,' Nisri said, rubbing his scalp hard. 'What do we have that we can use?'

'We have enough rations to last twenty-three days, and water for twenty-five.'

'Ration them both out,' Nisri said. 'That's a meal per soldier, per day, two for the sick. We'll switch to night operations to stave off dehydration. Sergeant Ballasra?'

'Um, yes,' Ballasra said, stroking his white beard. 'By your will and the Emperor's providence, my squad can see what the desert provides.'

'Very well, search the area for edibles, preferably something more appetising than sand. Duf'adar Sarish,' Nisri said, turning his attention to the stable master. 'We may need to slaughter some of the animals if they cannot graze, or if there is no water for them to drink.'

Sarish scowled, but he nodded. Turk and his officers straightened; they seemed ready to say something, but Nisri was quick to interrupt them.

'Which of your men do you recommend to help Sergeant Ballasra?' Nisri asked.

Turk bit his lip for a moment, before nodding to the olive-skinned man next to him. 'Captain Toria and his men are fine trackers and hunters.'

'The same Captain Toria that Captain Abantu saved?' Raham asked.

Of Nisri's men, all but Captain Abantu chuckled at the jibe, but Nisri silenced them with a harsh glare. He was not pleased, his look cruel, like the drawing of an assassin's blade from its sheath. Even Raham reddened and looked away.

Turk, meanwhile, had forcibly grabbed Master Gunner Nubis by the arm and pulled him back. Kortan noticed all this, and took measure of where the lines were being drawn.

'And for that,' Turk said, keeping his eyes on Nisri, 'Captain Abantu has my thanks. Captain Toria was searching for Major Anleel, First Company's commander, during the storm.'

'And have you found him?' Nisri asked.

'No sir. Five men went missing last night, from both companies. The electric discharges may have rendered them senseless long enough for the storm to get the better of them.'

'I sent two Sentinel squadrons searching for them,' Major Hussari said. 'There's no sign of them.'

'Unfortunate,' Nisri said. 'Very well, Captain Toria and Sergeant Ballasra will coordinate their efforts to locate food and water. What else, Captain Kortan?'

'Plasm-tins,' Kortan replied, 'to cook the food, we have enough for twenty days.'

'Perhaps we can siphon vehicle fuel?' Nisri asked, looking at Abantu.

'What's mine is yours, but we were only sent half of what we needed. The storm robbed us of the other half, and we're low on power cells for the vehicles.'

Nisri thought for a moment, before sighing. 'Ration the fuel as well. The command Chimera has priority on the power cells–'

Lieutenant Osam Djeer, the command staff's engineering officer, quickly interrupted. 'We can tether the command vehicle to the solar generators.'

'Do so. Major Hussari's squadron receives priority on the fuel, whatever is required to stretch our reserves to two months. Regular patrols will use any dromads and mukaali that Duf'adar Sarish can spare. Now tell me, good quartermaster, and for the love of the Emperor make it favourable news, is there anything we do have in good supply?'

'Yes,' Kortan replied with a smile. 'We have plenty of sand.'

2

'Put yours backs into it,' Nubis barked at his men as they struggled at the lip of the plateau. He wiped the sweat from his face with his forearm. The night air was graciously cool, and he was happy to be away from the sun. He watched as his men struggled to pull open the collapsible wire-frame cubes. The articulated mesh expanded to form interlinking baskets ten metres long. These would form the battlements atop the plateau. Once they'd riveted them into the hard rock, the companies would fill the layered rows of baskets with sand, creating walls that could absorb heavy bolter fire and shelling.

Nearby, a Turenag work detail was laying the foundations for the command bunker, and singing about their beautiful wives and the children they had left at home. A couple of men in Nubis's group began singing the praises of their wives in retort, when Nubis pushed through his men and slapped one across of the back of his head.

'What are you doing?' Nubis said, spittle flying from his mouth. 'Singing with them? These are Turenag! They killed the Orakle Murha and they've ambushed our fathers and our uncles. Go on, then! Sing! Sing like women, because you certainly aren't acting like the men of the Banna!'

The men hesitated, and then returned to their work, their prides stung and their skin flushed with heat. Nobody spoke, and even the Turenag work detail watched in silence.

'Well?' Nubis shouted at the Turenag. 'Keep singing! My men deserve to be entertained by women.'

The Turenag exploded into curses and insults, and several men moved forward with their pickaxes ready. Nubis and his men positioned themselves to face the enemy, pry bars and shovels in their hands. They were only metres apart when a white las-shot, instant and lethal, lit the night and scorched the earth between them. Two more landed in quick succession, for emphasis, stopping everyone in their tracks. Duf'adar Sarish held two dissimilar laspistols, one trained on each group of men.

'Get back to work,' the Sen'tach rider told them. 'You are frightening my animals.'

Nubis eyed Sarish and motioned his men back to work. Slowly, the work crews returned to their details, but none of them sang any more. They glared at one another and at Sarish, who was watching them carefully in return.

3

MAJOR IAS'R DASHOUR stood at the opening of the tent, waiting to be acknowledged by Nisri. He was a dour-looking man, his brow constantly knotted in some distant thought. He was light skinned with a pale olive complexion, and he kept his face clean.

Nisri sat at his desk, a folding table with thin, spindly legs. Stacks of data-slates and print-sheets covered the surface in neat, ordered piles. The colonel shook his head and motioned to the information.

'Useless,' he said.

'Sir?' Dashour said, taking the opportunity to step into the cool dark of the modular tent, with its open peel-back front and peaked roof.

'All this information, and it tells me nothing. You know what nearly killed us at Absolomay?'

'The tyranids?' Dashour asked. He suppressed a shudder at the thought of firing round after round into the advancing wall of screeching, chittering xenos, their claws scrambling at the rocky terrain, their strength undiminished despite the steady, winnowing salvos. The tyranids operated as an organism, sacrificing individuals to advance the whole. They leapt into lines of dismembering fire, protecting those behind them like living shields of carapace armour. Dashour felt humbled by the purity of their… faith. Faith was the only word that fitted, Dashour decided. He couldn't stop thinking about them.

'No, the tyranids took advantage of our weakness, but what almost killed us was lack of useful intelligence, stretched supply lines and poor support. Now where are we? We have a mind-witch's word of a massacre, and no evidence to support it; we have a ghost of a regiment with two meagre companies that are at each other's throats; and we have limited stocks with no guarantee of resupply. We're back where we started.'

'Not exactly true,' Dashour said. 'At least there are no tyranids.'

'That we know of,' Nisri said, laughing. 'But, after Absolomay, I expect the whoresons to pop out of the ground again.' He shook his head. 'You came to see me about something?'

'I wish it were good news.' Dashour took a quick breath. 'Some of my men found Major Anleel's body. He was murdered. It looks like lasburns to the chest and shoulder.'

Nisri shook his head and leaned back in his chair. 'Do you know who did it?'

'No sir.'

'Would you tell me if you did?'

'I would tell Prince Nisri of the Turenag, and perhaps even Lieutenant-Colonel Dakar of the 351st who it was that made his tribe proud, but, no, I wouldn't tell Colonel Dakar of the 892nd. His loyalty to the Aba Aba Mushira would humble me.'

'I see,' Nisri said, chewing on his lip. 'Do Turk's men know?'

'No sir. We hid the body until we could speak with you.'

'Very prudent.' Nisri closed his eyes, a scowl pulling at his face. 'Bury the body,' he said, his decision a heavy weight, 'as far from here as possible. Major Anleel vanished in the storm and that is the end of it. Oh… and tell your men to keep their mouths shut. They do not celebrate. They do not speak of it, even to each other. Tell them this. Tell them I'll keep my blade sharpened just in case they choose to wag their tongues.'

Dashour nodded.

'I can trust you to do this, Dashour?' Nisri ask.

'I serve you, prince-colonel. I am therefore doubly loyal to you.'

Nisri dismissed Dashour with a nod of his head and returned to his work.

* * *

4

KORTAN NODDED TO Dashour as he left the tent, though he received no recognition in return. He waited at the tent flap for Colonel Dakar to bid him to enter.

'More bad news?' Nisri asked, looking at the reports.

'No,' Kortan said, smiling. 'In fact, it's a small blessing, my good sir.'

Nisri looked up, the veins on his forehead strained and a glint in his dark eyes. 'I do not appreciate your familiarity with me.'

'Of course, sir,' Kortan said without missing a beat, 'but the Emperor blesses.'

'No praise for your Orakle this evening?' Nisri asked.

'The Orakle is a man,' Kortan said with a smile, 'a rather humourless one at that, no sport for drink or gambling, or women.'

'Are you trying to get on my good side?'

'Certainly not,' Kortan said. 'I'm merely charming by circumstance. I cannot help who likes me and who doesn't.'

'So the Emperor's blessing? What form might that take?'

'In last year's case, it took the form of a beautiful daughter of a salt merchant of Abusida Rehan. I was very blessed that night, and by morning, blessed twice more, but,' Kortan said, holding up his hands to forestall an irate looking Nisri, 'today, our blessing comes in the form of this.' Kortan held out a data-slate.

Nisri snatched the data-slate from the quartermaster's hands and studied the information. It was a topographical scan of the region with three triangular glyphs marked at the extremes of the map.

'What are these?' Nisri asked, studying the map.

'The location of three emergency orbit-drop containers, courtesy of the fleet before it weighed anchor.'

'They sent supplies?' Nisri said. A broad and cautious smile snaked across his lips.

'It appears so. The storm jammed their torch beacons until half an hour ago. I just confirmed their locations, though one... that one' Kortan said, tapping a glyph on the screen, 'appears to have been damaged in the drop.'

'Do we know the contents?'

'Some food, water and clothing... ammunition; enough to extend the rationing for a couple of extra weeks.'

'No fuel?'

'Too volatile for an orbit drop.'

'We'll take what we can get, eh? I'll send three squads to recover them. I want one of your men with each squad to make sure there's no pilfering of supplies. Coordinate with Duf'adar Sarish for the pack animals. Make several trips if you have to. We can't waste fuel for this.'

5

KORTAN WAS ON his way to the supply tent when Captain Lornis Anuman and a handful of his hard-nosed cadre stepped in the quartermaster's way. Anuman was a boorish looking man with a thick growth of peppered stubble on his jaw and a bulging chin. He was squat with a permanent tan to his flesh and a crooked bulge to his nose. He scratched at it his jaw with lazy disinterest.

'Captain Anuman,' Kortan said, spreading his arms. 'The Orakle delights me with your company.'

'I'm sure he does,' Anuman said. 'You were in Nisri's tent. I hope you're not getting too comfortable with the new colonel.'

Kortan laughed. 'Ah, captain, you're too ugly to be my wife, so why are you meddling in my business?'

Anuman and his men stepped forward, their hands resting casually on the pommels of their scimitars. 'Take care, Kortan. You should never turn your back on your own tribe.'

'Trust me, the last thing I'd do around you is turn my back. Now, out of my way,' he said, shooing them away. 'I have work to do. And, if you find yourself in my way again, I'll make sure some broken glass finds its way into your rations, or have you forgotten who handles your food?'

Anuman's grip closed around the pommel of his blade. Kortan could see the anger in his eyes and a tremble at the corner of his lips, but the quartermaster's smile never diminished. After a moment, Anuman stepped to one side. The captain's men followed suit, and Kortan brushed past them with no further trouble.

6

'HOW IS COMMISSAR Rezail?' Turk asked. He continued walking among the cargo containers atop the plateau, watching chains of men tossing box after box to one another down the line. Tyrell walked alongside him.

'Better,' Tyrell responded, speaking in tribal cant. 'He is resting in his tent. By day, he's in the command Chimera. It is the coolest place I could find.'

'Good. Should he need anything, let me know.'

'Of course.'

'One other thing,' Turk said, stopping to face Tyrell. 'Has he heard about the incidents?'

'The incidents, sir?'

'Don't play me the fool,' Turk said, a friendly smile on his face. 'The fights, the two companies almost coming to blows?'

Tyrell looked around. 'I am not comfortable discussing this behind the commissar's back.'

'But he hasn't heard about them, correct?'

'No,' Tyrell said, 'not yet, not with his heat exhaustion.'

'Good, then I have a great favour to ask of you.'

'You want me to lie to the commissar. I cannot do–'

'Yes you can, just for now, for the sake of the men. The two companies need time to adjust to their new conditions. They are Guardsmen, and they are good soldiers, but their hatred runs deep. They need more time. If Commissar Rezail starts executing men, they will not only despise one another all the more, but they'll also come to despise the commissar. How long do you think he'll last then?'

'Not long,' Tyrell admitted.

'Give us time,' Turk said.

Tyrell bit his tongue for a moment and privately mulled over the matter. 'You have two days, at best,' Tyrell said, finally.

'That's not enough–'

'Are we speaking as soldiers, lieutenant-colonel? Or are we speaking as tribesmen, Prince Iban Salid?'

Turk straightened. 'I am a prince of my people, first and foremost, but my duties as prince require that I serve my people as the Emperor's soldier. You are speaking to both.'

'Then may I be honest, as Hawadi and as a soldier?'

Turk nodded.

'You want more time? You and the Turenag have had generations to settle your differences. I could give you a year, two even, and it would solve nothing. Your men are soldiers; they should follow your example and act like it. The same goes for Colonel Dakar's men, but he hasn't asked for my council.'

'What are you saying?' Turk asked.

'I am saying I will not tell the commissar what has happened in his absence. But when he returns, rest assured I will report everything that happens from that moment forward. I have no other choice. If reason will not rule your men, then perhaps fear will.'

7

Day Five

The large bonfire was weak, the growths of dry brush found on neighbouring plateaus being poor fuel for the flames. The animals refused to eat the bone-white branches and thorn-brush leaves; all that was left was for the fire pit.

The half-finished base camp was clustered around the bonfire, just beyond the skirt of light. The command centre and the barracks were nothing but sandbag walls, and were still being built. Tents with peaked roofs, box frames and black cloth, designed to absorb the heat, littered the interior compound. A grid of solar panels plastered along the walls of one tent glistened under the stars, quietly awaiting morning.

The camp's modular, sand-filled walls were completed. They measured seven metres high, with an interior ledge for the gun emplacements, and barbed wire topping the battlements. At the base of the wall rested funk holes, alcoves to protect troops during shelling.

The atmosphere around the bonfire was quiet, the men finding little reason to socialise or interact beyond their small circles. As always, the Turenag sat on one side, the Banna on the other, and the command staff in the middle. Angry glares passed between the two tribal alliances, but with Commissar Rezail sitting there, still pale, but ever fierce in his vigilance, nobody exchanged words or pursued feud-oaths.

SERGEANT NUBIS RECLINED on his prayer roll and stared at the fire. Captain Anuman was at his side, his tone decidedly venomous.

'I'm sure of it,' Anuman said. 'Kortan is an opportunistic snake.'

'Yes,' Nubis said, 'but he is our snake.'

Anuman shook his head. 'Aya, but you can be sure of one thing, a snake always bites. It has no friend. It has no master.'

'Perhaps.'

'Listen to me; I'm sure Kortan is giving more supplies to Nisri and his dogs. We're on strict rations so they can keep themselves fat. Sabaak was on recovery duty with Sergeant Raham's squad.'

'So?'

'Let me finish. When the squad returned, Majri saw one of Raham's men pay Sabaak for extra meals, and Baloos says that neither the squad nor the animals looked particularly dehydrated after their trip. His father was a Mukowwa'en, a dromad driver, and he knows the look of thirst and water rationing. What do you think?'

'I think your men gossip like old women at the market... but there's use in that. Keep your eyes open. Let me know if you find anything else.'

COLONEL NISRI DAKAR and Lieutenant Colonel Turk Iban Salid sat on a large carpet with Sergeant Ballasra, Major Hussari and Captain Toria. The bonfire crackled gently, and they were studying the samples of things that Ballasra had wrapped in cloth strips, and was now unfolding for them.

'This desert is not entirely without hospitality,' Ballasra said. 'These small animals are meagre on meat and taste, but at least they are not poisonous.' He showed them several small strips of brownish meat, all cooked, and all looking dry and tough. 'Take it,' he said. 'Eat. It's cooked.'

Reluctantly, the men each took a strip and bit into the meat; grimaces all around. They chewed harder to force their meals down, the slightly rancid flavour filling their mouths with unwanted tastes and coating their tongues. Major Hussari chuckled at his compatriots' expressions while fighting to control his own. Finally, he burst out laughing.

'By the Emperor,' Hussari said, 'it's like eating feet.'

The others chuckled as well. Only Ballasra appeared indignant.

'I'll need all my water rations to wash that taste from my mouth,' Nisri added, slapping Ballasra on the back.

'Speaking of water,' Toria said, swallowing his meal hard. He struggled a moment to retain his composure. 'I found more river beds scattered throughout the area, all dry. I also found a small oasis. It's three metres wide, at best. It's being fed by an underground spring.'

'Good news,' Turk said.

'Maybe,' Toria said. 'It's a fair distance from here and I'm not sure the spring will yield much. I fear we may be wasting more water trying to get at it.'

'Still, we have to try,' Turk replied.

'No,' Nisri responded. 'I agree with Captain Toria. Our resources are thin to begin with.'

'I think we have enough breathing room,' Turk said.

'What happens if the fleet doesn't return when they're supposed to and we squander our water?'

'Exactly what happens if the fleet doesn't return and we've squandered our water while waiting? We'll have nothing. We should do this while we have the luxury to gamble.'

'I do not gamble. We'll search for another oasis, a larger one.'

'And while we search, we lose precious time.'

'Lieutenant-colonel,' Nisri said, his voice low to avoid drawing attention. 'The matter is settled.' He turned to Hussari and Toria. 'Find me another spring, something larger.'

Turk rose to his feet, his face flushed. 'Excuse me,' he said. He shot Toria an angry glance and walked away.

Toria sighed under his breath and rose as well. 'Am I dismissed, sir?' he asked Nisri. Nisri nodded. Somewhere nearby, people began playing small drum jars, and more men were clapping their hands in rhythm.

'Locust?' Ballasra asked, holding out a cloth with small blue insects. 'For an indigenous species, they're quite flavourful.'

* * *

COMMISSAR REZAIL AND Tyrell Habass sat with a group of men. Two Guardsmen, older members of the unit, played clay drums and slapped the animal hide stretched over the drum's hollow top. Four more men with bare feet, their puttees wrapped around their ankles and under their heels, wielded glittering scimitars etched with the tribal markings of the Banna. The dancers moved slowly around one another in a slow dance pantomime, while the rest of the men clapped their hands in time to the beat.

'Literacy is not widespread on Tallarn,' Tyrell said. 'Many tribes remember history through oral traditions, and battles are recounted in war dances.'

Rezail nodded. 'The Turenag were once part of the Banna Alliance, but then, something about the Orakle divided them?'

'The Tallarn,' Tyrell said with a wistful smile, 'are always hot-blooded, always fighting, except in their duty to the Emperor. We almost had a civil war. The two greatest alliances, the Doraha and the Makali, grew very angry with one another, and they threatened to draw their vassal tribes into the conflict. If that happened, then over half of Tallarn would still be in blood.'

'But a psyker brokered the truce,' Rezail said. 'Right?'

'Yes. In his honour, the tribes created an Orakle of the Emperor, a supreme scholar who would speak the Emperor's wisdom. Throughout the galaxy, he would merely be an astropath, but among my people, the greatest of the astropaths becomes the Orakle, a mouthpiece for the Emperor's guidance through the holiest of bonds, the Soul Binding.'

'You believe in the Orakle of the Emperor?'

'Believe? No, but we respect his elected position. He is a man, no more, no less.'

'But some Tallarn venerate him, don't they?'

'The same way you venerate your Living Saints. The Orakle is a conduit of the Emperor's will, no more, no less.'

'But the Turenag don't see it that way. When the Banna tribe agreed to the creation of an Orakle of the Emperor, a few tribes split from them on religious principles.'

'Yes, and they formed the heart of the Turenag tribe. Then others joined, all of them believing the Orakle is a false idol. The Turenag and Banna have been quarrelling ever since.'

Rezail nodded, and continued watching the war dancers. He was exhausted, his mind still throbbing from the heat. He could have slept where he sat, but there were far too many unanswered questions.

'Tell be about the Orakle... the one that was murdered.'

'One hundred years ago,' Tyrell said, whispering, 'the Orakle of the Emperor was chosen from the Banna, the first of them to receive that honour. He was a strong man, beloved, and a son to all Banna. But the Turenag alliance not only refused to recognise him, they said he was warp spawn… corrupted.

'The Turenag sent assassins after him and killed the Orakle. It was a blow against all Banna. They retaliated, slaughtering entire tribes of Turenag in vengeance, and the Turenag retaliated in turn. At first, the war was only between Turenag and Banna, but then Banna raiders attacked and supposedly killed a village belonging to Doraha.'

'Supposedly?'

'It was never proven. Some say it was Turenag posing as Banna, to gain more allies. Some say the Doraha were already helping the Turenag, and the Banna retaliated.'

'So, how did the Commissariat become involved?'

'My tribe, the Hawadi, it was our suggestion.'

'You suggested the Commissariat mediate the matter?' Rezail said. He was surprised. Most people feared the Commissariat and its rulings, for the fate of worlds often hung in their decisions.

'Tallarn worlds were on the verge of civil war. There was much fighting, much murder, far too much. Even the Hawadi could not bring peace. The only thing the two tribes respected was the sovereignty of the Aba Aba Mushira. The Commissariat served the Emperor as men of war, not men of religion.'

'I see,' Rezail said. 'So you gambled. You thought that if the Commissariat ruled, then both sides would be forced to submit to the ruling.'

'Yes, but the Commissariat remained neutral. They executed the agitators on both sides and issued a Writ Nonculpis for the surviving Banna and Turenag, saying the matter was settled.'

'Not the answer you hoped for.'

'No.'

'Even if the judgement had put an entire tribal alliance to the flame?'

'Better an alliance than the planet. Both Banna and Turenag so believed they were right that they were willing to risk Exterminatus. The Commissariat was very clear, though, saying that the Writ Nonculpis was to stop the fighting. There was to be no more civil war; but the fighting remained, hidden, but there.'

'Aren't they disobeying the Commissariat?'

'It's like the promise of salt, commissar. The Writ Nonculpis does not make men honest.'

'I see your point,' Rezail said, watching the dancers swing their blades with poetic grace. 'I see your point.'

* * *

8

TURK STOOD ATOP the battlement, the fire at his back, and watched the stars. He tried to pretend he was home again, staring at familiar skies, but the self-deception wouldn't hold. This sky was too perfect, too unblemished, to pass for Tallarn's polluted vistas. It was beautiful, but he could sense its strangeness. None of the stars called to him as old friends.

At the very least, it dampened the sour knot in his stomach. Turk was argumentative to begin with, he knew that, and he enjoyed the respect that occasionally accompanied his position. Nisri, however, seemed determined to undercut him, to remind him that his voice held no sway in decisions. It was expected given the bloodshed between the two alliances, and while Turk could justify and reason through his situation, the fact that he was raised to despise the Turenag coloured his views. The thought of being subordinate to Nisri, a hated enemy, gnawed at him.

'It's not home, is it?' a woman's voice asked. 'Not quite?'

Turk turned to find Kamala Noore walking up the duckboard ramp that led to his ledge. A chill ran down Turk's spine... had she read his mind? Could she do that without him ever knowing?

'I'm not reading your thoughts,' she said quietly. 'Your face, however….'

'I apologise.'

'I don't need an apology,' she said. 'I'm used to the reactions. But some company, I'd like that.'

Turk hesitated.

'We don't have to talk, I promise. Just let me enjoy your company. I'm tired of hiding in my tent.'

Turk nodded and went back to studying the stars. He could almost feel Kamala sighing, her body relaxing. She was beautiful, he knew, but she caught him staring before he could look away. 'The Turenag,' he stammered. 'How do they–'

'You don't have to make conversation for my benefit,' she said, blushing.

'I want to know,' Turk said, facing her. 'Do the Turenag treat you fairly?'

'No,' she admitted. 'I am a vessel through which corruption flows.' She turned to Turk. 'How do I explain this? Ah… do you know the Turenag are so absolute in their faith that they possess no images of the Emperor? To paint him, sculpt him, or illustrate him in anything but words is to worship the image and not the power. To record his image is to deny his boundless nature. Omniscience, omnipresence, they cannot be recorded, and to do so is to imply that the Emperor has limits. It is the Turenag mark of absolute humility and absolute submission.'

'What's that got to do with you?'

'The Turenag decided that to suggest that our power makes us greater than anyone else is also to suggest that we are closer to the Emperor in power. That implies that we are somehow closer to He that cannot be qualified. We become a point of definition, and you can't have that in respect to the Emperor.'

'I can see why that can be confusing. Perhaps if you read their minds,' Turk said, straight-faced, 'then it would make more sense.'

Kamala laughed. 'A joke, lieutenant-colonel, thank you.'

Turk shrugged, a modest smile on his lips.

'But no,' she said. 'I wouldn't want to read a Turenag's mind. Some tribes murder their baby daughters, and I know they kill psyker children when they have a chance.'

'How did you escape?' Turk asked.

'The Inquisition's Black Ships found me first. I returned to my tribe when they drew up the regiment. I was battle-trained by then and more than capable of defending myself.'

'Indeed,' Turk said. It was easy to stare into her black eyes and forget her power. Despite himself, Turk found he was swimming in her gaze, and she in his. It was a pleasant distraction from the road that he knew lay ahead.

CHAPTER FOUR

'As the passage narrows, there is no brother, there is no friend.'

– *The Accounts of the Tallarn*
by Remembrancer Tremault

1

DAY SEVENTY-THREE

'You think they forgot about us?'

Sergeant Ballasra knelt down and checked the tracks again: more of Khadar's indigenous rats, but a large pack this time.

'The commissar lashed another five men. It's getting worse at the camp.'

Ballasra sighed and ignored the nattering Guardsman keeping him company in the open desert. He examined the tracks. There were at least eight different indents in the ground, the only indication of direction a spray of sand from where their feet kicked back as they moved. He followed the tracks, and spotted them walking up the slope of a distant dune. They were too far away to determine their numbers.

'And water,' the Guardsman moaned. 'What I wouldn't give to fill my bladder with water.'

Ballasra motioned to Private Ignar Chalfous to join him. Chalfous pulled the two dromads by their reins and approached. They bayed and snapped their hooked beaks in displeasure.

'More of the rats?' Chalfous sighed. 'I'm tired of the rats.'

Ballasra scowled at the young soldier. 'No, young idiot. We're not hunting these rats for food.'

'So why are we following them?'

Ballasra turned to the younger soldier and shook his head. 'You're from the city, aren't you, boy?'

'Yes. Dasra City in–'

'Yes, yes, fascinating. What do the rats eat? What do they drink?'

'Well, I assume, food and water,' Chalfous said, laughing at his own cunning. Ballasra simply nodded and waited for him to finish the thought.

'Oh!' Chalfous said, finally understanding. 'You're following them to see if they lead you to water or scrub.'

Ballasra shook his head. 'Your parents must cry themselves to sleep every night,' he muttered.

'Pardon?' Chalfous asked.

'We'd best follow them before night comes,' Ballasra replied, shouldering his lasrifle.

2

KORTAN STUDIED THE officers as he offered his report. Nobody smiled, and Kortan knew better than to bring levity to the moment. Everyone appeared on edge and dangerously quiet, trapped in their own thoughts. He noticed a few angry glances being tossed about… they were losing patience. The last two months had taken their toll, and they were looking for someone to pay.

'We're not much better off than before,' Kortan replied. 'We're down to a week of food and two of water.'

'Water reclamation?' Nisri asked, his gaze fixed on the grey washed wall of the single storey command bunker. Most of the equipment had been turned off, with the exception of a vox and a single auspex device. It was dark, the lights turned off to conserve energy.

'The solar stills are only collecting eighty quarts a day. That's twenty gallons, enough drink for twenty men, forty with rationing,' Kortan said.

'Is someone pilfering water?' Nisri said, exasperated.

'No sir.'

'Then how is this possible?' Nisri barked. 'We've built over two hundred solar stills. That's–' Nisri struggled, trying to think through the maths; he, like everyone else, however, was dehydrated and unfocussed.

'Two hundred quarts, fifty gallons,' Turk said impatiently.

'I know,' Nisri said. 'Don't interrupt me again.'

Turk mumbled something, his face marred by an ugly scowl.

'What was that?' Nisri said. He looked predatory, dangerous.

'I said,' Turk replied slowly, 'we wouldn't be in this predicament had you listened to me two months ago.'

'This again!' Nisri said. 'You would have had us wasting precious resources trying to get at water that might not even be there. Instead of running out of water in two weeks, we'd be dying of dehydration now, all to suit your pride.'

'Excuse me, sir,' Turk responded. 'If you want me to agree with your decision, then you'd better make it an order. Until then, you made a mistake. You decided that cutting my authority was worth more than following a valid suggestion. And now, we might be months away from dehydration, not weeks!'

'On my father's blood, lieutenant-colonel, you will keep your mouth shut or I will shoot you for insubordination.'

'Your father's blood,' Turk said, sneering. 'The same coward who raped and murdered the women of my tribe?'

It was an instant flashpoint, the room moving from stunned silence into heated action. Nisri and Turk drew their weapons simultaneously. Men kicked over chairs as they reached for scimitars and guns. Nubis and the other Banna officers stood in front of Turk, while Nisri's men guarded him. Bolters and laspistols were pointing in both directions. Kortan did his best to shrink into the wall. He didn't want to take sides.

The room was quiet for a moment, filled only with ragged breathing and angry glares. Knuckles whitened, and fingers slowly pressed on their triggers.

A pair of las-shots punctured the silence.

COMMISSAR REZAIL AND Tyrell stood their ground, each one pointing a laspistol at one of the groups in the command bunker. They had everyone's attention, the two holes punched into the far wall still smoking.

'Enough!' Rezail said. His voice was a snarl, perfectly controlled and modulated, as per the Schola Progenium lessons on speech-craft and intimidation. It was enough to keep everyone's attention on him. The angry stares did not diminish, but he could see realisation slowly creep into their expressions. They were on the edge of a precipice. They knew that, but they didn't know how to back away from it.

Rezail finally understood that the purpose of the Hawadi tribe wasn't just to mediate. It was to offer both parties an exit from their predicament without losing face. The Tallarn were too proud for their own good. They dug themselves into deep holes without thinking, and then relied on the Hawadi, or someone else, to defuse the matter without appearing the fools.

What the two factions needed right now, Rezail realised, was a greater concern. If they really wanted to fight, there was little he could do to stop them from pulling the triggers. But, until then, he could offer them a greater threat: himself.

'All of you, out!' Rezail barked. 'One word of this to the men, one more outburst, and I will execute you like dogs.'

The Tallarn tribesmen hesitated, but eventually, they sheathed their weapons. Rezail and Tyrell, however, did not.

'Colonel, lieutenant-colonel, you two stay,' Rezail said. He nodded to Tyrell to leave with the others.

When the three men were finally alone, Rezail said, lightly tapping the pistol against his thigh, 'Any other unit... any other unit, and I would have you both executed for that pitiful display of soldiery.'

'Nobody insults my father,' Nisri began.

'Both your fathers are dogs,' Rezail snapped, 'and they should have mounted better mongrels than your mothers.'

Both Nisri and Turk looked at the commissar aghast, their faces working through the insult.

'Now that we've dispensed with the petty idiocies,' Rezail continued, 'you will not interrupt me again. Make no mistake, gentlemen, we commissars have executed generals before now for dereliction of duty and gross incompetence. Rest assured, neither of you would be the first regimental officers that I've shot.'

Nisri and Turk both bit their tongues, but some of the colour had certainly left their faces.

'In this case, I choose not to plant a las-bolt in your collective skulls,' Rezail said, almost sneering at them. 'I need you both to keep your mutts in check. If I shoot one of you, I might as well kill every member of your tribe, but, make no mistake, I brought enough clips for the task. Cross me once more, just once, and I swear your men will suffer the consequences of your pitiful leadership.'

Rezail remained quiet for a moment, waiting to see if they still had any defiance left in them. They didn't appear to, however, their tempers cooled for the moment, and their duties as soldiers remembered.

'I want you to speak to your men,' Rezail said calmly. 'Remind them of their duty to the Emperor. When the supply ship comes, and it will come, I want the fleet to find a proper, by-the-book operation. They will not find a rabble of men ready to kill each other. They will not find our faith in the Imperial Fleet, or the Emperor, lacking, is that understood?'

Nisri straightened and brushed the creases from his tan uniform. 'Perfectly, commissar.'

'Yes, commissar,' Turk said, regaining his composure. He still looked haggard, his thick frame winnowed by the rations, but his eyes were clear. 'Do you also wish to speak to the men?'

Rezail tapped the laspistol against his thigh. 'No,' he said, finally, 'I leave that to you.'

3

THE WINDS PUSHED at the sand, sending small ribbons across the compound. The camp appeared deserted; the Guardsmen stayed out of the heat or, if on sentry duty, sat in the shade of the covered watchtowers along the walls. Kortan could see the broken, distant gaze in the eyes of the Guardsmen. They were going through the motions, their actions mechanical. They'd grown anaesthetised. There was little to draw them away from the hunger lingering in the pits of their souls.

So much for the grand mission to investigate the mortis-cry, Kortan thought. For a month, the camp had been paralysed under the heat and restrictive rations. The med-hall was already filled with soldiers suffering from chest colds, fevers and even pneumonia, in one case. The rigours of rationing had weakened men to the point where ordinary ailments became extraordinary problems. The medicae were coping, but barely. Medical supplies had run out, and without water to help clean and sterilise the med-hall, the number of infections soared.

Kortan walked past the med-hall, into the assembly ground where rested the self-propelled Basilisk artillery piece, a massive gun fitted to the frame of a Chimera. Four recoil braces extended from the corners of the Basilisk, each anchored to the plateau rock with heavy pins. Kortan glanced into the vehicle stables on his way past; the giant sliding hangar doors were open and the vehicles inside covered by tarps. They'd been sitting quietly for weeks now, to conserve fuel. That didn't stop Captain Abantu from keeping his men busy with regular vehicle maintenance.

Kortan continued for the orange door of the supply shed. The shed was made of plascrete and provided some cool relief from the sunlight. He walked through the door, anticipating the flush of cool air of the storage facility, but instead came face to face with Captain Anuman and two startled Guardsmen. They stood near one of the stacked crates, its lid torn open, stuffing rations into a rucksack. Sabaak was on the duck-board floor between two metal shelving units, lying face down, and bleeding from the head.

Anuman was the first to react, and drew his laspistol. Kortan barely had time to duck behind a metal container before the las-shots peppered his location.

4

'WHERE ARE THEY?' Chalfous asked. The dunes had subsided into a ribbed plain of sandy-grey loam, broken by mounds of weather smoothed white limestone. 'I'm starving. I could do with a bit of rat.'

'Here,' Ballasra said, holding out his hand. A thumb-sized insect with a black and red carapace struggled between his fingertips, its legs high in the air.

Chalfous made a face and waved off Ballasra. 'Too bitter,' he said. 'They make me thirsty.'

Ballasra shrugged and peeled off the insect's carapace before sucking out the meat and entrails. They continued moving between the limestone mounds, Chalfous pulling at the dromads, and Ballasra searching the ground for tracks. He motioned to a large formation of limestones, a series of soft-faced pillars measuring at least ten storeys high.

'Was this ocean once?' Chalfous asked, staring at the limestone around them.

'No, perhaps a sea or a mighty river near the ocean. But there was life here once. She must have been a beautiful world, rich and green, like Tallarn of old.'

Chalfous nodded, half interested in Ballasra's meanderings, if the fatigued expression on his face and stifled yawn spoke of anything else. Ballasra shook his head. He hated the 'domesticated' Tallarn, those who'd eschewed their tribal ways to live in the hives. They'd grown soft and easily distracted.

Without another word, Ballasra continued forward, towards the formations. The sign of limestone was good, as were the multiple tracks in the sandy loam, far more tracks than the family of rats they followed. There was life here, more life than they'd seen on Khadar before, probably tucked into the niches of the shady outcroppings. While the others searched the small cluster of shrubs for signs of water, Ballasra preferred to listen to the rocks. The loam seemed fat with moisture. If nothing else, solar stills built here might pull more water from the ground. It was a pity they were so far from camp. It would take them half a day to return, weather permitting.

'What's that?' Chalfous asked, staring at the formation. He was standing to Ballasra's far left, which gave him a better vantage of the limestone clusters.

Ballasra sighed and wished the boy would keep his mouth shut. He joined Chalfous, just to see what had his subordinate gawking. He stopped short of chastising Chalfous, however, when he found himself staring at something completely unexpected.

'Well, well,' Ballasra said with a smile. 'This planet is far more interesting than we anticipated.'

'We should go back and report it?'

'Report what, boy?' Ballasra asked. 'No, we find out what "it" is first. Then we go back.'

Chalfous didn't seem eager, but Ballasra was already moving forward, a grin on his weathered face.

5

SERGEANT RAHAM WAS running for the supply shed and the sounds of fighting when the orange door burst open. A Banna Guardsman stumbled outside, firing his laspistol back inside at someone. He dragged a heavy rucksack along the ground, and turned to flee. He spotted Raham and fired wide in panic.

Raham dived for the ground, laspistol in hand, and fired back. The Guardsman took the blow to the upper chest, and fell silently to the ground.

Everything seemed to go quiet at that moment. Raham barely had time to pick himself off the ground when he heard the shouts.

'He killed Barakos! The Turenags killed Barakos.'

The fury of two months found its crack in the disciplined but flagging wall of soldiers, and the crack spread like a lightning bolt. A handful of men quickly surrounded Raham, all of them Turenag to the sergeant's relief, all of them trying to protect him, regardless of the reason. Before Raham could order anyone to stand down, several Banna tribesmen rushed Raham and his defenders.

It only took Raham a second to realise that he was in a brawl. All the ugly, tribal, sectarian violence spilled out in shouts of anger and clenched fists. This wasn't the kind of fight where punches were thrown, it was the kind of violence where centuries of hatred found howling release. Men strangled each other, driving their thumbs into eye sockets, biting, smashing heads into the rocky ground.

NUBIS WAS LEAVING the vehicle stables and trying to reach the commotion at the supply shed when someone leapt on him. Nubis reacted, throwing the Turenag off his back. As quick as a flood, the fight had overtaken him. He backed away, trying to put some distance between him and the mob of grabbing hands. Somewhere, he heard the whine hiss of laspistol fire followed by bolter fire. Daggers and sabres flashed in the light, and Nubis saw Turenag and Banna fighting. Men screamed and fell to the ground, where boots silenced their cries.

Nubis hissed a curse. A Turenag brandishing a curved dagger lunged at him. Nubis grabbed his wrist and moved to the side, exposing the man's elbow long enough for the master gunner to break it.

The next two adversaries didn't have the opportunity to attack. Nubis darted forward, driving a fist into one man's nose and breaking it flat. The second man earned one boot to the gut, and a second to the jaw.

More Turenag tribesmen advanced on Nubis, all intent on satisfying old debts.

REZAIL, NISRI AND Turk all emerged from the command bunker, into the full onslaught of chaos unfolding in the centre of camp. It was all a blur, a horrific vista of tribal violence and anger. At this moment in time, it did not matter who had started the fight or the rightness of it. A dozen men already lay on the ground, and Guardsmen, both Banna and Turenag struggled in each other's grips. More men were trying to rush in to help their compatriots, the reason for the skirmish unimportant. Turk and Nisri immediately began pulling men back or off each other, but only Rezail knew a heavy price was demanded of the moment.

'Protect my back,' Rezail said calmly.

Turk and Nisri both nodded, their faces pale. They both knew what came next, but neither could do anything against its inevitability.

Rezail drew his chainsword, and revved the spinning links into a roar. Those who heard and stopped, scurried away at the sight of a commissar hell-bent on enforcing the law. Those who didn't were locked in deadly combat. Rezail moved past them, decapitating the arms of those wielding weapons, or firing a las-bolt in the heads of those standing over dead bodies.

'I am the Emperor's dark angel!' Rezail shouted, his voice carrying above the noise, as he executed one soldier after the other. Those Guardsmen who heard and stopped were spared. All those who watched were stunned into silence, their mouths open.

'I dispense the will of the High Lords of Terra. I am the keeper of the regiment's fire, and I alone can spill the regiment's blood. Those of you who murder your fellow soldiers are no better than dogs! And I excel at executing dogs.'

'Stop fighting!' Turk roared, winging a couple of his own men for emphasis.

Silently, Nisri did the same, with gritted teeth.

The fight was quickly breaking up, but there was a cluster of men still brawling near the supply shed. Rezail knew that bloodlust had overtaken reason. There was only killing to be had.

NUBIS HEARD THE commissar and Turk shouting, but he could not disentangle himself from the fight. He seemed surrounded by Turenag. One bearded man charged, but Nubis sidestepped him and sent him headfirst into the ground. Three more converged on him, two with knives, and one with a laspistol. Nubis tried to mutter a prayer, but the pistol came up too quickly.

Suddenly, the hissing whine of a las-bolt rang out. The tribesman with the laspistol fell to the floor, his face blackened. The remaining men turned to run. Another shot caught one in the back of his head, cratering the skull and punching through the other side. The acrid scent of burned hair and meat filled the air. Nubis turned to find a wild-eyed and bleeding Captain Anuman pointing a laspistol at the fleeing men. Before the master gunner could stop him, Anuman fired wildly into the crowd, killing kinsmen and allies alike in battle lust. More men fell. Some tried to fire back, but Anuman seemed possessed and felled opponents one after the other. Others scrambled for the door or dived out of windows.

Nubis grabbed him by the wrist, pushing his arm up.

'Stop!' Nubis snarled. 'Stop!'

Anuman struggled with him, his face contorted in a pitch of rage. 'Let me kill them! They're dogs! They're dogs!'

Half of Anuman's face vanished under the flash of a las-bolt, and Nubis stumbled back, his front painted in blood and viscera. He turned, expecting the next shot to end him, but Commissar Rezail was staring down. Nubis followed the commissar's gaze, until it came to rest on Sergeant Raham's body at his very feet. His blond hair was matted with blood and a knife was lodged in his chest.

ANUMAN'S RAMPAGE AND death undid the knot of fighting, but Nisri seemed intent on revenge. He strode forward, his pistol pointed at Nubis.

'You killed Sergeant Raham,' Nisri said, his voice shaking.

'I did no such thing,' Nubis said, staring with fierce defiance. 'I tried to stop the fighting, and my knife is still sheathed.'

'You lie,' Nisri said.

'Colonel,' Rezail shouted, 'stand down.'

'I want satisfaction for Raham's murder.'

'Over my dead body,' Turk snapped back. 'Nubis had no–'

'That can be arranged!' Nisri shouted.

A bursting roar came from the commissar's chainsword, and links sparked and skipped over the rocky ground.

'Battalion Commander Iban Salid!' the commissar said. 'You will take First Company and retire to your barracks. I want details on what happened. Tyrell, escort Second Company to their barracks and get their side of it. Colonel Dakar, with me.'

THE COMMAND BUNKER was emptied, left to Rezail and Nisri as they shouted. The only people left outside were the medicae, who were tending to the wounded.

'Colonel Dakar,' Rezail shouted, 'I shouldn't be the one reminding you about your duties! The mere fact that you'd have me shoot Nubis, who clearly had nothing to do with Raham's death, proves to me that you've forgotten your duties to the Emperor.'

Nisri's face contorted into a hateful scowl. 'I know my duties as a soldier better than you, political officer. Sergeant Raham's record as an NCO was peerless. Sergeant Nubis's record, if you'd taken the time to examine it, is earmarked with disciplinary actions. He could have been a lieutenant or a major by now, but he always finds trouble.'

'And yet,' Rezail said, 'Sergeant Nubis was stopping his own man from shooting your tribesmen in the back. And how do you repay him for saving the lives of your men? By demanding his execution! Your judgement is impaired. Battalion Commander Iban Salid's judgement is impaired. Frankly, I would execute the whole lot of you for putting your petty, vindictive feud ahead of your duties to the Emperor. Since we've been stranded here, we've already lost three qualified officers and at least a dozen men… and none to the enemy! We've fought nobody except one another! One another, damn it!'

The anger left Nisri's body. He seemed to deflate, the life vacating him in a rush. He steadied himself against the desk. Rezail had to stop as well, his head swimming from dehydration, from hunger and from the fatigue. Neither of them said anything. There was nothing left to say; the situation seemed hopeless. They were trapped on a desert world with no apparent hope of rescue. For the moment, it felt like they'd come here to die.

6

THE COMPOUND SEEMED deserted. There was no unauthorised movement, and all off-duty personnel were confined to their barracks while Commissar Rezail spoke to each platoon in turn. A Guardsman sang a prayer-hymn to the love and devotion of the Emperor, over the loudspeakers mounted on the building. His throaty voice echoed in the lonely desert, and his words melted into one another to form the river of a melody that washed the ears and soothed the jagged heart.

Turk did one last sweep of the two barracks belonging to the Banna, before heading to the lone tent tucked at the foot of the wall. After a quick glance around, he ducked inside and immediately fell into the arms of Kamala Noore. There was nothing to say at the moment. They fell into each other's embrace.

NISRI SAT IN the darkness of the command bunker. The solitary lights of the only two remaining active control slates bathed him in their blinking wash.

'You're overdue by several hours,' Nisri said, not bothering to look up. 'I can't afford to send out search parties.'

'The desert provides me with all I need,' Sergeant Ballasra said, coming down the three stone steps. 'I heard what happened. Raham dead?'

'Saving the quartermaster's life. I wish to be left alone.'

'I know, but this is not the time for such privileges, not when your tribe needs you.'

Nisri shook his head. 'My tribe... I'm in danger of losing my command. Commissar Rezail would be within his rights to assume command. Do not speak of such things, not now, not after what's happened.'

'Was it not said,' Ballasra said, 'that we would find a new world... a paradise free of the heretic Orakles and iconoclasts? Here,' Ballasra said, handing Nisri his canteen, 'taste the waters of paradise.'

Nisri stared into Ballasra's eyes and saw, for the first time in ages, the spark of joy. Something had enraptured Ballasra, and it sang to Nisri as well. He took the canteen and was surprised at its weight. He hadn't felt a full canteen in months. He smelled the clean water and drank its cool freshness. This was not distilled water; this was not stale drink. He could taste the rock over which it had flowed in the heavy minerals that clung to his tongue. Ballasra smiled at Nisri's mystified expression, and produced a curved red knobbly fruit. Ballasra sliced off a piece with his knife and offered it to Nisri.

'Here, eat from the gardens of paradise.'

The fruit was meaty and succulent, and thick with red juice that dribbled down Nisri's chin. He laughed, a quick bark that echoed off the walls, and devoured the fruit down to the rind.

'I have found us our world,' Ballasra said. 'All that remains is for you to lead your tribe there.'

CHAPTER FIVE

'Thank the Emperor for His blessings,
And surely you must thank him for your misfortunes.'
— *The Accounts of the Tallarn*
by Remembrancer Tremault

1

DAY EIGHTY

The limestone rock formations seemed incongruous in the surrounding desert. They simply appeared, as though alien, displaced. They were massive, ten storeys tall and thick in girth. Red, green and orange shrubs grew around their base, in thick clusters, and the air carried an earthy musk. It was the smell of moisture.

A wide tunnel mouth nestled at the roots of the pillars, almost shielded by them, as if Khadar had started to yawn, and had forgotten to stop. The tunnel mouth was large and pressed into the earth like a thumbprint. Three Chimeras could drive into her, shoulder to shoulder, with little risk of bumping against one another. As it was, one Chimera was already sheltered inside the cavern's mouth, gathering food and water for transport back to camp.

The tunnel branched into a delta of smaller passages, some large enough to accommodate the chicken-legged Sentinel walkers under the command of Major Hussari. Bio-phos paint and lume-tubes illuminated the main tunnel, consigning the remainder to darkness. The corridors eventually stopped, leading back up to the surface, or reconnecting to the main passages. A mere handful dug down deep into the stone, eventually ending in what the Guardsmen had designated 'Cavern Apostle', and that was only the beginning of the network of giant caves.

Apostle was huge, like the grand hall of the battle fleet's cathedral ships. The ceiling arched high above the floor, while stalagmites and stalactites reached low and high. In a few places, thick columns that tethered sky and earth broke through the deep deposits of loam covering the ground.

Captain Toria, who possessed some skill in caving, explained that the caves were formed from water passing through soft limestone, eating away at it until it formed chambers. He called them solution caves, and theorised that, given the dry river beds that scarred the surface, Khadar was once a water-fertile world. Over time, the rivers ate through the limestone, forming an underground network of tunnels, exposing reflective pyrite flakes that glittered and improved any ambient light. Over the millennia, erosion turned the tunnels into caves, and any water that evaporated from the heat condensed on the walls and ceilings and dribbled down in thick rivulets. Given the strength and thickness of the larger streams, Toria theorised that there were more caverns such as this, filled with a sea's bounty in mineral-rich waters.

What Captain Toria was at a loss to explain, however, was how the cavern could hold a rich, verdant jungle, an eco-system unlike any the Tallarn had ever seen.

2

KAMALA NOORE STOOD on a high ledge overlooking the jungle canopy of Cavern Basilica. The cavern remained largely unexplored and partially dark, save for patches of bioluminescence. Thousands of light strings, which seemed to shine a soft white, glowed along the ceiling. Someone told her they were creatures that used their light to lure insects in for the feast. Kamala hesitated; did someone tell her, or was it another random thought plucked from their minds? She couldn't tell. It was hard to focus.

Several metres below her, the canopy glowed slightly, the fronds tipped with yellow glow bulbs that sent a sparkle across the jungle. Foliage rustled and the trees shifted, the bulbs dancing. She could hear the whines of the Sentinels' servo-motors as they explored their new environment, their guide torches flashing through the breaks in the canopy.

Unable to pierce the gloom with her eyes, her mind seemed to scramble wildly through the caverns, unfocussed, untethered. Since arriving on Khadar, Kamala had been searching for some sign of an Imperial presence, of a massacre, but there was none. With the exception of a survey team that had made a cursory examination of the planet ages ago, Khadar remained pristine and inviolate.

It wouldn't be the first time a psyker had received distorted images and misidentified them, but this felt different. There was a ghost of something in the air, and it was maddeningly elusive. It slipped through her fingertips and haunted her with the haze of dead faces. She could almost see an Imperial banner half-buried in sand. She could almost see the vague faces with their dead eyes that stared up at the sky, but, like a name that was on the tip of the tongue, it remained formed and unformed. It was never complete, and without it, she felt incomplete.

Whatever it was that Kamala believed was missing, she felt that the caves were critical to it. She reached out and sensed the enormity of the cave system. They spread out for dozens of kilometres, maybe more, and they pulled at her, stretched her thin. As always, the answer rested just beyond her grasp.

A brush of boots against the ground brought Kamala out of her reverie. She didn't need to turn around to know that it was Turk. With a nod, he dismissed the two Guardsmen watching her. Nisri wouldn't allow her anywhere unescorted, the fear of psyker corruption a steady refrain in a psyker's life.

'Found anything?'

'No,' she replied, staring out across the jungle. 'Some animals, and I – I wish I knew more.'

'Well, all we need to know is that the Emperor has delivered us from harm. There is enough food and water, to last us for forever.'

'Praise be to the Emperor,' Kamala said, her voice barely a whisper.

Turk stood next to her. He glanced around, ensuring they weren't being watched.

'What is it, my love?'

'I – I don't know. I feel stifled, suffocated. I can't focus. Something is pulling at my senses.'

'What?' Turk asked. His fingertips touched her hand.

'I don't know,' she said. She quickly squeezed his finger before letting go. 'I feel like I'm enjoying the last peace I'll ever know.'

'You can't know that.'

'Can't I?' she asked. A flicker of psychokinetic electricity flickered across her skin. She seemed embarrassed. 'I'm sorry, but whoever sent the mortis-cry... he stood here as well, looking out across the same jungle. It's as if he was here a few seconds ago. Did I just miss him?'

'You've found the expedition?' Turk asked.

'Just the whispers of their ghosts. No, not even that. It's as if I'm see-ing... hearing the echoes of their ghosts. It's as if whatever killed them didn't even leave behind enough of them to matter. Please, don't leave me alone.'

Turk nodded and held her hand gently.

3

THE SENTINELS CRASHED through the jungle, using their cannons to push branches and swathes of vines out of the way. Their torch lamps burned brightly, illuminating their surroundings. Major Hussari and his pilots marvelled at the jungle with its thick green trunks, giant fronds that brushed against the cockpit's open frame, vines that girded the massive columns and walls, and thick roots growing from the soft loam. Captain Toria had surmised that the surface rivers had left behind thick deposits of fertile earth. In some places, where the vegetation was barest, rock and limestone peeked through, but in the places where trees were thick-est, Toria estimated that the soil was dozens of metres deep.

The major was under strict orders not to burn or clear any paths through the jungle, a point Colonel Dakar seemed feverishly adamant on. Hussari did as instructed, though the going was far too slow. At this point, they were better off on foot, like Ballasra and Toria's squads.

'Runner Two, what's on auspex?' Major Hussari called into his micro-bead.

'Runner One, the jungle's thick, but we're coming up on a shallow stream forty metres ahead. After the stream, there's a wall with what appears to be a large cavern opening. It's a big one. Shall I designate it Devotion?'

'Negative, not yet,' Hussari responded. 'Toria warned us we might encounter maze caves with wall segments and partial half-walls. Let's make sure it's another cave first and not part of Basilica.'

'Understood, Runner One.'

Suddenly, 'Nobody move, nobody move!' Runner Two shouted.

It was too late. Runner Three, moving ahead of the pack through a small gap in the trees, had entered what appeared to be a clearing. Hus-sari was almost through the gap when a sharp crack echoed across the cavern. Runner Three vanished in an instant as the ground disintegrated beneath his bird's feet.

The clearing was a crevice covered by a thin layer of limestone. Run-ner Three screamed in his micro-bead as his walker fell. Seconds later, his bird crashed to the ground and exploded.

Major Hussari managed to pull on the steering levers in time, back peddling from the chasm that was opening at his feet and barely avoiding Runner Two.

'I'm sorry, major,' Runner Two said. 'Auspex didn't pick it up until it was too late.'

'This is Runner One to base.'

'Acknowledged, Runner One. Did we just hear an explosion?'

Hussari sighed. 'Confirmed. We lost a bird. Warn the other squads to watch their step. Auspex doesn't pick up crevices until it's too late.'

'Acknowledged. Return home, Runner One.'

Major Hussari switched off his micro-bead. Both Sentinels lowered themselves to the ground, kneeling on reverse-articulated legs until their cabins were a metre off the jungle floor. Hussari and Private Amum Bak flipped open their canopy frames and dropped to the jungle floor. They approached the lip of the chasm, carefully, and peered down. Smoke billowed up from the wreckage of the fallen bird while the fire lit the surroundings. It wasn't just a chasm, it was a rift in the ceiling of another jungle filled cavern. Fortunately, the forest was too wet for the fire to spread.

'By the Orakle's beard,' Amum muttered. 'How big is this place?'

4

THE TROPICAL FOREST in Apostle was thin in comparison to the deeper jungles. The air was also more humid the further down one ventured, but with water rationing at a cautious end, Commissar Rezail gladly indulged his thirst and hunger. He sat on a rock at the treeline, staring into the yellow bulb-lights that seemed to float in the darkness. He chewed on one of the peeled fruits, relishing its freshness and aroma, both of which filled his nostrils and coated his taste-deprived tongue.

Everyone at camp was clamouring to see this so-called paradise, but for now, the camp would remain where it was. Only when the fuel shortage turned absolutely critical would they establish another camp within the caves. At least, that was Turk's wise contribution to the discussions. Nisri, however, seemed pensive and rather territorial about the entire matter. He wouldn't commit to any answer, and instead loosened the water and food restrictions to just shy of luxuries like showers and laundry.

Rezail was lost in thought when Tyrell cleared his throat. Colonel Nisri was standing, waiting.

'A moment of your time?' Nisri asked, smiling and calm.

'Certainly,' Rezail said, wiping the juices from his mouth. 'Alone?'

'No, your adjutant may be helpful in… facilitating an explanation of my request.'

'All right,' Rezail responded, intrigued. There was still considerable tension between him and Nisri, but the colonel seemed oblivious to the events surrounding Raham's death and the riot... a riot that had left others, including Quartermaster Kortan and his assistant, Sabaak, recovering in the med-bay.

'I would like to formally announce my tribe's interest in colonising Khadar.'

Rezail was not expecting that. He glanced at Tyrell, who looked equally surprised.

'But, service in the Imperial Guard is a lifetime commitment,' Rezail said, cautiously.

'I know that, of course, but the High Lords of Terra have rewarded a home world with sister planets before. I am asking that my tribe, the Turenag Alliance, be allowed to colonise Khadar on behalf of the Imperium.'

'That only happens under extraordinary circumstances: extended campaigns, meritorious service so far above the call of duty that the war is entered as a Holy Action in all Remembrancer accounts, and in the official history of the Imperium.'

Nisri shrugged and smiled broadly. 'I would call these extraordinary circumstances, would you not?'

'No,' Rezail responded, 'and the only times the High Lords have done this is in recognition of the efforts of the Adeptus Astartes, never for a regiment.'

'Almost never,' Nisri said.

'You're splitting hairs,' Rezail said. 'The fact is, colonising a world is such a monumental undertaking that it's hardly done. And, whether I agree with you or not is beside the point, it is not my decision to make. Coming to me first carries no weight.'

'Yes, but they would listen to a political officer more than they would a colonel, correct? Besides, there is a greater consideration here.'

'And what's that?' Rezail asked cautiously.

'What I'm proposing would end the struggles between the Turenag and the Banna Alliances. I'm offering you the opportunity to end the threat of civil war on my world, something not even the Commissariat could do.'

5

NISRI HAD ONLY just left when Rezail threw a cautious glance at Tyrell. 'What do you think?' Rezail asked.

Tyrell looked around. 'I think that this is a very dangerous thing.'

'A chance to end the violence? How bad is the fighting on your worlds?'

'We skirt civil war constantly. The Banna and Turenag cannot battle openly without risking the wrath of the Adeptus Arbites, the holders of Imperial Law. But they can induce others to draw blood for them, and they've grown adept at manipulating proxies to war on their behalf. It is a civil war fought in back alleys and in assassination. But, nothing can stay in the shadows forever. This will not remain hidden.'

'Would this be perceived as taking sides? Or favouritism?'

'Indeed, yes,' Tyrell responded. 'By giving the Turenag this world, you are rewarding them for their actions, for killing the Orakle, for every Banna they killed. The Banna would never allow this, and they are on the same expedition. Iban Salid has as much claim on Khadar as the Turenag has.'

'If the High Lords of Terra agree,' Rezail said, shaking his head, 'which I highly doubt, the undertaking would be massive: the ships, the logistics, the formation of a planetary governance, the inclusion of the Adeptus Arbites to ensure the colony is being built according to Imperial Law, a military presence to protect the planet, the redrawing of naval patrol routes to include Khadar... even to call it mammoth is to treat the matter casually.'

'Of course, commissar.'

'But, wouldn't the Banna want to be rid of the Turenag?'

'They would be sharing Tallarn, not owning it, so to speak. By the blessing of the High Lords of Terra and the Munificence of His Golden Throne, the Turenag would settle and colonise this world.'

'And the Banna's pride prevents them from allowing it.'

'All the alliances would take umbrage. They would all be demanding a world to settle on this precedent. But for the Banna, it would say that the Turenag are right. More important, it means the Banna would be admitting that they are wrong, in the eyes of the Imperium.'

'Damn,' Rezail said. 'Your people are stubborn.'

Tyrell nodded without hesitation. He was a patient man, which the commissar appreciated, especially in light of the tricky manoeuvring to be undertaken between the Banna and Turenag. Whenever Rezail felt like handling the situation with the rough bluster of the commissars, he looked to Tyrell for a calmer response.

'Can I ignore the request, and contribute to the growing violence between your two tribal alliances?'

'There is another consideration,' Tyrell said, scratching his chin. A sly smile crept across his lips, and Rezail knew he wasn't going to like the suggestion, if only because it would be the prudent course.

* * *

6

'I HAVE TO admit,' Nisri said, standing next to the commissar at the jungle's tree line. 'I didn't expect an answer so soon.'

'I don't have an answer for you, not yet,' Rezail replied. 'I recognise the importance of this world in saving Tallarn from civil war, but I also recognise it as a shrewd move to legitimise your assassination of the Orakle and your conflict with the Banna.'

'I assure you, that I'm only interested in obtaining this paradise for my people.'

'Even if it required you and your tribe to "admit" that you made a mistake in assassinating the Orakle?'

Nisri's smile remained, but there was a ruthless edge to his admission. He understood the game, far better than the more straightforward Turk. 'Our assassination of the heretic Orakle was righteous. To admit otherwise is to renounce our claim of serving the Emperor and, more importantly, our claim on this world.'

'I understand that,' Rezail said, 'but as an official representative of the Imperium's interests, I must appear impartial.'

'Of course,' Nisri said, 'and as an official representative of the High Lords of Terra, you must also protect the security of the dominions of man. By giving us a home, Tallarn is made peaceful. Is that not in the best interests of the Imperium?'

Rezail chuckled aloud, something Nisri was not expecting. It was obvious that Nisri enjoyed a position of power, and people followed his word, often without question or criticism. The laughter ruffled his feathers, and he appeared indignant.

'Colonel Dakar,' Rezail said, still chuckling, 'you're trying to argue the politics of the Imperium with a political officer. You are a savvy man, I respect that, but I was trained by the Battle Orators of the Schola Progenium, so I'd appreciate not being "handled". The fact is, you are making a request for consideration under the articles put forth by the Master of the Administratum, the ancient right of an Imperial Guard regiment to claim an uninhabited or conquered planet for colonisation by their homeworld, is that correct?'

'Yes,' Nisri said, trying to curb his impatience. 'And–'

'And, under those articles, your regiment is composed of elements of the Turenag and Banna tribes. So consider your course very carefully, because, as it stands, both the Banna and Turenag have an equal right to make a claim for their people.'

'You have no right to make–'

'Don't interrupt me again, colonel,' Rezail said, his voice even and cold. 'You have one option for your people to settle this world, Colonel

Nisri, if the High Lords of Terra even entertain the matter, and that's through the Administratum, after the High Lords' blessings, of course. Now, seeing as your regiment is composed of Banna and Turenag, I would bet my life that you never even discussed your plans for this world with Lieutenant Colonel Iban Salid. Am I mistaken?'

'I am his superior. I do not need to discuss anything with him.'

'You do when you're using Imperial law to favour your tribe above his. We've been through this, colonel. You have no tribe when you wear that uniform, and all soldiers are equal in their duties to the Emperor. If you truly wish me to treat this matter seriously, you will include the lieutenant-colonel in any discussions involving colonising this planet.'

CHAPTER SIX

'Look to the sky too often and you open your throat to the knife.'

– *The Accounts of the Tallarn*
by Remembrancer Tremault

1

DAY EIGHTY-FIVE

The mood had lifted considerably at camp in the last couple of days. The fresh fruit, meat and water reinvigorated the soldiers, and different squads were allowed to help explore the caves in shifts. So far, they'd uncovered seven caverns spread out over nineteen kilometres, with new tunnels and passages discovered daily. There was no telling the extent of the network, but for certain, they had only touched upon a fraction of the true paradise beneath.

The tunnels and caverns continued descending deeper into the earth, where the jungles grew thicker and wilder. The Sentinels couldn't navigate the jungles of Caverns Cathedral and Emperor, while the trees of Golden Throne grew in such tight clusters that the squads could only advance a few metres every ten minutes. Nobody had yet found the cavern where the Sentinel had fallen, and one squad reported discovering an underground lake. Unfortunately, their pathfinding skills proved insufficient to find it again through the maze of tunnels.

Still, it was all done in high spirits, the lack of supplies and the events of last week ignored in favour of the recent good fortune.

Both Sergeant Ballasra and Captain Toria were on extended patrol, venturing so far underground that they couldn't be reached by voxes and micro-beads. Sergeant Ballasra's last report indicated that he had found the head of a beautiful waterfall that plummeted into the dark mists below. Meanwhile, back at the camp, the Guardsmen had built a fire pit from collected shrubs, and were enjoying a rare feast of seven Khadar pigs, hairless albino-like creatures with snouts and no eyes, slaughtered and mounted on spits.

2

TURK, NISRI, REZAIL and Tyrell sat in the shade of the command bunker. The door was closed and two Guardsmen waited outside. The laughing and the revelry of the men drifted through the walls, and the smell of succulent roasted Khadar pig tickled the nostrils. Nobody wanted to be inside, but the argument was too heated to walk away from it.

'Absolutely not!' Turk said. 'My tribe has as much claim to this world as the Turenag.'

'This paradise is not befitting idolaters,' Nisri said, growing more heated.

'Oh, but it is promised to murderers and butchers?'

'We kill the undeserving. You should thank us for saving you from–'

'The undeserving? You misbegotten–'

'Keep it civil,' Rezail warned, casting an eye on both men.

'Fine,' Turk responded, throwing his arms in the air. 'What of the ruling of the Commissariat, Colonel Dakar? This means nothing to you? Some would say that is treason!'

'The Commissariat already commended us on the execution of the Orakle–'

'And on our just actions against your tribe!' Turk countered.

'Oh yes,' Nisri snapped back, 'because the murder of innocent women and children is the kind of nobility I'd expect from–'

'Don't speak to your betters about nobility–'

'Gentlemen,' Rezail said, briefly entertaining the idea of shooting them both, 'we're not here to argue who's in the right. You've been doing that for… how many generations?' he asked Tyrell.

'Forty.'

'That many?'

'No, commissar, not forty specifically. Among the tribesmen, forty means many. It means too many to count.'

Rezail nodded. 'You've been fighting for countless generations with no end in sight. Back to the matter of this planet.'

'The Banna Alliance will never agree to the Turenag's claim on this world,' Turk said. 'It is either shared, or it belongs to no one.'

'No,' Rezail said, correcting him, 'actually, it belongs to the Emperor. Who acts as custodian, however, is another matter, one that makes this entire debacle moot.'

'Commissar Rezail,' Nisri said with a grand sigh. 'What is the purpose of this meeting?'

'The purpose of this meeting, gentlemen, is to demonstrate that neither of you holds any legitimate claim to this world. At best, and that's a highly slim "at best", you may be able to make the request as a regiment, but not as an individual tribe. By doing that, you're splitting your nonexistent odds even further.'

'I am fine with that,' Turk said with a smile aimed at Nisri.

'We would no longer be at each other's throats,' Nisri said.

'Fine, admit your mistake in murdering the Orakle, and apologise.'

'No,' Nisri said, sitting against a console. 'We were just.'

The room was quiet for a moment, both men spent of their argument. It was long enough to realise that everything was too quiet. The noise outside had abruptly died. One of the Guardsmen hammered on the door.

'Sirs, you need to see this....'

The four men quickly exited the command bunker.

3

THE DREAM THREW Kamala into a storm's pitch of images. A silence pressed her against the wall and did obscene things to her. She fought it, her fists connecting with nothing, her body wet with blood. For a moment, she forgot about her powers, her ability to defend herself. The shadows whispered at her and encouraged her to fight back.

'Here,' they said in disjointed chorus, 'take more power. We have more to give, much more, enough to split open your skin.'

Kamala fought the siren allure of their voices. She struggled against their promises, and recited a Canticle of Purity. The silence was trying to worm its way into her brain through her ears and eyes, nose and mouth. They shoved it into her mouth, that raw, moist thing that empowered her.

Energy flared within her breast, and she shattered the silence for a moment. The static of stars washed through again, if only for a moment. The quiet rushed back in, the way blood fills the empty heart. It was inevitable.

Kamala Noore sat straight up from sleep, her sheet soaking wet, the ghost fire of remnant psychokinetic energy pulsing around the tent. Clothing and personal articles were strewn across the room, scattered by her poltergeist mind. Kamala rose and dressed quickly. Something was terribly wrong. She could feel the panic welling up inside the minds of everyone around her. They battered her, and she stumbled. She pulled the psyker hood over her head, drowning out the fear.

A moment later, Kamala pushed past her tent flaps. Everyone gathered around the fire pit stared at the north-eastern sky.

A grey moon of oddly spiralled craters hung in the heavens and neared the horizon at astonishing speed. Its underbelly glowed with a near-incandescent white light.

4

MAJOR HUSSARI LED the two other Sentinels through the night-blessed desert. The Sentinel was an ungainly vehicle with a cockpit box mounted over two reverse-joint legs, and was armed with a single weapon. The squadron affectionately referred to them as 'birds', because they didn't seem all that graceful until they were in a full run, like now.

Their long, fast strides kicked up a dust storm and filled the air with the steady hiss-thump of their gait. It was among the few times in recent months that they could bring their vehicles to full sprint, and their fast run through the desert felt incredibly liberating. Still, while the wind that blew through their canopy was deliciously refreshing, the men were eager to reach camp and partake of the feast.

'Runner One, does Khadar have a moon?' the new Runner Three pilot asked.

'What?' Hussari asked into the micro-bead. 'Negative.'

'Then what the hell is that over there?'

Hussari checked Runner Three's co-ordinates before he turned to his left and slowed his bird to a stop. The others followed suit and stared at the north-eastern sky, where the grey moon's fast orbit brought it to the horizon.

'Emperor's Light,' Hussari muttered. 'Runner Two, get on the vox and ask them to confirm.'

'Yes, sir.'

'Sir, is that a meteor?' Runner Three asked.

'No, no... it was a moon,' Runner Two exclaimed, 'and it was on fire.'

'It wasn't on fire,' Hussari replied. 'It was entering the atmosphere.'

'Oh, Emperor's Love,' Runner Three said, whining. 'It's going to impact. It's a meteor strike.'

'No it isn't!' Hussari barked. He watched the moon dip below the horizon. He was almost whispering into his micro-bead. 'It was decelerating. Whatever it was, it just landed. Runner Three.'

'Yes, sir.'

'Mark its relative position. Dust Runners, back to base camp, full gait.'

The squadron of Sentinels lurched forward again, their movements almost ungainly until they finally opened their strides into full-out runs.

5

THE CAMP WAS in full motion. Guardsmen ran to their positions along the compound's battlements, and lined up at the quartermaster's shed where Kortan and Sabaak worked through their injuries. Over the vox, a priest offered one Canticle of Courage and another of Devotion. Three birds with the Dust Runners squadron strode into the courtyard, through the main double gates. Soldiers automatically moved clear of them, the ballet of warfare fully choreographed and in motion. Nobody seemed to pay attention to one another, and yet they avoided each other with practice and near-subconscious fluidity.

The Sentinels slowed their gait and stopped at the vehicle stable where Captain Abantu and Armoured Support were getting the vehicles fuelled and ready. Tech-crews ran to Hussari's Sentinel as the legs folded beneath it and dropped the cabin close to the ground. Hussari leapt out and headed for the command bunker.

'Full complement of fuel and ordinance on all my birds,' Hussari called back to the squadron crew. 'We're not here long.'

'Yessir!' someone snapped back.

Soldiers ran past the major with a stack of ammunition crates between them. Hussari smiled; no tribesmen or tribal politics here today. Only soldiers were invited to this party. He entered the command bunker into the full-blown chaos of organising warfare, and offered Nisri a sharp salute.

'REPORT,' NISRI SAID as Hussari saluted him. 'Did you see what crashed?'

'No sir,' Hussari responded, 'only what you saw, and it didn't crash. I swear it was decelerating before it vanished.'

'Auspex,' Turk called out, 'anything yet?'

'Negative,' the operator called out. 'We picked up a slight impact tremor, but nothing even close to a meteor or orbit strike. Whatever it was, it made a controlled landing.'

'It was guided down, sir,' Turk told Nisri. 'Anything on vox?'

'Negative,' a vox operator responded. 'More background static than normal. Whatever fell or landed disturbed the sand and generated an electrical field like the ones we've experienced. If there's a vox signal anywhere in there, they can't hear or receive.'

'No contact,' Nisri instructed. 'There's no reason to alert them to our presence just yet.'

The command bunker was bursting with activity. All the operating stations, including vox and auspex, were on active sweeps, not to mention the command staff waiting on intelligence, and the platoon leaders waiting for their orders.

'Options?' Nisri demanded.

'Send scouts to uncover what landed before the invaders can mobilise; if there is a "they",' Turk said.

'Anyone else? Sergeant Noore?' Nisri said, talking to Kamala, who was standing in the shadows, her hood covering her face. 'Sergeant Noore?' Nisri repeated.

'Sorry, sir,' Kamala finally replied. 'I was trying to pierce the silence.'

'Silence?' Nisri asked.

'It's nothing. Whatever landed, it's invisible to me. But, I can tell you this, the ghosts of those who died here before are growing more restless.'

'The ghosts?' Nisri repeated. 'I thought you found no evidence of an Imperial presence before.'

'Nothing… tangible,' Kamala said, her voice distant, 'but their spider-web echoes linger. Whatever killed them was powerful enough to wipe away everything around them, and while I can hear nothing from whatever it was that landed, the echoes of the ghosts are growing stronger, despite the silence.'

'You mean death?' Turk asked.

'No,' Kamala said, 'I mean silence.'

Again, the room fell quiet. A collective chill passed through the spines of everyone present, and a few Guardsmen spat on the ground to ward away the evil spirits. Kamala turned back to the shadows. After a moment, the noise seemed to return to the command bunker, much to everyone's relief.

'Major Hussari,' Nisri said, 'I want you to take your squadrons on reconnaissance. Find out what landed.'

'How many, sir? I have twenty at full strength and one at half-strength.'

'Take six squadrons just in case. I want the remainder on picket duty until we know what we're dealing with.'

'We'll be ready to leave in less than thirty minutes.'

'How long to get there?'

'I'll have to check the terrain, but I'd say a few hours. Whatever landed did so two hundred kilometres away, I'd estimate.'

'It was that big?' Turk asked.

'We could only triangulate between two points… our patrol's

position and base camp. Still, it indicates something mammoth.'

'Find out what it is,' Nisri replied. 'Meanwhile, the camp is on alert. I want scout snipers five kilometres out, and I want regular vox contact. Nothing sneaks up on us. Nothing surprises us again.'

6

MAJOR HUSSARI'S SQUADRON of three Sentinels, the Dust Runners, took the lead. The other five squadrons, each three birds apiece, assumed arrow-head formation behind the Dust Runners.

The blue sun was beginning to break over the horizon, throwing cobalt spears of light through the distant cloud cover. It was a clean, crisp morning, a fine day for a run. The squadrons followed the dry bed of an ancient river that measured kilometres across. It was a circumspect route, but it allowed the birds to move faster than the dunes permitted, and it minimised their dust trail. Nobody spoke. The pilots wore their kafiyas over their mouths and noses, and their oculars over their eyes.

At about two horizons out from the estimated landing zone, the squadrons left the river bed and began threading the dunes at reduced speed. By midday, they could see the wall of dust, agitated by whatever had landed. It was an orange clot on the horizon, masking all particulars of whatever had newly arrived. Lightning sparked and flashed inside the cloud, briefly illuminating the silhouette of a gigantic dome.

An hour later, the Guardsmen disembarked, and Major Hussari and his two best spotters proceeded on foot. Private Harros Damask was a hawk of a man in features and attitude, while Private Shanleel Qubak was short, squat and quick, both on his feet and with his tongue. Qubak was one of the few Turenag Sentinel pilots in Hussari's squadrons, but Hussari liked him just the same. The Turenag carried the vox on his back.

The three men remained low to the ground as they threaded their way around the dunes. The two scouts carried their lasrifles in swaddling cloth while Hussari kept a grip on his plasma pistol. The sand was coarse of grain, and there was very little of the fine dust to mark their passage, not that anyone inside the storm was likely to see out for the time being. At the crest of the first dune, they could see more, if barely.

A mountain of rock had fallen to the planet, but it was too spherical to be natural. The storm of sand shrouding it was highly localised and appeared to be in wild flight. No currents or direction guided it. It seemed agitated and unsettled, yet never lifted from around the dome. Lightning sparks manifested from thin air and arced in upon the enormous rock-like structure. The electricity was keeping the sand in flight, sheathing the dome in a turbulent orange mist. The wash of heat watered their eyes and prevented them from properly identifying the rock, although there seemed to be strange patterns etched into its surface. Even through the oculars, heat shimmers and vapour clouds masked its design, but it was huge, the size of a battle cruiser and easily a factorum tower in height. The area was still heated from its entry into the atmosphere. The nearby dunes appeared as though melted away.

'Whatever's in there won't be coming out yet,' Hussari whispered. 'I bet you a week's pay the surrounding sand's still molten.'

'I'll take that bet,' Qubak said.

'It was a rhetorical bet,' Hussari whispered.

'Closer, then?' Damask asked.

'Closer,' Hussari agreed, 'but not close enough to be struck by lightning.'

Four kilometres from the crash site, the three Guardsmen encountered their first black river of molten glass. The top of the dune had melted away and poured down the steep slope. It collected in the trough between dunes, and bled a small river of glass. Sand insulated heat efficiently, and the pool looked as if it was in no hurry to crystallise. It could well remain liquid for days.

As the three advanced, the heat soared and a foul smelling miasma penetrated the air with a mixture of rotten eggs and spoiled meat. Hussari covered his face and wet his kafiya with water from his canteen to keep out the stench; the others followed suit. They continued closer into the furnace-like heat of the landing zone and into the periphery of the storm. The dunes were smaller, their tops melted down along their slopes. Melted silicate collected in large pools and streams. The scouting team couldn't approach any closer; the ground was melted and the heat suffocating. Even the particulates in the sand storm felt hot, a shower of heated glass spray. Still, in the distance, they could hear a strange cracking thunder, like thinning ice. The men glanced at one another, and Hussari pointed them up the nearest dune.

They clambered up the partially melted dune, its shallow side apparently free of molten glass. The heat pummelled them and rose with each increment that they scaled the slope. Suddenly, a section of sand slipped away under Damask's feet and he fell forward to steady himself. Hussari realised their folly in one sickening moment. The glass hadn't slipped down the opposite slope... it had collected into a small caldera atop the collapsed dune.

The shifting sand broke the lip of the crater and a deluge of melted glass broke free. Hussari and Qubak barely leapt out of the way, but the avalanche swept across Damask, who was caught off guard and off balance. His howling scream was lost against the dunes as the molten river covered his arms and legs. His clothing combusted into flame, and in pulling his hands out of the glass, he sloughed the flesh off his own muscles.

Hussari and Qubak could only stare horrified as Damask fell backwards into the glass and was carried to the bottom screaming. He stopped crying when the glass poured over him at the bottom and burned off his face and throat. He stopped jerking a moment later.

The two Guardsmen remained sitting where they had landed, lost to the shock of their friend's brutal death. Finally, Hussari pulled the vox from Qubak's set and reported the tragedy, and their findings. Nisri encouraged them to investigate further.

Hussari scaled the dune from another spot, alone this time, and tentative in his steps. When he reached the top, he motioned Qubak to join him.

They could see more clearly now. The dust storm was thinner, the air melting the sand in flight into a steady rain of glass. Ghost flickers of lightning sparked and snapped, but it was diminished. The landscape around the ship had been flattened for a kilometre. Through the haze, it looked like a giant snail shell, organic and glossy, sitting in a huge crater lake of obsidian glass. Tiny dune islands slowly melted into the crater's great cooking pot, while vent spumes along the ship's spiral spine jettisoned streams of fetid-smelling gas, cooling and hardening the lake. Giant steam columns rose into the air, and the sound of cracking glass peeled like thunder off the crater's walls.

Hussari and Qubak stared at the sight dumbfounded. Well before tube-like orifices opened along the shell's bottom and disgorged their cargo; long before the chittering, snapping mass of beasts collected at the glassy base of their ship; long before the assembled host of thousands roared and waved their scythe-like appendages at the desert sky, Hussari was already on the vox, his voice strangled.

'Tyranids,' he whispered back to the outpost. 'It's the accursed tyranids.'

CHAPTER SEVEN

'As the dromad falls to its knees, more knives are pulled
from their sheaths.'

– *The Accounts of the Tallarn*
by Remembrancer Tremault

1

'Close those doors!' Nisri snapped. 'Nobody leaves.' Tyrell and Turk
quickly sealed the command bunker doors. Nisri was quiet for a
moment, waiting for the men to calm down, waiting for the fervour to
die.

Tyranids, Nisri thought, his mind numb with mortified reflection. Of
all the races to strike the heart dead with fear, the tyranids were the most
frightening.

'Not a word of this to the men, not yet at least,' Nisri said, and for once
Turk nodded his quiet assent. Idle speculation would only fuel the
panic, and they didn't want to reveal anything until it was confirmed.

Commissar Rezail paced a small corner of the sand strewn, rockcrete
floor, while auspex and vox compiled crucial data. Nisri and Turk, two
veterans of the intolerable waiting that afflicted all military operations,
stood by the vox operator and received reports as they came in.

'You're sure about the numbers?' Nisri asked.

'Certain,' Hussari's voice crackled back. 'We're looking at several thousand tyranids. They're milling about, waiting for the lake of glass to cool.'

'So they're trapped?' Nisri asked.

'Relatively. Some are capable of flight, but none have ventured far from the ship.'

'They're preparing,' Nisri said. 'The tyranids always act as a consolidated force. Any sign of other ships?'

'Negative, sir. But, if this is part of a splinter fleet, it could explain why we haven't seen any supply ships.'

'A good assumption,' Nisri said. 'Keep a watch on them. Let me know if they start to move.'

'Yes, sir, I will.'

Nisri shook his head and sat down at the planning table. Topographical etchings covered the table's clear surface, along with a designation rune for the tyranids' landing zone. The outpost appeared too small and too close to the swarm. Nisri tapped the glass.

'I wish it was orks,' Turk said. 'I could tell you what to do.'

Nisri looked up at his subordinate and nodded. 'I wish it were orks as well. They'd be easier to fight.' He noticed Turk raising an eyebrow. 'No offence meant, but orks are predictable.'

'Tyranids aren't?' Turk asked, sitting in a chair across from him.

'Not in any way that can help us,' Nisri responded with a sigh. 'They don't respond to our tactics. Worse, they learn from them. We can trap them in a pincer manoeuvre, and still they'd break through. We can box them in a canyon, and they'd scale their own dead to reach us.'

'Actually, the tyranids are like orks in some ways.'

The two men turned to find Major Dashour standing there.

'Forgive me,' Dashour added.

'No, speak,' Turk offered. 'I've never fought the tyranids before. I've fought orks and the dark eldar but not tyranids.'

'Sit,' Nisri said, offering Dashour a seat.

'Dark eldar?' Dashour said quietly. 'I've never faced them.'

'They are graceful,' Turk said. 'So graceful and so terrible it almost hurt to look at them. I've never seen such agonising death at the hands of such elegant looking weapons. What were you saying about the tyranids?'

Dashour nodded. 'They are like orks in that they're scavengers. Nothing is wasted on the battlefield, and blood only fuels their thirst. Orks may strip and rebuild equipment, but the tyranids let nothing organic go to waste. Smaller creatures wait behind the front line and digest the dead, theirs and ours. They return to their flesh factorums and rebuild their forces anew from the raw materials.'

The entire room had gone quiet, Nisri's men heavy with the memories of their last exchange, Turk's in frightened rapture of an enemy no Guardsman ever hoped to confront.

'We faced a splinter fleet at Absolomay Crush,' Nisri said. 'The battle was fought and won by the noble Adeptus Astartes, the Blood Ravens. We were sent to clean up the remainder; not a difficult task, supposedly.'

'But,' Dashour continued, 'the planetary governor forgot to mention the secret underground factorums he'd kept hidden from the Imperium, factorums to build and equip a heretic army.'

'The tyranids were hiding in the factorums,' Nisri said, 'feasting on the private army and factorum slaves, rebuilding their strength until they came flooding out of the very soil itself.'

Nisri and the others remained quiet, the screams of allies still fresh in their thoughts.

'What happened?' Turk asked gently.

'The fleet admiral thought our position was lost. So, they scoured the surface from space, and when they finally ran out of munitions to throw at us, they used the fleet's hooked chains, the ones they use to disembowel ships, to drop orbital debris on us.'

'I'm sure the fleet admiral did what he thought was best,' Rezail said.

'Perhaps,' Nirsi sighed. 'All I know is that the rain of fire and molten steel did little to stop the tyranids. They went underground, and we held our position for weeks against attack. Absolomay Crush earned its name on the day of our rescue, the entire world of Absolomay crushed and lost to us forever.'

After a moment, Dashour interrupted the heavy silence, trying to shift its direction, for which Nisri was grateful. Absolomay Crush had ripped out his regiment's heart, and it was a wound that would follow them to the grave.

'The tyranids are singular in purpose,' Dashour said. 'We are born to serve the Aba Aba Mushira, but our lives are one of distraction. Not them, they are bred with one aspiration, and it is an aspiration without diversion, without division. They are remorseless, they are driven and they fear nothing. Why would they? They are reborn again and again, ready to fight and die, and to continue on.'

'You admire them?' Commissar Rezail asked, his voice questioning, but with an element of an accusation lingering.

'I admire their capacity to die,' Dashour said. 'Any man can oath-swear his fealty to the Emperor, but whether he lives or dies by that oath is what makes him true. I have faced down death before and never once hesitated in my allegiance to the Golden Throne and the High Lords of Terra. I see the same in the tyranids, as perverted as their cause may be. I cannot help but admire them, for if I can weather my faith against theirs and stand unbowed, then I have proven my loyalty to the Emperor. I ask that I die strong.'

Nisri and the other Turenag nodded.

'What can we expect from the tyranids, colonel?' Rezail asked, joining them.

'What can you expect of any storm? You can expect a portion of it to sweep over you while the remainder continues on its path, somehow undiminished. You cannot run and engage them in moving battles, you will only die tired. They are relentless.'

'There goes our advantage,' Turk said.

'Unfortunately. The best we can hope for is to bunker down and weather their onslaught.'

'We need more time to prepare,' Dashour said. 'Once the tyranids start moving, they will not stop. They'll be on top of us within hours.'

'Agreed,' Nisri replied. 'We must fortify this position. Meanwhile, I will buy us the time we need.'

Nisri stood and went to the vox operator. He took the handset. 'Major Hussari, this is base camp.'

'Yes, sir,' Hussari's voice crackled back.

'How close are the tyranids to moving, in your estimation.'

'I wish I could say, sir... a few more hours.'

'Then I have a great task to ask of you; I need your squadrons to engage the tyranid host before they move, and draw them in the opposite direction.'

The line went dead for a moment, the weight of the request heavy in the air. Finally, the line crackled. 'That's eighteen birds against legions of enemies, sir.'

'I am aware of that,' Nisri said. 'The camp needs more time to prepare. We need you to bait the enemy away from here. Do so and you will be saving the lives of hundreds of men.'

Another pause. 'Understood, sir. We'll engage the enemy the moment they appear ready to move.'

'Acknowledged, Major Hussari. Fight with the Emperor's grace.'

Nisri put down the handset, half-expecting an argument from Turk, but Turk simply nodded. He understood the necessity of the feint and the sacrifice.

'Tell the men what's happening,' Nisri said. 'Tell them to prepare for a large-scale assault. We need to fortify our positions.'

Officers hurried out of the command bunker to relay the orders. Turk, however, hesitated before leaving. He drew in close to Nisri.

'We're exposed out here, sir,' Turk said. 'Surely you can see that. The caves–'

'The caves are off-limits,' Nisri said, quietly. 'Have Captain Toria and Sergeant Ballasra returned yet?'

'They're due to arrive shortly,' Turk said.

'Good. We'll need all the help we can get.'

'Yes, sir,' Turk said, snapping to a salute before leaving.

2

THE TYRANID HORDE milling about at the edges of the snail ship seemed to grow larger by the moment. The more Major Hussari watched them through his pair of magnoculars, the more certain he was of his impending death.

The tyranids seemed diverse and uniform at the same time. He could identify various species, but the strata seemed many, far too many for his eyes to identify. They moved in and around one another, like currents in the ocean, never colliding or trampling one another underfoot; a great choreography of organisms with one shared thought. The smaller swarms knew when to shift and move around the larger, tank-like creatures. There was no hesitation in their steps. They scuttled around impatiently on clawed feet, pereopods bristling with thorns or on their bellies. None slept. None waited. They were eager to be unleashed, and the din they made grew steadily.

A glossy carapace covered their bodies, their heads and ribcages plated with thorny bone shields. Barbed tongues darted from between rows of spiked, needle-like teeth mounted in powerful jaws. Some slavered, their spittle scorching the glass lake upon which they waited. And still, Hussari could not help but stare at their limbs, multiple arms that flowed into wicked-looking scythes, curved talons for hands, chest tentacles with hooked suckers, and tails that ended in stabbing lances or elongated stingers. They offered so many horrible ways to die, and all while staring into their black, impassive, abyss-like eyes.

Hussari also noticed that some of them carried organic-looking cannons, powered by pulsing veins and piston-like muscles. The cannons melted into their arms and backs. That alone frightened Hussari beyond reason. Better to think of them as animals, with no thought beyond the basest instincts. The weapons implied cold calculating intelligence. The weapons implied tactics and planning, and an agenda.

Hussari privately cursed the magnification strength of his magnoculars, which showed him far too much detail. He grabbed the vox that Qubak held for him and deliberately sighed before speaking.

'So what am I looking at?' Hussari asked.

'You see the weapons?' Dashour asked, his voice crackling over the line.

'Some sort of organic gun with cable feeds tied back into their bodies?' Hussari said. 'What do the guns fire?'

'Horror,' Dashour replied. 'If you're lucky, they'll fire spines with deadly poisons that cripple and kill.'

'And if I'm unlucky?' Hussari asked. He looked at Qubak and shook his head. Qubak mirrored the sentiment.

'They'll fire a wad of worms that will bore into your body and eat your nerves until you die screaming, or a cluster of beetles that will devour clothing, armour, flesh and bone.'

'Wonderful,' Hussari muttered.

'Don't underestimate the small ones. They are the fastest on the battlefield. They will try to overtake you and swarm you. They'll drag you down. If they cannot kill you off, they'll slow you down long enough for their allies to finish the job. The larger ones kill and sow terror by wading into the ranks of enemies. The largest are there to break through defences.'

'Understood, major,' Hussari said, trying to push the fear from his thoughts, trying to find something to inspire him and his pilots. 'Do we have any advantages over them?'

'Range,' Dashour replied after a moment's consideration. 'They have some weapons that can match ours, but not the fast ones, not from what I remember. The small ones are deadly within close range, mostly.'

'Are there any… commanding officers in their ranks? Something we can kill to sow confusion?'

'Nothing you can easily identify. Already, by your descriptions, these tyranids seem different from the ones we faced, but that's to be expected.'

'Different?'

The line crackled. 'The ones we faced,' Dashour said, 'were mostly subterranean dwellers, diggers. They used boring horns, dirt eaters and acid to burrow through the earth. I suspect the ones you described are better adapted to the desert. Their colouring matches the sand, yes?'

Hussari stared through the magnoculars at the tyranids' pigments, the orange and tan mottling. It was a perfect mirror to the surrounding sands. 'They do.'

'I've heard of splinter fleets quietly orbiting planets for weeks, reabsorbing their own biomass to create new warriors suited to the planet below.'

'Understood,' Hussari said. The news was growing grimmer by the moment. Not only were they smart, but they had also adapted to Khadar already. How long had they been up there? It didn't matter, Hussari realised. The advantage was theirs in every way.

'Major, listen,' Dashour said, a little more quietly. 'The tyranids possess shared thoughts, but from what I've heard about them, they have masters... a link through which their thoughts flow.'

'Would it be on that snail ship of theirs?'

'Perhaps. I can't say with any certainty, but yes, I believe a master tyranid would remain on-board ship for safety. If it dies, the tyranid link is shattered.'

'Thank you, major,' Hussari said. 'I have an idea, but I'll need to speak to Colonel Dakar first.'

'Certainly, but one more thing: I suggest you withdraw back to the Sentinels. Some tyranids are capable of flight, but others... they're chameleons.'

3

'I WON'T LIE to you,' Hussari said, 'we face a grim task.'

Sixteen men stood in a semi-circle around Major Hussari. Their Sentinels waited behind them, close to the ground and idling, ready for action at a moment's notice.

'The outpost needs more time to shore up its defences, and they need us to buy them that time,' Hussari said.

'My father would disown me if he knew I was saving a bunch of Turenag,' Corporal Ziya Rawan, one the men, quipped. The others laughed.

'My mother would shoot me for helping you Banna,' Qubak said, taking the joke in his stride. 'She's done it before.'

More laughter followed, and Hussari allowed the men their moment. He was asking much of them, and a little levity was the least he could do to repay their sacrifice.

'You can tell your fathers and mothers,' Hussari said, finally, 'that you were protecting the men of the Banna tribe. The Turenags just happened to be hiding behind us.'

The men roared with laughter or nodded their appreciation. This pleased Hussari; they were ready.

'Many of you have participated in the desert races of Škakar or Harneel. This is no different. Your priority isn't to engage the enemy; it's to outrun them, while keeping them close enough for them to continue chasing you. Use your weapons to draw their attention or to save a fellow pilot. Do not stand your ground. Race, and race as a squadron. Use cross-patterns to draw enemies away from you and to create the mother of all sandstorms. The Aba Aba Mushira willing, I will see you when this is done.

'But,' Hussari added as a sombre afterthought, 'if your bird is brought to the ground and escape is impossible... nobody will think less of you if you save the last shot for yourself. Just don't tell Commissar Rezail I said that.'

The men nodded, their enthusiasm dampened by the gravity of what lay ahead. But, they remained steady.

'Who do we war for?' Hussari shouted.

'We war for the Emperor, aya!' each man shouted back. Without a word, Hussari sank to his knees and faced east with his men. They prayed, opening their arms to the sky to receive the Emperor's blessing, and kissing the ground where they believed His feet rested, in absolute submission to His will.

4

THE VENTING GAS from the snail-craft cooled the glass fields, solidifying them enough to support weight. Soon, more tyranids would emerge from the spawning chambers, and the horde would begin its spread across the planet, seeking out organic material to digest and add to their birthing factorums. The tyranids on the ground already seemed eager and skittish. They appeared to smell the air, drawing on some scent that drove them to a greater frenzy.

Major Hussari prayed they couldn't smell the fear impregnating every drop of his sweat. The tyranids remained in their clusters, however, agitated but otherwise disciplined.

The opening salvo caught the tyranids by surprise. Six birds from the various squadrons Cadian- and Armageddon-pattern Sentinels, swooped over the lip of a dune and opened fire with their long-range guns. The air crackled with the energy fire of the lascannons, while the fast revolving chambers of the autocannons spewed out a steady chain of rounds. The Sentinels continued running along the dune's ridge, their guns swivelled towards the tyranid mob and firing blindly with accurate devastation.

Tyranids exploded from the autocannon fire, the stream of shells stitching its path through their ranks and tearing craters in carapace, bone and glass. The lascannon unleashed steady beams into more creatures, vaporising smaller targets and punching searing holes through the larger ones. The tyranids were so tightly clustered, it was easy shooting. Almost every second drew its share of tyranid ichor.

Major Hussari could have stayed on the dune's lip for a long while, strafing the enemy lines and venting the lethargy of the last few months, but the tyranids were reacting far too quickly for his taste. From the moment the first shots landed, the tyranids shrieked in a cacophony of voices, and began moving as one. The glass field cracked and broke under the combined weight of the tyranids moving with a united purpose. Some were already firing back with electrically charged rounds.

Many shots landed comfortably short of the birds, but a cluster of tyranids with simian-like swaggers and limbs carried mounted cannons on their backs, their ammo sacs pulsing and throbbing. They braced, and the tendon pistons on their organic cannons contracted. Blue electricity enveloped the cannon muzzles as the creatures fired clustered spores at the Sentinels.

'Scatter!' Hussari said into his micro-bead. A volley of electrified shots sailed through the air, almost lazy in their arcs. The birds broke formation down the dune slope, each of them scrambling to rejoin their squadrons for the mad run.

Hussari silently blessed each man for his skill as the birds half ran, half skated down the dune's back. Pistons whined and contorted metal groaned as the Sentinels moved in ways they weren't meant to move. They should have tripped and fallen, but the pilots were trained for desert combat, trained to stay on their feet in the most uneven of terrains.

Behind them, the spores hissed and popped. Hussari glanced backwards and saw the spore pods explode on their descent. They unleashed a sudden rain of long needles that peppered the sand, missing all but one Sentinel, a straggler that had reacted too slowly to the danger. Hussari watched in horror as the needles imbedded themselves into the steel chassis of Corporal Kadi Y'dar's bird. Several shots breached the canopy and impaled Kadi's flesh with fifteen centimetre-long needles. Even from where he was, Hussari saw the needles spinning, drilling through steel and skin.

Kadi screamed and contorted in pain inside his cockpit. His bird toppled end over end down the dune, towards Hussari and others.

'Move!' Hussari shouted as Kadi's bird barrelled down on them. Hussari pushed his bird into a long stride and jumped down into the trough between the dunes. His actuators and pistons rattled hard, and Hussari was wrenched down tight by his safety harness. The birds scattered in tight turns along the trough, almost being upended in the process, but Kadi's Sentinel rolled past them, kicking up sprays of sand, and barely missing the other pilots.

Hussari groaned with relief before yelling into his micro-bead: 'Go, go, go!'

The Sentinels split to rejoin their squadrons. The dunes shed sheets of sand from the approaching tyranid stampede.

CORPORAL ELAPH CARTOUK, squadron leader of the Burning Falcons, lay on his stomach at the edge of the dune and stared through his magnoculars. He felt exposed outside his bird, so close to the snail ship, but as Major Hussari had promised, their attack was drawing the tyranid horde away. He watched as the swarm streamed over and around the dunes, in the opposite direction. Cartouk breathed a sigh of relief, and stared at the snail ship. Only a handful of the creatures remained.

'What now?' Private Dubar Iban Dubar whispered. He was a young man, barely a campaign old, but already familiar with fighting the tyranids.

'Emperor willing, Hussari will keep the tyranids busy long enough for reinforcements to arrive.'

'So we wait?'

'We wait.'

After a moment, Dubar whispered, 'I never thought I'd be hoping for a Banna to succeed.'

5

TO THE UNTRAINED eye, the squadrons didn't appear to be operating together, but then again, this wasn't tank warfare. The Sentinels used their speed to their advantage, weaving around one another and hopefully raising enough dust to blind the enemy behind them. The Sentinels were in contact with each other, each squadron watching out for its own, and the squadron commanders answering to Hussari.

Sergeant Cortikas Iath's squadron, the War Chasers, split to the east, taking a portion of the tyranid brood with them. He manoeuvred through the troughs of the dune sea, his general course already determined. At first the tyranids tried overtaking him by mounting the dune crests, but that slowed them even further. Eventually, the tyranids learned, and funnelled through the maze of furrows, following the squadron like the head of a flood.

'Sergeant!' a voice cried over the micro-bead. It belonged to Private Deeter Mohar, a spotty pilot with one campaign under his belt already. 'They're splitting off!'

Iath pivoted in his seat to look, the Sentinels moving and rattling too much for him to make use of rear-reflectors. Behind him, a group of creatures was veering off into a connecting channel. They were quick runners, their six legs barely touching the sand, their squat barrel bodies compacted with muscles. Every so often, they generated a burst of leaping speed that propelled them ahead of the pack.

'They're trying to outflank us,' Iath said. 'Mohar, on my left flank, and make ready.'

The three Sentinels shifted position, moving around one another with barely a break in their speed. Rounds whipped past their open canopies and slapped off their metal skins. Some shots looked jagged and barbed, and others consisted of super-heated matter. What distressed Iath were the *splat* sounds he heard as rounds struck his bird's chassis. He knew they were organic in nature, and prayed they didn't eat through the Sentinel's plate, or remain volatile for long.

Fortunately, it took almost all their speed to keep pace with the Sentinels, so whenever a tyranid fired at them, it also fell back.

'Get ready, Mohar!' Iath shouted. 'They're going to flank us.'

The squadron was just about to intersect a channel to their left. The pack of runners emerged around the shrinking edge of the dune, their toothy maws open and their long red cartilage tongues whipping around in their open maws. They were almost on top of Iath's squadron, their speed blinding, their piercing howls startling.

'Now!' he screamed, perhaps more loudly than he intended.

Mohar swivelled in his Catachan-pattern bird and opened up with his only weapon, his flamer, spewing out a gush of promethium fuelled flame. The gel fire washed over the runners and clung to their skin as it burned. They screeched and dropped to the sand, writhing in agony. One collided with another pack on the heels of the War Chasers, setting several of its compatriots ablaze. It writhed around momentarily, before a larger tyranid with cloven hooves and two scythes for upper arms sliced into the beast and dismembered it with a handful of blows.

The last thing Iath saw before turning his attention forward was the remaining tyranids devouring their dead compatriots. No living matter was left behind in battle. Everything was devoured, everything reclaimed.

6

SERGEANT UMAR HADOORI of the Heretic Slayers squadron played games with the tyranids, trying to keep them off balance. He had to continually remind himself that because of their hive instinct, the tyranids could transmit vital information to one another almost instantly. Any ploy he used would have to be quick... quick enough for him to fire a couple of rounds before veering away and running for dear life.

Private Damask's death had already put him at a disadvantage, his squadron of three birds now down to two, but Hadoori prided himself on his cunning and quick wits. At his signal, the other Sentinel split from him around a dune. The two birds raced parallel to one another, straddling and flanking either side of the dune as it rose between them. They succeeded in shearing the tyranids into two groups.

At the next channel, as one dune tapered away and another began, the two Sentinels suddenly wove past each other. The manoeuvre was so sudden that the tyranids stayed on their targets and tried to switch over.

The chasing mobs collided with one another, all manner of beast slamming into allies and tripping over each other. To their credit, only the front wave collided. The rear guard merely ran around or climbed over their companions, and began following the new targets.

Sergeant Hadoori was pleased. 'Well there's a trick that will never work again.' But it didn't need to for the time being. The tyranid mob had fallen back, giving Hadoori the breathing space he needed to concoct some other plan.

7

'NOT AGAIN,' HUSSARI moaned. He'd managed to pull up alongside Corporal Tanis 'Mad' Maraibeh's Sentinel. Mad was an apt description for the squadron's maverick and unhinged pilot.

Maraibeh was driving with his bare feet, pushing both steering levers forward and making minute shifts in direction with skilled practice. Hussari knew better than to chastise the grizzled old man with his dark skin and thistle of tribal scars knotted on his face. He had a well-chewed cigar in his mouth, unlit. He enjoyed the taste of them, he said.

'How far behind us do you think they are?' Maraibeh asked over the micro-bead.

Hussari peered back and adjusted his running path so that he was clear of his own dust cloud in a moment. They'd entered a long, wide river bed, and the running was smooth. After checking the green auspex screen to confirm, 'I'd say two minutes,' he responded, running close to Maraibeh again. 'Set the timers for two-and-a-half.'

Maraibeh nodded, and cranked the screw timer atop his home-made pipe bomb. He tossed it out of the open-topped cockpit and primed two more tubes, which followed the first.

About two-and-a-half minutes later, the three charges detonated in fifteen second increments. Hussari was far enough away from the squadron's dust trail to see the explosions blossom in the heart of the tyranid mob. Beasts were thrown into the air, and the remaining group spread out further across the river bed's width.

'Did I get 'em?' Maraibeh asked over the micro-bead.

'Confirm that. You can probably shave ten seconds off the first timer, but they've spread out. You won't snare as many next time.'

'Smart bastards,' Maraibeh grumbled.

'Too smart. How many bombs did you make?' Hussari asked.

'Eighteen… fifteen now.'

'Save them for when we really need them.'

'Yes, sir,' Maraibeh reported back. 'That should keep them angry for a while.'

Hussari strode back into formation, the striding rumble of his squadron comfortably familiar. He noticed, however, that Maraibeh was still steering with his feet, cradling the back of his head with his hands.

8

CORPORAL RAWAN LED his Holy Striders through the uneven dune canyons. His auspex was a collision of topographical information, a mess of orbital resonance taken when they landed over three months ago and the current data streaming through auspex. With an angry snarl, he shut off the old intel; the dunes shifted quickly around here and the orbital scans were no longer valid. He'd have to rely on auspex to navigate through the maze of dunes, regardless of how limited its range.

More shots screamed by Rawan's bird. He glanced back and realised that the tyranid swarms chasing him were only metres behind. The damn things were fast, and no matter what he did, his squadron couldn't shake them. The beasts were relentless, and for the past couple of hours since this began, they'd been gaining steadily.

The collective shrieks startled Rawan as six-legged runners launched themselves at the Sentinels. Rawan watched in horror as two of the creatures latched on to the rearmost Sentinel, piloted by Private Elma Taris. One of the creatures tried to grab an exhaust stack and pull itself up, but burned its hand on the super-hot metal. It let go with an angry cry, but held on to the multilaser cannon and its battery packs with its other three arms.

The second runner was already atop the canopy frame, unbalancing Taris's bird. Taris fought for control, and the last thing Rawan saw before turning away was the creature atop the canopy plunging two spiked pereopods into the cockpit. A geyser of arterial spray followed. The Sentinel fell, and Rawan prayed that Taris would be dead long before the devouring horde swept over him.

Rawan's auspex picked up more movement along the adjacent dunes. The tyranids were moving along the ridge crests, firing down at them. This time the pack consisted of larger creatures: cloven-hoofed, bone-crest swept brows, multi-jointed legs, upper arms that seemed to melt into scythes and pairs of lower arms that held bone-guns. What they lacked in speed, they made up for in range.

'No!' Rawan cried, giving voice to his worst fears. The Holy Striders were about to be overtaken.

The tyranids opened fire, peppering the Sentinels with a salvo of shots. Rawan managed to pivot his bird's cabin in time, allowing the twin exhaust stacks behind his cockpit to shield him. Private Damous Obasra, in the Sentinel ahead of Rawan, wasn't so lucky. He spun his frame around, but a round splattered against his canopy frame, and his face. He screamed as the acidic globules destroyed his oculars, and then attacked flesh and bone. Within seconds, his entire skull appeared to collapse, right before Obasra's death spasms sent his Sentinel crashing to the ground.

Rawan tried to avoid the fallen bird, but he clipped the Sentinel on his way past, tangling his legs with Obasra's. The steering levers whipped out of Rawan's hands and his Sentinel fell hard. It crashed and rolled a couple of times before finally coming to a stop.

Despite the safety harness locking him in place, the fall knocked the wind from Rawan's lungs. He was rattled and on his side. He knew enough to know that he was in trouble as he fumbled for the holster snap of his laspistol. The tyranids were bearing down on him, the critters running full bore on all six legs to reach him. They were a handful of metres away when Rawan managed to pull his pistol. Unfortunately, instinct took over when the creatures launched themselves at him, their mouths open wide and their cartilage tongues wet with clear mucus. Rawan fired two crackling las-shots that ionized the air with yellow beams. The first shot bounced off a beast's exoskeleton armour, but the second shot caught it in the mouth. The dagger of light punched through the back of its skull.

A large tyranid landed atop the Sentinel, rocking it with its weight. Its scythe arm stabbed through the canopy frame, and through the meat and muscle of Rawan's thigh. He tried to scream, tried to draw his pistol up to his temple, but the monster vomited on his arms. The yellowish mucus began to dissolve his body. Rawan's hand fell off, dropping the pistol, the caustic bile instantly disintegrating the exposed bone. It was breaking him down into bio-soup. Rawan continued screaming as the tyranids arrived to lap up the remains of his dissolving body, their heads fighting to push through the frame of his exposed canopy.

9

THEY WERE OVER a dozen kilometres away from the snail ship when the small caravan of two Hellhounds and six Sentinels came to rest. The Hellhounds were modified troop carriers, each equipped with an inferno cannon and a turret-mounted heavy bolter. The two squadrons of Sentinels consisted of Catachan- and Mars-pattern birds, short-range vehicles designed to spread terror through the ranks of an enemy that felt no fear.

Corporal Cartouk was at the crest of the dune, staring out at the tyranid ship through his magnoculars, when the vehicles arrived in the dune trough below his perch. He slid down the sand slope, demanding, 'Is this it? Is this our support?'

'It's all you're getting,' Sergeant H'lal Odassa of the Dust Marauders squadron said, standing up in his cockpit. He stretched out his back. 'And, as senior officer,' he grunted, 'you're my support, as of now.'

Cartouk ignored Iban Dubar's quick indignant glance at him. Now was not the time to indulge the typical Banna/Turenag rivalries. 'Yes, sir,' he said.

The two Turenag mounted their birds and wheeled them around to follow in step behind Odassa's Dust Marauders and the second squadron, the Blight Thorns.

THE PLAN WAS simple, conferred over micro-bead on their way to the snail ship. The Blight Thorns would strafe the small swarms still milling about the base of the tyranid vessel and draw them into giving chase. The Burning Falcons, the Dust Marauders and two Hellhounds would then attack the ship and attempt to gain entry. Given the size that some tyranids reached, Odassa reasoned that they could enter the vessel with their vehicles and destroy both it and any hive-mind driving the swarms.

Cartouk disliked the plan immediately and expressed his doubts, as one of the only veterans to have faced the tyranids. Nobody, in his experience, had ever entered a tyranid vessel, and nobody knew what to expect inside. Moreover, any number of the enemy could be waiting within, and only the Emperor knew what shapes and horrors awaited them.

Odassa had his orders, however, and he was dead set on killing the tyranid mind beasts, and proving the hero of the day. Not that Odassa said that, but Cartouk assumed as much.

So... just out of sight of the ship, nestled between the bosom of dunes, the squadrons and Hellhounds waited. The Blight Thorns' pilots, quiet to the last, streamed past the dunes and built up steam on their run for the ship. Cartouk listened over the vox, and to what he could hear within earshot.

'Contact!' a voice said over the vox.

The whoosh of promethium-driven flamers, and the steady pulse of las-fire being spewed out from the rotating barrels, sounded over the dunes, followed by the echoes of terrible screeches. A rumble filled the air, and the ground shook, the dunes sloughing off sheets of sand.

'We got them mad,' the vox chatter said. 'Disengage and run!'

Cartouk and the others listened, their collective breaths held and their plan hinging on this precise moment. After what seemed like forever, the rumble faded, the sand no longer shook and the shrieks grew distant.

'Report,' Odassa said, his voice hushed over the vox. 'How many did you pull away?'

'I don't know,' the voice rang back, 'a good number. There're far less of those bastards there now, I know that.'

Odassa waited another gruelling half-hour before deciding that the swarms were far enough away. The blue sun had dipped down to the horizon, but the air would not be cool for some time. The glass fields were still hot, despite the jets of gas belched out by the ship.

On Odassa's order, Cartouk and Iban Dubar followed the Dust Marauders around the dune and out into the open. The ship loomed into view, suddenly larger and more sinister against the setting sun. The glass field, cracked and broken by the weight of the tyranid swarms, reflected the dusk light like a thousand lakes. The pilots fumbled for the diffusion oculars and swung a wide arc around the ship, making it look as though they were going to strafe and run.

Small swarms of tyranids, numbering in the dozens, immediately moved to intercept from their nests around the vessels. These beasts were larger and slower than their comrades. They were scorpion-like with eight pereopods that ended in wickedly curved scythes that clacked against the glass fields. Their bodies were long and segmented, and measured up to the Sentinel in stature, when they rose on their back four legs and lunged to attack the birds with their front four. Segments of long bone-plate ran from their heads, down the length of their spines, and ended in long tails and bulbs of thorn barbs.

Several of what Cartouk called 'scorpions' lashed out with their tails, firing a spray of barbs at the Sentinels. A pilot screamed over the vox, and Cartouk turned in time to see a Dust Marauder tumble to the ground and crack the glass. The pilot was riddled with the spines and screaming, his skin bulging under the strain of the hundreds of welts that were merging and growing, and tearing the skin open.

Cartouk looked away. He had his own problems, more scorpions were chasing them, a good three dozen by auspex count. Two new runes also appeared on auspex, coming up fast behind the swarms. It was working, Cartouk thought. They hadn't spotted the Hellhounds sneaking up.

The Sentinels wove inbetween each other, trying to trip up their pursuers. This strategy was far easier when used against the orks, whose vehicles were not as nimble as the tyranids and more prone to collisions. It didn't matter in this instance, however. The two squadrons were merely the head of the snake, weaving back and forth, distracting the tyranids from the real threat behind them.

The two Hellhounds suddenly announced their presence. They pulled up alongside the rear most scorpions, flanking the train on either side, and fired with their inferno cannons. Sticky promethium flame swept over the swarms, engulfing them before they could react. Even ahead of the mob, Cartouk could feel the heat surge at his back, blistering the paint job on his bird. His ears ached with the death cries of his pursuers.

'Now!' Odassa screamed over the vox.

The four Sentinels broke formation and scattered in different directions. The swarm was distracted, trying to escape the hellish onslaught of the inferno cannons. The Sentinels decelerated and spun around, adding their own promethium to the mix, or opening fire with their multilasers.

Tyranids in flight made for good target practice, and for the first time since fighting the beasts on Absolomay, Cartouk laughed and whooped as his las-fire brought scorpions down, one after the other.

It was over all too quickly, however, and the sense of danger returned.

'Hurry, find a way inside,' Odassa ordered. 'The tyranids won't let that go unanswered for long.'

THE SUN HAD almost set, and everything was deathly quiet, the tyranid rock apparently casting a hush over the winds and the sands. Night was already throwing its starry cloak over the heavens when they finally found an accessible door into the ship.

Not a door… a sphincter, Cartouk corrected himself, and shivered.

The oval-shaped orifice puckered out against the skin of the vessel. Many like it honeycombed the ship's surface, but this was the only one level with the ground. It opened into an organic-looking tube that angled upward into the darkness. There didn't appear to be any lights inside the vessel. But then, Cartouk reasoned, the tyranids no more needed to see to navigate their ship, than blood did inside one's body.

'The Hellhounds can't fit inside,' Odassa grumbled over the vox. 'Stay outside and secure the door. Sentinels, with me.'

Odassa's beacon torch flashed on as he entered the dark tube. Cartouk followed, instantly cringing at his surroundings. The dark grey walls seemed to glisten and envelop him. The curved floors felt spongy beneath his bird's feet, and the air smelt humid and fetid in a way that dug deep past his nostrils. Cartouk pulled his kafiya over his nose and mouth, grateful that the stench he smelled was that of his own unwashed body.

They moved slowly through the tubes, past intersections, and up some steeply angled passages and down sharp slopes. What guided them wasn't any sense of direction, but the size of the corridors. No two tubes were exactly alike, differing from each other in dimension and composition. Some tunnels seemed to breathe, the air inhaled and exhaled, the vein-like walls pulsing and glinting. Other places seemed more like a proper ship, the walls and floors made from hardened resin with the coolness of steel.

Throughout it all, there were no signs of life, at least nothing that proved a threat. Small cockroach and crab-sized tyranids scurried about on mysterious business, moving from underfoot when approached, falling back in place when the Sentinels passed. For all that, Cartouk could not help but feel they were somehow witnessing some grand orchestra of purpose, a symphony they would never see or hear entirely. And, for that, he was grateful.

'By the Emperor,' Odassa whispered, stepping into a large chamber. 'This can't be.'

At first, Cartouk didn't understand Odassa's shock. It was hard to see the chamber's true size in the darkness, but it appeared no different than the corridors, fleshy walls and coats of hardened resin melting over everything. Then, Cartouk stepped onto the chamber's tilted floor and heard the metallic ring to his footfall. Slowly, the chamber came into focus in his mind as their torches swept the emptiness. The floor was grated, the holes plugged with detritus. Arched cathedral struts that extended high above them, protruded through the resin layers on the walls, along with the frames of arched windows, bits of stained glass windows floating in the resin.

'It's one of ours,' Odassa whispered. 'It's one of ours.'

'Not any more,' Cartouk said. 'The tyranids must have cobbled it together from the wreckage of a cruiser.'

'We're never getting off this world,' Odassa said. He continued staring at the chamber, gap-mouthed.

'There's nothing more to see here,' Cartouk whispered, urgently. 'We must leave.'

Almost on cue, the vox crackled and sputtered, the panicked Hell-hound driver screaming 'Enemy contact. Enemy contact!' The roar of the inferno cannon drowned out the voices. 'Too many of them... merciful Emper...' the signal died.

'We're trapped!' Cartouk said. 'They'll be on us now.'

Odassa stared up into the empty cavern of the vaulted chamber, unable to act. 'We're going to die here.'

'Sergeant Odassa!' Cartouk screamed. Nothing. Cartouk spat out a curse at the Banna for his weak blood, and voxed the other two Sentinels. 'We're trapped,' he said, 'but perhaps we can hurt them before we die. Form up on me.'

Iban Dubar and the other Sentinel fell in behind Cartouk. He regretted not knowing the name of the other Dust Marauder pilot, but right now, other concerns took precedence. The three Sentinels ran across the chamber, their torches sweeping from side to side, looking for an exit. They found a side corridor large enough for them to use, the metal walls and floor of the Imperium vessel swallowed up by thick growths of resin and tyranid bio-matter.

Cartouk cast a last glance at Odassa before darting into the tunnel. A moment later, over the vox, they heard him scream.

Where there was nothing before, the tyranid vessel suddenly surged into life. Tyranids appeared in the corridors, as though birthed from the very walls. They scampered along walls and ceilings, racing to overtake the squadron. They seemed to be everywhere at once. Iban Dubar had taken point, and was blistering enemies with his promethium fuelled cannon. His fingers seemed to be stuck on the trigger, the corridor heated to the point where it hurt to breathe, yet Cartouk knew he could never let up.

Cartouk took the rear, and back-pedalled through the corridors, unleashing streams of las-fire at anything that moved. Scorpions, runners, leapers and snakes darted towards him, but in the confines of the corridor, he held them at bay.

Their progress seemed interminably slow, each step a kilometre in the making, until finally, a terrible rending filled the corridor. The ceiling seemed to rip open behind Cartouk. He glanced back, the air filled with screams. An avalanche of white maggots spilled from the rent in the ceiling, drenching two Sentinels under its mass. The screams turned to agonised shrieks, and then to gurgles. Cartouk knew the pilots were being eaten alive. Maggots were already dropping into his cockpit, through the crack in the ceiling, and racing over him.

Cartouk screamed in pain, the maggots biting off fingertip-sized chunks of meat as they bored into his flesh. More rained down, on his face and arms. Cartouk spun his Sentinel towards the other two birds covered in maggots. Blood and pain filled his vision until the things burrowed into his eyes. He spasmed in agony, his finger clutching the trigger, and he opened fire on his squadron.

CARTOUK NEVER SAW his shots clip the Sentinels, or the promethium tanks of Iban Dubar's bird. The accelerant fuelled explosion ripped through the tunnel, detonating the engines and fuel tanks of the other two Sentinels.

The blast tore open the adjoining tunnels and pumped fire through endless corridors, flash-frying all manner of beasts in its path. Walls cracked and tunnels collapsed; perhaps not a deathblow to the vessel, but certainly a crippling blow that sent shockwaves across the hive-mind, enough to give the creatures pause... enough to pull several swarms back to the nest.

10

SERGEANT A'RTAR SHAMAS, squadron leader of the Orakle's Apostles, craned his neck to look around. They'd been engaging the tyranids for several hours, and night had firmly locked its place over the world. It was a beautiful, star-filled evening, but with the darkness came a sense of isolation. The night winds even sounded different, and Shamas jumped at the errant noises.

The tyranids had remained with them for the first few hours when, suddenly, they dropped back and kept their distance. Now Shamas knew they were out there, just out of sight, keeping pace and waiting for the Sentinels to misstep.

'Report,' Shamas whispered into his micro-bead.

'Orakle Three here.'

Shamas waited for another moment before clicking the micro-bead again. 'Orakle Two? Report.'

The subtle hiss of static played back. No answer. It was as though the desert had swallowed him up.

'All right… pull in formation,' Shamas responded. 'I want you in visual contact.'

'I have you on auspex,' Orakle Three reported. 'I'm heading your way.'

Shamas was sweating hard. He ran a dusty sleeve across his forehead and hailed Orakle Two again. There was still nothing on micro-bead or auspex. He tried listening to the desert, picking out sounds between the heartbeat thumps of his Sentinel's footfalls, but it was impossible to discern any noise over the servos or his rattling engine. Worse still, the fuel gauge on his Sentinel was dangerously low. He had enough left in the drums for a few more hours of this hellish pace, but that would mean stopping to refuel, and even a minute standing still seemed too great a risk.

In the distance, he saw the repeated muzzle flare of an autocannon on full bore. A second later, the flashes stopped and it was dark again. The *thump-thump-thump* of autocannon thunder echoed across the desert. Shamas glanced at the auspex, but no identity runes appeared. He seemed alone in a sea of green sensor wash.

'Orakle Three,' Shamas called, 'was that you firing?' That, of course, was an obvious question, since Orakle Three was the only one in the squadron with an autocannon. 'Can you still see me on auspex, Orakle Three? Because I can't see you.'

This time, it was Orakle Three's turn to remain silent. Shamas whimpered, the night hedging in on him. He was all alone, the last one still running. He switched channels on the micro-bead.

'This is Orakle One… is anyone out there?'

He heard nothing for a moment, until, 'This is Runner One,' Hussari's voice crackled back. 'Report.'

Shamas bit his lip and forced himself to speak slowly and clearly. He would not be seen as the resident coward, even though he was fighting the urge to soil himself. It felt as if his insides had suddenly liquefied, and he was struggling against his fear and the urgent need to let go.

'My squadron is gone and I'm running low on fuel.'

'What happened?' Hussari asked.

'For the love of the Emperor, I don't know,' Shamas reported, biting his lower lip against the squirming pain in his bowels. 'One minute they were there, and the next minute... gone.'

'Did the tyranids get ahead of you? Did you double back?'

'No... I don't know, sir. We've been running straight since this thing began. Oh Lord Emperor... I'm almost out of fuel.'

'How much remaining?'

'Ten minutes... less. I have to stop.'

'Not yet you don't. We'll do this together. Rendezvous with the Runners. We'll cover each other as we refuel.'

'And the other squadrons?'

'We lost contact with the Holy Striders a while ago... now yours.'

'I'm sorry sir,' Shamas said, genuinely regretting disappointing the major. Thankfully, the wave of bowel cramps was retreating and the night air flushed his skin with a cool breeze.

'Nothing to apologise for. Just rendezvous at 30.03N 31.15E. Can you make it?'

'Yes, sir.'

'We'll refuel there.'

'What about the tyranids?'

'We'll worry about that when you get here. Just get here in one piece.'

The micro-bead clicked off, and Shamas felt grateful for a moment... a short-lived one at that. The movement was rapid. Something darted across the sky and blotted out the stars for just long enough to draw his attention heavenward. Shamas barely caught the movement as it hurtled towards his Sentinel.

No other thought entered his head other than to click on the micro-bead.

The flying tyranid landed atop the Sentinel, its almost vestigial hook-like feet catching the frame of the cockpit. It nearly toppled the bird, but continued flapping its great leathery wings. Shamas screamed.

'Orakle One?' Hussari shouted.

Before Shamas could even react, the tyranid's long bladed tail lanced into the cockpit, impaling the sergeant through the stomach and out through the back of his chair. He shuddered, his bowels releasing in a warm, wet rush. The tyranid, however, didn't seem to care. It leaned into the cockpit with its elongated, ridged head, and opened its jaws to reveal its hard, cartilage spike of a tongue.

Shamas could feel the world slipping away, the wrenching pain of his gut wound submerging beneath a haze of darkness. In the back of his thoughts, there was one last thing to do. He wasn't sure what that thing was, at least not until he said it.

'Flyers,' he said, stutter-gasping into the micro-bead.

'Orakle One? Did you say flyers?'

The spike tongue shot out on pneumatic muscles, cracking through the bone of Shamas's skull and fishing out his final thoughts.

11

HUSSARI GROANED AS he stretched his back and cramped legs, and relieved his bladder. The blue sun was swimming on the deep azure horizon, and for the first time in hours, they had a moment's reprieve. There was time to tend to their aching muscles and to refuel. Qubak was standing nearby with a vox ready. He was downing a few ablative pills to ease the stiffness that had spread across his back and neck. Corporal Maraibeh stood atop his Sentinel, staring out through a pair of magnoculars.

'Confirmed, sir,' Maraibeh said. 'They're heading back.'

Hussari finished his business and motioned Qubak over. He took the vox handset and waited for Qubak to raise the outpost. He finally nodded; they had a signal.

'Report,' Nisri said over the vox.

'We kept them busy for most of the night. They finally pulled back. We have the Burning Falcons to thank for that.'

'Any losses?'

'Yes, sir,' Hussari said. 'We lost many Sentinels. The Orakle's Apostles, Burning Falcons, the Dust Marauders and the Holy Striders are gone. We lost another bird from the War Chasers. The survivors from the Blight Thorns are rendezvousing with us. That leaves us with ten Sentinels, sir. The tyranids have given up the chase, for now. All surviving squadrons report the beasts retreating.'

'Hmm,' Nisri said, musing over his options, 'probably to deal with the damage to their ship. But, we still need more time.'

'Sir, they have flyers. That's what killed the Orakle's Apostles. They might have ambushed us too had Sergeant Shamas not warned us. What I'm trying to impress upon you is that if you remain at the outpost, they'll have you on five sides, and there're too many to fight.'

'The next words out of your mouth better not involve the caves,' Nisri said, the warning clear.

'Of course not, sir,' Hussari said. He clicked off the handset for a moment to mutter a colourful string of expletives, before returning it to his mouth. 'I just hope you're very well prepared for what might be coming your way. What are your orders?'

'Don't let the tyranids escape. You've made the Emperor proud this day with your courage and dedication, but I need you to keep on them... keep them distracted.'

Hussari craned his neck back and stared at the sky. He shook his head and placed the handset to his mouth. 'Understood, sir. Runner One out.' Hussari tossed the handset back at Qubak and headed to his Sentinel. 'The colonel expects us to get massacred defending an exposed position,' Hussari barked. 'Let's not disappoint him.'

'Let's show him how the Sentinels fight,' Qubak said.

Hussari offered Qubak a grim smile as they both climbed into their waiting birds. Hussari dropped into his seat and ordered the remaining Sentinels to rendezvous for another thrust.

12

THE COMMAND BUNKER was silent. Nobody spoke, for Nisri didn't appear to be listening any more. He stared at the tactical slate, studying the possible approaches to the outpost and their best defence. The operators continued to monitor auspex and vox, Rezail appeared to be asleep on the cot in an adjoining room, while Tyrell simply watched everything with his quiet fastidiousness.

Turk couldn't stand to be inside any longer. Nisri's stubbornness was killing the finest squadrons of Sentinel pilots that Turk had ever known. Now they were being used as cannon fodder to protect an outpost with no hope of ever surviving the onslaught that awaited it. Turk was certain that Nisri knew this, but the colonel was committed to a course of action and unwilling to sacrifice the caves. Nisri was trapped. Turk actually pitied him, for a moment, because he knew that Nisri saw no way out of his situation. The sense of pity lasted but a moment, however. It was mostly his men that were dying in the desert, his Banna kinsmen, and soon, all of them would die. The urge to walk away was overwhelming.

'I'm going to check on the men,' Turk said, by way of an excuse to leave.

Nisri offered a distracted head nod, but continued staring at the indication runes on the tactical table.

Turk walked outside, and felt immediately grateful for the bright wash of sunlight and for the sounds of life, such as they were. Men were adding more sandbags and fastening tripod guns and grenade launchers to the parapets. Rows of mortars rested in the courtyard, ready to provide indirect fire, alongside ammunition crates protected under small plasteel bunkers, water drums to cool the mortar barrels and the hulking form of the self-propelled Basilisk artillery piece. The forward observer and fire direction centre for the mortars and Basilisk were sheltered in a plasteel observation nest on the floor above the command bunker. It offered a three hundred and sixty degree view of the desert, and it contained several turret-mounted autocannons, facing both the desert and the compound interior.

Turk stood watching the men scramble to prepare the base for a fight they couldn't win. He was surprised when Tyrell walked past him and whispered, 'We must speak. Meet me behind the vehicle stable.'

Turk continued stretching, pretending he'd heard nothing. Tyrell vanished behind the vehicle stable building, and Turk followed.

13

THE REMAINING SQUADRONS approached the tail of the tyranid horde, ten Sentinels against thousands that seemed hell-bent on ignoring them. Major Hussari's small task force was a couple of kilometres behind the swarm and blinded by their dust wake. The Guardsmen spread their formation out and steered by auspex alone, navigating the flat desert plains with cautious ease.

Another kilometre and the Sentinels were closing the gap fast; they would be in firing range within a few minutes. The rumble of the tyranid stampede shook through the soles of Hussari's boots, and he took deep breaths in anticipation of another long chase. He even wondered if their adversaries knew they were shortening the gap behind them, but the auspex returned one solid mass of enemy moving away from them.

They were less than a kilometre behind when Hussari gave orders over the micro-bead to go weapons hot. The guns swivelled in their mounts, the pilots blindly tracking the largest clusters of enemies, their fingers eager on the triggers. In a matter of moments, the autocannons of the Cadian-pattern birds and the lascannons of the Armageddon-pattern vehicles would be in range. Catachan- and Mars-pattern Sentinels with heavy flamers or multilaser weapons were paired with the long-range birds to handle any tyranids that approached too closely.

Half a kilometre away, and the dust storm was blinding.

Suddenly, screams and curses filled the micro-bead. New runes identifying enemy positions by the hundreds appeared among the Sentinel formations.

'Evasion, evasion!' Hussari cried, but it was too late. Tyranids burst from the ground with lightning fast speed. All that Hussari could see were multiple pairs of scythe arms and a snake-like lower body ending in a mandible stinger, all protected by carapace plating. It haemorrhaged a flood of smaller bugs, behind, electricity dancing between their mandibles.

'It's a trap,' someone screamed.

Hussari barely avoided the one that broke free of the ruptured earth ahead of him, its scythe arms slicing too close for comfort. A nearby Sentinel was not so lucky. Two snake-like tyranids sank their scythes into the bird's legs and brought it down. Hussari ran past it as the tyranids skewered and pulled the pilot out of the burst cockpit frame, snapping bone and rending flesh. The smaller bugs swarmed over the screaming pilot, burying him and his cries.

Auspex was a mess, the solid mass of tyranids ahead disintegrating into smaller clusters of skirmish groups that were doubling back to attack the Sentinels. Hussari cursed and hit the channel purge on his micro-bead, silencing all screams and cries for help for long enough to issue a single order.

'Retreat! Full retreat!'

The screams flooded back in, and Hussari cursed the cunning of their adversaries. He continued running through the dust wake, trying to find other Sentinels to help. He may have issued the retreat orders, but he was damned if he was going to leave his men stranded.

Hussari came upon Sergeant Hadoori's Sentinel, which was still standing, but running in a wide circle. Smaller tyranids were crawling up its frame, a bleeding Hadoori steering with one arm and screaming as he fired round after round from his laspistol at the creatures swarming his cockpit. One dropped inside and turned into a frenzy of whipping claws. Hadoori was done for. Hussari angled his bird straight at the other Sentinel and opened fire with his autocannon. The whine of the spinning barrels was followed by a steady volley of shots that ripped through tyranid, Sentinel and pilot alike. It exploded a moment later, the flying shrapnel lacerating the surrounding sand and anything unfortunate enough to be in the way.

Major Hussari never slowed. He continued running, raking the ground ahead of him with a burst of autocannon fire, when auspex revealed a ghost of a return, another snake-like tyranid hidden underground.

SERGEANT IATH WAS losing Mohar's rune among the throng of tyranid returns on the auspex. It was growing increasingly difficult to read the battlefield signals; the fight was one large, frantic skirmish in the thickening dust storm. Particles of energised sand were generating a static charge large enough to disrupt auspex and vox with ghost images and noise bursts. Screeches, howls and the thunder of autocannon fire or the crackling whip of las-fire saturated the air, as did the muted hiss of tyranid bio-weapons.

Mohar screamed over the micro-bead before his transmission cut. A moment later, the dust storm lit up with a long gout of fire from a heavy promethium flamer. Iath headed in that direction, firing a fusillade of shots from the rotating barrel of his multilaser into the tyranids that crossed his path. The razor beams of light shredded and cauterised any beast they caught, leaving behind smouldering, dismembered husks. Mohar's flaming Sentinel abruptly ran into view, the charred remains of Mohar slumped forward on the steering leavers, carbon-cooked tyranids fused against the hull like a thick coat.

Iath watched the burning Sentinel vanish into the storm, and headed deeper into the fray, trying to locate others. He arrived in time to see an energised plasma shot splatter against another Sentinel. The plasma salted the pilot and bored holes into his chest, before the super-heated material ate through the promethium tanks. The fiery explosion devoured Sentinel and tyranid alike, while the concussion wave toppled Iath's Sentinel. Iath screamed, the blistering heat and flame of the explosion flash-searing his exposed flesh and melting cloth to skin. It instantly fused his rubber-rimmed occulars to his face.

The agony overrode reason, and Iath fumbled for the cockpit's med-kit. It didn't matter that he was surrounded by tyranids; it only mattered that he reach the pain killers, that he numb the excruciating agony that lanced him. His nerves felt devoured by flame and his skin screamed its anguish into his brain. It killed him to move, his clothing melted into his flesh; every little movement pulled at the cloth, tore open a fresh wound and exposed him to some new profound torture.

Iath couldn't grab the med-kit, his gnarled hands burned into fleshy knots. He cried in agony, until he saw centipede tyranids snaking towards him, their thorny feelers twitching in anticipation, their hundred legs moving like waves underneath their bodies, their mandibles clacking. Iath watched them approach and screamed at them to kill him.

He never thought the tyranids would be his measure of mercy.

AUSPEX DIDN'T LIE, and it was telling him he was surrounded. 'Mad' Maraibeh could see the pockets of tyranids moving through the dust storm, some towards him and others in different directions. They were organised, each one to its purpose, and none deviated from its course. The Sentinels he could see on scope had either stopped moving or vanished from the plate altogether. Only one Sentinel appeared to have escaped the massacre, but it was a wounded bird and limped along at half-speed.

He was alone in the fight, but the thought did not bother him. He would die serving the Emperor, and the notion of that glory emboldened him further. Maraibeh opened the micro-bead channel with its dying voices and began to sing, not of the Emperor and not of his own children, but a popular melody back home. It was a song sung at the campfires, of men and the pretty women they loved. Maraibeh smiled at the memory of his wife, feeling her jab him in the ribs, indignant. And, for that, he loved her all the more.

A superior, Sergeant Hadoori perhaps, yelled at him to clear the micro-bead, but Maraibeh was too jubilant to comply. There was nothing interesting to hear on the channels... only cries of help and orders to retreat. So he sang, and opened the nozzles on his flamer to full. He headed to the largest mob, clearing a path before him by washing the desert with bright promethium flame. A series of handwritten runes on his auspex marked the different distances and the times to reach them.

Maraibeh pulled out one of his pipe bombs. When a large tyranid mob on auspex reached the sixty second mark written on his display plate, Maraibeh cranked his tube charge to seventy seconds. He dropped the explosive into the satchel resting in the cockpit's foot well and jammed his lit cigar into his mouth.

A minute later, he ploughed straight through the mob of tyranids, dancing his Sentinel in a circle and washing everything he could see in flame. The tyranids were a sea of screeching beasts that surrounded his bird for as far as he could see, and auspex said they stretched out further than that. They jumped up on the frame of his exposed cockpit, but he managed to fling them off with crazy spins that would have thrown most Sentinels on their sides. Shots whizzed by him, but they struck either air or thick metal. Finally, one of the creatures with scythe blades and clawing arms managed to latch on to the Sentinel and pull its head up to the cockpit. Maraibeh laughed and jammed his lit cigar into its eye.

The creature screeched and raised its cutting arms to kill Maraibeh.

'Too late,' the madman said.

The pipe bomb exploded and detonated the remaining charges in the satchel. The explosion engulfed the promethium in the tanks and turned the Sentinel into a massive fireball of sticky flame and shrapnel. Dozens of screaming tyranids were caught in the deadly blossom, and dozens more severely wounded.

HUSSARI'S SENTINEL WAS badly damaged and limping. The lights on his control panel fluttered, while alarms warned him of catastrophic failures and of the fuel leaks that had all but crippled his bird. He was also bleeding from a forehead gash, opened up by a creature that had got far too close to him before he shot it off. Still, he wasn't out of the danger yet. He'd managed to escape the battlefield through the confusion, the dust storm and the massive explosion that rattled the desert, but not without picking up a tail or two. Three runners, skipping across the sand with their six legs each, were overtaking his bird quickly. Hussari, however, wasn't toothless yet. He pivoted towards them and fired his autocannon, raking the sand. The hound-like runners were quick, dodging as best they could, but the major was faster on the trigger. He caught each one in a hailstorm of steel-jacketed rounds, and cut them down well short of his bird.

On the last shot, his cannon clicked and whined as the empty barrels spun. He had expended the last of his ammunition.

Hussari continued on his path. From auspex, he was glad to see the distance between his bird and the tyranids grow wider. He'd escaped for the moment, but there were a couple of things still left to do. Hussari flipped through the comm-channels, trying to raise his squadrons. No answers. He was the only one left.

'Home base, this is Runner One, respond.'

There was a pause, followed by Nisri's voice. 'This is home base. Report.'

'My men are all dead. We did all we could.'

'Confirm that,' followed by another pause. 'Did you manage to thin their numbers?'

'We pinched them,' Hussari answered. 'That's about it. I hope we bought you the time you needed, because auspex says they're heading your way.'

'Roger that,' Nisri responded, his voice strangely vacant. 'Can you make it back?'

'Not with this bird, sir. She's badly hurt. But we hid Private Damask's Sentinel after he died. I can reach it.'

'Get back with all due haste, major. We'll need you here. Colonel Nisri out.'

Hussari clicked the handset back into the locking cradle and swore under his breath. He pushed his Sentinel as fast as she would go and headed for Damask's bird. No tyranids followed him.

CHAPTER EIGHT

'The mind is for seeing, but it is the heart that listens.'
— *The Accounts of the Tallarn*
by Remembrancer Tremault

1

TURK LISTENED AS Hussari gave his report and signed off. The command bunker returned to its tomb-like quiet. After a moment, Nisri studied the tactical plate and issued terse orders to the operators, Major Dashour and himself. Commissar Rezail and his adjutant finally left the room to examine the abatis spear trench laid at the foot of the outside wall using strips of metal from the drop containers.

When Dashour left, Turk walked up to Nisri and made sure to remain absolutely calm throughout whatever would happen next. He couldn't get angry. All their lives pivoted on his ability to remain calm. Tyrell's advice was still fresh in his mind and he knew that this was the right course for both men, despite what it meant to their egos.

'I would speak with you as an equal, one prince to another... alone,' Turk said quietly enough for his words to pass only between him and Nisri, 'but I will obey your decision as one soldier to his superior officer.'

Nisri looked up, a flash of annoyance burning on his face, but Turk would not back down. This was a matter between two princes and the tribes they commanded.

'Now's not the time, lieutenant-colonel.'

Turk sat down in front of Nisri and continued whispering, low enough not to draw the attention of the operators. 'I believe it is. You can court-martial me, and you can execute me, but Commissar Rezail is not here. This is a matter between two tribesmen and not soldiers. Give me a minute. After that, I will follow your direction as your subordinate, praise the Emperor in all things.'

Nisri sighed and finally stared Turk straight in the eyes. The colonel looked fatigued, the weight of his decisions and the inevitability of their fate a sure toll on his spirit. 'Fine… as one prince to another, what is it?'

'The caves,' Turk whispered, 'you wish them to be a gift to your tribe, correct?'

'Not according to your views,' Nisri responded.

'What I think of the caves is not in question, is it, Prince Dakar? What matters is what the caves mean to you.'

Nisri thought about it for a moment. 'Yes,' he said, finally, 'very well. The caves are for my tribe… for staying true to our faith,' he added as a small jab.

Turk bit down on his words and allowed Nisri his petty moment. 'What, then, if you're being tested?' Turk asked. 'What if this is another ordeal? Choose between your duty to the Emperor or the gift He bestows? Which is more important?'

Nisri straightened, instantly aware of the argument's implications. 'It is no such thing, Prince Iban Salid. We have found a paradise worthy of the Turenag, and I will not be the ruin of it.'

Turk leaned forward. 'The Aba Aba Mushira would not give you a paradise, just to fill it with scorpions. He would not offer you an oasis, just to poison it.'

'What if it is a test to see if we are truly worthy of keeping it?'

'And what if it's a test to see whether it is greed or faith that drives you? Think, Prince Dakar, imagine the glory that would be promised to your tribe if you turned your back on paradise to fight His enemies.'

'A paradise neither you nor Rezail believes to be ours.'

'Did it ever matter to you what we believed?' Turk asked.

'No,' Nisri admitted.

'I know you Prince Dakar, and you know me. You do not spend this much time hating someone without knowing the truth of them. I am not asking you to surrender your garden of delights. If the Emperor truly meant for you to have it, then nothing can stand in the way of providence. If this isn't providence, then nothing can save it. In either case, our remaining here, on this plateau, is certain suicide. It is a waste of our duty to the Emperor.' And with that, Turk shut his mouth.

If Tyrell was speaking the truth, and Turk believed he was, then Nisri already knew the caves were their only hope. He'd fought the tyranids before, and he understood the dangers of remaining exposed on all sides. The trouble was, as in all things that afflicted the two tribal alliances throughout this civil war, Nisri needed a reason to change his mind without appearing weak or betraying his people. He needed a reason to retreat to the caves without appearing indecisive. He needed someone else to state the truth for him.

Nisri appeared to have a burden lifted from his shoulders, as though he were no longer shouldering them alone. He straightened. 'I hear paradise can be fattening.'

Turk smiled. 'Only when it prepares you for the slaughter.'

'Emergency council, all command staff and every officer,' Nisri said.

'Yes, sir,' Turk replied, snapping up to salute before he transmitted the order over his micro-bead.

2

THE COMMAND BUNKER sweltered with officers, everyone quietly listening to Turk speak as they stood surrounding him.

'We lack the firepower to protect us from an all-out attack on all sides, and once the tyranids swarm us, we'll be cut off from our supplies of food and water. We will not last the night,' Turk concluded.

The officers listened, some nodding their heads, while others shook theirs and looked to Nisri for support.

'We'd be leading the tyranids straight to the caverns,' Captain Abantu said, speaking directly to Colonel Nisri, 'to the future home of our–'

'They'll find the caves with or without our help,' Captain Toria responded, interrupting. 'Is that not true of the tyranids? They possess an unerring skill in tracking down bio-matter to consume.'

'They do,' Dashour responded, 'but I say we keep them as far from the caves as we can for as long as possible.'

'This isn't a discussion,' Nisri said, 'it is an order. The caves do not belong to us unless the will of the High Lords of Terra are in our favour. If the caves truly belong to the Turenag, then the Emperor fights with us, and the Banna, in protecting them. Let any man who doubts that speak.'

Nobody spoke; the root of the dissension between the soldiers was tribal in nature, but with Nisri and Turk supporting one another's decisions, nobody dared offer a dissenting voice.

'There is one thing,' a rough voice said. Everyone turned to discover Nubis standing up to speak. Turk groaned inwardly, praying that Nubis understood the delicate balance they'd achieved. 'If we are going to make our stand at the caves, then we should mine the entry tunnels and collapse–'

The Turenag officers exploded into argument, and even Nisri was vehement in his refusals. To despoil paradise with their fight was one thing, but to begin destroying the tunnels was too much to bear. Nubis, however, was never one to be cowed by officers screaming at him, and he effectively raised his voice to cut through the wash.

'If!' he barked, loud enough to be heard. 'If we collapse the larger passages, we force the tyranids through smaller chokepoints. We conserve ammunition that way, and if we're in danger of being swarmed, we can collapse the tunnels completely and seal ourselves inside the caves... with no damage to them. We save *your* paradise!'

The voices lessened in pitch, enough for Nubis to speak normally. 'If we collapse the tunnels, the tyranids would have to dig far and long to reach us, and even then, we could continue to mount a defence, perhaps for long enough to be rescued, if the Emperor so wishes it.'

The room was quiet before Nisri spoke. 'Very well... we collapse specific tunnels to funnel the enemy, and we mine the others. If we must, and only on *my* word, then we collapse the others to save ourselves... and to save our paradise.'

Turk allowed the order to sink in before he moved on to the next matter, one most terrible to ask, but crucial to their survival nonetheless.

'What I am about to ask,' Turk said, 'will require a great sacrifice from some of you. Major Hussari reports that the tyranids will be here in about seven hours.'

Turk paused for a moment, allowing the statement to sink in. He could see the officers glancing around. They knew what was coming, what was being asked. Some officers could not meet Turk's eyes, and their gaze fell to the floor.

'If they find nothing here and follow us directly to the caves, they will catch us before we can prepare an adequate defence,' Turk said. Each word felt bitter in his mouth, a poison that would surely kill him for speaking it. He continued nonetheless. 'We need volunteers to remain behind to man the fort and engage the tyranids. We need volunteers to buy the regiment more time to prepare. Major Hussari is already aware of the situation. He'll arrive before the tyranid assault and engage the horde with the remaining squadrons in the open desert.'

The room was uncomfortably quiet. Commissar Rezail rose to his feet, about to challenge the men to rise to the occasion. Turk caught the commissar's eye, however, and gently shook his head. Rezail looked shocked, but he held his tongue.

Finally, Major Dashour stood. 'I hate caves,' he said. 'Confined spaces bother me. I'll stay and fight beneath the open sky.'

Another moment passed, everyone's breath held hostage in that moment between waiting and acting.

'I'll stay as well,' Captain Abantu replied at last. 'You'll need a gunnery crew operating the Basilisk, and who knows, perhaps our sacrifice will move the High Lords of Terra to give our people this planet.'

'Thank you,' Nisri said.

Then, to everyone's surprise, Quartermaster Kortan stood as well, his eyes dark and haunted, the long scab of the fight still fresh on his face. 'I wish to stay,' he said, nodding. Everyone was taken aback; Kortan's gift for selfish action was legendary. At first they thought it was another joke, and someone chuckled needlessly, but Kortan neither cracked his customary grin nor laughed. The room went quiet.

'Thank you, quartermaster,' Nisri replied, 'but your expertise will be needed at the caves.'

'Actually, sir,' Kortan said, 'Private Sabaak is more than capable of managing the supplies. I recommend him for a field promotion, sir, and, truthfully, I… can't let the Turenag stay behind alone. Someone has to bring the Banna glory,' he said through a weak smile.

Several of the officers chuckled, and Toria patted him on the shoulder.

'Very well,' Turk said, 'and thank you. I want the remaining officers to seek out volunteers to man the base. We can't spare more than fifty men.'

'Dismissed,' Nisri said. 'Begin evacuations.'

3

KORTAN WAS SHAKING as he walked back to the supply shed. He stared at the bloodstained rock where two soldiers had died, and fought to stomach the queasiness that made his intestines and guts feel slippery. Officers were already barking orders to their soldiers, and everyone was getting ready to pull out with emergency provisions only. Their personal items would remain behind until they could return to retrieve them.

There was a line of soldiers already at the supply shed, with Sabaak trying to handle the flood of requests for survival gear. Kortan was about to make his way inside when a rough hand grabbed him and pulled him to the side of the shed. A few soldiers saw and watched, but nobody interfered.

Kortan met Nubis's piercing black eyes; the scar patterns accentuated his angry scowl. Kortan knew what was coming.

'Make sure you don't survive,' Nubis whispered. 'There is no home for you at the caves, I promise you that.'

'Why? Because I killed two of Anuman's men… who were trying to kill me?'

'You murdered two men of the Banna Alliance, two men of the Nasandi! My tribe!'

658   Hammer of the Emperor

Kortan pushed Nubis back. 'I saw no men of the Nasandi... only jack-als who set their teeth at my throat! And so, I shot them like jackals.'

Nubis reared back with his fist, but Kortan didn't flinch.

'Tell me, master gunner,' Kortan said, a crooked smirk on his lips. 'Is the Nasandi tribe a kennel these days? Strike me if you truly believe I killed two of your kinsmen that day, and not dogs.'

Nubis did not strike, but his fist wavered.

'I thought so,' Kortan said. He turned and headed for the supply shed, half expecting to get beaten. No blows arrived. The other soldiers parted way for him and he entered unmolested.

4

THE CAMP SEEMED to be in staggered uproar. The Chimeras were leaving the compound with soldiers packed inside and atop the vehicles. Friends wore sombre expressions as they shook hands, embraced and kissed the cheeks of those staying behind. They clasped arms and exchanged data-slates holding farewell letters written to loved ones. Others traded pieces of jewellery: devotion chains, lockets with pictures of their wives and medallions of saints. None of those staying behind said it was so their comrades would remember them. It was always 'for safekeeping'. The Guardsmen spoke quietly, the air filled with the noise of machines.

The Chimeras would make a couple of trips to get everyone, but the soldiers involved in cementing the defence of the caves went first; they knew this would be the last time they would see one another. The Guardsmen were dog-tired, their efforts spent over the last day on forti-fying the base camp. Now they were expected to lay explosives throughout the cavern's tunnels and secure the choke points.

Worse, perhaps, was that with the shift of attention from fortifying base camp to fortifying the caves, the men leaving felt a renewed sense of hope. They could collapse the tunnels and seal the tyranids out. That hope, Turk knew, also tore them apart with guilt. That hope came at the expense of the men they left behind, and more than a few wept quietly, shuddering to contain their grief as they left.

Turk watched as a squadron of Sentinels headed for the main gate car-rying men on their open-frame roofs. It was far from an ideal ride, but Captain Toria and his men were urgently needed to scout the remainder of the caverns, to uncover any additional passages leading underground: anything that the tyranids might use to bypass their defences. Already there was the worry of burrowing tyranids, but Nisri had expressed doubt that the diggers could create traversable tunnels for their allies to use. Whether he was lying to offer a glimmer of hope, Turk knew not.

But he noticed that Nisri spoke through clenched teeth, and that was enough to worry Turk.

Shaking the many thoughts from his head, Turk briefly watched two Guardsmen lower the regiment's double-eagle banner and roll it up reverently. The 892nd, such as it was, was already home to them. He ducked inside Kamala's tent. Her kit had been packed and she appeared ready to leave, despite sitting on her bed and staring at the wall in a daze. Turk took her hands and kneeled before her.

'My love,' he said, 'wherever you are, come to me.'

Her tired eyes riveted on him, her expression almost wild and panicked. 'Did – did I leave you?' she asked, frantically.

'What's the matter?' he asked.

'When I first arrived,' she replied, 'I was sure there had been no massacre on this world, no Imperial presence. Now I'm certain of the opposite. There were Imperials here, some forgotten expedition, and they died, cruelly. The sands have claimed them now, but they were here. Their ghosts cry out to be remembered, and I can't stop hearing them.'

Turk nodded. He asked the question, despite his discomfort. 'Can you hear them now?'

'Not clearly, but the tyranids have awakened their memories and given them voices again. It's hard to tell... the tyranids skew my perception of things. Silence them. Smother,' she said, touching her lips. 'It was the tyranids who killed them.'

'That no longer matters,' Turk said. 'What matters is that we survive. I secured your transport.'

'Yes,' she said, standing, dazed, 'I was about to... go? Is that where I went?'

Turk stood with her and cupped her face in his hands. 'My cherished, I couldn't let you leave without a suitable goodbye.'

Kamala focussed on his smile, and smiled in return. She leaned into his kiss and seemed anchored to it. They relished the tenderness of one another for a long, lingering moment, before Kamala's smile faded. She broke away reluctantly, apparently lost. She grabbed her kit and headed for the door.

Turk stayed inside the tent for a moment longer, absorbing the jasmine ghost of her scent, troubled by her visions. He could not help his thoughts, could not help the primal fear that something was eating her mind. But no... the tyranids, and the ghosts they brought with them, were troubling her. That was all. He walked back out into the wild bustle of the camp, fully confident that in the chaos of the moment, nobody would see him leaving Kamala's tent.

* * *

5

IT WAS DARK when the main gates swung open and Major Hussari's Sentinel strode into camp. He was shocked by the ghostly state of it, the fifty-odd soldiers rattling around inside a compound like a handful of loose coins in a large jug. The other Sentinel squadrons were already on picket duty, with instructions to help base camp for as long as they could before falling back to the caves. Major Hussari, however, had sworn to remain and help the defences. This was no time to hide behind rank, not that he ever had.

Major Dashour jogged up to the Sentinel as Major Hussari turned the engine off and dismounted. He offered a sharp salute before asking the question everyone was too afraid to ask.

'How far behind are they?'

'An hour,' Hussari replied, casually. He handed Dashour a data-slate. 'Their direction hasn't changed from the information here. They're coming straight for us.'

Dashour nodded. 'Yes, sir. The Fire Direction Centre team can put this intelligence to use. We should be able to drop a few shells on them before they get in range of the wall emplacements and mortars.'

'Good,' Hussari replied. 'We'll have plenty to shoot at when the time comes.'

6

THE FIRST SIGN of their arrival was the dust cloud that slowly devoured the horizon. Long-range auspex picked up the tyranids next, the approaching horde like a solid storm front. If they didn't know what they were facing, the operators might have mistaken it for a thick storm, but they knew what was coming, and they trembled at the magnitude of the signal.

That's when the Basilisk began to thunder, firing off a deuterium macro-shell every few seconds, the sweaty crew working feverishly to shove shells into the loader that automatically fed the breach. Each shot shook the courtyard and buildings, and sent out a shockwave of dust, but the soldiers ignored the deafening crump of artillery fire. They all wore ear-guards fitted with micro-beads to hear and relay orders, though this was a weak rejoinder compared to the artillery fielded in most other engagements.

Guardsmen gathered along the northern wall and watched as the distant desert grew dark with bodies. The Basilisk's shells registered in the approaching mass as impact clouds that flung pinprick bodies into the air and darkened the mass with plumes of black smoke. Only later, what felt like an eternity afterwards, did the air echo back the hint of soft impacts. But the fire seemed inconsequential compared to the approaching mass, like using a pin to stab at the body of a wolf.

Dashour let the men watch for a moment before sending them back to their positions. The heaviest defences were along the western wall, where a dune created a natural ramp to the plateau and the main gate. While it did not face the approaching tyranids, it would probably be the most heavily exploited avenue up to the walls. Dashour also placed men along the other walls to handle the tyranids that scaled the plateau. But, between the abatis thicket of metal lances and the thin lip of plateau between the compounds walls and the cliffs, Dashour hoped fewer men would be needed to hold those positions.

Major Hussari was in the command bunker, instructing the squadrons engaging the edges of the tyranid legions. Nobody was to venture closer than autocannon range; the tyranids reacted too quickly to risk sending them in closer. As it was, the enemy was sending out harrying parties to go after the squadrons, overtaking some and scattering others. This was a flood, and they were but a lone rock hoping to break the back of the storm, but Hussari continued to direct his squadrons, hearing them die one at a time. He doubted whether more than a handful of birds would ever reach the caves.

Kortan, meanwhile, was regretting his decision with every fibre of his being, but he stood his ground along the northern wall. He tried to ignore the thunder of the approaching mob, the undulating sea of bone-grey, turquoise, blood-red and black carapaces. The pressure of them seemed immense. How they didn't crush one another with their bodies, Kortan did not know. For each artillery shell that cratered a hole in their ranks, the horde surged to fill it again; there was no sign of their numbers thinning. They were endless. Kortan was on the verge of collapse when a steady hand found his shoulder. It was Dashour. He handed him a remote device with a single switch mounted on its face.

'Is this the magic button to make them go away?' Kortan shouted, nodding to the tyranids.

'In a manner of speaking,' Dashour said, missing the joke. He said something else that was swallowed by the explosive artillery shot. The air was already thick with the smell of cordite from the propellants. 'I said, once the tyranids draw in close, the Basilisk will be useless. This is one of four triggers to detonate the ammo sheds that are filled with deuterium shells.' He paused, waiting for another salvo to be fired. 'When the camp is overrun–'

'Don't you mean "if",' Kortan said, half in jest and all in hope.

'When,' Dashour said. 'It will be up to Major Hussari, Captain Abantu, me or you to detonate the ammo sheds and take as many of these bastards with us as we can.'

Kortan nodded, his head swimming with the truth of their situation. In most operations, he was well behind the front lines. He saw combat rarely, if ever. Today, however, was another matter entirely. The Basilisk fired again. This time, it was joined by mortar fire from the trench below, and by the gun emplacements on the wall.

The tyranids had reached the base of the plateau.

7

THE BATTLE WAS an ugly, desperate thing. The tyranids struck the base of the plateau and melted around it, the way water flows to find cracks. They surged up the ramp, the air filled with their insect-like chatter and their war howls. In moments, the base camp stood alone in a living sea of enemies, the desert forgotten. The tyranids nimbly scaled the cliff sides, using one another for purchase before leaping up higher, their claws and blade arms sinking into the rock wall. Others, reminiscent of centipedes and cockroaches with faces, scurried up the cliff and defied gravity with no effort. A few fired up at the Guardsmen, but they seemed frantic, eager to reach the humans within and kill them with their bare hands.

The swell of tyranids reached the compound's walls. The first wave crashed into the abatis spikes and skewered themselves deliberately. The almost suicidal run caught the Guardsmen off kilter, until they realised that the tyranids were using their bodies to cork the spikes. Others used the dead to scramble higher up the wall, but the Guardsmen fired down into the mob. The skirmish was in desperate and full swing. The whistle of mortars was as constant as the weapons fire, and every shot was promised a hit.

DASHOUR STOOD WITH his men on the western wall, certainly more composed than they with their desperate battle cries, but fighting just the same. With bolt pistol in hand, he chose his shots, aimed and fired. The mob on the ramp below was packed together and blinding in their uniformity, but Dashour fancied he understood the tyranid… respected their strengths, and capitalised on their perceived weakness. The tyranids were hive-minded, and each pack possessed an anchor to that unifying intellect. It was usually a larger beast, better armed and armoured than the rest. Dashour sought them out with his sharp eyes, firing grenade shell rounds into their bodies. The rounds detonated inside them and sent out a hail of shredding fragments into their closest allies.

* * *

KORTAN KEPT HIS head low as he ran along the various walls. The over-sized packs strapped over both his shoulders were heavy, but were quickly becoming lighter as soldiers grabbed frag and krak grenades from him. The grenades went over the walls quickly, and detonated with muted whumps somewhere below. Kortan did not linger, however, and focussed on keeping his head down.

HUSSARI WAS ON the eastern wall, the one with the highest cliffs. The tyranids were clustered far below, with swarms of them trying to scale the rocks. He aimed down the scope of his M-Galaxy lasgun, picking off the highest climbers with a mid-range charge setting. Too little power and the shot might bounce off the carapace, but too strong a charge would deplete the power pack.

The major sighted, and sliced through the tentacle arm of a climbing beast with a mouth set in its chest, when someone next to him screamed. Hussari turned in time to see the man on the ground, writhing in agony, his shirt torn open, and the blood blisters on his chest exploding; beetle rounds were burrowing into his skin. Nothing could be done for him. The major turned the lasgun on the poor soldier and shot him through the head. That was the only triage any of them could expect today.

He was about to fire at another enemy when another soldier was hit: a shot to the face that rocked him off his feet and sent pin-sized beetles running in and out of the crater-like wound.

Sniper, Hussari realised. *They have a sniper.*

Hussari peered over the edge of the wall for a one-second count and whipped his head back again. A shot screamed past him, the sniper quick with his aim. Unfortunately, there were too many opponents below for him to see the sniper, but that didn't matter to Hussari. He pulled three frag grenades from his webbing, adjusted them to a short fuse, pulled the pin on each and dropped them in different directions. The grenades exploded above the tyranids, the shrapnel dispersing over a wide area. Hussari moved to a different spot on the wall and peered over again for a one-second count. The mob below was devastated: carapaces split open, bodies spitting jets of ichor and yellow and red organs unravelling from bodies. No shots followed, but Hussari could also see the press of tyranids rushing in to fill the gaps and devour their own dead.

BACK ALONG THE western wall, over the main gate, the fighting grew more intense. With no cliffs to scale, the tyranids were at the compound's walls. Soldiers along the battlements fired directly down into the mob below them. The Guardsmen were efficient in their killing, but, unfortunately, were stacking a wall of corpses for the others to climb. Dashour continued to pick his shots, aiming at those tyranids that seemed unique among the throng of runners, leapers and warriors. He wasn't sure if his plan was working, but he liked to pretend it was.

Suddenly, something caught Dashour's eye: a row of simian-like tyranids. They were well armoured, with long, muscular arms and giant, clawed fists, the sharp knuckles of which they used to drag themselves forward. Biomechanical cannons grew from their backs, while under each body was the weighted udder of their ammo sac. Dashour's eyes widened; he remembered these creatures, remembered the horrors they could inflict within the ranks of their enemies.

'Gunbeasts! Shoot them!' he cried, pointing. A few of the soldiers looked confused, unable to distinguish one tyranid from another in these conditions. Those that understood Dashour's orders aimed and fired, but their shots fell short.

Dashour ran up to the autocannon gunner sheltered behind sandbags and pulled him off the weapon. He planted his shoulders into the recoil braces and fired at the tyranids, stitching round after round into the targets. Shots bounced off the heavy bone moulding of the cannon mounts and the heavily plated arms and legs, but Dashour kept his finger heavy on the trigger, his tracer rounds bringing all ranged fire along the wall to bear against the gunbeasts. Two went down, telling hits scored along the creatures' necks and heads.

It was too late. Three gunbeasts strained, their cannons flaring with electric sparks and heavy muscles contracting. They fired their spore clusters.

The first cluster sailed over the wall and struck the mortar trench. The spore exploded on impact, generating a cloud that engulfed four mortar crews and sent the others scrambling from the pits. They screamed, their pained howls a piercing cry that stabbed the heart. Dashour knew the effects: instant haemorrhaging, destruction of the soft connective tissues, disintegration of the internal organs. They died as their organs and arteries melted into pudding, and their skin, muscles, bones and tendons detached from one another. They turned people into bags of soup and bone.

The second spore struck the wall and caught two Guardsmen in the splatter. They didn't even have time to scream as the liquid melted their heads and upper bodies. They fell to the ground, their organs spilling out of the exposed cups of their chests. The fast acting molecular acids also ate through the wall, opening a large crater, but not eating its way through.

The third spore struck the upper wall, this time exploding out in a web of filament threads covered in filleting micro-hooks. The threads wrapped around three men and instantly contracted. They tore through their clothing and sunk into their flesh until stopped by bone. One soldier died with a gurgle on his lips, the threads having cut through his throat and wrapped around his spinal column. The other two cried out for help, the wires embedded halfway through their stomachs, arms and thighs.

Dashour ignored the screams for help and the pandemonium. He continued firing at the gunbeasts, raking them with the autocannon to stop them from firing again.

'Major!' he cried into his micro-bead, 'watch out for gunbeasts... the ones with the cannons on their back. Take them out first.'

'Will do,' Hussari cried back, 'but we have our own problems.'

QUICKLY SWITCHING CHANNELS, the major backed away from the ledge of the battlements and contacted fire-direction centre while staring through his magnoculars.

'They're approaching from the north-east. They're the only things in the air,' Hussari said. He was staring at what appeared to be several flights of the creatures, what Dashour had called flyers.

'I see 'em,' Captain Abantu reported.

'Take them out. We can't afford to have them drop in our laps or skip us and find the caves before the others are ready.'

'Yes, sir,' Abantu replied.

ABANTU WAS RELATIVELY safe inside the fire-direction centre, but the action was no less heated. They held a commanding view of the western slope and the base of the northern wall, while anything they saw to the east was out of range of their autocannons. Still, gunners waited at the three gun mounts that lined each of the four walls, either firing at the enemy they could see and reach, or waiting to fire at their own battlements the moment the tyranids began scaling the walls.

'Sir,' the forward observer said. He was a nervous looking boy who had been steady and clear in his instructions throughout the engagement. 'Those gunbeasts that the major warned us about, I see more of them approaching from the east. I also see something the size of a small building. It's moving around us with a sizeable contingent.'

'Is it now?' Abantu asked. 'Moving around us? To flank us, perhaps?'

'Sir, I think that group's avoiding the battle deliberately. I think they're heading to the caves.'

Abantu sighed. How the creatures knew about the caves, he didn't know, but if they managed to get inside, they could build a brand new army with all that rich bio-matter, and he doubted the others could do anything to stop them. They needed more time.

'Direct the Basilisk's fire against that large creature and his group. Alert Major Hussari to the approaching gunbeasts, and tell the heavy gunners to fire on the flyers when they get within range.'

'Yes, sir.'

THE FIRST TYRANIDS made it over the south wall at the same time the fliers swooped into the fray. All twelve ball-mounted guns over the command bunker began chattering at that moment, inbetween the heavy artillery salvos aimed at the large tyranid force that was north of the compound.

It was nothing short of spectacular chaos, with the fight disintegrating into a three hundred and sixty degree free-for-all. A bipedal tyranid with a scorpion's tail mounted the southern battlement and swung its scythe blades, disembowelling one Guardsman and amputating the arm of another. Two ball mounts above the command bunker swung towards the warrior and unleashed a fusillade of shots that dismembered it and chewed through the ichor and blood-soaked duckboards, before blasting chunks off the walls.

FLYERS SWOOPED DOWN at the Guardsmen on the battlements. Kortan barely managed to duck as the blade-tail of one sliced at him. Laspistol in hand, he fired at it as it swooped skyward again, but it moved too fast. Kortan checked the sky and headed for a group of soldiers shouting for more ammunition.

MAJOR HUSSARI WATCHED as a flyer with insect-like wings skewered a tripod gunner on its lance arms and raised him into the air. The man screamed as the tyranid lifted him up and sank his teeth around the man's face. There was a brilliant explosion of red as the creature's cartilage tongue burst out through the back of his skull. Hussari screamed in anger and fired his lasgun. Crackling shots tore through the creature's wings, and both it and its prey dropped into the compound below. The surviving mortar crews shot the creature with their laspistols until it stopped jerking. Grim-faced, they returned to their steady salvos.

Hussari ran to an abandoned tripod mounted cannon and fired into the unending sea of enemies that was scaling the battlement's walls. The cliffs were thick with tyranids.

DASHOUR BRIEFLY TOOK note of the chaos around him. The ball-mounted guns were filling the sky with tracer fire, felling several of the flyers, and doing their best to keep them away from the wall crews. One occasionally managed to dart past the screen of fire, however, impaling a Guardsman or knocking him off his perch into the forest of claws and stingers below.

We're losing through attrition, Dashour thought, before turning his attentions back to the west wall. Here, the litter of corpses served as a ramp for their compatriots, and the tyranids were getting close enough to swing their bladed arms at the Guardsmen. To Dashour's right, a trooper wielding a melta gun fired a hissing thermal blast of ignited gases, striking a frog-like creature with powerful leaping legs and hooks for arms. The blast vaporised it and flash burned several leapers around him. Before he could fire again, a dozen small tyranids, each with four clawing arms and reverse joint legs, managed to bound up from the ramp, to the backs of their dead companions and over the walls. One tackled the Guardsman with the melta gun and pushed him off the wall. As they fell, the leaper slashed at the soldier, shredding the man before either of them hit the ground.

The tyranids scattered through the compound like a small plague, going after mortar crews and lone Guardsmen.

'The walls are breached!' someone yelled over the micro-bead.

'The northern tyranid mass is inbound,' Abantu said over the channel.

Dashour realised they were being overrun, the western wall moments away from being swarmed. The mortar and artillery crews stopped firing as they dealt with the leapers that were tearing into them. Another soldier on the southern wall was impaled on the scythe blade of a large bipedal tyranid that reached the battlements. The creature pulled him over the side before anyone could react.

Dashour scrambled to grab the dropped melta gun and brought it to bear. He fired thermal blasts at the enemies, vaporising those about to scale the walls. Another one of his men simply toppled over, a buzzing tyranid round leaving a hole through the chest.

'Prepare to retreat to the fire-direction centre,' Major Hussari yelled into the micro-bead. 'We'll make our last stand there! Emperor love you all for your bravery!'

KORTAN BACK-PEDALLED along the wall, his bags empty of munitions and grenades, his laspistol depleted, though he was hard pressed to remember when he'd fired it and what he'd hit. He jammed in another power core, his last, and began firing to cover the retreat of the other men. Any notion of saving himself was somehow distant, and he felt invigorated by his actions.

He fired shot after shot, as tyranids scaled the battlements and threw Guardsmen to the ravening hordes below. All their screams melted together until they sounded like one unending cry that never drew breath. Kortan continued backing towards the fire-direction centre as men ran past him.

* * *

TYRANIDS OVERTOOK THE southern wall entirely, the last soldier torn in half between two snake-like beasts with four arms apiece. They slithered along the battlements and on the wall, clinging like spiders, as they rushed the other positions. Men leapt to the courtyard below, to escape the attack. The mortar and Basilisk crews, and other Guardsmen were fighting back to back in small clusters, shooting up at the walls as leapers and runners cleared the parapets.

'Retreat!' Dashour cried, though he had no intention of surrendering his position along the west wall. Men ran past him, some cut down by bone rounds or grabbed off the walls by harpoon lines. He continued firing his melta gun, even after tyranids scaled the walls on either side of him. He was determined to stand his ground, to match his faith against theirs. He knew he was dead… there was no other end today but death. But he wanted to die facing them. He wanted them to see the same conviction of purpose that he saw and so feared in them.

'Come on!' he screamed, his controlled mien finally broken on the back of his bloodlust. As he fought, the last man at the western wall, a pack of small, dog-sized tyranids leapt at him. They seemed to be composed mostly of a large head with overly-developed fangs, a long skull crest of bone plates and six legs to scuttle about on. They bit and latched on to the meat of his arms, thighs, back and neck. Dashour screamed in pain, trying to whip them off, but more of the creatures leapt at him, biting whatever remained exposed.

Dashour fired a melta round at his feet, his last act of spite for an enemy twice faced and twice feared. The blast vaporised his lower body along with his attackers, and his lifeless torso fell off the wall into the courtyard below.

MAJOR HUSSARI SAW Dashour plummet from the walls, and wished him peace in the Emperor's care. Hussari was one of the last Guardsmen left on the wall, with Kortan standing at the entrance to the fire-direction centre, trying to get the remaining men inside. The Guardsmen trapped in the courtyard skirmish circles were stranded, the tyranids pouring into the compound and cutting them off from retreat. One soldier pressed his laspistol to his temple and fired, dropping immediately. The others continued firing at anything that approached them. Runners, centipede floor skimmers and frog-like leapers rushed a smaller skirmish circle of three men, and dragged them down with claw swipes and tail stings.

'Go inside and close that door!' Hussari cried into his micro-bead. Kortan saw him and motioned him over, but it was too late, there were too many tyranids on the wall between him and sanctuary. He waved Kortan off and continued firing his lasgun. 'Go! That's an order!'

Not waiting to see if Kortan obeyed, Hussari made a run for the nearby roof of the vehicle stable. He'd planned this route out a few hours ago, not to save himself, but to inflict as much punishment on his foes as possible. He landed on the metal roof, a storey below the battlements, and continued running for the edge. He felt the roof shake and the metal groan as tyranids leapt after him. He didn't bother looking behind. Either he'd make it or he wouldn't.

Hussari glanced up once and was glad to see the door to the fire-direction centre close, the FDC's ball-mounted guns still blazing. He leapt off the roof and onto the metal frame of Damask's idling Sentinel, left next to the vehicle stable. With practiced ease, he slipped into the cockpit and revved the engine. The barrel of the multilaser began spinning, and within seconds unleashed a steady torrent of electrified las-fire. Hussari strode into the courtyard, crushing smaller tyranids underfoot, while raking the area with crackling blasts. For the first time, the tyranids scattered, the Sentinel a surprising arrival.

The Sentinel continued moving around, trying to help the three or four skirmish circles fighting for dear life. They fought with renewed vigour at the sign of the bird, its gun blazing, but the tyranids showed no hesitation as they clambered over the walls. Several leapt for the Sentinel's cockpit, but Hussari was faster. He sidestepped them entirely, or blasted them from the air. Still, it was growing more difficult to move, the tyranids swamping at his feet, many of them trying to clamber up the moving legs.

Hussari saw one skirmish circle overrun, a brood of tyranids breaking through the soldiers and cutting them down with their scythes and sprays of acid. The circle crumbled. There was nothing he could do, except continue holding down the trigger and obliterating as many of them as he could. He squeezed the trigger hard, his fingers aching. He squeezed it after his Sentinel could no longer move through the bodies of the enemies; he squeezed it as a half-snake tyranid pulled itself up to eye level with him, its pincer tail poised above its head; he squeezed it as the tail slammed into his chest, and broke through his sternum and spine with a loud crack.

Still the multilaser fired as the Sentinel pivoted, Hussari's dead fingers unwilling to release the trigger or the pivot lever. The tyranids had to rip him out of the cockpit, before the laser whined to a stop and the Sentinel stopped turning.

FIFTEEN GUARDSMEN, INCLUDING Abantu, were inside the centre when Kortan shut the doors. Several men, with nothing left to hold the strength in their legs, collapsed to the ground, exhausted. The gunners on the ball mounts continued firing at the enemy below. They were safe for the moment, but this was their end. Everyone knew it.

'The charges,' Kortan said, stumbling over to Captain Abantu.

'Not yet,' Abantu said. He pointed to the periscope at the centre of the room. Kortan stared through the rubber-ribbed eyepiece, and was startled by the giant tyranid that seemed to engulf the magnocular enhanced view. At first, he thought he was staring at something standing right in front of the hooded prism on the rooftop, but then he realised that he was staring at something that measured the plateau in height, something that was lumbering straight for them like some unstoppable juggernaut.

'We cannot detonate the charges yet,' Abantu said. 'We must wait.'

The creature was huge, its head topped with the wicked spike of a ramming horn. Rows of sharp teeth, each the size of a man, filled its distended mouth, while a thick shell from which protruded an assortment of bone ridges protected its back. It walked hunched over, two gigantic scythes on its upper arms capable of splitting a tank in two. Wicked-looking claws stretched out from its lower hands, which were opening and closing in anticipation of the slaughter. Tentacles writhed from the gaps in its armour.

Kortan's throat went dry, the hope sucked out of him. He stepped away from the periscope. 'How long?' he asked.

'A few minutes longer,' Abantu said, 'and then paradise awaits us for our great deeds.'

Kortan nodded and silently prayed that he was indeed meant for such a place. Unfortunately, the tyranids had other plans.

The ground shook and rumbled. Suddenly, the floor ruptured. Half-snake tyranids had bored through the rockcrete floor from the lower levels, and burst up to grab anyone close to them. Captain Abantu and two others vanished into the large hole, pulled down by long claws and scythes that skewered them through. The men resting on the floor scrambled to their feet, and opened fire on the tyranid centipedes skittering up through the hole. The ball mount gunners abandoned their position and followed suit. They pumped round after round of las-shot and bolter fire at whatever horror tried crawling up. Everyone was screaming, venting their anger and fury at what they knew to be their last stand.

Kortan backed up against the wall, his left hand with his thumb poised over the detonator and his right firing his laspistol. One of the walls simply melted, its edges gummed by some substance that hissed and popped, and several of the smaller tyranids dragged another soldier out. The room seemed to be haemorrhaging monsters from the floor, walls and finally, the ceiling.

Guardsmen died quickly. Several dog-like hunters ran for Kortan's corner. He fired his last-shot, bringing one down, before he brought the switch up, ready to flip it.

The floor evaporated from beneath him before he could, however, and something pulled him down with its sharp claws.

Kortan was dazed. He was distantly aware of some sharp, intense pain at his feet and a horrid shucking noise. Something was stabbing his legs with millions of needles, each one tipped white hot. His mouth opened to scream, but nothing came out. He squeezed his fingers, desperately trying to flick the detonator switch, but his hand was empty. The sickening realisation hit him, and the pain at his feet turned into searing agony. He looked, and through the wash of tears, realised that a giant slug-like creature with plated armour had devoured his legs up to his knees. Articulated lobster arms ringed the creature's head and slowly fed Kortan's body into its maw, piercing and pulling, piercing and pulling.

Through the haze of pain, Kortan could see large leathery pouches lining the creature's flanks. The pouches undulated and writhed, and Kortan saw the acid-eaten hands and faces of his fellow soldiers pressed against the skin. They were being devoured slowly while the other tyranids watched.

Kortan screamed and fought the blackness that tried to claim his senses. Something caught his eye, something familiar, in the rubble next to him. He grabbed for it, unable to remember through the pain what it did. A switch gleamed on the box. There was a loud rumble outside, the foot tremors of something huge.

Kortan remembered and forgot, and then remembered again through the fire that ate at his every nerve.

He flipped the switch, and saw the first explosion blossom. It seemed to erupt in silence, the light and heat driven through him, pushing away all sound. The bow wave of air broke him; the fire consumed him; everything went black and mercifully cool.

CHAPTER NINE

'Write your misery in sand, but carve your blessings in marble.'

– *The Accounts of the Tallarn*
by Remembrancer Tremault

1

TURK AND NISRI waited in the command Chimera, which sat inside the mouth of Cavern Apostle, alongside a handful of other vehicles. Two Sentinels stood guard over them, ready to provide heavy fire support when the time came. Drums of fuel stood nearby, alongside ammo crates, explosives and any other supplies deemed necessary to the defence of the caverns.

The two men listened to the vox-chatter coming from the Sentinel pilots still outside the caves. The explosion that engulfed the compound was massive, the stock of artillery shells enough to prove devastating. The top of the plateau looked like a burnt cigar, ash, smoke and all.

'What of the tyranids?' Nisri asked.

'They were dealt a heavy blow,' the pilot reported. 'Major Hussari and the others managed to anger a second group heading your way. The explosion destroyed over a quarter of their forces along with a giant beast that measured the plateau's height.'

Nisri and Turk exchanged glances, but Nisri nodded. Yes, he had heard of tyranids growing to such proportions.

'They're more siege engine than beast. It's good the creature was never allowed to reach us, or it would have peeled open this mountain.'

Turk nodded. 'What are the tyranids doing now?' Turk asked, speaking into the vox.

'Regrouping, by the looks of it, but it's slow going. They seem… sluggish.'

Nisri cupped the mouthpiece of the vox-caster. A smile crept across his face, some of the tension evaporating. This was a reprieve, a small one at best, but a reprieve nonetheless. 'The major must have dealt a blow to the tyranids' hive-mind by killing some of the lynchpins,' he told Turk. 'They are trying to reorganise, but it's bought us the time we need.'

Turk understood. 'I'll tell the men that the sacrifice was not in vain.' With that, he headed out of the Chimera and raced off to pass the word around.

'Let me know the minute they begin moving. Are you or your men in any danger?'

'Negative, sir. We're far enough away so that, even if they give chase, we'll reach the caves before they do.'

'Even from the flyers?' Nisri asked. He remembered the gargoyle-like tyranids, their quick strikes lightning fast and more than enough to scatter a properly mounted defence.

'Most of the flyers died in the explosion. We're more than a match for the handful we can see.'

'Very well. Keep your eyes and vox-channel open. Nisri out.'

He patted the vox-operator on the shoulder and instructed him to report every bit of data that came over the line. Nisri then left the Chimera to oversee the cave's defences. At the very least, a glimmer of hope was peaking through the storm of recent events. The base camp had given them breathing space to prepare, and they proved that the tyranids were not limitless. The regiment was fortunate that only one ship landed, and Nisri hoped that whatever battle had forced them to make planetfall alone would also be the source of their rescue.

2

TURK MOVED PAST the men laying down another bundle of explosives, through to the tunnel where Nubis was briefing the squad leaders on the planned defences for the cave, while sixteen Guardsmen milled about. Nearby, a group of men was sandbagging a gunnery nest pointing down the throat of a chokepoint. The new quartermaster, Sabaak, was moving past them when he spotted Turk.

'Sir,' Sabaak said, tapping the rolled up cloth tied to his back on Y-ring straps. 'I was given the 892nd's banner. Should I hang it in the cavern? You know, to inspire the men?'

'Killing your share of tyranids will inspire the men. We'll fly the banner when the time comes.' With that, he moved further down the corridor.

The tunnel was wide enough to fit a Chimera through, though the twists and turns, rise and fall of the passage would have prevented most vehicles from successfully navigating it. The chokepoint was a straight way that ended at an intersection. Turk knew, from the initial briefing, that this corridor and the one to the left of them branched away from the main passage. It was a 'Y' intersection with each side tunnel sandbagged, mined and protected by two tripod-mounted stub cannons. Any creature entering the junction would be caught in a lethal crossfire with no cover.

Nubis paused, but Turk nodded for him to continue his briefing. He was quite curious as to the defences Nubis's men emplaced. Nubis returned to the wall, where he'd painted a crude schematic to the tunnels in lume-paint.

'We know the tyranids have a sharp sense of smell, so we've slaughtered some of the dromad and muukali and left them in the dead-ends,' he said, pointing to several tunnels that simply stopped. 'Anything that goes after the carcasses will trip the explosives and collapse the caves on top of them.'

'Wouldn't it be easier to simply collapse all the tunnels before they get here and wait for rescue?' Captain Lakoom Nehari asked. He was a slight man with ebony skin, his frame more suited to keeping ledgers than fighting wars.

'Strange question coming from a Turenag officer,' Nubis said.

'I'm being practical.'

Nubis sighed. 'The tyranids have diggers? Collapse the tunnels and they'll dig us out. Only... we won't know where they'll be coming from. Which tunnel? Above us from the roof? Below us from the ground? This way, we control the fight for as long as possible, kill as many as we can in the collapse, and hope it's enough to frighten them off.

'Now, speaking of explosives,' Nubis continued, 'each of the four skirmish tunnels are marked at intervals. Look,' he said, shutting off the light perched on the sandbags next to him. Darkness fell across the corridor, the walls illuminated by green patches of lume-paint. Further down the tunnel, however, at intervals of ten metres or so, were painted rings. 'We've placed explosive charges at each interval. Two of my men will be with each platoon, to trigger the explosives if... when the tyranids advance that far.'

'Won't the tunnels collapse?' Captain Toria asked.

'Only if I want them to,' Nubis snapped. 'The charges are shaped fragmentation charges, designed to kill anything in their path. They have
nothing to do with the charges that we drilled into the walls.'

'And the last circle?' Toria asked, undeterred and pointing to the ring
a few metres from them.

'That's your signal to make your peace with the Emperor.'

Nubis dismissed the other officers with a nod, but held back the
group of sixteen soldiers. Turk did not know them by name, but he
knew them to be Nubis's anti-armour and mortar support squads, men
whose expertise in the caves was practically useless.

'You know what is expected of you?' Nubis asked.

The men nodded.

'I want you to operate in crews of two. Once the explosives detonate,
you'll be trapped outside with them... or worse.'

'We war for the Emperor,' one said. 'We understand.'

'Aya,' the others said quietly, almost as if they were sharing a joke.

'Good. Grab your gear and find somewhere to hide.'

Nubis dismissed the men and caught Turk's eye. He glanced away, his
eyes barely hiding the storm of his thoughts. He removed his shirt and
went to help the Guardsmen add more sandbags to the heavy stubber
nest.

'I heard,' Nubis said, adding a sandbag to the wall. Shirtless, his ebony
black skin glistened, and the old lash scars on his back stood out like
rough ropes. 'The camp bought us more time. Hussari and the others are
heroes to the Emperor.'

'Yes,' Turk said. 'Stop a moment. Let me see your eyes when you speak.'

Nubis sat against the sandbags, his fierce black eyes glittering. Turk
knew that there was no animosity in them, at least none towards him,
but he knew when the Master Gunnery Sergeant was angry or on the
warpath. His eyes shone with a fierce determination to get the job done
right, and to inflict as much pain as possible while doing it.

'What passed between Kortan and you?' Turk asked. 'Did it have anything to do with that night? When Anuman and the others died?'

'Sir,' Nubis replied, 'the quartermaster died a hero to the regiment,
and I am the last one who speaks ill of the dead. It invites bad luck.'

Turk nodded. 'I understand, my friend.' He sat down beside Nubis and
dismissed the other Guardsmen with a nod. After they'd left, he fished
a worn metal container out of a pouch on his belt rigging and flipped it
open. Three hand-rolled, brown ash sticks were tucked under an elastic
band.

Nubis smiled. 'You've been holding out on me, Iban Salid,' he said,
slipping out one of the offered sticks. 'Thank you. From that old man in
the Kufai bazaar?'

'He hand-rolled them just for me,' Turk said. He pulled out a small box of matchsticks.

'Ah,' Nubis said with an appreciative smile.

'The old man was specific,' Turk said, striking a long match, and letting it burn a moment. He cupped it and offered it to Nubis, who dipped his stick in the flame. 'Let the cedar-rose match burn for two seconds to draw out the flavour,' he said before bringing the match to his own stick.

'Mmm,' Nubis replied, drawing in a long drag of the rich flavour, and letting the smoke curl away. 'This is good. It tastes like–'

'Home,' Turk replied. 'I know… I miss it too.'

They smoked for a while, each man lost to his private thoughts, the smoky haze a pleasant diversion, and an even more pleasant reminder of better days. Finally, as their sticks approached that last pinch of breath, Turk said, 'I wanted to thank you, my friend.'

'For what?'

'For keeping your word, for stopping Anuman from shooting more of Nisri's men, for being a soldier I could rely upon and a man whose word I could trust.'

Nubis nodded and then slipped his hand over Turk's. 'You're welcome, but I could never marry you. You're just… too ugly for my tastes.'

Turk pulled his hand away. 'Bastard,' he said, laughing.

3

COMMISSAR REZAIL TOOK a deep breath of the limestone and jungle flavoured air, hoping to remember it forever before the smell of blood and cordite painted its stench over everything. Apostle was busy with the rumble of idling engines and men shouting orders to one another, but a few steps into the jungle, and all the noise seemed to evaporate. For a moment, just one tranquil moment, Rezail could imagine he was, in fact, enjoying paradise.

'Let me ask you something,' Rezail said, hating to break the silence. He faced his adjutant, a look of utmost gravity in his expression. 'Did you offer Lieutenant Colonel Iban Salid advice on how to address and approach Colonel Dakar? Their… understanding was too sudden given their history.'

Tyrell hesitated for a moment before looking down at his feet. He nodded. 'I am sorry, commissar, but I saw a way out of the predicament.'

'And you didn't trust me enough to speak with me first?'

'No no, commissar,' Tyrell responded, immediately panicked. 'It is only that… the advice I offered was from one tribesman to another. I would never go behind your back… I swear.'

Rezail shook his head. 'Never again, understood? If I was a lesser commissar, I would have shot you on the spot for toying with my trust.'

'No, commissar, thank you. I never intended to be disloyal.'

'Very well,' Rezail said. 'Apology accepted, on condition that this is the last time.'

'Yes, commissar.'

They walked further into the jungle, brushing aside the growth.

'But I am curious… what is it you told the lieutenant-colonel that you didn't think you could trust me with?'

'It is not that I didn't trust you, commissar,' Tyrell explained. 'It's just hard to explain.'

'Try,' Rezail said, stopping to face Tyrell. 'Take your time.'

Tyrell thought it through for a moment, trying to plot out the best way to address the matter. Finally, he took a deep breath and allowed the explanation to flow of its own accord.

'Understand, commissar, that for Tallarn tribesmen, whatever is learnt in the cradle is carried with them to the grave.'

'Go on.'

'The first lesson learnt by someone like Iban Salid, a Banna, is that the Aba Aba Mushira is the supreme ruler of all. Service to him is absolute. The second thing he learns is that the word of the Orakle is absolute, for he carries the word of the Emperor. The third thing he learns is that he must avenge any wrongs against his tribe.'

'That has been this regiment's problem from the beginning,' Rezail said with a sigh. 'They should remember their duty to the Emperor first and foremost.' The entire matter bothered him, and he felt like he was presiding over a family squabble rather than a regiment.

'Yes, commissar, but if I may speak frankly?'

'Go on.'

'Please don't shoot me.'

'Go on!'

'Yes, commissar,' Tyrell said, clearly nervous. 'You do not… appreciate the problem. You think that you can execute a few men to bring about discipline, but what are a few executions to a band of men who are willing to become martyrs? Hate your tribe's enemies from the cradle to the grave. That is what they know. It is the absolute law of their lives, handed to them alongside an imperative that rightly says they must remain loyal to the Emperor. They carry their blood feud with the same conviction that they must obey the Emperor. They could no sooner disobey one imperative than they could turn their back on the most Munificent Golden Throne of Terra.'

'Damn,' Rezail replied. 'Why didn't you tell me this before?'

'Because before today, commissar, you wouldn't have understood, or perhaps you wouldn't have listened.'

Rezail nodded; the implication of this was a devastating blow to the regiment's survival prospects. If they survived the tyranids, could they survive one another? Rezail wasn't sure and, frankly, he was facing larger concerns. There was, however, one last concern on his mind, a simple question really.

'So what did you tell the lieutenant-colonel? How did he sway Colonel Dakar's decision?'

'I told him to understand the truths of the Turenag, the convictions that drive them: Serve the Aba Aba Mushira, fight your enemies and struggle for the purity of your faith, and for this you will be rewarded. Perhaps the Turenag will not openly say this world is their reward for their service to the Emperor, but they want to believe it is. I told the lieutenant-colonel to treat this place as Colonel Dakar's garden of delights, and to be the voice of those concerns he dared not utter. I told him not to be the enemy or the rival, but to be the advisor.'

Rezail noticed the sadness in Tyrell's eyes. 'And that's it?'

'No,' Tyrell admitted ruefully. 'I told him the chances of the Turenag settling this world were impossible, and since that is the case, why argue over who is going to inherit something that neither is bound to receive.'

'Sage advice, but you don't appear happy for bringing the two sides to an accord.'

Tyrell offered a wistful sigh and a half-hearted smile. 'I have brought both tribes closer to any peace they've known, closer than the wisest men of my tribe could do, and there is nobody to see my small victory.'

'Come,' Rezail said, sitting upon the root of a large jungle tree. 'We'll celebrate your victory together.'

Tyrell sat down with the commissar and groaned at the pleasure of sitting and relaxing, if only for a moment.

'To the small victories,' the commissar said.

'May they be many.'

4

TURK MOVED THROUGH the jungle, pushing giant fronds and glowing bulbs aside, and nearly stumbling over the roots of trees in his rush. He finally reached a small stream, no more than a few metres across, cut into the rock, and edged with plant rich soil. A shirtless Nisri, his emaciated body pushing his ribs through his onyx skin, washed his upper body in ritual preparation for the battle to come. A rich tapestry of tribal scars laced his back.

'What was so important that it couldn't be said over the vox?' Nisri asked, dipping his wash cloth in the stream and passing it over his arm.

'I spoke with Captain Toria. He's currently assisting Sergeant Ballasra in finding surface tunnels.'

'And?'

'Captain Toria suggested a plan that I think holds merit.'

'So you came to plead your case in person... I'm not going to like it, am I?'

'No, sir, but I ask you hear my argument through.'

Nisri sighed and set the wash cloth down. He motioned for Turk to sit opposite him, and waited patiently as the lieutenant-colonel knelt.

'We know the tyranids are heading for these caves,' Turk said. 'Perhaps they were heading here from the beginning and we were simply in the way.' He waited to see if Nisri was following him. Nisri sighed and motioned for him to continue.

'If the tyranids entered the caves, they would add considerable bio-mass to their existing army, perhaps enough to launch an invasion of the neighbouring systems. We cannot let them have what is here.'

'I'm not sure I like where you're going with this, lieutenant-colonel.'

'Please... hear me. I am only talking about preparing for a possibility.'

'You're talking about collapsing the caverns!'

'If it came to that, yes, sir, I am.'

'Out of the question!' Nisri replied.

'Sir, we're already committed to a course that we can't control–'

'I will not gamble with–'

'Please, sir, let me finish,' Turk said, feeling brave enough to interrupt, 'and then the decision is yours. We cannot control our outcome, but, by the Emperor, we can control the tyranids' fate. I'm not talking about destroying the caves if we don't have to. I'm talking about sparing your virgin paradise from the tyranids' ravages, should our defences fail.'

'You're asking me to destroy my tribe's future.'

'No sir, I am putting the fate of that hope in your hands. You alone dictate what happens here... you, sir, not the tyranids. What would be the greater travesty here, today? That you surrendered paradise to save the Emperor's subjects? Or that you let the enemy despoil the Emperor's blessings?'

Nisri said nothing. He picked up the wash cloth and dipped it in the river again. For a quiet moment, he washed his hands and scrubbed his face clean. He was clearly in turmoil over the decision, his brows knot-ted by the decisions weighing him down.

'I'm not agreeing with you, yet,' Nisri said, finally putting down the wash cloth. 'What is Captain Toria's suggestion?'

'We call in the remaining Sentinels. We pack them with explosives and fuel drums, and send them to the cavern's weak points. Captain Toria believes that by detonating the Sentinels at these spots, we can trigger a chain reaction. The caverns will collapse with the weight, and those adjacent will fall with the shifting rock. At least, that's how he explained it.'

'Has he located these weak points?'

'Two so far, but he's keeping his eyes open.'

Nisri stood and donned his shirt and kafiya. He dressed slowly, considering the matter. Turk stood as well, and wondered what must be going through Nisri's mind. Both men considered themselves pious, both with regard to their tribe's needs and their devotion to the Emperor. He couldn't fathom what it felt like to hold the promise of the tribe's future in the palm of one hand, and to be the instrument of its destruction in the other. He didn't believe this to be a Turenag paradise, or even that the Turenags deserved one, but he did understand the hardship associated with making such important decisions. He was glad he wasn't the one making that choice. He wasn't even sure he could make the right one.

'Lieutenant-Colonel Iban Salid,' Nisri said, 'tell the Sentinel scouts to make haste for the caverns as soon as the tyranids begin moving towards us. Use the explosives and fuel drums to generate a maximum kill yield, but I alone will hold the trigger.'

'Permission to pull Captain Toria from exploration duty.'

'Granted, but keep word of this quiet for now. There's no reason for the men to think we've lost hope.'

'Yes, sir,' Turk said, snapping off a salute before heading back to the command Chimera.

CHAPTER TEN

'A house divided cannot stand.'
                    – *The Accounts of the Tallarn*
                    by Remembrancer Tremault

1

FOUR HOURS AGO…

The mass of tyranids began moving again, heading towards the caverns with sudden purpose. They'd been feeding on the dead and fallen for the better part of the day, reclaiming precious bio-matter for their ship's organic factorums. The swarms within the horde redistributed themselves according to the new hierarchy, their numbers strengthened by those that had lagged behind, their lynchpins bringing order to the mental chaos, and bearing to the inevitable flood.

The Sentinels signalled the tyranid advance and their direction, which remained unchanged, before heading to the caverns as ordered. None of the tyranids broke formation to give chase. They moved as a single mob.

2

TWO HOURS AGO…

The seven surviving Sentinels cleared the mobile picket of fourteen vehicles, Chimeras and Hellhounds, and arrived shortly afterwards at the caves. They were ushered through the main passage and parked in front of Nubis's demolitions squad.

Members of Nubis's squad then began wiring explosives and attaching fuel drums to the Sentinels via a makeshift cradle. It would take a few hours to complete the task, but as each was finished, a member of Captain Toria's group escorted the Sentinels to their positions in the caverns.

3

ONE HOUR AGO…

The charges were laid and the tunnels cleared of personnel. Colonel Nisri Dakar and the other officers watched quietly, as Nubis hooked the last wire lead to a main terminal box, offered a quick prayer to the Emperor and yelled, 'Fire in the hole!'

One by one, he detonated the explosives, leaving several switches untouched.

The caverns shook with the force of the explosions and the resulting cave-ins. Tons of rock and sand filled the larger tunnels that the vehicles had used to enter the caverns. The small passages were likewise collapsed, their numbers too great to defend adequately. It took fifteen minutes for the dust to settle and the teams to report back in, but Nubis's squad had done its job well. The tunnels that were meant to collapse had collapsed, and those that were meant to channel the enemy into deadly chokepoints remained untouched. He had the master artisan's touch for demolitions, and even Nisri gave a sombre nod of appreciation, high praise indeed, especially given that it was for Nubis.

Nubis's squad quickly mined some of the larger passages and the rock heaps, to deter any tyranids from burrowing through. The remaining Guardsmen manned their positions at the four chokepoints, their positions heavily sandbagged and supplied with ammo crates. A regimental priest passed at each location, offering prayers and benedictions to the Guardsmen.

4

FIFTEEN MINUTES AGO…

The mobile picket line reported the approach of the tyranids. They were no longer moving slowly, but running at full pitch. The sound of weapons' fire clattered across the desert. Chaser Chimeras, stripped for speed and armed only with pintle heavy stubbers, strafed the flanks of the tyranid surge. They managed to pull smaller broods away from the main force and draw them within range of waiting Hellhound squadrons. The ploy was working on too small a scale, however, and for all their tactics, the Guardsmen were essentially killing the enemy tank by peeling paint flakes off its armour.

5

Now...

Thick black smoke from smoke grenades covered the battlefield and mixed with the dust storm to further muddy everyone's vision. The tyranids were everywhere, either trying to avoid the fast-moving vehicles or to attack them. The Hellhounds and Chimeras broke through the enemy line in wedge formation, and then proceeded to spin, weave and drive erratically through the combat zone, their treads spitting up sand and the innards of their crushed enemies. The Chimeras used their front-mounted shovel plates to shield themselves against enemy fire, before barrelling into tyranid formations. The Hellhounds did what they did best and washed everything with fire.

'Squadron Three has picked up a tail of fast-moving tyranids,' the tactical cogitator yelled.

Corporal Bathras Euphrates sat in the commander's chair below the Hellhound's turret, just inside the cupola with its protected vision slits. He checked auspex and saw the marker runes of Squadron Three blinking.

'Tell them to shift to a bearing of forty-seven degrees,' Euphrates said. 'When we cross paths, we'll shear off anything chasing them.'

'Yes, sir!'

'Sarrin,' Euphrates said, 'head for them and be ready to evade.'

'Yes, sir,' Private Ibad Sarrin shouted, and he tugged the vehicle's steering levers hard, bringing it back around.

A moment later, Euphrates and the two surviving vehicles of Squadron Three were heading straight for one another. They couldn't see each other through the dust and smoke, but their identification runes on auspex were pinging loudly as they approached.

'Now,' Euphrates shouted, and grimaced as Squadron Three's Hellhound and Chimera passed on either side of him, almost rattling his teeth loose. Private Darha Lumak, the gunner seated below him, unleashed tendrils of flame into the dust storm on faith alone. A swarm of scorpion and centipede tyranids ran straight into the blaze. They bolted off in different directions, some aflame and others merely singed. The Hellhound drove over the badly injured with an audible pop as their carapaces shattered.

Despite being outnumbered, the Hellhounds wreaked havoc with the tyranid lines. The vehicles were too few to be in any danger of colliding with one another, while the tyranids were practically tripping over each other trying to get at their adversaries.

'Lost contact with Squadron Six command tank! Chimera two is in trouble,' the tactical cogitator yelled, half turning in his seat. 'He's getting swarmed!'

Euphrates stared through the shielded visors for a second, and spotted the Chimera through the smoke and tyranid bodies. It was driving erratically, trying to throw off the bipedal scythers, leapers and other myriad beasts that were climbing the transport. They were trying to pry the personnel and equipment hatches open.

The Chimera's heavy bolter still blazed, however, obliterating tyranids with each shot. Four of the six lasguns sticking out of her side were also spitting out a steady stream of crackling energy. The tyranids, however, were quickly damaging the lasguns, de-fanging their opponent one tooth at a time.

'I see it!' Euphrates yelled.

'Auspex is dying out on us... damn storm!' the tactical cogitator yelled.

'Warn the gunners on Chimera Two to close their gun ports now!' Euphrates tapped Lumak on the shoulder. 'Give her a kiss! Not enough to cook the hull, but bake whatever shouldn't be there! Sarrin,' he yelled, 'get us closer!'

Sarrin jammed the steering levers with little grace, throwing everyone to the side and pushing the Hellhound in a new direction. Static electricity sparked off its hull. The tactical cogitator, Private Trask Aba Manar, fired the hull-mounted heavy bolter into a group of tyranids that swung into view.

'Chimera Two is ready for its bath!' Aba Manar yelled.

'In range now!' Lumak said, spinning the turret's handwheels and swivelling the turret in the direction of Chimera Two. The promethium tanks in the rear of the Hellhound gurgled as the main cannon belched a thick spray of flame. The blast was just enough to lick the tyranids on the hull and paint them with sticky fire. Many leapt off, screaming and ablaze.

Chimera Two opened her gun ports and began firing with her three remaining lasguns.

'Sir,' Aba Manar yelled, 'we just lost Hellhound Four and Chimera Six from Squadron Five! The storm is also hampering auspex and vox!'

'How many left?' Euphrates asked.

'At last count, five Chimera and three Hellhounds, excluding us.'

'Sir?' Sarrin said. 'Our pocket is collapsing. We're surrounded!'

'All remaining units,' Euphrates yelled into his micro-bead, fighting to make himself heard, 'form up. We're going to try to punch our way out of this swarm... see if we can't shatter it!'

'Sir, Chimera Two!' Lumak yelled.

Euphrates managed to catch the Chimera through the cupola's visors. A large hole, melted into the armour plate, had opened up the Chimera's port side. Tyranids were pouring in, and filling the micro-bead with the screams of the dying crew.

'Burn her!' Euphrates said.

Lumak opened the flamer's nozzles on full, washing the Chimera in a blistering stream of ignited promethium. The screams ended. The Chimera slowed to a stop, her features melted. Internal explosions rocked her frame, her ammo bins ignited.

'What did that?' Euphrates demanded.

'A beast wielding a cannon on its back,' Aba Manar reported. He aimed and fired the heavy bolter. It struck the simian-like creature as it prepared to fire at Euphrates's Hellhound. The round detonated inside it, cracking its carapace out and flowering the beast like a bloom of flesh and muscle.

'Form up on me,' Euphrates said.

He received crackling acknowledgement from the various commanders, and within moments, three Chimeras and another Hellhound had joined his ranks. The other vehicles were too heavily engrossed in combat, encountering heavier resistance in the form of larger beasts armed with scythes and bio-cannons capable of splitting their armour plating.

Driving in wedge formation, Euphrates and his allies cut a path straight through the horde. The three Chimeras broke the crest of enemies, using their heavy shovels to deflect incoming fire, while the two Hellhounds ran at their wings and used their flamers to protect the wedge's flanks. The Chimeras' rear gunners were firing on anything that gave chase, while the storm generated licks of electricity that shot and played off their armour.

The tyranids were blistering the Chimeras' shovel shields, however, unleashing diamond-hard rounds and acid bolts that weakened the plating or punched through entirely. Three cannon-backed beasts stood in the way of the wedge.

'Cannon beasts!' Aba Manar cried.

'Shoot them, before they fire!' Euphrates said over the vox.

Bolter fire peppered the ground around the three tyranids as they took aim. One exploded from a shell that pierced its back-mounted cannon, but the other two fired before the Chimeras piled into them, shattering carapace and splattering viscera and bio-fluid across the desert. Their salvos, however, struck two Chimeras, melting the shovel off one and the forward superstructure armour plating off the second.

The driver of the first Chimera screamed over the micro-bead, the spray from an acid round melting the windshields and spilling a drizzle of lethal droplets through. The vehicle jerked out of control and slammed into the Hellhound next to it, their treads biting into one another, their links unravelling in a hail of sparks and rent metal. Both vehicles ground to a halt, and the tyranids swept over them.

'Close up formation,' Euphrates ordered, watching both vehicles vanish under a mountain of enemies, 'and barrel through them.'

The vehicles did as ordered, with two Chimeras and the Hellhound trying to drive their spear into the breast of the swarm. More shots whizzed past, this time from the rear: a group of bipedal tyranids armed with bio-cannons. Auspex sputtered and flared, the air electrified by the storm of movement.

More acid rounds struck the rear of one Chimera. While they did not eat through completely, they weakened the rear plating enough for the next solid-mass rounds to penetrate the troop cabin. Euphrates could hear the shots ricocheting inside the vehicle over an open vox channel, the Guardsmen screaming in pain or gurgling their last breaths. The Chimera slowed to a stop, and Euphrates watched helplessly as tyranids rushed the vehicle.

Euphrates turned in time for a large tyranid to loom into view. It towered over the vehicles, its four spiked arms spread in what seemed like preparation for a lethal embrace, and its mouth opened in a deafening roar that shook Euphrates. It lowered its head, its turtle-like shell absorbing cratering cannon fire, and rammed its bony horn through the front plate of the last Chimera. The Chimera bucked upwards, its forward momentum brought to an abrupt end, and the treads lifted high into the air before it came crashing down. The creature's four arms lanced into the vehicle, buckling the plate under the tortured cry of wrenched metal. With a flick of its mighty neck, it lifted and flipped the vehicle over on its back.

Euphrates's Hellhound speeded past, its flame cannon spinning to douse the great monster in thick coats of fire. The enraged beast spun and followed the Hellhound, its blows missing the tank. It flailed, trying to put out the flames, and Euphrates lost sight of it in the thickening dust cloud.

'What in the Emperor's name?' Aba Manar said, forcing Euphrates to turn back around. Directly in front of them, the tyranids parted to reveal a creature the crew had never seen before, not even during the Absolomay Crush campaign against the tyranid splinter fleet.

The tyranid that floated into the Hellhound's path appeared frail, its limbs vestigial-looking, its long tail like a withered spine and its large, elongated head swept back with plate ridges that protected an enlarged brain sac. It hovered above the battlefield, bluish tendrils of lightning snaking off its body and striking the ground. The storm's electricity seemed to dance around it, lending it a halo of static fire.

Something opened in Euphrates's mind, some protective cobwebs meant to shelter him from the horrors of the universe, brushed aside. He shrieked, his voice echoing in the screams of his crew. Euphrates found himself hanging over some unimaginable gulf of time and space, a point where sense of self is obliterated and scattered across the endless darkness. They all stared at something ancient, something whose very being opened their perceptions to the great devouring infinity of the hive-mind. It dwarfed them and held their speck-like intellects between the claws of its forefinger and thumb. It drowned them out the same way an ocean might drown one's thirst.

Sarrin jammed the steering levers in an attempt to escape the presence of the hive brain. Aba Manar and Lumak were pushing themselves away from their stations and writhing on the floor, crying. Only Euphrates continued staring at the creature through the cupola's visor slits, unable to shear his gaze or his thoughts away from it. Mind lightning slithered around the creature's body, building to a crescendo. It unleashed a coruscating blast from its forehead that ripped through the Hellhound's armour, and vaporised Euphrates and his men where they lay.

The blast dissipated, and all that remained of Euphrates was the lingering psychic scream that lay trapped in the ash shadow that had been scorched into his armour.

KAMALA NOORE WAS trying to hear the ghosts of the lost expedition, when fresh screams erupted in her mind, tearing through the veil of mental silence that suffocated her. She drew in a sharp gasp, the full breath of the drowning swimmer upon reaching the ocean's surface. Her mind was finally clear for a moment. She knew the voices that screamed, and saw their terror in the seconds before something obliterated them from reality and imprinted their thoughts into the debris of their vehicle. She caught the lingering image of what killed them, an apparently frail creature whose warped body contained unimagined power. She'd heard about tyranid psykers before, heard they were terrible foes, but this was her first brush with one.

She recognised nothing human in its thoughts, nothing familiar. It was an alphabet of xenos thought and words, something that would drive her insane for even uttering their tongue. The psychic scream dissipated and the images faded, the psychic veil pushed back in place. But she felt focussed, no longer distracted by the maddening elusive songs of the expedition's ghosts. She was grateful for the reprieve, and vowed to thank the creature personally. She donned her psyker hood and prepared for its arrival, eager to stretch her mind to this lethal exercise.

* * *

6

THE LAST SURVIVING Chimera crew, commanded by Sergeant Abasra Doori, careened off one of the limestone pillars at the mouth of the cave network. The pillar flaked and threatened to topple, but remained standing.

The Chimera was still rolling when the rear door popped open and the crew jumped out. Several soldiers looked back into the vehicle cabin, but the white-haired, white-bearded Doori waved them off. 'Go!' he shouted, 'I'm behind you.'

Doori turned, trying to help the driver, Private Apaul Wariby, from his seat. Wariby was a light-skinned man in his thirties, and his stomach was wet with blood.

'I can feel it inside me,' Wariby gasped. 'It's moving.'

'We'll get you to a medicae!' Doori said, trying to pull him.

'I won't make it,' he said, 'and neither will you if you try. Go, you stupid old man. You were a lousy commander.'

Doori grunted. 'Fine, but if you're going to die, then you might as well die useful.' Doori grabbed and pulled Wariby from his seat, dropping him into the cogitator chair next to him. Wariby grunted in pain, his breathing fluttering in rapid strokes.

'You know how to use this?' Doori said, slapping the textured grips of the Chimera's heavy bolter.

'Yes, sir.'

'Good… shoot at everything coming your way.'

Wariby grabbed the bolter's grips and stared out through the armoured visors, towards the approaching sandstorm. He was breathing hard, his eyes fighting for focus. 'Run, sir.'

'Die well,' Doori said. 'Emperor knows you've earned the rest.'

Doori ran stumbling for the tunnels when heavy bolter fire rang out across the desert. Three men were waiting for Doori at the mouth of the tunnel and picking off the tyranids that had pulled ahead of the packs with their lasrifles.

'Emperor take you for fools,' Doori barked. 'Run!'

A dozen metres or so inside the tunnel, the sand petered away, leaving uneven but solid limestone underfoot. Hot on their heels, screaming in hungered fury, were the waves of tyranids that had followed Doori and his men. They were minutes behind, their screeches echoing off the rock walls, but somehow seemed much closer than that.

The tunnels were dark, the only illumination the bright stripes of lume-paint that guided them. Doori pushed his men in the back, forcing them to run faster. They followed the glowing stripes until they hit a painted rune on the wall denoting 'one'.

'Base, this is Chimera Five. We're the last ones through! Passing marker one!'

'Understood,' the voice said. 'Marker one is primed.'

The men continued running, the sound of the tyranids growing louder and drawing closer. Suddenly, an explosion rocked the network and shook the heavens of all their dust. Doori and his men stumbled against the walls. Bits of rock and limestone fell, but the roof held.

'Go, go!' Doori rasped, pushing his men along. They followed the turning, winding strips of paint, feeling as though they were doubling back on themselves… until the passage split again. This time, the lume-paint marked a second path. Doori pointed to the passage and pushed two of his men down the second corridor. 'Draw them after you and vox in the markers!'

The two soldiers nodded as they vanished down the tunnel. The shrieks of the tyranids, quieter for the moment, increased in pitch again.

A moment later, one of the soldiers shouted, 'Marker three!' on vox.

'Marker two!' Doori rasped with his dry throat, followed by the confirmation that the explosives were primed. Moments later, one explosion rippled through the caverns, followed by a second and then a third. More dust poured from the ceiling, while flakes of limestone fell and shattered on the floor.

'That's one of the dead-end tunnels,' a voice said triumphantly over the vox.

Doori could only grunt his acknowledgement, his breathing turning into burning ragged shreds, his sides aching and his head swimming. He could hear the tyranids' shrieks over the thundering in his ears. He could feel them behind him, but he dared not turn around. The passageway split again, with paint stripes heading in either direction. Silently, Doori pushed the other soldier down the second passage. The man complied, too exhausted to argue.

He was alone, now, not that it bothered him. Doori continued running, despite two more explosions that rattled the walls and ground. He was slowing, his chest in aching pain and his sides stitched with hot needles. The tyranids were gaining, how could they not? He turned around, and saw nothing at first, but then the lume-paint further down the tunnel was flickering. They were coming.

Doori looked ahead and saw another marker on the wall. It was half a dozen metres away. It was a finish line he would never reach. That realisation drew its surrender from his body, and Doori stumbled to one knee, unable to move any further.

'Marker Five and every marker along this path,' Doori said.

'Un-understood,' the voice replied.

'Stupid old man,' Doori said, chuckling, falling to all fours. The rush of tyranids behind him drowned out the beating thunder in his ears. There was no reason to turn around any more.

THE TUNNELS ROCKED and shook at the explosions meant to winnow the tyranids' advance, but with each step, they grew louder and more frightening. It seemed like nothing could hold back their flood.

Two of the Guardsmen barely made it behind the barricades of Tunnel One before the firing started. The third Guardsman was cut down by Captain Toria's men in Tunnel Three, because the tyranids were too close at his back. He died screaming at the Guardsmen to wait, never realising that his execution saved him from a more brutal demise.

Suddenly, the four chokepoints erupted in simultaneous firefights, the screams and reports peppering the vox-comm channels.

The tyranids jammed into the tunnels, and into the line of fire of autocannon and heavy stubber nests, and the las discharges of staggered firing lines. When one soldier depleted all his magazines, he tapped the leg of the man standing behind him, or the shoulder of the man kneeling before him. He then swapped out of the line with a fresh soldier, while he rearmed himself.

At every tunnel, there was at least one heavy gunner, a member of Nubis's squad with a flame thrower, melta gun or plasma gun, vaporising any of the fast runners that managed to close the gap quickly. Elsewhere, the dull thud of detonating mines reverberated, claiming a snake or large tyranid that thought of burrowing through the collapsed tunnels. Still, while the chokepoints poured on a steady stream of fire, they realised they were losing through the attrition of centimetres.

The tyranid weren't merely suicidal, they continued throwing every breed and type of tyranid at the chokepoints, providing just enough cover to drive forward by the barest of margins. Even when they approached the lume-circle marks on the walls and Nubis's men triggered the shaped charges, the tyranids filled the holes in their ranks within seconds.

Nisri's men had seen the tyranids attack and regroup before, but the prize of the cave drove them forward with unparalleled frenzy. They had an objective in mind, and nothing would deter them from that goal. The Guardsmen weren't the goal, they were the obstacle.

Occasionally, an armed tyranid survived long enough to fire back with its bio-weapon. Sometimes the round splattered against the tunnel wall or the sand bags, and sometimes the shot struck a Guardsman. When that happened, the wounded Guardsman was pulled from the line and replaced, while medicae did their best to stabilise the patient. Unfortunately, most tyranid ammunition continued inflicting pain and incapacitating their targets, and the medicae could do nothing for the screaming soldiers that bucked and writhed in the crippling throes of agony.

NISRI KNELT ON the front line, shoulder to shoulder with his best Guardsmen, the ably trained men of E Platoon and the orphaned soldiers of Sergeant Raham. Corporal Magdi Demar now led the platoon that was assigned to protect Tunnel One. But he felt like he was only filling Raham's large shoes until someone better came along. Still, Raham had drilled his men well, and E Platoon fought with the same ferocity as though their beloved sergeant stood behind them, shouting orders in their ears.

'For Raham!' someone shouted for the fiftieth time, and for the fiftieth time, the squad responded with renewed fervour, filling every centimetre of the tunnel with punishing fire.

The tyranids seemed to be growing smarter with each salvo, however, and they skewered their own dead on their talons, scythes and spike-claws, propping up the injured and dying to act as shields.

As they passed one of the lume-rings indicating where the shaped charges were hidden, Nisri shouted, 'Blow them apart!' The shaped charges, angled away from the Imperial skirmish lines, exploded, shredding the shield wall and forward lines of tyranids. The heavy stubbers opened fire and flamer units followed up the attack, washing the exposed corridor with generous gouts of flame. The tyranids shrieked under the promethium blast, their exposed flesh wilting, and their carapace armour blackening. Their numbers seemed to dwindle for a moment, before they swelled forward on another suicidal surge.

It was just enough for Nisri to see what was happening. The chokepoint was a stoopway, which forced the tyranids through on their stomachs. It was narrow enough for some bipedal tyranids to get stuck as they squeezed under. After a while, only runners and leapers ran through, and they pressed forward, obscuring the chokepoint. For a brief instant, however, Nisri could see the stoopway again. Snake tyranids were eating through the rock, widening it and allowing more creatures to stream underneath it.

'For Raham!' Nisri shouted, and the volley of fire intensified. Nisri tapped the puttee wrapped leg of the soldier behind him and swapped out. He moved down the rough-surfaced tunnel, past soldiers waiting for their turn at the firing line, and around a turn in the corridor. The noise was staggering, the tunnels amplifying the thunder of weapons dozens of times over. Nisri activated the noise filters on his micro-bead and switched to the command channel.

'Lieutenant-Colonel Iban Salid, respond!'

* * *

TURK MANNED TUNNEL Four alongside B Platoon, one of several orphaned platoons, the one that had answered to Captain Anuman. Like Anuman, his men were gamblers, and quick with their knives. They were rough in an urban sense, loud drinkers and brawlers, and they loved getting their hands dirty by jumping into the middle of fights. They were perfect for the close-quarter, execution style action of their chokepoint.

B Platoon protected what Captain Toria had referred to as a chimney. It was a vertical cut in the rock between two tunnels. In the tunnel above, the floors had partially collapsed, revealing the corridor several metres below. Nubis had used explosives to seal one end of the lower tunnel, funnelling the tyranids into a dead end.

Turk and B Platoon stood on the ledge above, firing down at the tyranids as they streamed into the pit. The fighting was intense; the fast-moving enemy often got through the tunnel passage and scaled the walls before anyone managed to draw a bead on them. Regardless, Anuman's men did their work with ruthless efficiency, standing firm, wearing their best scowls, and firing down a steady hail of punishment.

'Lieutenant-Colonel Iban Salid, respond!' Nisri's voice called over the micro-bead.

Turk stepped back from the ledge and let another Guardsman slip into his spot. 'Yes, sir,' Turk responded, cupping one hand over his ear to hear better.

'What's your situation?'

'Tunnel Four is secure for the moment. We'll run out of ammo before they gain any real advantage.'

'Don't underestimate them,' Nisri said. 'They're widening the chokepoint. I'm not sure how much longer we can last after that. Make sure they don't find a way around you!'

'Understood!' Turk turned in time to hear the screams. A leaper managed to leap up to the ledge and grab a soldier's leg. It pulled him down into the pit. The platoon killed the tyranid under a pounding onslaught, but the Guardsman was already dead, impaled through the chest, stomach and neck on the spiked backs of the enemies.

'Fill that gap!' Turk ordered, but a fresh soldier was already on it. He took his place at the ledge and began firing down with his lasgun.

'Captain Nehari,' Nisri said over the micro-bead, 'respond.'

CAPTAIN LAKOOM NEHARI and F Platoon protected the chokepoint of Tunnel Two. It was supposed to be the easiest job of the lot, the chokepoint a 'squeeze', a tight tunnel that the Guardsmen jokingly called 'the birth hole.' At least they thought it was funny, until the tight hole birthed a steady stream of small tyranids: leapers and runners mostly. Nehari and his men thought they had a handle on the situation up to a moment ago, when snake tyranids tunnelled through and suddenly, two more 'birth holes' opened in the wall.

Now the horde was squeezing through three holes, and Nehari wasn't blind to the steady pounding of heavy stubbers and las-fire that further chipped at the walls surrounding the chokepoint.

'Captain Nehari, respond,' Nisri demanded.

'I heard, sir. The snakes are widening the chokepoint here as well. We now have three – damn it, four, four holes!' Nehari screamed as a snake smashed through another portion of the wall and scrambled up the tunnel towards them. The hail of blasts tore it to shreds, but it was too late. The damage to the chokepoint was done, the rock peeling away in large chunks.

'Our chokepoint won't last much longer,' Nehari responded into the micro-bead.

'Hold your position for as long as you can,' Nisri responded. 'Commissar Rezail, are you listening?'

Nehari returned his attention to the fight. It was becoming frantic. The Guardsmen of F Platoon realised they would be swarmed the moment the chokepoint collapsed.

'Blow the third and fourth rings of shaped charges!' Nehari shouted.

'...ARE YOU LISTENING?'

'Can barely hear you,' Rezail responded. He fired a bolt pistol, having swapped out his laspistol in favour of something with more kick. The tunnels shook from two distant explosions rattled off in quick succession.

'For the Emperor!' Rezail shouted in Tallarn.

The forces of Captain Toria's C Platoon and Sergeant Nubis's A Platoon shouted out a cheer at the commissar's near-fluent mastery of their tongue. Tunnel Three was, by far, the most heavily contested section. It was wider and higher than the others, with a chokepoint that split the passageway to the left, towards Toria's platoon, or to the right towards Nubis. The crossfire was whittling the tyranids down considerably, but the passages were clogged with their bodies.

Unfortunately, after an hour of fighting, the tyranids had managed to break down part of the wall between the two split tunnels that formed the inseam of the chokepoint, widening it considerably. Now tyranids filled the tunnel like a living plug, their numbers scrambling on the floor, scurrying on the walls and scampering along the ceilings.

While the creatures were no longer caught in the crossfire, the two passages were wide enough for the four heavy stubber nests to spit out thick ropes of tracer fire, while the firing lines of Guardsmen were staggered three deep. One group was on their stomachs, the second on their

knees, and the third standing. Occasionally, the sharp *crack* of an explosion filled the corridor with a deafening snap, pasting tyranids against
the wall and splattering viscera on the men. How many explosives
Nubis had planted played on everyone's curiosity, but they were definitely taking their toll on the enemy, and adding the stench of fyceline
to the already heavy aroma of ozone, cordite and tyranid entrails.

Commissar Rezail and Tyrell stood with the men of the last row, firing
their bolt pistols and shouting encouragements at the troops. The
commissar also carried his chainsword, waiting for the moment when
he would need it in close-quarter combat. Nubis also took his share of
the line, firing a heavy stubber with cycling barrels, and an ammunition
chain fed from the pack mounted on his back. He cycled through his
store of hollow points, delighting in the shrieks of his enemies, the near
solid stream of tracers cutting the enemy in half.

Kamala Noore stood behind the left stubber nest, biding her time,
which naturally set the gunnery crew on edge. She appeared dazed,
unfocussed as though the battle was an echo to some greater truth. She
was waiting for something, her fist clenching and releasing, the small
sparks of bioelectricity sheathing her wrist with each flex. That small
display of power occasionally found release when a tyranid ventured
too close to the skirmish line. Kamala's attention found focus, and she
lashed out with her mind, a flare of psychic electricity slamming into
the beast and bursting it open. Then she returned to waiting.

THE DESERT SEEMED empty again, the sand scored by millions of tracks.
The sound of screeching tyranids was loud, the host of beasts clustered
at the cave mouth, eager to get inside. A brood of tyranids each with
four legs, a scorpion's tail and the armoured snout of a war hound, ventured out further, sniffing about here and there, but the fighting quickly
drew them back to the tunnels.

On a ridge of dunes that overlooked the surrounding desert and the
pillars of rock, a small section of sand shifted and spilled away. Two
Guardsmen, members of Nubis's anti-armour squad, quietly crawled
out from under their blankets. They'd been watching everything, waiting for their time to strike.

One of the soldiers pressed his micro-bead twice, generating a burst
of static that squawked in his earpiece. A moment later more static
bursts rang back, each unit reporting its readiness, seven in total. Everyone was in place.

The soldiers retrieved their portable missile launcher from the pit and
unwrapped it from its swaddling cloth. It was a heavy device, a shoulder
mounted weapon that required a gunner to handle the tube-like
launcher, and a loader to carry three spare missiles strapped to his chest

via a weight distribution rigging. Both men belly crawled to the lip of the dune and gazed down at the cave entrance.

The swell of tyranids was staggering. They seemed to number in the thousands, the swarms restless and eager to get inside. Some were huge, larger than the smoking ruin of a Chimera that had been flipped over near the tunnel mouth, apparently larger even than the tunnels. The two soldiers exchanged glances, but said nothing. Instead, they quickly searched the desert for the three other anti-armour crews, but with their tan and orange uniforms and camo-painted launchers, they would be difficult to spot. That was for the best.

Both men quickly shook hands and embraced. There was never any illusion that they would survive this thing, and there was no lingering on their fate. What came, came. The gunner set about making himself comfortable and acquiring targets through the launcher's scope. The loader removed two pressure plate mines from his rucksack and buried them one side of him and the gunner. He planted a small twig to mark their positions. At no time did he stand, instead shifting around on his belly like a snake, careful to avoid being seen over the dune's crest.

A static squawk sounded over the micro-bead. Slowly, over a matter of minutes, seven static bursts filled their ear pieces. The two Guardsmen were the last to sound theirs. They followed it up with a four-burst squawk. Nobody replied. They didn't need to. They were too busy firing at will.

The metallic whump and whistle of mortar shells sounded first, four shots in all. From nearby crests, the thunder and rush of two missiles streaked a smoky path to the cave mouth. The tyranids barely had time to acknowledge the attack, the explosions of fire, smoke and sand bursting in the thick of them. The blasts flung tyranids and body parts through the air.

By the time the gunner fired his missile down at the mob, a second flight of mortar shells pierced the air with their shrill keening. A terrible roar followed and the projectile curled, careening towards one of the pillars. The explosion devastated the thirty metre high stack of limestone, bringing it crashing down across at the entrance, crushing more beasts under its weight.

The two men swore they could hear the other crews cheer, and allowed themselves a smile. The loader mounted another missile into the launcher and tapped the gunner's head. He fired again, his missile joining the other projectiles as they devastated the hordes of tyranids, sending more dismembered beasts flying. Instead of being frightened or cowed, however, the tyranids surged outwards, splitting into smaller swarms, each unerringly homing in on the different crews. Each knew its place, each its duty.

And, they were bridging the gaps fast.

Time for one more, the two men realised. The loader popped another missile into the launcher and tapped the gunner on the head before dropping down next to him and covering his ears. The tyranids were scaling the dune to reach them, but the gunner took his time aiming. His next shot, his last shot, arced over the heads of his attackers, towards the tunnel entrance, and a second missile rocketed down from another angle, the mortar shells raining down hard and persistent. Both missiles slammed into the cave mouth, blossoming into hellish explosions that caught the beasts trying to escape further into the tunnels. The entrance collapsed at the same time as the first tyranids, bipedal creatures wielding scythes, reached them. One inadvertently stepped on a pressure plate mine, adding to the thunder of the explosions.

'COMMISSAR REZAIL,' NISRI repeated over the micro-bead. 'Are you there?'

'I'm here, I'm here!' Rezail yelled back. 'We're holding our...' He stopped, his voice deafening in the cavern. The tyranid swarm had stopped advancing, the corridor filled only with their dead. The Guardsmen hesitated for a moment, terrified of the sudden calm, before they scrambled to reload their weapons. Rezail could see the fear on their faces. They could still hear the distant echoes of gunfire in the other caverns, but the deathly silence in Tunnel Three seemed oppressive.

Nubis flicked on his micro-bead and contacted C Platoon in the neighbouring tunnel, but they could see nothing either. Everyone exchanged quick, panicked glances, but mostly, they couldn't tear their eyes away from the chokepoint with its carpet of dead tyranids. Something was happening, and they were more afraid of what they couldn't see than of what they could.

'Steady, men,' Rezail said. 'Remain strong and the Emperor's light will shield you.'

'What's happening?' Nisri asked over the micro-bead.

'The tyranids,' Rezail said more quietly, 'they've stopped attacking.'

'Not here they haven't,' Nisri replied. 'All tunnels, what is your situation?'

'Tunnel Two... we're still getting swarmed,' Captain Nehari replied, his voice almost panicked. 'All shaped charges expended!'

'Tunnel Four... they're trying here, but we hold the advantage,' Turk replied.

'Same for Tunnel One,' Nisri said. 'Commissar, be on your guard!'

'Depend upon it,' he said. Rezail glanced away from the tunnel long enough to address Kamala Noore. She was standing straighter, her battle-hood with its cyclops-like eye piece and power cables crackling with psyker energy. She almost appeared to be standing on her toes, her powers levitating her from the ground.

'What is it?' Rezail asked.

'Something comes, something to surpass my prowess,' Kamala said simply, her voice echoing with a faint metallic ring, her head held aloft. 'You will quake in its presence, but whatever you do, do not flee. I will try to distract it and keep your minds free of its terror. Shoot when I tell you to shoot. I cannot kill it alone, and neither can you. We need each other in this. Together we have a chance. Now, steel yourselves for horror!'

The ghost flickers of blue bioelectric sparks leapt from the distant walls to the tyranid corpses. The air buzzed and hummed with power, and the lume-paint on the walls seemed to glow more brightly.

'The Aba Aba Mushira's light guides me,' Rezail said, trying to instil courage in his men. 'His beacon is the celestial chorus of the Astronomican, and so long as they sing, I will always be close to His Grace. We war for the Emperor!'

'Aya!' a few men cried, their voices strangled by fear.

'Any man that runs will be executed,' Rezail concluded.

A shadow crossed the passage ahead, a shadow moving among shadows. It produced its own light, and it approached the chokepoint.

'We war for the Emperor!' Rezail repeated, his voice stronger, more demanding.

'Aya!' more voices cried out.

'We WAR for the EMPEROR!'

'AYA!' the platoons cried across the two tunnels.

A tyranid floated into view, lazy tendrils of electricity dancing off its atrophied spine and enlarged brain sac. Its mouth was pulled back in a perpetual scowl, revealing a row of bloody teeth, while from its back tube-vents leaked a greenish miasma. It was more than a linchpin of the hive-mind, it was one of the axles that guided the tyranids. The hive-mind's thoughts leaked out through its very being, stray images like bullets that wounded the mind and injured the Guardsmen. Some of the men cried out in terror. A few others sobbed. Even Rezail stopped speaking. He felt like he stood on the shores of an infinite, black ocean, able to see further across its vastness. Some unnamed horror rose from the waters, its tentacles raised so high as to brush away moons, its voice sending out ripples of tidal waves across the ocean's surface, so dwarfed were he and the others by the staggering monstrosity of the alien sea that drowned them.

They were all paralysed. They saw nothing but the beast, heard nothing but its terrible whispers.

'Do not drown,' a tiny voice said.

Rezail heard Kamala's voice, feeble against the roaring waves of the infinite seas. Like a man drowning, Rezail grasped at the lithe hand stretched out to pull him away. As he closed his hand around hers, he could feel others do the same.

Absently, almost subconsciously, a few of the gap-mouthed men tried to fire at it, but their bolt and las-rounds struck a bioelectric barrier surrounding the creature. Their shots ricocheted, and hope seemed to leave them again.

'Don't drown!' a voice shouted in their minds, and Rezail knew that Kamala was trying to buffer them from the worst of the attack.

Behind the creature, tyranids followed slowly, cautiously: the pack behind the hunter, waiting to be unleashed.

The creature seemed to scream, although its mouth never opened, and the full brunt of the hive-intellect blasted through the minds of the Guardsmen. A handful of soldiers scurried back, abandoning their positions and stumbling, fleeing down the corridor, their minds stripped down to their primordial terror. Rezail was too locked in his nightmare to even consider shooting them for cowardice. Instead, he stared at the creature, unable to take his eyes away from it. He was only distantly aware of a few men sobbing, and watched in horror as energy crackled and built in strength around the tyranid. He recognised the signs of an impending attack, the signs of death.

'Not this time,' a metallic voice called, cutting through Rezail's terror. 'In the Emperor's name, I smite thee!'

A hammer of bioelectric energy appeared in Kamala's hands, her hood crackling with an electrified halo. She motioned, and the hammer flew from her grasp, striking the creature's shields. Electricity sparked and showered everywhere. The tyranids screeched in anger, but did not rush forward. The blow, however, rocked the creature, and it blasted back with a braid of bioenergy that barely missed Kamala, and incinerated a nearby gunner.

Kamala fired back, her mental energies slamming into the creature's shields. Electricity flared and sparked across the entire chamber. The tyranid's and Kamala's powers snapped and danced against one another like two wild animals. Bolts struck the wall, and slammed one soldier in the chest, blowing his ribs open. Kamala almost buckled to her knee, but the creature's shield also seemed to dim.

Suddenly, it wasn't so invulnerable. Suddenly, it wasn't so untouchable. A crack was all it took for panicked hope to surge through, that last kick for the surface before drowning.

'Fire, damn you, fire!' Kamala screamed.

The Guardsmen, shaken awake from their fear and briefly shielded against the hive-mind, unleashed a sudden avalanche of rounds. Some shots whined and ricocheted off the creature's bio-shields, but many found their way through the weakened barrier, striking the tyranid horde.

It was growing difficult to see, Kamala's electric storm clashing with the creature's powers, the points of intersection flaring with brilliant explosions of light and peals of thunder, but the Guardsmen kept heavy fingers on their triggers. Another trooper rushed in to take the place of the fallen gunner, bringing the second heavy stubber to bear. Another soldier on the line fell, a blast of electricity shearing his shoulder off. The creature shrieked, the attacks overwhelming it, rounds skipping off its bone plates, shattering two of its limbs and destroying a segment of its tail.

Kamala doubled over in pain. Even with the amplifier, it was difficult maintaining her powers against the creature, but she seemed to redouble her efforts each second, pushing herself even after she collapsed to one knee, and then both. Her hand stretched out, trying to push against its thoughts. She was taking the brunt of its mental assaults. One of the fingers on her outstretched hand exploded from the lashing psyker energy. She screamed, but did not buckle. Another digit was obliterated soon after.

'C Platoon! Now!' Nubis screamed.

A second later, sporadic fire erupted from the adjoining tunnel, catching the tyranids and the creature in the crossfire. The hail of tracers and las-rounds increased with each passing second, the Guardsmen regaining ground.

The creature was buckling under the assault, its agony setting the tyranids behind it into an animal frenzy. Some raced into the killing fields, where incoming fire punctured and lacerated them to shreds. Others turned on one another, completely feral, and unable to distinguish friend from foe.

Another soldier fell, a stray bolt obliterating his face. Nubis stepped into the gap, his war cry carried in the cycling whine of his heavy stub cannon. The creature screamed, round after round pounding through its protective field and shattering pieces of its body. Finally, Nubis delivered the killing shot, a stream of hollow points stitching the creature's face and blowing out chunks of greenish matter from its brain sac. It flared for a moment, a surge of bio-electrical energy and the hive-mind's psyker powers scorching rock and beast. Finally, it crumbled to the ground in a number of unceremonious heaps.

The tyranids were stunned by the creature's death, as were the Guardsmen, who were rendered senseless from the mental slap.

'Keep firing, keep firing!' Nubis cried; at the same time the pack of tyranids went completely feral and began fighting anything they could see, each other and the Guardsmen.

On the vox, soldiers were reporting the same thing; the tyranids were lashing out at everything around them. But this was not the moment to celebrate. The tyranids were turning into rabid berserkers, and some of them were reaching the firing lines before dropping, killing Guardsmen in their dervish dance of claws and scythes. More explosions rocked the tunnels; the shaped charges were being expended quickly.

THE LARGE BIPEDAL tyranid continued stabbing the Guardsmen with its spiked limbs, chittering madly as the nearest soldiers screamed back and shot it at point-blank range. It eventually stumbled back, its carapace cracked wide and a gut-wrenching miasma spraying the line of men. Captain Nehari continued firing at the tyranids charging the line, yelling to drown out their horrible, guttural screams. The tyranids fell metres from the skirmish line, and the chokepoint had partially collapsed, allowing more of the creatures to stream through.

The chatter over the vox was frenzied, the Imperial Guard losing control over the battles in three of the four tunnels. Only Turk and B Platoon were having any success in keeping the tyranids corralled.

A runner with tube-like protrusions on its back reached the Guardsmen. As it bit into the shin of a soldier, it blasted out a cloud of greenish gas from its tubes. The soldier screamed, his tibia shattered.

They shot the creature dead, and pulled the wounded soldier from the line, but not before everyone began coughing. The men closest to the wounded soldier fell out of line, vomit exploding past their lips, and many soiling themselves. More men took their places, but everyone was fighting violent stomach cramps and intestinal spasms; the smell of faeces in the air didn't help. Nehari wasn't a fool. He'd fought the tyranids before, and he understood what they were up against.

Nehari activated the command channel on his micro-bead. 'Colonel Dakar, we're about to be overrun! We can't hold the line much longer.'

NISRI HISSED A curse at Nehari's message. Nothing could be done about it, but fighting while retreating was no way to do battle the tyranids. Worse, Tunnel Two and Tunnel Three were connected further back. If Two fell, Commissar Rezail and the combined Platoons of C and A would be trapped. Moreover, the tyranids would then flood into the caverns.

'D Platoon will help you fall back,' Nisri responded, immediately switching channels and sending half of D Platoon to help Tunnel Two evacuate under bounding overwatch fire. The other half, minus Sergeant Ballasra's squad, which was still searching the caverns, was to remain in reserve in case any of the fighting spilled into Apostle.

'All tunnels, all tunnels, prepare for withdrawal on my mark. Blow the remaining shaped charges.'

'Confirmed,' Turk called back.

'Hurry!' Nehari yelled, the fight at his position obviously desperate.

'Ready!' Nubis said.

'C Platoon,' Nisri said. He paused as a roar of explosives filled the tunnels. 'On my mark, collapse your tunnel and shift around to help cover A Platoon's retreat!'

After receiving the confirmation reply, Nisri waited for a desperate moment that felt like an eternity. The fight in his tunnel was going badly. The tyranids had almost reached the skirmish line, and men were being cut down before his eyes. His men began backing away, the enemy close enough for them to spit on.

'D Platoon in position!' a voice said.

'Withdraw now. Go, go!'

On cue, the decibel levels in the caverns rose to deafening pitch and the caverns shuddered under multiple explosions.

'E Platoon, withdraw and provide overwatch!'

Dust and bits of rock rained from Tunnel One's ceiling, and the soldiers staggered their retreat, tossing grenades into the swarm to slow them down. The explosions ripped through the front lines, enabling the gunners and Guardsmen to pull out from their positions. The soldiers were back-pedalling, practically firing down at their feet as runners and dog tyranids raced towards them.

Corporal Demar, Raham's replacement, was on the last row, when one of the bipeds hit him and two other Guardsman with toxic rounds. All three men went down, their muscles tightening to the point of snapping tendons loose from the bones. Nisri, in grim horror, saw Demar's exposed bicep curl up into the flesh of his arm. Someone tried grabbing Demar to pull him along, but more muscles snapped loose from their bone moorings. The Guardsman let go in horror as Demar's muscles bulged grotesquely. Within seconds, the advancing enemy covered all three bodies, and E Platoon was fighting in full retreat.

In Tunnel Three, the scene was much the same, the tyranids at the feet of the firing lines and the Guardsmen dying by the lashing death throes of their kills. Everyone was still rattled from the collapse of the neighbouring tunnel, but C Platoon was already providing covering fire for A Platoon's retreat.

When the order to withdraw came, Nubis cried 'Go! We'll hold them back.'

The second gunner nodded and opened up with a full salvo, no longer caring whether or not his heavy stubber overheated.

'What about you?' Kamala cried. Her hood was off. She bled from the nose and mouth, her eyes scarlet from internal haemorrhages. Tyrell supported her, while Rezail used his chainsword to keep the odd tyranid at bay. He opened a runner with a disembowelling slice, but even fighting them one on one was too difficult, even for Rezail.

'Commissar,' Nubis pleaded, 'you'll be overrun if we don't cover your retreat. Go, damn you! Tell them to collapse the tunnels.'

Rezail nodded and backed out with the remaining men, firing at the tyranids to keep some of the pressure off Nubis and the second gunner.

TURK NODDED TO the Guardsmen to withdraw; three of them pulled frag grenades from their belts, yanked the pins, and simultaneously dropped them down the chimney. Turk withdrew from the ledge as the explosions rocked the tunnel below and the screams increased to frenzied pitch. The soldiers darted into the tunnel and continued glancing back the way they had come.

The lieutenant-colonel was among the last group of men to retreat, when a rumble shook the ground and pitched him against the wall. A flood of tyranids broke through the collapsed passage, crawled out of the smoking chimney and gave chase down the tunnel after them. Turk and the others opened fire, trying to stop the sudden onslaught, but the tyranids were on them fast.

'Collapse the tunnels!' Turk yelled into his micro-bead, firing into the snarling face of a bipedal creature with elongated snout and bone plating that was mere metres from him. Men screamed as the tyranids cut them down.

'Almost there,' a voice called back.

Turk continued firing his laspistol, watching as the number of men between him and the enemy dwindled with each second. There were six men between the swarm and him. The tyranids pulled one man to the ground, his head crushed under cloven hooves. Five men remained. A beast impaled two men on the same scythe, and then took a moment to shake them loose.

'Blow the tunnels!' Turk screamed.

This time another voice joined his. 'I'm being swarmed,' Nubis cried over the micro-bead.

Turk's heart sank when he realised that his friend was about to die, but he had to focus on his own survival. Three men remained. One man jerked and screamed as he spun, his face collapsing from an acid round. Turk shot him to spare him further agony. Two men remained. One convulsed as a hissing beetle round struck him in the chest and ate its way through his sternum.

One man remained. His body jerked and spasmed as a tyranid lance speared him, filling his body with carnivorous worms. Turk fired his last rounds into the man and into his attacker, killing them both.

'Detonate the explosives you Turenag sons of whores. Do it!' Nubis's voice cried over the micro-bead. He was obviously in pain.

'Charges are set!' a voice responded.

'Now, now!' Turk screamed.

'Fire-in-the-hole!'

The repeated crack of sharp thunder ran along the spine of the cave, shaking the very heavens. Turk watched in horror as the roof above his head broke and stone seemed to rush towards him. Before he could even shield his head from the falling debris, several sets of rough hands pulled him out of the way.

'That's it. We're sealed in,' a voice said over the micro-bead.

Coughing and lying on his back, Turk looked around at the dirty, exhausted faces of the men in B Platoon. He had never expected paradise to be his tomb.

CHAPTER ELEVEN

'Every day of your life is just another overlooked
sentence in history.'

— *The Accounts of the Tallarn*
by Remembrancer Tremault

1

CAVERN APOSTLE WAS filled with quiet bustle for the moment, the soldiers
in shock over their ordeal. Everyone slowly filed out of the debris-
choked tunnels, covered in dust, viscera stains and the blood of their
comrades. Some dragged their guns behind them, but the ever-sharp
glare of Rezail snapped them back into discipline. Everyone headed to
the edge of the jungle, where the loam was thin and the vehicles waited.
The tyranids had proved themselves capable of many tricks, and the
Guardsmen had little doubt that they still had quite a few more to
unleash. Until that time, however, the soldiers needed a moment to
catch their breaths, eat and see which of their friends had survived.

Turk dusted himself off as he headed for the command Chimera. He
checked on the various squads resting on the ground. Nobody slept, the
infusion of adrenaline and fear a powerful remedy against sleep.
Everyone had lost a friend in the skirmish, but for Turk, the most
painful loss was Nubis. Nubis was a friend, stubborn and arrogant when
he wanted to be, which was all the time, but true to his word. He was an

honourable man, and Turk was proud that Nubis had proved to be the great Guardsman that Turk had always known him to be, saving the lives of the commissar and the men of his platoon.

That was all the thought Turk wished to indulge at the moment. He walked past the two sentry Sentinels, which were patrolling near the tunnels, waiting for the tyranids to bore through. Given the number of creatures they had slaughtered, Turk hoped it might take them a while to regroup. The tyranids were, literally, single-minded in their determination, but even they had to stop and recover from their battle wounds, right? Turk decided not to ask Nisri. He didn't want to know.

Turk arrived at the command Chimera, which sat next to four waiting Sentinels and another Chimera being used by the medicae to perform triage on the injured. Corporal Adwan Neshadi, Nubis's protégé for demolitions, was speaking with Rezail, Tyrell and Nisri. He appeared nervous, his youth betraying his confidence. Kamala stood nearby, her brow damp with sweat, and her eyes swimming in and out of focus. She smiled at Turk. He returned her smile, instantly concerned at her injuries and the blood in her eyes, but unable to show it in front of the others.

'It took longer to affix the drum cradles,' Neshadi said. 'We need half an hour to arm the Sentinels.'

There was a pause. Turk realised that Nisri was staring at the cavern jungles; he almost appeared in shock that this so-called blessing might be lost to his tribe. Turk understood exactly what was happening. In his mind, it seemed incomprehensible to be surrendering this paradise, to believe it the salvation of your people, and then have it torn away. He was staring at the shredding of his convictions, the exodus of two million kilometres walked, and knowing that another two million were to come.

Unfortunately, if Nisri was distant, then everyone could see it plainly. Turk forced himself into the conversation.

'I'm sure Colonel Dakar would agree that the best course of action would be to send the Sentinels to their positions, and to equip them with their explosives there. We cannot afford for them to be caught in the fight when... if the tyranids attack.'

Nisri, who stirred at the mention of his name, nodded in agreement. 'Correct, Lieutenant-Colonel Iban Salid. Send the Sentinels on their way along with members of Sergeant Nubis's platoon, whoever's best to arm the birds.'

'Speaking of Sergeant Nubis,' Rezail said, 'he was a hero today. He saved our lives.'

'Sergeant Raham also trained his men well,' Nisri said. 'They held their ground until the very end. Raham fought with us today. Every man here is a hero.'

'Most,' Rezail said, 'yes, but some men fled from the enemy. I'll be dispensing discipline shortly. Unfortunately, the men who fled may have already hidden in these caves. '

Nisri removed his kafiya and ran his fingers through his puffy afro. 'Commissar, if you would offer the men encouragement, I'd appreciate it.'

'Of course.' Rezail and Tyrell walked away, making their rounds to various groups of men.

Nisri turned to Corporal Neshadi. 'Get these birds out of here and prepare the explosives.'

Neshadi saluted and spun around to organise the work details. There would be no respite for any of them today, Turk thought wearily.

'Situation report, lieutenant-colonel,' Nisri said, moving into the jungle.

Turk nodded. 'F Platoon took the heaviest casualties: twenty-eight men killed. The survivors, eleven of them, including Captain Nehari, were exposed to toxic fumes. Six of them won't make it through the day. The rest can barely stand.'

'Unfortunate,' Nisri said. 'And the others?'

'A Platoon and C Platoon lost half their men in the Tunnel Three skirmish. I suggest merging them into A Platoon and putting Captain Toria in charge.'

'Agreed.'

'B Platoon only lost seven men; they're still able to fight, as is D Platoon, which didn't lose any of its forty men. Sergeant Ballasra's squad is still on patrol.'

'We'll fold the survivors from F Platoon in with E Platoon. Even then,' he sighed, 'Sergeant Raham's squad was almost picked clean. They won't be at full strength until we receive reinforcements.'

Turk nodded and waited until the silence seemed almost unbearable. Nisri appeared to be lost in thought, again, and horribly morose. 'Sir?' Turk said, 'Shall I oversee preparations for the next attack?'

Nisri nodded, half-distracted by his surroundings. 'Hmm? Oh, of course... yes. See to it, will you?'

Turk offered a crisp salute, not that he thought Nisri noticed, and was about to leave when their micro-beads clicked on.

'Colonel Dakar,' said Sergeant Ballasra, 'I have found it. Thank the Aba Aba Mushira for his good humour today.'

'Found it?' Nisri asked. 'Found what? A way out?'

'Yes, sir. It's a bit of a walk, but I found our escape, and it's free of the tyranids.'

Nisri nodded to Turk. 'Get the men ready. We're withdrawing to the exit point.'

* * *

2

I<small>T TOOK</small> A couple of hours before Ballasra's squad returned and briefed the men of their escape route. The cavern designated Halo of Purity, which Ballasra had named, was a small cave overlooked in their initial search of the Golden Throne cavern. Ballasra's men managed to burn a path through the jungle for easier access, news that brought a pained grimace to Nisri's face. Ballasra, however, promised that when they emerged from this ordeal, he would personally replant those destroyed trees in atonement. That, at least, drew a half-hearted smile from the colonel.

With the platoons redistributed, Toria was organising his squads to accommodate Sergeant Nubis's demolitions experts. Their role was to arm the four Sentinels. He also found additional weak points that he thought could be destroyed with simple explosives, of which the squads had plenty. Meanwhile, the vehicles revved their engines, preparing for departure. The four remaining booby-trapped Sentinels were already on their way to the various weak points, which left the command Chimera, and the triage Chimera conscripted by the medicae. The latter was to transport the injured inside and on its rooftops for as far as they could go. Nobody wanted to consider what they'd do if the jungle grew too thick or too rocky to navigate.

Toria was checking the squads, ensuring they had all the necessary supplies, when one of his men, Private Lebbos Lassa, tapped him gently on the shoulder. Lassa, a young tribesman with sun-browned skin, was staring at a section of jungle, his eyes widened by fear, his hand slowly pulling his bolt pistol from its holster. 'The leaves are moving,' he whispered.

The men in the squad noticed the furtive glances of their compatriots, and slowly unholstered their weapons, switching off their safeties in the process. Toria followed Lassa's gaze and saw the fronds and their glowing yellow bulbs swing gently back in place. He activated his micro-bead, switching to the command channel.

'Colonel Dakar, can any tyranids become invisible?' he asked, almost whispering.

'Yes, they have chameleons.'

'In that case we have company, and they're in the jungle.'

'Chimera gunners! Open fire on Captain Toria's target,' Nisri said over the open channel. 'All units… tyranids!'

Toria and Lassa fired the first volley, the second volley unleashed by their men. A moment later, the heavy bolter on the command Chimera opened up, spitting out a pummelling salvo of explosive rounds.

The barrage of shots peppered a section of trees where the fronds had moved, exploding entire tree trunks and shredding giant leaves. The rounds also punctured the air, slamming into something before the bolter rounds detonated. The creature only appeared as it detonated and sent out a blossom of chitin, yellow viscera and body parts. Other soldiers were already leaping to their feet and arming themselves, but it was too late; two more chameleons appeared out of thin air.

Their forms were terrifying. Long, undulating tentacles covered their mouths, rows of sharp pereopods ringed with spikes and hooks arched from their backs and around their bodies, sharp, extended claws adorned their lower arms, while their tails ended in hooded stingers. And, they were fast. One struck a nearby Guardsman in the thigh with its stinger, sending him into apoplectic seizures before his heart exploded inside his chest. The other one struck repeatedly with both pereopod spikes in lightning fast stabs that gutted another Guardsman in a matter of seconds.

Then, as quickly as they appeared, both chameleons vanished, before either man hit the ground.

The Guardsmen swung their guns, trying to find their targets, but the chameleons appeared intelligent. They attacked in the thick of the enemy, and soldiers couldn't open fire on them without shooting one another. Panic spread through the Guardsmen, the swiftness of the attack blinding and shocking. Cries of 'Where are they?' and 'Where did they go?' abounded.

'Skirmish circles!' Toria shouted. His men immediately fell into tight circles, back to back, weapons pointed out.

'Get into skirmish circles,' the cry carried.

Toria watched as Guardsmen scrambled to protect one another and formed rapidly expanding huddles. He saw Turk pull Kamala into one, while the commissar, Tyrell and Nisri entered another.

A chameleon appeared, but whether it was a third creature or one of the first two, Toria didn't know. It didn't matter; the beast charged into a skirmish circle formed by Anuman's B Platoon, swinging its claws and stabbing with its pereopods. Five men were caught in its onslaught, their bodies cut to ribbons and vital organs slipping through their fingers. One man managed to fire his lasgun into the creature's torso at point-blank range. That single catalyst brought the other guns to bear, and Anuman's men opened fire.

The chameleon vanished, but it could not escape the indiscriminate rounds. Ichor and carapace fragments appeared in mid-air, and with a knifing shriek, it reappeared. It stumbled back under the weight of the attack and fell, its chest cavity open, its raw organs spilling out on the grass.

As one died, another made its presence known. It moved past two men, shredding the meat and muscle of their thighs with a single swing of its claws, before vanishing. Both men hit the ground, crippled by the attack and screaming for help. Nobody had a chance to fire. It was so fast, it left Toria breathless. Guardsmen broke from their skirmish circles to help, but Rezail fired his bolt pistol in the air.

'No!' he shouted. 'That's what it wants you to do.' With a coldness that always seemed to exemplify the commissars, Rezail grabbed Tyrell's laspistol, turned it on both wounded men and fired, executing them with precision shots to their chests. He turned the pistol back over to Tyrell and ignored the harsh, silent glares. Toria half expected someone to push him out of the circle.

The chameleon attacked again, this time on the other side of the groups. Toria turned in time to see it run through six Guardsmen of a skirmish circle who were too busy staring at the commissar to protect one another. Again, the chameleon's movements were a dizzying blur of claw swipes and the piston-like speed of its stabbing spikes. In an instant, it managed to trample, eviscerate and impale all six men before it tried to vanish.

A curl of lightning arched out of nowhere, and struck the beast. Toria barely had time to register Kamala Noore standing there, arms outstretched. Electricity curled around her body, and as quick as it takes the mind to realise a thought, she struck it again. The blows weren't intended to kill it, just to daze it.

Sure enough, the chameleon reappeared, just long enough for the closest Guardsmen to fill it with las-fire. The creature screeched its dying gasp.

The screech was answered by the angry cries of its kin.

'There're more in the caverns already?' Lassa asked.

'Merciful Emperor,' Toria said. 'Up! Above us!' he shouted.

Everyone looked up in time to see the holes appear in the cavern's ceilings. Waterfalls of sand cascaded down in thick pillars, but the holes also bled swarms of tyranids that dropped to the jungle below or began crawling along the ceiling. In seconds, it was raining death.

3

NISRI STARED, DUMBFOUNDED at the scene before him, struck senseless by the death of paradise. The walls opened up, disgorging tyranids into the caverns, while more dropped into the jungle. The tyranids attacked anything and everything that wasn't of their species, from the fleeing, scurrying animals in the vegetation, to the panicking Guardsmen. They were a devouring swarm of locusts, eating everything they came upon and fuelling the engine of their bio-factorums. With this prize, they could raise another army, invade more worlds. With this prize, it was conceivable they would no longer be just the splinter of a splinter fleet.

Turk slapped Nisri again, trying to get him to focus. It was an absurd moment, him striking a superior officer, a man he was much more comfortable killing in the midst of all their chaos. The Guardsmen fought a losing battle trying to stave off the tyranids that had taken an interest in them, but at least three squads were protecting Turk, Nisri, Rezail and Tyrell. Turk wanted to make sure that nobody died in vain.

Throughout the jungle, men screamed. They fell to scythes, claws, teeth and acid wombs. The command Chimera drove into the jungle to escape, the driver not realising or caring that he was shearing off wounded soldiers that were still on his roof. The medicae Chimera was only firing its lasguns on tyranids or Guardsmen that approached it. After a moment, it too roared away into the jungle under the control of its panicked crew, but there were already runners and dog-creatures on its roof, killing the hapless injured.

Duf'adar Sarish, rather than allowing his remaining camels to die in the slaughter, was shooting them in the head with his laspistols, and firing at any tyranid that ventured too close to their bodies.

At this moment, Turk understood what it meant to have looked into the mouth of the abyss and found madness there.

'Leave me,' Nisri whispered, his heart broken of its faith. 'Let me die here.'

'Coward!' Commissar Rezail said with a snarl. He raised his bolt pistol to fire, but Turk slapped it away and stared up into the face of the taller man.

'No!' Turk shouted. 'If he stays, his men will too. We need all the help we can get in escaping and collapsing the caverns! Shoot me later if you must, but I'm assuming command.' Turk and Rezail locked eyes, the message understood. The commissar wouldn't labour the point, but when this was over, Rezail would have his reckoning.

Rezail stepped back. 'You're in charge,' he said. 'What is your first order?' Everyone flinched as a Sentinel moved past them, firing its autocannon on a pack of runners trying to advance on the group. Three of the beasts exploded under the hammering blows, while the remaining four darted away into the jungle's underbrush.

'Better hurry, sir,' the Sentinel called over the micro-bead. 'I can't keep the tyranids off you for much longer!'

Turk looked at Nisri for a moment. He expected to see fire in Colonel Dakar's eyes, the indignation of having a Banna steal away his command, but Nisri merely nodded his assent.

'Captain Nehari!' Turk shouted, calling over F Platoon's commander.

Nehari, still coughing, ran up to Turk and saluted. He was pale, his eyes half-lidded and jaundiced.

'Protect Colonel Dakar. I'm in command until he's in a right frame of mind. Move out to Basilica!'

Nehari nodded and took Nisri by the arm. Immediately, a squad of Turenag Guardsmen surrounded the colonel and captain, and escorted them into the jungle under suppressing fire. The Sentinel fired another stuttering salvo before moving past a thicket of trees. It vanished from sight, but they could still hear it unloading its main gun.

'All units,' Turk said into his micro-bead. 'Withdraw to the first rally point at Basilica.'

4

THE RETREAT WAS anything but orderly. The soldiers moved through the jungle in rough groups, losing men to their wounds or to tyranid ambushes. The Tallarn were not accustomed to jungle warfare. It was claustrophobic for soldiers used to fighting and manoeuvring in the open desert. The jungle carried sounds differently, the ground was rough and filled with treacherous pitfalls, and the sightlines made it impossible to determine what lay mere metres ahead.

There was only one salvation, and that was the rich biomass of the caverns. The tyranids were following racial imperative, and the imperative of their species demanded they consume everything in their path. They still sent out skirmish packs to hunt the humans, but that was no longer the sole focus of the horde. Consuming this world beneath the world was. The caverns represented a far richer resource of organic material than the Guardsmen could ever provide. They were but table condiments for the feast.

Turk and the others moved through the strange world gripped in yellow twilight, trying to remain quiet while pandemonium howled around them. It soon grew difficult to distinguish between the screams of the dying animals and those of the conquering tyranids. The only familiar sounds that reached them were the cries of their own men, the chatter of Imperial Guard weapons, and the reassuring thunder of the two active Sentinels as they ran through the underbrush, autocannons blazing to assist the different groups. After a while, the gunfire grew more and more sporadic, and, finally, the Sentinels were heard no more.

A group consisting of Turk, Rezail, Tyrell, Sarish, Quartermaster Sabaak and a handful of survivors from the various squads reached the limestone ramp and grand jagged awning that separated Apostle from Basilica. A handful of soldiers manning three heavy stubbers waved them through, while the broken bodies of Guardsmen and over fifty tyranids littered the entrance. Turk found himself studying the faces of the fallen, and recognised two Banna tribesmen by name. They hurried up the ramps, their advance covered by Captain Toria's and Nehari's men.

'Are you the last ones?' one of the Guardsmen asked.

'By the Emperor I hope not,' Turk said. 'Booby trap the entrance just in case, frag charges and wires, but don't leave until you can't hold this position any longer.'

The men nodded. This was no longer a matter of military feints and tactics. This was adrenaline-fuelled survival, and decorum had fallen to the wayside.

A handful of squads sat resting on a small patch of rock between the jungle of Basilica and the cavern's wall, among them, Colonel Dakar. Kamala Noore stood off to the side, her hood crackling and her attention distant. Turk was glad to see her. He offered her a quick smile, but could not tell if she was with them enough to recognise the gesture. He turned and addressed Captains Nehari and Toria. Nisri quietly joined them, listening instead of leading, as did the commissar. Rezail did not seem fond of either Turk or Nisri, but Turk couldn't have cared less.

'How many reached the rally point?' Turk asked.

'Not nearly enough,' Nehari said before coughing. He was sweating, the toxins taking their toll. 'Not counting the two Chimeras that barrelled through here, fifty-two men, and the mind-witch.'

Turk swallowed the insult; now was not the time to defend his beloved's honour. 'Are the explosives set?' he asked Toria.

'Three are set. Four remain. I'm sorry, sir… with everything that happened, there wasn't time.'

'You did well,' Nisri said. 'You did nothing shameful.'

Toria offered his gratitude with a head nod, but he was discomforted by the compliment and by the Colonel's apparently softened temper.

'You still have the explosives?' Turk asked.

'Yes, sir,' Toria replied, 'and we have the men for it, but there's something else. The tyranids are in the other caverns as well. They've dug in from every direction. We still can't be sure if Sergeant Ballasra's escape route is secure.'

'And where is the sergeant?' Nisri asked.

'Making his way to the entrance of the Golden Throne,' Nehari responded. 'He's awaiting our arrival.'

A high-pitched shriek from the jungles behind them startled the six men. Everyone heard it, and anyone sitting down was rising to his feet. Turk could see the leaves of the jungle canopy in Apostle swaying.

'Captain Toria, the burden of our survival falls on your shoulders,' Turk said quickly. 'I need those Sentinels armed.'

'My men would like to help,' Nehari said. 'We have a demolitions specialist with us, and we know where the Sentinels are.'

'Very well,' Turk replied. 'Each of you take your best squad and get to those Sentinels. Make sure you coordinate your targets. Captain Toria, we need a tracker to guide us to the Golden Throne and I need a satchel of explosives.'

'Yes, sir, but may I ask why?'

'I need to collapse the last cavern to make sure nothing follows us. Now both of you, go!'

Both captains answered in the affirmative before running off in different directions. Likewise, Nisri, Rezail and Tyrell drifted away, making ready their escape.

'Everybody! They're coming,' one of the Guardsmen at the entrance to Apostle shouted.

'Prepare to withdraw to the Golden Throne cavern,' Turk instructed.

The squads prepared to leave, helping one another to their feet, the line between Turenag and Banna lost in the ordeal. Kamala walked up to Turk and removed her hood. Dried blood clotted her nostrils, and her eyes were swimming in seas of red. Nevertheless, she appeared focussed, intensely so. She stared at Turk, her last anchor in her sea of thoughts. She needed him, he could feel it pulsing off her skin in waves. Though they wanted to touch one another, embrace each other, they could not. Instead, they merely exchanged the briefest of smiles, his loving and encouraging, hers a terrible sadness, contained.

'Sir,' Captain Toria said, returning to Turk. He handed him a satchel and motioned to a well-muscled man, his face covered by his kafiya and the occulars over his eyes. 'Private First Class Venakh Mousar will be your scout. You'll also need this,' he said, handing over a black metal vox. 'It's keyed to the explosives. Send the signal and they all blow up, including they one you're holding… just in case we don't make it.'

'Understood. Good luck.'

Toria offered a smart snap of a salute before rejoining his squad. The survivors then split into two groups, with Toria's squad heading off towards Cavern Cathedral, and the main cluster of Guardsmen and Nehari's squad travelling towards Devotion.

5

JUNGLE OR NOT, alien world or not, the scouts of Toria's group were good at their job, and right now, that was to move quickly and quietly. The Guardsmen double-timed it through the clusters of trees, over root tangles and under nets of hanging vines. They did not speak; they motioned to one another through hand signals, and the loudest things from their mouths were their breaths. Even the demo expert, Neshadi, from Nubis's old platoon, was fitting in like a seasoned pro.

Captain Toria held up a fist, bringing the squad to a quiet halt. On cue, the men ducked behind trees or went low to the ground. They were less than ten metres away from the Sentinel, which was hidden near a thick column. By the slant of the ceiling above, Toria had chosen this location, because the pillar bore the weight of the rocky sky. A large explosion would not only collapse this section of cave, but the chain reaction would destroy the floor beneath them as well, sending everything tumbling into the cavern below. Toria hoped that all that shifting rock would cave in this section of the network.

Unfortunately, the only thing between Toria's squad and the Sentinel in question was a small pack of five runners that were crawling over the vehicle. They were smelling the bird and deciding what to do about it.

Toria designated the targets with both fingers and, after ensuring everyone was ready to fire, made a low sweeping motion with his hand. The volley of las-shots was relatively quiet, precise and totally lethal. The tyranids dropped from the Sentinel with hardly a sound.

Toria and Neshadi ran up to the Sentinel to begin setting the explosives, while Lassa and the others took up defensive positions. 'We need to hurry,' Toria whispered. 'The tyranids share a hive-mind. They'll know something happened to their patrol.'

Neshadi nodded and continued working, rushing to lay the explosive charges without endangering their lives needlessly.

6

THE PACK OF four bipedal tyranids with their scythe arms and bone-plated head crests moved effortlessly through the trees towards the sound of coughing. Nehari wondered if he should admire their skill and lethal precision, but decided that the appreciation was misplaced. These were not trained soldiers; they were beasts, their murderous traits a birthright.

The tyranids found the Guardsman sitting with his back against the tree, coughing up a storm. Blood flecked his lips, and Nehari suppressed the rattling in his own chest. The creatures slouched low to the ground, and hissed as they approached. The ailing Guardsman saw them, his eyes wide in terror. He jerked, as if to move, but stopped himself. He lay absolutely still.

Nehari admired his courage, and drew a bead on one of the beasts. Someone else coughed, however, and the tyranids' heads snapped up in unison. It was too late. Nehari and the others opened fire from the surrounding brush, catching the tyranids in their snare of las-shots. The air smelled of ozone and entrails as the creatures screeched and died.

* * *

'IT'S GETTING… GETTING.worse,' the Guardsman said. He was shaking as he stood, and coughing up blood.

'I know,' Nehari said, spitting his own blood on the dead tyranids. 'Whatever we inhaled–' he coughed, harder than before. It hurt like hell, and it was nestled somewhere deep inside his lungs. It felt like his joints would fly apart with each gasping rasp. 'Better get to that last bird,' he said. 'While we still… can.'

The Guardsmen nodded and, suppressing violent, shaking coughs, headed deeper into the jungle.

7

TURK FIRED HIS pistol straight into the outstretched mouth of the dog-like tyranid. It fell at his feet, dead, but the other beasts of the pack were certainly alive and unhappy, and they were many… at least twenty-odd of the small creatures. The branches and leaves rustled as they bounded through on their six legs, their sleekly armoured heads yelping and howling up a storm. Elsewhere in the tightly clustered jungle of Cathedral, another pack answered the call.

One of the beasts leapt for a Guardsman, braids of thorny tendrils unravelling from its open mouth. The tendrils wrapped around the soldier's throat and tightened, bringing him to the ground and making him easier prey for five other dogs. Blood flowed in thick rivulets over the thorns, and the Guardsman gasped for air as the tyranids dug into the soft parts of his body. Quartermaster Sabaak and Sarish managed to shoot two dogs off the soldier, but he was thrashing around too much.

Another beast leapt for the commissar, shrieking, and startling him so badly that he forgot to swing his chainsword. A bolter shot detonated it in mid-leap, spraying Rezail and Tyrell in gore and body parts. Nisri offered Rezail a shrug, his expression conveying the simple truth… *had you killed me; I couldn't have saved you.*

Kamala also stood her ground, sending out sharp tongues of electricity that fried two of the galloping dogs.

'Fire in the hole!' someone yelled, and Turk and the others managed to duck before a grenade detonated in the underbrush and took out half the advancing pack.

More las-shots and bolter fire erupted, and the Guardsmen shot the remaining tyranids that were reeling from the concussive force of the explosion. Nisri ran to the injured Guardsman, who was still alive despite his terrible wounds, and kicked one tyranid off him, while shooting the one with its thorn tongue wrapped around his neck. The booted tyranid landed with a yelp, and was instantly hammered with las-fire.

Nisri and Turk tried peeling off the creature's tongue, but when they pulled back one of the tendrils, they realised the hooked thorns had shredded the Guardsman's throat. There was nothing left for him to breathe through. The Guardsman's eyes rolled up as he continued choking and bleeding. Nisri apologised to the soldier, offering a prayer, before Turk shot the Guardsman through the head.

'The packs know where we are,' Rezail said, looking at the bodies of three dead soldiers.

'We go,' Turk said. He held the vox detonator in one hand, just in case it became time to send the signal. They continued their exhausted trudge forward, a handful of hours behind them, and a handful more ahead of them.

8

'THAT DOES IT,' Neshadi whispered, jumping down from the cabin of the second Sentinel. 'We're done.'

'How many explosives do you have left?' Toria asked.

'A few krak charges and plenty of frag grenades.'

'Enough to rig a couple more surprises?'

'Yes, most certainly.'

Toria called his men in. They silently moved through the underbrush, alert for any unusual sounds, and knelt at the foot of the Sentinel.

'I say we plant the remaining explosives,' Toria said, 'finally bury the tyranids for certain. I know of a good fault-point that the Sentinels couldn't reach… but we could.'

'We won't make it out in time, will we?' Lassa asked. The rest of the dirty-faced men were silent. They waited for Toria's answer, but he could already read their grim expressions. They didn't think they could make it out alive, regardless.

'I don't think so,' Toria whispered. 'The best we can hope for is to plant the explosives and head as deep as possible. Maybe we could find that lake that someone said they saw. If we're lucky, we'll find a cave with no tyranids, and plenty to eat and drink. Maybe the Emperor will let us retire there in peace.'

'Stuck in a cave for the rest of our lives,' Neshadi said, sighing. 'I knew I should have brought a book to read.'

The others grinned and patted Neshadi in the shoulder. With a quick glance, Toria tallied their votes by their nods. It was a unanimous 'yes'. As quietly as they had arrived, Toria's squad vanished back into the underbrush, and silently wished their compatriots and fallen comrades a safe journey, wherever that journey ended.

* * *

9

NEHARI AND HIS men heard the steady stream of crackling las-fire from a kilometre off. As they approached, wild shots flew high over their heads, scything through tree limbs and branches, and raining down leaves around them. They could see a smoke column rising in the air through the gaps in the canopy, and collecting at the ceiling, where it eclipsed the rock and fields of light-string worms. The only other source of light came from the flashes of las-blasts, several trees that had been set aflame and the dimming glow of the tree bulbs. It was as if the jungle was dying.

Nehari, however, instantly realised that the shots belonged to a Chimera-mounted multilaser. Nothing else they had carried that firepower.

The squad broke into two groups of three men each. The heavy coughers, including the demolitions specialist, continued on their way to the last Sentinel. Nehari and two others crept through the forest, suppressing their coughs and hoping the continued las-fire would mask their approach. They were weakened by the toxins running through their veins, but their curiosity had been pinched, and that was enough of a motive.

The medicae Chimera was half-wedged in a crevice, a fissure that had opened up beneath it. Its nose was jammed in the crack and rested against the crevice wall, while its rear was angled upward in clumsy balance. It had shredded its treads trying to dislodge itself, and tyranids were crawling all over its hull. They were trying to peel away the access points to get to the meal inside, and were ignoring the futile lascannon that was desperately firing in different directions. The column of smoke was rising from a wider rip in the fissure, possibly where the command Chimera had fallen during the mad rush to escape.

Nehari could see the litters still strapped to the top of the vehicle, as well as the ripped bodies of men who were trapped and gutted when the Chimera fled. Nehari shook his head, and quietly filtered through the micro-bead's comm channels. He finally found the one with the panicked voice screeching for help.

'Hello?' Nehari whispered.

'Thank the Aba Aba Mushira!' the voice cried back. 'My vehicle is wedged. We're trapped in here. Please, get these things off of us.'

'You're trapped? Like the way you left those injured men to die on your roof?' Nehari said, coughing. 'Rot in the warp.'

Nehari shut off the screaming pleas for forgiveness, and motioned the squad to move away. The Chimera crew was earning its just fate.

* * *

10

THE JUNGLES OF Emperor were the thickest any of them had known, or ever seen. The trees seemed to merge into one another, their trunks braided and their branches intertwined. The loamy soil was thick and reeked of sodden earth. They followed Sergeant Ballasra's instructions, keeping to the cavern walls where the vegetation was thinnest, but even this far removed from Apostle, the sound of hunting and devouring tyranids seemed ever-present. How they managed to spread so far remained a mystery. All Turk cared about was staying ahead of them and steering clear of their appetites.

The scout Mousar swept aside his kafiya for long enough to gulp a drink of water; his lower face was covered in the thick, ropy scars of a promethium burn. After returning the kafiya to his face, he consulted the data-slate Ballasra had provided as a way of pathfinding, and motioned the others to continue following.

Turk stumbled a few more steps, before something pierced his fatigued mind, something he had seen a minute before, but did not register until now. He looked again to the vox detonator in his hand, to make sure that he actually saw its blinking light, and then groaned.

Nisri and Rezail noticed Turk standing, staring up at the canopy of jungle and cavern rock, and shaking his head. They motioned for the others to stop, and approached him as a fit of laughter overcame him. This was all too perfect, Turk thought. This was the perfect conclusion to their sad and sordid expedition.

'What's the matter?' Nisri asked.

Turk said nothing. He merely held up the vox detonator to show them the blinking light. Nisri straightened and let out a fatigued laugh. Turk shook his head and laughed even harder. Rezail simply looked confused.

'It's a warning light,' Turk finally managed to explain. 'It means that we're too deep inside the caverns. Any further, and the signal to detonate the explosives we already planted won't reach the bombs.'

'It means,' Nisri said, his voice soft, 'that someone has to stay behind and detonate the explosives from here.'

CHAPTER TWELVE

'Every sun must set.'

> – *The Accounts of the Tallarn*
> by Remembrancer Tremault

1

NEHARI AND HIS two escorts reached the Sentinel as the others were finishing attaching the explosives to the fuel drums. Nobody was providing them with cover, nobody had the strength left to follow military procedure or even care. Instead, they finished with the Sentinel, and walked a few dozen metres away before one by one, they collapsed to their knees or fell on their arses, hacking and coughing loudly. Nehari tried to pull one man up, but he fell down next to him, completely spent and afflicted by a deep-seated exhaustion the likes of which he'd never known. His muscles felt like hard stone, numb and heavy.

The toxins deprived them of strength, leaving them weak and wracked with nausea. No, worse than that, Nehari realised, it ate at their wills, robbed them of the mental fortitude they needed to push forward. That they had made it this far was a testament to their characters, but they were done. They had completed their task, and thoughts of survival no longer ranked among them.

They sat where they collapsed in the underbrush, under the yellow glow of the overhanging bulbs. They pulled close to one another, hacking blood and black flecks of what they silently suspected were their lungs. Their stomachs hurt, the muscles taxed beyond exhaustion and feeling torn.

'How... how pitiful are we?' Nehari said, his voice raspy, 'Like old men.'

The others tried to laugh, but that only generated a new fit of coughing. They patted one another on the shoulders or grabbed each other's hands for support.

'So,' another man finally managed to say, 'this is paradise.'

Renewed laughter and renewed hacking followed. Nehari smiled and shook his head.

'No... never paradise,' he said inbetween coughs. 'Paradise was never... meant for the... the living. It's always been a promise for... the dead.'

The men grew quiet as Nehari spoke, comforted by the timbre of his voice and the certainty of their fate.

'Glory be... to the Emp-Emperor, and praise be to Colonel Dakar's wisdom... but we... we suffer through life so that our paradise is eternal. Paradise is earned... never given... never taken.'

The sound of hissing surrounded them, figures moving through the underbrush. The men could no longer stir, save to aim their weapons. Nehari quietly pulled the pin on his frag grenade and felt someone's grip tighten around his arm. A pack of runners moved into the clearing, sniffing the air and picking their kills. Cartilage lined tongues licked the air in anticipation.

'There can be no... no death in paradise,' Nehari whispered. He opened his palm and watched the handle flick off and spin as it fell.

The tyranids reacted by trying to bolt back into the cover of the jungle. They weren't fast enough.

2

'I'LL STAY,' NISRI said, reaching for the vox detonator.

'No you will not,' Rezail said. 'I'll be staying.'

Turk shook his head. 'Commissar, this is a military officer's duty, not a polit–'

'Spare me,' Rezail laughed. 'This entire expedition has been anything but military in its timbre and demeanour so don't you dare use that on me now. Trust me, I don't wish to die here, but you said it earlier, lieutenant-colonel... if one of you dies, your men die with you. Besides,' he said, adjusting his uniform, 'it took the both of you three months to finally see eye to eye and put aside your tribal feuds, and it took the bloody tyranids to do it. If you make it out of here, I expect you to beat some bloody sense into your bloody tribes so that this bloody disgrace never happens again. Is that bloody understood, Prince Iban Salid and Prince Dakar?'

'Yes, commissar,' both men replied, trying to hide the hint of their smiles.

'Fine,' he said, taking the vox detonator from Turk.

Turk also fished out one of the explosives from his satchel. 'I suggest you find a nice place for this, commissar. I'll plant the other one at the escape tunnel.'

Rezail took the explosive and handed it to Tyrell without a second thought.

'Of course, I will be coming with you,' Tyrell said.

'Bloody well better,' Rezail said. 'I'll need an adjutant where I'm going.'

Tyrell smiled and left it at that.

Turk and Nisri returned to the group, which was watching the exchange with morbid interest. This time, it was Nisri who spoke, his command instinct slowly returning.

'I need five volunteers,' he said, 'to help protect the commissar and Sergeant Habass until it's time to detonate the explosives.'

There was a pause as the men exchanged glances, uncertain if they wanted to die so close to escaping.

'I'll stay,' Duf'adar Sarish said, stepping forward. Two more Guardsmen stepped forward alongside him.

'I guess I'll stay as well,' Sabaak said. 'The only thing I'm protecting is this banner.' He stepped forward, and for a moment, Turk saw the same look in Sabaak's eyes as he'd seen in Kortan's. That resolute stare and grim hardness ready to face what came next. Sabaak fidgeted with his Y-strap and pulled the rolled-up banner from it. He presented it to Turk, who nodded his thanks and handed it to another Guardsman for safe-keeping.

When a fifth volunteer did not step forward, Turk whispered to Nisri. 'I think that's enough, don't you?'

Nisri nodded. 'Sarish fights like a devil with those two pistols; we'll count him twice.'

The Guardsmen paused long enough to bid one another goodbye. They were silent farewells, nothing to be said save for shaking one another's hands and squeezing each other's shoulders.

As Turk moved away from the men, Kamala drifted close to him. 'I would have stayed had you stayed,' she whispered.

'I know,' he replied. He watched Rezail and his five protectors turn back the way they had come, searching for some place to hide their explosives. He turned, shielding them from the others for long enough to squeeze her uninjured hand. With that, Mousar continued forward,

guiding the remaining survivors to their anticipated rendezvous with
Sergeant Ballasra's squad.

3

SERGEANT BALLASRA AND his four men were shocked by the sight that
greeted them at the mouth of the jungle-rich Golden Throne.

'Is this it?' the young tracker, Chalfous, asked. 'Are you the only survivors?'

'Quiet, boy,' Ballasra said. 'You can see it in their eyes.'

Neither Nisri nor Turk had the strength left for words, they merely
leaned their backs against the cool rock of the narrow fissure connecting Caverns Emperor and Golden Throne.

'Come... you don't have much further to go,' Ballasra said, offering a
helping hand to Nisri. Nisri accepted and grunted heavily as he pulled
himself up. He glanced at Ballasra and nodded to Turk.

'You too, sir,' Ballasra said, offering Turk a hand up.

'Thank you,' Turk replied. 'We need to move quickly, there's no telling
when this explosive will blow up.'

Ballasra's eyes widened as he looked at the satchel being presented to
him. 'Then we'd best move, sir.' He motioned for the others to follow
him through a tight corridor in the bramble of jungle trees and the thick
web of hanging vines. The corridor had been hacked and burned
through, its edges jagged and scarred, but by this point, Nisri no longer
seemed to care.

Kamala paused and raised her head to the air, her hair hanging freely.
She sighed, the weight of the world evaporating from her expression.
Turk moved to her and whispered, 'What's wrong?'

'The ghosts,' Kamala said. 'They've gone quiet. We're almost at the
truth of it, my love.' She sounded relieved, and truth be told, so was
Turk.

He took her by the arm and guided her to the path, earning stares
from the others in the process. He no longer cared; being charged for
fraternising with an NCO seemed horribly trivial. Almost in response to
his thoughts, Kamala smiled.

4

THE HOWLING SEEMED to be carried on many voices, all of which appeared
to be approaching quickly. The jungle rustled and buzzed, as though
someone were taking a chainsaw to the trees. The tyranids were drawing
closer by the moment, and Rezail found his fingers nervously caressing
the vox detonator.

Rezail watched as Sabaak scaled the giant stalagmite-toothed walls, some twenty metres off the ground, and shoved the explosive into a crevice shared by the wall of Devotion and Emperor. If anything, Rezail hoped, they could seal themselves off in Emperor and still escape. It was a thin expectation, admittedly, but it was always human nature to pray against all odds for the favourable outcome.

Rezail activated his micro-bead. 'We've planted the explosive. The tyranids are coming.' A wash of static greeted him in return. 'I suggest you get rid of your satchel.'

There was no response. Rezail sighed. The buzzing from the jungle was growing louder, and Rezail could see the trees quaking under some mysterious force. He held the vox-caster and revved his chainsword, spinning the teeth counter-clockwise for more cutting power. The other men pulled their weapons, and silently mouthed whatever prayers brought them the greatest solace. Each of them prepared in their own way, and then watched the wide tunnel leading to Devotion. The grinding, buzzing noise increased in pitch.

Sabaak clambered down and pulled out his bolt pistol and scimitar, while Sarish idly spun the two laspistols in his hands. The other Guardsmen pulled their lasguns and waited nervously.

'Well, commissar,' Tyrell whispered, 'any regrets?'

Rezail smiled, his attention focussed on the tunnel and the jungle beyond. He revved his chainblade again. 'You're joking,' he said.

'Not at all. A burdened mind weighs us all down.'

'My burdens are inconsequential,' Rezail said with a smile 'and nothing I can't shear away with my chainblade and my faith combined. Prepare yourself... here they come.'

'Hell!' Tyrell whispered, watching the tunnel suddenly fill with the enemy.

THE OTHERS WERE moving quickly along the cavern wall when Turk heard his micro-bead hiss.

'Hello?' he asked, but there was no response. There wasn't the need for one. 'We'd better hurry!' he shouted to the group ahead, pushing against their backs to move them more quickly.

Ballasra nodded and pointed to the end of their journey: a small fissure angled up into the wall. They hurried into the high, narrow passage, racing against time that they knew was long past spent. Turk dropped the satchel at the mouth of the corridor, and hurried after the others as they scaled the steep and rock strewn slope. He recited a prayer over and over again, in the back of his mind, hoping he wouldn't have his spine snapped in the inevitable explosion.

The tyranids screeched and chattered in the jungles behind them, and gave chase. The jungles were filled with them, probably thanks to the

snake breeds that were digging tunnels through every metre of wall, trying to reach the biomass.

THE GUARDSMEN FIRED their boltguns as they backed away, trying to stem
the wave of the dog-like beasts, small tyranids that attacked their targets
in numbers. With enlarged heads and overly developed fangs, six spiked
legs a piece, and elongated tails, they swarmed over two Guardsmen,
biting and spitting out chunks of flesh and muscle. The sight sickened
Rezail, but he'd heard of this in other furiously carnivorous species; it
took longer to chew and swallow than to chew and spit, so the creatures
had grown adept at stripping their targets first and eating later. Both soldiers succumbed in seconds, screaming and falling to the ground, where
more dogs tore into their messy carcasses.

Sarish was firing both laspistols at the larger runners and centipedes
that were heading for him and the others. With expert shots, Sarish
felled them two at a time, while Sabaak finished off the injured. Tyrell
tried intercepting those that slipped through by standing between the
commissar and the tyranids, but the fight was already so wild and
chaotic that it seemed as if they were under attack from all sides. The
commissar was already brandishing his chainsword like a true battle-
trained alumnus of the Schola Progenium, his blade revving and
whining as it cut through the carapace of a simian-like creature with
barbed arms.

A human cry pierced through the chainsaw's scream, and Rezail
turned to see Sabaak drop his bolt pistol and stare down at his chest. A
fist-sized alien seed had lodged inside his torso. It opened like a flower
in bloom, further cracking the sternum apart, but instead of blossoming with petals, tiny black beetles poured forth. Sabaak couldn't scream,
the agony so intense that he contorted into seizures. The bugs ran riot
over his flesh, burrowing holes into his skin.

Sarish drew his aim and levelled four shots into the tyranid gunner
that had fired the round. By the time he turned his guns on Sabaak, the
young soldier was already falling face first into the jungle soil. Without
a word, the Duf'adar continued firing at the advancing tyranids.

Rezail, meanwhile, swung the chainsword into a runner, severing half
its limbs. It convulsed on the ground, spraying yellow ichor on the commissar's boots. He grunted in disgust.

'Adjutant, shoot that thing, please!' he said.

Tyrell snap-fired a shot into the tyranid before firing on an advancing
biped.

'Thank you!' Rezail said, deflecting the biped's scythe as it swung at
Tyrell's neck, and opening its torso to Tyrell's laspistol.

The chameleon appeared out of nowhere, literally. Its two pereopods arched down and impaled Sarish through the chest, out through his back and into the soil. Sarish never said a word. He grunted in pain, and fired his two pistols into the chameleon's face before it could withdraw. Both he and the creature fell to the side, their mutual deaths equally silent.

'It's just you and me, commissar,' Tyrell yelled, firing at the incoming flood of dog-like biters. There must have been a hundred of them swarming towards the two men. 'Oh Holy Emperor!' he cried.

Rezail paused for long enough to cry over his micro-bead. 'Get out, get out!'

Then the tyranids swept over both men, sharp teeth biting through the muscles in Tyrell's and Rezail's legs. Both men toppled immediately, their voices shrieking in agony. The creatures tore into their faces, necks, arms and chests, never noticing Rezail's single arm held high above them; the one holding the vox detonator.

THE MICRO-BEAD clicked and hissed again, and Turk screamed for them to move. This was it, he knew it was. The tyranids behind him were closing fast, but the blinding sunlight above beckoned and promised safety. He couldn't see where they were going, but he pushed hard and dragged the stumbling Guardsman to his feet before he could fall.

And then… cataclysm.

THE VOX-SIGNAL reached all the receivers almost simultaneously. The receivers primed the detonators and the detonators triggered the explosives. The three small explosions did little, other than to collapse some rock formations. The explosions from the seven Sentinels, however, combined with the fuel drums, turned the birds into massive frag bombs, incinerating nearby tyranids that were focussed on their diet of the planet.

The pressure wave spread burning wreckage across the caverns, and hammered a mortal blow against the network. Giant slabs of rock tore away, shifting the weight above it. Limestone shattered and cracked for dozens of metres inside the rock strata. The tyranids heard the thunder rumble through the walls and tried to run… but there was nowhere left to go.

The walls could no longer support the weight of the desert above them, and the tyranids' network of tunnels had destabilised the area further. The caverns collapsed, bringing a fall of sand and giant limestone rocks plummeting into the jungle. The tyranids scrambled away from the falling sky and the cascading pillars of sand. The fall turned into an avalanche, and in moments, the ceilings over Apostle, Basilica, Cathedral and Devotion collapsed.

In turn, the weight of the buckling caverns cracked through the roofs of the many unexplored caves below. This precipitated a second cave-in that crushed the unexplored beauty of the lower network. Sand and debris rained into ancient underground seas, past kilometre high waterfalls, and onto fossilised jungles preserved and sparkling with mineral coats. The deep collapse acted like a drain, pulling at all the tunnels and connecting caves, until it tore the entire network down into ruin.

ONE MOMENT TURK was running, rumbling sand beneath his tired legs and the blue sun above his head, the next, he was falling, the world pulled out from beneath his feet. Turk slammed back into the sand after a terrible moment of freefalling, the drop a stomach-lurching ride, and then tumbled down the longest slope he'd ever experienced.

The ground levelled out, and Turk finally rolled to a stop. He was dizzy and sick, his senses reeling, unanchored. A dust cloud obscured everything around him, while static bursts discharged and dazzled him. Someone's scream forced him to focus; a Guardsman was being swallowed by a sinkhole in the sand, his hands frantically scrambling to find purchase. He was neck deep; nose deep a second later, his eyes impossibly wide in panic. Turk scrambled to grab him, but it was too late, he simply vanished.

The pull of the sand continued, and Turk felt the desert beneath his own feet drag him slowly to the same hole. The sand felt too liquid, robbed of its cohesion. More static discharged and flared against the choked air. Turk leapt to the side and crawled against the current, losing a metre to every one he gained. Finally, he dragged himself onto a stable patch, and turned to see sand spiralling around sand in a torpid whirlpool. There must have been an air pocket somewhere beneath him. Add the strange properties of the sand, and the drag was enough to pull men down to their doom.

Turk collapsed atop his small island, panting and exhausted. He felt like he'd been running for as long as he could remember being alive. He ached. He was tired in a way that made him dizzy. He wanted to sleep, but there was no promise that his ordeal was over. The tyranids, he realised, and that thought alone was enough to shock him with adrenaline.

He looked around in mad panic, trying to get his bearings, but saw nothing that made sense. A massive dust cloud hung in the air, slowly settling and sparking. The sand sloped upward and away into a massive dune that seemed to stretch to impossible heights. Streams of sand continued pouring down the slope. They were thick, at first, but thinned slowly to a trickle. The more the dust storm settled, and the more Turk could see, the higher the dune soared, until its stature proved too incredible to comprehend.

Turk's micro-bead crackled to life, the voice strained and broken by bursts of static. Others had survived, Turk realised, gratefully. Slowly, the survivors found one another and gathered together: Nisri, Turk, Ballasra and a handful of others. When Turk found Kamala, they embraced and kissed, ignoring decorum and scandal. They then found two more men, their bodies snapped and twisted by unkind falls, and another two with broken legs and arms. The scout Mousar was among the dead, his mouth and eyes caught in a gasp, his neck turned at an odd angle. Turk quietly covered his scarred face with his kafiya.

'Has anyone seen Chalfous?' Ballasra asked. They all shook their heads in quiet shock, although Turk suspected it was Chalfous he had seen drowning.

Turk claimed the 892nd's banner from one of the fallen Guardsmen, and then they waited for the dust to settle completely. As it did, what they saw made even less sense. The sand dune that stretched above their heads was at least a kilometre tall. They could finally see far enough to follow the dune's ridge by sight, before realising that it wasn't a dune, but the lip of a giant crater. It was dozens of kilometres in diameter, massive whirlpools of sand and giant daggers of upturned rock dotted across its surface. They were at the bottom of the giant bowl that had once been the caverns.

As they explored their surroundings, Ballasra whistled them over. A claw had appeared in the sand, followed by the upper body of a wounded snake. Turk drew his pistol and killed the tyranid before it could crawl free.

Over the next hour, the survivors found refuge in the shade of a giant finger of rock that broke the skin of the desert. It was encrusted with mud, its water long past drunk by the desert. They buried the dead as best they could, tended to the wounded, killed the occasional injured tyranid that had somehow crawled its way out of the ground, and discussed ways of escaping the crater.

5

IT WAS NIGHT, and the air in the crater was deathly cold. The survivors huddled together to keep warm, and they covered the two injured men in the Imperial banner. They'd found one brief hope in a small puddle of water that had trickled to the surface, but by the time dusk had arrived, the greedy desert had drunk the puddle back up. Now they slept the sleep of the dead, waiting for dawn before attempting to crawl up the crater's dune wall. Not that they believed they would have much success. The slope was too steep.

Turk started awake, Kamala's hand gently covering his mouth.

'What is it?' he said, instantly awake. The others did not stir, the deep chill of the early morning drawing them deeper into their exhausted lethargy.

Kamala's eyes were black under the night sky. Turk felt disquieted by the way her gaze seemed to reach and rifle through his very soul. She was searching for something, searching for an anchor. Kamala kneeled down next to him and waited for him to sit up.

'Beloved, what is it?' he asked.

'The stars are silent again,' she said.

'That's good, isn't it?' he asked, hoping no more would come of this.

'No,' she said, a sob escaping her lips. 'No it isn't. I always hear the stars… always… I hear them throb and ache. I hear the echoes of the Astronomican, the whispers of the warp trying to eat its way into my head.' She thumped her temple with her palm. 'The Black Ships… the Black Ships find us and teach us how to ignore all but the Emperor's voice, but the noise is always there. It never leaves us. Never! Except….' Her gaze flitted back up to the stars, her eyes suddenly lost in the silent heavens.

Turk grabbed her shoulders gently, forcing her to focus on him again. 'Kamala, why are the stars silent? The tyranids?'

'We killed them,' she said, her voice broken. 'We killed one ship. One.'

'One?' Turk said, dread like cold water washing through his limbs and organs. 'There was more than one?'

'We killed scouts,' Kamala whispered. 'All that terror… all that horror for one scout ship.'

'More are coming?'

'No,' Kamala whispered, 'more are here.'

NISRI FELT THE low tremor move through the ground, building in strength. Streams, and then rivers, of sand bled from the dune wall. Entire sections hissed as they collapsed and slid. Everyone was awake and standing, their fatigue robbing them of the will to run, to cry, or to hide.

It was Ballasra who pointed to the distant wall, where the starry sky framed perfectly the lip of the crater. A dust cloud rose to blanket the crater's lip, and tyranids began pouring over the side and down the slope like the seething dark mass of a living shadow.

They numbered in the thousands. They numbered in the endless.

'They're coming from the south,' Ballasra said.

'There was another ship,' Nisri said. 'Merciful Emperor, there was another ship.'

'Make ready,' Turk said, simply. 'We have more left to kill.'

Slowly, silently, the Guardsmen prepared themselves. The tyranids were several minutes away, but gone was the anticipation of battle or the frayed nerves of eagerness. There was only the quiet determination borne of a bone-aching weariness and a desperate yawning to be done with it. They had fought, better than they had ever expected to fight, and they had won against incredible odds.

Nisri watched them prepare. He was proud of them, despite their differences… even because of them. How different things might have been if he hadn't been so stubborn, if Turk and he hadn't fought. This was not the time for regrets.

He knew what he had to do, for himself, the Guard be damned, his tribe be equally cursed. He called Turk over, beckoning him to the other side of the rock to speak. Both men walked quietly, Turk perhaps sensing what was to come. When, finally, they were out of earshot of the others, Nisri straightened and spoke.

'I just wanted to say… it was an honour, Prince Iban Salid,' Nisri said, quietly, 'and I ask you lead them into battle one last time.'

'I shall,' Turk replied, grasping Nisri's outstretched arm, 'and the honour was mine, Prince Dakar. Journey well.'

'I still fear I may not see you in my Paradise, son of the Banna,' Nisri said, pulling Turk into his embrace. 'I still will not shake my beliefs as a son of the Turenag, but I pray that the Aba Aba Mushira has a Paradise for soldiers, so that I might welcome you there as my brother.'

The men embraced for a moment longer and kissed one another twice on each cheek, as they might kiss old friends and beloved family. Then Turk turned around and walked away, leaving Nisri alone with his thoughts.

Nisri fell to his knees and offered his hands out in submission and prayer. 'Forgive me, oh Emperor,' he whispered. 'Forgive my hubris in believing I would be the one to find Paradise for my people. Forgive me for proving unworthy of Your gifts.' With that, Nisri pulled his laspistol from its holster.

TURK DIDN'T FLINCH at the discharge of the laspistol, even when everyone else jumped. 'Stay where you are,' he ordered, stopping Ballasra from investigating. 'Leave him his dignity.'

Ballasra hesitated, but said nothing. Like Turk, he understood the burden of leadership and the dangers of brandishing a keen-edged faith. Sometimes it was a weapon to use against your enemies, and sometimes, it was the device of your downfall. No knife was ever crafted that could not defend you against all aggressors one moment, and then be held at your wrists the next. Turk did not blame Nisri for his actions; he wasn't sure if he could have stared into the face of paradise and hope, for so long, and then given the order to raze it. He understood the colonel's anguish, and he respected him for it.

Turk ensured everyone was ready for this last stand, and offered hushed words of encouragement, and words of thanks for their efforts. He even propped the two injured men up and armed them so that they could fight to the last. When he reached Ballasra, the two men merely clapped one another on the shoulder. They were soldiers, the oldest of the lot. Nothing needed to be said.

The tyranids were less than a minute away when Turk reached Kamala. They embraced and kissed more passionately than they had during their nights of furtive lovemaking. The ground shook beneath their feet.

'I can hear the ghosts again,' Kamala whispered, her forehead touching his. 'I can finally understand their words.'

'What are they saying?' Turk asked, curious.

'I love you,' she said, and kissed Turk on the lips. He looked confused, but the time for questions was over. The tyranid wave was almost upon them. 'Protect me to the last,' she said. 'I finally understand what I need to do.'

6

THE TYRANIDS SWARMED over the last survivors, ripping through them in a terrible collision. The Guardsmen fell, cut down one by one, by scythe, by claw or by bite. They died firing their pistols and swinging their blades, their last furious act to kill those that slaughtered them.

Ballasra and Turk protected Kamala as the energy crackled around her body, but she did not unleash it. It built up inside her, setting her nerves on fire and blistering her skin. Her nose and eyes bled, the blood cascading down past her psyker's hood and soaking her chest. She paused for long enough to watch Ballasra fall, a pack of runners dragging him down into the sand and lacerating the flesh from his bones. She took strength from his death, and continued to bottle it up inside her.

Turk turned to save Ballasra, but a round of green bio-plasm struck him in the back. She watched as he burned alive, the green fire devouring cloth, and burning away his hair. Their eyes locked, and she took strength from him, but there was no recognition left in his stare before the fire split them open. She shut her eyes. She'd seen this before without knowing it, had dreamt it without understanding it. The images rifled through her thoughts, threatening to overwhelm her and scatter her energies. The air was suffocated by the stench of ozone, cordite and discharged bowels, but she forced herself past the noise, past the smells.

Kamala saw the deathblow arrive before it landed, felt it coming with the certainty of providence. She sensed her end in the seconds before it struck. Her eyes flew open as a scythe struck her between the shoulder blades and sliced straight through her sternum. She stared at the blade for a moment, feeling no pain. It was exactly where it was supposed to be, exactly as the ghosts had shown her.

She focussed on the tattered, blood-caked standard half buried in sand. The wind tore at its frayed edges, and the double-eagle emblem of the Imperium poked out from beneath the bodies of her friends. It was exactly as she'd seen it, overlaid each time a million times over with no discrepancy in how it unfolded. Every image she saw was the same, each one superimposed by repetition of this single event, over the last. All of them together burned into the fabric of her consciousness as the scene was somehow repeated again and again in history.

Not history, she realised. *It is history only once.*

One point in time had become the fulcrum of her existence.

Bioelectricity surged out from every pore of her skin, electrocuting the tyranid beast that delivered the deathblow. It lit her body with a burning incandescence. Her thoughts flew towards the heavens, her fading consciousness propelled upward by her mortis-cry, a cry not even the tyranids could silence. She broke through the silence of the stars, shattering through the veil, and felt the noise flood back in. Kamala sent her thoughts home, back to where it all began. She knew this would work, because it had worked before. It was ordained.

As the light and suffering of the world closed, Kamala could see her thoughts twist and change as they flew through the distortions of Empyrean Space.

She did not fear where her cry would go, not when she already knew the 'when' of it all.

This time, she prayed, *let it turn out differently. Let me understand more quickly.*

EPILOGUE

'How much does tonight resemble yesterday's night.'
                    – *The Accounts of the Tallarn*
                      by Remembrancer Tremault

1

There was, there was not.

2

THE TRANSMISSION FELL like a carelessly discarded blade from the heavens, straight into his naked brain. The astropath's muscles seized into hard cords. His teeth snapped down, cracking the enamel. His skeletal hands gripped the cradle's iron grasp bars, cutting flesh with rust, and he bucked against the leather straps holding him fast. There wasn't enough time to mouth a litany of protection or to will a psychic bulwark into place against the buckshot rain of thoughts. From the heavens, tonight, fell death, and visions of history undone and ghosts unmade.

WAITING DEATH

Steve Lyons

BOREALIS FOUR.

Can't say it was the most distinguished campaign of my career. A jungle planet orbiting a red giant on the inner rim of the Segmentum Tempestus. A hundred and ten degrees in the shade. Serpents lurking under every leaf, stinging insects as big as a man's fist. Even the flowers coughed out a nasty muscle-wasting virus. It was a damned disappointment, I can tell you. I had hoped for a challenge.

Never did find out if Borealis Four was worth saving. Could be that its crust was packed full of minerals and precious stones. Could be it was as dry as a corpse's throat. All that mattered back then was that, when the explorators set foot on this green new world, they had found a surprise waiting for them: a Chaos-worshipping cult, proud of the fact that the Dark Gods had begun to pervert their flesh and deform their bones.

And that's where I came in: Colonel 'Iron Hand' Straken – along with three regiments of the finest damned soldiers in the whole of the Imperium.

Catachan Jungle Fighters.

THE CULTISTS ON Borealis Four were one of the worst rabbles I had ever seen. Yet again they came bursting from the trees, howling at the top of their voices, throwing themselves at us with no care for their own lives. That was fine by me – we didn't care about their lives either.

'Well, don't just dance with those damned sissies, Graves – use your knife, man,' I shouted. 'And Barruga, you're as slow as a brainleaf plant.

You idle slugs, you gonna let this filth spew on the good name of the Catachan Second? I could whip this bunch with my one good arm if you sons-of-groxes weren't in my way. Thorn, stop flapping about like a damned newborn – you still got one damned hand, so pick up that lasgun! Kopachek, you got a clear shot with that flamer, what the hell are you waiting for? Emperor's teeth, do I have to do everything myself?'

We tore through that scum like blades through a reed bed. They were ill-disciplined, ill-equipped, didn't know what had hit them. They'd wasted their damned lives dancing around altars in dresses, waving stinking candles. Should have spent a few days on my world; they'd have learned how to fight like men.

I'd made a bet with my opposite number, Carraway of the 14th, that we'd be done here in four months, tops. Two months in, it looked like I was going to collect on that bet. Until that one night.

That one night, when my platoon of some thirty hardened veterans – along with a certain General Farris – was cut off from our comrades, stranded in the darkest depths of the Borealis jungle. That night, when I faced one of the toughest, most desperate challenges of my life.

That night, when I had to fight my own damned men.

THE JUNGLE ON Borealis Four was nothing compared to Catachan, but the march was taking too damn long. Cutting a way through the high vegetation was slowing us up, and the men were tired. But sunset was coming soon, and things out here tended to get a whole lot worse after dark, so I decided to offer a few words of encouragement.

'Pick up the pace back there! What do you think this is, a newborn's trip to the mango swamps? Myers, put some muscle into those knife strokes. Levitski, Barruga, keep trying to kick some life into that damned vox-caster.'

Still the machine offered nothing but a metallic thunk and yet another blast of static.

'Emperor's teeth, it's come to something when you mommas' boys can't finish off a bunch of damned half-mutant freaks.' I shouted down the line. 'And in front of the general! Well, I don't care how long it takes, not one of you is slacking off for a single damn second till we're back behind our lines. I promised you today was gonna be a cakewalk, and the man who makes a liar out of old 'Iron Hand' Straken, I'll throttle with his own entrails. What...?'

I drew to a halt, and the march stopped all around me. The constant buzz of insects and howl of jungle creatures had suddenly been joined by another noise – the faint tinkling of wind chimes.

'What am I looking at here? Where the hell did this come from?' I asked.

Without warning, we had come to a clearing, at least half a kilometre wide. The jungle canopy opened right up, and I was dazzled by the final rays of the setting sun. The air was suddenly cool and fresh, scented with blossom. And, squinting against the light, I could make out dark, unnatural shapes: Buildings. Dark-timbered wooden huts.

My first thought was that we'd found an enemy bolthole. But these huts were sturdy and well-kept, arranged around a larger central hall. Our enemies could never have built anything so orderly. Besides, if the taint of the Ruinous Powers had been there, I'd have damn well smelled it.

Why, then, was my gut warning me of something rotten about this place? And why the hell didn't I listen to it?

As we stood gawping, a figure approached us from between the huts. A boy, barely into his teenage years – but, with the last of the blood-red light behind him, I couldn't make out much more than that. Of course, my men reacted as they had been trained to do, raising their lasguns and taking aim, but the boy didn't seem at all worried by the sight of thirty muzzles pointed at his heart.

He padded closer, as the sun disappeared and the clearing was washed in the faint blue light of a swollen moon. I could make out the boy's face now, round and gentle, his eyes bright and wide. His skin was sunbronzed to perfection, and the moonlight made his bald head shine like a halo. He was wearing a simple white robe, ornamented by a garland of flowers.

'Welcome,' he offered.

The boy cocked his head a little, his full lips pursed as if he found the sight of thirty bloodied vets on his doorstep somehow amusing.

'Welcome to safe haven.' He continued. 'I am Kadence Moonglow – and all that my people have, we offer to share with you.'

'So you say, kid,' I spat back. 'But before we break out the damned peace pipe, I got a few questions for you.'

General Farris stepped forward with a diplomatic clearing of his throat. It was the first time I'd heard his voice all day.

'What Colonel Straken means to say is that we weren't aware of any settlement in this area.'

'And seeing as how, in two months here we haven't found a single life form that hasn't tried to eviscerate us-'

'I assure you that nobody in this village would wish harm to another being,' interrupted Kadence. 'We have learned to live in balance with even this harsh environment. As for your enemies… yes, they were a part of our commune once, but no longer. They have been cast out of this place.'

Sounded like bull to my ears. But General Farris motioned to the men to lower their guns – and, with a few uncertain glances at me, they obeyed.

Farris introduced himself, and the rest of us, to this Kadence Moon-glow, and accepted his offer of hospitality.

'Now hold on a minute, Sir.' I said. 'I told the men I'd get us back to the camp tonight. Nothing has changed. We can still—'

Farris shook his head firmly. 'The men are tired, Straken.'

'And some of them need proper medical attention. You think they've got a damned hospital tent set up here?'

Kadence interjected again. 'We will do what we can for your wounded. We have balms and tinctures, and most importantly our faith in the healing spirits.'

'Yeah', I thought, 'cos a few herbal potions and a bit of wailing to the skies, that's gonna sew Trooper Thorn's damned hand right back on. But Farris wouldn't be moved on the subject.

'We'll keep the men in better shape by letting them rest than by force-marching them overnight through that jungle.'

I wondered if he was really talking about the men, or about himself. Farris had taken a scratch in the fighting today. His left arm was held in a makeshift sling. He'd kept up with the rest of us so far, and hadn't whined about it – but I'd been watching him sweating and stumbling for a while now, waiting for him to drop.

Either way, I couldn't fault his logic – even if he hadn't been my superior officer. So, taking my silence as a sign of assent, the general asked Kadence to lead the way forward, and ordered my men to follow. I caught Thorn's eye as he passed me. He was still holding his bloodied hand to the stump of his left wrist.

'Never mind, kid.' I told him. 'That hand's looking a bit green now, anyway. Probably too late to save it. Have to make do with an augmetic. Hell, I once had my whole damned arm ripped off by a Miral land shark, you don't hear me grizzling about that. It's character forming.'

Walking into that village was like stepping onto a different world. The jungle suddenly seemed a long way away, and I was surprised to see children playing on the grass between the huts. Some of them stopped to stare at us as we passed. There was excitement and wonder in their wide eyes, but not a trace of fear, although we must have presented a terrifying sight in our jungle camouflage, laden down with weapons.

Farris dropped back, falling into step beside me.

'How do they survive?' he asked. 'They let their children play outdoors, for the Emperor's sake, just a few hundred metres from the monsters and the poison and the sickness out there.' He shuddered at the thought. 'We have to evacuate them, Straken. First thing in the morning. They aren't safe here.'

General Farris, you might have gathered by now, was not one of us. He hailed from Validius, a world so in-bred that eighty per cent of its population belonged to the monarchy, and didn't they just love to let you know it. To be fair, Farris had posted himself to the front line this morning – he must have had some guts. Somehow, though, during the fighting, he'd been separated from his own regiment and ended up with ours. A scrawny, pasty-faced man, the general clearly wasn't used to jungle conditions. He had brightened up plenty now that we had found shelter.

Kadence led us into the spacious central hall. It was packed with more of his people, all dressed in white robes, talking and laughing and sharing out bowls of plump, ripe berries. They cleared spaces for us, on benches or on cushions, and handed us fruit, hunks of sweet-smelling bread and mugs of crystal clear water.

Farris was in his element, shaking the hand of anyone who looked like they might be important, thanking them for their kindness, promising to repay it. I was happy to leave all the jawing to him.

My men were approaching the villagers' gifts with caution. I'd have stuck my boot up the backsides of any of them who hadn't. As Catachans, though, we have good instincts about food and drink; wouldn't last too damned long otherwise. We were soon satisfied that no one was trying to poison us.

In fact, the fruits in particular were sweet and moist, quenching the flames in my throat. I couldn't help but wonder why I hadn't seen their like before on Borealis Four.

Soon, my men were mixing with the villagers as if they'd been friends all their lives. I listened in on their conversations, heard a lot of small talk about Catachan and life in the Imperial Guard, but not so much about our hosts. They were good at deflecting questions.

Then Farris introduced me to two village elders – white-haired, straight-backed and dignified but with the same glint of humour in their eyes that I'd seen in Kadence's – and it seemed he had pried some information out of them, at least.

'They've been telling me of their people's legends,' Farris began. 'They believe they came to this world in a "great sky chariot" a thousand generations ago.'

'The Stellar Exodus?'

I knew that some of the first colony ships had strayed beyond the Segmentum Solar, and so in those pre-warp days had become lost to history. It had even been suggested that one of those ships had seeded human life on Catachan.

'Their ancestors were born on Holy Terra. They're the Emperor's people, like us.' Farris said.

'It seems we have a great deal in common, and much to talk about on the morrow.' One of the elders spoke up. 'For now, you and your men must sleep. We can clear this meeting hall for you. I see you have bedrolls. We can fetch more cushions and pillows if you wish.'

'That would be more than acceptable.' Farris responded. 'Thank you.'

As Kadence and the elders left, I grumbled something about making the men soft. Farris let out a sigh. 'You know, your men don't all have your... advantages, shall we say. You can push them too hard.'

I didn't bother to answer that. No outsider could understand the bond between me and my men. They'd have crawled through a Catachan Devil's nest on their bare bellies if I'd asked them to. That much I knew.

'All right, you milksops, that's enough damned pampering for one day. Get out there, start laying traps around the village's perimeter. Go easy on the mines, we're running dry. I want toe-poppers, lashing branches, anything that'll kick up a damn good racket. Graves, put that cushion down! Hop to it, you slackers, or do I have to do everything myself? And once you're done, I want four volunteers to join me on first watch. McDougal, Vines, Kopachek, Greif, you'll do.'

IT DIDN'T TAKE me long to find a good sentry position, in an old tree right on the jungle line. Its star-shaped leaves gave off a eucalyptus reek that would mask my scent, and my camouflage would be more effective here than against the buildings behind me.

I lowered myself onto my stomach along a low, stout branch, and shouldered my plasma pistol.

I was almost invisible now. So long as I didn't move a muscle, or make a sound. But then, I had no reason to do either.

Something was wrong.

It was nothing I could see, nothing I could hear. But I knew there was something. Something out there, at the edge of my senses.

I held my breath, straining to catch the slightest sound. There was nothing. Just the night-time breeze. Without turning my head, I refocussed my gaze, through my pistol's sights. I re-examined my surroundings through an infrared filter, but again there was nothing.

My damned comm-bead was still dead. I couldn't sub-vocalise a warning to the other four sentries, couldn't shout to them without giving myself away. It didn't matter, I told myself. They'd have sensed it, too.

For the next fifteen minutes, I stayed frozen in place – as did my unseen opponents. A waiting game. That suited me. I could wait all night.

Of course, I knew I wouldn't have to.

They made their move, at last. If I'd blinked, I'd have missed it. I knew then that these couldn't be the same cultists we'd been fighting these past months. They were too damned good.

But I was better.

There was a subtle shift in the texture of the darkness, the crunch of a leaf on the ground. I had already teased a frag grenade from my webbing and thumbed the time-delay to its shortest setting.

It plopped into the jungle grass just where the disturbance had been, and it lit up the night.

I had hoped to hear screaming, but instead I saw shadows streaming from the impact point, just an instant ahead of the earth-shattering blast. These were lumpen, gnarled shapes that could have belonged to nothing entirely human. I squeezed off ten shots, until my pistol was hot in my hands. I couldn't tell if I had struck true. The explosion had shot my night-vision to hell. I knew one thing, though. I had to move.

I rolled out of the tree, hitting the ground running beneath a barrage of las-fire from the jungle. Whoever – whatever – was out there, like the cultists, they had Imperial weaponry. At least I had made them reveal themselves.

I feigned a stumble, faltering for an instant, making myself a target. I was hoping to make the hostiles bold – and careless. A few steps forward, and they'd hit the tripwire that I knew was strung between us.

No such luck. I heard a soft thud at my heels, and I leapt for the cover of the line of huts ahead of me. The grenade that had just landed exploded, the blast wave hitting me in midair, engulfing me in a broiling heat but buoying my flight. I was propelled much further than my legs could have carried me. I landed hard, and instinctively rolled onto my augmetic shoulder, letting it take the brunt of the impact. I heard something break inside it, and a servo sputtered and whined, but I felt no loss of function as I pushed myself up and put a charred hut between myself and my attackers.

The sound of las-fire across the clearing told me that Kopachek had also engaged the enemy. I thought about going to his aid, but knew I had a line to hold.

I swapped my pistol for my trusty old shotgun: primitive, in some people's eyes, but reliable, and suited to firing from the hip. My eyes were readjusting to the dark, and I peered around the hut's side. The jungle was still again, silent. As if nothing had happened. But that silence was a lie.

The hostiles were still out there. Chastened, maybe; tonight, they had learned that Colonel 'Iron Hand' Straken was no pushover. They would be regrouping, redrawing their plans. But they hadn't retreated. I could still feel their presence, like a stench of old bones in the air.

They were waiting.

A second burst of gunfire took me by surprise. This one came not from one of the other sentry posts, but from the meeting hall at the village's centre. I hesitated for about half a second before I turned and pelted towards the sound. When I got there, the men were spilling out of the hall. They were still shrugging on jackets, tying bandanas, checking their weapons, but were already awake and alert to their surroundings, looking for a target. I grabbed the nearest of them – Levitski – and ordered him to replace me at the jungle's edge. I sent the next to relieve Kopachek – I wanted him back here with a situation report.

Trooper Graves was nursing a fresh wound. Snatching his hand from his temple, I saw the familiar red welt of a glancing las-beam hit.

'What the hell's been going on here?' I shouted.

I pushed my way into the hall, where I found the remains of my platoon in disarray – and two of them dead on the floor.

Standing over these two, with his laspistol drawn, was General Farris – and as he turned to me with a regretful slump of his shoulders, I realised what he must have done. He had shot them. A tense silence filled the hall before Farris leapt to defend his actions: 'I had no choice. They were lashing out, screaming, firing everywhere. This one, he came at me with his knife. He was saying crazy things, calling me a monster. I think… I think the cultists must have got to them.'

'No!' The protest came automatically to my lips. 'No damned way!'

It was one thing to see a comrade cut down in battle, dying for what he believed in. This… This was senseless. I felt cold inside. I felt numb.

I felt angry.

I remembered how Myers had fought so well that morning, laughing as he'd sunk his knife arm up to the elbow in cultist guts. I remembered how Wallenski had been so proud, last week, when the men had honoured him with an earned name. 'Nails', they had called him.

'They were good men, *my* men. You had no right.'

Farris's eyes darkened.

'Do I have to remind you, colonel, that I am the ranking officer here? You weren't even present. You don't know what—'

'I knew them, *sir*. I know my men, and they were two of the best.'

A heavy silence had fallen upon the hall. All eyes were fixed upon the general and me. Still, my words provoked a ragged, defiant cheer from the dead men's comrades.

'Either one of those soldiers would have given his last damned drop of blood for the Emperor.' I continued. 'It must have been… They must have come down with some virus. A fever. It made them see things.'

'Whatever the cause of their behaviour, they were threatening us all. I had to act.'

'You didn't even know their damned names!'

And the silence returned, almost a physical force between us.

It was broken by a quiet voice. Kadence Moonglow had entered the hall, and walked right up to my shoulder without my being aware of him. That, as much as any of the night's events so far, disquieted me.

'The covenant has been broken,' the boy said.

'What the hell does that mean?' I rounded on him.

'Blood has been shed. Now, they will not rest until they have blood in return.'

'Who will not rest? The cultists?' Farris asked.

Kadence shook his head. 'The jungle has bred far worse than those misguided souls. There are monsters out there. Monsters that the eye cannot see, but whose presence is felt nonetheless.'

'Yeah, well, thanks for the warning,' I said, 'but those "monsters" of yours already tried to blow me into chunks.'

Kadence shot me a sharp look – and, for a moment, his calm facade slipped and I caught a glimpse of something darker beneath it.

'They would not have attacked you except in self-defence.'

Then, composing himself, he continued.

'We welcomed you into our village, our home, because we sensed that you were noble souls. We only prayed that, in return, you could leave your war at our doors.'

'I don't know if you're aware of this, kid, but your monsters have this village surrounded.' I replied.

'And now they are free to enter it as they please. By sunrise, all we have built here will be ashes. No one will survive.'

'In a grox's eye!' I spat. 'Those things out there, whatever they are – they aren't dealing with a bunch of tree-hugging pushovers any more. If they want this village, they'll have to go through us to get it.'

'Colonel Straken has a point.' Farris cut in. 'We will do everything in our power to protect you.'

'There are less than thirty of you. Their numbers are legion.'

'But we have the defensive advantage,' I said. 'My boys can keep those hostiles at bay till dawn, or I'll want to know the damned reason why.'

'And once the sun is up, we'll be able to lead you – all of you - to safety. We have an army, not twenty kilometres from here.' Farris said.

Kadence bowed his head.

'As you wish.'

THE NEXT HALF-HOUR was given over to frenetic activity.

I trebled the guard around the village, this time counting myself out of the assignments. I wanted to be free to go where I was needed. I sent Barruga and Stone around the huts, telling people to pack their things and move to the central hall. They would be safer there, harder to reach. General Farris stayed in the hall, too – his choice. Someone had to organise things in there, he claimed.

I debriefed Kopachek. His story was similar to my own – except that, in his case, the enemy had fired first. Like me, he hadn't managed to get a good look at them. I sent him, along with MacDougal, Vines and Greif, to grab an hour's sleep in one of the vacated huts. Farris had been right about one thing: my men were the toughest damned sons-of-groxes in the Imperium. Sometimes, it was easy to forget that they didn't all have chests full of replacement parts to keep them going.

I hadn't forgotten about Wallenski and Myers. There would be a reckoning for their deaths, and soon. Meantime, I had warned every man to keep an eye on his watch partner – and to call for a medic if he felt the jungle sweats coming on.

THE QUIET OF the night was broken only by the occasional squawking bird, and the deeper cries of much larger and much more dangerous jungle creatures. Trooper Thorn was sprawled on his stomach, alongside a small, square hut, his wiry body masked by the long grass. His lasgun barrel rested on a mound of dirt, waiting for a target. I hurried up to him, keeping my head down, and dropped to my haunches beside him. He gave me a situation report without my even asking.

'Nothing, sir. Not a sign of the hostiles. Perhaps you made them realise what they're facing, and—?'

'They're out there.' I interrupted. I had rarely been more sure of anything in my life.

'Do you think…? That boy, sir, what he said… was he right? Are we facing… monsters? Daemons, or…?'

'Trust me, kid, I've seen enough monsters in my lifetime, and nothing – not a damned one of them – would last two minutes in a scrap with a Catachan Devil, or make it through a patch of spikers alive. So, don't you dare start shaking in your boots just 'cos you've seen a few drops of blood today and heard some damned fairy tale.'

'No, sir. It's just that… Colonel Straken, sir, is something wrong? You… you're sweating.'

'What the hell are you talking about?' I asked.

'What… what did you say?' asked Thorn.

Suddenly he was clawing at the ground with the bandaged stump of his left arm, pushing himself away from me and to his feet. His eyes had widened with fear, and his voice was loud – too loud. He had blown our cover for sure.

'Trooper Thorn, to attention!' I snapped. 'You're behaving like a damned newborn yourself. Hell, I know you're not long out of nappies, but—'

'Take that back, sir. Take it back!'

'I beg your damned pardon, trooper?'

We were both standing now, and Thorn had managed to grab his lasgun and was pointing it shakily at my head. I had brought up my shotgun in return – an instinctive reaction - but the image of a comrade in its sights shocked me to my core.

I lowered my gun, brought up my hands.

'Listen, kid.' I said. 'You're not yourself. You're sick. Like Wallenski and Myers, they were sick. But you can fight it.'

'I don't want to believe... This is a test, right? Tell me it's a test. Don't make me–'

'Why do you think you're here? Do you think I make a habit outta taking every snot-nosed brat fresh out of training into my command platoon? "Barracuda" Creek back at the Tower reckons you're the next damned Sly Marbo. You gonna prove him wrong?'

'The fever!' he cried and, for a moment, I thought I'd got through to him.

'It must be the fever, making you say those things. Please, sir, just... drop your weapons. I don't want to have to shoot you – not you – but I swear in the Emperor's name, if I must–'

His sentence was broken by a barrage of las-fire, which provided just the distraction I needed. I tackled Thorn before he could say another word, and the lasgun fell from his grip as we hit the ground together. I'd saved his life, my instincts and a keen ear keeping me a half-second ahead of the fresh salvo of enemy fire that had just erupted from the jungle.

In return for that favour, Thorn was trying his damned best to kill me.

I had him pinned with my knee, keeping him from drawing his knife. But the fingers of Thorn's one hand were locked tight about my throat. He was stronger than he looked.

No match for my augmetic arm, of course. I fought out of his grip, breaking a few bones in the process. Thorn was screaming curses, thrashing about wildly as he tried to unseat me, foaming at the mouth. In the meantime, I knew the hostiles wouldn't exactly be sitting around making daisy chains. They couldn't have asked for a better distraction, or easier targets, than these two damned fools brawling in the open.

I had no choice but to finish this. Fast. I could already hear my men returning fire, and this one was going to get ugly, and quick.

I twisted my shotgun around, trying to jam the barrel up beneath Thorn's chin. I had no intention of shooting him, of course. If he'd been in his right mind, he'd have known that. Instead, he fought with all his strength to push the gun away from himself. I let him succeed, even as I blindsided him with my metal fist.

The punch knocked Thorn spark out, and left a dent in the side of his skull that would probably take a metal plate to straighten out. The way this kid was going today, he was liable to end up like me.

While we had been grappling, the hostiles had made their move.

They came running, screaming, firing out of the jungle, somehow managing to evade all of our traps. My men were shooting furiously at them, but Thorn's little turn had left a gaping hole in our defences – and the hostiles knew exactly where our blind spots were.

I was a damned sitting duck. I didn't know why I wasn't dead already – but, seeing as I wasn't, I figured I could spare another second to hoist the unconscious Thorn across my shoulders before I ran for cover. No one gets left behind if I can help it.

My men were closing with the invaders, yelling for the rest of the platoon to back them up. I deposited Thorn on the ground behind a hut. I didn't stop to check how he was. No time for that. I had a battle to get back to. I raced back to join my men, running at the hostiles with my shotgun blazing. Emperor's teeth, but they were ugly! It was all I could do not to puke at the sight of them.

They had been human once, that much I could tell. Cultists, no doubt, some of them still wearing the tatters of their black robes.

Kadence had been right about them. They were monsters, now, no two of them alike. Their flesh had run like wax, set in revolting shapes. Arms had been fused to torsos, fingers melted together, heads sunken into chests. Some of the monsters – the mutants – had sprouted new limbs, from their ribs, their spines, even out of their heads. Some of them had six eyes, four noses, or mouths in their bellies. They were bristling with clumps of short, black hair, with blisters and blood-red pustules.

And they outnumbered us about five to one. There was no way we were going to survive without some discipline, so I started spitting out orders.

'Barruga, aim for the slimy one's eyes. No, its other eyes! Emperor's teeth, this one has a face like a grox's back end, and it stinks as bad. Greif, wake the hell up, you'd have lost your damned head if I hadn't shot that one behind you. Move it, you slowpokes, I want you up close and personal, right in their damned faces. Marsh, stop holding that knife like you're eating your breakfast. It only takes one hand to hold in your guts, so keep the other one fighting. Kopachek, where's that damned flamer? I want the smell of burning mutants in my nostrils!'

One thing I have learned about mutants over the years: they might be strong – damned strong, some of them – but it's rare that they're fast. They're clumsy, unwieldy. Comes from fighting in bodies they hardly know. That, and having the brain power of a blood wasp on heat.

And, at first, it appeared that these mutants were no different.

I was right in the thick of them. It was safer that way. It made it impossible for their snipers, on the edge of the melee, to keep me in their sights, or to use their grenades without decimating their own ranks.

So, the mutants were swiping at me with poison-dipped claws, straining for my throat with misshapen fangs, and I can hardly deny it, this is one battered old warhorse who has started to slow down himself. I always figured that, what I've lost in speed, I make up for by having a tougher damned hide than most. Even so, in a fight like this one, I'd have expected a few cuts and bruises. Not this time, though. This time, it felt like I was charmed. Like those damned freaks couldn't lay a hand on me.

And yet...

And yet, somehow, my knife thrusts weren't hitting home either. The mutants were ducking and weaving like experts. And whenever I thought I had a clear shot at one, as I started to squeeze my trigger, my target was gone, spun away, and there were only comrades in my sights instead.

My men were faring no better than I was. They'd slashed at a few of those melted-wax faces, cracked a few twisted skulls, but no more than that. And they'd taken surprisingly few wounds in return, just a shallow cut here and there. It was almost like... like the mutants were playing with us.

Insulted, enraged, I lashed out with my feet and my elbows, widened the arc of my knife swipes, turned my shotgun around and used its butt as a cudgel, but nothing got through. So, I took a calculated risk. I did what every nerve in my body was screaming at me to do.

I leapt at the nearest mutant and I slashed its throat, my frustration bursting out in a cruel bark of laughter as its hot blood spattered my face. My first kill of the night. But to make that leap, I'd had to drop my guard, leave my right flank exposed.

I expected to feel a talon in my ribs, to die in agony, but no such blow came. My instincts had been right. The mutants weren't trying to kill us. It was worse than that.

'They want to take us alive!' I shouted. 'Well, they can't have met a Catachan Jungle Fighter before. Time to step up your game, you goldbrickers. Show these mutant scum that we don't lie down and roll over till we're damn well stone cold dead!'

With a roar of enthusiasm, the men followed my lead. They fought with abandon, not caring what risks they took with their own safety as long as they hurt the enemy.

The switch in tactics took the mutants by surprise. They were thrown off balance, reeling, falling like tenpins. I knew it couldn't last.

They must have identified me as the leader, because now they were swarming me, grasping at me with filthy hands. I landed a few good blows, but then strong arms encircled me from behind, and a cold, clammy tentacle seized my left wrist and twisted it almost to breaking point. My shotgun fell from my numbed fingers. My knife hand… that was stronger than my opponents had bargained for.

For a moment, it looked like the struggle – my augmetic arm against three of those freaks – could have gone either way. But then, a flailing limb – or a tail, I suspected – whipped my legs out from under me, something blunt and hard struck the back of my head, and I was toppling backwards.

And the first thing I realised, as I blinked away stars, as I fought to keep awake and on my knees at least, was that my blade – my Catachan Fang – had indeed been wrenched from my grip.

Someone was gonna pay for that!

The mutants were looming over me. Seven of them, I counted. Or maybe just six; I wasn't sure if one had two heads. They were shouting at me in a language I couldn't understand, but one that made my every nerve jangle like the strings of a grox-gut harp. I had no doubt that they were screaming blasphemy of the vilest kind, and all I longed to do was to shut them up, to stop those awful, hateful words escaping into the world.

The grenade felt cold in my hand, and reassuringly solid. It gave me strength, put me back in control. I knew it would rip my body apart. I knew that this time not even the most skilled surgeon would be able to stitch me back together. But a glorious death was far preferable to defeat. And a death that took six – or seven – of my enemies with me…

Then, just like that, the mutants were gone. Withdrawn. Swallowed up by the jungle once more, with hardly a ripple to mark their passing. The quiet rhythm of the jungle settled in again as I unsteadily picked myself up. I saw a number of my men doing the same, looking as confused as I felt.

'How many wounded?' I asked.

There were only a few, and nothing a can of synth-skin couldn't fix. It didn't make any sense. The mutants had been winning!

They had left a handful of misshapen bodies behind them. I glared down at one as if it could tell me in death the secrets it had kept in life. The mutant was lizard-like in appearance, a forked tongue lolling from its open mouth, a thorny tail tangled about its ankles. It hurt my eyes to look at it. I blinked and shifted my gaze along the grass until it found a more welcome sight.

I didn't dare believe it at first. My knife. My Catachan Fang. Half a metre of cold steel, its early gleam dulled through a lifetime of use but still the most precious thing in the damned world to me. An extension of myself, a part of my soul. And the mutants had left it, standing upright in the ground. Almost… respectfully.

I spent a long time kneeling beside that knife, looking at it, before I picked it up, wiped it down and returned it to its sheath.

I spent a long time thinking about what it might mean.

TWENTY MINUTES LATER and I was back in the central hall butting heads with Farris.

'We gotta ship out of here.' I told him. 'We can't wait till morning.'

General Farris shook his head.

'We've been through this before, Straken. I won't have us marching through that jungle at night.'

'The men can cope with the jungle.'

'Maybe they can, but the villagers…'

'If we stay here, and those mutants attack again, I can't guarantee we can hold them back. Our best hope is to take them by surprise, punch through their lines and keep on going.'

'With the hostiles at our heels?' he asked.

'We only have to reach base camp, then the odds'll be even.' I said. 'With a couple more platoons, we can turn back around and blast that damned Chaos scum to—'

'But the villagers, man! Some of them are old. There are children. They won't be able to keep pace with us.'

'So, we lose a few civilians. Better that than—'

'No,' he insisted. 'We stick to my original plan. You said yourself that there were no casualties of the first attack.'

'Because the mutants weren't trying. They thought they could take us alive. Now they know better.'

'If I didn't know *you* better, I'd be starting to wonder if you'd lost your nerve.'

And for the second time that night, I had to fight down the urge to punch this damned Validian upstart in his smug damned mouth. Through gritted teeth I said: 'You're asking me to sacrifice my men, my entire command platoon, for a lost cause.'

'You have your orders, Colonel Straken,' he said coldly.

ONE HOUR TILL dawn, and a forbidding bird call broke the morning silence. The cold crept into my old bones as I lay waiting, and I longed to feel the warmth of the sun – any sun – one final time.

In the jungle, nothing had stirred. Still, I was sure that the shadows had grown longer. And darker. A deep, unnatural darkness. The mutants – the monsters – were gathering their forces, increasing in number.

There were butterflies in my stomach. That wasn't like me. A Catachan's patience is his greatest strength. But tonight, it didn't feel that way. It felt like we were only postponing the inevitable.

My mind flashed back to my talk with Farris, and I felt my blood heating up at the memory. But I realised something now. The general had had a point. Not about my motives – 'Iron Hand' Straken is no damned coward. But I *had* been reluctant to face the mutants again. I still was.

I couldn't explain why. It was a churning in my gut. An itch in my brain. An instinct that there was something wrong here, something I'd missed. Thinking back, I realised that the itch had been there all night. Ever since I had first clapped eyes on this damned place.

So, what was I doing out here? Waiting for an attack that I couldn't defend against, waiting to die? I was following my orders. But the Emperor knows, I've defied enough fool-headed generals in my time. I'd have stuck my knife in Farris's damned heart and been glad to do it, if I'd thought it would save a single one of my men. The problem was, this time, I didn't know if it would. I didn't know what to do for the best.

Or maybe I did. Maybe, at some level, I had known all along.

Maybe I just had to listen to my gut.

I climbed to my feet, and I walked towards the jungle, grass rustling beneath my feet.

As I passed the outermost huts of the village, I could almost feel the sights of a hundred lasguns upon me. I was out in the open now, at the mercy of those guns – but not one of them fired. I stooped and laid my guns on the ground, then I shrugged off my backpack and webbing, and set them down too. Finally, I raised my hands to show that they were empty.

I almost choked on the words I had to say, the last words I had ever imagined would come from my throat. I didn't raise my voice; there was no need.

'My name is Colonel Straken, and on behalf of the Second Catachan regiment of the Imperial Guard – on behalf of the God-Emperor Himself – I offer you my unconditional surrender.'

It was a minute – a long, anxious minute – before anything happened.

Then, I heard a whisper of leaves to my left and a near-human shape detached itself from the foliage. It padded towards me, lasgun raised, and I felt my fists clenching involuntarily.

The mutant was beside me now. I recoiled from its rancid breath. It spoke to me, in the same unholy language as before, and I wanted with all my soul to lash out. I wanted to punch, to kick, to spit, to pull my knife and to carve my name in that abomination's chest.

Instead, I just watched as the mutant signalled to its comrades. One by one, they stepped out from the jungle behind it. Each was an abomination, and the sight of them gathered together just made the violent urge grow even stronger.

From behind me, a single lasgun shot rang out. A mutant fell to the floor, clutching its shoulder.

'Hold your damned fire! That's an order!' I cried. 'No one is to engage these... the hostiles. It's not us they want.'

The mutants had brought up their own guns, but now they lowered them again. I couldn't meet their eyes, any of them. I felt sick inside, and my flesh was crawling like I'd been dipped in fire ants.

And now the mutants where shambling past me, a score of them – two score, three – and into the village. Towards the meeting hall.

I saw MacDougal and Stone springing to their feet, getting out of the mutants' path, drawing their knives but resisting the urge to use them. I was grateful to them. They trusted me. Even though, for all they knew – for all any of my men knew, watching this scene from their vantage points – I must have gone out of my tiny mind. Maybe I had, too.

But, somehow, this felt good to me. It felt like the smart thing to do. For the first damned time in this forsaken night, something felt right. From behind me, I felt the familiar rush of heat and flame as the mutants' grenades blew the meeting hall apart.

The villagers must have heard them coming – but for most of them, there had been no time to escape. The survivors came charging out of the fire and the billowing smoke. I saw old men and young boys, their faces darkened and twisted by hatred and rage. It was hard to believe they were the same peaceful people whose food we had shared. The villagers moved towards the mutants with an angry roar, lasguns firing wildly as they sought to kill the intruders.

The mutants showed no mercy. Half the villagers were shot down before they could take two steps. The remainder closed with their attackers, but they were unskilled in combat, quickly shredded by mutant claws. Their screams filled the clearing, drowning out the sounds of lasfire and conflict. This was the last thing I wanted to see, but I forced myself to pick up my feet, to get closer. Because I *had* to see this. I had to know.

Even transfixed by the unfolding horror, my old battle instincts hadn't deserted me entirely. Someone was coming at me from behind. I sidestepped his charge, threw him over my shoulder. The figure regrouped quickly, scrambling back to his feet. I was horrified to see that it was General Farris. The left side of his face had been burned away. He must have been in incredible pain. He was cursing at me, calling me all the damned names he could think of, and his fury gave him a strength that I'd never have expected. I may have hesitated too, because he managed to plant his foot in my stomach and push me into the wall of a hut.

'This isn't what it looks like,' I forced out. The words sounded pathetic, even to me.

Farris was marching on me with his pistol levelled and eyes bulging white with fury.

'I knew it would come to this. I've been watching you, Straken. You're undisciplined, insubordinate. I put up with your backchat because this was your regiment. But I always knew you were one step from turning, from betraying us all. I should have put this bolt between your eyes hours ago.'

The fighting suddenly seemed very far away, and in that moment it was down to just me and him.

I could have taken him alive.

But a pair of lasgun beams struck Farris from behind, and he stiffened and gasped, then crumpled to the ground.

Emerging from the shadows, Trooper Vines crouched over the general's fallen body, and pronounced him dead.

'I had no choice,' Vines said dryly. 'He was lashing out, screaming. He was saying crazy things, calling you a monster.'

I remembered that Vines had been close to Wallenski. I acknowledged, and dismissed, his actions with a curt nod.

The fighting was almost over.

The villagers were struggling to the very end, but there were only a handful left standing. It would be – it had been – a bloody massacre. One for which I could take much of the credit. And in that moment, I was filled once more with a crippling self-doubt.

But only for that moment.

The meeting hall was still alight – and where the blaze flickered across the faces of the last few combatants, native and invader alike, a transformation was taking place. I blinked and I refocussed, unsure at first if I was imagining things. But I couldn't deny what I saw.

In the glow of those cleansing flames, the lies of the moonlight were dispelled at last, and the truth stood revealed.

It wasn't till some days later that I heard the other side of the story. Colonel Carraway came to see me in my hospital bed, where I'd just been patched up once again, and he told me how lucky I'd been.

The explorators, it seemed, had left a survey probe in Borealis Four's orbit – and the tech-priests at HQ had tapped into its scans of the planetary surface. The aim had been to produce a tactical map, locate a few cultist strongholds. Instead, they had discovered a whole damned settlement, where a moment before there had only been trees.

Carraway and I worked out that the village must have shown up on the scans about the same time my men and I found it. As if, by crossing its threshold, we had broken some kind of foul enchantment.

Anyway, the upshot was that Carraway needed someone to investigate – and, since half my regiment was already in that area searching for me and my platoon, they were quick to step forward.

Kawalski, one of my toughest, most experienced sergeants, led the recce. He found the village soon enough – but his first impressions of it were quite different from mine. In his report, he described tumbledown shacks standing on scorched earth, twisted trees bearing rotten fruit, and a putrid stink in the air that made him want to retch.

I don't know why Kawalksi and his men saw the truth when I couldn't. Maybe Kadence's mind-screwing mumbo-jumbo could only affect so many of us at once. Maybe that was why it hadn't worked so well on Wallenski and Myers, or on Thorn. Or maybe that damned psyker meant for things to turn out just as they did, Catachan at war against Catachan.

Kawalksi sent a pair of scouts along the village's perimeter. They returned with reports of booby traps, and sentries hiding in the trees. Even when some troopers exchanged fire with one sentry, they weren't able to identify him. I had just been a shadow to them.

It was only when Kawalksi's men broke cover and attacked us that they saw who we were. That was why they had fought so defensively, trying not to hurt us, though we were trying to kill them. Kawalksi himself took me down, with some help. He was trying to get through to me, but he couldn't seem to make me understand.

We thought we were fighting Chaos-infected mutants. Instead, we were the ones infected. I'll always be haunted by the fact that it was me who killed Trooper Weissmuller, and laughed as I ripped out his throat. Standing orders say that Kawalksi should have shot me there and then.

But he had more faith in me than that.

It was a damned relief to be back on my feet again, and to have my time on Borealis Four done with.

Or so I'd thought.

We were all sat around a warming fire, with the sights and sounds of the jungle around us. But this wasn't the familiar scenery of Catachan – this was still a world marked by Chaos, and the ruined village around us was just another reminder of that.

I was the only one who saw him.

I don't know what made me look, why I chose that moment to tear my eyes away from the dying fire. But there he was, standing in the shadow of a hut – a ramshackle, worm-eaten hut, I could now tell. After all that had happened, he appeared unscathed, his robe still pristine and white. Kadence Moonglow.

He was watching me.

Then he turned, and he slipped away – and I should have alerted my men, but this was between him and me now.

I followed him alone.

TROUBLE WAS, THE boy was faster than I expected. We were already a good way into the jungle when I caught up with him. Or rather, I should say, when he stopped and waited for me.

'Colonel Straken. I knew it would be you who came after me. Leading from the front. You always have to do everything yourself.'

I was in no mood for talking. My knife was already in my hand. I only wished I hadn't laid down my shotgun in the village.

I leapt at my mocking foe. And missed.

I hadn't seen him move. One second, Kadence had been in front of me, and now he was a few footsteps to the left. I almost lost my balance, having to grab hold of a creeper to steady myself. It was bristling with poisoned spines. If I'd gripped it with my good hand, instead of my augmetic one, I would have been on the fast track to a damned burial pit.

I tore the creeper from its aerial roots and snapped it like a whip, but again, my target wasn't quite where I'd thought him to be.

'Your men aren't here now, colonel,' he said. 'You were overconfident, strayed too far from them. They won't hear your cries.'

And suddenly he threw out his arms – and although he wasn't close enough to touch me, I felt as if I had been punched. The impossible blow staggered me, and Kadence was quick to press his advantage. More strikes followed – once, twice, three times to the head, once in the gut. I was flung backwards into a thorny bush, caught and held by its thin branches. A thousand tiny insects scuttled to gorge themselves on my blood.

'You wanna hear crying, kid?' I yelled, wrenching myself free from the clinging vegetation. 'How about you get the hell out of my head? Stop making me see things that aren't damn well there, and face me like a… like a… whatever the hell it is you are.'

Kadence just smiled. And he gestured again, and my left leg snapped. It was all I could do not to gasp with the pain, but I refused to give him that satisfaction. I just gritted my teeth, transferred my weight onto my right foot, and continued to advance on him.

'I didn't ask for this fight,' said Kadence. 'I was content with my tiny domain, and a handful of followers who would do anything for me. For centuries, we hid from the outside world. Until, by the whims of a cruel fortune, you came blundering into our safe haven.'

I thrust at him with my knife. I missed again, his dodge too quick to even register.

'Your followers were mutants. Perverted deviants. And you tricked me into eating with them. You made me think... You made me see my own men as...'

I roared in frustration, my rage getting the better of me. I was swinging wide now, hoping to nick my target wherever he might be. My blade whistled through the empty air, and he was suddenly behind me.

'I knew that, once you had found us, more of your kind would come.' he said. 'I could not cloud so many minds at once. I hoped it would be sufficient to make you few see my followers as friends, your comrades as the thing you most despise.'

'You didn't count on me.'

'No. No, I did not. But for all you have taken from me this night, Colonel Straken, you will pay with your life.'

He made an abrupt slashing motion with his hand, and my leg broke again. A flick of his fingers, and my left shoulder dislocated itself. Kadence extended his right arm, formed his fingers into a claw pattern and twisted his wrist, and something twisted inside of me.

I was buckling under the pain, straining to catch my breath, but determined to close the gap between me and my tormentor, even if I had to do it on my hands and knees.

'Think you can finish me?' I struggled out. 'Good... good luck, kid. Better monsters than you have... have...'

I felt my ribs crack, one by one. My augmetic arm popped and fizzed, and became a dead weight hanging from my shoulder. I was on the jungle floor, not sure how I had got there. There were tears in my eyes and blood in my throat. And as I looked up, trying to focus through a haze of black and red spots, I saw Kadence making a fist, and it felt as if he had reached right into my chest and was crushing my damned heart.

And that was when something miraculous happened.

I felt the warmth of the rising sun on my back, saw the first of its light piercing the jungle canopy above me. And where those red rays touched the slight form of my assailant, like the flames of the fire back in the village, they exposed his deceptions for what they were.

Kadence Moonglow – the boy in the white robe – faded from my sight. But a few steps behind him, exposed by the sunlight, was a twisted horror.

I couldn't see the whole shape of the monster. The parts still in shadow were invisible to me. But I could make out a rough purple hide, six limbs that could have been arms or legs, and a gaping, slavering maw that seemed to fill most of the monster's – the daemon's – huge head.

I could make out a single red eye, perched atop that great mouth. And it blinked at me as it realised that I was returning its glare.

As my Catachan Fang left my good hand.

As it flew on an unerring course towards that big, bright target.

It was the shot of a lifetime. My blade struck the dead centre of the daemon-thing's eye, piercing its shadow-black pupil. It buried itself up to the hilt. And the daemon that had been Kadence Moonglow gaped at me, for a second, with what I took to be an expression of surprise.

And then he exploded in a shower of purple ash.

I DON'T KNOW how many hours I lay there, face down in the jungle.

I couldn't lift my head, couldn't move my legs without my broken bones grinding against each other. My insides felt like jelly, and most of my augmetics had failed. I was dying.

And if I didn't go soon, I knew there were any number of predators gathering in the brush, ready and eager to help me on my way.

I wasn't worried. Far from it.

I knew that my men were nearby. I knew they would never stop searching for me. And I knew that, whatever it took, they would find me. They would carry me off to the surgeons, as they had done a hundred times before.

I could trust them.

And when I heard their distant footsteps, I was still able to force a smile.

ABOUT THE AUTHORS

Lucien Soulban has authored and co-written over 90 roleplay supplements, and has helped launch three roleplay games. He wrote the script for *Warhammer 40,000: Dawn of War* and *Winter Assault* computer games. He currently works as a script writer for videogame giant Ubisoft Montreal.

Steve Parker was born and raised in Edinburgh. Scotland, and now lives and works in Tokyo, Japan. As a video-game writer/designer, he has worked ontitles for various platforms. In 2005, his short fiction started appearing in American SF/Fantasy/Horror Magazines. In 2006, his story The Falls of Marakross was published in the Black Library's Tales from the Dark Millennium anthology. His first novel, *Rebel Winter*, was published in 2007 and his latest book, *Rynn's World*, is the first book in the Space Marine Battles series.

Steve Lyons has written novels, short stories, radio plays and comic strips for characters including the X-men, Doctor Who, Strontium Dog and Sappire & Steel. He has written several non-fiction books about television shows, and contributes to magazines. His work for the Black Library includes *Ice Guard*, *Death World* and the audio drama *Waiting Death*.

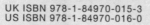

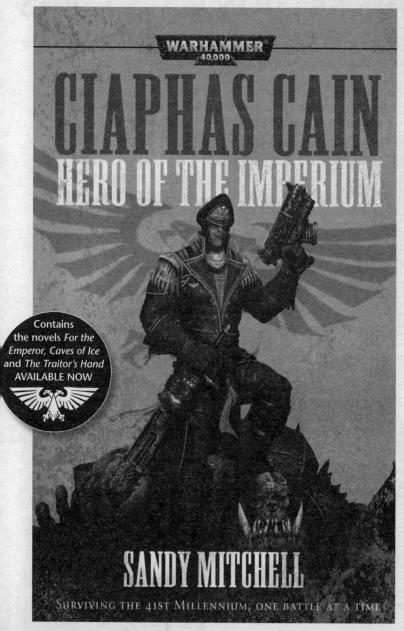

WARHAMMER
40,000

CIAPHAS CAIN
HERO OF THE IMPERIUM

Contains the novels *For the Emperor, Caves of Ice* and *The Traitor's Hand*
AVAILABLE NOW

SANDY MITCHELL

SURVIVING THE 41ST MILLENNIUM, ONE BATTLE AT A TIME

ISBN 978-1-84416-466-0

WARHAMMER 40,000

CIAPHAS CAIN
DEFENDER OF THE IMPERIUM

'An engagingly roguish hero, and realistic combat at both the strategic and very personal levels. First-rate Military SF!'

– *New York Times* bestselling author David Drake

Contains the novels *Death or Glory*, *Duty Calls* and *Cain's Last Stand*
AVAILABLE NOW

SANDY MITCHELL

DEATH OR GLORY • DUTY CALLS • CAIN'S LAST STAND

UK ISBN 978-1-84416-882-8   US ISBN 978-1-84416-883-5